D1528565

JUSTICE

**A CHOOSE A HERO ROMANCE™
WHERE THE READER CONTROLS
THE ENDING!**

BY

TRACY TAPPAN

Edited by:
Jessa Slade
Faith Freewoman

Proofread by:
Maria Connor

Cover by:
Christina El-Haddad

ALSO BY TRACY TAPPAN

CONTENTS

JUSTICE'S STORY...
Sometimes love comes in three…

Readers' Favorite Gold Medal winner, 2021 Kindle Book Award Semi-Finalist, JUSTICE is a standout romantic adventure where you decide which bold and fearless hero will win a happily ever after.

Star athlete and master thief Justine "Justice" Hayes was taught by her notorious father never to say no to a challenge. So when the commander of United States Special Operations Forces offers her an elite job no woman has held before, she can't turn down this supreme test of her abilities. But an impossible obstacle stands between her and the career of her dreams.

She has to survive the Navy SEALs' most brutal training program: BUD/S.

Despite a hostile admiral gunning for her, she soon finds herself wearing the rank of Navy ensign and fighting through grueling torture alongside some of America's toughest and most irresistible men. Distractions are not an option – she boots her tantalizing teammates solidly into the Friend Zone.

But ignoring her attraction to three of them—the leader, the gentleman, and the bad boy—turns out to be harder than she expected.

She ends up bonding with all three in the kind of soul-deep way only military comrades who have survived hell together can.

Until one of them betrays her...

In this Choose A Hero Romance novel, you have the one-of-a-kind opportunity to read three entirely different endings, with three unique heroes, each with its very own breathtaking happily-ever-after.

"Warriorship is as much a tempering of the spirit as a physical rendering. Even if toughness were measured in terms of a bar-fighting brawler or some Hollywood-generated macho facsimile, that conduct has no place in military society or in the company of true warriors. In fact, a warrior who has depth—one with sensitivity, compassion, and a strong spiritual sense of self—has a decided advantage. He enters the arena from a firm moral grounding."

Dick Couch
The Warrior Elite: The Forging of SEAL Class 228

To special operators, humble and brave,
who put their lives on the line for
freedom in unfathomable ways.

CHAPTER ONE

January
Coronado, California
Naval Amphibious Base

SAND IN THE Vagina.

This wasn't the name of a new alternative music group. It wasn't a bizarre beauty treatment, either, or the latest cure for maladies in sensitive places. Ridiculous on all counts. Female genitalia were already sensitive enough—Ensign Justice Hayes was rediscovering that today times ten.

Sand in the vagina, as it turned out, was the sleeper challenge of BUD/S, and considering the company Justice was keeping, a challenge unique to her.

She hadn't been prepared for it—hence the "sleeper" reference. She'd prepped for the rest: pain, sweat, constant yelling, hostility, prejudice, exhaustion, hunger, unfairness, and being stared at in every possible way, including the leers. Just not all the damned chafing.

All around her on the grinder—the fifty-by-thirty-foot asphalt rectangle that was rapidly becoming the seventh circle of hell—she heard the rest of her First Phase BUD/S class fidgeting, adjusting their weight.

The class was being held in the front leaning rest position of their push-ups for—in Buzz Lightyear's quotable words—infinity and beyond.

Justice rotated her hips from side to side, teeth gritted against the pain. Her soaked camouflage uniform pants were binding her crotch—adding to the sand in the vagina will-breaker—and her combat boots were cold and soggy. Her bun, still miraculously bound, felt like it'd gained five pounds of water weight, and her arm and chest muscles were jellified, as if she hadn't spent the past several months doing some of the most intensive upper body workouts of her life to prepare for this training.

Somebody two rows back groaned.

The candidate on her right angled his butt in the air.

Justice's head swam. When were the instructors going to recover them? Or were more push-ups on the way? How many sets had they done already? She'd lost track in the pain of—She cut off the thought and squeezed her eyes shut, sand grains grating against the backs of her lids.

Don't think about how many. Just do them.

Stay in the moment.

"Recover!" Instructor Hill shouted.

Everyone heaved a huge breath.

"RECOVER!" the class parroted back at the required deafening blare.

Justice lurched upright and came to attention, making sure to plant her boots squarely on the white swim flippers painted on her spot of the grinder.

Instructor Hill stalked up and down their ranks, glaring like he was hunting for something to eat.

Owner of the porn industry's cheesiest mustache, Hill was out to get her. Not paranoia. Truth. And since he clearly knew that all her extra cracks and crevices were housing sand in a soul-destroying way, he stopped right in front of her and bellowed, "Get wet and sandy!"

Fuck. Just fuck.

"You got sixty seconds!" Hill foghorned.

One hundred fifty-four SEAL hopefuls exploded into action.

But sixty seconds to run down the beach, climb over the fifteen-foot sand berm, run into the surf, get completely wet, run back out, roll around in the sand until not a single patch of skin or clothing showed, then run back over the berm to the grinder wasn't happening.

Which meant they were going to be punished—or receive a "beating"—for their tardiness.

"Drop!" Hill brayed the moment they stumbled back onto the grinder.

"DROP!" they sounded off.

Justice went down into the push-up position, squinting against a blinding tide of seawater and sweat. A lot of sweat. The weather was unnaturally warm for January, the infamous Santa Ana winds blowing in hot from the sea, sucking all moisture from the air, shrinking up sidewalks, and swirling sand into thin arabesques.

"Push 'em out!" Hill hollered.

On Justice's left, Ensign Brayden Street, one of the class officers, led them through the next set. "Push-ups! Ready!"

"READY!"

From the corner of her eye, Justice tried to reconcile the sand monster Ensign Street now was with the man she'd met a few hours ago in the officers' barracks.

Street was in full possession of the kind of blond-haired-blue-eyed-plus-dimples looks that would've been almost cherubic in handsomeness if not for him being such a studmuffin. He was on the tall side—six-two, six-three—and well-muscled without being bulky.

His lean jaw had been flexing vigorously when they first met, as he fought, she suspected, not to swallow his tongue. Not in a *help-me-I-need-the-Heimlich-maneuver* way, but more of an *oh-shit-I-can't-believe-this-hot-chick-with-the-nice-rack-is-going-to-be-my-roommate* strangle.

And she did. Have a nice rack, that was. And since she

didn't like to restrict her movements or risk snagging her clothing on a trip wire, an alarm, or a sensor—a lesson learned practically from the cradle—she wore fitted T-shirts. So, her nice rack was unavoidably obvious.

Street's body could be included in the splendid department. He had the type of physique that would be both fast and strong...although right now he'd been transformed into a liquid pile of quivering jelly muscles, like the rest of them.

Not that anyone would admit it.

"Down!" Street yelled.

"ONE!" Justice performed the push-up. The knotted muscles in her biceps stretched painfully.

"Down!"

"TWO!" Her triceps quavered.

"Down!"

"THREE!" The sand between her hands and the asphalt ground into her palms.

"Down!"

"FOUR!" Her elbows popped with—

A combat boot stomped down on her back.

She slammed into the asphalt, belly first, face second, cracking her nose against the hard surface. Pain speared through her cheeks, and she sucked down a moan.

"Your *chest*," Instructor Hill thundered down at her, "touches the ground on every push-up, Ensign. You need more of a cheat than your tits are already giving you?"

"No, Instructor!" She shoved back into a straight-arm position.

"FIVE!"

Down-up. Down-up. She watched blood drizzle out of her nose and make doodle art on the asphalt. *Eleven. Twelve.* The pool of blood grew into a sizeable blob. *Down-up. Down-up.* Into the Blob That Ate California... *Fifteen. Sixteen.* Ate all the beaches and the grinder so they couldn't do push-ups anymore… *Eighteen. Nineteen.*

"TWENTY!"

End of the set.

Ensign Street did a call-out to mark it. "Instructor Hill!"

"HOOYAH, INSTRUCTOR HILL!" the rest of them chorused.

"Recover!" Hill ordered.

Justice swayed to her feet, coming to attention with her shoulders back and—

Hose water drilled into her chest—her breasts, specifically, which seemed to be the nonmilitary objects of the day to hate.

The man directing the hose at her was Chief Tanner, a good ol' boy from Georgia with a light brown crew cut leveling the top of his head and very white teeth showing extra-bright against a late-season tan. He probably had a terrific smile…not that his facial muscles knew how to make one. He was wearing khaki UDT shorts, spit-shined black military boots with white socks folded over the top, and a navy blue T-shirt plus a ball cap of the same color embroidered with the SEAL trident in gold thread.

"You know what you are, bleeder?" Tanner leaned forward, as if to share something conspiratorial with her, even though his voice remained loud enough for the others to hear. "And when I say bleeder, I ain't talking 'bout the shit coming out your nose, hear?"

She maintained her forward-facing, thousand-yard stare and concentrated on breathing through the collateral spray of water flying up into her face and nose.

"You're the girl whose mama died," Tanner said, sideswiping her with the personal intel—though it shouldn't have surprised her. Of course, he'd read her personnel file.

She locked up every muscle in her body to keep from flinching. *Don't let the fucker get inside your head.* Unfortunately, the lock-up ended up looking like a flinch.

Ensign Brayden Street shifted a micro movement to glance at her.

Without taking his attention off her, Tanner angled the hose over and blasted Street in the throat.

"You're the girl," Tanner continued, "whose poor papa never had no sons, and so now you're here at BUD/S trying to be his boy. Ain't that right?"

Not exactly.

But this wasn't a psychiatrist's couch, or the local neighborhood haunt with Tanner as the cheery bartender ready to lend a sympathetic ear, or the inside of a romance novel with lazy, crooked smiles and Tom Cruise dialogue. This was grinder PT, and the instructors were all about feeding her boots-first to the other candidates to drive her *the hell outta my Navy*. Share time wasn't happening. Concentration was best reserved for things like not letting her knees buckle.

She spat water, careful not to hit the chief.

Tanner stepped back. "Drop!" he commanded.

"DROP!"

The class assumed the push-up position.

"Push 'em out!"

"Push-ups!" Ensign Street barked. "Ready!"

"READY!"

They thumped out the requisite twenty.

Tanner recovered them.

They stood.

Water flung into Justice's face again, but this time it was kickback from the chest of the man on her right. He had nostrils arched to such an extreme it looked like he was perpetually disgusted over something.

"Christ almighty," Tanner swore at the guy. "Were you just whelped out your mama's pussy yesterday? Name, candidate!"

Everyone in the class had their names stenciled on their helmets and white T-shirts, but last names only.

"Seaman Brantley Shaw!"

"*Brantley*." Tanner sneered the name as if a bird had crapped it into his mouth. "Brantley ain't no frogman's name. Drop!"

"DROP!"

They dropped.

"Push 'em out!"

Tanner pounded Shaw in the back of the head with water while they did their push-ups.

"*Brantley* sounds like a guy who… Hey, Warren," Tanner called up to Instructor Hill, who was now overlooking them from a raised wooden dais on the north side of the grinder. "What's that drink your wife likes?"

"Down!" Street yelled.

"Appletini."

"ONE!"

"That's right." Tanner hardened the stream of his hose water at Shaw.

Shaw grunted.

"Down!"

"TWO!"

"You're the type a guy," Tanner taunted, "who drinks appletinis, probably not even man enough to go down on his woman. Ain't that right?"

"THREE!"

"Gonna run and hide behind a rock soon as the shooting starts, ain't you, pussy?"

With a sulky huff, Shaw did his next push-up.

"FOUR!"

Justice swallowed against her raw throat. Her count-offs were beginning to sound hoarse.

"FIVE!"

Tanner stepped over to the man beside Shaw and missiled water into his nape. He kept up the drenching until the class reached twenty push-ups.

They boomed the required call-out. "HOOYAH, CHIEF TANNER!"

"Recover," Tanner clipped.

They stood.

Justice gulped for air.

"Name!" Tanner demanded of his newest victim—Shaw's neighbor—the hose directed at the guy's belt.

"Quartermaster First Class Gale Colgate!"

"What?" Tanner stood unmoving, water running off his elbow, clearly astounded. "Gail? What the hell? That's a *girl's* name." Contempt dripped from his words. "It's fucked. Push 'em out!"

Drop to the asphalt. Twenty push-ups. Stand.

Tanner strode back the way he'd come, his hose aimed at faces as he passed—Appletini Shaw, Justice, then Ensign Street.

Justice didn't close her eyes quickly enough, and a thin shaft of water darted under her eyelids and stung.

Tanner stopped in front of the candidate on Street's left. "Name, candidate, and it had better be a good one."

The guy hesitated.

Beefy man. Bull-necked. Should've gone by Krog.

His silence earned him a blast of hose water between the eyes.

The guy scrunched his face against the pelting water and yelled, "Seaman Ludlow Hornsby!"

Tanner froze.

Instructor Hill laughed from up on the dais, his mustache rippling, joining in on the fun.

"Un-be-fucking-lievable." Tanner exhaled a hard breath. "*Ludlow Hornsby*. Sounds like an asshole drinking English fucking tea with the Queen." He glanced over at Instructor Hill. "Did I wake up on the wrong planet this morning? SOF sending us only pussies and *women* for candidates this time?"

"It's fucked!" Hill agreed at high volume.

"Damn right it is." Chief Tanner growled. "Push 'em out!"

Drop to the asphalt. Twenty push-ups.
Wait in front leaning rest position.

"Now, see, Instructor Hill has the name of a fine, upstanding American male. *Warren*. And me? Bobby." Tanner pronounced his own name with smooth reverence. "This is due to the fact that our mamas and papas aren't stupid fucking crackers." Tanner sniffed in disgust. "It is infinitely clear to me that y'all's parents are idiots. They produced nothing but morons."

Justice hard-stared the blood design in the puddle of water beneath her. Her nose was still bleeding but had slackened to drips *pit-patting* into the small pool.

Tanner moved his hose over to the man next to Hornsby, jetting water against the guy's darkly stubbled skull. "Name!"

"Petty Officer Keith Knight!"

From up on the dais, Instructor Hill laughed again. "You hear that, Bobby? One more K in this piece of shit's name, and he's in the Klan."

"That," Tanner said in a severe tone, "is a seriously fucking problematic situation."

Justice's burning abs started to spasm. She flexed her butt muscles to take some of the pressure off.

Keith Knight. He was her boat team leader. Solid handshake, steady stare, vitality bursting from every pore. She'd met him only briefly this morning, but those things had stood out. That, and he had the same aqua blue eyes as his half brother Brayden Street. From what she could tell in the dawn light, the brothers didn't look anything alike other than their eye color. Keith's hair—what she could find of it—was dark brown, and he was a far cry from cherubic or godly.

More like ruggedly handsome.

The entire Amphib Base was, in fact—as The Weather Sisters liked to sing it—raining men, specifically those who'd received more than their fair share of allotted testosterone. Every one of the candidates should come with a warning label: hot bods known to inspire spontaneous orgasms in women between the ages of eighteen and forty—make that fifty—if stared at for too long.

Not that it mattered. Justice wasn't here to speed date these guys. The exact opposite. Impressions were everything in the small SPECWAR community, and the hell if she was going to become *that* woman—the one who slept with men she worked with.

Tanner snarled at Knight, "Your name is as fool as you are. Push 'em out!"

Justice thought it would be a relief to finally move. Not quite. The tendons in her elbows had frozen, and they snapped and popped through all twenty push-ups.

"Recover!"

She struggled upright, exhaustion making her feel like she was on a merry-go-round. Her vision narrowed down to a long, dark tunnel. Her body was gouting so much sweat, dehydration was probably reaching dangerous levels of—

She caught back a breath as Tanner was suddenly nearly nose-to-nose with her, the bill of his ball cap pressed against her forehead.

"Do you know what you are?!" he grated at her from between his beautiful white teeth. "You, bleeder, are the female making a *joke* out of these fine American boys who deserve to be here—who ain't here because of some politically correct bug up a senator's ass. They *earned* their way."

Justice stared past Tanner's ear and didn't respond. The chief had clearly watched the movie *G.I. Jane* too many times. Justice's presence here had nothing to do with politics or a senator's ass-bug. She *had* earned her way here with her unique skillset. The Navy recruited her, for Christ's sake— albeit one man did so grudgingly.

"You hear me, bleeder?"

She maintained her mouth-shut posture. Tanner's breath smelled slightly of donuts, although she might've been imagining it because she was hungry. No way could a man with Tanner's physique keep up his build by starting every day with a bear claw.

Tanner eased back—but only so he could quick-nod his head forward and thunk his bill cap into her brow. "RING OUT!" He roared the order.

Her next breath hit bottom, refusing to leave her lungs, while, alternately, her heart tried to run away from her ribs. She almost glanced over at the ring-out bell. *Almost.* Three clangs on that, and her misery would be over. Half a morning into this, and the bullshit being shoveled her way was already as bad as one of the worst acts of bullshittery ever perpetrated on her—her dad's lie about her mother.

But quitting wasn't an option. Quitting equaled failure, and failure would sully the family name. Justice had besmirched the Hayes rep once with a trip to a holding cell in juvey when she was sixteen. Once was enough. She would die here on the grinder before she let anyone think she couldn't hack it.

"You're headed there anyway," Tanner ground out, "might as well save yourself the hurt."

"Negative, Chief Tanner!" She hurled her shout into his

merciless face.

Tanner's mouth flattened to a hard, dark line. He directed his water hose at her feet, flooding her boots.

She kept her focus pinned on the sky. Three H-60 Seahawk helicopters out of the neighboring Navy base, NAS North Island, flew across scattered clouds in loose formation.

Tanner moved back. "Secured for chow!" he yelled, finally dismissing them.

Someone behind her hissed, "Thank fuck."

"Form it up!" Ensign Street directed them. "Running ranks!"

The class rotated in formation and jogged in the direction of the chow hall, where—

"WHAT THE FUCK IS THIS?!" Instructor Hill barreled off the dais, veins popping out all over his forehead from his screaming. "When you're told to go somewhere, you run! Do you hear me, you lazy scum? PUSH 'EM OUT!"

Justice's stomach shriveled. In a broken-jointed motion, she dropped down onto the blacktop into push-up position.

"Push-ups!" Street's voice was gravelly.

Maybe if she did something spectacular, like give birth to a fully realized Navy SEAL, trident proudly gleaming on his smooth, pink chest, the instructors would actually let them stop.

"Ready!"

"READY!"

"Down!"

"ONE."

"Cocksucker."

"Shit a brick."

"Fucking hell."

"Down!"

"TWO!"

"Shitballs."

"Motherfucker."

"Ass-wiping bag of crap."

A steady barrage of curses followed every push-up, the gritted oaths expressing pretty damned clearly how especially demoralizing it was to be released for chow, then yanked back.

"TWENTY!"

"Instructor Hill!" Street called at the end of their set.

"HOOYAH, INSTRUCTOR HILL!" they shouted by rote.

"Start over for Hayes," Hill fumed. "Because she didn't do a single push-up right."

Justice came close to shaking her head. So untrue.

A candidate behind her snarled. "Plant your arms wider, Hayes, you weak cunt."

"Shut it, Chalmers," another man snapped.

She focused with cold precision on the pile of spit beneath her. She'd jogged over to someone else's painted flipper-prints, and whoever had been here before clearly didn't own a whole lot of drool control.

Don't think about it. Just do it.

"Push-ups! Ready…"

Chapter Two

THE NAVAL AMPHIBIOUS Base mess hall was standard-issue: food in shiny metal containers presented under clear glass, utilitarian tables and benches made of uncomfortable plastic, unforgiving fluorescent lighting, unadorned white walls, and easy-to-mop linoleum in a hideous gray-speckled pattern.

The food looked surprisingly good, although the rich aroma of hamburgers and grilled chicken was being somewhat drowned out by the collective stench of the candidates: seaweed, sweat, and wet clothes.

Half a day of BUD/S, and they already stank like swamp beasts. They likewise looked as bad as they smelled: bruised, worn, some bloodied, and most of them still so sandy they resembled sugar cookies.

Justice endured a few elbow jabs in the food line, but mostly was hostilely ignored.

Fine. She wasn't here to make friends.

She headed to an empty table, marveling at how a tray with a single plate of food, a small carton of milk, and a water bottle had somehow managed to break all laws of physics and take on the poundage of two watermelons. She sat, managing not to groan during the journey from upright to ass-plant. As soon as her butt hit the bench, she grimaced. There was so much sand down her pants, it felt like she was sitting on a super-sized Kotex.

She chugged her bottle of water, then slowly cut a bite of chicken and ate it. *Chew. Swallow. Repeat. Focus on the basics.* There was broccoli and rice on her plate too. The burgers had looked tasty, but a bit too greasy, and she needed to eat as healthy as she could during BUD/S. She didn't have the testosterone advantage the male candidates did. Compensations had to be found and exploited where they could. *Chew. Swallow. Repeat.* Her nose throbbed and was swollen to the size of... She couldn't tell exactly how big it was, only that if she glanced cross-eyed down at her own face, she could see it.

She was on her fourth bite of chicken when a sand-encrusted boot slapped down on the bench beside her. The owner of the boot propped a forearm on his thigh and leaned toward her. His forearm was very hairy. His head was not; black dots littered his skull in lieu of actual hair. His appearance was average, his body, exceptional—Iron Man muscles bulged against his camo pants.

"Here's a thought, Haaayes." Hairy Arms elongated the *ha*-sound in the first part of her last name, succeeding in sounding like he surely wanted to sound: snotty. "Just a small fucking suggestion—next time you blow Instructor Hill, maybe you could *not* cheese-grate the poor guy, huh? Give the rest of us a break."

Some of the other candidates glanced over.

Justice's nape prickled. She pinned her focus straight ahead and kept chewing. Across the room, Man-With-Girl-Name strode into the head. Maybe he also had a doodie-sized log of sand in his crotch in need of tending. "Thank you, candidate," she replied formally. "I appreciate your advice on how to properly fellate an instructor."

Straightening, Hairy Arms clunked his boot down. Sand tumbled off it onto the linoleum. "Well, hey, you wanna dick to practice on, I'm here for you."

Chew. Swallow. Cut the next bite. Why couldn't men ever be original? Although she supposed a part of her should be grateful Hairy Arms had brought this exchange solidly into well-travelled territory.

Men hit on her. A lot.

That hadn't always been the case. Her junior year of high school she'd been a zit-faced, lank-haired, gangly track star, boys wanting nothing to do with her. Over summer break she changed into a cat-eyed brunette with a lot of curves supplementing her athletic physique, returning for her senior year having to beat 'em off with a stick.

With no grandfathering-in period to teach her how to manage this sudden male attention—and without a mother to guide her—she'd been wildly experimental while figuring out what to do. During the process she made an interesting discovery—when a man was faced with the return attention of a truly beautiful woman, he froze up.

Just went completely into terror-lock.

How long he remained in *oh-shit-what-do-I-do-now?* mode was the tricky part of the equation. Two seconds? Or forever? This unknown had thrown her off her game a bit...until she learned how a certain "look" could help to keep power in her hands.

She turned toward Hairy Arms now, smiled too bright-ly, and gave him her psycho eyes.

He blinked so hard he knocked loose some sand from his lashes. He stepped back, frowning, then walked away.

She took a satisfied bite of chicken. *Another evolution of torture secured.*

She was almost done eating when another visitor dropped by.

Petty Officer Keith Knight.

He sat down across from her.

During his pre-chow brush-down he'd missed a few spots—two silver-dollar pancakes of sand were plastered to the side of his neck. He was holding an apple in his hand

and rolling it as he gave her a thorough perusal. "So a man walks into a library and asks for a book on how to commit suicide. The librarian says, 'Fuck off, you won't bring it back.'" Knight grinned, presenting straight teeth supported by a solid, sand-dappled jaw.

"Sick," she remarked.

He chuckled. "How you holding up?"

Good question. And one she was in no way going to answer. If she started cataloguing her complaints, she'd pay closer attention to them. "Ready to rock," she lied. "You?"

"Livin' the dream."

She almost smirked at his own lie. Or maybe it was the truth. Despite all the physical abuse he'd endured with the rest of them, there was still something spring-coiled about him, like his body hovered on the edge of exploding into violent action.

"I used to do some really extreme shit growing up in Jackson, Wyoming," he told her. "This is like that, only on speed." The apple stopped. "You got any issues, Hayes, I want you to come to me right away. Okay?"

Issues? Why was he mentioning that? Had he overheard Hairy Arms being a pervy jerk? She shot her focus over to the douchebag.

Knight caught the look. He glanced over his shoulder, observed Hairy Arms for a moment, then turned back around. His pupils seemed to narrow in on her. "You need to report something?"

"Nope." She opened her mini carton of milk with a pinch of her fingers.

Knight watched her. He rolled the apple again. "Don't try to be Superwoman and wait till you're on the brink of breaking before coming to me."

"Got it. Right. No sweat." She downed a few glugs of milk. "Thing is, Knight, I don't recall hearing myself ring out this morning."

He exhaled. "You're taking this the wrong way."

"Am I?" She set down the carton. "Have you told the other men on your boat team the same thing?"

"In fact, I did." His mouth tilted. "Minus the Super-woman part." His focus roved over her face, lingering on her turnip-bulb nose.

The man earned credit, at least, for not trying to talk her out of being here.

She thrust her tray aside. "Anything else?"

"No." He stood and peered down on her. "I just hope you've got a damned good reason for doing this."

She shrugged. "Simple enough."

Mr. Dawson had told her this was the challenge of a lifetime, and since when did she ever pass up a challenge? Testing herself was her compulsion, her religion.

She grinned up at Knight. "Wouldn't it be awesome if I actually pull this off?"

CHAPTER THREE

May, eight months ago
Langley, Virginia
CIA Headquarters

"EXCUSE ME, ARE you Miss Justine Hayes?"

Justice's heels clacked as she came to an abrupt halt on top of the CIA's emblem—an American eagle on a blue background—set dead center in the CIA headquarters' foyer.

She hated heels, but Mr. Garcia, the agency exec who'd hired her, hadn't told her what to wear on her first day of work. Low heels plus a nice pair of black slacks and a blue blouse seemed like the safest bet.

She turned around.

Three men were striding toward her, two in white-washed Navy uniforms, each with a white hat tucked under his arm, and one civilian in a perfectly tailored, dark gray suit.

She didn't know any of them. "Yes?"

The suit extended his hand with a smile. His body was slim in a way that made age difficult to gauge. She'd guess mid-forties, even though there wasn't a speck of gray in his neatly trimmed, cinnamon-colored hair.

"I'm Conroy Dawson," he introduced himself. "Owner and CEO of Sevette Security and Investigations."

She shook his hand without reaction. The *security* part was interesting. The name *Dawson* was meaningless.

"This is Lieutenant Adrian Baskin." Dawson gestured at

the younger of the two Naval officers, blond and freckled. "Naval Special Operations Recruit Directorate."

Special Operations *Recruit?* More and more curious. She shook Baskin's hand.

The third of their threesome was a distinguished older man, a splash of gray at each of his dark-haired temples. He had a chest full of medals—*way* more bells and whistles than the young Baskin.

Commander, Naval Special Warfare Command, Rear Admiral Joseph Sherwin, according to Dawson's introduction.

The admiral gave Justice a steely look and didn't offer to shake her hand.

Rude, but also interesting.

"May I help you gentlemen?" She checked the wall clock. She'd made sure to arrive early on her first day, but that was to *arrive early*, not stand around playing guessing games with a trio of stiffs.

"We have a proposition for you," Dawson told her amiably. "Would you mind joining us for a cup of coffee?"

Proposition electrified the hairs on the back of her neck. People used innocuous-sounding words like that just before they asked her to do the type of work her father used to do. *Like father, like daughter* seemed to be the natural assumption made by those who knew about the infamous Grayson Hayes. And it was sort of true.

But only *sort of.*

"I'm sorry, Mr. Dawson," she returned courteously, "but I don't have time for coffee." *Or your dubious shenanigans.* "I'm on my way to work right now."

Dawson's amiable expression remained solidly in place. "That might not be necessary, Miss Hayes, if you would give us a moment of your time. We'd like to make you a job offer." He gestured at the metal detectors guarding the way in. "A better one."

She smiled, polite and patient. "I doubt it." Being a covert operative was probably the only way to keep at bay the boredom that'd been plaguing her ever since she moved out of her father's house of tricks.

Dawson shook his head. "CIA intelligence-gathering techniques would not properly utilize your skillset."

Intelligence gathering… What the hell? Justice quick-checked on the people passing through the foyer. How did Dawson know what she'd been hired to do at the agency? "I'll be working in admin," she informed him in a banal tone.

Dawson's faint smile was knowing. "The job of a CIA covert operative," he went on, anyway, "rests primarily on forming relationships with, shall we say, those who are unsympathetic to the America way of life? Not so with us. Our job would entail *only* clandestinely procuring or destroying information. For someone like you, it's a dream job."

"Someone like me?" she echoed. *Someone who has a very dangerous compulsion?*

"A person with your skillset. Like your father's."

So here we are. Arrived at the dubious shenanigans. As suspected. "Thank you, sir, but I'm not interested." She started for the metal detectors.

She heard Mr. Dawson follow. "Please, Miss Hayes—"

She swung back around. "*Miss Hayes* is about as distaste-ful to me as Jus*tine*. I go by Justice, and I'm sorry you wasted your time, Mr. Dawson. I don't do my father's type of work. I'm legit." And, oh, hadn't she paid for *that*.

"Of course, you are. We"—Dawson indicated the two Navy men—"wouldn't be here if you weren't."

Valid point. "All right," she said. "What's this about? The short version, please."

Dawson hesitated.

The crowd was thinning in the foyer, the sound of footsteps made by various heel types receding, conversations fading away.

Dawson obviously figured he wasn't going to land the coffee date he wanted, so he forged ahead. "Technology is growing increasingly complex, as you're well aware, and this has affected how secrets are hidden and stored. Consequently, intelligence gathering has become a new game—the days of Navy SEALs sweeping mounds of paperwork into knapsacks are over.

"To operate effectively in this new, sophisticated environment, United States Special Operations Forces is creating a program under the heading Special Missions: three units of three—two enlisted led by one officer—plus a helicopter and flight crew. These units will be sent into some of the most secure locations in the world, nearly impossible places to breach, and tasked with technologically advanced intel collection."

Justice dragged her tongue across her lips. *Nearly impossible places to breach…*

A small smile hit Dawson's mouth, a frolicking twitch at one corner suggesting that he knew exactly the carrot he'd just dangled in front of her—steal lots of shit, but *legally.*

Dawson nodded at the admiral. "Admiral Sherwin, as commander of all Special Warfare, is overseeing the military side of standing up these units. I'm the civilian contractor who's been brought in to help get the more technical aspects of the program on its feet. We'd like you to lead one of these Special Missions units, Miss Hayes."

"You'd like me to…?" Her tongue went ungainly. *Lead… What?*

"You're extremely computer savvy, but more to the point, you have an indispensable skill for…shall we say, infiltration?"

Justice nearly snorted. *Diplomatically put.* "I appreciate the compliment, sir, but last I heard, women aren't allowed into Special Operations Forces. *And* I'm not even in the military."

"Correct. You'd have to join the Navy."

She blurted out a laugh. Her father would go apoplectic. Admiral Sherwin stared at her coldly.

Dawson pressed onward. "These units are noncombative. Ideally, Special Missions will only be sent into cleared areas." He straightened his tie. "Think about the opportunity we're truly offering you. There are plenty of female agents in the CIA, but not a single woman has ever worked for Special Operations Forces in the field. If you head up a Special Missions unit, you would hold the distinction of being the first, maybe the sole, woman to crack that inner sanctum. It's the opportunity of a lifetime."

Her heart raced over its next two beats. That would add a nice shine to the Hayes name.

The admiral growled. "She's not in yet, Dawson."

Justice glanced at the admiral, then smiled thinly at Dawson. "There's a catch, isn't there?" There always was.

"Not a catch," Dawson corrected, "rather two requirements. One, you'll have to go through Special Operations training."

She raised her brows. "Which is…?"

Dawson faltered a moment, clearing his throat. "You'll have to graduate from BUD/S."

She had half a mind to choke. "You mean *SEAL* training?"

"You're fit enough," Dawson hastened to assure her. "You were NCAA champion of both the 100-meter and 200-meter sprints in college, with times fast enough to make the U.S. Olympic—"

"I know my own résumé, thank you." Or maybe Dawson was reminding Admiral Sherwin. "The part I don't understand is the need for SEAL training. BUD/S is designed to mold men into warriors, and didn't you just say the Special Missions units will be noncombative?"

"Yes. But…" Dawson's eyes flicked sidelong to Sherwin.

The admiral's expression was stubborn and set, and— *ah*. Now Justice got it. Sherwin wanted the Special Missions program to fail. A means to this end would be to make the members of these new units have to pass the most difficult training program in the world.

"You'll still be going into volatile areas," Dawson reasoned. "You'll need to be prepared for anything." He smoothed a hand down his tie, flattening it to a point at his belt. "But even before BUD/S, you'll have to pass the Special Missions' test."

"Which is?" she asked again.

"It's an obstacle course of sorts but constructed for our specific training needs: half a dozen buildings, multiple objectives, numerous kinds of intel to steal—*if* correctly assessed as valuable—all wrapped in an array of booby traps."

A tide of warmth washed through her pelvis, and her core pulsed a couple of times. *Booby traps? All on the way to stealing stuff?*

"Admiral Sherwin has agreed to offer you the position of Special Missions leader, but *only* if you make it through our obstacle course cleanly." Dawson's playfully twitching smile reappeared, like he knew that what he said next was going to reel her in. "You should know, however, that no one else has made it through without at least one mistake. Not even the men we've already selected to lead the other two teams. No one at all," he repeated quietly.

It was the ultimate *gotcha!*

She drew in a deep breath through her nostrils. "Will I be allowed to use my own tools?"

CHAPTER FOUR

DAWSON ARRANGED TO fly Justice to San Diego, specifically to the town of Oceanside, where the Special Missions Obstacle Course was located in the middle of some extensive desert terrain on the Camp Pendleton Marine Corps Base.

Testing day was an absolute blast!

Kudos to Dawson and his minions—they came up with some extremely tricky stuff for their course: hair-thin, nearly invisible trip wires running through windows, alarms deactivated on a delay, locks with angled insertion points, and more.

She hadn't been so thoroughly challenged in a long time, and *hah!* It was so much fun! When she hopped off the last fake building in a puff of dust and strolled over to the control shack, she was grinning hugely.

Dawson was grinning back, a whole lotta *I knew you could do it!* in his expression.

Admiral Sherwin regarded her flatly, then with a smartly executed military heel pivot, he marched away without a single word of praise.

Pout if you want. She felt too great to care. Times like these she was on solid footing with herself—like she could unequivocally answer a resounding *Yes!* to the question, *Are you worthy of being Grayson Hayes's daughter?*

Dawson gave her hand a congratulatory shake. "Well done, Miss Hayes. I'll draw up the paperwork."

Justice was fast-tracked into the SOF pipeline, but *not*

before first signing a contract guaranteeing her the right to withdraw from her military obligation if she didn't make it into Special Missions. Ending up on a destroyer, planted in front of a computer ciphering endless strings of code if this gig didn't pan out for whatever reason, could be termed the exact opposite of a dream job.

She flew through the entry-level requirements, passing the Physical Screening Test, or PST, with flying colors. The Physical Screening Test required applicants to perform a certain number of sit-ups, push-ups, and pull-ups, plus do a run and a swim to a designated distance within a specific time limit. The C-SORT, the Computerized-Special Operations Resilience Test—basically a psych eval—was a breeze. Finally, she went through MEPS for a general physical and military in-processing.

Once all this rigmarole was secured, she was matriculated to OCS, Officer Candidate School—or boot camp for officers—in Rhode Island.

A few days before she shipped out, she drove from San Diego to Bel Air, California, to have dinner with Dad. As it happened, he wasn't as freaked out about her joining the military as she thought he'd be. He could appreciate the immensity of the challenge she was undertaking. He was the one who'd bred the obsessive need to conquer the unconquerable into her, after all. Tell a Hayes something wasn't doable, and he or she would turn themselves inside out to contradict that—and then would do the undoable.

Officer Candidate School was a trip, basically twelve weeks of drill instructors trying to make recruits go Bambi-eyed by harassing them and assigning them senseless tasks.

Built compact and hard, with faces like icebergs and voices that could be heard over a sold-out Army-Navy game plus the Marine Corps Marching Band playing at the same time, the drill instructors were fearsome men, several positively menacing.

And who would've guessed these guys would be put to shame by the BUD/S instructors? Downright Mary Poppins look-alikes, those OCS drill instructors were by comparison.

At any rate, Justice graduated OCS without much more trouble than a bad case of athlete's foot.

She promptly flew back to San Diego. This time her destination was Coronado Island, a sunny, elegant beach city, with well-manicured palms, lawns, and storefronts. It was a paradise for the comfortably rich who offered but a façade of welcoming tolerance to bikers, beachers, and surfers.

Justice was stashed in PTRR—Physical Training, Rest, and Rehabilitation—for three months of pre-training while she waited to class up at BUD/S. Once she began Basic Underwater Demolition/SEAL, this would put her on a twenty-one-week training path, the program broken into three phases of training, each lasting seven weeks.

She used the time at PTRR to immerse herself fully in military culture so she could embody a true-blue sailor *and* to train her brains out.

Impossible challenge? Hah! It shall be met! By the end of each day, she'd sweated so much she was dizzy. But she was about to go head-to-head with some of the best and strongest men in America.

No amount of working out ever seemed like enough.

The other candidates at PTRR—medical rollbacks from prior BUD/S classes and stashed officers like her—didn't know who she was or what to think about her, so after an initial check-out, they mostly left her alone.

Until word got out that she was The BUD/S Woman.

Then from one day to the next, the men were gaping at her.

Let them stare. Justice had plenty of practice dealing with stares—for her height, her looks, her rack, her athleticism, and for the infamy attached to her family name.

Finally, she was classed up, but before she could even grab her sea bag and walk from one side of the Amphib Base to the other, she hit a brick wall of bureaucracy.

BUD/S officers' quarters didn't have a female head.

The Navy higher-ups were apparently in a tizzy over figuring out how to accommodate Ensign Hayes's bathroom needs in a way that wouldn't potentially earn them a publicity nightmare or a sexual harassment charge.

So while the rest of her classmates went into Basic Orientation, she was assigned a SEAL mentor to teach her the ropes—how to do call-outs, how to get completely wet and sandy, and the like.

Three weeks went by.

The day before First Phase arrived, and she was still tangled up in red tape.

That morning she put in a request to see Captain Miles Eagen, Naval Special Warfare Group One Commander.

By the afternoon, she and her SEAL mentor, Chief Fred Jowdy—a standoffish man, but fair-minded—were led into a bland office, painted the mandatory white, two armless chairs facing an austere steel desk, a row of gray metal filing cabinets behind it.

Captain Eagen was currently in front of an open filing cabinet drawer, fingering through several folders.

He wasn't especially tall, standing a few inches under six feet, but he had the broad shoulders and long, tapered waist of a natural athlete—his torso resembled an upended pyramid balanced on his hips. Whatever he might lack in height, he made up for in sheer impact. He was a man who commanded the space he occupied.

Justice came to attention in front of the captain's desk.

"At ease," Eagen said.

Justice relaxed into parade rest.

Eagen closed the drawer and sat. "What can I do for you, Ensign Hayes?"

"Sir, request permission to join my BUD/S class."

Eagen took a moment to absorb that. He then shifted his focus over to Justice's mentor. "I wasn't aware that Hayes hadn't joined her class." His expression cooled. "Why is that, Fred?"

"Your XO has been handling this, sir."

Eagen's brows slowly lifted.

Justice was *the* first female to go through BUD/S for *the* most important new program SOF would stand up this century, and his XO was dealing with everything.

"I see." Eagen gestured at his door. "Ask Commander Sachs to step in here, Fred."

"Sir." Justice's mentor left.

She waited silently in parade rest, gazing at the captain's filing cabinet.

A moment later Chief Jowdy returned with an officer wearing overly pressed camouflage BDUs, his buzzed ash-blond hair cut into a triangle on top of his head.

The XO and Jowdy came to a stop on either side of her.

Eagen leaned back in his chair. "What's the snag with Ensign Hayes classing up, Harold?"

The XO laid out the bathroom issue.

"How many officers are in Class 684?" Eagen asked.

"Two. Three"—Harold Sachs, the XO, nodded at Justice—"including Ensign Hayes."

"Not a lot of personnel to juggle around one bathroom, Harold. Do you think we could trust in three college-educated individuals' ability to figure out a rotating bathroom schedule?"

"Yes, sir," the XO said after the barest pause. "It's just that the people over at PR are—"

"Are not in command of this base." The captain snapped his chair to an erect position and addressed her. "Ensign Hayes, are you comfortable sharing a bathroom with two men, as long you are provided with appropriate privacy when you need to use the damned thing?"

"Yes, sir." She met the captain's gaze. "I will sign a document to that effect if required, sir."

Eagen expelled something between a snort and a grunt. "That just might be required. Very well, Hayes, pack your gear and be here at zero-five-hundred tomorrow. I'll accompany you to the officers' barracks myself."

"Yes, sir." Heat flushed through her, then a wave of cold. Excitement or nerves? Probably both.

Holy shit, she was heading to BUD/S.

"Dismissed."

She did a sharp about-face.

"Hang back a minute, Harold," she heard Captain Eagen say to his XO as she strode out of his office with Jowdy.

CHAPTER FIVE

THE BUD/S OFFICERS' barracks consisted of two four-man bedrooms grouped around a community room and a small, open kitchen area.

The community room—located across about twenty feet of open space from the main door—was carpeted in serviceable brown ugly and outfitted with a TV, an L-shaped black faux leather couch that sagged in the middle, a square glass pedestal coffee table, and a ceiling fan, which was retired from use in the winter months. A sliding glass door was tucked into the right corner of the room, just beyond the couch.

To the left of the carpeted space was the open kitchen area built on a four-by-six rectangle of gray linoleum. What color the floor was before thousands of SEAL candidates had tramped over it was anyone's guess. A countertop about the size of an air hockey table pointed outward toward the open space. Behind it, facing the wall, was a fridge/freezer and a small oven topped by a four-burner stove. Past the kitchen countertop, there was a four-seater dinette set.

The bedrooms and bathroom were located off the main entrance. The latter smelled of urinal cakes and would have to be shared by those with testicles and those—*oh, my*—without.

The two class officers had clearly been warned of their new roommate's impending arrival. They were waiting at attention this side of the kitchen area, wearing the training uniform of the day: multi-pocketed camouflage pants, a white T-shirt, and black combat boots.

"At ease," Captain Eagen told them.

The two men settled into parade rest, widening their stances and tucking their clasped hands into the small of their backs.

Both of them shifted from a forward stare over to Justice to check her out, and—

Pa-zow!

Clearly she wasn't what they'd expected—probably some sort of ManCur.

Man-wise, she *was* very muscular.

Her recent months of working out extra hard had packed on an additional ten pounds of sheer strength, especially on her upper body. But she was tall, and so her muscles were long and graceful, and that meant, in fact, *no*, she didn't look manly.

And as far as being a dog went…

Not even on her worst day.

Her breasts—a solid C cup—and the feminine shape of her features didn't leave the nature of her sex in question.

The one introduced as Ensign Brayden Street noted her attributes by trying to swallow his own tongue.

Ensign Rudy Dunbar flushed lobster red and blurted out, "I have a girlfriend."

Captain Eagen was in Dunbar's face in two strides. "Is there a reason you felt compelled to inform us of that, Ensign Dunbar?"

"No, sir, I…" Dunbar's eyes rolled around in their sockets like dice in a Yahtzee cup. "I-I…" Any minute the poor guy was going to need CPR. "No, sir!"

The CO stepped back, his brows down. "Assign Hayes to a boat team."

"Yes, sir." Street tugged a laminated card out of his rear

pocket. "We did a height-line yesterday." He glanced at her. "How tall are you?"

"Five-eleven."

Street consulted his card. "Keith Knight's crew." He nodded approval. "He's my half brother. He'll take good care of you."

"Is there some reason," Eagen asked coolly, "that you think Ensign Hayes needs to be *taken care of*, Ensign Street?"

Street stilled. "No, sir." He slowly slid the height-line card back into his pocket and gave her an uneasy look.

She edged up one side of her mouth. Like, *we're cool.*

"Ensign Hayes is here to *train*," Eagen emphasized. "She's an officer, yes, but not here in a leadership role, so it's the job of you two men to set an example for the others to follow. You see petty rivalries starting up, shut 'em down. Ensign Hayes isn't in competition with any of you candidates. She won't be heading into SpecOps, only The Missus."

Justice somehow managed not to roll her eyes. Yeah, *The Missus.* The SPECWAR community had already adopted a pejorative term for the new unit. After all, pecking order and hierarchy must be maintained. Everyone needed to know exactly where they stood at all times. No one could be allowed to forget that Special Missions—or "The Missus"—sat below Special Operations.

The captain scowled at Street and Dunbar. "You two bone this up, and you'll be cleaning the latrine with your own livers. Understood?"

"Yes, sir!"

Dunbar's throat pumped like a beer tap pulling on the last dregs of a keg.

"Carry on," Eagen snapped.

"Sir, yes, sir!"

Eagen left.

No one moved until the door *clicked* shut.

Then the only things they moved were their eyes.

The three of them darted glances at each other.

During the check-out, Justice noted that Street was one helluva handsome guy, even with his hair all but sheared off.

Rudy Dunbar...not so much. His features were squashed together around the rather largish focal point of his nose. It gave him the appearance of permanently sucking on a lemon. He was shorter than she was, running about five-eight.

A full thirty seconds went by.

"Well." Justice adjusted the duffel bag strap on her shoulder. "Awkward, anyone?"

Another beat passed, then a grin split across Street's face.

A dimple winked at her. *Oh, Lord.*

"Fuck." Dunbar scrubbed a hand over his brow. "I think my sphincter swallowed itself."

"Nice, Dunbar," Street drawled.

"Hey, the captain said he wants us to treat her like just one of the guys." Dunbar brought his focus back to her. "And I said what I said about having a girlfriend to make you feel better, okay? Like I wouldn't think of you, uh, that way."

"No worries," she said. Although Dunbar would've been more convincing if he hadn't made the explanation directly to her breasts. She indicated the two bedroom doors behind her with a backward lean of her head. "So which one's mine?"

Street pointed to the door closest to the main entrance. "There." He walked past her, slipping her duffel off her shoulder. "I'll show you."

She quickly grabbed the strap back. "I've got it, thanks."

Street stopped. "Ah." He smiled as he let go. "Oops."

He opened the door to her bedroom and held it for her.

She flipped on the lights. The walls were painted the base-typical stark white, the floor tiled in gray. Next to the same wall as the door was a dresser and one set of bunk beds. Across from the door and jammed in the left corner of the room was another set of bunks—this one had a metal desk at its butt end. The desk had a stack of three drawers on one side, a metal leg on the other. A nightstand was positioned in between the two bunks.

Justice walked in and dumped her duffel by the desk.

Street observed her from the doorway.

He seemed to fill the frame, although he wasn't especially bulky. He had the build of a triathlete—athletically multi-talented. His body could probably do a lot of things very well, and, *hmm*. A thought best avoided.

"Man, you… The instructors are going to try and eat you alive." Street gave her a head-to-toe appraisal.

It was a clinical assessment of her capabilities to withstand such a devouring, and also… Not. But at least he wasn't being overly blatant about his attraction to her, so he earned a few points.

"So, what brings you here?" He chuckled as soon as the words came out of his mouth, probably realizing it sounded like a trite pickup line.

"We should muster now, shouldn't we?" No offense to Street but getting chummy with a man who would be stripping naked and showering right next door to her bedroom didn't seem like the brightest idea.

"Uh, yeah." He glanced over his shoulder. "Right."

It was still dark outside when they exited into the early morning, only a thin line of whitish pre-dawn stretching the length of the horizon. Shreds of fine mist hung over the base, and a breeze blew in from the Pacific Ocean, carrying briny traces of seaweed and also a dry desert scent hinting at the Santa Ana headed their way.

Justice and her two roomies trotted over to a large dirt hole known as "the pits."

The candidates were lined up in formation next to it, four men wide and as many back as it took to hold the entire class—in this case, one hundred fifty-four candidates.

"Keith!" Brayden called out.

A man with K-N-I-G-H-T stenciled across the back of his T-shirt broke from the ranks and jogged over.

"This is Ensign Justine Hayes," Street introduced her.

Knight was her height, although it was difficult to believe he was. The breadth of his shoulders probably created the illusion that he was taller, layers of muscle straining against his T-shirt in hard slabs—he was more thickly built than his brother Brayden. Although...maybe it was also the energy pouring off him making him seem so much bigger.

Knight reached out to shake her hand, some of the dark stubble on his head glinting under a haloed building light.

A strong grip accompanied by direct eye contact.

Petty Officer Keith Knight was a man who knew how to check out a woman's chest with only his peripheral vision. A rare specimen, this one. He should be studied in a lab.

"So the rumors are true," he said, his smile cutting deep grooves into both sides of his mouth.

"I'm afraid so," she returned.

The rest of the class watched the exchange avidly, all expressions represented: shock, indifference, disgust, lust, anger...and, of course, there was always the requisite super asshole.

"Hey, look! That sailor comes with her own buoys!"

Some of the other men snickered, while sour-faced Ensign Dunbar stalked off to find the culprit.

A muscle in Street's cheek jumped. "Hayes," he continued to Keith, "is going to be on your boat team. She'll be an extra," he added quickly. "You won't lose any of your regular seven men."

"Roger that."

"And it's Justice," she clarified. "When I hear Justine, I want to punch a screwdriver into my ear."

"Duly noted," Knight said with a low chuckle, then glanced at the brightening horizon. "Let's do this," he added to Brayden.

Street called to the class, "Line up!" Then to her, "Come stand next to me."

She fell in where Street indicated, nodding a greeting to the arched-nostril guy next to her.

They marched off at double-time, Street calling the cadence.

"To my left!"

"HEY!"

"To my left!"

"HOOYAH!"

"Pumped up!"

"PUMPED UP!"

"Hey!"

"HOOYAH!"

"Motivated!"

"MOTIVATED!"

"Driven!"

"DRIVEN!"

"Hey!"

"HOOYAH!"

"Bust it out!"

"BUST IT OUT!"

"Hooyah!"

With a final bellowed "HOOYAH!" they each found a pair of white-painted flipper-prints to stand on and came to attention.

Directly in front of them on a wooden dais stood two

instructors: one with a mustache—Hill—the other wearing a ball cap—Chief Tanner.

Both were glaring at her.

The instructors are going to try and eat you alive.

They weren't going to be nice to her, no. Nor did she harbor the hope they would be particularly fair. But she hadn't expected quite the level of animosity radiating from the two.

Hill came off the dais on a direct rampage for her, his jaws bunching into thick knots.

Beside her, Brayden Street hissed something.

Under the heat of Hill's vicious glare and his unbridled charge, her throat rapidly squeezed down to a circumference that prevented comfortable airflow. Keeling over in the first two minutes of standing on the grinder would be one bummer of an embarrassment. But if she did, she did. Because the hell if she was going to do anything visible to check the problem with her throat.

Like swallowing.

Hill slammed to a stop in front of her, leaving no more than an inch of space between them. "Do you got 'nads, Hayes?"

She stared blindly at the bridge of the instructor's nose and kept her own counsel on the matter. Because, yes, biologically speaking, she did have gonads. They were her ovaries. Probably Hill wouldn't appreciate her pointing out this scientific fact.

"No one without a set of nuts is going to be in *my* SOF." Hill's mustache spasmed like a caterpillar superglued to his upper lip and not too fond of the scenery. "You hear me?"

They all knew she could hear him. He was directly in front of her and yelling.

Proper response? "Hooyah, Instructor!" she shouted.

Sneering, Instructor Hill called up to the dais, "Let's drum her out of our Navy right now, Bobby."

Nodding, Tanner scrutinized her through the narrow slits of his lids. "Lotsa places for sand to get into on a female." He crossed his arms. "Lots."

"Damned right," Hill agreed caustically, then he thundered at the class, "Get wet and sandy!"

And so it began…

Until her Sand In The Vagina was epic, and they were finally secured for chow.

Things will be better after lunch…

Not even close.

CHAPTER SIX

THE WHOLE THING about Justice not looking like a dog even on her worst day?

She was going to do a take-back on that.

After her run-in with the apple-bearing Keith at lunch, she'd jogged to her barracks room to change her T-shirt—the one her abused nose had bled all over—then went to the bathroom to pee and deal with the sand load in her crotch.

She'd made the mistake of looking in the bathroom mirror.

Her nose was a walnut, dark brown and lumpy, her sand-tortured eyes rimmed in red, her complexion as a whole, pasty, though her lips were especially white, and her hair was… It was a disaster, snarled up with several different species of seaweed, her half-bangs matted to her brow.

This morning she'd secured her hair to her head with about twenty small, metal snap barrettes, first twisting the length of her hair into a rope, then clipping it, inch by inch, into a bun. Her contraption had proved sound—her bun had managed to stay intact through this morning's beatings. But it was going to take forever to tug it all apart in the shower tonight.

She would save herself a good deal of time and effort if she cut off her hair, but short hair coupled with her height and physique *would* make her look manly. Her appearance generally wasn't her first order of business, but she wasn't completely immune to such things either.

Plus, hadn't Demi Moore shaved her head in *G.I. Jane*?

Justice hated to be unoriginal.

After making a quick pit stop in the community room to give her muscles a rubdown, she re-mustered on the grinder.

Tanner and Hill were back on the dais, and if possible, the two instructors looked even more pissed than they did this morning. Steam was dribbling out of Chief Tanner's ears, and Hill had gnawed off half his mustache.

It was Hill who stomped to the edge of the platform. "Not *one* candidate rang out before lunch," he gnashed at them. "This has never happened in all of BUD/S First Phase history."

Tanner stalked off the dais, padlocking Justice.

"Oh, fuck me," she hissed.

Brayden stiffened.

She braced herself, bolstering her courage with one of her dad's adages. *If you have to, fake it till you make it.*

Tanner strode up to her and rammed the bill of his cap against her forehead again. "*You*, bleeder, are seriously fucking with the proper evolution of my program." He showed her his teeth, not so pretty when bared like fangs. "No one wants to quit in front of a female."

Well, what the hell did he want her to do about it? Stick a finger down her throat and barf up some estrogen?

Up on the dais, Hill lifted a megaphone to his mouth. "We will not secure this next round of PT," he trumpeted, his voice metallic and shrill, "until someone rings out! Man your boats, you worthless pieces of shit!"

The entire class hit the beach at a run, sprinting for the flotilla of rubber boats parked on the sand.

"Knight's crew to me!" Keith yelled.

She charged for her boat team leader.

"Grab the firmest boat possible," Keith ordered them,

breathing heavily. "A floppy boat is fucked to carry on your head. The firmer the better."

"That's what she said," a voice chirped.

Justice rolled her eyes. *Great.*

Pervy Hairy Arms was on her boat team.

A LOT COULD be learned about a man by spending too much time with him under a waterlogged, unstable rubber boat.

That was "Land Portage."

The evolution required a seven-man boat crew—in Justice's case, eight—to carry a thirteen-foot, one-hundred-seventy-pound rubber IBS, *Inflatable Boat, Small*, on their heads over every imaginable kind of terrain: hard-packed sand, sand so soft it swallowed combat boots, berm sand on an incline, and knee-deep water.

Pervy Hairy Arms—Brad Ziegler—for all the boundary issues he suffered from, proved his worth with his Iron Man leg muscles. He was a workhorse under that punishing boat...although, unfortunately, the noises he made when he strained sounded like sex noises.

Coincidence?

Dog Bone, a round-faced, gentle giant—Justice's height but twice as wide—was also a rock.

Zack Kilgour was mouth-seamed silent through every hardship. He had the beady stare of a sniper. 'Course he'd also *told* them he wanted to be a sniper in the Teams.

"Hold the boat straps at the base, dammit! You gotta pull forward!"

This came from Travis Chalmers, a former firefighter, who apparently knew everything there was to know about how to succeed at BUD/S and was all about telling them how to do those things correctly.

Every time Chalmers berated them, the bones in

Knight's jaw stood out extra prominently.

Keith was showing his stripes as a great leader, keeping his crew in line, properly rotating everyone through different positions on the boat—except for her; she stayed at the easiest spot in the rear—all the while dealing with his own pain.

"Get your head back under the fucking boat!" Keith growled this order for about the hundredth time at Appletini.

Yeah, just as Chief Tanner had predicted, Seamen Brantley Shaw was a pussy.

When the weight of the boat became too much—and when wasn't it?—Shaw would lean his head out. The moment he did this, the pressure on Justice's head, *everyone's* head and spine, increased exponentially.

Her cranium crackled, and her cervical vertebrae compressed. Her teeth splintered while her eyes bugged out. "Boat ducking," she decided after the first two times of experiencing its repercussions, was the worst possible sin a man could commit against his teammates—cardinal, mortal, and venal sins all wrapped into one reprehensible act.

Her own spinal cord would snap in two before she ducked boat.

"Quit already," English-Fucking-Tea seethed at her, "would you?"

"You mind your program, Hornsby," Keith grated. "Hayes will mind hers."

"You're not keeping together!" Chalmers bawled. "Everyone has to run in unison!"

A low snarl rumbled out of Knight.

Appletini groaned and leaned out.

Maybe *he* should stick a finger down *his* throat and upchuck some estrogen.

English-Fucking-Tea cursed, "Fuck this!"

Hairy Arms went, "Oh, oh, oh, ah, ah, ah."

And the sun steadily sank toward the horizon.

THE SKY WAS streaked with the orange and rose hues of impending sunset when English-Fucking-Tea's sixth "Fuck this!" heralded his actual departure.

"I'm done, Knight." Hornsby bowed out from under the boat—leaving the rest of them staggering to compensate—and clomped over to the bell.

Three rings.

Clang, clang, clang.

It might as well have been a cowboy call to head out west.

A stampede ensued.

Hornsby's DOR had apparently cleared the way for others to Drop On Request.

Justice wasn't exactly sure how that worked. It must be written in some deeply entombed definition of manhood that as long as a guy wasn't the first one to paint his balls pink in front of a beautiful woman, he wasn't an unmanly squish. Being second was okay. Being tenth or fortieth…as long as he wasn't *first*.

Really, guy rules were so asinine.

Twenty-two men rang out in rapid succession, decreasing Class 684's numbers to one hundred thirty-two.

The boat team leaders scrambled to reorganize their teams. Height-line cards were out, and the leaders were shouting back and forth to each other.

"Colgate over here!"

"You get Parker!"

The teams were redistributed.

A new candidate to join theirs was a handsome Black man, name of Boyd. His shoulders were wide and sloping like a boxer's, and a small mole resided near his upper right lip—"beauty mark" on a woman—that drew attention to his ready smile. He reminded Justice of a guy she'd dated in high school—yes, clear down to the mole. Unfortunately, her high school crush bolted her senior year, when she turned beautiful. He was one of those guys whose terror-lock lasted forever.

The class jogged up and down the beach for another ten minutes, then Instructor Hill ordered them to secure their boats.

In college Justice dated an Irish guy—complete with the cool accent—who she didn't have anything in common with, but she couldn't stop seeing because he was so damned good at oral sex. Whenever he went down on her, she came lots and lots.

One time, it was just *crazy*, like, a dozen times right in a row...but that mega-multiple was nothing compared to the pleasure of removing the IBS from her head.

And it left her just as weak-kneed.

She tottered around in the sand, spitting out a mouthful of bile. Her eyeballs rounded up toward her hairline. *Uh-oh...*

A hand grabbed her upper arm and steadied her.

Knight.

He'd come up behind her.

He released her almost immediately, so she didn't have time to think about him helping her...determine *what* to think...figure out even *how* to think. The five-hour crush of the IBS had suffocated the electrical impulses in her neurons. Like a skipping record player, her brain seemed to be processing only every third input of environmental data.

"Shoulder to shoulder!" Chief Tanner commanded.

The candidates gave each other *what-the-fuck?* looks. They were going to have to endure "surf torture"?

"No way," someone breathed.

Yes way. This was BUD/S. Just because Instructor Hill said they *wouldn't* end before someone rang out, didn't mean they *would*.

A four-wheel-drive ambulance drove onto the sand berm.

They all veered around to watch it park.

Ambulance...

Never a good sign.

"SHOULDER TO SHOULDER!" the class repeated as they staggered down to the surf in a line.

"Lock arms!"

"LOCK ARMS!"

Knight offered Justice his arm.

She blinked at his muscular forearm, unable to figure out what to do. It was just so funny, seeing Keith's arm proffered to her, like he was asking her to dance.

"Forward, march!"

"Come on, Hayes," Keith urged her.

She linked up with him. On her other side, she hooked arms with the high school crush lookalike Black guy.

"FORWARD, *MARCH!*"

They plodded into the surf in a wavering line. Hisses and curses competed for decibel ranking with the crash of the waves. The unseasonably warm weather hadn't translated to the ocean. The temperature sat in the low- to mid-fifties: cold as fuck.

Justice's toes convulsed and her skin shrank.

They waded farther in, water rising above their waists. Icy needles pierced her stomach and crotch.

"Well, there go my balls," someone gritted, "frozen completely the fuck off."

"Stop!" Tanner instructed.

"STOP!"

Next should have come, "Take seats!" but Hill and

Tanner had sensed weakness in the first stampede of DORs, and they were maliciously gleeful for more.

"About-face!"

The entire line of candidates groaned.

Tanner and Hill were upping the torture by forcing the candidates to sit with their backs toward the ocean—this meant they wouldn't be able to see incoming waves and so couldn't prepare for the hits.

Justice gave the gleaming ball of the sun sitting puddled in the Pacific Ocean one last, longing glance, then turned around. A wave crashed into her lower back, shoving her forward with the rest of her class. Her tired legs moved in a strange underwater waddle-walk.

Her teeth started to clack together. *Already*. And she hadn't even sat all the way down in the water yet.

"Take seats!"

Maybe if she did something spectacular, like vomit up a smoke jumper in full fire-retardant Kevlar, the instructors would secure this exercise immediately.

No such luck.

CHAPTER SEVEN

"TAKE SEATS!"

They sat.

Wham!

A wave slammed into them. They ass-skidded around on the sandy bottom.

Up and down the line men coughed and choked.

Wham!

Now Justice didn't close her mouth in time and gulped saltwater down her windpipe. She wheezed and gasped.

"Listen, everyone," Chalmers called out in his know-it-all tone. "I can tell when the waves are coming, okay?" He was seated on Knight's other side.

Wham! Another wave.

Sand filled Justice's eyelids.

"Watch for my signal!" Chalmers put out his hand, pinkie and thumb stretched outward, and made a swimming-fish motion with it.

Two seconds later—*wham!*

Chalmers hadn't signaled the wave.

"Nice one, Chalmers," someone snarked.

"No, no, I got it, just—"

Wham!

Seawater surged up to their chins. They sloshed and bumped.

Chalmers did his swimming-fish signal again.

"Put your damned hand down," Knight bit out. "I can't

stay linked with you when you keep lifting your fucking hand."

Wham! Wham! Wham!

The instructors finally called them out.

Not to stop, though. *Oh, no.* That would be nice. That would be Reasonable Man thinking.

Two corpsmen hiked down from the ambulance to med-check them for hypothermia.

The medic who stopped in front of Justice examined her pupils with a penlight.

Justice's eyes were so full of sand, she could barely blink, and her teeth were chattering so hard it was like they were trying to escape her mouth.

"What's your name?"

"Ensign Hayes."

"Where are you?"

"In my own backyard, Aunt Em."

The corpsman met her gaze.

Justice smiled shakily. "One can always wish."

Back into the surf they went. The sky was now an orchid purple, stars beginning to peek out.

The pain was almost out-of-body…

Ring. Ring. Ring.

Seven more men DOR'd, and finally, *finally*, the instructors secured their remaining one hundred twenty-five for evening chow.

They humped to the decontamination shower and hobbled through the spray—like going through a car wash for the hygienically challenged.

Which they all were.

From there Justice headed directly to the mess hall.

Most of the other candidates went to the enlisted barracks to put on dry clothes before eating, but she didn't have that luxury. By the time she untangled her hair, showered, and changed, the chow hall would be closed.

She chose a burger this time—using a knife and fork seemed way beyond her current capabilities—and slogged over to her lone table. She sat carefully, aware of sensitive places rubbed raw by sand.

Bite.

Chew.

Swallow.

She hunched over the table, water steadily dripping off her hair and nose onto her tray. She concentrated very intently on eating. It wasn't going so well. The tendons in her jaw had gone slack from all the teeth chattering.

Gradually other candidates roamed into the cafeteria. The noise increased, but not by much, as if none of them had enough juice left in them to talk.

A man sat down across from her. "Patch 'em up time," he said to her.

She closed her eyes—*ouch*—then opened them again and inched her chin up to see who dared.

Keith Knight.

He was fresh and clean, *fucker*, and it was odd to see him looking so appealing. She was used to seeing him dirty and wrecked...except for this morning. This morning he'd seemed attractive, but the lighting was poor.

Here and now, under the mess hall's bright lights, Keith was showing off a strong outdoorsman's face, his features chiseled into tough lines by wind and weather. Not in a craggy way, but in a ruggedly awesome way. It worked on him. Very nicely. What hadn't changed from morning to evening was the aggressive energy rolling off him. He carried himself like he constantly expected a punch to come his way and planned to stay on his feet no matter how brutal the hit.

"You should change out of those wet clothes," he told her. "You're shivering."

She slashed a smile at him. It felt grotesque on her mouth. It no doubt was. Seaweed was probably hanging from her teeth. "Want something?"

"Patch 'em up time," he repeated.

As if that was supposed to mean something to her.

"You've got a cut on your back," Knight informed her. "Probably from when Instructor Hill stomped on you this morning on the grinder. It's been oozing blood all day." He waved a box at her. It had a red cross on the lid. It was a first aid kit. "I can bandage it for you."

She laughed. The noise sounded like a chainsaw going down a garbage disposal. A new sound. "No."

He considered her, busying his tongue in his mouth for a moment. "If you're wondering if I offered other team members the same thing, I did. Ziegler had a cut on his shoulder I patched up." Knight gestured in the general direction of her back. "You can't reach the wound yourself."

"I'm not lifting my shirt up in the middle of the mess hall, Knight."

Keith's brows rose, then he chuckled. "We're talking about your *back*, Hayes. It's nothing we're not all going to see when you hit poolside." Deep lines of amusement played at the corners of his mouth. "Unless you plan on going through Pool Comp in a tank."

Oh, such a funny guy. What the comedian didn't realize was that no way in hell was she letting him touch her. Not with her on the verge. Of what, she couldn't tell exactly. Not of hysteria. She'd never suffered a hysterical moment in her life. Not of tears. She didn't cry, either—or rarely did. She just felt a weird, on-the-verge-of-something tension inside her, like her body had broken down about an hour ago, and her mind hadn't caught up yet—but any minute it would.

"All right," Keith said. "Let's go to the officers' quarters, and I can—"

"No."

Keith set the first aid kit on the table and rested his hand on it. "You know why SEALs call themselves Team Guys, Hayes? Because we're a team. You're not going to make it through this if you go it alone."

She ripped a vicious bite out of her burger. He didn't think she *wanted* to be a team? She'd left everything she had on the grinder today trying to prove herself to the others, but no one had bothered to let her know she'd passed muster and made it into the club.

Did they, Knight?

Swallowing the lump of bread and meat, she stood abruptly. The backs of her knees hit the bench, and she almost tipped over onto her ass. She stepped over the bench. "*I'm* not the one failing to be a team player, Knight."

He peered up at her. "No?"

She turned sharply and stalked out of the mess hall.

AN HOUR AND a half later she was clean.

She'd taken a long, hot shower, which helped to relieve some of her muscle cramps, but unfortunately also softened up other things.

Like her will and determination and strength.

Now it felt like there was a gushy pile of rawness inside her, oozing up and trying to take over. She was holding it down with both hands and both feet and maybe a knee, but some of it still squished up through her fingers.

Sleep it off. That's what she needed to do. *Just sleep.*

She prepped for the ten-foot trip from the bathroom to her bedroom by pinning her wet hair into a loose bun—no one was going to see her hair down during her time at BUD/S—and putting a bra on under her T-shirt—no one was going to see her braless while she was at BUD/S.

She set off, trudging toward—

"Hey." Street materialized in front of her with a big, friendly smile. "Rudy and I went to the Surf Mart and bought ice cream." He balanced a gallon of Dreyer's on his fingertips. "Rocky Road. We weren't sure what flavor you like, but figured everyone likes chocolate, right? Dunbar wanted to go for something minty for you, but, you know, it didn't seem very SPECWAR." He laughed.

She stared at him. His laughter was allowing a second dimple out. Apparently the dominant one showed itself with only a smile, while the secondary one...*crap*.

She couldn't handle this right now.

Screw Brayden's stupid-ass dimples. What was she supposed to do with dimples when she was barely holding down a ton of raw glop and hovering on some kind of verge? Dimples were for a *woman* to admire, maybe even lust after, and she wasn't even female anymore. Not here. She was...she was...

Frowning, Brayden lowered the ice cream container. "Hey, are you okay?"

She swallowed, hearing the moisture in her own throat. Sentences formed. Not a single one was coherent.

His concern deepening, Brayden reached out a hand. He probably meant to give her an encouraging pat on the shoulder, but she bowed out of it.

His expression froze.

"I just need to hit the rack, Street."

His expression unfroze and immediately turned Nice Guy sympathetic.

Her heart lurched past her defenses and rolled into a slow somersault of longing. *Wonderful.* She needed comforting looks from Street about as much as she needed Knight touching her.

Street gestured at the sliding glass door. "Why don't you come out on the deck, sit and stare at the beach for a bit?

Down some extra calories and decompress. Today was an extremely shitty day."

She clutched her bag of shower supplies in taut fists. She was reasonably sure that spending time with Mr. Nice Guy would flood her with so much raw glop it would make Hurricane Katrina look like a leaky bathtub. And in addition to not seeing her hair down and her breasts in a braless state, no one was getting a gander of her raw glop during her time at BUD/S.

Be like a duck was another one of her dad's maxims.

Translation: no matter how frantically you might be paddling underwater, above the surface you should appear as nothing but gliding serenity.

Most would say, *Never let 'em see you sweat.* But Dad liked to be colorful.

"Thanks," she said. "But I'm going to have to take a rain check." She edged past Street and aimed for her bedroom door.

"Hey," he called after her. "Your back is bleeding."

She closed her eyes and cursed under her breath.

Crashing into her bedroom, she fumbled with her bra strap, trying to unhook it, then gave up.

She collapsed face-first into her pillow, bringing day one of BUD/S First Phase to a miserable conclusion.

Chapter Eight

THE REST OF the week was just as miserable.

The morning bugle would sound Reveille, and whoever remained of Class 684 would muster on the grinder and stare with dull inevitability into the distance against the instructors' predictable first order of the day.

Get wet and sandy!

After that, more inevitable would commence; they would PT until all their tongues were hanging out.

Continuous rounds of Land Portage—Appletini relentlessly fucking them over by ducking boat—were followed by more grinder PT and surf torture—Chalmers relentlessly annoying them with his fish-waggle hand signal—interspersed with classroom lectures.

In the classroom, they all struggled not to earn the instructors' wrath by dozing off.

Sometimes, in the middle of a lesson, the instructors would combat the candidates' ennui by PTing them indoors. Instead of saving them from the cold, this punished them in a new way. The steam wafting off their sweaty bodies would permeate the small space with humidity and make it nearly impossible to breathe.

Get wet and sandy! would be called out, again and again, making it so all evolutions were conducted with sand packed into ears, eyes, ass cracks, and, for Justice, her labia. By day three, she was coating her vagina and nipples with Vaseline. This attracted more sand but cut down on the actual chafing.

During it all, whenever the class was about to be recovered from an exercise, the instructors would drill them through *another* set and always blame Justice's incompetence.

It was colossally unfair.

She might not be at the top of the class, but she damn well wasn't at the bottom, either.

She stored the unfairness away and kept slogging.

Knight kept her under constant surveillance.

Street watched her too, half the time looking like he wanted to give her a big hug, and the other half the time like he wanted to give her a big hug…but for a different reason.

At the end of every day, muscles throbbing, weak with exhaustion, soaked and half-frozen from surf torture, she would plod to the mess hall and grab a sandwich or a burger or something else portable to eat on the way back to her barracks room.

Private shower time had become her favorite part of the day. Hot water. Sand removal. Alone time. Pep talks. After her shower, she would chat briefly with Street or Dunbar, then close herself inside her bedroom and study her hacker books. Or sleep.

You're not going to make it through this if you go it alone.

Right.

Still waiting, Knight—to hear a fellow teammate holler an inspiring *Get some!* or to receive a *you-got-this!* back-slap. Until then, she was going to *mind her own program*, as Knight once said to do, and *embrace the suck*, which was another one of Knight's wise old sayings.

The man was full of gold nuggets.

Friday arrived—testing day.

The morning kicked off with the Obstacle Course, an evolution Justice should've absolutely crushed. Her whole life had been one big obstacle course, climbing buildings, swinging from rafters, and slipping through tight spaces, not to mention that running was her forte. But she let herself be bounced around and nearly trampled by the horde of other candidates and ended up with a time in the bottom third.

All candidates below the top third were put on the "Goon Squad" and received extra love from the instructors.

"Push 'em out!"

Justice and her fellow shamefaced bottom-two-thirders dropped to do push-ups while the top performers sprinted off to the next evolution: Timed Swim.

After the Goon Squad was done with their push-ups, they joined the others at the surf.

Candidates for Timed Swim were paired based on their entering Physical Screening Test scores.

Street and Knight were the top two, so the brothers were given the lead position.

Justice's PST score had earned her the fourth spot—an amazing place to hold in this crowd. She was put with Donnie Cogan, a guy off Brayden's boat team, which meant he was tall.

He was less than thrilled by the pair-up, probably figuring Justice's lackluster O-course time would translate to the Timed Swim. And since swim buddies weren't allowed to get farther than six feet away from each other, her failure would be his.

The instructors inspected everyone's wetsuits, fins, and gear, then set the class loose with a "Bust 'em!"

They dove in.

The Timed Swim route ran parallel to the beach one nautical mile north, up to a collection of large rocks at the historic Hotel Del Coronado with its recognizable red, conical roofs, then one mile back south to the start point. Swim pairs were required to do the combat sidestroke facing each other, one man pointing toward shore—the guide—the other aimed out to sea. The most efficient pairs periodically switched places—the guide expended more energy—and Justice and Cogan decided their rotation before setting out.

They rocked it.

By the turnaround point, they had progressed to third place. Halfway back to the start, they were in second, close enough to the lead pair to hear Knight and Street arguing.

Brayden was currently in the guide spot, and Knight was complaining, "This isn't String Lake back home, Bray. You've got to compensate for the waves."

Brayden glared at his brother. "Don't fucking tell me how to swim, Keith."

"I'm not fucking telling you how to swim. I'm fucking telling you how to navigate. If you veer too far toward shore, we—Shit!"

Yeah, heh-heh. Justice and Cogan had caught up. The two of them gave it their all, but ultimately weren't able to take Knight and Street.

Still. Second place was very respectable.

Splashing out of the surf, Justice smiled at Cogan. "We almost had 'em."

Cogan responded by flatly staring at her breasts, then hiking off to the decon shower.

She stared at Cogan's retreating back and felt her chest tighten. What the hell did it take to win with these guys?

Putting her head down, she stalked for the mess hall. *Did it matter?* She'd spent her whole life on the perimeter of normalcy—as the girl raised without a mother, as the daughter of an infamous cat burglar. Loner status was her comfort zone—right?—and she'd be damned if she was going to let the opinion of a bunch of men who suffered from a hyper-secretion of testosterone needle her.

That evening she grabbed a BLT in the chow hall and

did her usual—after a long, hot shower, she closed herself inside her bedroom and slapped open a hacker book.

Elbows propped on her desk, she listened to a group of candidates gathering in the community room, getting ready to head out on the town and party.

A knock sounded.

"Yeah," she called out, spinning her chair toward the entrance.

The door opened on Street.

He was wearing civvies, khaki pants, dark shoes, and a blue polo shirt that turned his eyes so aqua they looked like they'd been stolen off an idol to the gods. His hair had grown out over the past week, and the rich, tawny gold—though still ridiculously short—was now long enough to counterpoint facial structure that was truly some of Mother Nature's best work.

Like a cat waking from a nap, warmth and awareness stretched lazily in Justice's belly. She carefully pushed her hacker book higher on the desk. It was a testament to how badly beaten down she felt that her detachment over Street's yumminess would slip so considerably, especially when— *Oh, dear God.*

He flashed her his dimples. "Hey, Justice, it's Friday night. Time to secure the week with alcohol. Come out with us."

It took all her willpower not to jump up and rush Brayden, to throw her arms around his neck and give him a sloppy cheek kiss. To bake him cookies and change out the shoelaces in his combat boots to something brand-new and shiny, and altogether, you know, be weird over his offer to include her.

The truth was, five days straight of shutout *had* taken its pound of flesh, even on an only child who was used to a lot of alone time and should be in her damned comfort zone.

Underneath her *it-doesn't-matter* attitude, she did kinda care what the guys thought of her.

But this evening's inclusion was being offered by Street alone, for which he earned even more Nice Guy points. As far as the rest of the candidates were concerned, a bar scene wasn't going to change how they'd already categorized her: as the weak link in the class who earned them extra rounds of PT.

"Nice of you to ask, Street, but no guy wants a chick around when he's out to get laid."

Street propped a shoulder against the doorjamb, as if he was taking a moment to consider how easy it would be for him to get laid tonight.

Answer: *pshaw!*

"C'mon," he coaxed. "*One* drink."

Some of her raw glop oozed up between her restraining fingers. It was a warning: in her current state, dimples plus alcohol plus broad shoulders plus Nice Guy could potentially add up to succumbing to stupid temptations...like dancing with this man and laughing and...running fingers over dimples and seriously considering a *kiss.*

Tension pulsed through her head. "Better not." She gestured at her hacker book. "I still have some studying to do."

"You're always studying."

"After BUD/S I've been assigned to crypto school." She summoned up a smile. "I'll be fine, Street, and thanks again for the offer."

"All right. But before I head out..." He stepped into her room, bringing a delicious hint of aftershave with him. "Here." He slipped something out of his pocket and held it out to her.

She eyeballed the rectangular object. It was about the size of a bar of soap. "What is it?"

"Soap."

No, really?

"Some French kind. Rudy says Sable recommends it. Says it smells good."

"Sable?"

"Rudy's girlfriend."

Justice mouthed *Sable* at Brayden. What kind of name was that?

Street's eyes crinkled.

"Why?"

"What do you mean, *why*? What is soap used for, Justice? Jesus Christ."

She'd meant, *Why are you giving it to me?* Gifts had the potential for multiple layers of meaning. Was Brayden trying to ingratiate himself to her for a later seduction? Or was this another way he was attempting to take care of her, like when he held the door open for her and pulled out her chair?

Acts of gentlemanliness weren't good. Good on a date, yes; she was all for chivalrous behavior in a man she was seeing. Not good when a woman was trying to convince future operators to take her seriously.

"Uh, thanks." She accepted the soap—she couldn't come up with a good reason to refuse—and read the label: *Fer à Cheval*, lavender-scented. *Sheesh*. He'd probably spent too much. "All right, now begone." She flicked her fingers at him in a shoo-away gesture. "Off you go to get laid."

He laughed. "That might be difficult. I think I froze my balls off in the Pacific several days ago. But yeah. Enjoy your studying." He turned and strode toward the community room, the easy movement of defined muscles beneath his clothing emphasizing the natural power of his body.

"No shortage of testosterone from where I'm sitting," she muttered, pulling her hacker book forward. She tried to read, but the words swam into squiggly blobs. A windblown emptiness opened up inside her belly, tumbleweeds rolling across the deserted landscape of her life. She sank her forehead into her palm.

You're fine; you're in your comfort zone. She sighed. *Yeah, yeah, keep saying that, ten times, fast, and maybe—*

"Going it alone again, are you?"

She bolted her head up and snapped her focus over to the door.

Keith Knight.

CHAPTER NINE

KNIGHT WAS STANDING cross-armed in the doorway.

In a pair of dark-washed jeans.

That were subtly hugging an incredible package in front. *Oh, fuck me.*

Wait, no, no... She didn't mean it that way. *She...dammit.*

She banged her book shut and slammed to her feet. Anger was such a pal. So much better than hanging out with loneliness and isolation, self-doubts, and one's own inadequacies.

"You'll excuse me for not joining you," she said tartly, "but I like my Mai Tais extra heavy on the dark rum, decorated with a fancy umbrella, and sans elbow jabs and hostile stares."

He shook his head. "The men aren't pissed at you. They're just miserable in general out there, like you are, and fed up." Keith's tone was infinitely reasonable.

He was such a level-headed guy, wasn't he? Wholly sensible. She could just fucking hit him.

"They've got nothing against you personally," he added.

"No?" She stalked over to him.

He came out of his cross-armed posture.

"Then maybe you can explain why Donnie Cogan looked at me like I was fecal matter," *fecal matter with tits*, "after Timed Swim today. And that was *after* a great performance. I deliver a subpar performance, I'm scorned. I deliver a great performance, I'm still scorned." She threw her arms in the air. "How do I win, Knight? Tell me. Do I offer a blowjob to any man in the class who will pretty please like me, and, oh, don't worry, I never cheese-grate dick?"

The muscles in Keith's neck rippled.

"I'm everyone's pain in the ass," she went on, hurling the full force of a glare into his face. "The outsider. The SOF member who'll never be a warrior. The candidate who carries her gonads in the wrong place, *not* on the outside, but on the inside—which, by the way, protects them from being a blatant weak spot on the human body, like men have, but far be it from me to mention such a thing to any of you ego babies."

Keith's eyes narrowed, but other than that he didn't move—he didn't step back, he didn't step forward, although she sensed he would've preferred to do one or the other.

Action, that was Knight.

Thing was about no one doing a step-back... They were standing very close. Close enough for her to feel the heat of his body, and who knew the swamp beast could smell so good—two things her labia majora enjoyed with a shivery tingle.

Easy as pie! That's what her dad used to say about any job. That's how Justice was rating the difficulty factor of Keith getting laid tonight too.

She sneered at him. "You suck."

Keith breathed in, slowly and deeply. "I'm doing my damnedest to create a solid boat team out there, but the task is made exponentially difficult with you locked down tighter than a drum."

She jutted her jaw. "Just minding my program."

"When was the last time you ate in the mess hall?" he asked quietly.

The back of her neck grew hot. *Shit.*

"When," he continued, "have you come to me for help when you were struggling?"

She took a step back now.

"I can't help you if you don't tell me what's wrong."

"What kind of help are we talking about, Knight? You stealing weight from my backpack and redistributing it to the rest of the boat team?"

Keith's brows lowered.

Yeah. Caught ya!

"The packs are *sixty* pounds," he defended himself, "and what are you? One forty, one fifty? The ratio of pack weight to body weight should be—"

"Knight," she cut him off, "you're not winning me any friends by doing that."

"You're never going to be an operator," he volleyed back. "The men know that."

Out in the community room, one of the men *hooyah'd!* over something. The others laughed.

"I'm still going to be out in the field someday, potentially working with you guys. How far do you think my career in Special Missions will go if I'm pegged as the team member who has to be taken care of?" She could just see Admiral Sherwin now, all his suspicions about her being a big mistake shining nastily in his cold eyes. "I'm making a reputation for myself *now*, and I can't have the men thinking of me as deadwood on a future op. I need you to treat me like a regular candidate."

Keith made an irritated sound, air passing between a corner seam of his lips, then he dragged a hand over his short hair. "All right, I'll do my best. Even though you'll never be an operator, I definitely respect you as a top athlete."

The tension inside her chest eased a bit. *Respect*—just like a grubby-fisted child wanting candy, she craved that from Knight. His compliment, admittedly, felt really damned good. "Thank you, I appreciate it."

"Hey, Knight!" someone called from the community room. "Let's go, man."

"Yeah!" he called over his shoulder. "Be right there." He turned back to her and stroked a hand over his chin. "So, I, uh...I take it the blowjob offer was only a joke?"

She brought her chin up with a jerk.

His smile was amused, friendly only.

"Aw, crap. I owe myself a dollar." *No sex talk in front of fellow candidates.*

He chuckled. "So are you coming out with us?"

"Go ahead without me." She smiled. Didn't entirely feel it, but she smiled anyway. "I need time to process." Moreover, a fair amount of heat still lingered between them because of their argument, and she would owe herself a lot more than a dollar if she let herself fully explore it.

Keith stepped backward through the doorjamb. "You're doing good, Hayes. Just keep working hard, like you are. The men will come around."

Her breath hitched for a second. "Okay."

Nodding, Keith turned and left.

CHAPTER TEN

JUSTICE SHELVED HER hacker books for the night.

She might not be securing the week with alcohol, but she could still indulge in some relaxation. So she lounged on her bunk and started up a Netflix movie on her laptop. One of the *Mission Impossibles*.

Halfway through, she got a hankering for popcorn, and strode into the kitchen to—

"Holy shit!" She nearly jumped out of her own feet when she saw Street in there. "What the hell are you doing back so soon?"

Brayden was standing in front of the open freezer door, the gallon of Rocky Road balanced on his palm. He'd changed into a pair of long gray cotton shorts, a plain white T-shirt, and flip-flops. Obviously he was in for the night.

"What happened to getting laid?" she demanded.

"What are you, my pimp?" He set the ice cream on the counter and wedged the lid off. "I happen to value my equipment. I don't just loan it out to anyone." He opened the silverware drawer with a rattle and pulled out an ice cream scoop. "Want some?" He asked the question like he didn't expect her to accept.

She never had.

I'm not the one failing to be a team player, Knight.
No?

She watched Brayden fill his bowl with Rocky Road.

You're locked down tighter than a drum... "Sure, thanks."

He smiled broadly and grabbed a second bowl.

They both threw on windbreakers before taking their ice cream out on the deck and sitting next to each other in cushioned lounge chairs.

A partial moon hung in the sky, casting shimmering light over the gentle ripples of the ocean. Waves lapped languidly at the shore. A cool, crisp marine layer was in the air, the incongruence of beauty and cold.

Licking the end of her spoon, Justice turned toward Brayden...and found herself staring at him. Soft porch light bathed his face in gold, highlighting the nobility of his profile: a straight nose, a sleek but sturdy jawline, high cheekbones, silken hair. He had the kind of features that belonged on someone handing out tickets to heaven.

Her face, by comparison, was the kind generally found on a Wanted poster.

"What?" he asked, catching her staring.

She lifted a single shoulder and turned back to her ice cream. "I don't know. I was just thinking about the question you asked when I first arrived. Why am I here?"

"Ah." He waited. "And?"

She poked at the Rocky Road with her spoon, hunting for a mini marshmallow. "Do you think a person has to know the answer to make it through BUD/S?"

"Yes," he answered simply.

She scooped up some ice cream, but then just tipped her spoon over and let it plop back into the bowl. "What if it's not a good reason?"

"As long as *you* know what's motivating you, it's proba-bly enough."

She nudged her tongue at a couple of her teeth. "How bad would it be if I said I'm here for the challenge?"

He chuckled. "You'd sound like Keith."

"Really?"

"Yeah. Keith and I grew up in Wyoming together doing all kinds of wild-ass sports—rock climbing, deep-forest camping, hiking the Grand Tetons, whitewater rafting, cliff diving. Nothing was ever hard enough for Keith. He's talked about becoming a SEAL since he was ten." Brayden popped a bite into his mouth. "He could've been an officer, too, you know. He has a college degree, same as I do—it's why he entered the Navy as a petty officer. But he enlisted because he didn't want to end up pushing papers."

"You don't care about the paperwork?"

"I want to be in the thick of the fight too, yeah, but I want to *lead*. There have been times in my life when I should've stepped up, but I..." He trailed off and shook his head. "Never mind. I just want to become a better leader is the main thing. Prove that I'm good. But then, you know what I mean."

I do? Well, yeah, she did. But how did he know that? "So you and Keith were raised in the same town?"

"Yep. I'm best friends with all the Knight boys—four total. We did everything together."

Five of these high-impact men, charging through life. "The poor townsfolk," she said with a brief laugh. "You five must've been a force to be reckoned with." And if all the brothers were as good-looking as Street and Knight, then... "Especially with the ladies."

Brayden chuckled. "We created our fair share of earthquakes."

She gazed at the stars, uneven clusters, whole populations. "I can't imagine it. I'm an only child."

He brightened. "Hey, so am I."

She *tsked* at him. "You just admitted to spending all your time with *four* half brothers. That doesn't count."

"But at the end of every day I went home to only my mom, and it was always so...so fucking quiet, you know?"

She snorted softly. "I do know."

"Besides, my dad never treated me like his own son."

She stopped with her spoon partway to her mouth. "What do you mean?"

"Whenever I was over at the house, I was just another one of his sons' friends."

She frowned. "Why?"

"Beats the fuck outta me."

She slowly ate the bite of ice cream. *Well, huh.* "Did your mom ever say anything to your dad about the way he treated you?"

"Nope." Peering down at his feet, Brayden scrunched his toes in his flip-flops. "She either didn't see it or didn't want to see it." He looked up. "What about your mom? Do you remember much about her?"

Justice blinked twice, thrown off guard by the question. She set her spoon in her bowl and rested the bowl in her lap.

Brayden's gaze softened. "You don't have to talk about her if you don't want. On the first day of BUD/S Chief Tanner mentioned your mom had died, and I've just been curious about it."

"Oh. Yes. Um, but...I don't remember her. She died giving birth to me." A familiar grief broke over her in a wave of pain.

"That sucks."

"It does." She looked deep into Brayden's warm eyes and...*crap.* The two of them were *connecting* over everything they had in common. Two only children, brought up in tomblike households, maybe holding onto daddy-slash-mommy issues...probably too easily drawn into cozying up next to each other... Oh, this was bad. Things like shared commonalities and mutual understanding were complications she didn't need right now.

Brayden took her bowl from her, stacked it with his,

then stretched over to set both bowls on a round patio table. His T-shirt tugged flush against his side, revealing the defined lines of his abs and lats.

She licked the residual ice cream off her lips, caught herself, then stood abruptly. "I should probably get some rest now."

Brayden hastened to his feet.

"Thanks for the ice cream."

"'Course." He gave her a sideways smile.

A school of dolphins broke the surface of the ocean, moonlight gleaming on their silky silver flesh, the different noises flaring from their blow holes creating a symphony of whispers, *huussh* and *chush* and *shush*.

She could hear Brayden's soft breathing, too, *feel* it, like a soft breeze stirring her hair follicles.

"I don't think you're in this only for the challenge, Justice."

She paused. "No," she admitted.

He waited.

"It's the endgame—the job on the other side of this horror. It's something I *need* to do." She was the daughter of one of the most brilliant criminal minds of all time, and she'd gone legit. Working a dangerous job like Special Missions was about the only way to prove to Dad her choice wasn't an easy path.

"Why's that?" he asked.

"The explanation is complicated," she evaded, edging away from the intimacy that'd already sprouted between them. "My father is Grayson Hayes. Google his name, then you'll understand."

Brayden searched her face. "I think I'll wait till you're ready to tell me."

Chapter Eleven

Monday morning—Extraction Swim.

It wasn't starting out promising.

The exercise was being overseen by two instructors: Terrell Clark, a sleekly built Black man with a golf ball-sized wad of Copenhagen bulging against his cheek, and her arch-nemesis, Warren Hill.

The swim was one mile long, straight out to sea in combat clothing, the end marked by Instructor Hill sitting on a jet ski. From the jet ski, paired swimmers were supposed to haul themselves into an idling Zodiac speed-boat—a "static" maritime extraction. At this point, the boat would take them farther out into the Pacific Ocean, drop them in the water again, then circle back around, this time with a rubber ring hanging off the side. Each candidate was required to loop his arm through this ring and use momentum to vault his body into the boat—an "active" maritime extraction.

The Zodiac had already carted off the first swimmers on Justice's boat team, and the next pair was closing in on the jet ski.

Meanwhile Justice and aspiring sniper Zack Kilgour, her swim partner today, had drifted to dead last.

A knot twisted inside her chest, and her breathing be-came more strained. Their last-place position was her fault. She'd practiced plenty of swimming exercises in her prep workouts at PTRR, both in the pool and the ocean, just none while wearing combat boots. Now she couldn't seem to make her kicks work right. It felt like she was lugging her body through the water instead of gliding.

Kilgour glanced back at her to check her position—like with the Timed Swim, her partner wasn't allowed to get more than six feet away from her. Frowning, Kilgour slowed down *again*.

Argh!

Spitting salt water between her teeth, she continued her combat sidestroke while simultaneously reaching down to untie her boots. Wresting off one shoe, then the other, she knotted the laces together, then hung her boots around her neck, shoving the toes down her shirt so they wouldn't dangle and create drag.

She got going then. *Yes!* Speeding up to Kilgour, she tapped his boot.

He looked at her with surprise.

She made a forward-chop motion with her hand.

He nodded and took off. They passed the other swim pair and arrived at the jet ski *not* dead last.

Kilgour hauled himself into the waiting Zodiac.

She followed, taking a seat on the side of the boat.

Instructor Clark turned from where he stood at the helm and glared at her boot necklace. "What the fuck is this, Hayes?" His cheek quivered around the Copenhagen bulge.

"My boots were slowing me down, Instructor, so I—"

Pain exploded in her lungs as the sole of Clark's boot found her chest with force, sending her whipping over the side of the boat in a violent summersault. She hard-splashed in the ocean, seawater pouring into her mouth—because she had it wide open in a silent, screaming *OW!*

She came up spluttering and gasping, clawing at the line of shoelace now wrapped around her throat like a garrote. Clark's kick had knocked every molecule of oxygen from her lungs.

"You think when you're evading the enemy, he's just gonna hang around while you take your fucking boots off, so you can escape all comfortable-like?" Clark hawked a vicious stream of tobacco juice over the side of the boat.

Justice's only answer was a wheeze.

"Put your boots back on," Clark growled.

The last two members of her boat team climbed on board the Zodiac.

She treaded water while she fumbled on her boots. Her face kept dipping below the waterline, and she spit saltwater, struggling to breathe.

"Now swim to shore," Clark ordered her, then gunned the Zodiac.

Foaming wake hurled into her face, and the chop tossed her around. Still catching her breath, she watched the Zodiac speed off, the men on her boat crew blank-staring her from the stern.

The Zodiac shrank smaller and smaller until the engine noise faded completely away, leaving only the slap of water against her face and the screech of a couple of seagulls overhead. She treaded in a half circle and examined the shoreline. The cars seemed Matchbox-size and the buildings like they belonged on a toy train set.

A one-mile swim.

In freezing water.

Wearing combat boots.

Her will started to slink away, but she squashed that nonsense and bucked herself up—*hey, at least no one is yelling at me*. Her teeth started to chatter. *Just get to it.* She set off at a steady swim, then stopped and floated upright.

The Zodiac was roaring back.

CHAPTER TWELVE

JUSTICE WAS REASONABLY certain Instructor Clark hadn't suffered a crisis of conscience and, no…

Keith Knight was standing near the helm, his solid legs planted wide for balance, his wet T-shirt clinging to the deep grooves of muscles on his chest. He had a steely blue gaze locked on her.

The rest of her boat team was gathered in the stern behind him.

The Zodiac surged to a halt, and Justice bobbed up and down from the resulting swells.

"Get in the water with your teammate," Knight barked at the others.

Every man splashed in—sniper Kilgour, know-it-all Chalmers, Appletini Shaw, Pervy Hairy Arms, High School Crush Lookalike, Gentle Giant Dog Bone, and Keith Knight.

Without a word, Instructor Clark gunned off again.

They bobbed some more, like corks being popped around on an old-timey fireman's jumping sheet, then the sea calmed. They drifted in silence…sort of a tense silence.

Justice angled her face up at the sky. There wasn't a cloud in sight to spoil the endless blue of the beautiful California dreamin' vista. It would've been a gorgeous day, if, you know, she was sunbathing on the beach with a daiquiri.

A mixture of emotions churning inside her, she looked

at her teammates again, but couldn't come up with anything to say. *Sorry, you're in the cold water again because of me* was an option. But coming into BUD/S, she'd promised herself never to offer up excuses for a poor performance. She would only fight to be better and never make the same mistake twice.

Keith pushed a tentacle of seaweed away from him. "So an operator is walking with a terrorist into the desert, right. The terrorist says, 'Hey, mister, it's getting dark out here and I'm scared.' Operator answers, 'How do you think I feel? I have to walk back alone.'"

High School Crush grinned, looking even more crush-worthy, and some of the other men chuckled.

Knight effectively broke the tension, and Justice felt a sudden and ungoverned upsurge of hero worship for the man. She bit into her numb lips, trying to bring sensation back into them, and worked to pin her heart back in its proper place. She'd never needed a man to make her feel safe—the idea was ludicrous—and she'd certainly never needed a man to *save* her. Except…

Down in her gut, deep in the glades and dells of her inner truth, she *had* been wanting Keith to save her—to do whatever it took to help her belong. To make her feel like a part of Team Knight.

And guess what? He'd come back for her while she was floating alone in the vast blue ocean and brought her teammates with him.

"You men pair back up," Keith told the others, "and head for shore."

As the rest of the team swam off, Keith turned to her.

"I—" She started and stopped. *No excuses.* But she was also supposed to ask Keith for help when she needed it. She gave him an *I'm-cold*, lip-quaky smile. "I don't seem to be able to swim effectively in combat boots."

Keith smoothed a hand over his face, sweeping water off. "The flutter kick doesn't work so well in those. With heavy boots on, you need to kick using your entire thigh, but you'll wear out your legs faster doing that. Your best bet is the dolphin kick. You'll use your entire body in a wave motion, so it's more difficult to combine with the combat sidestroke, but in the long run more efficient and less tiring. You want to give it a try?"

"Absolutely."

Keith showed her how it was done, and she followed his lead. About ten minutes into the swim, she had it down.

By the time they were slogging back onto shore a half hour later, all of Class 684 was waiting for them on the beach, standing at attention.

Instructor Hill was positioned in front of their ranks. His arms were crossed, his eyes filmed with an unsettling sheen. "Class 684! On your faces because Hayes can't follow a simple order."

Oh, for fuck's sake. Didn't she just pay for that with Clark's brutal kick and then a one-mile swim?

"Push 'em out!" Hill bellowed.

She assumed the push-up position, the lure of flipping Instructor Hill the bird on the way down dancing across the screen of her imagination. Somehow she resisted.

It was Dunbar who led them this time. "Push-ups! Ready!"

"READY!"
"Down!"
"ONE!"
"Down!"
"TWO!"
"Down!"
"THREE!"
Hill's boot slammed onto her back.

She splatted in the sand, barely keeping herself from a full face-plant.

"Tits in the sand!" Hill bawled at her. "How many times you gotta be told, Hayes!?"

She struggled back to a straight-arm position, swirled her tongue around inside her mouth, and spat out sand. *Misogynist motherfucking douche-whore.* She couldn't believe Instructor Hill had a wife. Who in her right mind would marry a guy like him? Probably a woman who swilled down too many of those appletinis she favored in order to deal with her husband's dirty-diaper overgrowth of upper lip hair at the end each day. And his seriously bunched-up attitude.

On the twentieth push-up, the class called out, "HOOYAH, INSTRUCTOR HILL!"

"Again!" Hill roared. "Hayes is *still* fucking up!"

Justice glared down at a desiccated, half-buried sand dollar and moved her teeth against each other, grinding sand, tasting acid. Fighting to improve a poor performance she would do. Watching her teammates continually pay for her mistakes—most of which were invented—had officially grown old.

"Push-ups!" Dunbar yelled. "Ready!"

"READY!"

"Down!"

"ONE!"

Justice shouted, "Tits in the sand!" after "One!"

Some muffled laughter rolled through the ranks.

"Down!"

"TWO!"

"Tits in the sand!"

"Down!"

"THREE!"

"Tits in the—"

"Recover!" Hill hollered.

The instructor was right in front of Justice when she came to her feet, his mustache bristling up his nostrils.

"You think," Hill said in a low snarl, "that I want to hear someone on *my* Teams saying 'tits' over and over?"

She was reasonably certain his question was rhetorical. She kept her tongue between her teeth.

"Fifty push-ups!" Hill thundered, "Only Hayes!" He made her move out of the ranks to stand facing the class. "And if I hear you say *tits* one time, it's the men who'll pay."

Hooyah, ass-fucking douche-whore! Another temptation she barely tamped down, screaming that at Hill. She dropped to the sand and counted off—normally—while the rest of the class stood at attention.

By forty push-ups, the muscles in her arms and chest were volcanic quiver-blobs. On her last push-up, Instructor Hill grabbed the back of her skull and mashed her face into the sand.

"Recover," he barked.

She shoved upright. "Hooyah, Instructor Hill," she gulped out, blinking owlishly to get the sand out of her eyes.

BUD/S was never fair, and it rarely made sense. It was a test of resolve and fortitude in the face of anything. The instructors notoriously invented failures just so they could beat the class more, throwing in extra sets of PT and additional time spent in surf torture for wildly improbable reasons. The instructors weren't nice, and they weren't here to be anyone's friend, but they'd never been outright mean to her.

Until now.

As Justice stood there, working to store the unfairness of it away, probably looking absolutely pie-in-the-face with sand, she felt the other candidates' sentiment toward her change.

A dark ebb of anger rolled off the others, her boat team

radiating the worst of the murderous vibe. Knight stood at attention with his jaw hammered down tight; Sniper Kilgour's lids were thinly narrowed; High School Crush's nostrils were flared; Hairy Arms' complexion was a dull red; and Dog Bone's shoulder muscles were bunched into small dunes.

But it was Brayden who ended up surprising her the most.

When Instructor Hill released them to Land Portage, Brayden made a brief detour to their IBS on the way to his own. He discreetly passed out a supply of Power Bars he'd stowed in the pockets of his camos—Knight's boat team had missed lunch.

Keith gave his brother's shoulder a brief squeeze. "Thanks, Bray."

Justice brushed the sand off her face while watching Dog Bone unwrap three bars, stack them on top of each other, then eat them as a bundle in two bites.

When Street came to her, his eyes were a deadly shade of stormy blue. He handed her a bar. "Get that down you." His voice was gravel and fury. "Quick."

Who would've thought the nice guy gallant of the group was capable of such rage? "Understood," she said.

THE DAY DEVOLVED into the usual endless round of PT and beatings. Hill and Clark got creative, sending them off to *get wet and sandy* by making them combat crawl the whole way to the surf. By the time Justice made it over the grinder and down to the ocean, the skin on her elbows was mostly rubbed off. Miraculously, the day didn't end with them freezing their assess off in surf torture.

When she went to the mess hall that evening for chow, she was *not* soaked in seawater. So instead of to-go food, she grabbed a tray and stocked up with spaghetti, salad, a chocolate pudding cup, milk, and water. She found her lone table and sat, tugging a napkin from—

Pervy Hairy Arms sat down across from her with a tray of food.

She blinked.

High School Crush sat next to Hairy Arms, and Dog Bone settled his bulk on her right.

"Uh…" she said. "Hello?"

Crush showed all his teeth when he smiled. "You're not doing as bad as you think you are, Hayes. Keep humping it."

"Okay." She knuckled one of her eyes. Crush was probably just a figment. "Thanks."

Crush came halfway out of his seat, offering her his hand. "I'm Omar Boyd, by the way."

She shook his hand.

"So, hey, Hayes…" Hairy Arms cracked open his water bottle. "You ever munch carpet?"

"What the fuck, Ziegler?" Crushy Boyd snapped, sitting back down.

"What? I need a new fantasy for my whack-off logbook, all right?"

Dog Bone grunted. "Who has energy to rub one out at the end of the day?" He scooped up a forkful of spaghetti the size of a boxing glove and shoveled it into his mouth.

Hairy Arms was appalled. "You *always* make time to whack, man."

Justice once read about the largest ball of twine. It was in Cawker City, Kansas, and spanned eleven feet in diameter. That was the size of Dog Bone's second bite of spaghetti.

Hairy Arms picked up a piece of garlic bread. "I gotta have details. Taste. Smell. The color of—"

"Ziegler," Boyd cut in again, gesturing at Justice. "You know she's an officer, right?"

"Hah, yeah, college—experimentation time." Hairy Arms' leer grew. "Maybe you—"

"Move."

They all turned to find Knight standing at the end of their table, holding a tray of food. His expression was stony.

Hairy Arms started to scoot over.

"Up and out," Knight corrected in an icy tone. "You're disrespecting a member of the team."

"It's all right, Knight," Justice interceded. "Ziegler was just shutting up now."

Ducking his chin, Hairy Arms shot her a quick grin while scooting over. Crushy Boyd scooted over too.

Knight sat across from her. He rolled a bite of spaghetti onto his fork—a perfectly sensible amount.

She almost pointed at it for Dog Bone to take heed.

What was *not* sensible was the number of chocolate pudding cups on Keith's tray: six.

Dang, what was the deal with the Street/Knight brothers? One was an ice cream fiend, the other a pudding addict.

Hairy Arms ate more garlic bread. "So, hey, Hayes…"

Knight's chewing slowed.

"Is it true what Chief Tanner said? Your dad wishes he had a boy, and it's why you're here?"

"Nope." She slugged some water. "What about your dad? Does he wish he had a boy?"

Knight's head swung up, laugh lines bracketing his mouth.

Crushy Boyd openly guffawed.

"Great." Hairy Arms rolled his eyes. "We've got two fucking comedians on this team."

Dog Bone finished his dinner. An entire man-sized plate consumed in three bites. Maybe his jaw unhinged.

Keith scooped up another forkful of spaghetti. "I hear we're doing surf passage tomorrow. As soon as the instructors release us to the evolution, hustle ass to grab a firm boat. Once again we're going to need a firm one—shut up, Ziegler—otherwise it'll be fucked trying to get over waves in something that'll bend in half at every hit."

Everyone agreed, then settled into general bitching and moaning.

Listening to them, Justice steadily ate her spaghetti and was ridiculously glad for their presence. She had the beginnings of a team. It was a small one, but here they were...and if Team Knight's rugged leader had seen her expression just then, he would've caught The Almighty BUD/S Woman looking moony-eyed with gratitude.

Dog Bone pointed at the chocolate pudding cups on Keith's tray. "You gonna eat all those?"

"Touch one," Keith warned, "and you die."

She offered her pudding to Dog Bone. "You can have mine."

Dog Bone eagerly took the cup and peeled off the foil top. Setting the opening at his mouth, he quick-squeezed the plastic cup with his fist, rocketing the entire blop inside and slurping it down in one gulp.

Justice considered Dog Bone closely. Maybe he didn't have an esophagus. Maybe food went directly from his mouth to his stomach, and he'd been written about in all kinds of medical journals.

Dog Bone saw her staring. "What?"

"Um...nothing." Picking up her tray, she stood. "I just gotta go hit the books."

"Make sure you see to those scraped elbows," Keith said to her without looking up. "And your back is bleeding again."

She hovered tableside.

Keith forked up more pasta.

Hairy Arms tucked the last corner of garlic bread in his

mouth and observed her.

Well, shit. She cleared her throat. "I could actually use some help with that."

Keith glanced at her. "Officers' quarters in fifteen?"

"Better make it thirty. My shower routine is a bit...complex."

Ziegler's ears perked up into little fluffy points. "Really? Got details?"

Boyd didn't scold Hairy Arms this time. He was too busy staring unblinkingly at his tray.

Knight returned to eating, but...*hell.* Even the back of his neck stained a little red.

Her *shower activities* were clearly being expanded upon in everyone's imaginations to include more than the normal soap and shampoo.

"Fucking men," she muttered and strode off.

CHAPTER THIRTEEN

IF A LOT could be learned about a man by spending too much time with him under a large, unstable rubber boat, even more could be learned about him from the touch of his hands. Or maybe it should be said, a lot could be *confirmed*.

Justice already knew that Keith was strong, solid, confident, and full of unstoppable energy, but when he took hold of her wrists, she *felt* those things: in the muscular solidity of his palms, in the power of the fingers wrapping her wrist bones and pressing against her pulse, in the no-nonsense way he directed her limbs where he wanted them to go, rotating her arms this way and that so he could inspect her scrapes.

She knew these things, yet...feeling his power through a wrist-grab was a bit...heart-quickening.

It was a dominant hold. Not at the present moment, but generally a man captured a woman's wrists when he was all about making her submit to whatever he wanted to do to her.

Pin her arms above her head while he explored the deepest reaches of her mouth with his tongue.

Hold her down on the mattress to make damned sure she stayed in place so he could pound hard and uninterrupted between her thighs.

The scenarios were endless, and Keith suddenly taking a starring role in some surprising honey-butter fantasies. All from the touch of his hands.

She wasn't even remotely into being dominated or

BDSM play, but she did love a strong man, and when it came to power and aggression, Knight was incredibly well-endowed with these traits. Give Petty Officer Keith Knight something to do, and it got done. Always.

Action Man.

He turned one of her arms over, pulled her forward a bit, and applied antibiotic ointment to her elbow...with gentle strokes of his fingers. Heat stirred a pulsing arousal in her loins, and a small gasp slipped out of her.

He glanced up. "Does that hurt?"

God, no. "A little."

He softened his touch.

Oh, yeah, that worked out *much* better for her.

"Let's leave the elbow scrapes open to the air for now," he said as he finished with her left arm. "Okay, shirt up."

She swiveled around in her chair—she was at the four-seater dinette set located between the kitchen and the couch—and grabbed the scruff of her T-shirt, tugging it up in back. The front partially went up, too, gathering under her breasts.

Keith made a *humph* sound.

"What? Is it infected?"

"No."

"Is it worse than you thought?"

"No."

"Well, what then?"

"You're just ripped as shit, Hayes."

She cranked her head around to look at him.

His smile was cute. "Sorry. I know I'm not supposed to notice. Lean forward."

She turned back around and set her forearms on the table, careful of her sore elbows.

Keith lightly applied antibiotic ointment to her cut. She shivered. He said sorry for hurting her. She rolled her eyes at herself.

"Hey," Dunbar called out, entering the room. "What's going—" He came to an abrupt halt and gawked at them.

"Just patching up Hayes here," Knight said.

Justice *allegedly* wasn't supposed to be showing any more of her body than she would poolside—at least according to Knight's original claims about this process. But strictly speaking, that wasn't true. If her bare midriff was to be taken into consideration, and judging by where Rudy was staring, it was.

Dunbar did his lobster act again. "What the fuck are you doing?" he demanded of Keith.

Keith tore open a packet of gauze. "Didn't I just say?"

"But…you two are *alone*."

Keith laughed. "I didn't realize I needed a chaperone to give Hayes first aid."

Dunbar scowled. "Well, you do."

Keith laughed again as he set the bandage on her back.

"I'm serious." Dunbar's lemon-sucking face went into overdrive. "Captain Eagen said he'd make me and Street clean the latrines with our livers if we didn't take care of Hayes."

Justice whipped her focus over to Rudy. "He most certainly did not."

"Yes, he did," Dunbar countered.

"I was standing right there, Rudy. Eagen said the exact opposite."

Keith started to tape the bandage in place. "Rest easy, Dunbar. Dealing with Hayes's bloody injuries hasn't worked me up in the least."

Justice glanced toward the ceiling. She was obviously a hard-up loon because the process had, er, worked her up a bit.

"Done," Keith said.

Justice yanked her shirt down.

"Hey." Brayden Street walked in, a grocery sack in his arms. "I bought a new flavor of ice cream."

Dunbar pointed an accusing finger at Keith. "Knight was in here alone with Hayes, his hands all over her."

"Hey!" Justice slammed up from her chair.

"Chocolate chip and…" Brayden froze with a gallon of Dreyer's halfway out of the sack. "Wait, what's happening?"

"She was half-naked," Dunbar reported.

"Rudy," Justice seethed, "if you don't shut your trap, you'll be worrying about what *I* do to your liver."

The veins in Rudy's temples bulged. "I'm trying to defend you!"

"What you're doing," she said between her teeth, "is dragging my reputation through the mud. I'm the one woman among more than a hundred men. If you keep saying shit like that, then no one will ever take me seriously as a team member." And when it came to blabber-mouthing, Rudy was worse than a washerwoman.

Knight snapped the lid closed on the first aid kit. "She's got you there, Dunbar." He started for the door.

Dunbar glared after him. "Where the hell do you think you're going?"

"To the White House. I was invited for dinner."

"I'm not done with you, *Petty Officer*."

Knight came to a slow stop—heel, toe, then boots to-gether.

"Rudy," Street uttered. "Don't."

Keith pivoted toward Dunbar. "Yes, sir?" he inquired coolly.

Rudy didn't speak for a long moment, a tic twitching beneath one eye. What could he say? He was an officer and Keith was enlisted, but the men respected Knight more than they did Dunbar—and Rudy knew it.

"Watch yourself with her," Rudy sniped, "or I'll report your behavior to Captain Eagen and have Hayes yanked off your boat team." Wheeling around, he marched into his bedroom and slammed the door.

Justice's heart was suddenly right next to her tonsils. "Can he do that?" She skidded her gaze over to Street. "Can Dunbar have me removed from Knight's team?"

Street shrugged. "If Eagen gets involved."

Ice flooded her veins. She didn't think… She'd finally made some strides with the men…was becoming a team and… She really wasn't sure if she could go back to doing this alone and still make it through. "Can you stop it?"

Brayden started to speak.

Keith overrode him. "You're not getting pulled off my team." His words were weighted with all the power that made him a conqueror of domains, a stormer of hills, the kind of man others followed into the breach.

Brayden closed his mouth and turned away abruptly, shoving the new ice cream in the freezer.

Keith kept his focus on her, his expression as firm as his tone had been, yet also tempered with sympathy and understanding.

Well, yeah, he'd caught her being a 'fraidy girl.

She blew out a noisy breath. "What the hell is wrong with Dunbar, anyway?"

"Isn't it fucking obvious?" Knight retorted. "He likes you."

Chapter Fourteen

Who would've thought there was something on Planet Earth able to make a woman want to get back under an uncooperative, ten-ton rubber boat doing Land Portage?

That there was a thing making her pray for it, in fact.

Log PT was that thing.

Please, God, I'll do anything to stop this…ANYTHING.

Each log was eight feet in length, a foot in diameter, and weighed one hundred fifty pounds. Unwieldy and rough-hewn, the log was incredibly painful to carry, even while wearing long-sleeved fatigue shirts buttoned to the collar and cuffs, like they all were for this evolution. Sand still ground agonizingly against the soft skin of the inner arms.

To meander at a light stroll with such a log would've been bad enough, but the instructors had invented a staggering variety of ways with which to torture each seven-man team: do squats with the log, jumping jacks, toss the log into the air then catch it, dead lift the log overhead, hold it out in front of the body at arm's length—*ow!*—now do these same things during surf torture, now hump it up and down the sand berm, now hold it against the chest while doing lunges—*aaaaahhhh!*

Whole teams were collapsing on top of their logs in exhaustion. Men were shouting at each other, vomiting, pissing themselves.

"Come on, Hayes!" Know-it-all Chalmers sniped at her as they huffed and puffed, doing lunges in a race against

Brayden's team. "Stay with us!"

Dammit, it wasn't *her* slowing them down. It was fucking Appletini again. Every time they dropped into a lunge, Appletini would slouch over the top of the log for a rest. Which meant that on the way back up, the rest of them were lifting Shaw's weight in addition to the log's.

Down.

Up.

Wheeze.

"Hayes!" Chalmers groused.

She made a glottal noise in her throat.

They busted their asses, hissing air between set teeth, but ended up crossing the finish line second to Brayden's team.

"Losers!" Copenhagen Clark yelled, taking a swig of Red Bull around his lump of chaw. "Push 'em out!"

They dropped, planted their boots toes-down on the log, did twenty push-ups in that horrid position, stumbled upright, and hefted the log again.

Pain ripped along Justice's arms. *Really, God…anything…I mean it.*

"Lunges again!" Clark used the back of his hand to swipe a dribble of tobacco juice off his chin. "Down to the sea!"

Breathing was horrible. Justice's lungs were on fire, and her body was an inferno. Her shoulder and back muscles were in a pissing match over which was in more pain, and her knees were all like, *yo' mama,* contradicting them.

"Embrace the suck!" Keith growled at them. "Come on! Go!"

Justice's college track buddy, Anne, got married and had a kid right after graduating. "Come over to my house for Stevie's third birthday party," she said when Justice was in Bel Air before going to Officer Candidate School. "You can drink wine in a corner while the kids play. No biggie."

It *had* been a biggie. The noise all those kids made was astronomical, and Justice developed the worst headache of her life. *That* headache was peanut-sized compared to the one she had now. Her brain was over-boiled from the San Diego sun, the veins in her temples shrunk down to filament thread from dehydration.

"Get it together, Hayes!" Chalmers banged his shoulder into her shoulder.

Rage hardened the skin across her face. *Screw you, Chalmers, you little shit! It's not me!* All the unfairness she'd been storing away ruptured out of her as an intact grenade.

Snarling, she stepped back and seized Appletini by the shirt collar, yanking him off the line. "Stay away from this fucking log, Shaw, you no-load douche-whore!" Kicking his feet out from under him, she sat him down, then shoved her way back into place.

"Reposition!" Knight ordered.

The rest of the men spread out along the log.

Shaw scrambled to his feet, but when he tried to get back on the line, there wasn't room for him.

Instructor Clark was on Appletini like a shark on chum. "What's this I see!?"

The rest of Team Knight continued toward the sea. Minus Appletini, their lunges were now smooth and coordinated. They moved at a good clip.

Chalmers grunted in surprise.

Yeah, Travis, you can kiss my ass.

"So, Hayes," Crushy Boyd gasped, "what exactly is a douche-whore, anyway?"

She didn't have spare oxygen to laugh.

They reached the ocean, then were directed to secure Log PT.

Justice helped heft the log on top of the stack of others,

then stood by the rack, panting. It still hurt to breathe.

It hurt to stand.

It hurt to walk.

It hurt to blink.

"Man your boats!"

She closed her eyes, good and tight. She had prayed for Land Portage. Now her wish was being granted. But she really, really didn't want it anymore.

"HOOYAH!" The class ran to their boats.

She claimed a strap at the rear of the Knight Team IBS.

"Come on!" Chalmers started in. "You guys gotta grab the straps near the base or—"

"Cut the chatter," Knight growled.

"You know what?" Chalmers threw down his strap. "Up yours, Knight! I can't deal with your screw-ups anymore." He stomped off.

Ring. Ring. Ring.

"Good fucking riddance," Hairy Arms grumbled.

Knight called for another man, but too many had DOR'd during Log PT.

Justice was going to have to stand in as a regular.

Appletini sulked back over to the team.

Together the seven of them hefted the boat onto their heads and jogged toward the shoreline. After three revolutions of position changes, it became clear that Knight wasn't going to treat Justice like a regular.

He wasn't rotating her into the middle spot.

The typical manning of an IBS during boats-on-head consisted of two men in front, two in the middle, two at the rear, and one at the very back—the coxswain. Strategically, it was best to put the fastest men in front—they were in charge of constantly pulling forward on the straps—and the strongest at the back—they pushed up the berm. But the toughest spot for the toughest men was the middle spot. It was here the water-logged boat sagged the most and was heaviest.

"Put me in the middle," she gritted at Knight. "I'm not an extra now. I need to take a turn."

The sides of Knight's jaw bulged.

On the next switch, she forced her way into the middle.

Hol-lee shit. Now she knew the answer to the question: could her headache grow worse?

The middle spot accordion-collapsed her forehead into her chin and dumped all her teeth out of her mouth. *Joking,* although only half-a-joke because *fucking, seriously.* An unequivocal *YES!* to the worst headache ever part. *I'm going to die.* But she damn well didn't duck boat, not once.

When the instructors secured Land Portage, and Team Knight dumped their IBS in the sand, her boat crew stood with hands on their hips or knees, chests laboring, and stared at her.

With new eyes.

She hadn't been the one to fuck up Log PT, and she held her own as a regular man during boats-on-heads.

She would've smiled at them if she had any teeth left.

"Hydrate!"

"HOOYAH!"

A tub of water bottles was brought over to the class.

Justice downed two, vomited them up, then downed two more.

The class was secured for evening chow.

What? No surf torture first?

Nirvana.

She aimed toward the chow hall and spotted Knight just ahead. He'd taken off his long-sleeved fatigue shirt, and his regular T-shirt was plastered to his torso, revealing an endless terrain of hard, carved muscle.

She veered over to him, betrayal burning like a fireball in her chest. "What happened to our arrangement?" she demanded as she drew even with him, her voice chafing her throat. "You agreed to treat me like a regular candidate."

He stopped and turned toward her. Nasty red wheals covered his arms, and his cheeks were a little sunken in, but his eyes were sharp. "I have an entire boat crew to consider when making decisions about the success of any evolution, Justice, and whether you want to hear it or not, you're not as strong as the men."

The statement hit her like a medicine ball to the stomach. No, she didn't want to hear that right now—because it was brutally true. But also… *Screw you, Knight.* "I did it, though, didn't I?"

"Yes," he said. "You did. But I didn't put you in spot two, and I need you not to defy my orders out there."

Orders? She curled her lip. Although, unfortunately, yes, he had the right to give them. She might outrank Keith in real-world military, but on the BUD/S boat team, he was the boss.

She deepened the curl of her lip. Hopefully toward a sneer. But maybe toward a quivery, girlie thing that would've been monstrously horrible at this precise moment. "Sure, Knight," she drawled. "But just to clarify—when I need your help, I'll ask for it, like with the dolphin kick, like with the first-aid patch-up job. Otherwise, I would appreciate it if you would let me fail before you assume I will due to my unfortunate estrogenic load-bearing capacity. Are we clear on that too?"

Knight's eyes bored into hers with implacable steadiness, his pupils dilating as if to take in more of her body without requiring him to move. "No, ma'am," he returned, dangerously soft, "we are not clear. The middle position on an IBS is notorious for causing back injuries, and the fuck if I'm going to see you put in a neck brace because I *let* you fail."

"Who says my neck is more valuable than the guys'?"

she challenged.

"That's my call to make."

They stood immobile, gazes clashing.

The world contracted, tunneled in on itself, narrowed down to only the two of them.

Knight stepped closer to her, so close she could see the budding black whiskers trying to push up along the masculine curve of his upper lip.

Justice's pulse hammered. There was somehow now an edgy, belly-dropping quality to the way Keith was looking at her…an almost sexual undercurrent to it.

Keith's focus slipped to a rip on the shoulder of her shirt.

Her heart went freight train on her. She dragged a hand over her mouth and stalked off.

SHE WAS STILL moving in long, ground-eating strides when she stormed inside the officers' barracks.

Brayden was in the kitchen, digging the chocolate chip ice cream out of the freezer. He hadn't showered yet, and his inner arms were caked with dried blood from the abuse of Log PT. Sand clumped his eyelashes together and salt water was crusted in his hair, and yet somehow he still managed to look less dirty than she did. It was like no matter how much sweat and sand got ground into this man, he would never lose all that was upright and good and honorable about him. Whereas all the polish in the world couldn't hide that she hailed from grimy thief stock, unfit even to shine the shoes of Golden Boy here.

"Why do you men have to be so damned difficult?" She planted her hands on her hips, but the bent-elbow position spiked pain through her own raw arms. She dropped her hands.

Street closed the freezer, one of his eyebrows inching up.

"Did I do something?"

"Oh, you're the worst, always the consummate gentleman around me, pulling out my chair, standing when I stand. You even gave me a gift."

He set the gallon of ice cream on the counter. "It was soap," he responded in a *what's the big?* tone.

"Yeah? Did you give soap to the men?"

He lip-twisted that. "They don't get sand in hard-to-reach places." He chuckled.

She flushed. "So glad you find this entertaining."

"Sorry, Justice, I just feel like I've come in on the second half of a conversation." He dished ice cream into a bowl. "Want some?"

"No, dammit."

He glanced at her through his matted lashes. "Maybe you can fill me in on the first half."

She chopped a hand out. "I've got Boyd trying to protect me from Ziegler's dirty mouth, Dunbar championing me in an imaginary harassment case, *you* holding doors open for me, and now Knight's treating me like I belong on a fainting couch rather than under an IBS."

Street tossed the scooper into the sink. "You need to cut Keith some slack. He has an issue with people under his watch getting hurt." Brayden sucked a droplet of ice cream off his thumb. "And besides, what kind of man do you think goes into the Teams? The kind who *doesn't* like to look out for others?"

"I don't need protecting," she stated, her words terse and cold. "I've arrived at BUD/S with a full complement of functioning limbs, thank you. I'm perfectly capable of doing a job."

Brayden smiled.

The hairs on her nape bristled. Oh, the man's dimples weren't bailing him out of this one. "You don't think so?" If he said anything about substandard upper body strength, she was going to sock him.

"Of course, I think so. I see you sweating your heart out every day on the grinder, and I'm proud of you—if I can say that without sounding condescending." He stuck the chocolate chip back in the freezer. "My mom's a very strong lady, too, who goes her own way. I mean she never did anything BUD/S-like crazy, like you. She just…defined life on her terms."

He searched the silverware drawer for a spoon. "When she got pregnant with me, my dad asked her to marry him—begged her to—but she didn't want domesticity. I mean, she wanted *me*—she even gave me her last name—but she's a painter, and she needs to control the world she creates in." He gave up on the silverware drawer and tugged a spoon out of the dish strainer. "My mom is the most determined woman I know, but she's always a *woman*. It's no insult being female, Justice."

Her face burned. "I don't have any problems with being a woman," she retorted. "Just not at BUD/S." She stepped up to the kitchen counter and braced her palms on it. "I need you to stop treating me like a woman."

He scraped up some ice cream and put it in his mouth. "You *are* a woman."

Her scalp boiled over at his banality. "Are you listening to me? Not *here*, I'm not. You and I aren't at fucking cotillion, Street, and you bending over to kiss my hand every morning at muster actually does me damage." A breeze wafted in through the open sliding glass door and fluttered her bangs. She shoved her hair aside.

He leaned back against the stove. "My mom raised me to treat women a certain way, and I can't change. Sorry."

She stepped swiftly around the counter and brought herself nearly nose-to-nose with him. "*Try.*"

CHAPTER FIFTEEN

THE WAVE BROKE with shocking thunder and roared at the IBS, the churning white froth violently jouncing and jolting the small rubber boat.

Today was surf passage day, not yesterday, as Knight had heard. Yesterday the swells had been small. Today they were big—the instructors were obviously keeping an eye on the surf report. The waves weren't *The Poseidon Adventure* big, but in a thirteen-foot unstable rubber boat, even a seven-foot wave felt humongous.

Sea spray flew at Crushy Boyd and Pervy Ziegler—seated up front—hitting them full in the face, while Knight and Sniper Kilgour, in the middle spots, ducked below the worst of the spray. Appletini and Dog Bone were in the rear—no one, by the way, missed Chalmers—and Justice was manning her usual coxswain position in the very back.

The boys were serving as the grunt power, while she held the dual jobs of keeping the crew paddling in sync by calling the strokes plus steering the craft, using her oar like a rudder.

They all wore orange life vets over camouflage combat gear.

She shook water out of her eyes and focused on the ocean ahead. "Stroke!" she called out. "Stroke! Stroke!"

Hairy Arms groaned. "Christ, this is killing me. Is anyone else popping a chub from hearing Hayes say *stroke* over and over?"

Knight lifted his oar out of the water and smacked Ziegler on the side of the head.

"Ouch! Shit, man, just saying…"

A wall of seawater rose up in front of them. They'd just paddled into the break zone, and—*holy crap!*

"Dig in!" she yelled. "Come on, we've got this!"

The men rowed harder, creating a vista of rippling, bulging muscles in front of her that she didn't have the luxury or time to fully appreciate—or a sanity checklist nearby to test if she even should.

"Stroke!" she bellowed. "Stroke!" Arms straining, she fought to keep the boat straight as one of the rowers lagged—any guess who? The boat skidded a little sideways, and she cursed. Cresting a wave even slightly off-center was asking for disaster.

The boat went vertical.

Justice saw blue sky.

The men hunched over, putting all they had into the rowing, but—

The boat flipped over backward.

The sky smeared by and collapsed into palm trees and institutional buildings, then the men were tumbling from front to back, crashing down on top of Justice in a clobber of boots and muscles and flying oars. She lost her next breath. A paddle whacked her on the head, and a hot slice of pain cut across the upper left side of her forehead, and—

Whoosh!

She was underwater, skidding, bumping, and scraping over coarse sand, whirling, flipping, and rolling in the savage white surf. She went numb behind her solar plexus, a sort of distant warning-fear of how bad this could get if it didn't let up soon.

Cold seawater went up her nose. She pawed at the ocean and broke the surface, gagging, half-blinded by red stuff.

Blood? Another wave slammed into her and drove her back under. She rag-dolled through a second spin cycle, her limbs going lax and slushy. Someone was hammering a board of nails into her temple. A black curtain passed over her mind.

She wasn't sure how she made it to shore—she was suddenly just lying limply on her back, her limbs starfished out at odd angles. The tide sloshed her around like so much loose kelp. She stared up at gray thunderheads.

"Hayes!" Hairy Arms appeared in a crouch at her side. "Holy fuck, are you all right?"

The image of his features was distorted, but she could still tell his eyebrows were veed together. Water dripped off him and pattered onto her face.

"Yrdribwazeronme," she slurred.

Crushy Boyd's legs appeared above her. "Whoa, that's hosed up, man. She's not even speaking English."

Hairy Arms held up three fingers in front of her. "How many fingers am I holding up?"

"Three."

"Nope."

No? Crap.

Ziegler dropped his hand, then put up three fingers again. "How many?"

"Three."

"No."

She squinted. Pinpoints of bright light skipped across her vision.

"Quit messing with her, man," Boyd said. "Look at her head."

Hairy Arms grinned.

"You're dripping water on me," she repeated.

Hairy Arms lifted his focus and scanned the area. "Where the hell is Knight, anyway?"

Dog Bone jogged up. "Getting a new bunghole ripped

open by Instructor Clark for our wipeout." He frowned down at Justice. "That's not good."

"Help her to her feet," Hairy Arms said.

Dog Bone frowned some more. He looked unconvinced about the wisdom of that idea.

Hairy Arms stood and offered her a hand.

She clasped palms with him.

He tugged her upright.

She stood and pitched forward, not stopping until she was sagging against Ziegler with her nose smashed against his orange life vest. She couldn't seem to push herself upright.

Boyd made a noise in his throat. "Oh, now, that's just embarrassin'."

Ziegler chuckled.

Why did it have to be the pervert she was pressed against?

A new person arrived behind her. "Hey, what's going on?"

Brayden. That was Brayden's voice.

"Hayes messed up her head bad," Dog Bone reported.

Her shoulders were grabbed from behind. She was pulled vertical and turned around. Ah, yes, there was Mighty Dimple Man.

Brayden's eyebrows shot up. "Messed up bad and then some. You okay, Justice?"

"Absolutely superb," she lied.

Brayden released her. She swayed. He grabbed her again.

"No biggie." She mustered a confident expression. "Just still riding the waves is all." The left side of her face felt wet. Not runny-wet, more like viscous-wet. She glanced down and saw blood covering her life vest. "Uh-oh. Thassa lotta blood."

Brayden gave her a reassuring smile. "Head wounds

bleed a lot, right? I'm sure it's not as bad as it looks."

Crushy Boyd made a face. Clearly he disagreed.

"Why don't you grab her some water?" Brayden suggested to Hairy Arms.

"Roger." Ziegler jogged off, sidestepping around Keith, who'd just arrived.

"Fucking Clark," he growled. "You'd think the asshole had never been in—Jesus! Justice, what the hell happened?" Keith focused on her forehead, and then he did something she'd never seen him do before.

He blanched completely white.

"I'm all right," she said. She didn't mean it, but maybe she should try to mean it or at least put on a better game face in case it *was* as bad as it looked. It felt bad. Like she was back at Stevie's birthday party and a second busload of toddlers had arrived.

"No, you're not," Keith countered sharply. "Get your ass over to a corpsman."

What? And risk a medical rollback? *No way.* "No, no. Thanks." She stepped away from Brayden. "I'm good."

"The fuck you are." Keith grabbed her arm and aimed her toward shore, where several of the instructors were using paddles to heap sand onto the backs of candidates who were working hard to secure their crafts. More sand went into their boats.

She pulled her arm from Knight's hold.

Keith's eyebrows lowered into a thunderous frown.

"Keith," Brayden said in an even tone. "Why don't you just give her a second?"

She looked between the brothers. Had Street/Knight passed through the Phantom Tollbooth or Calvin and Hobbes' transmogrifier when she wasn't paying attention and switched brains? The cosseting gallant was currently the calm one, while the steady leader was completely off his cork.

Hairy Arms trotted up and held out a water bottle.

She stared at it. Just stared. And stared.

"Dammit, see?" Keith bit out. "She's acting weird."

Right. She needed to not do that. She flung a gesture at Hairy Arms. "It's just because this is Hairy—" She cut herself off.

"Harry?" Ziegler repeated—or *thought* he was repeating. He slashed a brow at her. "Hey, I'm cool with you calling me by another guy's name, Hayes, no problem."

"This is *Ziegler* we're talking about," she pronounced carefully. "He probably rimmed the bottle."

Dog Bone scrunched his forehead at Ziegler.

"I didn't." Ziegler laughed. "No shit."

"Justice." Keith's words were tight and succinct—he was obviously putting a great deal of effort into holding onto the last vestiges of his temper. "The cut on your head is severe. You need stitches."

Stitches! She would definitely be outed for stitches, and if she got stashed at PTRR again, she might never make it back out. "I'm good, really."

"That's for a corpsman to decide. Go to the—"

"Jesus, I'm *fine*."

"I'm not making a suggestion," Keith all but snarled, his expression livid. "Check in at the ambulance. *Now*."

Her stomach trod over her heart on its way into her throat. She cast a desperate glance at Brayden.

"Don't look at him," Keith snapped.

"He's a class officer." *And you're being a complete pig-head.* "Shouldn't he have a say in this?"

Keith took an aggressive step closer. "I'm your boat team leader."

Brayden raised a peacemaker's hand. "Listen, Justice, Keith's right. You need to have your injury treated. If the corpsman tries to insist on stitching you up, tell him you *only* want it butterflied." Pointedly, he added, "Stay calm while you're dealing with him."

It was then she realized how hotly she was glaring. The skin on her face was also pulled so taut she probably looked like she'd been dead for two days.

"If you stay level headed," Brayden went on, "you'll convince medical you're self-assessing correctly. Clear?"

She locked her jaw and gave a short nod. She didn't trust herself to speak right now. If she did talk, a lot of *Fuck you, you fucking overprotective fucks* would come spewing out.

She stormed off.

Chapter Sixteen

By the end of the day, Justice could no longer tell if her headache was from the wound on her temple or from having her jaw clenched in rage and frustration for the better part of four hours straight.

No one was listening to her insist that she was *perfectly fine*. She was still nauseous, dizzy, occasionally saw spots, and Stevie and his maniac three-year-old friends had taken up residence *inside* her head, the frenzied horde of them battering her skull with their little fists, and…

So, okay. She felt like crap.

Worse, her game face apparently sucked—something that could mean her demise in a place like this. It took the fight of her life to convince the corpsman to forgo stitches and only butterfly-close her laceration. At last the guy did, and after some more unnecessary dicking around, she was finally sent back to duty.

By then, the surf passage evolution was over.

But, hey, she was lucky enough to rejoin the gang for end-of-the-day PT, which she did in stoic silence. Keith watched her through narrow eyelids, clearly not too happy about her refusal to speak.

If her attitude made her seem like a pouty prima donna in his opinion, well…he could go suck his own dick about it. She'd come way too close to getting completely screwed over today, and just *maybe* he should've kept his mouth shut and his opinions to himself.

Wasn't it only yesterday she'd reminded him to treat her like a regular candidate?

Perhaps pigheads needed lots of reminding.

When the day was secured, she stalked over to the enlisted barracks—walking sideways on a tightrope—and planted herself at the flagpole outside, waiting with her temper on high boil.

A few minutes later, Hairy Arms and Sniper Kilgour strolled by.

Ziegler's eyes rounded on her. "Whoa, Hayes. Your head looks like a plum."

She compressed her lips into a flat seam. Yes, she'd seen it, thank you. Her temple was swollen into a healthy knot, the flesh of the wound staining into the kind of dark bruising that made it look like a squid had taken a dump on her head. "Could you tell Petty Officer Knight I'd like to speak with him, please?"

"Uh, okay." Ziegler bolted inside, Kilgour following.

Ziegler must have warned Knight about her eat-shit-and-die expression. When he stepped outside his face was already set.

Well. Since he was braced for it... "Do you realize how close I came to a medical rollback today, and all because you couldn't mind your own damned business?"

He crossed his arms and spoke with an edge. "I didn't realize the welfare of my boat team wasn't my business."

There was enough sarcasm in his tone to make her want to rip it out of his larynx. She gave him an acid glare. "You need to learn to pay attention when I say I'm good."

A muscle jumped in his jaw. "A flap of your skin was hanging down."

"I don't give a fuck!" she yelled.

"I do!" he thundered back. "It would've been grossly negligent of me not to send you to medical."

She clenched her teeth, nausea bubbling at the back of her throat. The length of her esophagus felt like it was covered in road-rash. How *awesome* would it be if she puked, then fainted in the middle of this argument?

Keith shook his head. "Look at you, Justice. You're fucking *gray*."

She thrust a tautly knuckled fist against her lips. *Get through this…get through this…* "Before I lose my mind," *and consciousness,* "I need to make sure you understand something. On my completely fucked journey to BUD/S, I almost didn't make it out of PTRR. If I'm rolled back there a second time for an injury, I might not ever escape. So I need you to stop being an overprotective jerk and treat me like a regular candidate—like we *agreed*—and I need you to do it right fucking now—like I told you *yesterday*."

He regarded her flatly. "No."

"No?" Her head pounded so hard, she saw double for a second. She was getting really sick of this man acting like her basic human rights were optional. "You can't say *no*. I'm not asking you to pass the fruit salad. I'm telling how I want to be treated as a human being."

"If I see you wavering, I'm not walking by. If I see you on the ground, I can't just step over you. That's not the man I am. So the thing that needs to happen *right fucking now* is for *you* to chill out."

She dragged air through her teeth. The pigheaded dick wasn't even making a pretense of caring about her needs. She stood in place, bile in her brain and anger in her throat—or something like that. "Now I *really* need you to pay attention. Are you, Knight? Listening? Carefully?"

He gave her a burning look.

"If you end up sabotaging my career out of some misguided notion that your chauvinistic pampering is actually *leadership*, then I will hack into all your accounts and destroy your life. Do you understand *that*?"

"We're done here."

Are we? My, how the wrangler did enjoy bossing her around. "If you say so. You're the boat team leader." She cut around him, circumnavigating a bush. Her legs were trembling. This fight with Keith was definitely a fight-fight. There wasn't a single sexual underpinning to how she felt right now—like she wanted to smash his face and bash his head and feed him his own balls.

"By the way," she threw back at him, "pudding is for girls. Be a man and eat a candy bar for once, you fucking pussy." Storming across the grounds to the officers' barracks, she thundered into her bedroom and slammed the door. Stalking over to her bed, she gripped the top bunk, pressing her forehead against the railing to—"Ouch!" She jerked back. "Dammit!"

She spun around and sank heavily onto her bottom bunk. A soggy lump pushed into her throat. It felt like a wad of tears, but that was stupid. She snagged her trashcan and set it between her legs. She was about due for a trip to the vomitorium.

Cradling her head carefully in her palms, she thought about things for a long time while she did battle with her nausea. As she gradually calmed, she came to the conclusion that she just might be cracking up. Keith was one of the most solid men she'd ever met. He looked out for the people under him, and even though he might be more protective of her than was warranted, it didn't make him a pighead who was actively trying to screw her over.

You need to cut Keith some slack. He has an issue with people under his watch getting hurt.

She could've handled things with a bit more finesse. One didn't crack a safe by bashing on it, after all. Sighing, she stared at her pillow. She would just go to bed and hope come morning none of this had actually happened, if Stevie and his fiendish friends would let up on her skull for a bit.

A soft knock sounded.

"Come in," she called, still slouched with her forearms draped over her thighs.

Keith stepped inside, holding an ice pack in one hand. His other hand was closed into a fist. "Hey," he said, nudging the door closed with the heel of his boot.

"Hi." She peered up at him. With her sitting and him standing, he appeared taller than usual.

"I brought you some contraband." Crossing to her bed, he hunkered down in front of her and put out his fist. He opened it. Three pills sat on his callused palm. "Ibuprofen," he identified them. "I had some stashed in my car."

"Holy crap," she moaned. "Lifesaver." Only corpsmen were supposed to dole out pain meds at BUD/S. She leaned over sideways, grabbed the water bottle off her nightstand, and slugged down the pills. "Thank you."

"You bet." He seemed just now to notice the trashcan between her legs. He gave it an arch look, then put it off to the side. "I would also like to go on record as being a big fan of Snickers."

"Oh, God," she moaned, covering her face with her hands. "Please don't make me feel worse for saying that than I already do." She spread her fingers and peeked at Keith through the split. "Have you ever heard how only children can sometimes lack conflict resolution skills—no one else in the house to fight with over the Pop-Tarts 'n' all?" She dropped her hands. "Would it surprise you to know I'm an only child?"

He chuckled. The smile reached his eyes, which were no longer dark with temper but back to being a gorgeous aqua blue—a much better shade.

"I'm sorry," she said.

He nodded. "This place is getting to us all. Here." He handed her the ice pack. "Put this on your lump."

Keith Knight, the patch 'em up guy. She lightly pressed the ice to her bump.

For a moment it looked like he wanted to adjust how she was doing it, but he kept his hands to himself. "I've been pacing the beach, thinking about everything you said, and I'd like to clarify a few things, if that's all right?"

"Go ahead."

"The idea that I might be trying to sabotage you—even subconsciously—was really bothering me. So I took a hard look at it, and I'm one hundred percent sure I'm not."

Guilt stabbed at her. She'd flung out the accusation in the heat of the moment. "I know you're not."

"I *want* you here. Okay?"

The depth of color in his eyes sent a trickle of warm honey down her spine. *Want...* "Uh, okay."

"I'm also one hundred percent certain I treated you exactly how I would've treated anyone else. If Ziegler or Dog Bone or Kilgour had been bleeding like fuck from a severe head wound, I would've told him to get his ass to medical too. So we might have to agree to disagree over whether or not my actions today counted as chauvinistic pampering."

She winced. Wow, she'd lacked finesse in their argument by a long shot. "In all fairness, I have no idea how bad I looked."

He paused, then his expression eased. "Nice of you to say that. And...if we're being completely honest here, you may not be entirely, completely off base about *some* overprotectiveness on my part. You're just doing really well, Justice, and I want to see you succeed."

She believed him about that too. He looked out for her too much sometimes, yes, but he'd also worked tirelessly to make her a part of Team Knight.

She tucked up one side of her cheek, feeling surprisingly sappy all of a sudden. After weeks of enduring so much unfairness, having Keith be entirely fair was…extremely nice. He could've viewed her as not worth the effort of pacing the beach and thinking about, but he'd clearly put a great deal of thought into all this.

"Thanks, Knight. I appreciate you talking things out with me."

Irony tugged at the corners of his mouth. "Not usually my strongest suit," he admitted. "But we're friends, right?"

She lowered the ice pack and carefully set it on the bed beside her. *Friends*. Was that what they were? It felt like more, but she wasn't sure what. Comrades? That sounded kind of silly, although if they both made it through BUD/S, they might end up working in the field together someday.

She searched Keith's face for a way to explain it, but as a smile steadily curved a mouth constructed for much more than *friendship*, she didn't know how to describe him at all…except in goofy, sentimental ways—

And she was probably concussed.

Chapter Seventeen

YOU MUST LEARN to listen with your entire body, Justine, not only your ears…

Her father's words echoed hollowly through her head.

Feel a situation to truly know it…

"Down!"

"FIFTEEN!"

I heard you moving again, Justine.

Her father was sitting in a folding chair, his back to the main part of the family living room.

Try again. Remember—total silence.

"Down!"

"SIXTEEN!"

"Y'all will not be recovered until Hayes collapses!" Chief Tanner threatened.

"Down!"

"SEVENTEEN!"

"She doesn't have to ring out, just fucking fall over s'all."

Justice stared down through fractured vision at the floor in front of her as bile ran out of her nose.

Tanner's statement? Total bullcrap.

This endless beating was *all* about making her quit. *For good.* She was scheduled to leave BUD/S tomorrow for two weeks, and the instructors damn well didn't want her coming back—were hugely hacked off that they hadn't driven her to DOR already. So today's beating was colossal, endless, a huge fucking standoff that would only end with someone on a stretcher or—

"Argh!"

The man on Justice's right collapsed, splashing to the floor. Yes. Correct—*splashing*.

So much sweat and seawater was on the floor of the mess hall at this point, Justice's bloody hands were partially submerged where they were braced on the linoleum. The walls were also crawling with droplets of humidity and the windows weeping. Hours ago the available, breathable oxygen had been reduced to nil.

Hours and hours…

"Down!"

"EIGHTEEN!"

Sometimes you can tell which wire to cut by feel alone…

Now it was Uncle Alistair guiding her, his smile wide and encouraging.

Which one is the hot one? Cut it!

The colossal beating began after noon chow: push-ups, flutter kicks, mountain-climbers, eight-count body builders—like burpees, but with extra pain—pull-ups, hit the surf, more push-ups, sit-ups, get wet and sandy, more flutter kicks, back/belly/feet, leg levers, combat crawl over the sand berm, push-ups, get wet and sandy, surf torture, Egyptian push-ups…

Which was where they were stalled out now.

The Egyptian push-up position was not unlike Down-ward Facing Dog: butt stuck straight up in the air, feet and knees together, hands on the floor in front of the eyes. On the down part of the Egyptian push-up, the front of the head briefly touched the diamond formed by the fingers. Over and over.

Bump, bump, bump.

As Justice's brow hit her hands repeatedly over *hours*, the injury on her forehead went back to feeling like a throbbing knothole—yeah, okay, she'd needed stitches a week ago—and an old scar on the back of her hand reopened. First it turned red, then swelled and bubbled up, then split open and bled.

That's how long they'd been doing Egyptian push-ups.

For so long that Justice's mind had slipped, a piece of it going far away, back in time to her childhood, while another piece was still here with the rest of the class in the mess hall.

Where she didn't want to be.

"Down!"

"NINETEEN!"

Appletini Shaw edged over to take the place of the man on Justice's right who'd just splashed over. Shaw glared at her around one of his planted arms.

"Down!"

"TWENTY!"

Justice's nose and sinuses burned as another stream of bile ran from her nostrils onto the floor.

"Chief Tanner!"

"HOOYAH, CHIEF TANNER!"

"Again!" Tanner roared. "If y'all can't outlast a bleeder, you don't belong on my Teams."

Justice observed with shaky vision the swill of water on the floor, discolored from passed-out men having shit and pissed themselves, the surface coated with a layer of oil from all their sweat.

Now the bile from her nose was adding to the mire, plus the blood on her hand...

Look at this safe, Justine! The Ward-Lock 2000 is an antique! It will take a special touch to open it...

"Push-ups! Ready!"

"READ—"

Justice went flying into her left-hand neighbor—

Sanchez.

She bowled him over, then kept tumbling over the top of him to collide with the next guy, Hooper, knocking him to the floor too.

Hooper hit the linoleum with a ground-out, "Fuck!"

She lolled to a stop on the slimy floor in a state of torpid discombobulation. Jagged lightning forked across the ceiling—er, probably cracks in the plaster—and she stared at the squiggly design in such acute and complete pain, she lost all connection with her body. Thank God for her medulla oblongata. If not for the autonomic functions that part of her brain was performing, her heartbeat and respiration would've stopped altogether. *She* certainly didn't have any energy left to keep them going.

"Recover!" Chief Tanner belted out.

Men groaned, shouted, cursed.

Boots sloshed; more bodies splashed to the floor; some candidates stumbled into each other with fleshy whacks.

All the sounds rode an acoustical rollercoaster in Justice's ears, like someone was manically spinning the world's volume knob.

Tanner released them, shouting, "Dismissed to decon!"

To hose off the sewage. Better just to abandon their group to a nuclear waste site and be done with them.

All right, now tuck yourself in there, Justine. You mustn't be afraid of small crawl spaces. Maintain control of yourself at all times, my girl.

Crushy Boyd's features smeared into view above her. If not for his dark complexion, she might not have seen him against the backdrop of white ceiling.

He held out his hand to her. A clown hand. A monster claw. A chicken drumstick.

"Come on, Hayes," Boyd croaked, bending over, and—he fell down, skidding out beside her.

Tiny waves of sludgy water rippled against her sides. She sagged her mouth open. *Breathe in—one, two. Breathe out—three, four.* Circumstances were so dire even her medulla oblongata couldn't be depended upon anymore.

Boyd was standing again, stumbling. "Help me get her up."

Someone grabbed her under the armpits and hoisted her to her feet.

Thanks for the help, man. She started a smile on her mouth but couldn't seem to make it spread any further than a tic along a nerve.

Keith appeared in front of her. His sweaty face was a daguerreotype of the original, caved in at the hollows beneath his cheekbones, his flesh sepia-toned. "Huddle up," he told his boat team in a hoarse voice.

Her guys formed a box around her. Someone took her by the shoulders and physically turned her toward the door—and the image of Chief Tanner rolled past her vision.

He was glaring with predatory intent at…

Not at her.

At…

Appletini Shaw.

So *that's* what happened during Down Dog push-ups—Appletini had kicked her over.

Now the instructors had a new person to hate. Not so good for Appletini. Better for her.

Outside, the sky was a sullen gray. There was an angry bite to the wind, and it flapped a lose louvre on one of the mess hall's outer window blinds like a semaphore, white then beige then white again.

Her team led her toward the decontamination shower, and she bumped and jostled between the men like a ricocheting pinball. When she zigged one way, a teammate was there to steer her back on track. Zag the other way, another man was there, using his shoulder to keep her from falling over.

"Way to hump it, Hayes," Boyd told her, still croaky.

They arrived at decon.

Appletini was just ahead of their group, and Knight shot forward, juking between men like a running back heading for first and ten.

"You weak-tit little coward." Keith choke-rammed Appletini against the shower wall.

"Hey," Appletini gasped. "Get off me." He tugged at Keith's arm, but Knight wasn't going anywhere.

His legs were braced solidly, muscles all over his body punching up against his flesh.

The class surged closer to watch, boots squishing, lungs sounding like rusted-out hamster wheels.

"You ever do anything like that again," Keith warned darkly, "and I'll smoke-check your ass off my boat team."

Appletini's face flushed red and bright. "You can't do that."

"Watch me. Every time you try to do something with my team, I'll bounce your fucking head."

Justice weaved on her feet, blinking repeatedly at Knight. Where the hell was the man finding the energy for this fight? It was amazing. *He* was amazing. *Good ol' Hero of the Day.* Her smile felt goofy. Whittled down to nothing but visceral feeling, her raw glop was getting the better of her. *Man 'o the Hour and all 'round Hunk-a Chunk-a.*

Appletini was turning an asphyxiated shade of blue.

Off to the side, Dunbar hissed at Brayden, "Should we stop this? We're officers."

"Stop what?" Street drawled.

Increasing levels of pain were chasing numbness from Justice's body. The all-over hurts were emerging in oddball patches, spots of numbness interspersed with spots of heat and knives. Like she was a Horror House leopard.

Finally, Keith released Shaw, giving him a hard shove as he stepped back.

Appletini sucked in air. Massaging his throat with one hand, he pointed an enraged finger at Justice. "*She* kicked *me* off Log PT."

Keith sneered. "Because you *weren't* performing, you cowfuck. You kicked her over because she *was*."

Weebles wobble, dah, da, da. It was a song from Justice's childhood, a commercial for a toy… How did it go? *Weebles wobble, but they don't fall down.* That was her…teeter-tottering on her roly-poly base, but not falling down…somehow.

Knight rounded on them. "BUD/S is the ultimate mind fuck," he blasted at the entire class. "You *know* that. The instructors have been trying to turn us against Hayes from the start. Don't you think they've been watching us for that?" He chopped a hand at Justice. "You go against her, you're not a Team Guy."

The leopard spots on Justice's body were splotching together, converging to coat her body with more and more pain. Ligaments leaked out of her patellas. She didn't know how she didn't fall. Maybe it was the blanket of warmth and triumph around her heart holding her up.

All around her, the other BUD/S candidates were nodding in agreement with Keith. It was a supreme moment. No matter what happened from here, these men considered her a teammate.

Relief, unfortunately, vacated the last germs of Saving Grace adrenaline from her system. Vertigo cartwheeled her brain into her chin. Her stomach rose up like a helium balloon, fast and inevitable. She said, "Urp," and listed out of the circle of men, taking off at a tottering limp.

"I've got her," she heard someone say.

Inebriated-sounding footsteps followed.

She put her head down and moved forward with a sense of purpose motivated solely by the blinders-on goal of getting horizontal in bed. Mere seconds away if—

She began to puke violently. She didn't bother stopping, just leaned sideways and spit vomit as she went. A pigeon waddled across her path, its neck bobbing. A high-frequency whine played in her ears. A hum built in her throat.

With a harsh cry, she arrived at the officers' barracks and flung herself inside.

Chapter Eighteen

"Hayes—"

It was Brayden who'd followed her, Dunbar stumbling along not far behind.

"Go away," Justice squawked. "Let me die in peace."

She whirled on Brayden, a move her shoddy equilibrium was in no condition to handle. She went down on one knee, her teeth clacking together.

"Oh, great," Dunbar whined, putting on his most sour lemon face. "*Now* you collapse."

"Shut up," Brayden snapped.

"Fuck you." Dunbar careened into the bathroom.

"Shoot me," she entreated Brayden. Her tongue was a swath of cardboard, and it came out, *Schut me*.

Brayden grabbed her elbow and worked at pulling her upright.

She shoved at him on the way up, but her nonexistent stability couldn't deal with sudden forward motion either. She went down again. Her fingers slid along the front of Brayden's body and caught in the waistband of his pants, taking him down with her.

Brayden crashed onto his ass, cursed once, then splatted flat onto his back.

She landed on top of him, her tits in his crotch and her cheek cradled on his sweaty upper abs. His stomach muscles were very hilly. He really was a well-defined son of a gun. He also would've been hell to smell if bile hadn't singed away the majority of scent receptors in her nose.

Brayden moaned. "My kingdom for a horse."

She didn't budge from between his splayed thighs. She couldn't. She was done. Cooked. Go ahead and carve her up for Christmas dinner.

She heard the shower turn on. It stayed on for about three seconds, then there was a booming crash. The water turned off. Dunbar bumbled out of the bathroom stark naked—beyond caring what Captain Eagen would have to say about it, apparently—and further blundered into his bedroom.

Brayden lay in place, breathing in short bursts.

There was a very nice-sized penis beneath her breasts, but she stank and this was ridiculous. "Somebody needs to untangle." The unspoken addendum would be: *you.*

She couldn't.

Grunting, Brayden shoved up a little. He hooked one of his arms through one of hers and towed her backward, like one wounded soldier dragging another across a field of battle. He hauled them to the kitchen, his breathing heavier, new sweat glistening on his salty brow.

He leaned her against the cabinet below the countertop while he slouched across from her next to the refrigerator. Groping the door open, he tugged out two Gatorades. He opened one bottle and handed it to her, then proceeded to open another and down it.

It was something directly out of Comedy Central, her trying to drink her Gatorade. Her hand was shaking so badly, Arctic Blitz went sloshing everywhere—onto her T-shirt, the floor—going everywhere except inside her mouth.

Brayden came up for air, saw what was happening, and scooted over to her. Putting his hand over hers, he guided the drink to her.

She managed to get the rest of it down, but couldn't tell

if she felt any better. She was still shaking a lot—her leg bones rattlin' against her knee bones; her knee bones crackin' against her thigh bones; her thigh bones splittin' apart her hip bones. Now she was a Horror House children's song.

The hum in her throat started up again.

A furl appeared between Brayden's eyes. He struggled to his feet, making a wreck of it by bashing his knee into the cabinet beside her head, finally managing to steady himself enough to offer her a hand.

"Please, no," she begged. "Don't make me move."

"Come on."

"Brayden…"

"It's either up on your own, or I carry you." His pale lips slid off-center. "Like a damsel."

He was as thoroughly cooked as she was, or thereabouts—too spent to follow through on a threat such as carrying her. But then again…this was Brayden. Maybe she shouldn't call his bluff when it came to damsel-saving.

She somehow managed to assume a vertical position, and…you know, it probably wasn't good that she had no recollection of how she did it. Her expression must have shown her concern.

Brayden led her only as far as the community room couch. He made her lie down on it, then joined her, tucking himself behind her body.

"What are you doing?"

"It's just till you stop shaking." He spooned her within the strong cup of his body.

She tried to wedge an elbow under her. "I need a shower…"

"Don't argue." He draped an arm over her waist and released a long, stuttering breath.

She fell back on the cushions, the fight completely out

of her. If Brayden wanted to take care of her, she was too weak and tired and sick of it all to stop him. Besides, even stinky and sweat-soaked, he felt good, his entire muscular body vastly immovable...a physical reliability that was also *him*, and quite heart-twisting.

Brayden's breathing slowed. He tucked his knees snugly into the curve of hers and ducked his head to her shoulder, curling himself around her like he needed to hold onto her as much as he needed to stop her from falling off the earth.

It made things better.

The surf pounded a lulling rhythm, and within moments she fell into a deep coma-sleep.

It was dark when she woke.

Stars glittered brightly outside the sliding glass door, littering the sky by the millions. A soft *wazz* vibrated off the TV, and Rudy's muffled snores came through his bedroom wall. Otherwise, the Amphib Base was blanketed in quiet, shop having been shut up for the day.

She moved to stretch, then knocked off that idiocy, a groan spilling out of her. She was stiff enough to be made of plaster.

Brayden's nose pressed into the back of her neck. "Can we just stay here, please?"

"I'm starving." She rolled out from under his arm and off the couch, trying to put her legs under her. Total fail. She landed on her rear with a loud *thump*. It was jarring.

Brayden exhaled a breath—a laugh.

She stood, then immediately sat, propping her butt on the edge of the couch. "Do you think the mess hall's still open?"

Lifting himself onto an elbow, Brayden reached up to the lamp beside the couch and snapped it on. "I have lasagnas in the freezer."

She peered sideways at him. "Man, you're a regular Boy

Scout when it comes to provisions, aren't you? First the Power Bars on Extraction Swim day. Now this."

"I also have extra actuators." He jogged his eyebrows up and down. "If yours rusts on your UDT dive vest, you know who to come to."

Please don't be delightful right now. Not when I just slept in your arms.

She forced herself to stand and put some distance between them. "Um…should we maybe talk about the weird nap-thing we just did?" *Weird, as in quasi-intimate.*

Mutual understanding and shared commonalities plus intimacy were *all* complications she didn't need.

"We could." He squinted against the light, still sleepy-eyed. He would've been sexy in a rumpled sort of way if half his face wasn't browned out by…she dared not think what substance. "But I'm actually having trouble standing the sight of you right now."

She snorted. "Oh, and you're just a daisy." He was trying to un-weird it, and she appreciated it. Still… "Maybe I should give you my Don't Get the Wrong Idea speech."

"Only if you want me to laugh at you." He groaned himself to a full sitting position. "Trust me, Justice, you were wholly gross the entire time I was completely unconscious."

True. Except she'd noticed him at the height of feeling her worst: his package and his broad chest and his gentlemanly silliness that today hadn't been so silly. But then…maybe he was made out of the proverbial *sterner stuff* than she was. Maybe he should give *her* a Don't Get the Wrong Idea speech.

Maybe she needed to go with a temporary insanity plea.

He creaked to his feet like a ninety-year-old man. "We need to bandage your hand."

She checked on her old scar, still open and bloody.

"Why don't you shower first while I get the lasagnas going."

"All right, thanks." She headed off to the shower—and caught Brayden slanting a speculative glance at her.

BUD/S WAS RUTHLESS, unforgiving, and brutal. She hated just about all aspects of it: the perpetual filth, the constant psychological bludgeoning, the never-ending, unrecoverable physical pain, the absence of basic comforts, and sometimes even the lack of inalienable dignity.

She was being trained, yes. Would she have made it through yesterday's colossal beating if not for everything that had come before? Probably not.

But she still loathed BUD/S more than she'd ever thought possible, so it wasn't as if she *wanted* to stick around for the infamous fourth week of BUD/S training—Hell Week.

It was just...

The men.

She was going to miss the knuckleheads. They accepted her, and she'd grown attached to them. And the worst part...? She was never going to see a good portion of the candidates again. When she returned, a large percentage would be gone. It was a statistical fact.

Such was the massive weeding-out power Hell Week wielded.

Regret and something that felt like a close cousin to dread shot through her all at once. She should've said a better goodbye to Brayden last night, instead of silently eating her lasagna in stupefied exhaustion. What if he wasn't here after—

No.

She couldn't allow herself to think that.

Shoving her worries aside, she glanced at the eastern sky,

where the first rosy spears of dawn were streaking through cirrus clouds. The air carried the smoky perfume of someone's beach campfire. A couple of brown leaves drifted across the dais just as Chief Tanner and Instructor Hill climbed it.

"Ensign Hayes!" Tanner called out, looking at her directly. "You are cleared to depart."

"Aye, aye, Chief!" With a hole in her chest and a wide-open space in her belly, she toe-heeled a step off her painted flippers.

How bad would it be if she rushed onstage and gave the peckerhead a playful bop on the schnoz? *Thanks for the memories, Chief. It's been swell.*

Nonsense-talk. Tanner's memories sucked booty.

"Class 684!" Tanner called to the rest. "Fall out!"

"AYE, AYE, CHIEF!"

Justice did an about-face.

The members of her boat team gathered around her.

She gave them all a full dose of Mama Bear stern, arms crossed, eyes narrow. "Be here," she told them firmly, "when I get back."

Crushy Boyd grinned. "Affirmative."

"You shouldn't go." Dog Bone looked at her the way a child would if he'd been denied dessert—no small thing for Dog Bone.

Well, it wasn't up to her. Admiral Sherwin insisted that Hell Week was a quintessential SEAL rite of passage, and since Justice would never be a SEAL, the admiral had been unmovable on the point of booting her for the week of Hell Week and the week of recovery afterward. So she was being temporarily reassigned to NAS North Island to train with her Special Missions team, both the enlisted men she would command and the flight crew.

"I'm afraid I have to," she said, then individually met

each of their gazes.

She lingered on Keith, pretty much deciding in this stolen moment that women who gushed about tall men hadn't thought the matter all the way through. There was something very…provocative about looking a man directly eye-to-eye. It provided a sense of perfect-placement fit. Like a woman could just step straight forward and there she'd be, hip to hip, breasts to chest, no adjustments required to rub nipples, no going up on tiptoes for a kiss. Automatic Lego-lock, whole-puzzle excellence.

Keith's eyes warmed on her—had he just read her mind? "You're not going to go soft, are you?"

"That's what she said."

Keith cast a look skyward.

Justice laughed. "I'll stay fit," she told Keith, then punched Ziegler in the left pec.

Hairy Arms clasped a startled hand over the spot, then kept his hand there, covering the area she'd punched like he wouldn't wash it for days.

Considering the week ahead of him, he probably wouldn't.

She lingered some more, staring at Knight again, a hard knot wedging into the hole in her chest. This man…Keith…he was everything she so highly respected in a man. Confident and smart, unyielding in his convictions, a team player down to his core…how could she return to BUD/S and last a single day without him around to teach her how to be better?

He *had* to make it.

Her heart was well into her throat when she finally managed to speak. "Don't fuck up Hell Week."

Keith did a *fuggedaboutit* thing with his mouth. "Not an option."

"Good," she tossed back curtly, drawing herself up. She

needed to watch herself. How easily could hero worship morph into blubbering lovesickness?

Maybe too easily.

Forcing her gaze away from Keith, she addressed the rest of her boat team. "All right, you dickheads." She snapped them a salute with her bandaged hand. "See you in two weeks."

She turned and jogged off.

She'd only gone a few feet when her team gave her a call-out. "HOOYAH, ENSIGN HAYES!" they yelled. "TITS IN THE SAND!"

She cracked up, and when she darted a peek at the dais, she saw that Tanner's lips were twitching, and even the crumb duster residing on Hill's upper lip seemed to be grudgingly at peace for once.

CHAPTER NINETEEN

LIFE FROM THERE took on the feel of suspended reality.

Justice stayed in a nice room at the North Island BOQ—that she inhabited *alone*—enjoyed a decent wake-up time—arriving at work by oh-seven-hundred felt like vacation hours—drove her car to work instead of marching there, and ate what she wanted to eat, when she wanted to eat it. She accomplished all of these luxuries without sand in her vagina.

But having these surface comforts was like floating on a tranquil sea, experiencing beauty and peace, a cushiony weightlessness, and all the while below her sharks circled, ready to shred her the moment she dipped too low. BUD/S lurked, waiting for her return, and the not-too-distant future held a lot of unknowns for her: would she get along with the men of her Special Missions unit and flight crew? Would she pass the upcoming test of her skills as a leader? Following the *fake-it-till-you-make-it* rule for this phase of her training was not the optimal path to take—she wanted to actually *be* good.

Especially now that the eyes of the nation were upon her.

Yeah, weird thing…when she drove off the Amphib Base—her first time out since starting BUD/S—two TV news vans were waiting for her. They chased after her, reporters hanging outside windows, waving and shouting to hail her for an interview. *The BUD/S Woman* had apparently become a media phenomenon over the three weeks Justice was getting wet and sandy every day.

She drove fast and left the reporters behind. The public eye wasn't a good place to be as either a thief or a member of SOF.

She still felt like a bit of a "media sensation" come Monday morning when she was traversing the hallway of the HSC-85 *Firehawks* squadron—aviators started poking their heads out of doorways to watch her pass.

The heat from their stares prickled along her spine. She was out of practice at being gawked at, and besides, these stares weren't merely curious, but evaluative. She was *The BUD/S Woman* the news was spouting off about, and these elite airdales wouldn't be especially forgiving in their assessment of whether or not she was up to snuff.

If only she knew herself.

Having a bunch of sadistic instructors bent on destroying her every day had a way of shaking a woman's confidence.

So, absent truth and knowledge, she kept her boots full of bravado and her back straight as she passed open doors.

The function of each workspace was designated by a small plastic sign sticking out from the top of the door: Operations, Maintenance, Safety, etcetera. The general décor was minus the trappings most civilians found improved the daily grind, like plants and carpet and furniture that didn't look laminated.

A few framed posters decorated the walls, a picture here of a Seahawks helicopter landing on the sloping deck of a Navy ship, a picture there of the home guard helo sporting the full regalia of its logo on the tail—a garish red bird. A "show" bird, only. Helicopters used during normal operations were painted solid gray, the whole don't-wanna-provide-a-bright-red-target-for-SAMs thing being a major factor.

Snapping a smart right-face into the CO's outer office, she checked in with the yeoman and was waved right inside.

Justice came to attention in front of the CO.

Commander Benjamin Quinn was seated behind an institution-grade desk, but even though his body was half-hidden, Justice could still tell he was of medium build, maybe a little wiry. He had the kind of curmudgeonly face that regularly gnashed on cigars, probably even on the golf course—there was a bag of clubs leaning against the wall behind him. His bald head shone under a blaze of sunlight streaming in through half-mast window blinds.

The CO let her stand at attention a few beats longer than necessary. There was a creep-factor to that.

"At ease, Ensign. We don't stand on ceremony here."

No? She didn't go into parade rest, then, but merely relaxed and looked at him.

He smiled. Yellow teeth. Those choppers definitely gnawed on cigars.

She nodded a greeting. "Sir, it's a pleasure to train with your squadron over the next couple of weeks."

The CO's sallow smile narrowed off, and he sniffed. "The Missus crew isn't mine, Ensign. They primarily answer to Captain Eagen." Narrower and narrower. "They just occupy space in my hangar and take up my mechanics' time."

She didn't know what to say. She hadn't been briefed on the territorial intricacies between SOF and their aviation support squadron, so she wasn't sure how to respond to a man who was grumpy over factors completely outside her control.

But Commander Quinn seemed to expect something out of her, so she said, "Yes, sir." And suffice it to say, some wrinkles probably still needed ironing out in the new Special

Missions program.

"Your team's down in the hangar." Commander Quinn stood, and as he came to his full height, he didn't look entirely pleased to discover he was shorter than her.

He led her back down the unexciting hall.

They passed a female pilot along the way. The woman was slim and outfitted in the aviator's customary uniform—an olive drab flight suit.

Justice nodded with a professional smile. Other women were like a box of chocolates when it came to Justice; she never knew what she was going to get.

This one nodded and smiled back.

The hangar was a massive, cold, steel-encased space, stocked with all the clutter needed to keep mechanical monsters in full working order: grease guns, hydraulic jacks, tools of every shape, nuts, bolts, screws—you name it. The place stank of transmission fluid, and somewhere a pneumatic tool was *rrrrrrring* repeatedly.

Double doors were shoved wide open, exposing the flight line outside—an expanse of concrete painted with white circles at regular intervals: parking spaces for helicopters. The wind sock was snapping in the breeze. Weak sunlight streamed in through the open doors, illuminating two helos to the left of the personnel door that Justice and the CO had just passed through. These birds were at rest, rotor blades folded back.

A third helicopter was off to the right in a private corner of the hangar.

Three men in the requisite olive drab flight suits were inspecting this bird. One guy had his head jammed inside the belly of the creature, another man with bright red hair was balanced on top of the bird near the rotor blades, a third was standing under the tail out in the sun, sunglasses on, peering up at the rear rotor.

The *rrrrrrring* noise stopped abruptly as Justice passed a guy in mechanic's coveralls. He came to his feet, his chin resting on his chest like an open drawbridge.

The guy on top of the aircraft noticed them next. "Hey," he called to his buddies.

The pilot near the rear rotor straightened and strode toward them.

Justice's first thought was *holy shit, he has hair!*

It was cut to meet Navy regs, but she was so used to seeing men with extreme buzz cuts that the stuff on this man's head seemed luxurious. Pure black in color, rich and lustrous—hell, it *was* luxurious.

His flight suit was decorated with patches of eye-catching Americana, and clung impeccably to a form that was tall—an even six feet, she'd say—and athletically lean: a strong man, but with his strength distributed economically. The sleeves of his flight suit were shoved up on forearms displaying some impressive vein-work.

He had the smokin'-hot pilot-jock look down to absolute perfection. Aviator sunglasses hugged a face that was obscenely handsome, and he sauntered with a gunslinger's rolling stride, a supple ease deceptive about how relaxed he truly was. As he drew closer, Justice could feel a vitality equal to Keith's radiating off him—though where Knight's energy held an aggressive edge, this pilot's was totally of the *let's party!* variety.

After living in survival mode for so long—imprisoned with men doing the same—the vibe was oddly refreshing.

"Whoa!" the pilot exclaimed as he swept off his shades. "They working you out much over there at the Amphib Base?" Laughing, he offered her his hand to shake. "Lieutenant Pete Robbins, head pilot."

Diamond dust clearly had been ground into this guy's tooth enamel—his movie-star smile visibly sparkled—and

Justice's second thought about him didn't exactly come from her brain. More like her heart and her lower regions, the first went *thump!* the latter, *jumping Jehoshaphat!*

Was this guy for real?

Or had too many weeks spent around nothing but sweaty, dirty, tension-ridden men smacked a pair of hot-to-trot glasses squarely on her face? Her nipples were actually tingling.

She shook his hand. "Ensign Justice Hayes."

"Justice?" Robbins's brows slid up. "As in, fight for?"

She shrugged. "If that's what smokes your shorts."

Robbins laughed again, deep and barrel-like, his chin dipping down just low enough to give her the impression that the things that *smoked his shorts* were plentiful and diverse.

And why such a thought should raise prickly little hairs of curiosity along her arms was a curiosity in its own right.

"Is the Missus crew here yet?" Commander Quinn demanded.

"No, sir. Those boys had to touch base with their day jobs first." Tucking his sunglasses into a breast pocket, Robbins added for her benefit, "Your crew has been temporarily assigned to IT while they wait for you to finish BUD/S." Back to Quinn. "They should be here any minute, sir."

Frowning, Quinn checked his watch. "You have a launch time to make, Lieutenant."

"Yes, sir. My guys"—Robbins gestured at the other two flight-suited men—"are just finishing up pre-flighting the aircraft."

"Very well. See that you don't jam up my flight schedule." The CO stalked off.

Robbins gave Justice a sardonic look. "Benny Boy doesn't like us very much."

"So I gathered."

"Ah, here are your guys now." Robbins gestured to a spot over Justice's left shoulder.

She turned around, catching her first glimpse of her crew.

The two men were both dark-haired—basic brown—and wearing the Special Missions uniform of the day: black T-shirts and black-and-gray camo combat pants bloused into black boots. They wore fatigue caps but removed them as they entered the hangar, tucking the bills into their back waistbands.

Justice would wear the same uniform once she officially joined Special Missions, but when military etiquette demanded a cover be worn on her head, she would don an all-black narrow hat, known as a "piss-cutter," instead of a fatigue cap.

The taller of her two guys wore a pair of black-rimmed glasses secured in place by a strap around the back of his head, his hair cut a little more high-and-tight than the Navy required. He was thickly built, but his muscles were of the smooth type that generally came from winning a genetic lottery ticket rather than the result of much actual physical effort. The glasses added to her assessment of him being *techie geek* rather than *weight room warrior*.

The second man was short, and after one look at Justice, he tripped and fell.

He didn't fart around about it either but landed flat on his face.

She tensed but didn't move forward. Rushing over to help the poor guy up would probably make him feel worse.

"Judging by your lack of reaction," Robbins drawled next to her ear, "I take it this is a common male response to you?"

She cut Robbins a sharp glance.

He only smiled, lavishing her with a full blast of Bradley Cooper.

She walked over to the two men as 6'3" helped up 5'6".

Robbins stayed by her side, gesturing at the tall guy. "This is Petty Officer Ron Glinski and"—the shorter one— "Petty Officer Charlie Morris." Whose cheeks were now fire-extinguisher red. The metaphor worked on several levels— he could've used one to put out his face.

"You okay?" she asked him as she shook his hand. Miraculously, his nose wasn't bleeding.

"He's just nervous," Glinski explained when Justice shifted over to shake his hand.

She smiled at Morris. He had the puppy eyes of a dyed-in-the-wool follower, and the current loose-jawed expression he was aiming her way said that he'd been really worried his new female boss wouldn't be able to pull off Alpha Dog for him. But now…maybe she could.

"The boys have been…hmm, how to put it?" Robbins reached sideways—didn't even look—stuck a finger under Morris's chin and snapped the man's mouth closed. "They've had their skivvies in a knot over being the only Special Missions team with a female leader."

Now *both* Morris and Glinski needed a fire extinguisher.

She gave Robbins a glib look. "Maybe you shouldn't have put it at all."

Robbins laughed, a boisterous, swashbuckling sound this time. "Aw, no big deal. We're going to be one big, happy family, right?"

This was said just as the other two flight-suited men arrived.

"Here are my guys. My AW, Ketchup"—Robbins gestured at the redheaded Aviation Warfare specialist who'd been on top of the aircraft—"and my copilot, Willie."

Willie had brown hair and was pretty much nondescript

in every way: not tall, but not short; not handsome, but not ugly; not thin, but not built. He was chewing gum with lively vigor, his mouth set at full smile. His expression reeked of *I'm-just-so-glad-to-be-here.* He probably made a very bouncy sidekick.

"Nice to meet you." Justice shook the hand of each man, reading their nametags: LT. Nate "Willie" Wojno and Petty Officer Jett "Ketchup" Murphy.

Ketchup made sense in light of the red hair, but *Willie?* "Why do you go by Willie?" she asked the beige copilot.

He snapped his gum and widened his smile until the sides of his mouth were in danger of disappearing into his ears. "It's my call sign."

Well, yeah, she knew that much, but why that name in particular? She checked out Robbins's nametag. "And yours is Bingo?"

"Correct-a-mundo."

"Like the dog?"

A smirk toyed with Robbins's mouth. "I bring to mind a dog?"

Her nipples having been hard as bullets throughout a lot of this exchange would lend itself to a *no* answer on that. "I mean like the song—Bing-O was his name-O."

Robbins shook his head slowly—back, then forth, one time—a mischievous light in his eyes. "Nope."

"You're not going to tell me?"

His brows came together sagely. "The origin of a call sign can only be divulged in places with low lighting and the plentiful distribution of alcoholic beverages."

Hmm, one of the smoother ways she'd been asked out for a drink. "Oh, well, shucks," she said. "Shall we go brief our training run now?"

Robbins chuckled, clear traces of *resistance is futile* in the rumbling noise. "Now? Yes. Tonight? First round's on me."

He headed deeper into the hangar. "Ready Room's this way."

She kept pace with him while the others followed.

"Aw, hell, you know what?" Robbins chin-nodded *hello* to the mechanic with the pneumatic tool. "I might as well give up Willie's call sign now. He used the relief tube in-flight and forgot to zip up until after he stepped out of the aircraft…"

Chapter Twenty

THEY FLEW NORTH to Camp Pendleton, a Marine Corps base set on a sprawling 125,000 acres of desert terrain—plenty of space to play sandbox in—located between San Diego and Los Angeles. The Special Missions Obstacle Course was situated at the southern end of the base, and Justice's team was scheduled for later training runs there to fast-rope onto the tops of buildings or into the middle of a "village," then practice infiltration and extraction, complete with lots of orgasmic booby traps to disarm.

But today's training was a simple fast-rope to the ground, more of a team-building exercise than anything else, designed to help them learn to work together.

Robbins brought the helo to a steady hover sixty feet above an open dirt field and told her through the earpiece in her helmet, "You're a green light."

The fast-rope was basic enough in premise: unfurl a long, nylon rope out the side door of a hovering helicopter, then have team members deploy one by one to the earth below. Main goal was to descend fast to avoid becoming a target for enemy ground troops—a real threat in actual-world situations.

Justice gestured for Morris to go first.

He hooked the rope to the metal rappelling ring on his belt, then moved eagerly into the side door, his back pointing outward, the balls of his feet poised on the edge of the aircraft.

"Now, now, now," Justice called to him. "Go!"

Morris leapt out the door with the kind of *livin'-large!* daring that'd probably seen him through his own BUD/S training.

Leaning out the door, Justice watched Morris ride the rope like he was on Thunder Road, *whooshing* into the massive curls of dust being thrown up by the rotor wash.

Landing in a crouch, Morris unhooked his rappel ring, then slung his M-4 rifle from back to front, holding it in a two-handed "ready" carry, muzzle down, as he ran to the side and took a knee.

Justice went next.

She whizzed down the rope, her bandaged right hand twinging slightly beneath her steel-reinforced gloves. She likewise landed in a crouch, then met up with Morris and knelt beside him. No rifle for her, though. She needed to keep her hands free for her sticky-fingered tasks. Same reason she didn't wear bulletproof clothing—the added weight hindered her movements.

Her sole weapons of choice were a KA-BAR knife on her left hip and a Sig Sauer P226 on her right. A fanny pack full of the tools of her trade sat at her lower spine. Every pocket in her combat pants was also crammed full. She never knew what she might have to tackle on any job, so she arrived ready to deal with almost anything.

Next came big guy Glinski.

No Thunder Road for him.

No whizzing.

Justice stared up at the taller of her crewmen in incredulity. He was progressing down the rope like a cross between a sloth and an inchworm.

Several eternal minutes went by.

"Dear parents of everyone on board this aircraft," Pete Robbins's voice sounded in her earpiece. "We regret to inform you that your sons are all *dead* because they were left hovering over an enemy drop zone for so long they took on massive enemy ground fire."

Justice's nape burned. Like she couldn't see what was happening without Robbins sitting front and center in the Peanut Gallery. She jabbed her fingers into the speak button located at her throat mic. "Stand by."

"Uh-oh. An extremely pissed off woman just threw a melon at us. She had plenty of time to line up her shot."

Justice ground her teeth together. *With any luck, it rammed right in your big mouth, Robbins.*

"FYI," he added, "too much sand in the intake heats the engines. Helicopter pilots kinda sorta don't like that."

Justice squinted. An F-5 level sandstorm *was* roiling around the drop zone. Glinski was no more than a hazy blob.

He finally arrived at the bottom of the rope and stepped off.

Not hopped.

He didn't pounce, spring, caper, or gambol off. He didn't do the merengue.

He *stepped.*

"What the hell?" she muttered.

The helicopter immediately banked into a turn, roaring over the top of them as it flew off and gained altitude. She ducked her chin and closed her eyes against the whip-up of sand, then stood and strode over to Glinski.

Morris trotted at her heels.

Glinski was red-faced.

She tugged off her helmet. "I can tell by your expression you know that didn't go so well."

Glinski nodded stiffly.

She kept emotion out of her voice, trying to sound curious rather than critical. Piecing this together was what needed to happen. "You did the rappelling training at BUD/S, correct?"

Special Missions wasn't sent to Air Assault School as a part of their training—even though they probably should be—but they all worked the sixty-foot rappelling tower at the Amphib Base.

"Yes," Glinski answered.

"And you passed?" A question designed more for its probative value than for actual informative content. Because the answer was already known: of course, he passed. He was here, wasn't he? But there was something he wasn't telling her.

"Yes."

She waited. So much for him catching the drift. "Do you have anything you'd like to add?"

"It wasn't my best exercise," he admitted.

"Why?"

He shrugged. Shook his head. Looked off to the side.

Not a lot she could do with that. Maybe he was just out of practice. "All right." She jammed her helmet back on. "Let's go again."

And again.

And again.

They worked at it all day, and if Glinski's speed increased, it was merely from an inchworm to a mouse—a mouse on 'ludes. She tried several times to persuade him to tell her what the holdup was, but he remained vague. This was probably how Glinski survived BUD/S: He didn't complain. At all. About anything.

By the time they arrived back at HSC-85, Justice was hot, sweaty, covered with dust, and all the patience in her attitude had shuffled along to make room for frustration and grouchiness.

She, Morris, and Glinski jogged into the hangar while

Robbins and his crew shut down the helo on the flight line.

She stood in front of her men, her hands on her hips, her tongue balled up with indecision. What should she say? What was the correct thing?

Nothing?

Should she let the day slide for now and hit the exercise again tomorrow? That didn't feel right.

The training evolution had gone extremely poorly. It was up to her to figure out why and fix it; she was the officer.

But she knew what it like to be burdened with the demands of pure performance. It was very stressful. Very isolating, and the hell if she was doing that to Glinski. Talking to him rather than pressuring him was what would coax the best out of him.

If only Glinski *would* talk to her.

"Have you two been keeping in shape?" she asked, since saying *nothing* wouldn't be very confidence-inspiring.

Morris and Glinski exchanged looks.

Silence: the guilty man's answer.

She lowered her brows, using a stern expression to hide her belief that their conditioning—or lack thereof—had nothing to do with the current problem. "Just because you two are riding desks right now doesn't mean you can slack off on your physical fitness. You're still Special Operations Forces." True enough, which made *something* out of the *nothing*, and she felt a tad better for it.

"Yes, ma'am," they both intoned.

Robbins and his men tramped by the three of them into the hangar. The AW, Ketchup, disappeared through the personnel door while Robbins and Willie attended to paperwork.

"Tomorrow we start the day with a five-mile run," she told her guys. "Then we'll go to the shooting range." She needed to assess their other skills. With luck, Glinski would be an expert marksman, and she could give him some self-confidence-building *attaboys*.

"Yes, ma'am."

She dismissed them.

Robbins strode over. "Rough first day."

It was a neutral comment, expressing facts in evidence only. He'd shut up making fun of their slowness after the first failed run, probably recognizing a real problem.

"You look like you could use a drink." Robbins scratched the underside of his jaw. The skin was a little indented from his chinstrap. "You want to join Willie and me for happy hour?"

"Uh, I don't know. I have to…" She gestured in an indefinite way. She had to…*what?* Go sit in a forlorn BOQ room and stare at a hacker book that would be impossible to read right now.

"There's a place called the I-Bar on base," Robbins told her. "It's a pilot hangout, a come-as-you-are joint. We all go there after work, wearing flight suits and stinking of JP-5 jet fuel. So—" He gestured at her dusty combat clothes. "You won't stick out at all."

A *yes* hovered on the tip of her tongue. She could really stand a drink right now. But big mistakes often followed a woman speaking that one little *yes* syllable to a man, especially when she found herself staring into eyes gone unnoticed before—sunglasses' fault—brown with gold rings around the irises, unique, striking, and as gorgeous as the rest of him.

"The I-Bar is located in the BOQ complex, so you can just walk to your room after a few."

She glanced at the personnel door. *Well…*

"We could put our heads together over the Glinski problem."

Hell. Pete was just making it too impossible to say no.

And resistance, after all, was futile.

CHAPTER TWENTY-ONE

THE I-BAR, SO named by virtue of it being located in Building "I" of the North Island Base—hey, if you want creativity, don't join the military—was definitely, unapologetically, a pilot hangout. Besides the sole fashion statement being the olive drab flight suit, with aviators displaying patches from squadrons all over North Island, the interior left no doubt as to its primary clientele.

Model aircraft of every stripe dangled by fishing line around a U-shaped center bar, and the entire ceiling—and it was, truly, *every* square inch—was covered by beige aviator mugs. The glassware hung lip-to-butt flush against one another and were monikered with pilots' names plus golden wings.

The place was packed, the happy hour crowd spilling out into an outdoor courtyard.

Aviators stood in small groups, talking with their hands and laughing with the ease of men who knew what they did for a living was really fucking cool. Most stood with one knee cocked forward in the self-assured gunslinger way—although none carried it off as well as Pete.

When she and Robbins first arrived, his promise did not bear fruit. Justice did, in fact, stick out.

Of course, she did.

Anywhere she went, she was stared at, and the idea of working for the CIA was starting to seem sillier and sillier. She never disappeared innocuously into a crowd.

On the way across the courtyard, Robbins greeted a few fellow pilots, then stepped inside the dark interior and bellied up to the bar. He hailed the female bartender. "Hey, Pam. The Robbins bottle of mezcal, if you would." He held up three fingers and dazzled her with some glittering Zac Efron.

Pam blushed to the roots of her hair and fumbled a bottle of tequila off a shelf. She set it in front of Pete along with three shot glasses.

Robbins filled the glasses, naming each as he went. "Willie, me, Justice." He reached over Justice's shoulder to give Willie one of the shots, then handed her the one he'd labeled as hers. "If we reach the bottom of the bottle on your shot," he explained, "you have to eat the worm."

She glanced at the bottle. It was only a quarter full.

Robbins set a salt-shaker and a slice of lime on the bar in front of her. "'Course, if fall-on-his-face Morris happens to be here when we empty the bottle, he'll eat the worm for you. One day into training, and the kid is already willing to take a bullet for you. *Wants* to."

Willie slugged back his drink, then sidled off to talk to a civilian female. Willie might be unbuttered-toast bland on the outside, but he gave off a lot of zest-for-life energy. He engaged the woman with surprising skill.

Robbins downed his shot. No flinching. Then he sucked on his slice of lime with a lip skill that sent heat flushing through the pit of Justice's belly.

What is it about this guy? She swiftly took her own shot.

Pete ordered a Budweiser.

"Budweiser." Justice arched her brows. "That brand seems too vanilla for a guy like you. Dos Equis, maybe, or…no. St. Pauli Girl."

One corner of Pete's mouth hiked up. "Because of the sexy woman on the logo? Am I already so transparent?"

"Tragically, yes."

He laughed. "You're not too far off from the truth, actually. I judged a Budweiser bikini contest back when I was in flight school. And such experiences tend to leave their mark on an impressionable young man. What are you drinking?"

"Tom Collins."

He ordered for her. When her cocktail arrived, he handed it to her, then gathered the mezcal bottle, their two shot glasses, and his beer. "Let's head outside."

They angled through the crowd and exited onto the courtyard. Not as many people were outside.

Pete snagged a four-seater table near a two-layer white fountain surrounded by well-manicured potted plants teeming with colorful offerings. The evening was mild, dusk just settling, fluffy popcorn clouds drifting across a lavender sky.

Justice sat in a chair kitty-corner to Pete's.

He lounged back. "So they're beating you up pretty badly over there at BUD/S, are they?"

She plucked the garnish off her drink and tossed it on the table. "What makes you say that?"

"Bandage on your right hand, nasty cut on the left side of your forehead."

Not to mention the problematic wound on her back from Instructor Hill's stomping boot—being wet and sandy all day didn't lend itself to proper healing.

She shrugged. "Comes with the territory."

Pete's focus remained on her forehead. "That's going to leave a scar."

"Adds character."

He chuckled. "Good to know."

"You have a few?"

"More than."

"Ah. The life of an aviator can be rough too."

"More like I had a rambunctious childhood."

"Now why doesn't that surprise me?"

He smiled and drank. "So why are you doing it?"

A small dirt clod was stuck to her knee. She flicked it off. "That seems to be the question on everyone's mind."

"Damn. I hate being a cliché."

She almost laughed—that idea defied imagination. "Why did you want to become a pilot?" she asked instead of answering.

He rested his beer in his lap. "I was the kid always at the top of the tallest tree or jumping off a roof. My whole life, I wanted to fly."

"That's cute."

"What every man wants to be called." A smile curved his lips.

Snorting, she drank more of her cocktail. "So has the life of an aviator worked out to be everything you dreamed it would be?"

"Mostly." He went quiet for a moment, staring at the fountain. "Not always."

She observed his still profile, sensing a surprising ebb in his vibrant energy. Such moments of somberness probably came few and far between for Pete Robbins.

"Combat flying is a dangerous game," she offered. "I'm sure you've been in some scary situations."

"Yeah, but that part's no big." Coming out of his brief reverie, he looked at her. "If you're not the type of person who gets off on pushing the envelope, you don't belong in Naval aviation." He took a sip of beer. "It's losing good men that's the sucky part."

Now she looked at the fountain, watching water burble sluggishly up from the top, then drizzle downward. Here was a side of being in the military she hadn't fully worked through: the death factor. If Glinski or Morris died, she wasn't sure how she'd handle it. As their leader, she was in charge of more than their training—she held their lives in her hands.

Pete spun the beer in his lap. "Last cruise I was on before joining Special Missions, a helo off my detachment was shot down during a hostage rescue mission in Pakistan. A young pilot was killed." He gave his head a small shake. "Just a damned kid."

"I'm sorry." Justice's throat went dry. "How do you go back to work after something like that?"

"It hits hard, for sure. You cruise in close quarters for six months with a bunch of guys, and they become your family. Or at least they do for me." Pete sloshed more mezcal into both their shot glasses. "Bottom line, though, you can't overthink it. No one would ever hop into a cockpit—or go out in the field—if they did. Pilots, we follow safety protocol. We trust our training and our instincts. You can be the same way. Listen to your gut and trust it. You wouldn't be here if you didn't have good instincts."

While stealing? Her instincts couldn't be topped. *In other ways…?*

"If I'm so good, how come I can't figure out Glinski?"

"You're really bothered about him, aren't you?"

"No one likes to fail." Someone needed to increase the water pressure on that stupid fountain.

"You haven't failed. It's only been one day."

She picked up her tequila and tossed it back. "Problem is, I'm not sure if I know how to help him. It's foreign to me—being responsible for others. I've only ever had to look out for myself."

"Apply the same concept."

"What do you mean?"

"Whatever you've done in the past to take care of yourself, do it for Morris and Glinski."

Like, encourage my guys to steal stuff so they can feel a rush of self-confidence? "You're going to have to be more explicit, Robbins."

Pete downed his second shot. "Put yourself in their shoes. Whatever problem Glinski has with fast-roping, it's something you've experienced in your life, too, or something similar."

"Hmm, I don't think so."

"Probably so. You're just not coming up with it right now." Pete studied her, his eyes reflecting the glow of the setting sun. "You know what I think? I think you're too caught up in the BUD/S mentality. All day long, instructors are telling you what to do and think, how to act. You've become so programmed to do everything their way, you've lost touch with how to do it your way. And your way is better."

"Hah! Yeah. I'll just inform the instructors of my greatness when I get back."

Pete's eyes danced. "I'd like to see that, actually." He picked up the mezcal and checked the level of tequila.

"No more for me. I have an early call in the morning. A five-mile run with my guys, plus a broken crew member to fix so he doesn't end up killing himself and/or everyone else on the team." *And all that.* "Thanks for the drinks." She stood. "I guess I won't see you tomorrow since it's a no-fly day."

Pete looked up at her, squinting one eye against the lowering sun. "Oh, you'll see me." A lazy smile played at the edge of his mouth.

She couldn't tell exactly what his expression meant, but the skin across her pelvis tightened.

CHAPTER TWENTY-TWO

"LONELY, ARE WE?" Robbins lounged against the doorjamb of Justice's BOQ room, the bottle of mezcal dangling indolently from his fingertips. He was smiling. Ryan Gosling was out in full force, maybe with a dash of the other Ryan—Reynolds—thrown in to make sure Justice's heart fell *all the way* out of her chest.

How did a woman forget in a mere twenty-four hours this level of impossible handsomeness? Her jaw was currently trying very hard to drop down to the carpet. If she hadn't just taken a bite of apple, it probably would have.

Minus his flight suit this evening, Pete was doing his drop-dead gorgeous impression in black jeans and a blue striped button-down, the sleeves rolled up on his magnificent forearms. Three buttons on his shirt had been left undone, exposing a wedge of tanned flesh and a sprinkling of black chest hair.

For a long moment she just stood with her hand on the doorknob, checking out Robbins and chewing her apple—then finally it registered what he was referring to when he'd said, *Lonely, are we?*

Behind her, seated in one of the hotel chairs, was a dummy she'd fashioned out of old clothing—pants and a shirt stuffed with nearly one hundred eighty pounds of weight.

After she'd spent the day working with Glinski and Morris, she trained some more on her own, prepping with special intensity for the upcoming Buddy Carry at BUD/S, an evolution that would require her to transport a "wounded" comrade *and* his gear. She was pretty sure everyone expected her substandard upper body strength to earn an F grade on the exercise.

Whether you want to hear it or not, you're not as strong as the men.

Maybe not. But she was going to give it her all.

Swallowing her bite of apple, she hooked her thumb at the dummy. "Meet Ralph." Because that's what a woman did after running too many miles with him slung across her shoulders.

Amusement stirred in Pete's eyes. "Would Ralph care to join us for a drink?" He lifted the tequila bottle. "The mezcal is likewise lonely."

She waved the alcohol away. "The tequila is going to have to find another friend tonight."

Robbins slanted a brow at her. "Scared of the worm?"

She *pshawed*. "I've eaten much worse."

Pete straightened off the jamb. "Oh?"

"*Oh*, nothing. That story remains with me." She turned to set her apple on the—

"Whoa!" Pete exclaimed. "You've got long hair."

Startling, she jerked back around, self-consciously sliding her fingers over her wet ponytail. She'd forgotten her hair wasn't in a bun.

"Damn, Justice. Put a little makeup on, and you might actually be good-looking."

She snorted. *Yeah?* "Hit the weight room on occasion, and one could say the same about you."

He burst out laughing. "Spoken by someone who only hangs out with SEAL mongos."

She lifted one side of her mouth. "Jealous?"

"Let's see…" He rasped a hand over the black stubble

on his jaw. "I regularly operate a forty-five-million-dollar aircraft, flying into low-level, hairy situations, so far without a single mishap."

"So that would be a *no?*"

He angled a devious glance at her. "See how much fun we're having already? Let's go get a drink."

She sighed noisily. "I can't go out drinking every night, Pete."

"Why not?"

She opened her mouth, but…it was actually a good question. Behind her, her room expanded out into a vast, echoing emptiness, devoid of all human habitation. No Brayden Street, waiting with ice cream and dimples and easy conversation. No rugged and solid Keith Knight, tossing out off-color jokes or the next piece of strategy to help her improve.

There was only one overweight and very silent Ralph.

"Come on, Justice. Tomorrow we're heading out to the ship—a strictly booze-free zone."

Specifically, they were checking onboard LHD-6, the *Bonhomme Richard*, a Wasp-class Amphibious Assault Ship.

Over the course of Justice's two-week break from BUD/S, her Special Missions crew was scheduled for two overnight stints on the *Bonhomme Richard*, what would eventually become their primary underway vessel.

Known as a "bird farm," the LHD, or Landing Helicopter Dock, provided care and feeding for twelve H-46 Sea Knights, four H-53 Sea Stallions, three small Hueys, and the bitchin'-est bird of all, the H-1 Super Cobra—four of those. With so many helos on board, the Special Missions Navy H-60 Seahawk would blend right in, which was the very reason an LHD had been chosen for Special Missions.

Whenever SOF went anywhere in the world, they liked to do so inconspicuously.

"This is our last chance for a little fun," Pete reminded her. "And I want to hear about your day."

Hear about my day? Who was this guy's mother, anyway? Someone who should have her picture hanging in a Greatest Parent Ever Hall of Fame, that's who, candles lit and shrines built to honor the mother who'd brought up her boy to ask about a woman's day.

"All right." She wrapped her ponytail into a bun, jamming a couple of bobby pins into it as she headed for the bathroom. "Wait a sec while I change."

Back at the I-Bar, they settled down at the same fountain-side table as yesterday, a repeat of a Budweiser and a Tom Collins in front of them. The bottle of mezcal sat ready to continue its steady dwindle toward a date with the worm.

"So what's the deal with you being called Bingo?" she asked. "You never told me."

"Aw, come on. We just sat down."

She hiked a shoulder. "I could just go on thinking of you as Bingo the dog."

"All right, all right…" He chuckled. "Hold your bladder." He poured them each a measure of tequila, then picked up both his beer bottle and shot glass. "*Bingo*," he began, "in pilot-speak refers to the minimum fuel required to return to base. When an aviator hits bingo in his aircraft, it means he has to come off station immediately and head for home. If he doesn't, he'll be standing tall in front of his skipper and explaining why." Pete knocked back the tequila and set the shot glass down. "I've flown past bingo two times."

"You ran out of gas *twice*?"

"I did not run out of gas. I was below the mandatory reserve when I landed."

"So what happened with that? Your gas gauge break? You go color-blind in the middle of the op?"

Pete's diamond teeth sparkled at her.

How much was the monthly upkeep on those? Probably a lot.

"First time it happened, I was on scene after an aircraft crash. My SAR swimmer was still carting people out of the ocean when I hit bingo. No way was I flying off with survivors still in the water." Pete tapped the bottom of his beer bottle against his thigh a couple of times. "Luckily, my skipper agreed with my call. My ass stayed out of a sling."

He took a short sip of his beer. "Second incident, I was on a VBSS mission. A merchant ship was being taken hostage by pirates, and I fast-roped the rescuing SEALs down to the deck. A firefight broke out right as I hit bingo, but I had the SEALs' sniper on board—I was circling the ship with him for air support. Do you think I should've just left those guys to fend for themselves?"

Justice picked up her shot glass. The courtyard was growing more and more dim with the setting sun, Pete more and more fascinating. "No."

"Me, either. But unfortunately, I pushed fuel limits so low I almost had to ditch in the water. In fact, we were just preparing for an emergency water landing when I spotted a Group 3 cargo ship. I landed on the back of that boat, but it's super difficult to get a helo with an empty tank off the deck of a cargo ship—fuel has to be flown out to the bird, etcetera. People weren't happy with me. It was also my second offense, so the skipper couldn't just pardon me."

"Ass in a sling this time?"

"Ish. I had to stand tall, dressed in my spiffiest whites, in front of a FNAEB."

"What's a FNAEB?"

"Stands for Field Naval Aviation Evaluation Board. Basically a bunch of higher-ranking officers gather facts on an aviation incident. They send their recommendations to whatever admiral is in charge of the Wing at the time, and he decides if a pilot should lose his flight status or not."

"Doesn't sound like a party."

"No. My fun-meter definitely wasn't pegged. But—" A spark ignited in his eyes. "Bad things led to good in this case. After the FNAEB determined my reasons for breaking the rules were mission-critical, I was given a slap on the wrist, tacitly labeled 'reckless,' and openly given the call sign 'Bingo.' And then, guess what happened a few months later? I'm called into Special Warfare Command to meet with Admiral Sherwin, Howdy Doody the Recruiter, and some overly caffeinated civilian dude. They offered me my own flight crew on one of their new Special Missions units. Apparently, my reckless, balls-out flying was exactly what they were looking for in their OICs."

"You know that 'reckless' and 'balls-out' kind of make you sound like you're the Wreck-it Ralph of the skies."

"Hey—" He pointed the neck of his Budweiser at her. "You and your guys ever land knee deep in shit, you're going to be damned glad I do things balls-out."

"I think I'm just going to drink my way through that imagery." She downed her tequila.

Pete chortled. "All right, now tell me about your day. How'd it go with Morris and Glinski?"

She set her shot glass next to his on the table, then told him about the morning five-mile run. Morris and Glinski both performed well, but she was still going to up their workouts over the next two weeks, then leave them a plan to follow while she was at BUD/S. Both had done well at the rifle and pistol range, too, but Livin'-Large Morris put up expert scores, earning himself the *attaboys*. She also took them to practice fast-roping at the Amphib Base's rappelling tower.

Morris moved like greased lightning.

Glinski like frozen wax.

"So you still haven't connected the dots on the Glinski problem?" Robbins asked.

She finished off her Tom Collins. "No."

A group of aviators on the other side of the fountain laughed—someone must have told a funny.

"Ron's a good guy, Justice, worth the effort to figure him out. BUD/S let him in even though he wears glasses because he's some savant-level computer genius."

"Yeah, I get that." She plonked down her Collins glass. "A suggestion for *how* to figure out Glinski would be more helpful, thank you."

"Like I said before, you need to see the problem from your own perspective."

"What the hell is my perspective?"

"You tell me."

She slouched back in her chair. Sometimes it felt like Pete was asking her to fill out a Mensa crossword puzzle, but with too many nebulous clues and not enough direct answers.

"Who are you?" Pete pressed.

"The BUD/S Woman."

"You're more than that."

"Does this have to do with me being a thief?"

"You being a—" Pete perked straight up in his chair, his eyebrows leaping. "A what?"

CHAPTER TWENTY-THREE

WHAT THE FUCK? Justice glared accusingly at the dregs of her Tom Collins. *What the fuckity fuck did I just say? Dammit.* Alcohol was nothing but stupid juice.

"Look—" She powered to her feet. "I should be going."

"Ho, I don't think so." Pete was right up on his feet next to her. "I'm not letting you go anywhere after dropping that juicy morsel on me."

"I'm not here to be juicy for you, Pete." *Dear God.* She needed to stop talking. This minute.

Pete's eyes danced.

No wonder she couldn't do the Mensa puzzle. She didn't have any IQ points left at all. She took a step—and caught her shoe on the leg of her chair. *Crap.*

Robbins chuckled. "Careful, Ensign. I do believe you're half-crocked."

"How's that possible? I drank as much tonight as I did last night." Although standing upright now, her center of gravity did feel a little sloshy.

"Did you eat anything today other than an apple?"

"Breakfast." *Oh.*

Pete nodded. "Empty stomach." With a hand on her elbow, he steered her safely around the table. "I know a great place on the Island for burgers…"

Robbins pulled to the curb in a 1969 candy apple red classic Ford Mustang convertible. Top down, aviator sunglasses on, he was factory-strength hotness and yum, and

Justice's heart went *whammity!-wham!-wham!* She couldn't even begin to describe what was going on down south, but her poor, underused vagina seemed like it was getting pretty fed up with collecting dust around him.

Careful, Ensign. I do believe you're half-crocked.

Right. She needed to be careful. Any more liquid inhibition-reducer in her system, and God knew where she'd go with all these sex thoughts.

She climbed in.

Robbins told her to buckle up.

She did, and he peeled down the street with the speedometer needle jumping.

She leaned back in the plush black leather interior and let the wind whip her bangs into a wild tousle, enjoying the sea scents gusting across her face. A sense of freedom sang in her blood.

Pete took her to Nicky Rottens, a bar and grill on Coronado's main drag, Orange Avenue. He miraculously found a spot to park on the busy stretch of road not too far from the front door.

As they headed in, a reporter flagged them down.

"Excuse me! Excuse me, Justice Hayes…"

"What the hell?" she muttered.

"We picked him up coming out of North Island's gates," Pete said.

She ducked inside the restaurant while Pete flashed his smile at the guy and tossed out meaningless sound bites about The BUD/S Woman.

The interior of Nicky Rottens was mostly wood, with bottles of booze lining about five shelves on a brick wall behind the glossy bar. TV screens of all sizes—one nearly taking up an entire wall—played sports from every vantage point. Most of the staff was bleached-blond and tan, looking like they were just bidding their time till they could hit the surf again.

A hostess led Justice and Pete to a table near the long bar.

On the way over, Justice indulged in a lingering gander at Pete's backside. His ass had to be one of the top ten in the state.

The waitress arrived with a friendly smile. Feminine appreciation lay in the smile she gave Pete, but not outright suggestiveness. *A tip-saving maneuver, that.* Was there anything more tacky than a woman who hit on a man while he was with another woman? Then again, maybe the waitress was behaving herself not out of upstanding character or tip-greed, but out of pure survival instinct.

Justice *looked* like she could easily flatten a rival, even though she would never get into a cat fight. The idea was absurd. Why would she ever fight over a guy? If a man didn't want her, he was welcome to find the door out of her life.

Pete said, "The Reuben sandwiches are great here. You good with one?"

"Sure."

"What do you want to drink?"

"Whatever you're having."

Pete ordered two drafts.

The waitress left.

Pete jumped right in. "So what's this about you being a thief?"

She rearranged their coasters, swirling them around, making one chase after the other.

"Here you go." The waitress dropped off their foaming drafts, putting an end to Justice's fidgeting.

A clear advantage of possessing one of the top ten asses in the state was fast service.

"Has the fact that you can have any woman you want

turned you into a base whore, Robbins?"

"About the same as it has for you, probably."

She *hah'd.* "Is that supposed to be a touché?" She rolled her eyes. "Puh-lease. You get laid way more than I do."

His eyes quick-tracked over her. "The point is you could." He put his napkin in his lap.

She slouched back. "Maybe I *should.*" *A twenty-three-year-old woman has needs, you know.* "Last time I was with a man was over a year ago, when I was visiting my dad right before I left for OCS. I hooked up for a booty call with a guy I used to date in college. He's very good at—"

She stopped short. *Wait, what am I saying?*

One of Pete's eyebrows flickered upward.

"Uh...something I like."

"Good." The halos around Pete's irises took on a brighter, more golden sheen. "Liking stuff is good."

The waitress dropped off their Reubens.

Pete thanked her, then picked up his sandwich, strong fingers wrapping around the bread, vein-worked forearms flexing.

Justice watched him take a bite.

Some sauerkraut leaked from between the two pieces of bread, and he somehow managed to make it look sexy. *What is it about this guy?*

"Why do I always feel like you're seducing me?" She slapped her palm on the table. "How do you *do* that?"

He munched a few fries, his gaze alight with all the fun the bastard was having. "I'm just sitting here talking to you, Justice." He casually licked his fingers.

She struggled with a sudden and violent urge to tear his clothes off. "I all but tell you I need to get laid, and you don't do the blatant, gross thing and offer your services to me. Most men would have me halfway out the door by now. Hell, Hairy Arms would already have me pinned against the wall around back."

Pete sat there, quietly amused.

"But the offer is still there"—she pointed a finger at him, circling it around the vicinity of his nose—"oozing from every pore."

"Why *aren't* you getting laid?" He ate another bite of sandwich, speaking from the side of his mouth as he chewed. "Aren't you sort of fat with choices over there at BUD/S?"

She laughed. "The reputation I'm trying to build for myself isn't *that*. If I smeared the Hayes family name that way, it would put my father on a soft diet." Her dad probably wouldn't care less if she banged every swinging dick in BUD/S Class 684 if that's what she wanted to do. The unacceptable part was being evaluated for anything other than her skills as a thief.

Pete aimed his chin at her plate. "Eat your sandwich. Then tell me about being a thief. You obviously slipped up when you said that, and you're trying to avoid talking about it. But too bad. There's no going back. I want to hear."

She downed a few good glugs of beer.

"You couldn't have a record," he commented for her. "You wouldn't be in the United States military if you did."

Her belly made a sick burble. She put the beer down, then sighed expansively. Why should she care about spilling to Robbins, anyway? A few keystrokes on the computer and he could find out everything about her. Mostly.

"The real thief is my father. Grayson Hayes—a man universally and internationally considered to be the most successful cat burglar of all time. He stole millions over a thirty-year career and never *once* saw the inside of a courtroom or a jail cell."

Pete's eyes lit. "No way. You're joking."

"The police knew exactly who he was and what he did, but they could never catch him."

A full-throated laugh launched out of Pete. "That's awesome."

She gave him a droll look. "Most people would mention the illegal part."

"Forget that. You have the coolest dad on the block. Was your mom in the business too?"

She flicked her gaze aside. "No."

"But your mom was okay with what your dad did?" Pete took another bite.

"I never asked her." True, but designed to evade bigger truths. "Dad put together a stellar team: Stanley Zappatosi, driver and lookout, Ken the fence—known as 'Bandit'—and Alistair Russell, alarm specialist—Uncle Alistair to me. He was Dad's best friend and right-hand man for the first twenty years of my father's career." *Until...*

She quickly buried the memory of Uncle Alistair before it could fully form. Thinking about him was nearly as bad as thinking of Mom.

"And your dad groomed you to take over the family business, I'm guessing?"

Until a trip to juvey derailed that plan...

Boy, Pete was scraping scabs off *all* her shittiest memories this evening. She studied her fries. There was a lot of pepper on them.

"You called yourself a thief too," Pete reminded her.

"Yes," she said at length. "Dad was grooming me to be his partner. He built an amazing house to train me in, with traps and crawl spaces and ladders and a mishmash of monkey bars hanging from the ceiling. My daily homework consisted as much of conquering his challenges as actual schoolwork."

Pete's eyes were as bright as the overhead lamp. He was totally digging this. "What kind of stuff did he have you do?"

She raked back over some of her memories, but it wasn't the most pleasant undertaking. Remembering her obsessive need to please Dad awakened the dangerous hunger that always tingled her fingertips. "Uh, well, one time he didn't let me walk on the floor for three days. He told me once I made it into a room, I could use the floor, but to get there I had to figure out another way."

Pete threw back his head and hooted. "What a blast! I bet you were never bored in your crazy house." He released an envious sigh. "I hate being bored."

She snorted. Another thing she totally believed about him.

Pete grabbed more fries. "You ever steal anything big?"

"No. Whenever I was out with Dad, he only had me to steal low-key stuff. He wanted to test me but make sure I couldn't get into big trouble." The one time she got caught was all *her* fault.

"Like what?"

"Like, one time Dad had me climb up a five-story fire escape in New York City to steal a pencil from someone's random apartment."

"Ho, that sounds—"

"I was ten years old."

Pete paused with some fries partway to his mouth.

"*Ten*, and my dad made me climb five stories."

Pete set down the fries.

"I got a scar on this hand"—she held up the bandaged one—"by failing to properly disarm one of his booby traps." She could still feel the metal claw snapping shut on her flesh. "That's not a blast, Pete. Or if it is, it shouldn't be. Life shouldn't always be a game or a challenge."

She looked at one of the TV screens. Baseball. The next batter was performing some serious testicular adjustments before stepping to the plate. Maybe that's where he kept his

Home Run Secret Sauce and he needed to release it—like the kraken. Maybe he'd forgotten he was on national television, millions of people watching him jiggle his junk.

She closed her eyes in an extra-long blink. "Nothing ever felt real when I was growing up. Not my upbringing. Not the flashy, notorious man my father was. That's not right for a kid. Living like that messes up a person." She met Pete's gaze. "I walked away from my childhood with an unhealthy need for excitement—a compulsion to leave no challenge unmet, the riskier the better. To this day I struggle with feeling like I'm not worth a dime if I can't steal shit better than everyone else." She hefted a breath. "It's also a lonely way to grow up, feeling so isolated from everyone who's *normal*."

And what about those times when her dad would shut himself away in his study if she screwed up a challenge? Her rational mind knew he was strategizing how to improve her lessons. The rest of her had felt like the only person on the planet. Although the worst came after her stint in juvey— Dad went away to Monte Carlo for three months, abandoning her to her guilt.

Pete wiped his hands on his napkin. "I sort of know what you mean. My mother and father subscribed to the hands-off method of parenting, figuring that my sister and I would learn lessons more effectively if we just worked everything out on our own. But that left me running around like a hooligan, fucking everything up."

"And getting lots of scars?"

His mouth angled into a half-smile. "Exactly. I'm surprised I'm not dead." He ran his tongue along his inside lower lip. "I remember looking around at other kids my age—who were regularly getting hammered by their parents—and wondering why their experiences were so totally different from mine. A lot of times my life didn't feel real either."

She nodded, then abruptly sat back, holding on to the edge of the table. She was doing it again, allowing a commonality to develop between her and a man.

Why the hell did she keep letting this happen? She was supposed to be avoiding complications, not repeatedly running headlong into them.

Damned suspended reality.

That's what it was. Relaxing here in a comfortable restaurant, the sun setting in orange shades across the windows, with a handsome, fun-loving man offering her movie-star smiles and a no-stress good time—who accepted her bad side—made her feel like she was inside a bubble.

It was muddling her boundaries.

She gazed at Pete again. At the strong arch of his cheekbones, the chiseled jaw, and the flawless turn of his lips. *Beautiful*, that's what he was.

And *bad*. This man would know how to get into all the most exciting kinds of trouble.

Trouble, trouble, trouble… She shouldn't love it, but…

Releasing a slow breath, she planted one elbow on the table and propped her cheek on her fist. "You know what you are?" Her eyelashes sagged a little, and she brought them back open. "You're like a cross between Zach-Galifianakis-*Hangover* and Chris-Hemsworth-*Thor*." *Look how Pete Robbins so cavalierly puts his life on the line for others, going past bingo on fuel, and…stuff.* "Lieutenant Pete Robbins, helluva guy." What in the world was she going to do with him?

"Uh-oh, heart-eyes-emoji look." Pete tossed his napkin on the table. "Not totally in character for you, I'm guessing." He rose. "Let's have your Reuben wrapped to go."

She peered up at him. "Why? What's going on?"

Pete took her by the elbow and eased her to her feet. "Come on, little drunken sailor, time to take you home."

CHAPTER TWENTY-FOUR

THE TRAINING RUN to the USS *Bonhomme Richard* wasn't going to go well, and Justice was having a hard time being a duck about it. Below the surface, she was paddling as fast as a turbojet in afterburner, and the tension on her forehead suggested she wasn't hiding her concern so well.

Take one glance at Petty Officer Ron Glinski, seated across from her on the Special Missions helo, and the reason for her anxiety would be obvious.

Poor Ron looked gray.

To date, Glinski had bombed all his fast-rope exercises, and those drills had been over stable terrain. Today they were expected to drop onto the swaying deck of a ship, and the likelihood of Glinski pulling that off well was about as likely as a hamster winning the Triple Crown.

He knew it.

Justice knew it, and a lot of her internal frenetic paddling was stress over failing to help her guy resolve this issue.

You need to see the problem from your own perspective.

Does this have to do with me being a thief?

You tell me.

Justice blew out her cheeks. Still not grasping the relevance.

Over near the helo's open side door, Ketchup the AW waved to get her attention. She, Morris, and Glinski were wearing passenger helmets today—ear protectors held in place by a stretch of netting over the top of the skull. No mic and no earpiece meant that only Ketchup had contact with the cockpit.

The AW shouted something to her.

She strained to hear him, squinting at his moving mouth. "Blah blah blah"—lots of thunderous rotor noise—"blah blah blah."

Ketchup concluded his speech with a big smile, obviously happy about what he'd told her.

Wouldn't it be nice if she could be in on the celebration? She turned to Morris on her right. "You catch any of that?!" she yelled.

"Not really!" he yelled back. "I only heard him mention Fighter Alley."

"Fighter Alley?" She frowned.

Fighter Alley was an area of designated airspace off the coast of San Diego where pilots went to practice high-risk maneuvers—combat flying and dogfighting and all other manner of unauthorized acrobatics.

"I thought that was an urban legend!" she said.

"No!" Morris answered. "It's real!"

"Did we brief Fighter Alley?!"

"No!"

She glared at the cockpit. *You better not be sidetracking off our training run, Robbins, you—*

The helo unexpectedly banked into a hard right turn, the lean of the aircraft so steep Justice had to clutch the side of the aircraft to stop herself from taking a header into Morris's lap. As it was, she rammed shoulders with him pretty hard.

Making another sudden move, the helo plunged toward earth in a screaming dive.

The soles dropped out of Justice's feet. Oxygen *whooshed* from her open mouth.

Livin'-Large Morris let out a "Whoop!"

Glinski's gray complexion turned anemic.

She braced her boots on the floor and pressed her shoulders back against her seat. *Pete, you maniac!*

She tried to get Ketchup's attention to—

The helicopter swooped out of its plunge like it was on a runaway rollercoaster, only to make things worse by lurching ninety degrees nose-up.

Justice choked back a gasp.

Hello out there! Does no one besides me realize that the idiot at the helm learned every lesson in his life by almost dying?

The bird twisted sideways and dove again, resuming horizontal flight while the *whop-whop* of the rotor blades stuttered out of sync for a disconcerting moment.

Ketchup leaned out the side door, peering backward and shouting excitedly into his mic.

Noise and speed increased, like they were in a car chase—or the aviation equivalent of one.

The horrendous nose-up-and-over maneuver was repeated.

Blood emptied into Justice's legs. Her hangover sent Fizzy Pop stomach acid sizzling into her nose.

Glinski bent over and outright vomited on the raft bag.

Ketchup frowned at that, then said something into his mic.

Disneyland security arrived and escorted all of their wussie-selves off Space Mountain. Speed, noise, forward motion: everything returned to normal.

Lungs pumping, Justice kept a knuckle-bulging grip on her seat for the rest of the flight. The discordant rasp of her breathing was still loud in her ears when they arrived at the ship ten minutes later.

Robbins brought their bird to a hover forty feet above one of the helo landing pads lining the black runway.

Justice and Morris unbuckled their restraints and

wrenched off their ear guards.

When Glinski moved to do the same, Justice stopped him. "Why don't you disembark when the aircraft lands, Ron?"

Glinski gave her a hurt look, even though it was the right call and he knew it.

This fast-rope exercise would be difficult enough for him after a good night's sleep and a hearty bowl of Wheaties. It didn't bear imagining how it would go post-upchuck. Not that a SOF team member shouldn't be able to perform in *way* more adverse conditions. But this was training, not real-world, and their current reality was unavoidable: fast-roping for Glinski on this hop would be a guaranteed fail.

Justice told Ketchup to pass on to Lieutenant Robbins that only two would be fast-roping down, then she gestured Morris into the helo's side doorway.

The AW gave Morris a thumbs-up, and away he went.

When Morris was safely on deck, Justice dropped his duffel bag down to him, then her own. Grabbing the rope, she hooked up and waited for a thumbs-up from Ketchup.

He gave her the go-ahead.

She jumped out, speeding the whole way down with her heart aching over Glinski's hurt look, her teeth gritted hard enough to rupture her mandible, and her mind busily writing an epic ballad to Pete's imminent demise, lots of blood and gore and—*Shit!*

She landed wrong.

She turned her ankle out on the deck, but luckily muscle memory kicked in—she'd taken plenty of falls in her father's house of tricks—and her body automatically went with the rotation instead of fighting to stay upright. She hit the deck with her shoulder and rolled through the fall, springing immediately to her feet. She managed the whole evolution smoothly.

But still.

That wasn't the way a fast-rope was supposed to finale, and all around her the flight deck crew laughed.

Her stomach went into ulcer-boil. So much for making a good first impression on her new ship. *Fucking Robbins.* She devised another couple of stanzas to the epic ballad of his butchering, adding a jinx and a pox to his penis, maybe something in verse. *Hey Diddle Diddle, your penis is little, and shriveled and shrunk like a prune...*

The plane captain gave her the all-clear sign to cross the flight deck. Throwing her duffel over her shoulder, she jogged toward the tower rising up from the starboard side of the vessel. Her ankle twinged, but she forced herself not to limp.

She and Morris joined a Marine Gunnery Sergeant wearing jungle utilities and a billed cap.

Count on a gunnery sergeant not to have cracked even the merest hint of a smile in the near vicinity of his face. Normally Justice adopted a strict, no-stick-up-the-butt policy about men, but the sergeant had just become her new drinking buddy.

"Ma'am." He saluted her. "Gunnery Sergeant Walck."

"Gunnery Sergeant." She returned the salute. "Ensign Hayes."

They watched the Special Missions Seahawk land and spin down.

Glinski, Ketchup, Willie, and Robbins emerged from the aircraft and jogged across the flight deck with duffels slung over their shoulders.

Robbins's gait seemed extra buoyant, and when he joined their threesome, Justice saw why.

That top-ten ass in all the state... He was laughing it off.

Willie, on the other hand, had opted for a *live-to-see-my-*

next-birthday choice about his reaction to Justice's fall; he was checking her out first.

He took one look at her expression and kept his face straight.

As the Grail Knight in *The Last Crusade* said to Indiana Jones, *You have chosen wisely.*

Robbins, blind to anything but his own good time, didn't let up. "For her next trick, Ensign Hayes is going to trip over nothing, then look behind her to see what she tripped over."

The Gunnery Sergeant's left nostril lifted. Apparently laid-back jokester was not his preferred language.

Justice secretly sent Walck a hug emoji. Something she'd never done in real life, but this moment seemed perfect for it.

"Sirs." The sergeant saluted the two pilots. "The skipper is on the bridge at present and will meet with you at his quarters prior to noon chow. A stateroom has been assigned for Lieutenant Robbins and Lieutenant Wojno to share— the room next to the six-man. Ensign Hayes will bunk with our female meteorological officer, First Lieutenant Tesarik."

Positives: no absurd bathroom issues to deal with on board this ship.

"Tesarik is on duty right now, as well," the sergeant aimed at Justice. "You can meet her in the wardroom at chow."

"Roger that," Justice said.

The sergeant turned back to Pete. "Do you require assistance finding your stateroom, sir?"

"Nope," Robbins answered, adding an extra pop to the *P.* "Been around the block a few times, Gunny, thanks."

It was up for grabs who was more annoyed with Pete Robbins right now.

"Yes, sir," the sergeant responded tightly. "I'll check

your crew into their racks." His nod included Ketchup, Morris, and Glinski.

The three enlisted men followed Walck through a personnel door.

Justice likewise followed Pete and Willie through the same door, but they went in a different direction, traveling left down a corridor that smelled like being inside the Tin Man's oil can: empty of oil, but still stinking of it.

They walked a maze of corridors—Justice trying to catch bulkhead numbers—for some minutes and finally ducked through a steel portal labeled "Officer Country."

Several Marine Corps pilots passed them in the corridor, then several more. All wore severe haircuts—more skull showing than hair—walked like their flight suits still had the coat hangers stuck in them, and smirked derisively at their Navy group.

The *Richard* served as a launch platform for Marine Corps Expeditionary Forces, and the Navy was way underrepresented.

One Marine knocked shoulders with Pete on the way by, snickering, "Nice haircut, squid."

Pete gusted a long sigh. "My restraint may not be rock-solid over these next few days."

Justice rolled her eyes. "You wouldn't know *restraint* if it walked up and took a huge shit on your face."

A muffled sound came out of Willie.

Pete smirked over his shoulder at her. "Wake up on the wrong side of the hangover this morning, did we?"

Actual lightning bolts might have shot out of her eyes. She couldn't be sure...but the degrees Fahrenheit her eye sockets were registering was very high. A deep growl roiled in her throat.

Willie sped up.

"What the fuck, Willie?" Pete called after his buddy.

"You're running from her?"

"I happen to hold the firm belief that she's stronger than either of us, Bingo."

Two more whitewalled Marine pilots headed down the hallway in their direction.

Christ, it was beginning to feel like Justice, Pete, and Willie had been put on this vessel like kids bused into a magnet school outside their normal neighborhood zone.

A pilot with a scar slicing along his right nostril stopped in front of her. "Well, well, look what we have here."

Praise the Lord! The requisite super asshole has arrived. Yum. He would make a tasty pre-Robbins snack.

Scar Nose checked out her body. "Damn, woman, you're taking my breath away."

"How funny. Your breath is pushing me away." She dished up an extra helping of Christmas fruitcake into her psycho-eyes.

Super Asshole took a prudent step backward.

Willie gaped.

Pete laughed silently into the front of his flight suit.

"Hustle up, Patterson!" Super Asshole's friend said.

Scar Nose seemed all too happy to comply.

After the Marines went wee wee wee all the way home, Justice slammed past Robbins, making sure to knock into him good and hard with her duffel.

"Very mature," he drawled.

Maybe not, but satisfying all the same. She powered down the hallway, and Willie scurried ahead through the next portal.

"Willie!" Pete shouted, exasperated.

Next passageway contained the officers' staterooms.

Their group arrived at one labeled *First Lieutenant Tiffany Tesarik*: Justice's quarters.

She threw open the door, confirmed the space was

empty—yes, her roommate was on duty—then flung her duffel bag inside. Whirling back around, she yanked Pete's duffel off his arm and hurled it at Willie.

He stumbled back a step.

"Time for me to hand you your ass, Robbins, you fucking dick."

Pete's mouth tilted into a lazy lean. Widening pupils squeezed out the gold of his irises in sort of a carnivorous look, like a lazing wolf who'd been happily roused to the task of eating his daily maiden.

Reaching over to Willie, Pete patted his trusty sidekick on the shoulder. "Don't wait up," he said and sauntered into Justice's stateroom.

Chapter Twenty-Five

JUSTICE FOLLOWED PETE inside and banged the door shut. Loud noise: generated for reasons of temperamental satisfaction. She stood rigidly in place, lungs working hard. Beyond words. If the appearance of her eyeballs was anything like her vision, they probably looked like they'd been dunked in Red Dye Number Forty.

A man who knew what the fuck *restraint* actually was would've handled a woman in her condition—like a stick of dynamite on the tail end of its fuse—in a conciliatory fashion.

Maybe, *All right now, what's wrong?*

Or, *Come on, let's work this out.*

But no.

First thing out of Pete Robbins's mouth was a Scottish accent. "She cannae take any more, Captain. She's gonna blow!"

Astounded. Then murderous. Many more things, but Justice's brain was actually spluttering. Robbins was mimicking Scotty from *Star Trek*. "You're going to make a joke out of this?"

He shrugged. "Until I know what's wrong, sure."

According to the pressure in her ear canals, she was currently standing eight leagues under the sea. "What's wrong," she gritted back, "is that you're dangerous."

He perked up. "Oh, we're doing *Top Gun* now? Cool." He rolled into mimicking Maverick. "That's right,

Ice…Man. I *am* dangerous." He gestured at her face. "Now you bite your teeth at me."

She totally lost it.

Grabbing the collar of his flight suit in both fists, she slammed him back against the bulkhead. The metal wall rattled as if all the rivets were coming loose—she'd gained an unrealized amount of strength over the past months.

She added a snarl to the overall drama of noise she was making, so damned sick of this man's blasé attitude and his juvenile refusal to take responsibility for his actions. "You're nothing but a spoiled, delinquent child."

Pete's eyes stained black. "Uh-oh." He surged off the wall. "Now you've done it." A strong arm clamped around her waist. "I also like biting." He jerked her tight against him and crushed his mouth down on hers, his—

There was no honeymoon period.

No pre-initiation phase into the ways of Pete Robbins.

He devoured her from the moment his mouth locked onto hers, kissing her with a consuming and unrelenting hunger, his lips slanting hers apart and his tongue invading her mouth. The intoxicating feel of soft on soft socked her in the knees, and she almost favored the bastard with a moan.

He tasted like mayhem and decadence and lust.

Lust for life.

Lust for all things female.

Lust for *her*.

With a ragged exhale, she twisted her fingers into his flight suit, her grip still clenched in his collar. *To push or to pull?* She couldn't tell. She shouldn't be doing this, but she hadn't been kissed since the Ice Age—where her southern regions had been hanging out, incidentally… though not now. Now, moist heat was welling between her legs, the flood of sensation discharging all important decision-making into the care of her vagina. *That* piece of bothersome equipment was ready to provide All Very Good Reasons why she should strip naked and fuck Pete silly.

You're not going to make it through this if you go it alone. Top-of-the-line Knight wisdom that could—no, *should*—be applied to her personal life. What benefit was there in solitude? What person operated more effectively all by herself?

It's no insult being female. A Street admonishment that was spot on—she *had* been suppressing her feminine side too much. But right now she was very much in touch with her femininity, and it didn't feel weak. It felt wonderful.

Decision made: don't push.

Pull.

She did, dragging Pete closer while upping the heat of their kiss, melding their lips together into one never-ending stroke and counterstroke, wet warmth and hot breath…and a dangerous craving for beautiful, bad Pete and his exciting brand of Big Trouble.

Trouble, trouble, trouble…

She slid her hands over his strong shoulders and clasped her arms around his neck, pressing her breasts against him, and now a little moan did slip out—she had *way* underestimated the quality of his physique.

Humming his approval against her lips, Pete edged her backward a few steps toward the bed.

She went willingly.

A few more steps and—

They were tumbling together onto the stateroom's lower rack, Pete's mouth easing away—no teeth bonking with this man. He landed right between her thighs with expert agility, and she gasped softly when he pressed his lean hips forward, bringing her into full contact with a solid erection. Excitement was like a charge of adrenaline. Her breathing quickened. Her heartbeat drummed against her ribs.

He nestled his lips against her throat, using his tongue to sketch patterns of fire along the length of her neck. It was like a caress to every nerve ending in her body. Tingles tripped along her flesh.

She floated her fingertips down the channel of his spine, feeling his back muscles ripple as he moved to burrow a hand beneath her shirt. His touch on her bare flesh released another huge wave of liquid warmth into her groin. She edged her knees higher, clutching his hips, so lost to the anticipation of welcoming him inside her body it was especially jarring when the ship's loudspeaker blared—

"Relieve the watch! Relieve the watch!"

"Oh, crap." She exhaled a hiss as sanity came rushing back. "*Shit*. Pete, get off."

He set his elbows on either side of her body and peered down on her. "Don't leave me now," he murmured.

"Come on, Pete." She gave his shoulders a push. "Off."

"Screw *off*."

"Pete!"

He gave her a grumpy look but climbed off her, backing up a couple of steps to give her room to duck out from under the top rack.

She scooted to the edge of the mattress, the movement wadding up a non-Navy-issue blanket—Tesarik's.

Wonderful. Justice had nearly fucked a man on her roommate's rack.

She shoved to her feet. What the hell was wrong with her? If she kept doing stupid shit with Pete—drink, laugh, cavort, *kiss*—under the illusion she was inside some sort of bubble, she'd hose up her future. When she left Pete to return to BUD/S, she *would be coming back*. Back to work with him.

He was a military colleague.

Here, now, this: it *was* the real world.

You're not going to make it through this if you go it alone.

It's no insult being female.

No excuses this time. Only reality checks. Alone? No, the idea didn't appeal. But what she needed right now were teammates, not a bedroom complication. Female? She had plenty of time to be a woman later. During training, she couldn't allow the softer sides of herself out. This was her original conclusion on the matter, and she needed to stick by it.

She tucked her shirt back into her waistband, her gestures stiff and brusque. "Dammit, Pete, we're on a Naval vessel."

He stared at her, his dissolute mouth moist, the lower half of his flight suit stretched to capacity by his raging boner.

"Not only that," she added, "but I don't even particularly like you right now."

He sighed demonstratively.

"You deviated from the flight plan today to go off and play. You may not care about your reputation in the Navy, but I care about mine." And if he laughed his top-ten ass off over that bit of *yeah-right-your-undies-are-currently-soaked-you-little-tart*, she would commit another act of violence against him. "How do you think it looked today, us arriving late to the ship?"

"We weren't late," he countered. "The ship contacted me and said they couldn't man flight quarters at the prearranged time. I used the delay to go practice combat flying at Fighter Alley."

She yanked her belt buckle back into place. "And you didn't think to inform me?"

"I did. Through Ketchup. I told him to tell you."

Well…crap. She firmed her mouth. "You shouldn't have

done it, anyway."

He planted his hands on his hips. "I'm not going to lull my balls to sleep flying endless circles in Starboard D just so you can fulfill some anal need to keep a schedule."

She narrowed her eyes. *Anal?* "God forbid you should ever be bored, even if it means looking out for a crewmember."

"I didn't—"

"Glinski barfed because of what you did!"

He exhaled sharply. "If you and your guys can't handle a few rotor-overs, Justice, your team doesn't belong operating in Special Forces. Shit gets real in the field."

"I'm aware of that," she retorted. "But I'm using a crawl, walk, run approach to train my guys—it's the same way the BUD/S instructors deal with us. Glinski was already facing a tough time fast-roping down to a moving target, then you go and bounce him around the back of an aircraft. You *knew* I was struggling with an unsure crewmember, but you went to Fighter Alley anyway."

Pete paused. "All right. You might have a point. I probably shouldn't have diverted to Fighter Alley."

If that was his way of apologizing, she was accepting it. "Okay. Thank you for saying that." She owed him an apology too. "And I'm sorry I slammed you against the wall. It was uncalled for."

"Aw, well"—he swept a hand across his heart—"internal injuries only. We *did*, however, break the pilot credo."

"The pilot credo?"

"Three absolutes." He ticked the points off on his fingers. "Never pass up the opportunity to get gas, never miss a chance to go to the bathroom, and *never* waste a boner." He clucked his tongue at her.

She blinked, then—*Ho, boy*. She shot air out of her nostrils. *Boy-oh-fucking-boy*. Planting her feet wide, she crossed her arms beneath her breasts.

A prison matron's pose.

A listen-up-good-you-fool pose.

"Do I need to give you my Don't Get the Wrong Idea speech?"

Pete's brows soared into a high arc. "That actually might be fun to hear."

She firmed her jaw. "Does everything have to be fun with you?"

"As much as I can make life fun, yeah. For some reason I've never been able to figure out, most people like to wallow. Like you."

"Excuse me?" Was this another *anal* accusation?

"You don't let things go, Justice. Like the Fighter Alley thing. Me? Okay, I blew it. Shouldn't have gone there. Lesson learned. I've already moved on. You? You were so torqued up during the whole trip to the ship, you let it undo you. It's why you fell on your ass on the flight deck."

Heat unfurled up the back of her neck.

"Life's hard enough"—a knock sounded at the door— "why make it worse by sweating shit?"

"Uh…" Willie's uncertain voice came through the closed door. "Sorry to interrupt you guys during, um, you know, whatever it is you're doing in there."

Justice's blush spread from her nape into her face, scorching all the way down to the subcutaneous layer of her skin. Willie thought she was doing exactly what she'd almost done, and, hey, just curious, what happened to her not being *that* woman?

"But, er, guys…we're due at the skipper's quarters now."

CHAPTER TWENTY-SIX

THE SKIPPER'S STATEROOM was wood-paneled and carpeted in navy blue, with about half a dozen brass wall sconces providing light. Bookshelves of highly polished mahogany flanked a bed with a bedspread also in standard-issue navy, a picture of the current American president on the wall above the headboard. Directly across from the door was a wood desk, as shiny as the shelves, the rest of the stateroom opening up beyond.

Currently seated at the desk was the skipper. Whittled features, ropey muscles, salt-and-pepper hair, fortysomething-ish, Commander Abe Cardoso looked like the type of man who just grew tougher when life handed him tough shit.

He was, thank God, die-hard Navy.

The three of them—Willie, Pete, then Justice—formed a line in front of the skipper's desk and came to attention.

"As you were," Cardoso told them.

They settled into parade rest.

Cardoso's attention beelined onto her. "I heard you took a spill on the flight deck, Ensign. Are you all right?"

She drew in a secret breath. *Remain calm.* "Yes, sir. Thank you, sir." *And here's me letting it go, Pete.* "Unfortunately, the extra acrobatics I'd planned to impress my new ship backfired." She lifted one side of her mouth in a half-smile.

Cardoso sat back in his chair and lifted the same side of

his mouth back.

Next to her, Pete practically vibrated with interest.

What could she say? She wasn't the one who'd invented the rule, but the fact remained that men excused beautiful women of just about anything.

"At any rate, welcome aboard." Cardoso included Pete and Willie in that. "Lieutenant"—he held out a sheet of paper to Pete. "This is when the ship can man flight quarters over the next two days. Plan your fast-rope ops along these lines."

"Yes, sir." Pete accepted the paper.

Justice's mouth went dry. If the ship had been less than impressed by her landing, wait till they saw inchworm-sloth Glinski in action—or *in*action.

"However, we won't be conducting any fast-rope ops on this short cruise," Pete added.

Justice stilled. *What?*

Cardoso's brows speared together. "Are you not onboard to train?"

"We are, sir, yes. But seeing as this is a new team, we're taking a crawl, walk, run approach to becoming a well-greased unit."

Ka-thunk. Justice's heart tumbled out of her chest and rolled down the passageway. Did Pete actually just say that?

Cardoso stared hard at Pete, a tic jumping in his leathery brown cheek. "I've put myself at great risk volunteering to allow an untried team—no, *concept*—onto my ship." The commander's tone was composed but overlaid with steel. "Do *not* fuck this up."

Justice heard Willie gulp. Two people down the line, and she still heard it.

"Roger, sir. Message received." Pete smiled, the expression not so much movie star this time as smooth operator and car salesman. "This trip is for running landing drills.

Next time we embark will be for fast-roping. We'll also use the pre-deployment workups to fine-tune our tactical coordination and teamwork. By the time we hit the Med, we'll be your most valuable asset on board."

One of Cardoso's eyebrows raised askance.

A sizable boast, considering the present company of Expeditionary Marines onboard.

But Pete's powers of seduction did not discriminate by sex, race, creed, or rank.

Commander Cardoso gave a mollified nod. "Very well. You have the ship's schedule. Use it as best suits your program." He waved them off. "Dismissed."

They left-faced, departed the commander's stateroom, and aimed down the passageway in the direction of the wardroom for noon chow.

As she walked, Justice stared at Pete's wedge-shaped back, her throat full. She still couldn't believe Robbins had relieved her guys of fast-roping. Maybe her reputation wouldn't be in complete ruins by the time she left the ship, after all.

Pete took the paper Cardoso had given him out of his breast pocket and began to tear it into neat strips. "All right, Willie, time to announce the Naval presence to the wardroom. Hell if I'm going to be ass-fucked by a bunch of devil dogs for months on end." He tucked the ribbons of paper back into his pocket. "Back me up."

"Always. Let 'er rip, man." A true-blue sidekick, that Willie.

The wardroom was an officers-only, all-purpose space, used for eating, relaxing, and pow-wowing. A rectangular table of dark laminate surrounded by armchairs on rollers dominated the main area. Just off the head of this table was the galley, separated from the wardroom by a waist-high wall and countertop, plus a glass window on a slider. At present, the window was open, letting in delicious food smells—baking bread and sizzling bacon.

Mess cooks were inside, busily making final preparations.

A lounge area on the side of the room farthest from the door was furnished with four cushioned chairs, indigo blue but speckled white from wear, for TV watching and chilling out. Near to the lounge was a built-in buffet with a coffee urn—always full—mugs, and a basket of snacks.

Pete, Justice, and Willie stepped into a rabble of Marine officers, wearing either flight suits or jungle camouflage.

All conversation stopped.

All eyes turned toward their Navy threesome, or more accurately, toward Justice.

She's the one—whisper, whisper—*The BUD/S Woman.*

"Okay, folks," Pete said in a jaunty tone. "Step right up to get your tickets." He produced the strips of paper he'd created and slapped them across his palm. "Five bucks apiece to stare at our intrepid Special Operations female."

The crowd froze as one, tension closing like a fist around the room.

"Single line. No pushing."

No one moved.

"Come on. Don't be shy. In fact, I know you're not."

Willie pointed at one of the Marine pilots. "Hey, Bingo, he owes twice."

"Ah, that's right." Pete sauntered over to the man—it was Super Asshole from earlier. "*Homo Erectus* here already had a run-in with Ensign Hayes, wherein he rightfully got his dick stomped."

The scar on Super Asshole's nose whitened.

"Fork it over," Pete told him. "Ten bucks."

Super Asshole just glared.

"Don't have your wallet on you? No prob. We'll just

take it out of your mess dues."

"Overpriced bullshit," another pilot piped in nastily. "Considering the low-level performance we saw on the flight deck."

Sniggers rippled through the crowd.

Justice remained blank. *Be a duck, be a duck.*

Pete strolled over to New Dick and eyed him up and down. "Clearly, what we have here is a case of cranial-rectal inversion. Because only you having *your head up your ass* would explain how you didn't see that Ensign Hayes was simulating an under-fire landing...drop and roll...as she was *ordered* to do."

Justice's pulse tripped out of rhythm. *Why, Pete...you little devil.*

The mood of the crowd turned uncertain.

"So next time, before you start armchair quarterbacking team tactics you neither know about nor are capable of understanding, recommend an internal ten-second pause prior to opening your suckhole." Pete *tsked*. "No wonder the Corps has such a high aviation accident rate, stupid fucking jarheads."

The aggression and hostility needle twanged erect. Not a favorite epithet of the Marines, that one. The tangy reek of sweat suddenly seemed overpowering.

The glowering mob surged toward Robbins.

Willie protected Pete's right flank.

Justice took a solid stance on Pete's left...and didn't *that* give the Marines pause.

She was already such a strange ranger to these men— *Stay back! View only under glass!*—they had no idea what to make of this new oddity. Thought bubbles formed above many a sheared head: could this chick fight?

She could.

Her father had wanted her to be able to escape any

situation, even if that meant violently. None of the grace and beauty of martial arts for her, though—her dad made her take lessons in Krav Maga, the Israeli technique for aggressive street combat.

So even though the Marines vastly outnumbered the Navy, no one moved.

And Pete, being Pete, messed with them even more.

"Yeah, men, watch your six with this one." He slung an arm around Justice's shoulders. "Ensign Hayes trains with SEALs, so, you know, she could kill you with just her pinkie." Pete's gaze drifted to the ceiling in mock perplexity, and he stuck a finger to his chin. "Or was that bake a pie?"

A blurt of laughter brought everyone's attention toward the female Marine who'd made the noise. She was standing on the opposite side of the table from their knot of belligerence, a huge smile on her face.

She was a pretty young woman, with green eyes and short, red hair styled into a pixie cut. She didn't look much like a Marine—aside from the jungle utilities. She seemed too perky, her smile too open and friendly.

She waved at Justice.

Her pocket nametag said *Tesarik*.

The XO barged inside, calling out, "Attention on deck!"

They all snapped to attention as Commander Cardoso entered.

The skipper told them to take their seats.

Tesarik beckoned Justice over to her side of the table.

It took some gear shifting to change from ready-to-fight into glad-to-meet, but by the time Justice rounded the table, she had a smile firmly in place and a *nicetameetcha* hand extended. After they introduced themselves, Tesarik and Justice sat next to each other.

Conversation resumed in stutter steps, everyone else also struggling to change from skirmish to social.

Across the table, Pete divided his attention between the skipper on his right and the Marine on his left, skillfully drawing out the second man. Now that the Naval presence had established itself as a non-scrape-and-bow service, why not be friends?

Justice picked up the menu in front of her. Chicken Kiev or Salisbury Steak? The paper fluttered. She was shaking. Not from nerves. Her heart was thumping so hard, it was passing through her hands into the menu.

We won't be conducting any fast-rope ops on this short cruise… We're taking a crawl, walk, run approach to becoming a well-greased unit… Ensign Hayes was simulating an under-fire landing—drop and roll—as she was ordered *to do.*

Teeter-totter, see-then-saw… One minute Pete was acting like a delinquent jokester, mimicking *Top Gun* and *Star Trek*, and the next he was supporting her with the skipper and fixing her reputation with the wardroom.

Who *was* this guy? She couldn't pin him down. When she was around him, it was like she was dangling from one of the monkey bars in her childhood home, one-handed and off balance, scary but exciting as she came close to falling…

Falling for what? Or…

For whom?

Sliding her eyes up the menu, she found Pete over the top of it.

He met her gaze and dropped her a wink.

CHAPTER TWENTY-SEVEN

YOU MUST BE careful not to fall, Justine.

I know, I know, Dad, but… Wait, fall from where?

Or…for him?

Fall for whom?

Which man…? Hold on…!

If you grip the bar too tightly, you'll tire your hands and then you'll run the risk of falling.

She peered up. Her arms were stretched high overhead, her biceps pressed against her ears, and her fingers were curled around a monkey bar.

She was at her childhood home, hanging above the living room. Except…where was the furniture? Beneath her swaying feet, she could only see a hazy conglomeration of blobs.

Justine, you mustn't go too high!

Too high, Dad? How is that possible? I can't go any higher than the ceiling…

Careful!

She gasped. *Dad!*

Whatever was below her morphed into a scattering of surreal specks. She couldn't even see the floor! She cycled her legs mid-air. Her fingers were slipping. Terror came in a blinding explosion of spots behind her eyes.

Dad, help!

If she fell, there was nothing to stop her from dying! No net, no harness…

Pete's voice thundered out of nowhere. "Don't fall, Justice!"

Justice bolted upright in bed, gulping for air and blinking rapidly. The room came into focus.

Her North Island BOQ room.

That's right. Jesus. She was no longer on the *Bonhomme Richard* and….

A dream. She'd only been having a dream.

She rubbed her eyes, chasing away the last images of the monkey bars. She'd forgotten how frightening her dad's house of tricks could be, clambering around high places without a safety net or a—

The realization hit her full in the face. *Without a safety net…* "Holy shit," she breathed.

Snapping on the light, she found Pete's number on her cell phone and called him.

He answered on the second ring. "Where are we headed?"

She pulled her chin in. "Didn't I wake you?"

"Of course. It's three a.m. So did you find an all-night speakeasy or something? I'm in."

"No. I…you don't sound sleepy at all."

"That's how I roll. So?"

She exhaled broadly. "You never cease to fascinate me, Robbins. Look, I think I figured out what's wrong with Glinski. I need your help in the air tomorrow."

"Name it. I'll come up with a flight plan."

She told him what she wanted to do.

"Roger that. Alrighty. Since we're turning and burning in a few hours, I need to get my beauty rest." *Click.*

She glanced at the front of her phone, then grinned and turned off her light.

THE SUN WAS a true gold at zero-seven-hundred the next

morning, the weather still a bit nippy but holding the promise of reaching the low 60s later. Sea scents swirled through the HSC-85 hangar, overlapping with the stench of jet fuel.

Robbins, Willie, and Ketchup—all splendidly flight-suited—were busily prepping the Special Missions bird. Metal clanked on metal as compartments were opened, checked, then closed, and the pilots kept up a steady chatter, businesslike but amicable.

Morris and Glinski arrived, and she gestured for them to step just outside, out of earshot from the others but not too close to the noise of the flight line. Two helicopters were already turning with muffled thunder, far enough away that the steady drumbeat of their rotors was no more than militarily pleasant background noise.

She looked between Glinski and Morris. "What we're about to discuss doesn't go beyond this team. Clear?"

Her guys exchanged a glance, their expressions slightly wary, then nodded.

Justice zeroed in on Glinski.

Whatever problem Glinski has with fast-roping, it's something you've experienced in your life, too, or something similar…

Dad, help! If I fall, there's nothing to stop me from dying! No net, no harness…

"You're afraid of heights," she said, "aren't you, Ron?"

Glinski blanched white as salt and didn't answer.

Understandable reaction. If word leaked out about this, he would be immediately dropped from SOF—exactly the reason he'd been so close-mouthed about it.

Naval Special Warfare Command might've overlooked Glinski's glasses because his eyesight was only slightly out of range—he could operate without specs if absolutely required—but no way would they ignore a phobia that directly affected his ability to perform a mandatory operational skill.

"I'm not going to report this to Captain Eagen, Glinski, not yet, so keep a cool head." Here Justice was, a baby ensign, and she was already making a choice that could tube her career. Maybe her leadership style was going to be taking care of her men above all else.

She could live with that.

"I *want* you on my team," she went on. "You're a computer genius and a good man. Fast-roping with a fear of heights has to be incredibly terrifying, but you've been trying to do it. That impresses me."

Glinski's throat moved.

"But the bottom line remains: you have to be able to fast-rope effectively to do this job."

Threads of sweat slid out from under Glinski's fatigue cap. "I know. I just…" He trailed off.

He'd been trying, but just *couldn't*.

"Okay, so here's how our team will operate." She pointed at Morris. "First man down the rope is Charlie. Always. Once he's safely on the ground, you and I will go down together."

"Together? What do you mean? How?"

"Well…sort of hugging."

Glinski blushed bright red.

"Yeah, I know. It sounds weird, but it'll only be weird if we let it be. The key to making this work is for you to look right here"—she stabbed two fingers toward her eyes—"at all times. I'm your anchor. You don't look down at the ground. You don't look up at the hovering helicopter. You eye-lock me. Copy?"

Glinski's expression remained uncertain, but he said, "Copy that."

"All right." Justice set a hand on Ron's shoulder and

smiled. "Let's crush this."

CRUSHING IT, THEY did not do.

Not at first, anyway.

They began the fast-rope exercise over a grassy field—dust blow-up made things scarier for Glinski—and he and Justice performed the initial drops in a clumsy jumble. Every time Glinski moved to stand in the helo doorway, he would naturally check to see where he placed his feet. But that meant he would look down.

Then he'd get scared, and his inner sloth-inchworm would take over.

Justice finally started grasping Glinski by the chin strap and *making* him look at her during the crucial positioning phase. This required Glinski to place his feet by feel alone. No small thing. But he learned quickly, and he actually worked more smoothly once he wasn't in fear for his life.

The fast-rope fell apart again on the way down, mainly because…well, it *was* weird, her practically sitting on top of Glinski's lap, the two of them gazing steadily into each other's eyes.

Glinski kept breaking eye contact with her, shifting his focus past her to the sky…or to the underside of the bird…or to wherever. It didn't matter where. Wherever it was, once Glinski confirmed where he was—dangling many feet above the earth from a hovering helicopter—he would screech to a halt.

And then Justice would crash into him.

This problem she solved by lightly cuffing Glinski whenever he started to off-shift. She had to take her brake hand off the rope to do that, so…more collisions ensued.

They collected a fair number of bruises, but eventually they got their jam on. The more times they went, the more they perfected their timing. They rode the rope faster, from higher altitudes, and down to different terrains.

And they got over the weird.

Glinski's confidence visibly grew, and wasn't that a helluva thing to see?

Like watching a baby colt take its first wobbly steps. Or your kindergartner bravely board a school bus for the first time. Or…something. Justice didn't know motherhood from Adam, but Glinski was *her* guy and she'd figured him out and helped him, and…she hadn't needed to steal a single damned thing to do it.

By the end of the day, her grin was so wide it was a wonder she didn't knock Ketchup out into the big blue with it.

When their group gathered back at HSC-85's hangar, everyone was hot, sweaty, covered with dust—and grinning as gigantically as she was.

Gazing around the circle of men, Justice stood with her thumbs hooked in her belt and was ridiculously glad for them. They were becoming a team. Still a shaky one, but a team, nonetheless.

Their group disbanded…except for Pete. He remained standing in front of her, his expression full of pride.

"Look who's large and in charge," he sing-songed. "Nice job with Glinski."

She widened her smile. Pete's pride in her felt good, no two ways about it. "Top-notch flying today," she complimented back.

Pete had hovered the helo for a lot of hours today during their exercise, and that was no easy thing. To the untutored observer, a hover might look like a helicopter was merely floating airborne at idle, the pilots playing gin rummy in the cockpit or sipping cups of tomato soup, only occasionally glancing out the windshield to make sure a midair collision wasn't imminent.

Very far from the truth.

Maintaining a hover required a coordinated effort of micro-inputs applied to the collective, the cyclic, and both pedals at the same time. Everything had to work in concert, and it required constant concentration. And Pete had done it all day—first hovering at twenty feet, then thirty, then forty, and so on. Every time Justice, Glinski, and Morris fast-roped to the ground, Robbins would lower the aircraft to retrieve them, then up he'd go again into a hover.

And repeat.

And repeat.

"Thank you," she said.

Still smiling, Pete answered with an "Oorah."

She snorted and rolled her eyes. "Christ, Robbins, did the other side get to you while we were on the *Richard?* 'Oorah' is what the Marines say. Navy says 'Hooyah.'" Despite her razzing, a seltzer ball of joy popped apart inside her tummy. Today had been her best day in the Navy so far. "Maybe I need to hit you," she tossed at him.

His eyes glittered. "Expect the usual consequences if you do."

Consequences immediately brought up the memory of shoving Pete against the wall in her stateroom and their follow-on kiss. And thank God her mind didn't have a view window into it. Otherwise, Pete would've been able to see some real doozy images. "I refuse to be riled by you being you. Today was too good."

"It was," he agreed. "Maybe now my balls won't get barbecued."

She picked up her gear bag and swung it over her shoulder like an overcoat. "A bizarre thing to say."

"No." He laughed. "The whole time I was telling Commander Cardoso our team would be doing fast-rope ops on our next trip to the ship, I figured I was lying my ass off. After today, maybe I wasn't."

She smiled, and the seltzer ball popped some more. Pete had really put himself on the line for her.

"We need to celebrate," he said, "and I have just the thing for us to do. I'll come by your place at eight." He told her this like tonight's date was a done deal.

The man was too well-trained by women never denying him.

"Wear black clothes," he added.

Well, hmm, *now* she was incredibly curious…too damned curious to do the proper thing for the dignity of womankind and deny the cocky bastard.

Chapter Twenty-Eight

"PICK A BAG!" Pete sang out as he barged into Justice's BOQ room.

He was holding up two Walmart sacks. One was already crinkled from whatever adventures it'd been on with beautiful, bad Pete; the other looked like it'd been through just as much—the asterisk in the *Wal*Mart* was stretched into a diagonal.

Pete waited with the devil dancing in his eyes.

She smoothed her tongue across her lips, already tasting Big Trouble ahead.

Trouble, trouble, trouble…

Uh-oh. Now her fingertips were tingling.

Stop and breathe.

Don't get amped.

Pete Robbins was a Naval officer. His brand of trouble—while exciting—would be of the perfectly respectable, law-abiding type.

"That one," she said, pointing to the bag in his right hand.

"Excellent choice!" He upended the sack on her bedspread.

The contents tumbled out with a *clonk* of heavy glass on glass—the bottle of mezcal plus two shot glasses.

He slid a wicked glance at her. "Initiation time."

He set the shot glasses on her nightstand and poured the last of the tequila into them. When the bottle of mezcal was empty, he shook it.

The worm slithered into one glass.

He offered it to her. "*If* you're gusty enough to eat this bad boy, that is."

"Ah," she drawled, "peer pressure at its finest." She took the shot glass and knocked it back. The tequila slid easily down her throat while the worm settled on her tongue. She moved the little larva around in her mouth.

Pete watched her avidly. "I'd be happy to share the worm with you." His smile gleamed. "'Course now that the little beastie is in your mouth, a lip-to-lip transfer would be required."

Jeez. Kiss a guy one time, and he thinks it's going to be a regular thing.

Probably because all the other women he'd ever kissed raced back for an extra helping—hordes and hordes of perky, top-heavy snack treats, wanting more and more.

She peeled her lips back. "You suck."

His eyebrows hiked.

Edging the worm into a gentle clamp between her teeth, she showed it to him, then chomped it in half. Licking it into her mouth, she swallowed it down.

A resonant purr sounded in Pete's throat. "Oh, little sailor," he warned in a silky tone. "No challenge goes unmet by me, either. You may find that out the hard way."

"Doubtful," she threw back but with more bravado than actual substance. Inklings were growing in dewy spots on her brain that she just might be out of her league with this man. "What's in the other bag?"

"Good question! Tonight we'll be taking advantage of your special talent." He upended the second sack.

A colorful pile of women's lingerie spilled out: lacy bras and panties in a variety of shades and sizes.

Justice gave him an arch look. "Just what do you think

my specialty is, Robbins?"

"Being sneaky." His laugh was a low, pleased rumble. "Tonight we're going to break into Benny Boy's office and decorate it with these." He swept a hand over the lingerie.

Break into...

A warm, pulsing sensation spread upward into her diaphragm. "Breaking and entering is illegal, Pete." *Not* the respectable-and-law-abiding trouble he was supposed to be offering.

"Nah. It's only a prank."

She held herself still and tense. Words like "self-disciplined" and "ethical" drifted across her conscience—desirable character traits to own; things decent people wanted to possess.

Meaningless drivel next to the thought of a good old-fashioned B&E.

"So grab whatever you need and let's boogie." Pete stepped toward the door, again operating off the precept that this was a done deal.

"Hold on a second," she protested. "I can't do a job I haven't cased first."

Delight glinted in Pete's eyes. "Listen to the way you talk."

"We could get into a lot of trouble." *Trouble, trouble...* A shudder contracted her spine.

"Only *if* we're caught. And we won't be. This job is chickenfeed for a woman of your talents." One dark brow tilted. "Isn't it?"

She hefted a sigh. "*More* shameless peer pressure. You're really becoming a boor."

"The argument lacked finesse, true. But..." His smile was pure male confidence. "Effective nonetheless, I'm guessing."

Well...fuck. "What would we be dealing with?"

"The CO's office has one deadbolt and a keypad alarm," he told her, all business.

"Personnel?"

"A duty officer mans the premises around the clock, but at this time of night, he'll mostly be kicking back in the hangar."

It *was* chickenfeed. "Too easy," she pronounced in a last attempt at a getaway…an attempt as feeble as the job itself. "It'll be a snooze."

"I know, I know," Pete soothed. "But Commander Benny Boy Quinn deserves to be fucked with. He's a complete dick to us."

Anticipation surged into her blood and made her nerves whir. Both of her hands were now tingling, palms, fingertips—everything—and her heart was stomping around inside her chest, knocking into her ribs, wanting free of its strictures.

An apt analogy.

She vented another big sigh, like Pete was asking her for a kidney instead of offering her a primo sweet-sauce good time, a *show-me-the-money-then-let-me-roll-in-it* rage-a-thon.

"Let me get my tools," she said.

JUSTICE MOVED IN complete silence down the squadron hallway, and—surprise—so did Pete.

Not bad for an untrained hack.

She'd thought she would have to keep Robbins under careful surveillance—untrained hacks were notorious liabilities—but he was proving to be a good accomplice. He wouldn't add any sticky-fingered skills to the job, but he wasn't proving to be an encumbrance, either.

More surprising, Pete didn't offer any suggestions on how to deactivate the alarm when she popped the hatch on the keypad. She was reasonably certain he didn't know dick about alarms, but a lot of men couldn't seem to stop themselves from giving a woman their "expert" advice, even on things they knew nothing about.

It was probably some sort of mating behavior.

Which was probably why Pete didn't do it. He had enough of those behaviors down pat, the cool ones, without degenerating into being a poser.

She studied the keypad's electronic guts, found the connectivity wire, then clamped it off. *Easy as pie!* She focused on the deadbolt. For an organization that was infamous for wasting thousands of taxpayer dollars on asinine sundries, like toilets and ashtrays, the military had clearly spent very little on the CO's door lock.

She picked it in under thirty seconds.

Setting her hand on the doorknob, she prepared to enter, then paused when she heard metal clattering and a man talking. The sounds were muffled by distance, but she still glanced at Pete.

He gave her a *don't-worry-about-it* shake of his head. "Just maintenance," he told her quietly, "working down in the hangar. They won't come into the office spaces."

She nodded, then the two of them slipped inside.

By the light of a streetlamp coming through the open window blinds, Justice checked out Quinn's office. It was the same as it'd been the day she checked in with him, except now, behind his desk, there was something the skipper's golf clubs had hidden before…something incredible.

A large metal safe.

Not chickenfeed. Not in the slightest.

It was a Ward-Lock 2000.

Waterproof, fireproof, advertised as *bar none, the best protection for commercial businesses*, it was one of the last of the great dinosaurs—this ancient monstrosity wasn't even manufactured anymore. She'd only ever trained on a Ward-Lock at home with Dad, never once opening one on a real job.

And now here one was.

Calling to her…asking for it.

Oh, this caper had just taken on an entirely different flavor.

Padding over to the beast, she crouched down in front of it. *Hello there.*

"Hey, what are you doing?" Pete stage whispered.

Breathe in. Breathe out. Savor it. "Opening this."

"The hell you are," Pete countermanded. "There's classified material in there."

"I won't read anything." She inspected the hash-marked knob and the door handle. Both were careworn, but still solid and impenetrable. *Supposedly impenetrable.* A thrill of excitement cascaded through her groin. She was practically pre-orgasmic.

"Justice—"

"Hey." She abruptly swiveled around on her heels. "*You* brought me here—a woman who confessed to having a compulsion to leave no challenge unmet."

"Yeah, and if you'd recall you said it was an unhealthy compulsion."

"Well…*deal.*" No way was she walking away from a Ward-Lock 2000. She'd have an easier time shooting her father in the face—ironically enough, he would understand the choice.

She wiped her hands on the butt of her pants, then reached inside her fanny pack of tools, finding her small listening cone by feel. Her fingertips were on fire. Setting the cone against the safe next to the dial, she pressed her ear to it and listened carefully as she turned the knob.

Clothes rustled—Pete was flinging women's lingerie

everywhere.

A pair of underwear flopped over the top of her head. She released a breath—*delinquent*—then brushed the garment aside and blocked out the sound of Pete.

You must listen with your entire body, Justine, not only your ears.

She quieted the working of her lungs and calmed the rhythm of her heart. The tumblers whispered to her. Another wave of exhilaration curled through her belly. There was something so…raw about this. No electronics, no complicated wiring, no fancy tricks, just her against the volcano.

First one tumbler murmured into place, then another. She almost missed the third, then—

Bump.

She straightened, grabbed the handle—and stopped.

Bump?

Not a murmur, but a bump. That didn't seem right.

No fancy tricks…

Shame on her. *Every* job had the potential to deviate from the norm. Forgetting rules wasn't permissible. Mistakes killed a thief or got her imprisoned.

Listen to your gut and trust it, Justice. You wouldn't be here if you didn't have good instincts…

Exactly. Trusting anything beyond your own gut shortened survival.

"What the hell are you doing over there?" Pete hissed.

"Be quiet, I'm thinking." She glowered at the safe. *You shitty little trickster, you…* The beast had nearly duped her with a decoy tumbler. She cracked her neck, then leaned forward again, listening through her cone. She slowly turned the dial, paying close attention. Another tumbler settled. A murmur.

Not a bump, a murmur.

Straightening, she held her breath and pulled on the handle.

The safe door swung wide on a stack of files, several computer discs, flash drives, a box of cigars—she was staring at it all. A kind of unearthly ecstasy rippled over her.

I did it!

Pete came to stand over her. "Dear parents of everyone in this room, we regret to inform you that your son and daughter will be taking an extended vacation at Leavenworth due to turning a harmless prank into a Class One Felony."

She peered up at him. "Do you have any idea what I just did?" She smiled. "The best of thieves would've needed a stethoscope to hear those tumblers—probably an electronic sound enhancer. I only used this." She held up her small cone. "*And* I caught a decoy tumbler."

Pete paused, then his mouth quirked. "Everything you just said was pretty much a dog whistle to me."

Justice beamed at him. "This was such a blast, Pete."

He huffed a quiet laugh. "Okay, you're really cute right now, Punky Brewster. You kind of look like how my sister does when she faces down chocolate." He gestured at the safe. "But maybe you could close the door before orange coveralls become our uniform of the day."

"Roger that." She grabbed the handle, but as she moved to close the safe, a file on top of the stack caught her attention. She pulled it out. "This one has your name on it." She held it up to him. "Do you want to read it?"

Pete stepped back. "No." He hesitated. "What does it say?"

She flipped it open and glanced at the top page. "It's the first draft of your FITREP. Says you're a great leader and an exceptional pilot."

He didn't react.

"It also says you'd go far in your Naval career—if you

took your job more seriously."

His see-sawed his head, then he shrugged. "Take life serious and life gets serious."

"Ah." She tossed the file back inside the safe. "The world is clear to me now, thank you." She closed the steel door and stood. "Let's go. We've been here a while, and *not* lingering at the scene of a crime is one of those sacrosanct thief rules."

Pete nodded sagely. "I can see how that would be the case."

They did the sneakers thing back down the hallway, making it outside and into the squadron parking lot without incident.

The moon was brilliant, the stars sparkling.

She flung her arms wide and threw her head back, pirouetting under the magnificent sky. "I'm high as a kite on adrenaline right now."

A Ward-Lock 2000! And she'd opened it. Only one other safe on earth was considered more difficult to open—a Ward-Lock 2000 *Class A*, sold exclusively overseas—and a scant handful of thieves in all the world could claim conquest of either.

And she was one!

Chuckling, Pete swept her up and kept spinning with her, turning and turning—right into the shadows of the *Firehawks'* building. He set her on her feet, and their legs churned together for a few steps as he backed her against the wall.

His strong arms holding her close, he bent his head, his mouth an aching inch away from a kiss.

She parted her lips under the warm stroke of his breath on her mouth, her will to resist eddying away. Her nipples peaked against the contours of his chest. Her breathing quickened. Caught up in the exhilaration of the mini-heist, the power of her adrenaline, maybe even the trippy aftereffects of eating the mezcal worm, she leaned into Pete, pressing against the full muscular length of his body.

A lambent glow of need shone in his gaze.

Her belly did a warm rollover at how he looked in the moonlight, soft shadows defining his cheekbones and adding a harder chisel to his jaw. He was so gorgeous, all flash and shine. It was almost like he wasn't real.

Maybe he wasn't, here inside her bubble.

The damned bubble.

She let her eyes drift into a slow blink. "Pete," she groaned softly. "I'm not in a bubble."

"You're not in a bubble?" he murmured.

No. And she was careening fast toward a decision that offered no take-backs. Only real-world consequences and aftermaths.

She straightened and tried to pull away.

He didn't let go.

"Come on, Pete. I need to think."

"You already think too much." But he released her.

She stepped back and stared down the side of the *Firehawks'* building. The reflection of moonlight turned several windows into a glossy shade of silver. "We shouldn't have done that."

"It was only a prank," Pete repeated, maintaining the company line.

She met his gaze. "We broke into the skipper's office. That's not a prank, at least not for me." The drugging effects of her adrenaline were still doing cartwheels in her system. *One* heist, and she already itched to do another. "I'm holding on by the skin of my teeth here, Pete, trying to stay out of trouble long enough to start my Special Missions job, where I can steal shit legally. A job, by the way, that would've gone right down the crapper if we'd been caught tonight."

"I had several excuses ready to go," Pete assured her. "We would've been fine."

A man who can remove the threat of consequences by talking himself out of anything… That wasn't extra-bad for her at all, was it?

"What you just said only makes it easier for me to give into temptation," she said. "You're flashy and larger-than-life and being around you pings the side of me that wants to be flashy and impressive too. You…you're not good for me."

He shook his head. "You're wrong. I'm actually the best fucking guy who could be in your life right now to keep you sane."

Her throat swelled. "Even if that were true, you're a complication I can't deal with. I don't know how to explain it, and I'm not sure if you can understand…just…BUD/S is the toughest thing I've ever had to do. There's no room for me to think about anyone but myself. I have to stay totally focused on making it through. I can't be running off to play with you."

He stared at her through the shadows. "You're right, I can't even begin to imagine what a monster BUD/S is, but I can understand everything you just said about needing to stay focused. So if that's what you really want, I'll respect it."

"It is." Her lips felt strangely elastic. Setting Pete aside was proving harder than she'd thought. "I'm sorry, but not everyone has the luxury of adopting a take-life-serious-and-life-gets-serious approach."

"They do. They just don't realize it."

CHAPTER TWENTY-NINE

JUSTICE SAT IN her car in front of her North Island BOQ room. The trees in front of the building were loud with birds, the occasional blue jay swooping off a bough, sailing on an updraft for a moment of weightless freedom before flapping off into the cool, cloudless late morning.

There was no other activity.

It was Saturday.

Her temporary assignment with the HSC-85 *Firehawks* was over. She was heading back to the Amphib Base today to be ready for an early Monday morning muster at BUD/S. *Hooyah* and all that… or *Oorah*, if you were Pete.

A smile tugged at the corners of her mouth.

Lonely, are we?

Pick a bag!

She was going to miss his antics.

She was going to miss *him*.

Pete Robbins, helluva guy.

He'd kept to his word during the remainder of the time they trained together and gave her the space she wanted. He'd stopped flirting and stirring up trouble, but he was nice about it, never depriving her of his devil-damn-the-world side. He was alternately a colleague, a Happy Hour drinking buddy, and—yeah, still sometimes—a delinquent pain in the ass.

He still wanted to see her, so when they'd said their goodbyes Friday afternoon in the hangar, he plucked her cell

JUSTICE   2 1 5

out of her hand and inputted his home address.

"Drop by any time!" he crooned.

Doubtful she would. She needed her weekends to recover.

But the final curtain had not dropped on Lieutenant Pete Robbins. She would be back.

Starting her car, she drove out of the lot.

All right… Time to fully pop the bubble and get back in the game. Prep herself for constant abuse, unrelenting cold, and psychological warfare. She would return to BUD/S better…stronger…faster.

Yes.

The Six Million Dollar Man.

Gentleman, we can rebuild her. We have the technology.

She will crush Pool Comp, conquer drownproofing, master knot-tying, kick the unholy shit out of the Obstacle Course. The O-course especially, dammit. There was no reason why she shouldn't put up a top-five time. With her experience and background, she shouldn't be struggling. She should—

She startled. *My experience…*

She inhaled deeply. "Well, I'll be damned."

You've become so programmed to do everything their way, you've lost touch with how to do it your way. And your way is better…

Tonight we'll be taking advantage of your special talent…

She did a U-turn and pulled over. Finding Pete's address on her phone, she brought it up on her GPS.

Pete was in the middle of eating a sandwich when he opened his door to her knock—a turkey, lettuce, and tomato on wheat by the looks of it.

He gulped his food down and said, "Holy shit."

"Hi."

"Hi back." His eyes lit. "Come on in." He stepped aside to let her pass. He was wearing loose black nylon basketball shorts and a T-shirt with "Stone Temple Pilots" on it in neon yellow writing.

She'd never seen him in short sleeves before, and, wow, his arms didn't disappoint. The masculine swell of two *very* sculpted biceps bulged at the hems of his sleeves.

"I thought you were going back to the Amphib Base today," he said.

"I was. I am. I was headed that way, but…I need to tell you something first."

"Uh-oh. Am I in for one of your infamous speeches?"

She laughed. "No, nothing like that." She paused. "I don't think so, at least."

Chuckling, he crossed to a side table next to a dark brown Barcalounger that was aimed at a television set. The History Channel was playing quietly.

"A man more interested in King Tut than baseball," she commented dryly. "I didn't know your kind existed."

"I never cease to fascinate you, right?" Pete set the sandwich on a plate, then walked back over to her. "Okay," he said, dusting crumbs off his hands. "You have my undivided attention."

She met his gaze, smiling…then her smile blopped over. Staring at the aching handsomeness of his face and into his lively eyes, it was suddenly all she could do to produce a single syllable.

"Well," he murmured. "This *isn't* a typical speech."

"No." The one word came out a little hoarse. She cleared her throat. "I want to thank you. And also to apologize."

Curiosity flickered across his face.

"I've been unfair to you, saying you're a bad influence on me, when…you actually…you really helped me, Pete. You showed confidence in me at a time when the BUD/S instructors were more interested in breaking me than inspiring me. You knew from the start I'd be able to figure out Glinski, and…I did. Then the night of our caper in Quinn's office, you believed in me then too. I drew on some of my best skills that night because of you, and now…I feel like I'm back in touch with who I really am. I can return to BUD/S smarter and tougher, so…thank you."

His mouth tipped sideways. "Your speeches are really growing on me."

She exhaled a breathless laugh.

He stepped closer, his eyes soft and warm like liquid chocolate. "I'll give you BUD/S, Justice. When it's over, we're revisiting the issue of dating."

Her throat tightened around a conflicting turmoil of emotions, all of them churning up to tug her in different directions.

Push…pull…

Pete's playful to her serious.

Her need to think things through versus his let's-just-do-it, balls-swinging-free manner.

His oil to her water.

Or…?

Was he the best fucking guy who could be in her life right now?

She really didn't know. "I haven't even decided if I'll ever date a military man," she said. "Especially one I work with."

"I guess you have four months to figure it out." He led her to his front door and stopped in the jamb. "But I want you to remember something while you're gone. When all those BUD/S assholes are shitting on you, everything's way too stressful and you're going insane for a break from getting your balls busted, I want you to remember me. I'm here, and I'm ready to make things better."

She swallowed hard, but it was no use—a solid lump

was now wedged in her throat. She hadn't felt her raw glop in a long time, but suddenly it was squelching relentlessly past her restraints, ballooning the lump in her throat to an atrocious size…

She cannae take any more, Captain. She's gonna blow!

She laughed, a sort of soggy sound. "Okay. I'll remember."

He smiled, just a little, just a twinkle of almost-boyish Chris Pratt.

Justice's eyes burned. Ugh, now she was on the verge of crying. Who knew this last-minute trip to see Pete would turn her into such a wreck?

He wrapped a hand around her nape and tugged her forward, planting a firm kiss on her brow. "Go be tough now, little sailor."

She took a lurching step backward, nodded mutely, then turned around, her legs barely working as she walked away from that sweet, adorable bastard.

CHAPTER THIRTY

THE SIX MILLION Dollar Man wasn't feeling entirely bionic when she drove into the officers' barracks parking lot on the Amphib Base fifteen minutes later.

More like sick with dread.

Back to constant abuse, unrelenting cold, and psychological warfare…

No lumps or tears or raw glop, though.

Justice had taken control of those on the drive. Which was good practice. She needed to get back into the habit of storing shit away, shoring herself up against the kind of emotions that wouldn't benefit her at BUD/S.

Like lust and yearning and femininity…maybe a wee bit of infatuation.

Hopping from her car, she swung a duffel bag and a grocery sack out of the trunk. She started for the barracks, and her heart skipped a couple of beats.

She was going to see Brayden Street and Keith Knight again—at least they'd *better* be here. She hadn't thought about them much during her time in the bubble, needing a break from all things BUD/S so badly when she left two weeks ago. But seeing the officers' barracks got her—

"Hey!"

She turned around.

Brayden!

He was crossing the parking lot toward her, wearing polished black boots, camo pants, and the brown shirt that marked him as a Hell Week grad.

Limping slightly, he came to a stop in front of her, the sun catching in his blond hair, his dimples out in full force.

Lord. She'd forgotten how toe-curling those were.

His face was animated with pleasure at seeing her. "You're back!"

She freed a huge smile. "And *you* made it through. Although clearly not without some damage. What's with the limp?"

"Ah. I got stress fractures on my shins from all the running during Hell Week."

"Shit. Bummer." Running with stress fractures had to be a serious ouch.

"Yeah. An old injury of mine's acting up."

"Football?"

He made a scornful sound. "Real Wyoming men play ice hockey."

She held up a hand. "Hey, sorry."

He smiled. "No," he went on. "I got into a rock-climbing accident when I was seventeen. Some unstable terrain crumbled away, and I fell from way too high up and snapped both my shins on the landing."

"Jesus." She snapped her head around and stared at him. "Double ouch."

"Yeah, it was bad. There were five of us climbing that day, and everyone was seriously injured, except for Keith. He just dislocated his shoulder on a hard rollout. Walt, another one of my brother's, fractured his arm and got a concussion. Another guy broke his pelvis in three places, and another…" Brayden glanced aside. "He died."

"I'm so sorry," she said quietly.

They passed a flagpole, the stars-and-stripes doing a languid flap-and-flutter number, the metal clasp *pringing* against the pole. Palm trees swayed in the background.

"Did Keith's shoulder act up during Hell Week too?" she asked.

"What? You mean from the rock-climbing accident? No. The only thing still bothering Keith from that is his conscience." Brayden raked a hand over his hair. "He was leading us on the climb that day, so he blames himself for what happened. I don't think he's ever gotten over it. He didn't even go to the funeral, and Ryan was one of our best friends from hockey." Brayden coughed a little. "But, hey, you look good."

"Well, I was out drinking and carousing the whole time you had a boat on your head."

A disbelieving laugh shot out of Brayden's mouth. "Yeah, right."

No? You ever hear the one about the rakehell gunslinger who came into town, a bottle of mezcal in one hand, lacy women's panties in the other, a smile that could make you feel snake-bit?

"So I assume Keith made it." She spoke this as a statement of fact—best to presuppose the desired outcome about something so important.

"'Course. We got each other through, actually. Every time we sat down for chow, we'd start up with shit like, this is no big deal, come on, we've done this before. I would say, we've frozen our balls off worse than this, right? Remember the snowstorm we got caught in along the Owen-Spalding Trail without our winter gear? Then the next time, Keith would say, we've been fucked up worse than this, remember? Like when we were lost in the Paintbrush Divide for two days. A lot of the other guys started gathering around us, too, just to hear the bull we were spouting."

Justice smiled, imagining it. "So who's left from my boat team? Zack Kilgour?" *Sniper wannabe.*

"Yep, he made it."

"Brad Ziegler?" *Pervy Hairy Arms.*

"Absolutely. The guy's a serious sled dog." Brayden cast her a sidelong glance. "You happy about him or not?"

"Aw, sure. Ziegler needs reprogramming, but he's basically harmless. Dog Bone?"

"Still here."

Good. "Omar Boyd?"

"No."

She stopped short. "What?"

His lips twisted. "Medical rollback. He came down with pneumonia and kept falling unconscious out of his IBS. He'll have to join a later class after he recovers at PTRR."

So he could still become a SEAL, but still... *Damn.* No more High School Crush.

They started walking again.

"Oh, shit, what about Shaw?" *Fucking Appletini.*

"Gone."

She made an approving sound in her throat. "About time. What a waste of skin."

"The guy was doomed from the moment he kicked you over during Egyptian push-ups. No one lives through a Keith Knight vendetta."

She snorted. "Anyone left on your boat team?"

"Donnie Cogan."

Justice's Timed Swim partner. *Meh.* Cogan had never taken a shine to her.

"Seven rollbacks from other classes who were stashed at PTRR joined the class," Brayden told her, "so we're at a total of forty-two now."

Which equaled thirty-five originals. That *was* a serious Hell Week weed-out.

They were almost at the barracks.

"Oh, hey, I have a gift for you." She stopped again and held up her grocery sack.

"Really? Wait…" Brayden smirked. "Is it soap?"

Hah! She should have thought of that. "No." She rattled the grocery sack at him. "It's ice cream. A very un-SPECWAR flavor."

"Uh-oh. Mint chocolate chip?"

"Funfetti!" She whipped the gallon jug out with a ta-da flourish. "I think it's even pink."

He laughed. "Hell, I'll eat it."

She grinned. "I'll share."

His eyes crinkled at the corners. "Good." He took the ice cream from her.

They arrived at the barracks, and Justice leapt forward to grab the knob before Brayden could open the door for her.

He *humphed*. "Take advantage of my slower speed while you can." He came in behind her, holding the door open with a hand high up on the frame. "It's the only time you'll—"

Female laughter chimed through the air.

They exchanged glances.

What the hell?

The main door *clacked* shut, and a second later Rudy Dunbar leaned partially out of the community room. Catching sight of them, he jumped up from the couch. "Hey! Look who's back!" He was clearly happy to see Justice.

And *that* brought a woman immediately to his side.

She was wearing a dress of unseasonable white stretched taut over gigantic breasts, ones that were way out of proportion to her small stature—it was a wonder she didn't spend all day fighting not to fold in half. Mouse brown hair was pulled back to reveal young features, although somehow lacking the bloom of freshness. Probably because her makeup was puttied on like frosting.

"Hi, I'm Sable." She introduced herself with a smile. "Rudy's girlfriend."

Justice dropped her duffel and grocery sack by the door and walked toward the community room, hopefully keeping a straight face. She'd never gotten used to that name.

Brayden followed.

"So you're The BUD/S Woman we've all been hearing so much about on the news." Sable's smile didn't waver, but the slight narrowing of her eyes as she checked out Justice added an edge of bitchery to the expression.

"My," Sable chirped, "you must consume a lot of protein."

Chocolate-covered cherries.

If other women were like a box of chocolates when it came to Justice, Sable was a chocolate-covered cherry: delicious-looking on the outside, but too syrupy—and, honestly, a little gross—on the inside. Moreover, chocolate-covered cherries gave Justice heartburn. Meaning, they didn't like her.

"Nice to meet you," Justice said, and *oh, your consume-a-lot-of-protein double-entendre didn't slip by me.* Rudy Sour Face could have this one.

Another woman stepped into view. "Hello," she said.

If there was something in this world that could be goosed up a man's ass to make him go into full rigor while he was still alive and standing, that thing had just been shoved up Brayden's butt.

What the hell was wrong with him?

"I'm Charlotte." The second woman offered her hand in a genuinely welcoming gesture. "Brayden's girlfriend."

Ah.

CHAPTER THIRTY-ONE

CHARLOTTE WAS THE epitome of everything Justice was not: petite, well-dressed, perfumed, with taffy blond hair exquisitely coiffed. She smelled like roses, and when she shook Justice's hand, she partially bent her grip, the way women of genteel hospitality and feminine charm always did their hand-shaking.

What a perfect woman for Brayden.

Not a smudge of grubby criminality about her.

The two of them should have lots of babies together. Perfect blond offspring. Right here in this room, in fact. Wouldn't that be a jollification?

"Well." Justice slapped a hand down on Brayden's shoulder—very hard. "Gotta run."

Brayden's eyebrows knifed into a scowl.

"Don't be ridic," Sable objected. "You should stay."

Response options to something so insincere? Justice idly scratched behind her ear, drawing a blank. She had very little experience dealing with this type of confection.

"Yes," Brayden agreed in a steely voice. "Stay." His nostrils were wide and stiff.

Last time Justice had seen him this enraged, she was wearing a pie-face of sand, care of Instructor Hill.

"That's okay." She'd sooner get wet and sandy in the nude than hang out with this crowd. "You all need to catch up, and I want to go say hi to my guys." She started to pivot toward the door, and in the moment her face was aimed solely at Brayden, she whispered, "You suck."

Brayden grated a sound in his chest. "Wait a minute—"

Not even waiting a second. "It was nice meeting everyone." Justice lobbed this last artificial nicety as she beat a fast retreat for the door, picking up the grocery sack she'd left by her duffel on the way out.

JUSTICE'S NOSE HAD never been jammed precisely and directly into a dirty jockstrap, but if it ever had been, the stink would probably rival what she was smelling inside the enlisted barracks. What the stench had been like when candidates packed the room to capacity, she didn't dare imagine. On the bright side, it drowned out the lingering aroma of Charlotte's rosy perfume.

She searched for Keith among the milling brown shirts and spotted him—bottom bunk, fifth over on the right.

He was lying with one arm bent behind his head, and the soles of his booted feet pressed together so that his wide-open, bent legs formed a diamond shape. The position displayed thick thighs and a crotch Justice forced herself not to admire.

He was engaged in an activity rarely seen in the natural male habitat—the reading of a paperback novel. A Tom Clancy something. Maybe Keith read the classics when he wasn't at BUD/S. Maybe she didn't care. Reading the written word outside of *Sports Illustrated* was impressive enough.

She strode to the foot of Keith's bunk, quipping, "So this dyslexic guy walks into a bra…"

The book dropped down.

Pleasure blazed across Keith's face. "Well, look what the fucking cat dragged in." He swung out of bed and came to his feet, giving her a once-over. Then another one, slower. "Damn, Hayes, you look different."

Well, damn, Knight, you do not. He'd lost a little weight, but otherwise he was the same Keith, with the kind of rugged handsomeness that look like it'd been peeled right off the cover of a *Bold Frontiersman!* magazine. His body radiated its typical massive amount of energy.

She smiled. It was good to see him.

"Relaxed," he defined. "That's what it is. You look—"

"Like she got laid," Hairy Arms inputted as he rounded her.

Dog Bone and Sniper Kilgour followed.

"Hey!" she exclaimed. *Her guys!* All wearing their victorious brown shirts. Come Monday morning on the grinder, she'd be the lone white shirt in a sea of conquest. "So Team Knight busted it! Hooyah! All of you made it through." She swept her gaze over them. It was so great to be back with her team again. "Everyone okay?"

Kilgour canted his head forward an eighth of an inch. His version of a nod.

Dog Bone gave her a shy smile.

She jerked up her eyebrows in mock horror. "Good God, Dog Bone, you've lost weight." *Not an ounce.* "You're a mere shadow of your former self. Here—" She tugged a box of Ding Dongs out of her grocery sack and handed it to him. "You'd better take these."

His face illuminated in pure delight.

"Don't eat them all in one…" *Sitting?* "Bite."

Hairy Arms pointed a finger at a small nick on his chin. "I cut myself shaving."

"Aw." She *tsked*. "Poor Ziegler. You'll never be the man your mother is."

Keith guffawed.

Sniper Kilgour smiled.

Dog Bone's mouth was already full.

"Great." Ziegler rolled his eyes. "The other fucking

comedian's back."

Keith leaned an arm on the top bunk. "So you cool with your Missus Team?"

"Oh, yeah. They're a great bunch of guys."

"Hah!" Ziegler triumphed. "Told ya she got laid."

Only almost on the USS *Bonhomme Richard...*

Keith kept talking as if Ziegler hadn't. "Shaw and Boyd didn't make it. You hear?"

She nodded. "Brayden told me."

"We took on two replacements from another boat team. Sanchez and Giddiup." Giddiup had earned his nickname because he ran with a weird skip in his step. "Our team's back to seven."

Seven, not eight? She raised her brows. "I'm still not an extra?"

"Nope. You're a regular guy."

"Uh-oh. You can't be happy about that, me not being as strong as the men 'n' all."

"Ouch." Keith made a show of rubbing his ribs. "I felt that elbow dig from clear over here."

Dog Bone waved the empty Ding Dong box at her. "These were good."

She did a double take. What...? Wait, how long had she been standing here?

"Guys!"

The four of them turned around.

Giddiup was skip-jogging toward them. His color was high and his brows low. "Good," he clipped at Justice. "You're back. I need your help."

"What's going on?" Keith demanded.

Giddiup's lips flattened against his teeth. "My sister's boyfriend got drunk last night and knocked her around. The douche knows I'm gunning for him, so he's holed up at his parents' mountain cabin." Giddiup addressed Justice again.

"Can you come with me and lure the cocksucker out?"

She didn't have anything else going on today, so she said, "Sure, why not?" Teaching an abuser a lesson was as good a way as any to spend her time.

Keith inserted himself again. "Ziegler, Dog Bone, and I are coming along as backup."

CHAPTER THIRTY-TWO

THE CABIN TURNED out to be located in the foothills of the Mountain High Ski Resort, a good two-and-a-half-hour drive from San Diego. Their group of five arrived just before one in the afternoon, shortly after making a pit stop at In-N-Out Burger for lunch.

Keeping hidden next to a row of tall pines, Giddiup stopped just before the start of a dirt driveway, rock salt clattering against his car's undercarriage. He shut off the engine, pulled on the parking brake, then turned around and rested an elbow on the seat divider.

Justice was in the back next to Dog Bone and Ziegler. Keith was riding shotgun.

"The four of us will get the car rolling for you, okay?" Giddiup told her.

The idea was for her to fake a breakdown, then once Bruce the Abuser came out of the cabin to help her, Giddiup, Keith, Ziegler, and Dog Bone would rush him.

And at that point you wouldn't want to be Bruce.

"But then you'll have to push it the rest of the way up the driveway," Giddiup warned.

"Not a problem," she said. The driveway was only few yards long.

She climbed out of the car, catching a face full of brisk air. The sky was clear blue, and the sun was sparking diamonds in the patches of snow littering the ground and clinging intermittently to tree boughs.

She inhaled a deeper breath of delicious air. Mountains were one of Mother Nature's best ideas. Nothing against the beach, but there was something about the smell of pine and the crispness of mountain air that settled into her soul.

She rounded the back of the car and strode up to the driver's side door.

Giddiup was waiting for her. He set his hands on his hips and inspected her. "Can you make yourself look hot?"

Ziegler nearly went into spluttering cardiac arrest. "You don't think Hayes is hot?"

Giddiup flipped a hand in the direction of her head. "She's just too bunched up wearing a bun. Take your hair down, all right?"

"No way."

Giddiup gave her an irritated look. "You need to come across as a party girl. Bruce sees a hot woman at his mercy, he won't be able to resist coming outside." He flung a gesture at her chest. "At least unzip your jacket so the ass-fuck can check out your tits."

"You think," Ziegler mimicked Instructor Hill, "that I want to hear someone on my Teams saying tits?"

Keith laughed.

Giddiup scowled. "This isn't funny."

Justice did a palm-up. "Don't worry, I'll get this guy to come out."

The men gathered at the trunk.

Justice moved to hop into the driver's seat, then hesitated. She undid enough of her hair to make a ponytail.

Hairy Arms groaned. "Okay, now *that's* going in my whack-off logbook, for sure."

Justice glanced back at Hairy Arms. "You know that being a dick won't make yours bigger, right, Ziegler?" She leaned inside the car and popped the brake.

The boys grunted the vehicle into motion.

Cranking on the steering wheel, Justice turned down the drive and kept the momentum going while the boys scattered into the surrounding woods.

Immediately up ahead she spotted a simple, one-story log cabin with a square-paned window on each side of a front door. Thin wisps of smoke were drifting from the chimney—someone was home. In the distance beyond the cabin, a mountain rose up like a snow giant, lumpish on the sides, but smooth down the middle, where she could just make out a ski lift. On the left side of the cabin a smaller version of a mountain flowed smoothly upward to a flat top.

Probably there was an amazing view at the summit.

The front door of the cabin swung open just as Justice muscled the car to the end of the drive.

A man of medium build in dark ski pants, unlaced snow boots, and a red anorak stepped onto the porch. He had short black hair and a black goatee, although not a full goatee, more like a mustache accompanied by just a stripe of vertical beard down his chin.

The latest fashion in Hades no doubt.

"Hi," she called out and waved cheerily—because that's what a hot party girl would do, right? *Be cheery.* She jumped in the driver's seat, yanked on the parking brake—paused to unzip her jacket nearly all the way—then jumped back out.

Bruce crunched through patchy snow up to her.

"Sorry to bother you." She smiled radiantly. "But my car quit on me."

"No bother." Smiling back, Bruce checked out the number the cool air was already doing on her nipples. "Hey, I got some hot coffee inside." He hiked a thumb at the cabin behind him. "You want to come in and warm up a bit?"

Somehow she managed to brighten her smile even as prickles crawled up her spine. Bruce was *supposed* to be ogling her breasts—it was why she'd unzipped—but her lizard brain was still warning her that here was a man who didn't take kindly to *no*.

How glad was she that a bunch of SEAL candidates were secretly surrounding her?

"Great!" she enthused. "But would you mind taking a look under the hood first?"

"Well…I don't know much about—*Shit!*" Bruce's attention zipped to something behind Justice a millisecond before he whipped around and hauled ass for the cabin.

Giddiup rampaged past Justice and performed a flying tackle, taking Bruce down into a snowdrift, puffs of flakes cascading into the air.

"You fuck!" Giddiup snarled.

Bruce wrestled and fought. "You know what, dickwad? I'm not the fucking problem. Peggy's a real bitch sometimes, and *she's* the problem."

Red-faced, Giddiup threw a punch.

Bruce tried to hit Giddiup back.

The two were stirring up quite a racket.

Keith stalked up to the writhing bodies, combing the area. "Get him inside," he ordered.

Hairy Arms and Dog Bone hoisted Bruce to his feet, muscling him into the cabin, boots scuffling and everyone cursing a lot.

Keith glanced at her. "You coming?"

"Think I'll pass on the main show." She pointed at the hill. "I'm going to go for a hike while you deal."

Keith headed toward her. "I'll go with you."

"Not necessary."

He smiled. "You know the SEAL motto—one is none, two is one."

Team Guys never went anywhere alone.

The hill was a steeper climb than it'd appeared, and she and Keith had to concentrate a bit on where and how they placed their feet. They hiked without speaking, although it was a relaxed and companionable silence, and very different.

Justice had performed any number of physical activities beside Knight, but every grueling task they'd done had been under orders and duress. Now here they were on a challenging hike *by choice*, moving at their own pace, enjoying the surrounding beauty, and growing more and more...what?

Companionable?

They made it to the top, and the view was as spectacular as Justice had predicted.

She puffed vapory breaths as she panned the vista, miles of soaring, snow-covered peaks and an endless expanse of crystal horizon.

Keith peered up at the sky too, tracking the drift of a few wispy clouds.

What did a man like Keith see when he gazed at clouds? Surely not unicorns.

"What kind of woman," he asked quietly, "goes on a tough hike on her last day off from BUD/S?"

She startled a bit, then shrugged, playing it casual, even though something in his tone had warmed her. "It's a beautiful day."

"How about whitewater rafting?" he asked, meeting her gaze. "You into that too?"

She arched a brow. "If we're talking Class Five rapids."

He smiled. "Deep-forest camping?"

"Absolutely."

"Rock climbing?"

"Puh-lease." She'd been scaling the sides of buildings since age five and was an expert climber by thirteen.

"Sky diving?"

She narrowed her eyes a little. "Am I being auditioned for some role I'm unaware of?"

He tipped his head briefly at her. "You and I just seem to have a lot in common. I was thinking we should stay friends after BUD/S."

Friends. Here was that word again.

Alexa, define friend: Friend is usually defined as a person attached to another by feelings of affection or personal regard.

Not altogether off, but not quite right either. Where was the mention of *hunger*? Like her craving for Keith's respect. Her need to be near his high energy. Her base desire— always such a sideswipe when it got the better of her—for his well-built body.

Maybe when it came to male-female friendships she stood firmly on Team Harry: *men and women can't be friends because the sex part always gets in the way.*

Quite the expounder of social wisdom, that Harry Burns from *When Harry Met Sally.*

Pete? She'd definitely been tempted to add a *with-benefits* cherry on top to her friendship with him. Brayden? The appearance of a girlfriend in the community room earlier today had cut her surprisingly deep. Keith? Out here, free of the militaristic Amphib Base, away from BUD/S and its horrors, she was as captivated by Wyoming Man as she was by the snowy wonderland that suited him so well.

"How about skiing?" Keith half-smiled. "I'm guessing you're a pogue at that, you being an L.A. girl."

"I'm probably not as good as you, Wyoming Man, but I can keep up. My Uncle Alistair used to take me skiing to Mammoth Mountain for a week every year. Until I was eighteen. Then he…" She cut herself off, the simple explanation suddenly veering toward the complex, general information turning into a confession.

"Then he what?"

Then he left.

She shoved her hands in her jacket pockets. "Not really important. He wasn't an actual uncle, anyway."

"Seems like the guy was important if he took you on ski trips for so many years."

"Yeah." Her voice box squeezed her next words down to a low volume. "But this is where the secrets come out."

Keith looked a little surprised, then said, "Ah. No problem. Circle of trust here. Total cone of silence."

She smiled at him but remained quiet. *Never completely trust* was not only a Hayes family rule but a standard every good thief followed. And yet…the need to open up pulled at her, which meant, God knew, she wasn't thinking clearly…or she was decision-making from her feelings of loss— from saying goodbye to Pete and her Special Missions guys…from finding Crushy Boyd gone.

It was so easy to lose a team, wasn't it?

Like when her dad's crew had fallen apart.

She huddled into her jacket, a nip of frost sugaring the air. "Alistair was my dad's best friend and colleague…until he screwed up a job and my father showed him the door." *Just like that.*

"What did he screw up?"

She gathered words into her mouth but couldn't push them out.

"Something to do with a robbery, I'm guessing."

She fixed Keith with a sharp look.

He was expressionless. "I was Googling your college track record and came across your dad. Grayson Hayes, right?"

Tugging her zipper higher, she tucked it under her chin. "That's Dad. Alistair was his alarm specialist."

"So what happened?"

"The team was on a heist to snatch a cache of rare rubies from the Coventry mansion in Atlanta—old Southern family, money going back to antebellum times. I was along for the ride, to observe and help out where needed, and…I'm still not sure what went wrong. Suddenly sirens are wailing, and the whole house is going into lockdown. Everyone was trapped inside, about to get caught by the cops—and my dad had never been caught. In fact, he would've been mortified if the authorities even came within a whiff of having evidence against him. So I acted fast to save the team.

"We all knew that Dale Coventry, lord of the manor—if you want to call him that—had a reputation for being a man-whore. So I stripped down to my bra and underwear and draped myself across the bed in the master bedroom."

Keith's brows shot straight up.

"And you can wipe that image from your mind right now, Knight."

Keith grinned.

"Anyway, when the police arrived, Alistair pretended to be my pimp, smoothly explaining how Mr. Coventry had reserved me for the night's entertainment, but unfortunately neglected to disengage the alarm. Because of Coventry's rep, the cops believed the story. But because of Coventry's standing, they didn't want to stick around to verify it, put themselves into the unenviable position of having to arrest the city's wealthiest magnate for soliciting sex. They satisfied themselves with hauling me and Alistair in. This allowed my father to sneak out of the house and get away. So Dad's name remained unsullied, but *I* was arrested for prostitution."

Keith exhaled in a rush. "Shit, really?"

"Unfortunately, yes. Luckily, the charges were dropped for insufficient evidence, although I'm still in the process of expunging the incident completely from my record. Anyway, the whole ugly episode was disastrous enough that my dad sent Alistair packing. His best friend of twenty years. Poof. Gone." *No more ski trips for her.*

No more love of a man who was like an uncle to her.

Keith's mouth drew down. "Seems harsh."

She shrugged, but the gesture felt manufactured. "Being the best of the best comes at a cost. Mistakes aren't permitted."

The wind picked up for the length of a few sporadic gusts, rustling the tops of the trees. Snowflakes plumed off needle tips. Her coat collar flapped, and her ponytail tangled.

Keith turned to face her fully.

She returned his stare, and her heart started to beat an erratic rhythm. His features were so roughly masculine no one would ever consider him handsome in the traditional sense, but how could such a bold and fearless face be described as anything but good-looking?

Keith's focus skated to her ponytail, and an expression stole into his eyes that sent an electrical bolt through her.

She breathed slowly for several seconds as a ripple of heightened awareness rolled down her spine. A heated tension coiled in her pelvis.

Oh, Harry Burns…

He'd really been onto something, hadn't he?

ROSY PERFUME AND Chocolate-Covered Cherry were gone by the time Justice returned to the officers' barracks and thank God for that.

She collected her duffel bag, still by the door where she'd left it, and lugged it into her room. Hunkering down, she began to unpack, tugging out one of her hacker—

"Where the hell have you been?" Brayden demanded.

She pivoted.

He was standing in her open doorway, his posture rigid.

"I had something to do with my team."

"You've been gone all day," he accused testily.

"It was a big something."

He stepped into her room, his face taut. "I've been wanting to talk to you about something."

Justice rose from her crouch. "What about?"

"I wanted to tell you that Charlotte is *not* my girlfriend. Okay? She's my ex. I broke up with her before coming to BUD/S, but she didn't agree with the reason I did, so she hasn't accepted it and keeps pursuing me."

"Oh. Sorry. But…you don't really owe me an explanation." Justice didn't hold any claims on Brayden, even though…er…sometimes she acted like she did.

"I just wanted to make sure you knew that I'm not the type of man who would lie with you on a couch"—he chopped a hand toward the community room—"if I had a girlfriend."

"Whoa." She lifted a palm. "Hold up there. I thought we discussed the nap incident and decided it was nothing. I was wholly gross. You were completely unconscious. Remember?"

He planted his hands on his hips. "I don't want you thinking badly of me." Behind the anger, his eyes were raw and earnest.

She heaved a sigh. "For crying out loud, I *don't*. You're the damsel-rescuer. If a guy like you ever cheated on his girlfriend, someone would have to call God and ask Him to remake mankind. Everything would be wrong."

Brayden was somewhat mollified, but not completely. "You said I sucked."

"Um…" *Shit.* "That was nothing. A Freudian slip."

"A slip about what?"

"If I knew, it wouldn't be Freudian, right? Subconscious drives and all that, you know…" She trailed off. *This must be what babbling sounds like.*

Brayden's eyes narrowed.

"Maybe I don't want you to know."

"Tell me anyway."

Really? Was he allowed to insist on that?

He waited.

She made a face, privately to herself—or half-privately. "Sometimes I get a little territorial."

His eyebrows flew up. If he'd been a cartoon character, they would've soared all the way off his forehead.

"In a totally sisterly way," she rushed to add.

"Are you sure?"

"Yes!" *As far as you need to know.* "You're a fellow candidate, Brayden. Don't get weird on me now."

He hesitated. "All right. I won't." His shoulders finally relaxed. "But I prefer to think of you as a friend, not a sister."

Friend—again with the *friend*. Why did this keep coming up? Maybe it's like what Inigo Montoya said to Vizzini in *The Princess Bride*, "You keep using that word, I do not think it means what you think it means."

Brayden gestured toward the kitchen. "So do you want to go dig into the Funfetti now? We could talk shit about Sable, be a couple of dirtbags."

"Yeah." She laughed. "Sounds good."

They headed into the kitchen.

Brayden opened the freezer. "I'll start by saying *both* Sable and Rudy are a pair of whiny gossips." He pulled out the new ice cream container. "While you were away, I had to sit though those two trashing everyone with a pulse."

She laughed again. "Sorry."

Brayden clattered in the silverware drawer for the scooper. "Did you know that I once caught Rudy opening my mail? He said he thought it was his." Brayden pried off the ice cream lid. "Like *Brayden* and *Rudy* are similar names. Fucking liar."

She leaned her elbows on the counter and watched Brayden dish out the Funfetti. It was all so familiar.

Tomorrow she would have to face down abuse, cold, a sandy vagina, Chief Tanner's beautiful white fangs, and Instructor Hill's woolly-lipped rage.

But for now it was good to be back.

CHAPTER THIRTY-THREE

"BUST IT!"

Justice launched off the mark at full power, letting her body flow into a pure, muscle-memory run.

No strategizing about how to best manage a soft-sand run—which was, by the way, to follow in the pre-packed footprints of the man in front of you—or how to run with less bounce during Land Portage—the less bounce the better when you have a heavy boat on your head.

She just stretched out and went.

Your way is better....

Hah! She all but flew through every challenge on the O-Course.

Parallel Bars—*Easy as pie!*

Tires: like those used for football practice—*Fun!*

Low Wall… High Wall—*Hot damn!* It was like hopping a backyard fence.

Barbed Wire Crawl—she'd wriggled through sewer pipes plenty of times.

Cargo Net: a fifty-foot-high grid of rope—just like climbing up that five-story fire escape in New York. *Yeah!*

Balance Logs: three weathered trunks that rolled when stepped on—how many times had she light-footed across a tiny ledge? *Balance was her thing!*

Hooyah Logs: a short log pyramid—she could practically skip over those.

Rope Transfer: climb up a rope, swing over to a ring

and grab it, transfer to another rope, climb down—remember the time she hadn't been allowed to use the floor at home? *Simple!*

Dirty Name: throw the body from one log hurdle to a higher log hurdle—like jumping from city building to city building.

Hooyah Logs again…

The Weaver: like a sideways ladder—*Neat!*

Burma Bridge: rope handholds on each side, with a single rope to walk across—like the night of the double-whammy break-in when she'd walked the tightrope between the Walkers' house and the Haywoods'. *Gimme a break!*

More Hooyah Logs—*Hooyah!*

Rope Swing: swing via rope up onto a balance beam—*Tarzan Woman action, cool!*

Monkey Bars—*Her whole life!*

Balance Beam… More Tires…

Incline Wall: jump onto a wall angled at forty-five-degrees—like scrambling across a slanted rooftop. *In my sleep!*

Spider Wall: use hand and footholds to scale three levels of a wall—she'd mastered wall climbing by the age of five. *Is this all ya got?*

Last obstacle—Vaults: hop up onto straight arms, swing over with legs.

Keep running…

End with a fifty-foot sprint across the finish line.

Jump up, fist pump, and yell, "Hooyah!" because—

She came in third place!

Ziegler was first—no one could beat his Iron Man legs—and Keith second.

Brayden might be able to take her once his shins completely healed, but for today…

She was *third!*

She belted out another "Hooyah!" *No Goon Squad for her today.*

Some candidates gaped at her. Most smiled. They knew her reputation as a track star, and there was no shame in coming in behind an athlete who'd once put up Olympic level times.

Chief Tanner shook his head as he made notes on a clipboard. "Never thought I'd see the day. Best you be passing your next drug piss test, bleeder. Push 'em out!" he ordered the Goon Squad, then secured the class for chow.

KEITH SLAPPED HIS food tray down on the table across from Justice, and the rest of her guys formed up around her.

Dog Bone sat next to her, Sniper Kilgour next to him, Ziegler sat on the bench next to Keith. Brayden even joined them this time, sitting next to Ziegler.

Stares all around.

Justice scanned their faces. "Yes?" she inquired innocently, catching back a smile. "May I help you, gentlemen?"

"What happened to you while you were away?" Keith demanded.

She took a bite of her tuna sandwich and chewed with gusto. *Heh-heh-heh.*

"I keep telling you, she got—"

"Shut up, Ziegler." Knight kept his focus on her.

She set down her sandwich. "I just solved some shit about myself is all. I realized that this whole time at BUD/S I've been trying to compete *with* you guys, instead of doing things my own way." She grinned openly. "I guess you could say I got back in touch with who I really am."

Sniper Kilgour declared that to be "Weird."

"And do you know who I really am?" She pushed languidly to her feet. "I'm a thief." She dug into the right-side pocket of her camos and produced a wallet. She tossed it onto the table. "Chief Tanner's." Left side pocket. Another wallet. "Instructor Hill's." She reached into the lower pockets of her pants and came up with four more. "Clark's...Byrne's...Malton's... Simon's."

Dog Bone stared at the pile of wallets in open shock.

"Holy fucking shit," Ziegler hissed. "How the hell did you get all those? I never even saw you near those instructors."

She planted her palms on the table and leaned forward. "Because, gentlemen, I'm not some average, run-of-the-mill thief. I'm world-class."

One of Keith's eyebrows rose while the other dipped. Amused. Curious. Maybe just enjoying her.

"We're so screwed," Ziegler groaned. "The instructors are going to put a hook through all our nuts and drag us around the beach behind a four-by-four."

Justice straightened. "Not lingering near stolen goods is one of those thief rules written in stone." She slid her hands into her pockets. "I suggest you follow it. See ya." She turned and swaggered off.

From the side of her vision, she saw Brayden perform a swift butt-spin on his bench. "I'm outta here."

In the next second, the rest of the men followed Street's lead and scattered.

Justice whistled a lilting tune as she left the chow hall.

Things were going to be okay from here...

INTERLUDE CHAPTER

FOR THE NEXT sixteen weeks of BUD/S, things *were* okay.

Life still sucked most of the time, the days loaded down with plenty of hardships and discomfort, but Justice held firm to her new *my-way-is-better* attitude, and she steadily made it through.

She spent the last week of First Phase doing OTB—Over The Beach insertion training—then it was on to seven weeks of Second Phase, where the class learned to dive and do badass stuff while underwater. The drills started in the CTT, or Combat Training Tank—ahem, the *pool*.

As a self-described landlubbing runner, she hadn't expected to do as well as she did, but it turned out she was a gazelle—or the aquatic equivalent thereof—in the water. Drownproofing wasn't as bad as she'd feared. Candidates were tossed into the deep end with hands and feet bound, but she stayed calm and bobbed smoothly to the surface whenever she needed air. It helped that she could hold her breath for a long time. The candidates who ran out of breath easily suffered a drowning panic that led them to act in ways the instructors didn't like. The men who were the most solidly built—with no body fat to help with buoyancy—likewise struggled to pass.

Staying calm was actually the key to all underwater exercises, especially the dreaded Pool Comp. During this exercise, Justice had to crawl back and forth along the pool bottom wearing twin-80 dive tanks on her back, breathing through a Jacques-Cousteau-era double-hose regulator. Various instructors beat on her, simulating "hard surf" hits and creating malfunctions with her rig that required a careful sequence of actions to resolve—all which had to be done while short on air from a malfunctioning rig.

But rigid procedure sat directly in her wheelhouse—the alarms she'd disarmed at this point in her life were beyond counting. And after being stomped on so many times by Hill, what was a bit more stomping?

She had the worst trouble with the lifesaving practical. The "victims" didn't particularly want to be saved and attempts to do so degenerated into all-out brawls. Keith exited the pool with a bloody nose. Brayden came out with his shirt ripped and gagging up a gallon of chlorinated water. During her turn, Instructor Simon dragged her under in a bear hug. After several times of this, she realized she was heading for a fail. She didn't have the comparative strength for a mano-a-mano battle.

So on the next round, she dove deep and swam between Simon's legs, the plan being to pop up behind him and catch him by surprise. But on her way through, she accidentally head-butted his balls. When she swam to the surface he was bug-eyed and gasping, and, well...it would've been stupid not to take advantage. She hauled him to the safety of poolside.

Any instructor other than Nigel Simon would've had Justice doing push-ups with twin-80s on her back till the sun set. But Instructor Simon had always viewed her with nothing but thin-lidded suspicion, like any minute she was going to yell "Rape!" and ruin his Naval career. The contact with his balls went unmentioned. She passed.

Her highest achievement was the Buddy Carry: a 100-yard sprint where she first humped her partner and his combat load, then her partner carried her and her combat load. She was paired with Ziegler. He was ecstatic. Whether that was because she had to loop her arm through his inner thigh to hoist him onto her shoulders, or because she—while no cotton ball—was the lightest candidate, who would guess?

But Ziegler, while completely out of touch with today's sexual realities, was one of *her guys*, and he called out encouragements the whole time he was draped across her shoulders. She made it to the end, though not especially prettily. Hobbling knock-kneed the final few feet, she collapsed in a heap, Ziegler tumbling off her shoulders, laughing the whole way down. Pouring sweat, she lay on her back, her lungs practically convulsing as she wheezed for air.

Chief Tanner appeared above her, growling that her wounded partner would've *bled way the fuck out* by the time she got *his damned fool ass some help*. But she *did* carry him to the designated point...and speaking of bleeding. Tanner stopped calling her "bleeder" that day.

Brayden asked for Justice to be issued an honorary brown shirt for her performance.

The instructors agreed.

It was her crowning victory.

Third Phase arrived. The class moved into their final seven weeks, with the first week spent in the classroom studying land navigation, then the next week at the Naval Special Warfare Group One Mountain Training Facility in the rugged Laguna Mountains. There, they put the essentials of land navigation into practice.

This was her best time at BUD/S, the week spent strolling through beautiful forestland, finding plot points on a map, and camping out with the guys. Although Justice's femaleness did create another one of those absurd bureaucracy scrambles—this time about where she would bed down. Finally the tall foreheads agreed that she could erect a private tent, separate from the men, which actually ended up saving her from a lot of nighttime hassles. When the instructors made their occasional midnight raids to harasses the candidates, she was often forgotten.

Throughout these weeks she met with her Special Missions crew on three different Saturdays for training ops, so she saw Pete, radiant and dazzling, full of vim and swagger. She didn't go out drinking with him after training days, but they joshed and played during their exercises, and he remained a temptation.

Interaction with her Special Missions team had to be discontinued completely during the last month of BUD/S. The candidates were sent into seclusion at San Clemente Island, known as "the rock" for its boulder-covered landscape and sparse vegetation, with picturesque crabgrass, ice plant, and cactus predominating. The misery factor for this final training cycle shot right back up. Every day, seven days a week, was a full workday from zero-six-hundred to twenty-hundred.

All evolutions were also on subjects unfamiliar to Justice: pistol and rifle shooting, demolitions, and IAD. During the Immediate Action Drills, the candidates were taught how to shoot and move at the same time in a very choreographed manner. For safety reasons, the standards were exacting. Any mistake, real or perceived, was punished by a visit to a seven-foot-tall vat of water, known as the dip tank. *All* candidates made trips there for their transgressions, and since the water was never changed, the dip tank became increasingly vile. Justice spent most of her time on San Clemente Island wet and reeking.

If any fellow candidate still secretly harbored sex thoughts about her, she couldn't imagine that lasting through her stink-time on the rock. For the most part, though, the sexual tension had disappeared a long time ago.

The guys were close to her, but in an almost indescribable way—not intimate and not indulgent sisterly and not like full inclusion into the warrior brotherhood. It was just like...they loved her in their special grunt-manly way. They'd also grown very protective of her, but since this attitude didn't affect her reputation as a viable SOF team member, she didn't try to do anything about it. They definitely saw her as a solid performer, and their protectiveness wasn't over the top. She came to accept that it was actually kind of sweet.

She loved the adorable knuckleheads right back, and her insides grew more and more achy as BUD/S steadily wound down to a close. Who knew which, if any, of her guys she'd ever see again? The men were going into six months of SEAL Qualifying Training following BUD/S graduation—a private, in-house ceremony on the grinder—while Justice was due to head off to Pensacola, Florida, to attend cryptology school. After crypto, she would report to the USS *Bonhomme Richard* for workups with her Special Missions crew, then real-world deployments. Whether or not she would run into one of her guys in the field was still a big question mark.

So the last day of BUD/S brought up a jumbled bag of emotions for her, poignancy and sadness mixed with a lot of relief and pride. And excitement—she could hardly wait to accept her Certificate of Completion at the graduation ceremony. It would mark the ultimate culmination of all her hard work and sacrifice, a message to herself and to everyone else, *I did it!* She was good enough to be part of the most elite team in the world.

So her spirits were high at the end-of-class party on San Clemente Island at the Hell Box—the instructors' lounge, heretofore off-limits to lowly non-graduates. Class 684 had lost three additional candidates for medical reasons over the course of Second and Third Phase, but the thirty-nine who remained celebrated the conclusion of BUD/S by chowing down on barbecue and slugging back beer.

The CO of Naval Special Warfare Group One Command, Captain Miles Eagen, showed, but not to kick up his heels.

He came to make an announcement.

"BUD/S has been extended for two weeks." His hand came up to stop any complaints before they could begin. "You're not being given *additional* work, just rescheduled work."

The tall foreheads wanted Justice to attend SERE School.

SERE, Survival Evasion Resistance and Escape, was required training for all military personnel who would serve in a forward position—pilots, door-kickers, line officers, and special operators, for sure; anyone who could one day be taken prisoner by the enemy.

Normally SEAL candidates attended SERE at the end of their six months of SQT, but since Ensign Hayes would eventually be working near the field of combat, she needed to learn how to handle herself in a POW situation. The schedule had been revamped to allow her to attend SERE with her BUD/S classmates. It was as simple as that.

Not so simple, as it turned out.

It ended up profoundly changing everything.

CHAPTER THIRTY-FOUR

July
Warner Springs, California
Navy Remote Training Site
SERE (Survival Evasion Resistance and Escape)
Level-C training

JUSTICE STRODE BRISKLY into Commander Wallins's office and—

She paused a micro-second with her bootheel suspended midair.

The room was full of Navy bigwigs.

Wallins, the commander of SERE School, was there, of course, but he'd been ousted from his rightful position behind his desk by the man whose presence never portended anything good for Justice.

Admiral Joseph Sherwin.

His expression was stern and cool. As usual. As always. Same as his orgasm face, she'd bet.

What the fuck?

She set her boot down.

Was her training about to be delayed? She'd just spent the first week at SERE in the classroom, learning the Code of Conduct and SERE techniques. Tomorrow she was scheduled to go into the field with her classmates to practice survival and evasion skills, plus resistance training against various interrogation methods in a mock POW camp. Had a problem arisen?

Not another bathroom issue…

Captain Eagen said, "Take a seat, Ensign."

The captain was standing off Admiral Sherwin's left shoulder. Behind Eagen was the only man in the room not wearing a military uniform. Tall and muscled, with a chest as wide as a Buick's hood, a swarthy complexion, and black, wavy hair hanging to his shoulders, this man was wearing dark, worn clothing.

Justice had never seen him before.

She sat in the chair in front of the desk, putting herself at eye level with Sherwin.

The admiral didn't waste time getting to the point. "As I suspected, allowing you into a BUD/S class has adversely affected the attitude of the men." His glare was accusing. "I *warned* the board about this."

She maintained a neutral mask. Behind it, she was a whole lot of *what? What attitude? What warning?* "I'm afraid I don't follow, sir."

"Your BUD/S instructors report that the candidates have grown protective of you, Ensign Hayes." Sherwin leaned forward. "This makes you a future liability in the battle space."

Beneath her mask she was still way the fuck confused. How was she a liability? She wasn't even going to work with SEALs *in the battle space*. Run into? Maybe. Work with? No. "It's my understanding, sir, that I'll be operating primarily with my Special Missions team, having very little contact with SEALs."

Sherwin sat back. His jaw was hard. His upper lip hinted at a sneer.

Clearly she was a dunderhead of the highest order.

Eagen picked up the conversation. "The Missus program is still in its infant stages, Ensign. We can't fully predict how it will evolve over time. There's already been talk about attaching some Missus units to SEAL squads."

Really? How cool. She'd have a better chance of seeing her guys again.

"The protective attitude Admiral Sherwin is referring to," Eagen went on, "presents a potential difficulty in a POW situation. If you and the men are ever taken prisoner together, our worry is that your classmates' feelings for you could be used against them. To save or protect you, they might say and/or do things they otherwise wouldn't."

She frowned. "I certainly don't want that to happen, sir, of course not." Although she had no idea what she was supposed to do about it. The ship had already sailed on the issue—she and the men were close. That bell couldn't be unrung.

Eagan nodded in approval. "Glad to hear it. Because with your cooperation, we'd like to train the men here at SERE to deal with the contingency we just described."

"Yes, sir. How, sir?"

"Our plan is to expose your classmates to a situation where you're in serious danger, observe how they react, then debrief them on their actions afterward."

"Yes, sir. I see." Although she didn't, not entirely. *Serious danger* could mean a lot of things. "What kind of danger?"

Here Eagen hesitated. He glanced at Sherwin, almost as if he was hoping for a sign he didn't have to continue.

Nope. Sherwin was stone.

Eagen resettled his weight. "We're given a great deal of latitude in Level C training. SERE instructors are allowed to make enhanced physical contact with SEAL candidates, for example, but not with others. The situation with you is unique since you're the first female member of SOF. We need your permission for the instructors to make physical contact with you."

So that's what this is about. The Navy's PR wonks were worried about her "female sensibilities" being bent out of joint if she was slapped around at SERE. "Yes, sir. I can take the hits." She offered up a professional nod. "I'm sure the instructors here won't dole out any worse than I've taken already." *Fucking Hill.*

Eagen hesitated again for a beat. Two beats, three beats.

Too many beats.

From the side of her vision, she caught Wallins wiping sweat off his brow.

A whisper of tension touched her spine. *What's going on?*

"Our plan entails more than hitting." Eagen gestured at the Buick behind him. "This is Lieutenant Gavin."

Justice shot a look at the guy in the corner. *He's military?*

The Buick inclined his head in greeting.

"Lieutenant Gavin is an instructor here at SERE, and we'd like you to allow him to pretend to sexually assault you."

She slammed her focus back to Eagen. "What?" she snapped, her heart stopping.

Wallins's complexion turned the color of potato salad left out in the sun too long.

Eagen forged on. "We believe the mettle of the men won't be truly tested unless they see you go through something horrendous. Rape is one of the worst things a woman can endure, and one of the worst things a man who cares about a woman can be forced to watch."

Her stomach turned to ice. A full block of it.

She glanced again at Wallins—sweat was practically boiling off the commander's scalp now.

Admiral Sherwin gave her a frosty glare. "The rape of a female prisoner of war would present your classmates with a real-world POW situation. The training would be invaluable."

She held the admiral's stare. *Real-world, huh?* Rape was what Justice had waiting for her out there, was that it? *You trying to scare me off, you slimy fuck? Get what you've always wanted and keep SOF as an all-boys club?* A stain of red bloomed behind her eyes. *What do you think I've been doing these past months at BUD/S? Knitting? Writing my memoir?* Guess what, Admiral She's-Not-In-Yet-Dawson? *I've been taking gut-checks along with the rest of the men—and hardening.*

"Training of this sort could save the lives of those men," Admiral Sherwin went on in a clipped tone.

She gripped the armrests of her chair. Blatantly manipulative much? What was she supposed to say now? *Nah, let 'em swing. I might break a nail while being pretend-raped...*

Eagen added hastily, "You and Lieutenant Gavin would be able to work out the specifics ahead of time—to choreograph the evolution."

She checked in with the Buick. What did he think about all this? Was he secretly happy over being able to play-rape a beautiful woman? Or did the idea make him squeamish? Probably not much made a Buick squeamish. He didn't look happy—although he didn't look much of anything. Except big. And an awful lot like a scary terrorist.

Maybe Justice would break more than a fingernail.

A lot of *no-thank-you-sirs* battered their way up her throat. Except, blatant manipulations aside, if what these senior officers proposed was even slightly correct—that if she agreed to a fake rape, her guys would receive potentially life-saving training—then there was no question about what her answer would be.

She'd just have to buckle down and think of this as one more crappy BUD/S exercise. *Embrace the suck*, as Keith always said.

"All right, sir," she said. "Yes. I'll do it."

"Are you sure?" Eagen asked. "You have to be one hundred percent on board, Ensign. If there's even the slightest reticence on your part, we can't proceed."

Well, what woman *could* be one hundred percent on board with something like this? It wasn't like she would be walking into a bedroom rape fantasy with a man she knew and trusted. A quasi-violation lay ahead, and just how high the yuck-factor would go during it was impossible to predict or imagine.

And, hey, was no one aware of Commander Wallins having a stroke? Because, see, if Justice was cornered into this and then the hare brained scheme went awry, it was Wallins' career that would go down the dumper.

"Yes, sir," she assured Eagen. "I'm sure."

"Very well." Eagen indicated the SERE instructor again. "You and Lieutenant Gavin may proceed to the briefing room to work out the specifics of tomorrow's fieldwork."

She came to her feet, nodded to the superior officers, and left Wallins' office with Gavin.

Traveling one door down, the two of them entered a room with five rows of folding chairs stretching back from a large screen, no doubt for PowerPoint presentations covering subjects of varying degrees of lid-sagging tedium. A rectangular window let in plenty of sunlight, but Gavin flipped the light switch anyway. Fluorescents sputtered on.

The SERE-instructor-cum-terrorist-cum-rapist held out a hand to her. "Michael Gavin."

She shook his hand but didn't provide her own first name. He knew her as *Ensign Hayes*. That was enough.

He noticed the lack and exhaled a breath as he drove a hand through his long hair. "Look, I want to be clear upfront. This is a training exercise only for me. I have a wife and two daughters."

That should matter.

Somehow it didn't.

The tall foreheads undoubtedly chose Gavin to do this unsavory training exercise for the very reason that his estrogen-rich family unit would look good to the press if this ever leaked out. But the fact was, it didn't matter how Gavin appeared on paper. Because since when did being a family man stop wayward perversion from overtaking plenty of the Y-chromosome-carrying faction of the population?

"So what's the plan?" Justice asked abruptly. Pleasantries over, and ten-hut!

Gavin paused, looking like he was considering taking another stab at becoming buddies, but then asked, "How naked can I get you?"

"What?" She reddened. "Not at all!"

Sighing, Gavin wearily scratched the side of his scruffy face.

Her blush deepened. *Right.* Sexual assault couldn't be perpetrated on a fully clothed victim. "I understand we have to make this rape look real, Lieutenant, but I've fought tooth and nail to earn the respect of my classmates, and all that will fly out the window if they see my bare breasts bouncing around. Truth is, I don't know how to work this out."

Gavin kneaded the back of his neck.

An A/C vent rattled with cheap parts.

"Okay, so how about this?" he said. "The men will be detained in a row of standing wooden cages, and in front of those cages is a big, open-slatted crate. I can lay you on top of the crate, facing away from the men, then only take your pants off, not your shirt. Your breasts won't be bare, and no one will see your crotch in that position."

Her heart ground through its next few beats. *No one but you.*

"Will that be okay?" he asked.

No. "Yes. Fine."

"From there, I'll undo my pants and position myself between your legs. I'll thrust my hips, but I won't enter you, of course."

Her mouth went dry. *Of course. Everything's going to be just swell.*

"I'll try to keep this part short, for you, and, uh…I would prefer not to…" He left the rest unsaid.

He didn't need to go further. A body sometimes did what a body did, and what could a mere human do about it, except look himself in a mirror afterward and assure his reflection he'd done his best. Probably poor solace to a married man, who at the end of the day would have to face his little wifey asking him, *So how was work, dear?* The details of "accidentally" popping an erection between another woman's legs while terrifying the fuck out of her probably wouldn't find their way into the inventory of his workaday activities. No need to go further on that point either.

"To make it look real," Gavin continued, "I'll need to hit you. I'll try to make it just slaps." He seemed to startle a little. "I mean, not *just*—"

"I know what you mean." *We're both feeling awkward here. Let's finish up.*

"I can't exactly predict how this whole thing will play out because I don't know what your classmates will do. We'll both have to be flexible." He waited. "Do you have anything you'd like to add?"

Yes. I'd like to add that I don't want to do this.

She shifted to stare out the window. She didn't know what suburban Warner Springs looked like in July, but the Navy Remote Training site was mostly large scrub brush, desert weeds, and dirt clods, all surrounded by a chain-link fence, beyond which she could just make out a TV news van—The BUD/S Woman was still being stalked. Even a clear blue sky couldn't cheer up the terrain, and nothing could temper the images careening through her mind right now—

Dog Bone, never able to eat the world's biggest sandwich; Kilgour, his sniper dreams lost; Sanchez, denied the chance to watch his baby daughter grow up; Ziegler, no Miss Right coming along to fix him; Keith Knight...Brayden Street...their stunning aqua eyes frozen forever in sightless stares.

This training could save the lives of those men.

"I have nothing to add," she said.

Attention: Chapter 35 and 36 contain intense content. If you have triggers, please consider skipping ahead to Chapter 37.

CHAPTER THIRTY-FIVE

HIGH-PITCHED SINGING SQUEALED from hidden loudspeakers in a foreign garble, and the shouting climbed to ear-aching decibels. Smoke reeking of cordite still lolled across the earth from the firefight that'd just gone down to capture the "prisoners," and the stink of sweat blanketed the POW compound in sour nausea. Swamp rot from an algae-covered pond added to the sickening stew, along with the cloying, oddly sweet aroma of blood.

Seven tall, wooden cages stood in a line off the nose of a wood and tarpaper shack, bordering the west side of an open, dirt area where there was a slatted crate.

The crate.

Six men apiece were in three of the cages, five apiece in the other four, which equaled thirty-eight men total. The thirty-ninth man in their class was Brayden—but he'd been hauled off at the beginning of their capture for a "private interrogation."

Justice stood motionless in the last standing wooden cage. Her cagemates were Sanchez, Atkins, Schlesinger, and Kilgour. Except—

Thwack. Another punch.

Justice flinched.

Sniper Kilgour was currently being worked over by three bad guys.

The "terrorists"—a dozen or so—were all large, dark men: dark hair and dark eyes, although a variety of skin tones were represented. They spoke in either a guttural foreign language or accented English. Presumably fake accents, but maybe not. They seemed real in every way. Their rough appearance got the ball rolling on that, but having *mean* and *intimidating* down to the smallest nanoscopic detail closed the deal.

Especially Lieutenant Michael Gavin.

The SERE-instructor-cum-terrorist-cum-rapist stood near the tarpaper shack, his arms crossed and his legs planted wide, his eyes narrowed on sniper Kilgour.

His long hair was messier than yesterday, his scruffy beard scruffier, his muscles bigger—although how this last one was possible, Justice didn't know—and he'd stripped his expression of all feeling, mercy, or even the basest grains of humanity.

He didn't even look like Lieutenant Gavin anymore.

More like his evil twin.

The question of whether or not Justice would be able to pull off a pretend-rape believably no longer lingered as a concern. Not a single doubt or worry remained.

No *acting* required.

She was honest-to-God scared.

Her naïve hope that the lieutenant might go easy on her was long gone, and her efforts to mentally fortify herself against what was about to happen kept coming up snake eyes. Nothing in her past could compare to what she was about to endure—nothing she'd done as a thief or a track star or in her dating life. She'd dealt with plenty of unwanted male attention, yes, but nothing that ever threatened her with bodily violation. A flash of her psycho eyes had always been enough to deal with anything too bothersome—laughable against Gavin.

She just wanted to go home.

This was a big-pile-of-girlie-melt thought that'd never

crossed her mind during the entire six months at BUD/S.

But at BUD/S she'd been given a choice. It was *her* decision whether or not to put up with the instructors' torture: deal with it or ring out.

Here, she had no control.

She had no means of communicating with Gavin if things started to go too far—in retrospect, they should've decided on a "safe" word—and there wasn't a single organ in her body not shaking over the idea of such total vulnerability. Once the ugliness got going, she would be at Gavin's mercy—which, she'd already noticed, he'd forgotten to bring with him today.

So much for all the gut-checked nerve she'd developed, huh?

The door to her cage *womped* open and Kilgour was heaved inside. He came stumbling up to her, his teeth and chin painted with blood, his left eyelid raised into a horrible, dark hillock.

He grabbed her shoulders and shoved her down to her butt, urging her into a corner of the cage. "Make yourself small," he panted, his voice graveled with concern. "Be invisible."

Nodding, she scrambled backward, even though it wouldn't make a difference. *Poor, deluded Kilgour,* so blissfully ignorant of the inevitability to come.

We've obtained special permission to push Class 684 beyond normal SERE limits.

This was what they'd been told in their pre-fieldwork briefing. The strategy behind the statement—at least obvious to Justice—was to make sure the male candidates believed an actual rape was occurring when it occurred.

Still seemed like an unlikely stretch?

While sitting comfortably on your living room couch, drinking a beer and watching the game, you might scoff—

yeah, the whole idea required too much suspension of disbelief. But the Navy had created a real fucking award-winner with this POW compound. Everything tasted, smelled, sounded, and looked like an actual, hair-bristling enemy war camp populated with genuine terrorists.

Immersed in the authenticity of this place—being thrashed by rapidly escalating, *real* violence—that pre-brief warning would rise up and add an extra layer of doubt.

The question of *Just how far past the limits?* was already showing in everyone's expressions.

Even Justice—who knew what to expect—was babbling internally about how far this would go. Caught up in the noise, the stink, the fear, the thinking about it, the *wait*, she was having a helluva struggle keeping her state of internal chickenshit from becoming externally noticeable. She was losing focus.

Not good.

She pressed the heels of her palms to her forehead, but she couldn't seem to think straight.

There was just so much damned shouting.

It was totally different from the BUD/S instructors' yelling, which, though noisy and obnoxious enough to make a person wince, still left desires, motives, and annoyances discernible. This shouting was a loud, chaotic mess of aggressive syllables and slashing sentences that scrambled the brain over what to focus on, if anything at all. Maybe—probably—her classmates had dealt with this kind of shouting during Hell Week. *But for her, alas…*

"Dog Bone, you got this, man! Stay tight!"

Justice jerked her head up. *What, who…?*

Through the legs of her cagemates, she saw several ter-rorists muscling Dog Bone over to an incline board.

Justice strangled on her next breath. *The waterboard…*

One terrorist tugged a hood over Dog Bone's head, then two more slammed him down on the incline board. A fourth poured water steadily over the cloth covering Dog Bone's nose and mouth.

In seconds he was choking and struggling.

Justice stuck a fist to her teeth. "No." *Not my dear, sweet Dog Bone.*

Her classmates shouted protests.

It sounded like Dog Bone's lungs were being dragged through a pile of wet, sucking mud. His legs and arms convulsed, then went rigid.

Tears burned Justice's eyes. She bit her fist.

Be tough, little sailor.

I can't, Pete. It's Dog Bone.

After an inexorable eternity, Dog Bone was pulled upright and hauled off the waterboard, then manhandled over to a small bench set at the foot of the slatted crate. His hood was ripped off, revealing a dripping, red face, and purple lips.

A terrorist leaned to within an inch of Dog Bone's nose and bellowed, "You tell us aircraft carrier movements! Now!"

"I'm just an airman." Dog Bone coughed words out of a serious case of soggy lung. "I'm not told stuff like that."

The terrorist lugged Dog Bone to his feet. "Back on board."

Gavin barked something in the guttural foreign language.

The terrorist stopped.

Gavin made a sweeping, dismissive gesture, like, *there's no point*, and spoke in the foreign language again.

The terrorist dragged Dog Bone over to the first cage and thrust him back inside.

Keith was in that cage, and he gave Dog Bone a solid, encouraging pat on the shoulder before turning back to what was happening now—something everyone knew was very bad.

Gavin was moving toward the row of cages.

Justice's heart started to race so fast, she couldn't discern individual beats anymore. It was one, long *vrrrr* like an over-revved NASCAR engine.

Gavin stopped in front of Keith's cage and gestured at Dog Bone. "I believe it true this man know nothing," he said in a thick accent. "We need officer." He raked a flinty stare over all the candidates. "Which one of you officer?"

No one spoke.

The foreign music screeched to a higher note and went on screeching.

Gavin prowled up and down the line of cages. "Someone tell me officer, or I make tell." He came to a stop in front of the third cage, this one holding Dunbar and Ziegler along with others.

Gavin waited, nostrils flared.

In the sky behind him, the orange fist of the sun sat low in the sky, still cooking the earth.

Kilgour collected some saliva and blood in his mouth and spat on the ground.

Justice picked at a camo thread on one of her knees and felt her jaw spasm.

Gavin's upper lip lifted. "Okay. I make." He issued an order in the foreign language.

Half a dozen terrorists exploded into action. They charged the seventh cage.

Justice's.

Barreling inside, each terrorist took on a SEAL candidate, grappling, punching, and jabbing Sanchez, Atkins, Schlesinger, and Kilgour with pointed sticks.

In the turmoil of the fight, no one could tell what was actually happening…

Until it was too late.

Justice was dragged outside the cage and thrown onto the small bench.

She was now sitting at the end of the crate.

Chapter Thirty-Six

Justice gripped the bottom edge of the bench, blood pounding into her ears so hard, the influx felt like it was stretching her earlobes down. *Keep your shit together. Come on. If you lose it now, it's the same as ringing out.*

She forced herself to loosen her hold on the bench.

Gavin strolled up to Keith's enclosure, nonchalantly scratching the side of his face.

Keith watched his enemy with a penetrating stare, standing unmoving near the door. Not a single muscle twitched, but he was still coiled and poised with the capacity for instant, insane violence.

Gavin leaned a forearm high up on the cage, his wrist hanging loose. "So, hey," he said to Knight, his tone suddenly smarmily sexual, like he was planning on how to bag the babes with a drinking buddy. "I think you tell me who officer, or I make you tell me"—he cocked his head back toward Justice—"with *her*."

Keith's next words came up from the gutter regions of his diaphragm. "I wouldn't do that."

"Then point me who officer."

"What do you want to know?" Knight countered. "I'll tell you."

Gavin glanced around absently, like he was enjoying the scenery—fire-blackened scrub brush and broken trees, the stagnant pond and the bullet-pitted shack with its rusty window frames, sinkholes and feverish patches of weeds, trampled and hopeless—the smutty ravages of war, the vulgar stink of it.

I love the smell of fear in the morning…

Gavin looked at Knight again. "The USS *Harry S. Truman* is now in Persian Gulf. Where next port call and when?"

"I don't have that information," Keith said flatly. "None of us do."

"You lie." Gavin braced both palms on the cage, his arms straight, his chin low. "You deployed with battle group."

"Only as a detachment," Keith said, feeding Gavin the backstory they'd all been given in class. "We're based primarily in Afghanistan."

Gavin shoved off the cage. "You *lie*," he repeated, sharper. "And you know who pay for lie?" He stalked over to the small bench. "*Her*." He seized Justice by an arm, yanked her to her feet, and slapped her.

She sucked in a swift breath as her head snapped to the side, her loose bangs tumbling to the wrong side of her brow. Pain firecrackered on the point of impact, then streaked through the rest of her face. Her ears rang. That hadn't been an ordinary slap—the hit didn't even make a typical *crack* sound. Gavin had used the hard edge of his palm, and the blow *thudded* brutally against her jawbone.

Angry rumblings passed through the cages.

"I talk *only* to officer." A grinding impatience scratched across Gavin's tone. "Who is?"

Justice straightened, hot-faced. "Fuck this guy. Don't tell him anything. I can take whatever he dishes out." Fifty/fifty chance whether that was true or not.

No one spoke.

The screeching music switched to a wailing death song.

Gavin yanked Justice against his body, pinning her back

to his concrete chest. Fisting a hand around her throat, he propelled her, stumbling, toward her classmates. "I ask one more time," he bit out. "Then—" He grabbed Justice's breast with his other hand and squeezed it. Hard.

A raw, shocked tension charged the air.

Still no one spoke. The hell if anyone would give up a teammate but…

Ensign Dunbar shifted his feet. A man could give himself up.

"Don't," Justice grated.

A threatening bass note vibrated in Gavin's chest. He tore Justice's belt open and broke her zipper, then shoved his hand down the front of her pants.

Justice held her teeth tightly together.

Gavin wasn't pressing his fingers inward, but he was still cupping her *there*, his hand huge and hot and sweaty.

She ground her skull into his collarbone. *How's* that *for a signal to dial it the fuck down!?*

Keith eyed his enemy coldly. "Continue on with that, you motherfucker, and this shit"—he rapped a fist on the cage frame—"isn't going to be enough to hold me."

If a lot could be learned about a man by spending too much time with him under a large rubber boat, and more from his hands, then even more could be discovered when he showed his primal side.

And a deep blackness had entered Keith Knight's eyes, the kind that washed away the man who read paperbacks, told off-color jokes, and strategized all the best ways to win, leaving behind a man capable of anything. Of incredible sacrifice…

"Don't," Justice repeated, sounding winded. "Remember Down Dog push-ups? Remember the Buddy Carry? I'm not a fucking flower." *Maybe just a hybrid breed of flower, a cross between tulip and tough.*

No one spoke.

The shrieking music continued to bludgeon the camp.

Gavin exhaled through gnashed teeth. "Enough!" He started to drag Justice back toward the crate.

She dug in her heels, trying to stop him, but her open pants sagged down to her knees, limiting her range of motion. Her boot heels ended up troweling zigzagged troughs in the earth.

Then she was at the crate.

A terrorist leapt forward with a knife, slicing through the crotch of her camos.

Now her legs could be spread.

She emitted a low, wet noise, giving in to a rush of fear.

The tension in the cages thickened, grew spikes of alarm.

"*I'm* an officer."

Gavin stilled. He looked up with his psychopath's eyes, focusing on the Dunbar cage. But it wasn't Rudy who'd spoken.

"All right," Gavin said to Brad Ziegler. "Come out. Talk." He jerked Justice straight but kept her locked against his chest with that strong hand at her throat.

Her pant legs flagged all the way down to the ground, bunching around her ankles like a pair of camo-patterned '80s legwarmers. Goose bumps peppered her bare thighs, and a blush scalded her neck. Her classmates had never seen her so uncovered, not even poolside.

Whenever she'd been at the pool she wore a one-piece bathing suit made of industrial-grade rubber and a pair of loose-fitting UDT shorts.

Now she was in her underwear.

Her underwear was full-coverage nylon, resembling competitive running shorts more than an undergarment. *But still.* It was the most crotch the men had ever seen on her, and the exposure was upping the "real" factor of this even more. Taste, smell, sound, the ruthless fist at her throat—it was all very real.

"Put him on board," Gavin snapped when Hairy Arms was taken out of his cage.

Ziegler's brows lowered. Clearly he hadn't thought calling himself out as an officer would earn him a stint on the waterboard.

What *had* he thought? That he'd sit in a confession circle with these assholes, drinking Turkish coffee and smoking a peace pipe while he adjusted his balls and spun yarns about ship movements and security codes?

Apparently, nothing *but* that scenario was acceptable to Hairy Arms—he put his head down and bull-charged the two bad guys who'd released him. Bowling both men to the ground, he reared above them and got in several good shots before he disappeared beneath a grunting, writhing, roiling dogpile.

It was a regular slugfest, and the cages reverberated with deafening encouragement.

The keening music cried a wild counterpoint.

Justice's heart thundered.

Ziegler was finally overcome and yanked to his feet with one arm hammerlocked up between his shoulder blades. His nose dripped blood, and his shirt had been ripped off, his bare torso streaked with mud. His captors started to force him toward the incline bench.

"Hold," Gavin ordered.

They stopped.

"You have tattoo." Gavin gestured at the Navy anchor on Ziegler's left pec. "Officers do not have tattoos."

Blood drained onto Ziegler's upper lip. He licked it off. "I was prior enlisted."

"You too young," Gavin observed darkly.

Ziegler countered, "I got it before I went into the service."

"It is *Navy* symbol," Gavin seethed. "I sick of this! Too many lies!" Against Justice's back, the forbidding tension in Gavin's wrought-iron muscles tautened.

Alarm shafted through her. Her spine spasmed in instinctive resistance to the preparation she felt rising in him.

Gavin thundered at his men in the foreign language, and Ziegler was hurled back in his cage.

"*You* lie," Gavin snarled, "and *she* pay." With his grip on her throat, he whirled her around and threw her on top of the crate.

She landed painfully on her back, blood howling through her veins. Everything inside her rebelled against the act about to be perpetrated on her. She snapped to a sitting position, locking her hands into fighting fists.

Gavin slapped her back down, using the hard side of his hand again—hard as a punch. The crate rattled beneath her thumping spine. She saw fuzz.

Gavin unbuckled his belt. "I show you how she pay for the silence of all you." He unzipped his pants.

"What the fuck?" someone ground out.

Breathing violently, Justice made fish-like motions with her mouth as she tried to bring a recitation of the Hayes family rules to bear, like an armament. *Be a duck... Don't make the same mistake twice... Never completely trust... Fake it till you make it...*

The sayings tumbled through her mind like a singsongy mnemonic, none of it taking hold. Her adrenaline-soaked brain was too slippery with panic.

What would Keith do?

Action.

Gavin made a grab for her underwear, but she kicked him in the gut, landing the sole of her boot on the soft spot just above his groin. The force of the impact propelled him backward by several feet—enough room for her to maneuver. She jumped off the crate and belted him with an uppercut, clapping his teeth together.

He made a gusty noise as his chin popped skyward.

A bloodthirsty roar bellowed from the cages. *More!*

She followed with a cross-cut elbow, catching him on the side of the eye.

His head whipped sideways. He returned face-front almost immediately, his eyes fired with rage.

She surged forward, struggling to move nimbly with her pants bagged around her legs.

He stepped back, taking himself out of range—though barely. She misjudged it. He ducked under her wild swing, and as he straightened back to his full height, he plowed a fist into her solar plexus.

Air left her so fast and so hard, she gagged.

She'd endured plenty of hits in her Krav Maga classes, but this was a whale of a punch, and oxygen deprivation was uniquely destabilizing to the human body. Her brain paused for a half second to confirm system functionality.

Too much time.

Time enough for her attacker to take hold of her—by the throat again—and brace her against the crate while he hit her repeatedly across the face with those punch-like slaps, over and over. Lightning bolts electrified her left cheekbone and eye socket with pain, and stars mottled her vision. Sounds mashed together as one: shouts, music, the beating of a heart, the rushing of blood.

She wilted into her knees, dazed stupid, only semiconsciously aware of being forced down on the crate. Her underwear was ripped off and her legs wrenched apart.

"HEY!" Keith roared.

Her attacker forced his way between her spread thighs.

Holding her down with his brutal hold on her throat, he started to slam between her legs, the power of his hammering hips jolting her spine against the wood of the crate.

The music scratched off.

And in the sudden, haunting quiet, everything became real: the weight of her attacker's body on top of her, his burnt-mortar stink, his sweat dripping steadily from his brow onto her shirt, wetting the area over her right nipple, the bruising impact of his hips against her naked loins.

And the overwhelming sense of suddenly feeling very, very small.

Her vagina clenched protectively. A scream rose, and she opened her mouth. It trickled out. She clawed at the hand around her throat. Tears gushed down her face.

"STOP!"

The bellow startled several seed-pecking birds into the sky.

Her attacker stopped, panting hard.

"Stop what you're doing right now."

Justice craned her head back toward the cages, peering through stinging sweat and tears to see who'd spoken.

First cage, Keith Knight's: the five prisoners had made themselves into a human battering ram. Sprinting from the back to the front, they threw their combined weight against the door, then returned to the rear and raced forward again. *Crack! Snap!* If they had more room, they probably would've broken through. They hit the door once more before the lull in action finally caught their attention, and they stopped.

Keith grabbed the prison bars with bloody fists, his eyes wild.

Second cage: Giddiup was still yanking violently on the metal lock.

Next cage over: Ziegler, the designated vulgarian of the group, the infamously sex-crazed pervert. He was standing with both hands pressed to the top of his head, an expression of wholesale horror on his face.

Next one over, the fourth cage…

No.

Justice's focus slipped passed this enclosure as a man came into view.

He wasn't in a cage.

He was being shunted toward her crate, a terrorist holding each of his arms.

He was drenched in sweat, his muscular chest rising and falling rapidly beneath his clinging shirt.

His aqua eyes were murderous.

Brayden Street.

CHAPTER THIRTY-SEVEN

JUSTICE PUSHED AT Gavin, but she had no strength left, and kitten paws were no match for a Buick. Her arms flopped down, and she fumbled her fingers around several slats in the crate to keep from falling into the blackness and stars swimming around the edges of her vision.

Overhead, a few sparse clouds made monster faces at her.

"I'm Ensign Brayden Street, a no-shit officer. I'll tell you everything you want to know: the ship's schedule, rendez-vous points, communication codes. But you need to leave *her* alone."

One side of her attacker's mouth snaked up—the evil side. He wiped his chin clean of sweat, then hefted himself off her.

As he stood, a penis did *not* slide out of her body.

Dear God, it *hadn't* been real.

More tears slipped out of her eyes. Except it had been real in the way that mattered most. All choice had been stolen from her hands and put into *his*—a minor sideways shift of her attacker's hips, one moment of lost perspective, a single small slip of morality, and he *could* have been inside her. She wouldn't have been able to stop him.

How was *that* for sullying the Hayes family name?

Her tears wouldn't stop, and she couldn't hold back a small moan when Gavin hooked a fist into the front of her T-shirt and hoisted her off the crate. The length of her spine—rubbed raw on wood—protested the movement.

Gavin tossed her inside the crate and slammed the door shut. "Bring officer to me."

She curled herself into a tight fetal ball, folding her feet back toward her rear to cover her bare privates.

Feet shuffled. "I need to see if she's okay first." Brayden's voice softened when he spoke her name. "Justice—"

"You don't give orders." A loud *thump* on the interrogation bench. "You take."

"Fuck you," Brayden shot back, then again, gently, "Justice? Are you okay? Can you say something?"

Probably. But she was in no mood to try.

When things go to shit, fly under the radar. Grayson Hayes's rule number...some such.

She pulled her chin down to her chest and tucked her hands underneath her jaw. She could smell her own sweat. And fear. She slicked her tongue along her upper lip and tasted salt. Her whole body was shaking.

"You want I take her out for another go?" Gavin asked, smarmy again. "Maybe you sit right here, get a better view, eh?" *More scuffling.* "Or you start talk."

Justice swore she could hear Street's teeth grind together, but he did what he was told and talked.

She grew sick at heart, her trembling body sinking into the earth.

Her damsel-rescuing gallant had been broken.

To save or protect you, the men may say and/or do things they otherwise wouldn't...

Now here was Brayden, betraying his own country to keep her from further harm.

Damn you, assholes. Damn you all.

A bunch of scuzzbucket tall foreheads and superior officers had knocked her gallant off his white horse.

Fuck Admiral Sherwin and everything he stood for.

Fuck his ass and his dog and his car and…

But…

As she listened to Brayden talk, reality seeped in—he wasn't betraying his country. He was doing everything SERE school had taught them to do: he was weaving a clever blend of fact and fiction, telling the truth about things that wouldn't compromise ongoing missions or the lives of American soldiers, but lies about things that could hurt U.S. interests.

Justice crushed her eyes shut. *It's okay.* She drew in a chafing breath. *Brayden's doing everything right.*

Her mind floated away then, into a dazed slipstream of randomness: successful heists, childhood birthday parties, her honorary BUD/S brown shirt, drinks with Anne before Stevie came along, winning the NCAA championship, playing cards with Uncle Alistair, beach volleyball with her friend Chloe, her dad's proud smile whenever she conquered one of his tasks…

Through it all, the pain was there.

The left side of her face pounded, and a soreness between her thighs matured into a bruising ache. Her body wanted to go elsewhere. Her brain, on board with this idea, dragged her toward sleep. Her thinking mind tried to bob and feint around unconsciousness, but she was clobbered by it anyway.

Pow! And it was *lights out!*

Down she went, everything dimming to black.

HEADLIGHTS WOKE HER.

Justice crimped her lids barely open, peering through the slats of her crate at the long white shafts of light coming from a four-by-four idling next to the tarpaper shack.

It was nighttime, dark out, but still balmy.

She watched two pairs of camouflage-colored pants walk

toward her, the headlights spearing at intervals between the moving legs. Two corpsmen—a man and a woman—set a stretcher on the ground next to her crate. The female unlocked the small cell, pulled open the door, and hunkered partway inside. Gently unbending Justice's legs, she wrapped a blanket around Justice's nakedness, then the male corpsman joined the female to help maneuver Justice out.

They laid her on the stretcher.

A preternatural silence emanated from the cages.

Justice could feel her classmates staring at her, speechless in their devastation. She turned away from the row of enclosures.

"Twenty-three-year-old female," the woman corpsman reported, "suffering visible contusions." She took Justice by the wrist to check her pulse. "Ma'am, can you tell me your name?"

Tears seeped to the edge of Justice's lashes.

Maintain control of yourself at all times, my girl!

For once—just one damned time in her whole life— she'd like to know what a mother would've said at a crisis moment like this.

"Patient is unresponsive," the woman said.

"I'm not," Justice croaked. "I just don't want to talk."

"Geraldine," the male corpsman urged. "Let's just get her out of here."

The closest military hospital was at Camp Pendleton in Oceanside, a one hour and twenty-minute trip from Warner Springs.

Justice slept again during the drive.

Once at the hospital, she was put into an exam room, dressed in a gown, hooked to an IV, and treated for bruises and swelling on her face. She said she was fine "elsewhere" and wouldn't let anyone check under her gown. She wanted to take a shower, but no one would let her until she finished her bag of fluids.

It was almost an affront when her rapist showed up with his long hair freshly washed and brushed, the worst of his scruff shaved off. He was wearing well-worn jeans and a maroon Henley with the sleeves pushed up. He was Total Normal Guy. Gone was the psychopathic terrorist who'd raped her, and in his place was a walking-talking reminder of how she wasn't allowed to feel abused. What went down in the "mock" POW camp was a "training exercise" only.

It hadn't been real.

Gavin strode up to her bed and stood with his hands crammed deep in his pockets. "That," he said at length, "went roughly."

She crunched stiff fingers into her blanket, the muscles in her back pulling tight as nylon cords. If the tall foreheads expected her to debrief her non-attack with the man who had non-attacked her, then someone over at the Navy's Sensitivity Training Center needed a swift kick to the ass.

"Don't worry," she said perfunctorily, "I'm not calling the IG." Legal had already been by to question her. Captain Eagen, too, and a constant influx of other faceless people— and if one more person asked her, *Are you okay?* she was going to spit. "I *get* that you were just doing your job."

Gavin's brow knitted. "Is that why you think I'm here? To make sure my job is secure?"

I don't care why you're here. She bit her lips together. Was she allowed to say that? Did a non-rapist—who was Just Doing His Job—deserve to hear it?

What was she permitted to say?

Nothing?

What was acceptable to feel?

Anything?

"I came here to check on you and to apologize." Gavin took a hand out of his pocket to drag his fingers through his hair. "You fought really hard, and it was making things worse, and I didn't know what else to do to stop you. I'm sorry. I...we should've discussed the plan in more detail."

She studied her hands. She'd broken a couple of finger-nails on the crate slats. Was she allowed to laugh bitterly at the irony of that?

"There was...there was a point in it all when you..." Gavin paused, and she sensed him struggling. "I think you thought it was real. You got a look in your eyes..." He trailed off.

She stiffened the muscles in her face.

"I'll never forget it," he added quietly.

She pulled her lips in. How wonderful that this man had seen her so raw. Nothing like being stripped naked all over again.

She looked up. "Listen, Lieutenant. Your explanation, by nature, asks for an understanding of it. Which means this discussion...what happened between us...is about *you*—about *me* taking care of *you*—and I can't deal with that right now."

Gavin startled, then blanched. "That wasn't my inten-tion. I wanted to apologize, like I said, and, uh, suggest...I thought counseling might be a good idea. It's available through the Navy at—"

"No," she snapped. Becoming the first candidate in the history of all the world to head into *counseling* following BUD/S graduation wasn't a distinction she intended to add to her reputation. Besides, what had happened to her was a hoax. A fake. A mirage. A non-rape by a non-attacking Normal Guy.

"Okay." Gavin cleared his throat. "Anyway, uh, I should go." He glanced down and briefly touched a finger to his eyebrow. "One last thing—what you did wasn't for nothing. Your classmates were debriefed and taught what they did right and wrong. The next time it happens, they'll be better prepared."

She laughed in a phlegmy burst. "The next time? There won't be a next time, not for me. Ever. If there's one valuable lesson I learned from all this, it's that I'll never allow myself to be taken a prisoner of war."

She stared fixedly at Gavin as images spattered across her memory like spittle: her underwear being ripped off, her body trapped beneath a heaving, sweating bull of a man, a hand at her throat forcing her down, every act perpetrated against her stealing her dignity, respect, control over her own body.

So, *congratulations Sherwin*, the "training exercise" crushed her into insignificance. *You win!* She might never fully recover from this playacting episode, which meant for sure she wouldn't survive the real deal.

The rape of a female prisoner of war would present your classmates with a real-world POW situation...

"I'll eat a bullet first," she ground out to Gavin.

He went very still. His brows sank lower over troubled eyes. "I'm sorry to hear you say that. I'm especially sorry to know I contributed to you feeling that way. I...I'm sorry about everything." He turned to leave, then paused in the doorway, setting one hand on the jamb. "Everyone was so concerned about saving the men, we forgot about you, didn't we?"

Justice swallowed convulsively. There was nothing she could say to answer that. Nothing at all.

CHAPTER THIRTY-EIGHT

JUSTICE'S INJURIES DIDN'T warrant an overnight stay in the hospital, but the Marine Corps van wasn't available to transport her back to the Amphib Base till the next morning, so she spent the night on her exam bed.

Just as well.

She wasn't up to facing anyone till she'd applied some Bondo to the worst of her vulnerabilities.

She slept fitfully, waking the next morning with an apocalyptic wreckage in her gut. Looked like time alone in the hospital to make repairs hadn't done much good. Her raw glop had just oozed too far and too wide. Guess the glop hadn't received the memo that SERE was a training exercise *only* and Gavin was a non-attacking Normal Guy with a wife and two daughters who was *just doing his job*.

He probably volunteered at his church on weekends, while she was the type of woman who spent her time trying to figure out bigger and better ways to rip people off.

On top of that she made foolish decisions in her life. Like going legit. Like forming friendships with men she was attracted to. Like agreeing to let herself be *raped*.

What happened to her epiphany about the importance of doing things her way, anyway? Post-Hell Week, she'd gotten back in touch with her strengths: her speed and her agility and her wits. But she hadn't relied on any of those at SERE. No, she tried to go head-to-head in a fistfight with a Buick.

She supposed such was the underhanded outcome of panic—the inevitable rout of good sense and rationality by raw glop.

Was she allowed to make excuses about it?

She stared out the van window on the ride back to the Amphib base, watching images pass by in colors and shapes of it-doesn't-matter.

An hour later she arrived.

Climbing out of the van, she heard the muted sound of men's voices spilling from the open door of the officers' barracks, some rising above others, demanding to be heard.

Her guys were in there, waiting for her.

She stood unmoving. What would she see in their expressions? Pity over the hyper-estrogenic state they'd witnessed her suffer from at SERE?

Shame and embarrassment washed over her. Her guys hadn't seen her naked, no, but they saw her lose a fight, and in a community where winning was everything, it might've actually been better for them to have seen her bare breasts—as long as she'd won.

She kept staring at the front of the building.

It was a depressing concrete block with a spiderweb of cracks near one of the bottom edges.

The thought of doing anything but staring blankly at a wall felt like too much work.

"Everything good, ma'am?" the van driver asked her.

"Uh…yeah. Thanks for the ride." She closed the door.

The van drove off.

She finally got herself moving, humping her duffel inside. She dropped it by the door and walked into the community room.

Instant and complete silence.

The place was packed with men: her boat team was there, plus Dunbar and Street, and more besides. Every man stared at the left side of her face, discolored with mushroom patches of bruises.

"How *dare* you fucking do that."

She turned, searching the crowd, and found Keith.

He was glaring at her, his lips a rigid slash. "Don't you *ever* put yourself in danger for us again. Do you hear me?"

"Keith," Brayden admonished in a low tone. "Justice doesn't need to hear shit right now." The expression he aimed at her was drawn, like he hadn't slept in a month.

It was the kind of broken-soul tiredness a man felt when he'd tried very hard to keep someone he cared about safe, only to lose that battle.

A hiccup of relief burbled up in her. She almost sat down right there on the ugly carpet, crisscross-applesauce style, and hunched over. Her guys didn't revile her for being "weak."

She wasn't seeing pity or rejection, but genuine concern and sympathy. Even the emotion beneath Keith's fury was rattled alarm, similar to how he'd looked on surf passage day when she cut her forehead open. Of course, with a roomful of SEAL candidates behind him, he would only let his rage out.

"At the SERE debrief," Brayden said, "we were told it was fake, what happened, but—"

"It *was* fake."

"Was it?" Brayden looked deeply into her eyes.

She swallowed with difficulty. No, not really, which was the scrambled eggs part.

"There were times when it seemed like…" Brayden hesitated. "The expression on your face made it look like it was real."

Jesus, everyone needed to quit harping on that. The idea of so many people taking a gander at her raw glop was adding to her crazies.

Brayden went on, "You were taken away on a stretcher."

"The Navy was just covering their asses," she said. "Things got rougher than planned. Look—you guys were supposed to have learned something from the exercise. Even though you may never see me go through something like that in real life"—*count on it*—"someday you might have to watch your friend or comrade or best buddy or brother endure torture. If there's any takeaway at all about how to deal with that better after SERE, then it was worth a few bruises."

Silence dropped like a lead weight over the room. The droning hum of rubber tires on asphalt grew louder in the parking lot then softer.

"You shouldn't have done it," Dog Bone said softly, his head bowed.

Her knees shook. Here was the one shy voice with all the power to fell her. *Don't break down...hold on...fake it till you make it...*

But all the Hayes catechisms couldn't see her through Dog Bone's simple, honest love for her.

Her throat choked up. "They told me all of you could die in the field if I didn't do it." A single tear slipped down her cheek. She scrubbed it away. "This came directly from Admiral Sherwin and Captain Eagen. What was I supposed to do after they told me that?"

Brayden's eyelids sank shut.

Keith looked at the ceiling, his Adam's apple jerking. "Fuck."

Giddiup followed Keith's curse with a stream of imaginative oaths of his own. "We need to go get drunk. Because this blows."

"Best idea I've heard yet."

"Yeah, bro."

"I'm in."

"You in too, Justice?" Brayden smiled gently. "I bet you could stand to pound down a few."

Actually, the thought of a noisy bar with men hitting on her sounded unbearable. "Thanks." She smiled back, though she could feel it wasn't much. "But I think I'll save myself for tomorrow night, lift a few with you guys to celebrate BUD/S graduation. Tonight I just need to veg in front of a movie."

Keith gave her a long look. "This sure is one helluva way to go out, Hayes."

If he only knew.

CHAPTER THIRTY-NINE

JUSTICE NAPPED IN a half-sleep, half-waking state that left her feeling groggy and vague when she woke a few hours later, like she hadn't rested at all.

Dim light was creeping through her open bedroom door, setting the time at early evening.

Untangling herself from the sheets, she slowly pushed upright, stiff and sore. Her T-shirt was soaked with sweat, as if she'd spent the whole time in bed fighting her demons. She generally didn't have nightmares—her last one helped her figure out Glinski's fear of heights—but what was her poor psyche to do? She wasn't dealing with her feelings during waking hours, so her subconscious was having to step in.

Feelings, unlike food, were much better when processed.

Scooting to the edge of her mattress, she sat slumped over with her head buried in her hands. If someone would just tell her which feelings she was allowed to have, she would do her best to deal with them.

Maybe it would help to talk to someone.

Her dad?

No. Too icky.

Her former track buddy Anne?

Too busy.

Tiffany Tesarik from the *Bonhomme Richard*?

Too much of a stranger still.

One of the guys?

Too unhelpful. They'd just tell her to punch someone.

Although…that might not be such a bad idea. Maybe she *should* go out with them tonight, after all.

Stir up trouble…get into a bar fight…

But where was the satisfaction in hitting some nameless no-neck drunk? *He* wasn't the one who'd wronged her.

So she should go after the man who had.

Lieutenant Michael Gavin.

Except…he'd robbed her of the right to hate him by showing up at her hospital room as an apologetic and caring SERE instructor.

Everyone was so concerned about saving the men, we forgot about you…

All right. Then hunt down the other men.

Put on my running shoes…jog over to the opposite side of the Amphib Base…bust into Captain Eagen's office…call him out as a maggoty cockbite…

Except Eagen had always been on her side. He'd seemed genuinely uncomfortable with the fake rape—like he was only following Admiral Sherwin's orders—and losing Eagen as an ally would be a huge, tactical mistake.

All right—Sherwin.

Barge into Admiral FuckOver's office…denounce him for being a sadistic, manipulative dickasaurus…blush up a storm when he counters with, You fully agreed to the exercise, Ensign.

She *had* agreed.

So there.

Shut it.

She lifted her head from her hands at sounds coming from the community room. The men were gathering there, getting ready to go out to a bar and be stupid.

She saw Ziegler pass by her open door.

It was the first time ever she'd slept with her door open,

but there were monsters under her bed now.

Leaving her door open was also supposed to have created the sense that she wasn't alone in the dystopian landscape of her own innards.

Total illusion. Smoke and fucking mirrors. Pass a card through the window. Saw the woman in half.

She *was* alone.

Everyone had someone except for her.

The men out in the community room?

A lot of them would be getting laid tonight.

And the men who'd wronged her?

She could just see Gavin now, opening the front door of his home to find the wifey waiting to greet him after his hard day of rapine and torture. He would hug her close, bury his nose in her hair. *What's wrong?* she would ask. His only answer would be to shake his head. He couldn't confess to the woman he loved how he'd colluded with the plan to break another woman's spirit. He would just hold her…and heal in her arms all the same.

The perpetrator had a loving family to go home to and help him, while the victim had no one.

The unfairness of that was so massive, Justice could find no place inside her to store it.

Her vision blurred.

She was so sick of it all. Fed up with being the Navy's first-female-in-SOF experiment. Sherwin's lab rat. *The BUD/S Woman* media event spinning the nightly news cycles. The supposed badass. Always so fucking tough. An androgynous flesh pawn. The puppet master's toy. A magician's trick.

What happened to just being a woman?

She laughed soggily. *How ironic can it get?* She'd fought so hard to make everyone see her as other-than-female, and now all she wanted to do was act like a woman—smooth lavender lotion on her skin, get a mani-pedi, wear a dress, and put on makeup. She *liked* those stereotypical womanly things. She missed those things. Curl her hair. Drink a cocktail with an umbrella in it. Crawl in bed with a man and snuggle into his muscular arms...

She hadn't been with a man for ages.

She stared out her open door, listening to the rumblings in the community room, an achy longing weighting her chest.

She didn't *have* to be alone.

There were men out there who cared about her.

Like...

Keith—what about him?

Hunk-a Chunk-a, Man of the Hour, and *Good ol' Hero of the Day.* There was no dearth of mutual attraction between them—unless she'd misread his signals—and it would be sheer bliss to step within the circle of his power and vitality. Only one sticking point held her up, and not, incidentally, that she was an officer and he was enlisted. The UCMJ might frown on officer and enlisted fraternization, but she, *ahem*, never had a problem with being sneaky.

The problem was that she didn't know how he'd react to her coming to him for help. What if he saw her as easy or frail? After six months on his boat team, she probably should know better, but Keith tended to keep deeper thoughts to himself. She knew that he was a whiz at patch 'em up, at claymore mines and pop flares. He'd taught her the proper way to clean her rifle and the mechanics of a good flutter kick, but beyond those fundamentals, she didn't know him—not really. If she had a deeper understanding of who he was, she might've been willing to risk it, but Keith's respect meant everything to her. She wasn't sure she had the stamina to deal with losing it right now.

Brayden?

Her confidant, her ice cream-eating buddy, her only-child comrade...the man who always treated her like a woman in silk even when she was in camos. *Here* was a guy who could celebrate her femininity...cherish her...care for her. And Brayden wouldn't judge her for coming to him either. Over the past six months of hanging out with him on the deck at the end of every day, she'd gotten to know the more intimate parts of Brayden—*he* shared.

But what about entanglements? The Brayden Street who would treat her with such chivalrous care was also the gentleman who—she strongly suspected—didn't have one-night stands.

I happen to value my equipment. I don't just loan it out to anyone...

Would he try to make a *thing* out of her coming to him? That was the last thing she wanted—her moving-forward position was still *no complications*. She only needed a night of sex with a strong man. That was it.

So probably not Brayden.

How about...?

She glanced at her cell phone on the nightstand.

How about Pete?

Gregarious, full-of-life, drop-by-any-time Pete Robbins, the best fucking guy who could be in her life right now. She knew Pete too—she'd hung out with him at the end of her workdays—and he wouldn't try to complicate her life by making a *thing*—one-night stands were Pete the Penis's bread and butter. He could definitely deliver on her need for a night of great sex with a strong man, no strings attached.

Fun, laughter, orgasms galore! Yes, sleeping with Pete would give her just the sort of mind-blowing pleasure she needed to erase the abuse between her thighs—out with an old memory, in with the new. Hadn't he proved his skills in the sex department with a burning kiss on the *Richard*? A night with Pete would be a wild ride…

But…

Would it be too wild?

Too fun?

She dropped her focus to her torn fingernails.

A woman would have to be at her best before she tried to handle movie-star gorgeous Pete Robbins, and Justice wasn't that. She required tenderness right now more than anything else. And could she really count on a man who never took life seriously to take care of her in one of her most serious moments?

Moisture gathered along her lashes.

Probably not.

Dog Bone? *Oh, yuck.* He was like a brother. Ziegler? He'd probably pass out at the asking, and besides, *double yuck.* Sniper Kilgour? Quiet types weren't exactly her—

She heard the men start to clatter for the front door.

From the darkness of her room, she watched them leave.

She *let* them leave.

You don't need their help.

Store it away. Push it inside. Be a duck.

The barracks' door closed. Footsteps faded toward the parking lot.

She shoved and struggled, her chest hurting from the process, but as much as she worked to numb herself, she only succeeded in snuffing out the tips of her nerve endings, like matchstick heads—the fire extinguished, but still alive with a smoking pain.

She'd left something of irreplaceable worth on that crate in the POW camp. Her sense of self and power.

Her lower lip trembled.

She knew no way to cope.

Cars revved up and drove off.

Silence.

Just the distant pound of the surf and the occasional rustle of windblown sand across the deck, the rattle of dead palm fronds.

Utter solitude.

CHAPTER FORTY

THE BARRACKS' DOOR slapped open again, and Justice jerked her attention toward her bedroom door in time to catch Brayden stride by.

She froze on the edge of her mattress for two jolting pulse beats, then swayed to her feet and crossed to her doorway. Gripping the frame, she listened to rummaging noises. It sounded like Brayden was searching for something.

An achy warmth spread through her. She'd never realized how familiar he sounded…the weight of his tread…the cadence of his movements…

She stood with her weight forward and listened.

Other than Brayden's noises, the silence was still oppressive.

A physical enactment of isolation.

A sick bacterium infecting her heart.

You don't have to be alone…

Fate had air-dropped a man who cared about her back into her sphere, giving her a second chance to heal herself.

Brayden started to pass by her door again, tucking money into his wallet, heading for the exit.

He was dressed for a night on the town in summer beachwear: flip-flops, khaki shorts, and a red polo shirt. He was freshly shaved, a spicy hint of aftershave wafting off him, and his short, tawny hair was neatly combed.

Her confidant, her ice cream-eating buddy, her only-child comrade…

Maybe she *could* depend on Brayden to care about her enough to give her exactly what she wanted—not a thing, just a night.

Didn't she deserve some tenderness after what she'd been through?

Where was Gavin right now? In loving arms. And Eagen? Sherwin? They were probably both getting laid, too, although Sherwin while wearing starched pajamas and only through the dick peephole.

Was it really too much to ask to have someone help her through a rough time?

She flipped on her bedroom light.

Brayden stopped suddenly. "Justice! Hey, I thought you were asleep."

"No," she said quietly. "Not anymore."

He strode forward, a smile for her in his eyes. "Do you want to change your mind about going out with us?"

"Actually, I thought you might want to stay in with me tonight and watch a movie."

He opened his mouth.

But before he could respond to that boring option, she quickly tucked her hand inside the waistband of his shorts and slid the backs of her fingers lightly over the taut muscles of his abdomen.

Such a move should have made things obvious. But to make absolutely certain Brayden understood what she was offering, she tilted her head back—a very damsel position to tempt the damsel-rescuer—and peered deeply into his eyes, drenching her gaze with a message that couldn't be remotely misunderstood. As Marvin Gaye immortalized:

Let's get it on.

Points to Brayden. His terror-lock lasted only about one second.

He stood blinking while she smoothed her hands up his

solid pecs and linked her arms around his neck. She leaned full-length against him. "Take me to a hotel," she urged softly, "and roll around on the sheets with me all night."

There. A woman couldn't get plainer than that.

He hauled in a hard breath. "Christ, Justice, I'd be lying if I said I haven't dreamt of a moment like this." He clasped her forearms. "But the timing isn't so great. You're not thinking clearly after SERE." He gave her arms a small tug.

She held on. "I'm very clear about what I want, Brayden, and it's sex." She clutched him by the shirt collar and swung him around into her room, propelling him backward toward her desk.

She aimed him at her chair.

The backs of his legs hit the seat and rolled it across the floor until it bumped into the wall.

He sat abruptly. "Justice," he tried again. "Come on—"

She dropped onto her haunches in front of him and set her hands on his knees.

Tension rose in him, *more* when she prodded his knees apart, pushing his legs wide open.

He set his hands on top of hers. "This isn't what you need."

"How about you try *not* telling me what I need and instead listen to what I'm actually saying." She tilted forward onto her knees to put herself deeply within the vee of his spread legs.

The edges of his nostrils fluttered, like he was a bare decision point away from acting. To do what, she couldn't tell, but she was game to find out.

She stroked her hands up his runner's legs, the thick muscles of his thighs flexing beneath her palms.

His zipper twitched.

She nudged his polo shirt up enough to expose his navel. *Oh, yum.* He had a happy trail. A perfect one. She leaned forward and nuzzled it.

He rewarded her instantly with a full-on erection.

"I love your happy trail." She kissed her way down it, inhaling a deep breath to savor his scent, not his aftershave this time, but him. All Man. "I love where it goes." She arrived at the waistband of his shorts and began to work the button open.

His hand landed on top of her fingers, stopping her.

She looked into his fiery eyes.

"Don't."

She smiled playfully. "You don't think I can get you?"

A dark blue intensity entered his gaze. "You can't. Not like this."

Lifting her brows, she poked a finger into the center of her loose bun, pulling outward until she tugged her hair free of its restraining band. The mass cascaded past her shoulders.

"Jesus Christ in a hothouse." Brayden's lips pared back from the edge of his teeth. *Control* did not appear to be his highest achievement right now—it was hanging by a thin thread.

She gave him a sultry look from beneath her lashes. "Care to change your answer?" She rocked forward and crushed her breasts against his erection.

His cheeks sucked in on his next inhale.

My, the nice-sized-penis assessment she'd given him after Down Dog push-ups might've lacked proper generosity. Taking him inside her was going to *celebrate her femininity* more than she'd thought.

Dipping her head, she licked one of the knuckles on his blockading hand. "Let me in," she whispered.

His other hand came up and tucked under her chin. He urged her to look at him, managing to handle her gently even though his eyes were white-hot. "Whether you realize it or not, you're hurting right now, Justice, and I can't do this while you're hurting." He slipped his fingertips to one of the bruises on her face and caressed her sore flesh, his gaze holding hers, breathless heat and heart, for an eternal moment. "I'm in love with you."

"No, you're not," she shot back.

Complications are unacceptable.

"Yes," he countered, "I am. And I have been from the first day you walked into the officers' barracks."

She exhaled a hard breath. *Damn you, Brayden.* He wasn't just going to make a big thing out of this, but a *humongous* thing.

She shifted away from him, her stomach tight. Why did he have to say he loved her?

"I *am* here for you," he insisted. "Let me just tell the guys I won't be going out tonight, then we can grab a couple of bowls of chocolate ice cream, sit on the deck, and talk."

"*What*," she snapped, "out of all the shit that went down at SERE do you imagine I want to talk about?"

"What the hell's going on here?" a voice demanded from her doorway. "What are you doing with Justice?"

She jerked stiff and spun around.

Keith.

He was standing just inside her bedroom, his eyebrows furled together, a killing glare aimed at his brother.

"Nothing," Brayden retorted.

Keith's expression grew more thunderous over the obvious lie—a man with his legs spread, a woman kneeled between them, and his dick as hard as a plumber's wrench wasn't doing *nothing*. Then Keith shifted over to her and gave her a look of utter…*disappointment.*

Face hot, she slammed to her feet, her heart and chest shredding.

Well, there went Keith's respect, *gone*.

He'd caught her turning to Brayden for help, and now he saw her as weak. Oh, sometimes it was a real fucking pain, being right about people.

And the hits just keep on comin'!

Now Rudy Dunbar pushed inside her room, and seeing what there was to see—Justice with her hair down like a wanton little hussy of a Jezebel, Brayden sprawled in a chair like a sahib ready to get his cock rocked—Dunbar flushed so red, his complexion wasn't even in the ballpark of lobster.

More like the vicinity of Darth Maul.

"What the fuck?" Rudy blared.

Wouldn't it have been nice if Justice remembered *before now* that Brayden, Keith, and Rudy planned to carpool to the bar tonight? When Brayden had said, *Let me just tell the guys I won't be going out*, he didn't mean texting. He'd meant trotting out to the Navy van waiting in the parking lot.

And now Rudy Blabbermouth was making all sorts of wrong assumptions. "You've been boning her this whole time?" His sour face scrunched up like a toddler on the verge of a temper tantrum. "Right under my nose!"

Keith's skin stretched like dried plastic over his facial bones.

Brayden towered to his feet, his eyes molten steel. "Stay out of this," he bit out. "Both of—"

Keith vaulted forward and drilled a punch into Brayden's face, landing the blow between Brayden's mouth and nose.

Brayden's head jolted back, and he reeled into a stagger, crashing into Justice. She skidded sideways into her desk. Brayden's head snapped erect, the whites of his eyes showing with pain and surprise.

Teeth bared, he lunged at Keith.

Keith threw a real haymaker of a hook, but Brayden ducked under the blow and locked both arms around Keith's body, bowling his brother to the floor. The two men hit the linoleum hard and rolled across the room, swinging powerfully at each other with both fists.

Rudy danced around the two bodies, shouting.

The combatants came to a stop only by slamming into the bunk bed across from Justice's desk.

Keith popped to his knees, looped his left arm around Brayden's neck, and jerked his brother against his side, then started pounding him with one punch after another.

Actually, he only got in two—

Brayden grabbed Keith around the back of the neck and yanked down.

Keith's forehead rammed the edge of the bed frame, and he let go.

Brayden rolled free and lurched to his feet, his hands still balled into fists. He was breathing so hard his collarbone was popping against his skin.

On his feet now too, Keith hissed breaths between clenched teeth.

"What the *fuck's* your problem?" Brayden snarled.

Keith swiped blood off his upper lip with the back of his forearm, then stabbed a finger at his brother. "You crossed a boundary, Brayden."

"No," Justice butted in. "*I* did." She'd succumbed to a moment of weakness—*a pox on your balls, Lieutenant Gavin*—and wrecked her credibility.

And she'd come so close to making it through BUD/S with her reputation intact—*tomorrow* was graduation day. But now she was *that* woman: the type a guy bangs but doesn't take seriously.

Justice gripped her hands around the edge of her desk on either side of her thighs—at some point she'd hopped on top of it. Not only had she destroyed her reputation, but her actions had led to two best friend brothers beating on each other.

Pain ballooned inside her.

Sorry, everyone. I should've been a better duck.

She slid off her desk and started across her bedroom, her knees feeling like a runny omelet.

The three men watched her.

She left without a word.

Chapter Forty-One

ADMIRAL SHERWIN'S OFFICE exuded all the ambience of a mortician's workspace. No books on the shelves, no family pictures placed at strategically homey vantage points, no paintings or *see-how-great-I-am* plaques on the walls. An oak desk nearly black with age had nothing on it but a computer screen, a keyboard, and a single sheet of paper.

The lone adornment was an American flag standing in the far corner, hanging from a pole with an eagle stanchion on top.

The place was as austere and unappealing as Sherwin himself—even the temperature seemed several degrees cooler here than in the rest of the building.

But then…heartless creatures probably needed cold environments to thrive in, didn't they?

Justice snapped to attention in front of Sherwin's desk. "Ensign Hayes, reporting as ordered." Her feet felt like mud. Unstable. Her mind full of doubts.

Something very bad was clearly about to happen.

Keith had just been leaving this office as she was arriving, and his expression had been livid. He didn't even look at her.

"At ease," Sherwin said.

Justice assumed the position of parade rest.

Sherwin leaned forward, looking down at the sheet of paper on his desktop, taking several moments to read it.

Justice's nerves crackled. *A total psyche out*—the admiral

had read whatever was on that sheet long before her arrival.

"An eventful night of 'conduct unbecoming,'" Sherwin remarked coolly, sitting back. "Sexual indiscretion, brawling among the ranks, flagrant disregard of Article 90 of the UCMJ, assault of a superior commissioned officer—all over a *woman*."

Woman, derived from Old English, *wimman*, alteration of *wifman*, a compound of *wif* "woman" plus *man* "human being," meaning—*the candy-assed little spunk junkie bitch who has ruined my all-boys club.*

Or said as such.

Justice didn't respond. Just rubbed her molars together. Rudy Blabbermouth had made sure *all* the sordid details of last night reached the admiral's ears, hadn't he?

Jealous little pucker-face.

He'd never forgiven Justice for not becoming *his* ice cream-eating budding and falling madly in lust with him.

Sherwin sniffed. "You give my Navy a bad name, Ensign, and I want you *gone*. I will be bringing punitive charges against you."

She jerked her focus from the wall over Sherwin's head to the admiral himself. What the hell for? *She* hadn't been the one to get into a brawl, albeit she was the cause of it. "For what, sir? The sexual indiscretion you alluded to never occurred, and even if it had, it would've been with a fellow officer. I didn't break any code of the UCMJ."

"You lied on your Navy application," Sherwin accused. "That *is* an actionable offense."

She blinked. "Excuse me?"

"You have an arrest record, Ensign. You never mentioned it on your application, which is lying by omission."

"I do not have a record," she countered in an even tone. "With all due respect, sir, your information is incorrect. When I was sixteen, I was brought into juvenile hall for *questioning only*, not—"

"I'm referring to what happened when you were eighteen," Sherwin cut in. "You were arrested for solicitation."

She nearly stumbled out of parade rest. How the ungodly fuck did Sherwin know about that?

"Don't bother denying it." Sherwin aimed a knife-hand at his office door. "Petty Officer Knight just told me all the details."

She inhaled two quick breaths. *What—?*

Keith wouldn't...

No way would Keith throw her under the bus to save his own skin. That wasn't his style.

Steel edged Sherwin's mouth. "I am actively searching for ways to oust you from Special Operation Forces, Ensign Hayes. I will accomplish this task with or without anyone's assistance, but I informed Petty Officer Knight that if he could offer me information to help achieve my goal faster, I would drop the charges against him for striking Ensign Street. He was reluctant, but in the end realized you were on your way to being booted anyway, so he made the intelligent, career-saving choice." Sherwin paused to inspect her with a piercing stare, as if searching for a reaction.

She was giving him one.

All the blood was draining from her face as the memory came back to her in a violent rush: the two of them hiking up a snowy hill at Mountain High, their growing companionability, her breaking her *never-completely-trust* rule by telling him about Uncle Alistair's botched alarm job on the Coventry heist...

And how she'd thrown herself on her sword to save her father's team, resulting in her being arrested for prostitution.

Nobody but nobody outside of her dad's crew knew about her arrest record.

Only Keith.

This was an inescapable fact.

Sherwin couldn't know about her arrest record unless Keith told him.

Yes, Keith took great care of his people and was good under pressure, but she had no idea what he was capable of when something truly precious to him was threatened.

Keith's talked about becoming a SEAL since he was ten...

And hadn't he looked guilty a few moments ago when he was leaving Sherwin's office, unable even to meet her gaze?

A claw started to rip at her belly, but she flexed her abdominal muscles around it.

"You may proceed to Drop On Request as soon as you leave my office," Sherwin informed her.

She spasmed all over. "What?"

"Ring out," Sherwin all but snarled. "You know where the DOR bell is."

For a military man with a chest full of battle-won medals, Sherwin sure had made a huge tactical blunder. Justice might've been willing to leave quietly to avoid a court martial, but the hell if she was going to humiliate herself by ringing out.

Her humiliations were currently piled high enough, thank you. "I will not quit, sir. You'll have to bring charges against me if you want to see me discharged from the Navy." She held the admiral with a level stare. "But please be aware of this: the press will surely want to interview me about such a shocking turnabout. *The BUD/S Woman* has become quite a media sensation over these past months." She pointed to the swollen side of her face. "Questions about my bruises will certainly arise, and I'll have no choice but to tell them exactly how and where I received them, and by whose design."

The admiral's nostrils pinched, his face flushing a ruddy

shade of rage.

The temperature in the room lowered another degree.

"How Public Relations—or you, sir—will survive the fallout of my tell-all will be interesting to see. But I'd venture to guess the spin-out will make the PR wonks' former bathroom and camping worries an interdepartmental joke of the century."

"Leave," Sherwin ground out. "Pack your gear, be off the base before sundown, and I won't bring charges against you."

She stood in place with a rod up her spine, her toes solidly gripping the insoles of her boots. *Leave and miss BUD/S graduation?*

Sherwin swept up the paper and jammed it into his desk drawer. "Otherwise I'm sure the press will find equal fascination with your misconduct of last night coupled with a former arrest for solicitation. Do you want that to be your legacy, Ensign?"

JUSTICE HEADED DIRECTLY into out-processing from Admiral Sherwin's office.

Robotic and far away, she went through her final med check.

Cold to her marrow, she signed all necessary paperwork.

Half-anesthetized, she checked out with Captain Eagen.

As she traveled from building to building, a lump grew in her throat, then another—lump upon lump.

She'd been robbed of BUD/S graduation. The pinnacle of all her hard work. The brass ring she'd aspired to for six torturous months. Just a flimsy Certificate of Completion to some, maybe, but to her it meant *everything*. It was her career opus. Her freaking apotheosis. It said she belonged. It said she'd been weighed, measured, and tested, and she had *passed*.

She was good. *Really good.*

But Sherwin stole it from her.

There would be no victorious pinnacle, and her reputation would definitely be left in ruins—Sherwin cinched that outcome too.

Rudy Blabbermouth would joyously pass around all the gossip about last night, and Justice wouldn't be around to contradict it. If she'd been able to stand proudly on her white flipper-prints this evening, Rudy's version of events would've lost power. But now she couldn't show on the grinder, and her absence would confirm her guilt to the entire class.

Her hard-won reputation would crumble into an unsalvageable ruin.

Outside of ringing out at the eleventh hour, she couldn't imagine anything more devastating.

Lump upon lump.

Dusk was settling by the time she finally returned to the officers' barracks to finish packing.

She stuffed the last of her belongings into her two duffel bags, her movements clumsy and stiff, her whole body feeling like nothing more than a flesh sack full of broken bird bones.

Broken by the loss of her reputation.

Broken by the public humiliation.

Broken by the betrayal of two men she thought she could depend on, but who'd let her down so colossally she was missing the most important day of her life.

Fucking Brayden—if he'd taken her to a hotel room when she'd asked, the two of them never would've been discovered *in flagrante delicto.*

Fucking Keith—if he'd butted out and hadn't punched Brayden, Sherwin never would've had something to hold over him.

And so she was done.

Done with needing.

Done with trusting.

Done.

She didn't even have enough left inside her to confront her betrayers.

Hoisting her two duffel bag straps onto her shoulders, she made a final visual circuit of her room, ending on her honorary brown shirt. She'd left it neatly folded on her bottom bunk, the letters H-A-Y-E-S showing face-up.

She was leaving BUD/S as Class 684's biggest joke, exactly what she'd fought so hard *not* to become. She didn't deserve a brown shirt.

Outside, she heard the guys gathering on the grinder for graduation—loud male voices, call-outs to friends and arriving instructors, bursts of exuberant laughter.

Brad Ziegler, Dog Bone, Zack Kilgour, plus others… She wouldn't be able to raise a glass in toast to her guys now.

Lump upon lump.

Giddiup and Sanchez and Hooper and more… She wouldn't be saying goodbye to them.

More lumps…

By the time she was hefting her duffels into her trunk, it felt like she'd tried to swallow an entire head of broccoli and failed.

Climbing into her car, she gripped the steering wheel and stared straight ahead, fighting to store everything away…despair…defeat. Her raw glop hardened into a cracked, petrified shell. Rap your knuckles on it, and it would sound hollow and heavy.

She drove out of the parking lot and wended her way through the Amphib Base. Her lungs collapsed when she exited the main gate for the last time.

The sentries saluted her.

A wan half-moon rose into her rearview mirror, and the distant strains of a bugle mournfully called Taps.

ONE YEAR LATER

Post-SEAL Qualifying Training
Post-Cryptology School
Post-pre-deployment workups

CHAPTER FORTY-TWO

LIEUTENANT JUNIOR GRADE Justice Hayes was going to die.

Not after a long and illustrious career, either, but on her first real-world overseas mission as leader of her "Bat Three" Special Missions team.

Her only solace was that her squad could claim—posthumously, probably—a Mission Accomplished status before things went pear-shaped. One hour ago they'd successfully sneaked past several dozing lab techs into North Korea's primary underground uranium bunker on a mission to embed a Stachys Virus into the main computer.

Similar to the Stuxnet used against Iran, Stachys was a malicious computer worm, but where Stuxnet overspun uranium centrifuges, Stachys employed an electronic "spike" to disrupt the process altogether—like jamming a stick in the spokes of a wheel. Locking up the centrifuges in such a complete way would deliver a massive setback to North Korea's burgeoning nuclear program.

And bonus deal: while inside the network, Ron Glinski had spotted several interesting files.

After he'd downloaded the data, the three of them snuck back out, exiting the bunker and slipping past the perimeter fence undetected—*none the wiser*, as it were.

But five minutes into the four-mile trek to their rendezvous point—a grassy glen in South Korea where Pete Robbins and crew waited to fly them back to the USS *Bonhomme Richard*—a vehicle approached on the road they were on. They followed briefed procedure and deviated into the trees to let it pass.

And that's when the textbook mission went off script. Glinski's boot caught the edge of a ditch and down the hill he went.

"Crap," Justice hissed when she saw the night swallow up her guy. "Take a knee," she told Morris.

He instantly knelt, scanning the surroundings with his M-4 ready.

Kneeling too, she pressed the speak button on her throat comms. "Hey, Glinski, you good?"

"Yeah." Glinski's answer came through her earpiece. "But I think you should come down here and see this."

"What is it?"

"A shit-ton of North Korean soldiers."

She glanced at Morris.

Dealing with *a shit-ton of North Korean soldiers* didn't sound like it sat—you know, technologically speaking—inside Special Missions' job description. They also had a timetable to keep.

But then this didn't sound like something she should ignore either.

"Roger that," she said. "On our way."

The ditch wasn't too steep, and she and Morris were able to climb down quickly and quietly.

Glinski was refitting his fatigue cap back on his head when they joined him. He pointed toward a large, flat area artificially lit by overhead halogen lights.

It was maybe an acre's worth of grassy field surrounded by chain-link fence topped with concertina wire. Out in the field were, yes, a shit-ton of North Koreans wearing camouflage. Several hundred of them were divided into about a half dozen separate groups, and they looked to be drilling different combat maneuvers, some hand-to-hand fighting, but most were working with rifles. Each exercise was punctuated with an aggressive yell—the Korean version of *hooyah*, no doubt.

Justice whispered, "This is probably why there was only a nominal guard inside the uranium bunker." Every fighting man in the country appeared to be out in that field.

"They're a special forces unit of some kind, I think," Glinski said. "See their armbands?"

Justice nodded. The patches on the soldiers' uniforms weren't regular military insignia.

And if North Korea's insane leader was augmenting his ground forces at the same time he was expanding his nuclear program, then some serious shit was about to hit the world stage.

"Take pictures of this," she told them.

The three of them edged up to the fence, crouching in the shadow cast by a single-story wooden building running about as long as a football field—barracks?—on the north side of the field. They pulled out their cell phones and snapped what pictures they could from their limited vantage point.

Glinski also took a short video.

"All right," she said softly, "let's get out of here."

Such beautiful words, those—too bad she hadn't spoken them a microsecond sooner.

A North Korean man strode around the corner of the wooden building, the sound of his approach masked by all the *hooyah* shouting. Food-stained apron, wrinkled pants, stubble on his chin like licorice shavings—a cook, not a soldier, so the guy wasn't armed with anything other than his mouth.

But he put that to good use the moment he saw them. He opened it wide as the Holland Tunnel and howled loud enough to wake two generations of the dead.

Adrenaline flooded Justice's body to the tips of her ears. "Go!" she blasted at her guys.

They went.

Unfortunately, the shit-ton of North Korean soldiers also went, chasing after them and not being too shy about using their weaponry.

A barrage of gunfire roared, bullets whining by in all directions, slapping into tree trunks and digging small divots into the ground next to Justice's boots. She ran up on her tiptoes as tracer rounds dissected the night in streaks of light—pyrotechnically pretty but fucking terrifying.

Glinski and Morris chugged beside her in a zig-zaggedy race through the tall stand of trees.

The Special Missions units are noncombative. Ideally, they will only be sent into cleared areas.

Got that one wrong, Mr. Dawson.

Figured. Tall Forehead Bureaucrats never knew dick about how things worked in the real world.

And the situation was only going to go from bad to worse.

According to the map Justice memorized of this area, the woodland was about to end at a canyon. They'd soon have nowhere to—

There!

Cloaking woodland gave way to twinkling stars above and a lot of nothing below. The edge of a cliff came into view, dropping jaggedly into a dark abyss.

A less-than-comforting sight and—

A bullet whistled past her ear.

Fuck it.

"Jump!" she yelled.

CHAPTER FORTY-THREE

WITHOUT BREAKING STRIDE, Justice hurled herself over the edge of the cliff, fisting a hand in Glinski's shirt at the last minute to make damned sure he followed.

She caught air.

Lots of it.

*Fly...fly...*across the moon, through the immanent expanse of the universe. Her pulse thudded faster.

Wham!

She landed hard on her booted feet, jolting both ankles and the entire length of her spine. A couple of two-armed windmills kept her from tumbling ass over kettle down the hill—like Morris and Glinski did—and she slammed back onto her ass.

Both her guys somersaulted into a series of bone-bruising *thumps*—this hill *was* steep—clattering and grunting and cursing the whole way down, while she slid on her posterior into a high-speed, reckless chase after them, spewing dirt and pebbles from both sides of her hips, her fanny pack bumping against her lower back. She hissed air. By the time she skidded to a halt at the bottom, her butt was on fire and her lower back throbbing.

She paused for a wits-gathering moment—*ouch!* and *fuck!* and *holy shit!*—but didn't have the luxury of remaining on her derriere. The sounds of stomping boots and Korean shouts coming from a skyward direction told her the enemy was amassing on the ridge above.

She gathered saliva into her mouth and barked, "Trees!"

Thank God there was a small copse a few yards away—the only cover available—otherwise the soldiers above would've been able to pick them off with the ease of a turkey shoot. Or whatever the Korean equivalent of that was.

The two shadowed lumps that were Morris and Glinski staggered to their feet and took off with her toward the mini woods.

Huffing, the three of them hunkered down on their bellies inside the forest, lying side by side. The darkness was complete—the way no city could ever be dark—and also strange, like there was a palpable quality to it, the blackness shrouding her in something.

Probably foreboding.

No wind blew. The only noise was the discordant chorus of exhaling-inhaling of her and her guys, and the crowd-gathering noises of the North Korean soldiers. The leaves on the trees didn't even stir, each one looking etched in metal against the star-strewn sky.

"Everyone okay?" she checked in, sweat bleeding off her brow. "Besides bumps and scrapes." Broken bones or sprained ankles would considerably encumber their E&E…assuming they even *could* Escape and Evade.

Morris and Glinski grunted to communicate *we're basically okay*.

She tugged a pair of Night Vision Goggles out of her fanny pack and strapped them on to reconnoiter the area.

First she inspected the ridge above.

Green-coated human shapes came alive up there, several of the soldiers facing each other and gesturing wildly. No doubt they were discussing the best way to kill or capture the fugitives.

Next she scouted the canyon.

It was hourglass-shaped—fat at the east and west ends

and pinched in the middle where their small forest was. A stream ran along the south edge of the woods, or maybe it was a river. It was big enough and fast enough to be making a racket.

"What's the plan?" Morris asked breathlessly.

Excellent question. Too bad she didn't have a hard-and-fast contingency plan to fall back on. She'd briefed her team about what to do if they encountered resistance inside the bunker—neutralize it. Or if they ran into the scientist in charge of North Korea's nuclear program, Dr. Hyeong—apprehend him; the CIA wanted to have a little chat with the man.

But she hadn't discussed the possibility of running into an entire army of hostiles. Because they weren't supposed to. No intel chatter had warned that a massive training facility sat in the middle of nowhere, a mere four miles from the friendly side of the border.

What was happening right now shouldn't be happening.

Her stomach turned over. This was one of those times when it was better to be the follower than the decision-making Alpha Dog.

Her choices weren't plentiful or desirable.

Leave the cover of these trees to make a run for the opposite side of the canyon, and the turkey shoot would commence. The stream was a closer escape route, but even though she could hold her breath for a long time, it wouldn't be long enough. The moment she came up for air, the bad guys would pop her in the head.

Morris and Glinski too.

Stay put, and the enemy could either wait them out—easily, since among the three of them rations amounted to a couple of energy bars and one water bottle—or bring their superior numbers to bear with a full-on assault. It didn't take a genius to calculate how three against hundreds would play out.

She glanced up again and—

Pete.

He was the answer. The most viable means of escape was *up*.

Yanking the SAT phone off her belt, she pressed the speak button. "Chaos One, this is Bat Three Actual. How copy?"

"Loud and clear," Pete answered. "You ready for onload, Three? I don't have a visual on you yet."

"Roger. We are mission complete, but need to be picked up from a new extraction point. Mark these grid coordinates." She consulted her GPS and rattled off the LAT LONG numbers of their position.

Examining the canyon again, she checked west and east. Yes—at either fat end, there was enough room for a helo to land.

"Interrogative," she went on. "Are you able to fly in and exfil us from this new location?"

"The coordinates you gave us are inside North Korea." Pete's tone was deadpan, like he didn't know if she was kidding or not.

"Affirmative." *I'm not kidding.* "Be advised we're pinned down by a large force of hostiles and unable to move."

Pete didn't respond. The SAT phone merely *crackled.* The crackle seemed surprised and concerned, like Pete was holding down his speak button while not speaking. Probably his eyebrows were up high too.

"Chaos One," she said. "Do you—?"

"Stand by." A prolonged silence passed, then Pete came back online. "Bat Three, exfil is a negative. I've been denied permission to fly into North Korean airspace. Hold your position. There's a SEAL squad inbound to your location."

She licked her lips. Burnt gunpowder tasted hot on her

tongue. *How long will that take?* "Roger that. Standing by. Out." She hooked the SAT phone back on her belt. "We wait," she told her guys—unnecessarily. They'd heard the whole convo.

Morris turned to stare at her. With his own NVGs in place, he resembled a prehistoric insect, a half-man-half-bug Son of Mothra. She felt a chill of fear come off him. He wanted reassurances from her.

Unfortunately, she didn't have any to give.

She was putting their chances of survival in the low thirtieth percentile, and nobody wanted to hear those odds. Not even her. Not when dying would suck so badly right now. Dying on any given day wasn't good, but it was especially difficult to accept after having fucked up the past year of her life so badly.

Shoving her NVGs up, she rubbed the bridge of her nose.

Damaged down to her soul by the way BUD/S had ended—with the loss of two of her best friends *and* the chance to *hooyah* the most awesome success in her life—she'd crawled inside herself and shut out the world.

Be done with it all…

Done with needing.

Done with trusting.

Done.

She hadn't even stayed friends with Pete.

He'd been baffled and hurt by her rejection at first, but eventually *whatever'd* it, and proceeded to date, and probably fuck, every Southern beauty Pensacola had to offer.

Justice got weird.

Shaken, jealous, adrift, confused…more confused when she received several messages from Brayden asking her to contact him…she reverted to her old coping habits.

She began to break into places around Pensacola.

First place was *Fast Eddie's Fun Center*. She rearranged all their arcade prizes for no other reason than she could.

On the day an envelope arrived with her BUD/S Certificate of Completion inside—*mailed* to her—she upped the danger factor that night and broke into Pensacola Parks and Recreation. There, she hacked their computer, switched around everyone's SSNs, then felt bad about people not getting paid, broke back in, and put everything back. At the Pensacola Energy Operations Center she rewired their electric grid, causing rolling blackouts throughout the city, felt bad about that, too, and finally stopped bullshitting around.

But she remained twitchy, self-doubt and loneliness gnawing at her.

After finishing cryptology school, she reported to the USS *Bonhomme Richard*, but the new assignment didn't help her as much as she thought it would. She was away from sticky-fingered temptations—that was good—and the higher operations tempo of pre-deployment workups was a further distraction. But being on board a ship of hundreds did nothing to alleviate her isolation.

Captain Scar Nose, that big cockbite who'd treated her to a sleazy pickup line her first day on board, had spread his venom about her prior to her arrival. The other Marine pilots and Surface Warfare Officers gave her a wide berth.

She roomed with Tiffany Tesarik again, but when the pretty, perky First Lieutenant and Pete Robbins started to become overly chummy, Justice withdrew from the potential female friend. Whenever Justice was in her stateroom, she was, for all intents and purposes, alone.

Curled into an emotional ball.

Locked away from life, stuck inside a gulag of her own making.

Soul, insensate.

Done.

It'd been a miserable way to live...it was a miserable way to die, and her shoulders sank under the weight of regret. Hindsight was totally useless at this point, though. As much as she might wish, here in the dark with death a few yards away, that she'd done things differently, she didn't see how she could have pulled it off.

She'd been too hurt.

Too paralyzed by her pain.

Too lacking in the kind of knowledge that might've helped her figure herself out. Probably motherly wisdom stepped in at times like these...and yeah. No mom for her.

"Shit," Glinski cursed, cutting into her thoughts. "The enemy's flanking us, Lieutenant."

What? Justice slapped her NVGs back down and scanned the cliff. Her heart nearly went dead in her chest.

Glinski was right—the green images of the North Korean soldiers were spreading out along the ridge.

They were moving into attack formation.

Morris exhaled a thick breath. "Oh, fuck, we're so hosed."

Justice grabbed her SAT phone again and pressed the speak button. "Chaos One, Bat Three Actual. How copy?"

"Go ahead, Bat Three."

"Update on that Team rescue?"

"Stand by."

She waited. An eternity. An Ice Age.

Morris mumbled, "Fucking Bat Two."

Bat Two was Lieutenant Browning's unit—the team that was *supposed* to have taken tonight's mission. But today was Bat Two's last day in-country, and when Browning's wife had gone into labor back home, he'd asked Justice to take the op for him.

It'd seemed like the nice thing to do...

"Bat Three," Pete finally answered back. "That's a negative on info. Comms are dark."

Up above, enemy soldiers began to pour down three sides of the hill in a steady flow: six, eight, a dozen, more—a blitzkrieg.

Morris made a choked noise in his throat. "What are we going to do, Lieutenant?"

An icy sensation spread beneath Justice's belt buckle. Morris damned well needed to stop asking that. She pushed the speak button again, but then just let the phone crackle, same as Pete had done. Her voice was gone. Her hand was shaking.

There were so many enemy soldiers on the face of the hill now, their NVG images were merging into a giant green blob.

Unsteadily, she used her other hand to ease off the snap on her Sig Sauer, loosening the weapon for a smooth draw. Her guys probably thought she was readying to fight rather than preparing to keep the promise she'd made to herself over a year ago, right after SERE School—*I'll eat a bullet before I allow myself to be taken prisoner by the enemy.*

She swallowed heavily. *Sorry, Dad.*

"Bat Three," Pete said. "SITREP?"

Something inside her quivered. The feeling was... She knew what it was, and she greeted the reemergence of her unwanted emotions to the tune of Simon and Garfunkel's "The Sound of Silence."

Hello raw glop, my old friend, I've come to talk with you again...

An odd slip of the mind?

Yeah.

"Bat Three?" Pete pressed.

The Situation Report is that we're completely fucked.

Her heart pulled in on itself. Her guys were going to die

alongside her. Which really sucked. They were good men, skilled Naval petty officers.

"Chaos One," she rasped into her mic. "Overwhelming enemy forces are imminent on our position. This is my final transmission…"

Lieutenant JG Justice Hayes is going to die…

Unless a rescue mission can reach her in time.
But who will save her?
Which hero?

Keith? Brayden? Pete?

YOU choose!

To read **Keith Knight's story**, go to page 325.
To read **Brayden Street's story**, go to page 465.
To read **Pete Robbins's story**, go to page 605.

KEITH KNIGHT'S STORY...

If you burn him, you're out.

A man with a temper as red-hot as his looks, Petty Officer Keith Knight isn't about to forgive Justice for what she did to him after BUD/S graduation. Doesn't matter that he's still got the hots for her, and maybe – just maybe – he's totally in love with her. Okay, it does matter. A lot.

He doesn't hesitate to yank her out of hot water when her classified mission goes south.

Face-to-face with her for the first time in a year, his anger and hurt detonate in a scorching confrontation. Never one to back down, Justice lets him have it right back, and out of the fire he discovers what really happened at BUD/S.

His *the-hell-with-you* attitude goes out the door – turns out he got it all wrong.

His desire for this tough-on-soft woman jacks back up to turbocharge…but is Justice too wounded from their painful misunderstanding to let him in for a second chance…?

CHAPTER FORTY-FOUR

Late June
South Korea
Outskirts of Cheorwon

KEITH KNIGHT WAITED for three things: Nickelson to finish taking a crap and come out from behind a set of low bushes; the exfil bird assigned to transport his fast-action guys back to Camp Casey to arrive; and a call on his SAT phone informing him their extraction was once again being canceled, same as the last two times they'd been scheduled to head back to base.

Embracing the suck of a third cancellation wouldn't be easy.

He might be a big outdoorsman, but even he was sick of his own stink and living off MREs after a week straight in the field.

He shifted his shoulders, resettling his pack, the humidity like a suffocating blanket he couldn't throw off—even at night, the air was so oppressive it was like flypaper on his skin. Nickelson had a bad case of the runs, Digger breathed through his mouth like his sinus cavities were full of sediment, sweat ran like rainwater down Rick's temples, and Keith's shirt hadn't been dry for seven days.

Humping around a full kit only added more sweat to the equation. Besides wearing an armored flak jacket and carrying an M-4 rifle, his knapsack amounted to sixty pounds of dirty clothes, extra ammo, and three remaining days' worth of food in the form of prepackaged Meals, Ready-to-Eat, military field rations notorious for being unappetizing.

Sometimes Keith woke up with a phantom wad of crackers from a peanut butter snack pack—the bedrock of the MRE—globbed to the roof of his mouth.

"A hot meal," Rick said, throwing out what he was most looking forward to about returning to Camp Casey, the U.S. Army Base in South Korea closest to the DMZ, or Demilitarized Zone.

Due to its potentially volatile location, Casey was unofficial home plate for in-country special operators. Currently that included two of SEAL Team Five's units, Romeo and Keith's fast-action guys—call sign Whiskey—along with two Rangers.

A first tour guy like Keith—and clearly able to read Keith's mind about food—Rick Sickmeir had the kind of young, honest face that made grandmas want to pat him on the head—false advertising at its finest. Below the neck Rick had a shitload of scars. "Rowdy" Rick Sickmeir operated at one speed: full throttle. He fought hard, partied hard, and fucked hard. This last assumption was based on his taste for rough-living women: the tougher, the meaner, the better. Rarely did Rick come off a weekend without a fat lip or a black eye. Earned from man, woman, or beast, who could tell? Rick would fight anything.

"Nah," Digger contradicted. "A hot shower." He was standing on Keith's left, his Night Vision Goggles dropped down over his eyes and his forefinger resting on the trigger guard of his M-4. His head was on a constant swivel, even though they were in friendly territory.

SpecOps habit.

"My nuts have been stuck to the side of my thigh for two days," Digger added. He was black-haired and olive-skinned...and tight-lipped about his origins. Latino or Italian or American Indian? He could be one, the other, or a mix.

No one knew.

Keith panned the sky for the helo. "Don't see why you even bother bringing your nuts, Dig. Not like you use 'em."

Digger peered at Keith over the top of his strap-on NVGs—Digger preferred a boonie hat to a helmet—and lifted his lip into a sneer.

Keith just chuckled.

Digger's sneer wasn't real, or his complaints, either.

If his jaw-jacking had been real, Digger would've been a dick-ass Team Guy. But, nah, he bitched and moaned just to make it seem like he wasn't all about the job. Which he was—with a long history of ex-girlfriends to show for it. Why Digger didn't save himself the hassle and just go for the occasional one-night lay was a mystery. But he didn't. He kept trying for a girlfriend: landed one, ignored her in favor of his Team brothers, got dumped, then complained.

A shadow moved through the darkness, and Keith snapped his head around.

"Took your sweet time about it," Digger grumbled.

Nickelson's call to nature was finally complete.

Mitch Nickelson—a second-tour guy like Digger—looked as noble as he acted; every hair on his head was always combed neatly in place, and the required in-country beard he wore was barely long enough to pass regs. Honor, patriotism, and integrity weren't just intangible concepts to Nickelson; they made up the building blocks of his cells. As the sniper of the group, he should've been in charge of Whiskey, but he just wanted to fight the fight and didn't care about advancement. When Keith had done his usual and stepped in as leader, Nickelson had gladly let him.

All the men had problems. Nickelson's sister was married to an asshole who needed a serious head-pounding—but how did a noble guy like Nickelson pound his own brother-in-law's head? Rowdy Rick's father had been a violent asshole before he was murdered. Digger was—unintentionally—an asshole to women.

Keith himself?

He didn't know his asshole from a hole in the ground when it came to women, so who was he to talk? He was such a twisted mess on the inside these days—for a full year now, actually—he hadn't even gotten laid since…

When *was* the last time he saw some action? *Shit.* It was right after he graduated from BUD/S…probably trying to expunge a certain someone from his mind.

He'd picked up a woman at Danny's Bar, a SEAL booze joint on Coronado Island, off-limits, by unspoken rule, to all but full, trident-wearing SEALs. As an SQT candidate, Keith shouldn't have gone there, but *fuck it.* The hottest chicks hung out there.

He'd never learned his hookup's name and could hardly remember anything about her, except that at one point during the act he squinted down at her and was barely able to finish. She wore too much mascara, and her perfume made her smell like the type of dried flowers his mother set around the house in bowls. Not bad or cheap, just fake. Not natural. Why the hell did women gunk themselves up, anyway? They already had everything they needed to lure a man—indented waists and soft curves above and below. It made no sense to ruin it.

After the Danny's letdown, Keith had adopted a *why bother?* attitude toward women. He hadn't tried to bag another one until right before shipping out to Korea, figuring he better turn the engine over at least once before the battery died completely. But at Bar West in Pacific Beach—a notorious pickup joint, and, yeah, he'd gotten his

ass chewed by the SQT instructors for going to Danny's—
he wasn't able to muster excitement for any of the women.

He sat at the bar, letting his beer go flat, and came to
the conclusion that he was a twisted mess on the inside.
Complicated shit. All he could really say about it was it'd all
started and stopped on the BUD/S grinder.

And the current heaviness in his chest wasn't completely
due to in-country tension and humidity.

Nickelson reclaimed his position on Keith's right. "Foxtrot going to be at Casey when we get in?"

"Tomorrow," Keith answered.

Team Five's Foxtrot squad was Whiskey's relief—Keith
and his guys had come to the end of their six-month tour—
and the changeover would either add to Keith's overall life
shittiness or provide an opportunity to finally smooth out a
lot of regret.

Foxtrot was his brother Brayden's unit.

Keith saw lights winking in the sky over Nickelson's
shoulder.

He raised his NVGs, lifting the green away from his
vision. The lights were white and red. "Helicopter," he said.
"Inbound."

They waited in a ragged cluster as the exfil Black Hawk
out of Camp Casey drew even with their position. Engine
noise pounded the earth, and the downblast flung up dirt
and dust. The bird set down, and the four of them ran
toward it, ducking under the whirling blades.

The moment Keith's boots hit the metal floor, the lead
pilot was already twisting around in his cockpit seat and
jerking his thumb at the door.

Like—*Get the hell back out.*

What the fuck? Keith turned to the crew chief, the
enlisted guy manning the M-60 machine gun in back.
"What's the deal?!" he shouted over the thunderous noise.

"You're being ordered to return to Echo Outpost!" the guy yelled back.

Digger let out a string of curses vile enough to curl even the hairs in a drill sergeant's ears.

Keith shot a zip-it glare at Digger—the crew chief was only the messenger. "Why the ramp-up!?"

"Intel just came in!" the guy answered. "Your HVT is in Pyonggang!"

Keith strove for calm. He swung his rifle onto his shoulder and didn't shoot anyone. If that wasn't total horseshit, then Echo was logical. That outpost sat just this side of the DMZ—the borderline between North and South Korea—on the South Korean side, four miles away from the small town of Pyonggang in North Korea.

But last Keith had heard, Dr. Hyeong, the High Value Target his fast-action guys had been hunting all week, was in Changdo, catching a booty call from his mistress. That put the scientist over fifty miles away from Pyonggang.

Except now, once again, some intel geek, joystick in one hand, eyeglass cleaner in the other, was changing the story.

"How accurate is this new intel?!" Keith yelled. If he and his men were about to be denied hot meals, much-needed showers, and comfortable beds for another runaround—and all because some douche had confused Pyonggang for Pyong*yang*, over one hundred fifty miles in the opposite direction—then he *would* have to start shooting people.

"This isn't coming from two tin cans and a string!" the crew chief shouted. "The HVT has been spotted in Pyonggang!"

That fully engaged Keith's attention.

Dr. Hyeong wasn't likely to be misidentified.

Portly, with funky black hair sticking straight up at the front of his head, the scientist in charge of North Korea's nuclear program had the most recognizable birthmark in the world—a bright red oval on his right cheek resembling a creepy, bulging third eyeball.

"Word is," the crew chief went on, "the HVT is going to check on his uranium bunker, but first he'll go to one of his favorite restaurants for chow. Which restaurant is the big question—there's one on the east side of town, another on the west. Foxtrot is at Echo now, ready to man the east."

What? Keith's stomach bucked. Foxtrot was already in-country?

"Your men are needed to cover the west. The Rangers have been called back from tracking Hyeong to Changdo, but it's doubtful they'll make it in time. You're the closest SEALs."

Probably true—Echo Outpost was only a klick away.

"Roger that." Keith jumped out of the helo. "Drop the hammer!" he yelled at his men. "This is the real deal!"

Chapter Forty-Five

ECHO OUTPOST WAS a windowless shitheap of a shack embedded in the concealing woodland and rocky terrain common along the DMZ. It was little more than twenty feet square, with about half a dozen battery-operated LED lanterns hanging from ceiling hooks, and the same number of rolled sleeping bags lining the walls.

Whenever operators came to an outpost, it was an understood rule in the SPECWAR community that they should contribute something to the ready supplies. So a random conglomeration of crap lay around in no particular order, ranging from mosquito repellant and toilet paper to Korean porn and playing cards to all kinds of snacks out of the Camp Casey PX. Someone had gotten funny and thrown in a box of condoms rubberbanded together with a tube of Preparation H—okay, that might've been Keith. When he and his guys were at Echo earlier this week, he'd also dropped off a first aid kit.

Items you would never find left behind were ammunition of any kind or tobacco products of any brand. Too valuable.

Four camp stools were strewn about on the left side of the room. Right side, there was a card table and four folding chairs for sit-down chow, even though a cooked meal wasn't possible—no running water, no heat source, no electricity.

Situated a stone's throw from North Korea, Echo Outpost followed strict light and noise discipline.

Except, apparently, once it was time to party.

When Keith and his men entered through the one door, pushing aside the blackout drape and stepping inside, more noise was being generated than eight men would normally produce or was generally allowed.

The six men from Foxtrot and two Army Rangers were laughing, high-fiving, and hugging, although embracing SpecOps-style, with backs being slapped hard enough to knock the rust off a bad weld. It was pretty damned plain to see that they were in the middle of a victory celebration— Dr. Hyeong was clearly toast.

"What the *fuck* is this?" Digger blasted, still puffing from their one-kilometer sprint.

Wasn't it obvious? The Rangers had made it back in time to cover the west side of Pyonggang.

A roomful of faces turned toward Whiskey.

The men from Foxtrot—known around Team Five as the Brute Squad—looked like a hundred miles of bad road, one guy so ugly his face resembled a bucket of smashed crabs. How the newest blond and dimpled member was fitting in with all this unattractiveness was a mystery to Keith—he'd been out of contact with his brother for the whole year since BUD/S.

And if there was a regret worse than that, he couldn't name it.

"Foxtrot is in-country for five minutes," Digger kept on snappishly, "and *they* bag the kill we've been hunting for a *week*."

The complaint only earned more hoots, banter, razzing, and laughter.

"Hey," one of the Rangers called out. "We humped in sub sandwiches for everyone." He reached inside an open knapsack and pulled out a paper-wrapped hoagie. "Chow down." He missiled the sandwich at Digger.

It wasn't the hot shower Digger had been craving, but it wasn't an MRE, either. Digger's glower finally eased.

Whiskey was drawn into the celebration. Men separated into groups, opening a corridor of vision to—

Keith stared at the man across the room, who was likewise eye-locked on him.

Brayden.

Keith's heart jerked in a weird way.

His brother had fleshed out since Keith last saw him.

A never-ending year ago.

On the grinder.

At BUD/S graduation.

The day after Keith saw the woman who was supposed to be *his* primed to suck his brother's dick.

What the hell are you doing with Justice?

Nothing.

So said the man with a woman on her knees between his splayed legs, his shirt shoved halfway up his body, his shorts pitching a serious tent. Keith gritted his teeth. *Brayden's fucking huge cock.* Like the asshole needed it—Captain Shit Don't Stink always knew the exact right way to treat a woman to get her in the sack.

The soul-ripper of losing Justice to Brayden had led to another—Keith trying to beat the fuck out of the brother who'd only ever been his best friend—had led to *another*—the most well-matched woman in the world for him bailing without a word.

All told and collectively, this past year had been one of the worst of Keith's life.

He'd done his own disappearing act after those soul-rippers, taking off for SEAL Qualifying Training without working things out with Brayden first.

After SQT, he'd checked on board his new home at SEAL Team Five in San Diego and focused totally on the job—in perfect company for that.

Out of good luck or bad, Brayden ended up on the same Team, although he arrived much later than Keith. Following BUD/S graduation, Brayden, as an officer, had to go to JOTC, Junior Officer's Training Course, while Keith went directly into SQT, where he simultaneously trained as a medic. Keith had pinned on his trident and been assigned to Yankee Platoon, then worked up as one of Whiskey's fast-action guys and headed off on deployment by the time Brayden arrived at Team Five.

But teammates couldn't avoid each other forever.

Time was up.

Here was his brother, freshly arrived with Foxtrot, bringing with him all the fucked memories.

Brayden stepped closer to the sandwich knapsack and dug out a hoagie, throwing it to Keith.

He caught it with one hand.

Shouldering his way through the men, Brayden drew up to Keith. "You want to get some air?"

This last week of Keith's life had only been open air, but if Brayden planned on reaming out Keith for the way he'd handled this past year, then outside—away from witnesses—was better.

Keith left his knapsack by the door along with his helmet and SAT phone—he kept his rifle—then swept aside the blackout drape and stepped outside.

Brayden followed.

They stood side by side, staring up at the sky, the stars hazy from the humidity. The two of them had stood in a similar way countless times in Wyoming, listening to the reedy song of crickets, but this was different. Now a chasm was between them—a distance Keith had put there with his hurt pride.

He started to unwrap his sandwich in an abrupt motion.

"I'm sorry."

Keith stopped unwrapping. Those weren't exactly the first words he'd expected out of his brother's mouth. "Isn't that my line?" he countered tautly.

"No." Brayden transferred his own hoagie from palm to palm. "While I was going through JOTC, learning how to lead, I came to the fucked realization that I've let you down your whole life, Keith."

"What?" Keith tried to scowl at his brother, but the moonlight was thinly veiled and nearly colorless and he couldn't see Brayden's expression. His brother's features were vague shadows, but they were still the features that'd always belonged on the side of a coin.

How was it that Keith shared the same father's DNA with Brayden? Keith wasn't any kind of pig, but he'd never looked like *that*.

"What the hell are you talking about?" he snapped.

"Because Dad never treated me like his own son, I was never sure how to be with you and Walt and Thad and Adam. I didn't know if I could step up and be the big brother. So I never did." A muscle worked in his jaw. "So you did. But *I'm* the oldest, Keith. I should've acted like a big brother." His fingers flexed around his hoagie. "This goes clear back to the day of the rock climbing accident. I suspected the terrain was unstable, but I didn't say anything."

Keith stiffened his spine.

Here was a memory he kept in a dark pit of his brain where he never looked: the five high school friends thumping down a cliffside toward a devastating crash landing. Brayden had shattered both shin bones, his other brother, Walt, fractured an arm and cracked his skull, Matt broke his pelvis, and Ryan…

Never mind Ryan.

Brayden stared at him, his eyes dark holes in his face. "The accident wasn't your fault. It was mine. I should've said something."

Keith jerked his head sideways, a single small movement that was a howling denial. "*I* was the one leading the group, not you."

"But you shouldn't have been," Brayden retorted. "That's my point." He exhaled. "Over this past year I've wanted to text or call you a hundred times, but there was always too much to say that would never be enough. I'm sorry."

"Stop saying that," Keith growled. "I could've texted or called you too." *I should have.*

"Yeah, except…I don't think you really know how to deal with shit like this." Brayden rubbed the side of his head, his blond hair gleaming fresh-to-the-battlefield clean. "You know, I always envied you Dad, but this past year I also came to another fucked realization—you didn't have it so great with him either. After Ryan died, did Dad say anything to you? 'It wasn't your fault' or 'It was just a horrible accident' or something like that?"

Keith held his sandwich in a still fist. His heart was barely beating.

"Dad never helped you figure out how to deal with the hard shit in life." Brayden peered up at the sky, tracking a crescent moon that was drifting past some branches. "I think it's because Dad never completely got over my mom refusing to marry him," he added quietly.

Keith locked the muscles in his jaw. Here was another memory he kept inside his brain-pit. Because if he looked too closely at it, he'd have to watch an otherwise happy childhood replay where his mother had only ever come in second place to the woman his father truly loved—Brayden's mother, Marsha.

"Anything difficult comes along in life, Dad buries it. And now you do the same." Brayden's voice dropped. "I've never known you to hit someone without thinking, Keith, but that night you caught me with Justice, you laid into me over her like you'd come off your spool." He paused. "You'd fallen in love with her."

Only cross-eyed, kicked-in-the-kneecaps in love with her, but did it matter?

Brayden went on. "You didn't know how to cope with having your heart stomped on, and Justice stomped you good. Seeing her try to give me a blow job just about ended you."

The provolone in Keith's sandwich was probably melting from all the heat his fist was generating. "And doesn't that create a fucked brotherly situation?"

"What do you mean?" A frown was in Brayden's tone.

"*You're* in love with her too."

"No."

"Cut the shit."

"All right," Brayden admitted. "I *was* in love with her. But it was situational."

"Situational?" Keith repeated in a snide tone. "Really? How does that work?"

Brayden passed his sandwich back and forth again—right hand, then left, then back again. "Best I can explain it is that I'm the type of guy who needs a woman to take care of. I'd broken up with Charlotte before going into SEAL training, so Justice became my focal point. Concentrating on looking out for her got me through all the torture. It was only a BUD/S thing. I've moved on."

"A BUD/S thing," Keith parroted again, probably starting to sound emo, but could someone please explain how a man *moved on* from a woman he was batshit crazy about? He'd really like to know.

"Yes. I'm back with Charlotte now."

"For fuck's sake, Brayden." Keith looked skyward. "This has rebound written all over it." *Justice splits, and Brayden just so happens to get back with his ex.*

"No," Brayden repeated. "I initially left Charlotte because I thought she couldn't handle being with a SEAL, but she proved me wrong. She never left me, even when I left her." He pushed a hand through his hair. "I also want children someday, a traditional family, and I don't see Justice going that route. She's worked too hard to make it into SOF. She wants a high-impact lifestyle, same as you do, which means she isn't the right woman for me, but she's perfect for *you*. So go for her, man."

"Yeah," he drawled. "I'll jump right on that."

Brayden gave him a *look*, one Keith could feel more than see, but he knew his brother well enough to know when he was being visually smacked. "Don't let what happened between me and Justice hold you up. She was just reaching out to me for help to get through her post-SERE shit. That's all."

That's all.

Was that supposed to make him feel better? Like it was nothing when it was *everything*.

Justice hadn't come to *him*.

"Here are some reasons not to go for her," Keith clipped out. "One, why would I even want a woman who so completely ghosted me? Two, after spending the past year not thinking of her that way"—*liar*—"because my brother was supposedly in love with her, who says I can even shift gears? And three, she doesn't want me—refer back to one."

Brayden crossed his arms. "Point one: Justice bailed on BUD/S the way she did because she was understandably fucked up. I mean, first she came to me for help after SERE and I pushed her away—to do the right thing, yeah, but it still had to sting. Then you and Dunbar catch her in a compromising situation, blasting to pieces the reputation that meant so much to her."

A loud *thump* sounded inside the shack. Rowdy Rick was probably stirring up roughhousing.

"Point two: I repeat again, I am *not* in love with Justice. And point three: don't be an idiot about her wanting you. She's in awe of you, Keith."

Heat ran up his neck and into his face.

"*Talk* to her. Tell her how you feel."

He curled his lip. The idea of talking to Justice about his *feelings* sounded about as much fun as crying or puking—the first he never did, the second only under the most dire of circumstances. "I'm sort of on deployment right now, Brayden."

"So is Justice."

Keith swung his head around.

Brayden smiled archly. "Her Missus unit arrived on station a few days before Foxtrot."

Keith slowly turned to stare into the forestland.

There wasn't a breeze to be found in this godforsaken country tonight, but suddenly it seemed like the trees in front of the shitheap shack were tilting sideways. The sky went slushy, too…or maybe his knees were preparing to give him a nose-plant view of the ground. A vein in his brain was probably in the middle of exploding, offering him a way out of this unwanted convo via an aneurism.

Justice is in Korea.

"Hey, Knight." The shack door flew open, and Rick stepped outside. A belt loop was ripped off his camos, and he was holding up Keith's SAT phone. "An emergency exfil call just came in. A Missus unit is trapped in a canyon under heavy enemy fire. We've been ordered to yank 'em out, if we can get there in time. Sounds like they're about to bite the big one…"

CHAPTER FORTY-SIX

KEITH HAD NEVER run faster in his life—four miles in a little under twenty-five minutes, in full kit. He was breathing so hard his ribcage hurt, and liquid was leaking steadily from of his nostrils. Probably a mammoth amount of sweat. Hopefully not blood.

The south ridge of the compromised canyon came into view dead ahead, and he skidded down onto his belly at the edge, jacking his legs apart and snapping his M-4 up—stock snugged against his right shoulder, safety clicked off, right index finger resting on the trigger guard. He *ticked* over his rifle scope to night vision mode and peered through it at the north side of the canyon.

"Shit," he hissed.

"What we got?" Rick landed an arm's length away from Keith's left side, dropping into the same position.

"Ass-ton of enemy," he answered, "as promised."

A callback to base on the SAT phone had provided the eyebrow-lifting info that on the E&E op their band of twelve operators—Whiskey, Foxtrot's six, and the two Rangers—would be facing down a potential hundred bad guys. And not some Mickey Mouse faction, either, but a special forces unit spotted training at a nearby secret camp.

Digger settled next to Rick and casually vomited.

Idiot had eaten too many sandwiches.

Nearly silently, Nickelson slid into place on Keith's right, his head slightly tilted as he sighted along his sniper scope. "Got 'em," he said. "Small cluster of trees."

Keith had already spotted the three heat signatures. Two of the forms wore hats with brims, the third had a bun on the back of her head.

"Whaddya know," Rick murmured, peering through his own scope. "A female *is* with that Missus unit."

"The three are hurtin," Digger observed. "Missus would be fried already if the steepness of that hill hadn't slowed down the bad guys."

"Yep," Rick agreed.

Keith let out a low snarl. "Cut the chatter."

Rick popped his head up and stared at him.

Keith ground his teeth against the urge to start issuing orders. The vanguard of the advancing enemy had reached the bottom of the hill; time was critical. But he wasn't the officer here. "Brayden," he snapped into his mic. "You on scene?"

"Here," Brayden confirmed over comms. "Mark that tall tree at the top of the north hill, midpoint."

"Got it."

"Your men target the enemy to the west of the mark. My squad has the east."

"Roger that."

"Pepper a line of fire at the bad guys' feet first," Brayden instructed. "Let's see if we can drive 'em back up the hill before we go full hot."

"Copy that." Keith lifted his head, swiped the sweat out of his eyes on his sleeve, then looked through his scope again.

Brayden gave the command: "Execute, execute, execute."

Their ridge roared with gunfire.

Keith pulled his trigger five times. Through green-tinted crosshatching, he saw four puffs of dirt spout up on the north hillside around four soldiers' feet.

Bloody streaks spurted from the fifth pair of boots.

"Uh-oh, SpaghettiOs," Rick piped in.

Keith grunted. "Guy didn't want to get tagged, he shoulda stayed at home in his La-Z-Boy." He adjusted his position.

About a quarter of the enemy scrambled back up the hill. The rest didn't.

"Full hot," Brayden ordered.

Their ridge roared again.

Keith squeezed off another five shots. He didn't miss this time—five bodies fell. Not his first kills on this deployment. Shooting humans was worse than hunting deer back home, but he tried to think of it the same way.

More of the enemy retreated, clawing up the hill, dirt clods and pebbles avalanching in their wake.

A soldier closest to the bottom raised his weapon and sighted on the Missus.

Nickelson's sniper rifle discharged a round with a smart *snap*.

Part of the soldier's head blew off in fireworks of green.

"Nice shot," Keith said.

"Smokes!" Brayden barked.

From his periphery, Keith saw Digger smoothly push up onto one knee and heft a mini grenade launcher onto his shoulder. A ball of fire flashed from the nose of the weapon, followed by a *pff-zat*.

Keith looked up to track the arc of the smoke canister.

Down the line, two more grenade launchers went off. *Pff-zat. Pff-zat.*

All three canisters hit their marks true, landing between the small woodland where the Missus was pinned down and the north hillside where some of the enemy still advanced. The canisters spewed a steady billow of smoke, and within thirty seconds the patch of woodland was concealed from enemy view.

Brayden must've given the Missus a go-ahead order— the three jumped up and ran south toward a bridge spanning a small river.

Keith and his men laid down additional covering fire.

Brayden doled out more orders. "Foxtrot, make for the north side."

Brayden's unit was going to destroy the secret North Korean training camp.

"Whiskey," Brayden went on, "rendezvous with Missus."

Keith and his fast-action guys were charged with escorting the rescued threesome over the border into South Korea.

The Missus' bird waited there, according to base, ready to fly them all to Camp Casey.

"Roger that." Keith and his three guys edged backward on their bellies, far enough away from the lip of the ridge that they wouldn't create target-ready silhouettes when they stood.

Hopping to their feet, they dropped down their NVGs and ran in stagger formation.

Up ahead, the Missus topped the cliff and aimed for them.

Keith's belly changed from solid matter into warm water.

He would know that run anywhere.

No one moved like Justice.

She had an almost indescribable stride. Not feminine. Not masculine, either. Just...totally athletic, everything tight and in place and working together in perfect synchronization.

His group and hers met along the ridge, and everyone came to a halt, panting.

The warm water in Keith's belly sloshed into his groin, and his next breath required hard effort to pull into his lungs.

Here she was, right in front of him, her tall, lithe body in the flesh.

Some stuff happened to his heart, too, but he was in the middle of an E&E here, so whatever it was had to go on the back burner.

And *fuck it* anyway.

Justice's smile blazed out of the night. "Aren't you a sight for sore eyes," she said to him.

Not *him*. To the shadow-faced, helmeted SEAL who was rescuing her. If she knew it was him, she wouldn't be smiling.

Wouldn't it be nice to know what he'd done to deserve it?

His anger came roaring back over the shitty way she'd treated him—her dismissal of him as a man to help her through her post-SERE issues. Her uncaring bailout. The year-long silence that'd robbed him of her friendship, and how much, in spite of it all, he'd missed her: her can-do attitude, her grit and discipline, her jokes, her hazel-green eyes.

Those eyes had been his downfall from the start.

Day one BUD/S, shaking her hand at dawn muster, he'd looked directly into those eyes—and taken a concrete fist center-chest.

Her gaze had shone with all the confidence in the world...but also with tension and worries and uncertainties. It amounted to a mixture of tough-on-soft woman that got to him right off.

Then came the other looks.

The wrenching detachment she adopted the first week of BUD/S.

The self-deprecation she clearly felt the first time she'd asked for his help. *I don't seem to be able to swim in combat boots...*

The affection for "her guys" she couldn't hide when she left BUD/S during Hell Week. *Be here when I get back.*

The pride shining brightly whenever she achieved her biggest victories—her top-three O-course score, her honorary brown shirt, *I'm not some average, run-of-the-mill thief; I'm world-class.*

A solid fucking year Keith had spent trying to forget all those looks.

Impossible.

And how irritating was it that she still had such an effect on him?

Dammit.

Damn *her.*

Keith squeezed his rifle. Too much bullshit. Stacks of it. A crushing weight.

Digger adjusted his boonie hat. "There a reason we're just standing here scratching our balls?"

Rick was watching Keith closely.

The first full-bodied *boom!* of Foxtrot's explosives going off at the training facility sounded.

"Move it out," Keith ordered gruffly.

Their group took off at a steady pace for the DMZ, Justice falling into step beside Keith like it was the most natural thing for her to do.

Like it always had been.

CHAPTER FORTY-SEVEN

THE CAMP CASEY Ready Room had two doors.

One headed into a hallway leading to the mess hall. The other door opened directly onto the flight line. To the left of this door was a brown couch, its back against the wall. To the right, all the basic paraphernalia needed for briefing: a polished conference table surrounded by matching cushioned chairs, a white board—X's and O's drawn on it like football plays—and a pull-down screen. The whole room was lit by fluorescents above. Below was synthetic carpet stiff as plywood.

The pulse of the helicopter's rotor wash pushed at Keith's back as he tramped through this outer door into the Ready Room, his guys and the Missus following.

When the door swung shut, it hit Keith just how bad he stank. A mingled combo of sweat, dirt, jet fuel, maybe even a rotten peanut butter snack pack, and gunpowder wafted from him in—he wouldn't be surprised—visible waves.

Funny how he'd spent the majority of his time at BUD/S as a disgusting excuse for a man—sweaty, foul, plastered in sand and seaweed, tired and cold, riddled with aches and pains—but suddenly *now* he was aware of his own revolting-ness.

Were his balls stuck to the inside of his thigh too?

He muttered a curse. Since when did he give a shit about stuff like that? Why should he care that he was seeing Justice for the first time in a year resembling something in need of a scrape-down? Did it matter that she, besides being wind-messed and carrying some residual terror-pale in her complexion, was a knockout compared to his garbage-pail exterior?

No.

He came to a rigid halt by the conference table, his men dispersing in an uneven pattern around him.

Justice stopped near the brown couch with her guys on either side of her.

Keith assessed her up and down again and fumed. Not a lick of makeup on, and her skin was still honey smooth. And as far as scents went, maybe he wasn't even smelling things correctly in the first place, seeing as his heart was currently being ripped through his nasal passages over him *still being completely in love with this woman.*

He gnashed his teeth. She didn't deserve his love. Not after wronging him so deeply.

Didn't matter that she was the most well-matched woman in the world for him. Someone who could keep up on rock climbing outings, be happy deep-forest camping, snow ski the black diamond trails, and screw all day, moving from a bed to a counter to a shower to the floor, then back to the bed… All the things he liked to do. *Didn't matter at all…*

He ground his teeth harder.

Yes. It fucking did. It was actually everything, and damn him if he didn't want to bend her over a stack of O-course Balance Logs and spank her moronic ass for being so right for him.

Justice swept a gaze over Whiskey's fast-action guys. "God love the Navy SEAL," she said with another glowing smile. "I speak for my entire unit when I say thank you." She gestured at the taller of her two guys. "Ron Glinski." Then she indicated the short guy. "Charlie Morris." And finally she introduced herself. "I'm Justice Hayes."

Rowdy Rick—looking *way* too interested in this woman who could give him the best female ass-kicking of his life—jumped right in. "Rick Sickmeir."

Nickelson nodded. "Mitch Nickelson."

Digger stared at Justice from beneath the brim of his boonie hat in undisguised shock.

She was probably in better shape than she'd been at BUD/S—heaven help Keith's long-deprived dick. Her waist was a taut curve above hips that flared, but leanly, and her legs and ass were a miracle. Up top, her shoulders and arms were densely rounded and ridiculously cut, but also…refined-looking—for lack of a better way of putting it—which meant her muscle-rich body wasn't man-like. Her tits being another miracle didn't hurt matters in this regard.

Justice had always worn sturdy, concealing undergarments beneath her form-fitting T-shirts. Tonight was no exception, except…the shock of switching from the oppressive humidity outside to the Ready Room's air conditioning was too much for her bra to handle.

A slight pucker of nipples showed at the front of her shirt.

Keith whacked his rifle strap onto his shoulder with more force than necessary.

"That's Digger." Rick introduced the man who'd forgotten how to talk. "And over there is—"

"Hayes knows me." Keith tipped his head forward, rolling his combat helmet off his skull into his palm, then straightened, exposing his dark hair and a clear view of his face. He had longer hair and a beard, but still…

Justice froze.

As he knew would happen, her smile vanished. What he hadn't expected was the weird thing she did with her eyes. She blanked out completely, staring through him as if he was a hole in space.

He gritted his teeth so hard his cranium throbbed. *Fuck that noise.* She was welcome to either stick her horns in his ass over a selection of imagined slights or grovel for his forgiveness, but a blank-out?

He wasn't taking *nothing.* Not after a year of that shit.

"Lieutenant." He flicked an impertinent salute at her.

This out-of-nowhere insolence sent surprise buzzing around the room.

Rick set the stock of his M-4 on the floor and leaned a forearm across the nose of his weapon, settling in for the show.

"Petty Officer Knight." Justice acknowledged him in the kind of flat voice one usually reserved for a distant aunt with gin-soused breath and reeking of bargain basement perfume.

"Missed you"—shot out of his mouth—"at BUD/S graduation."

That cleared her gaze, although she still wouldn't look him directly in the eyes. She stared at his nose like maybe he'd stored his extra cash there.

"You had someplace better to be back then?" he asked, his tone like barbed wire scraping over chalkboard—*unpleasant.* Because the idea that he could mean so little to her when she meant everything to him took the twisted mess inside him by the balls and twisted harder.

She inhaled and exhaled a long, harsh breath, the kind that moved her shoulders up and down. Her focus finally shifted to his face. With eyes of pure flint, she ran a slow inspection over him—from his jaw, down his neck, across his shoulders, over his chest, lower...

Rick rubbed his cheek with his free hand.

Digger adjusted his boonie hat back on his head for a better view.

With that long stride of hers, she suddenly took a huge

step forward, bringing herself so close to Keith her nose almost bumped his—more to the point, her *breasts* nearly touched his chest.

A stabbing pulse shot through his balls. This in-your-face confrontation style of hers always put a rock in his pants, all the blood below his belt pooling heavy and hot in his groin.

She reached for him…

Tendons pulled taut in his crotch.

She flicked dirt off his shoulder, and a tic beat in one of his nostrils. *That* was some kind of a challenge.

"You need to police your uniform, Petty Officer."

A growl built.

"Not that you're anything but a disgrace in it." She pinched something off the side of his neck, her fingers briefly touching his flesh.

He felt his lips jerk against his teeth.

"Or should I say you're nothing but a *turncoat* in it."

He narrowed his eyes. *What?*

"In fact, would you like me to enumerate *all* the ways you've failed to live up to standard over the course of your Naval career?" She held the weed in front of his face and twirled it.

There was something distinctly aggressive about that.

Acidic gorge rose up and ate away his molars. "Yes, ma'am, please do. It would be a refreshing change from your usual gutless silence."

Her eyes flared and snapped. The grate of her teeth flashed.

Hurling the weed aside, she—

"So, hey," Digger interjected. "Important public safety announcement: everyone in this room is armed."

"Shut up, Dig," Rick said from the side of his mouth.

Justice went stiff and remained that way for several long

seconds, her whole body practically vibrating with the hostility rolling off her.

Keith kept his weight forward on the balls of his feet. Options for what she could effectively do to him physically were limited, normally nil, but he'd be stupid to underestimate this woman. Options for what he could do to her physically, on the other hand, were limitless—although what he was willing to do was still up for debate. A headlock with an ear-bite might be a good place to start.

Finally she stepped back, two hot spots of color sitting high on her cheekbones. She moved on from him dismissively, shifting over to Rick.

Rick perked right up, hoisting his rifle and stepping forward.

Keith arm-barred him back.

Rick's eyes drilled a couple of *how-interesting* holes into the side of Keith's face.

Justice's focus continued along the line of Whiskey guys, passing over Digger and stopping on Noble Nickelson. "Anywhere around here my men and I can get some grub?"

Nickelson pointed helpfully at the door leading into the hallway.

She nodded at her guys.

Glinski and Morris looked very happy to leave. They went through the door first.

At two in the morning the chow hall would be closed, but the mess cooks always left out something for mid-rats, if only the makings for PB&J—which at this point in Keith's culinary life would be the equivalent of eating a smear of diarrhea on pressboard. But he followed Justice anyway. The fuck if he was letting an accusation of turncoat go.

He'd never ratted on anyone in his life.

Tucking his helmet under his arm and swinging his rifle off his shoulder to carry it by the action, he stalked into the hallway after her, glowering at her bun, lopsided from her harrowing night.

The hallway echoed loudly with footsteps. He might've been stomping.

Up ahead, Glinski and Morris pushed through the double doors labeled *Chow Hall*.

As Justice arrived at the same doors, she braced a hand on the outer jamb, blocking Keith's path.

He drew up.

"My helicopter will be done gassing up for a trip back to the *Richard* soon, so why don't you find another time to eat, Knight?" She sniffed pointedly. "Preferably after you've made your way through all the base's sanitation stations."

He slashed a grin at her. There it was.

"This night has already sucked huge, and your selective memory about what happened a year ago isn't helping the blood pressure in my head. So take my suggestion, and fuck off."

The seals on the valves controlling his own blood pressure ruptured. Not a single apology was in sight. Not a moment's willingness to finally explain herself was sitting on the horizon. "My memory is fully intact," he bit out, so much heat boiling into his face he felt his skin peel off. "You and I bled, sweated, and suffered together for six hell-filled months, then you left without even a goodbye. You treated one of your best friends like dogshit for no good reason. *You* did that. Not me."

"*For no good reason*," she repeated, sharp and incredulous. "I can't believe you just said that, after what you did."

"What did I do?"

"This discussion is over." Her voice was stony.

"The hell it is. I'm not going anywhere until you tell me what happened."

Her stare froze to ice.

"Would you cut with the fucking dramatics. I honestly don't know. You called me a turncoat, but I've never turned on anyone—ever."

She released a guttural breath. "Are you really going to stand there and pretend you don't remember being called into Sherwin's office the morning after you hit Brayden?"

"I remember. What about it?"

"Sherwin threatened to bring punitive charges against you for striking an officer," she fired at him, a lot of iron in her spine. "*Unless* you helped him kick me out of SOF."

Keith paused for a blank moment. *What?*

"He told you he was going to find a way to oust me with or without your help, so—"

Wait... *What!?*

"—since I was getting the boot, anyway, you should make the right decision to save your career. You did."

Keith held up a palm. "Hold just a fucking second—"

"You proceeded to tell him about my arrest record, and because of that, Sherwin—"

"*Stop*," he cut her off. "What kind of weak-tit little nark do you think I am?" His throat clenched and released. This was one of the worst bitch-slaps his ego had ever taken. "I can't believe you would swallow such garbage even for a second."

A muscle in her cheek jumped. "I saw your expression when you left Sherwin's office. You were livid, like you'd just been manipulated into doing something you were ashamed of."

"I was pissed all right—at *Brayden*, for what I thought he'd done to you. For taking advantage of you." *For taking you from me.* "The meeting with Sherwin brought it all back."

"Then how did Sherwin know about my arrest record?"

"The fuck if I know how the douche found out."

"You were the only one who knew that about me, Keith."

"I don't give a shit."

"Yo!" Rick called out, walking down the hallway toward them, his thumb aimed back at the Ready Room. "Bird just arrived for the Missus."

"Thanks," Justice said stiffly, then yanked the chow hall door open and called to her guys. "Pete's here."

Glinski and Morris appeared and headed at a trot down the hall.

Justice let go of the door. It *woofed* shut. She met Keith's gaze. "You asked me a minute ago if I had someplace better to be back then. I *didn't*. There was no place I wanted to be more than at BUD/S graduation. But Sherwin *made* me leave before the ceremony due to my arrest record." Pain wedged deep in her eyes. "I missed graduation because of *you*."

Keith's heart began to beat too hard and too fast. This was horrendous.

"So, yes," she went on. "I left without saying goodbye. You didn't deserve it. Then or now." She stepped around him and jogged down the hall.

Keith watched her go.

The Ready Room door closed behind her.

She was gone.

Again.

With nothing resolved.

Shit…

What the hell did I just do?

He'd let hurt pride drive his actions again, that's what, getting so caught up in needing apologies and explanations he forgot to do what he'd set out to do.

Convince the woman he loved to love him back.

Tell Justice how you feel, Keith…

He hadn't done that.

He'd yelled and snarled, insulted, threatened, and criticized.

Dammit.

He squeezed his helmet so hard, he probably warped it from a circle to an oval.

Rick tucked his hands in his pockets and rocked back on his heels. "Blew it with her, Knight, didnya?"

Hissing a breath, Keith thrust his head back against the wall and gave his skull a good, solid clunk.

CHAPTER FORTY-EIGHT

SPECIAL OPERATORS WERE housed in a barracks building separate from the main part of the Camp Casey base, away from the prying eyes and ears of regular military—Top Secret Missions needing to remain top secret and all that shit.

But even racked out in Boondocks Sector, Keith could hear the sounds of a military installation coming awake: the muted workings of machinery and vehicles, a turbine engine spooling up in the maintenance hangar, and, closer, the rumble of voices coming from one room over in the SpecOps general living area.

Gray light pressed at the bottom edge of the window blinds, and birds—who took their lives into their own hands by hanging out near an airfield—squawked with the rising dawn.

Keith couldn't sleep.

Everything was upside down and backwards and different now. He'd spent an entire year stewing over Justice slighting him, only to find out that she left BUD/S the way she did because *he* had slighted *her*.

He hadn't, of course.

But if he really had betrayed her the way she thought, he could totally understand her hating him.

You were the only one who knew about my record, Keith… How else did Sherwin find out?

He didn't have an answer, and that was a big problem.

It meant Justice's opinion of him was operating off some pretty damning evidence. His bruised ego aside, he could see how just telling her, "I'm not that kind of man," wasn't enough to convince her.

He needed to serve up the real culprit to have a hope in hell of reconciling with her...although *when* he would score this miraculous reconciliation was also an issue.

His deployment was over.

Whiskey's relief was on-station, and he and his guys were due to transfer back to San Diego any day now. Being in California would put him over eight thousand miles away from Justice and for a period of six months—*her* deployment was just beginning.

Logistically, the geographical distance would make it impossible for him to convince her to fall in love with him, be his girlfriend, and proceed to have lots of sex with him.

Not that he was having any luck with those goals even while he was in the same room with her.

Lots of problems. Not a lot of good solutions.

His least favorite situation.

He kicked his covers off. The barracks' AC was either on the fritz again or he was.

Locking his hands behind his head, he stared at the underside of the top bunk's mattress, trying to clear his mind. He tried deep, even breathing. Tried several relaxation techniques. Nothing worked.

Enough.

Lying in bed wasn't going to infuse his brain with the right strategy. A man only solved shit when he kept moving.

Spinning his body off the mattress, he thrust to a standing position and jammed his legs into a clean pair of camo pants, then thumped his feet into his boots with equal force, and—

"Thinking about her, Knight, arencha?"

Keith narrowed his eyes on the man sacked out on the top bunk. "I'm seriously reconsidering rooming with you when we get back to the States, Sickmeir." He punched Rick in the arm.

Chuckling groggily, Rick rolled onto his side. Peckerwood was probably sleeping like a baby.

Keith stalked into the SpecOps general living area, a room of unfinished wooden walls, no pictures, only knotholes, except for a single Snap-On Tools Pin-Up Calendar from the late '80s. One couch with a nap like Q-tips and a color like vomit served as the token piece of furniture. Around it was a dumping ground for knapsacks, duffels, and various equipment. The room smelled of dried sweat, rotting carpet, and Dinty Moore Beef Stew.

Keith continued into the small attached kitchen. A short counter with a sink and stovetop was shoved against the far wall, three cupboards above. A microwave and coffee maker commanded most of the real estate. In front of the kitchen there was a pocked wooden table surrounded by four chairs of different makes and models. One of the table legs was duct-taped together, a casualty of Rowdy Rick and a Ranger landing on top of it during a wrestling match.

Keith made himself eggs, toast, and coffee, then sat down and picked up an old newspaper left on the table. He was alone, everyone else sleeping the day away—operators worked primarily at night.

I was thinking we should stay friends after BUD/S… He'd said this to Justice while standing on top of a snow-covered mountain with her.

What a joke.

He'd come solidly out of the Friend Zone with Justice Hayes on the day she sat in front of him in the officers' barracks with her scraped elbows propped on a dinette table and her T-shirt lifted in back.

It was the first time he'd seen her bare body—only her *back*, yeah, but, *fuck*. She had the type of figure that was in all respects constructed to take a starring role in his wet dreams—which it'd started doing after that day.

Later, seeing her on top of a snowy hill at Mountain High with her hair in a ponytail—a mere *ponytail*—he just about uncorked.

Dammit.

Damn *her.*

Damn you, *you stupid shit, for never telling her how you really felt.*

Would she have come to him after SERE if he'd been more open?

The question circled him like a shark.

Lots of *what-ifs* and *if-onlys*.

If only he'd told her…

But how could he? She'd hamstringed him in that regard by taking such a strict stance about being treated like just another candidate. She gave him no choice but to keep their interactions professional.

So he had.

While he was her boat team leader.

BUD/S graduation was supposed to have opened up all kinds of other possibilities.

Like the two of them getting together and having lots of sex…

Shit.

Jerking to his feet, he crossed to the sink and washed his dishes, leaving them to dry in the strainer. He headed to the bathroom, and after he took care of that need, he whacked off. Then he returned to his rack, hauled on a set of workout clothes, and went to the mini gym to lift weights. Afterward, he ate lunch, took off on a run, then hopped in the shower, considered whacking off again, went ahead with it, and finally made his way to the kitchen.

He scanned the cupboards for dinner options and pulled out a can of chili con carne.

By now the others were up.

Foxtrot and the Rangers were still in the field, but Digger and Nickelson were playing cards in the general living area, and Rick was crunching cereal at the kitchen table.

Hunched over his bowl, Rick was eyeballing Keith as if any second he expected his fearless leader to take a stand on top of the table and make an announcement to the room.

Okay, guys, I really actually have a lot of mush in my chest because I'm in love with that well-built chick, and I want to fuck her so-so bad, like, forshizzle, my poor balls and stuff.

Rick licked milk off his upper lip. Patience was everything here. Such a break in manly SEAL-ness was sure to come—it was only a matter of waiting for it.

Life, and the people in it, were nothing if not Rowdy Rick's playground.

"Tasker just came in," the lieutenant commander in charge of in-country SpecOps said as he strode into the kitchen.

Two guys from Team Five's Romeo squad were trailing him.

The commander, a competent man, last name of Diako, was holding a piece of paper in one hand and making a gather-'round gesture with the other.

Nickelson and Digger came in from the general living area, and the Romeo guys joined the group.

One was Giddiup, a late addition to Keith's boat team back in their BUD/S days, who'd never shaken off a bizarre hitch in his step. But since he managed to go wherever he was needed—fast—no one gave him shit about it beyond the nickname.

Second man was Bigfoot, a third-tour veteran whose

boot size was, yes, astoundingly large, but so was the rest of the man; six-six, broad as a semi, and hairy as his call sign implied. When Bigfoot first arrived in Korea—three months after Whiskey—he'd vowed to grow his beard long enough to tuck into his belt. He'd been well on his way...until Diako snipped it off while strolling by one evening.

Was it mentioned the commander had fast hands?

Bigfoot walloped Diako in the shoulder for the unsolicited barber action.

Diako hit Bigfoot back.

The next day Bigfoot resumed growing his beard.

Typical Team Guy way of communicating, even between officers and enlisted. All SEALs grunted, sweated, and fought together within a close-knit brotherhood, regardless of rank. So even though certain traditions of respect were observed in the Teams, officer-enlisted relations were mostly different among SEALs than in the regular Navy.

Still...might be better if they all played more cards whenever they weren't on patrol.

Diako checked in with his paper as he said, "Last night the in-country Missus unit extracted intel off a computer inside a North Korean uranium bunker. Analysis of the data unearthed a missile silo hidden in the hills of North Korea, about ten miles from Echo Outpost."

Diako glanced up. "This is the first time pencil-pushers at base have heard about it, so there are a lot of knotted-up skivvies right now. Missus is scheduled to go in and neutralize the situation, but considering the firefight that went down last night—plus the discovery of a new North Korean special forces unit—base wants SEAL backup." Diako nodded at the men in the room. "Whiskey's fast-action plus Bigfoot and Giddiup will be coordinating with Missus."

"What?" Bigfoot sneered. "With that gash?"

"Hey, man, no worries, Justice is great." Giddiup jumped right in to defend her. "Knight'll tell you. Me and him went through BUD/S with her. She's... You gotta..." He chuckled. "You just gotta see her."

"She could crack you between her thighs like you were no more than a swizzle stick." Rick sucked on his spoon and gazed off into space, probably imagining the joys of that.

Bigfoot snorted. "A real diesel type, huh?"

Rick popped the spoon out. "Nope."

Bigfoot looked between Keith and Giddiup. "Anyone ever tag her?"

Rick blinked winningly at Keith.

Keith put the can of chili con carne back in the cabinet. Any break in expression might give away how the thought of seeing Justice again was just about wrenching his heart down through his stomach.

"Nah." Giddiup shook his head. "She was nothing like that to us. I mean..." He frowned. "A rumor once flew around about her and another officer, but"—he glanced at Keith—"it wasn't true, was it?"

"No."

"Maybe," Diako cut in, "you assholes can knock off the Oprah grab-ass and get to work. This is a Level One Operation—enough missiles are at the new silo to meet the criteria of a first-strike threat. A Black Hawk is spinning up now to take you six to the *Bonhomme Richard* for a full briefing. Jock up and move your fucking asses."

CHAPTER FORTY-NINE

JUSTICE COULDN'T SLEEP.

She tried relaxing her body section by section. She tried meditating. She tried thinking of a blank space.

Nothing worked.

To make matters worse, the *Richard* wasn't exactly a peaceful place, especially during daytime working hours. With nearly two thousand troops onboard, the ship amounted to a small city, and it was never at rest. The floor swayed on a continuous teeter-totter—sometimes gently, other times not—and then there was the constant racket of bootsteps, loudspeakers, clanging bells, talking, pounding, whirring, beeping, and jangling.

Jangling could also best describe the state of her nerves right now.

Last night had been extremely rough...although she didn't know which was worse—taking on gunfire and almost dying trapped in a small woodland.

Or being on the receiving end of a full detonation of Keith Knight's aggressive energy.

Like having a car drive through her chest, that—not altogether the nicest sensation.

She hadn't exactly acted in ways to tame the lion, though. Maybe it was an only-child thing; she'd never tangled with a sibling, so what did she know of backing down? Or maybe—just, you know, maybe—she'd been holding onto as much resentment as he had all this time over his betrayal.

The Betrayal That Was No More—Today's After-School Special…

If she was willing to accept that Admiral Sherwin had outright lied to her about Keith's involvement.

Yeah, and how much of a stretch would that be, really?

From the start at CIA headquarters, Sherwin had made it more than obvious he didn't want the stink of her odoriferous ovaries anywhere near his precious SOF warriors.

So come SERE—when she was still around—the admiral had baldly tried to scare her off with a "fake" rape.

When that didn't work…

Why wouldn't Sherwin have sunk to a new low?

Thinking about it, Justice could totally see Sherwin calling Keith into his office for some bullshit reason just so Keith would be leaving at the same time she was arriving. That way she'd be susceptible to his lies.

Maybe if she'd been more like herself after SERE, Sherwin's con wouldn't have so successfully planted seeds of doubt in her. Except…

Except there was also reality to contend with—Keith was the only person who knew about her arrest record.

And that raised another question.

How could Sherwin have known Keith knew?

She opened her eyes and stared at the ceiling.

Forcing herself to replay every detail of that sordid episode, she heard Sherwin's words ring through her mind as clearly as if he'd spoken them yesterday.

Petty Officer Knight was reluctant, but in the end realized you were on your way to getting booted anyway, so he made the intelligent, career-saving choice…

Right after Sherwin spoke this, he'd observed her for a reaction.

She remembered feeling the blood leave her cheeks.

She groaned softly. *Crap.* She'd fallen for the oldest trick in the book. Sherwin had only been making an educated guess about Keith, probably figuring Justice had told someone about her record. Her boat team leader would be the most logical choice. The admiral threw out the guess to see if it would stick.

And she confirmed it with her reaction.

The fuck if I know how the douche found out.

So she'd come full circle, back to *if not Keith, then who?*

Her stateroom door eased open with a small *squeak.*

Justice rolled over and peered past a slit in her bed curtains.

A pair of green eyes were peeking at her through a crack in the doorjamb.

"Oh, hey, you're awake." Her roommate, First Lieutenant Tiffany Tesarik, opened the door all the way, revealing Pete and Willie in the corridor behind her.

Justice pushed up on an elbow. "What's up?"

"I was wondering, if, ah…" Tiffany grimaced sheepishly. "Would it be okay if Willie crashed in here on my bunk?"

Justice glanced over Tiffany's shoulder at Willie.

Willie rolled his eyes, aiming the end part of the roll at Pete behind him.

Ah.

Pete and Tiffany wanted some private time together in Pete and Willie's stateroom.

Justice sat up and slid down from her top bunk. "Just let me change into my uniform, and I'll go to the wardroom."

"Oh, no." Tiffany's brow crinkled. "I don't want to kick you out. I just thought…I mean…since you and Willie would be *sleeping*, I didn't think, you know, it would be a big deal to have him on the bottom bunk."

Yeah, and Captain Cardoso would surely be perfectly

fine with that arrangement.

"It's okay," Justice said. "I'm too spooled up to sleep anyway."

"But I…" The crinkles on Tiffany's forehead lengthened. "I don't want to…to inconvenience you or…"

Pete took Tiffany by the arm. "They can work it out on their own, Tiff. Come on." He trotted her off.

Five minutes later, Justice was changed out of the cotton sweatpants and T-shirt she wore to bed and into her Special Missions uniform: black boots and T-shirt and black-and-gray camos.

Plopping down in a cushioned chair in the wardroom's lounge area, she clicked on the TV.

True Lies was playing.

What was it with military men and Arnie flicks?

Slouching wearily in her seat, she somewhat watched the movie while her mind wandered to Pete. Underway for a week, and he'd already found a playmate to entertain him on the high seas. No surprise it was Tiffany—he'd been chummy with her ever since Justice rejected him.

That chumminess had perturbed the hell out of her at first, mostly during the period when she still lusted after Pete. But over time, the truth won out. Tiffany was better for Pete—she was wholly delighted and amused by Pete one hundred percent of the time, while Justice's amusement could be counted at about eighty percent. The other twenty percent of the time Pete drove her nuts.

He tried to joke her out of her intense moods when she didn't need that.

What she needed was for a man to help her blow off a head of steam—strap into a parachute and jump from an airplane, hop in a kayak and hit some rapids, throw on climbing gear and scale a sheer cliff.

A man who could go extreme.

Keith and I grew up in Wyoming together doing all kinds of wild-ass sports—nothing was ever hard enough for him…

She closed her eyes.

Great. She was pining after a guy who hated her.

You treated one of your best friends like dogshit…

She slumped deeper in her chair.

At some point she must have dozed off because the blare of the ship's loudspeaker jerked her awake.

"Flight quarters! Flight quarters! All hands man flight quarters!"

Groaning softly, she shifted positions. The order was a common one on a "bird farm" like the *Richard*, and she'd mostly learned to block it out. She got comfortable again and was just drifting off when—

"Lieutenant Hayes?"

She opened her eyes.

Standing in front of her was the *Richard's* Operations Officer, Major Virdel, bald, but working it.

He had a file folder in his hand. "Got a new mission for you." He offered her the folder.

She heaved herself to a better sitting position and took the folder without enthusiasm.

"It's a potential combat op," Virdel elaborated. "So half a dozen SEALs just landed on board as backup."

She sat bolt upright.

IN THE *RICHARD'S* multi-million dollar comm center, Justice studied the terrain of North Korea displayed on the illuminated map board and arranged a thoughtful frown on her face—portrait of a military professional reviewing the more critical points of the op she was about to brief.

While within the blessed secrecy of her internal fantasy world, she was playing out a scene of ripping fistfuls of Keith's hair out during the throes of a spine-breaking orgasm.

When had the stinking bastard grown so good-looking, anyway?

After a year spent trying not to think about the dick— *The Dick Who Was No More: A Lifetime TV Premiere*—she hadn't been prepared for the changes in him.

Same amazing aqua eyes and mouth-watering physique tempted her, but his longer hair emphasized the square shape of his jaw and the masculine thrust of his cheekbones in a way that the BUD/S buzz cut never had.

He wore a beard now, and the facial hair upped his ruggedness into something usually only found on a man who wrestled wild mustangs for a living, ate raw bear paws, and refused to sleep on anything more comfy than a boulder. His vivid power also had a new edge to it. More confidence? A certain lethality?

Washed, combed, and wearing a fresh set of camos, the obnoxious jerk looked even better than he had last night. His eyes, minus the rock-meets-face rage of yesterday, carried a heated intensity now, and every time she found his hot gaze across the lit-up map board, her lower regions went wild.

Good thing female genitalia did these things discreetly. Considering the extreme activity going on down below, she might've ended up rivaling the ship's wailing collision alarm, then everyone in comm would've gotten confused and "braced for impact."

Jesus.

She needed to take a breath.

So she lusted after Keith. *So what?* That was her normal stomping ground—she'd worked on fantasies of jumping Knight's junk all through BUD/S.

What she needed to ask herself was if she felt anything for him beyond lust.

She honestly couldn't tell. Her emotions had been tucked under a robo skin suit for so long, it was a mystery, trying to figure out what to feel for him or how to process the way they'd ended now that she suspected he didn't betray her after all.

Be sorry? Or still angry? Or feel hurt? Or blank out to nothing?

Actually, a state of nothingness wasn't going to work anymore. She'd tried to blank herself out toward Keith in the Camp Casey Ready Room, but—with him standing right in front of her—that'd been a fail.

How about regret?

You and I bled, sweated, and suffered together for six hell-filled months, then you left without even a goodbye.

Yeah. There was a lot of regret.

If she hadn't been drowning in a cesspool of anger and hurt at the end of BUD/S, maybe she would've talked to Keith before she left for crypto school, saved them both from an extremely fucked year.

But sometimes pain led a woman's boots where it would, and all other paths be damned.

It didn't bear thinking about anymore.

Planting her boots wide, she swept her focus over the Team Guys she'd met on last night's rescue.

Guy who was clean-cut as a British crew captain.

Guy who liked to do stare-a-thons.

Guy with a face like an elf.

Then she welcomed the new arrivals: Giddiup—*hey!*—and Bigfoot. One look summed him up: a misogynist, born and bred.

She commenced the operational brief.

Generally lengthy and intricate, the main points of the brief for Operation Urgent Fury were there: their target missile silo was brand new, and, with construction still underway, the computers in control of the missile launch codes were still located above ground—specifically on the top floor of a four-story building.

The first floor of this building was a guardroom housing five sentries. A shift change occurred every morning and evening at seven thirty. Prior to the changeover, the outgoing guards did a final circuit of the grounds, including all of the twelve-foot-high stone perimeter wall, as well as the underground silos. The cycle took between fifteen and twenty minutes, and during that time the first-floor guardroom was empty. This provided a window of opportunity for Special Missions to sneak up to the top floor, hack into the computers, and change the launch code sequences.

Voilà! Missiles rendered useless. *Free world continues to sleep peacefully in their beds at night.*

If all went well, the backup SEALs' sole job would be to hold position outside the perimeter watching for trouble, but hopefully doing nothing more than picking nits out of their beards—*pointed look at Bigfoot.* The key to this op was stealth: get in and get out undetected. No sounds. No exposure. No shit-ton of North Korean soldiers chasing after them, guns blazing.

Once Justice's crew reached Mission Accomplished status, they would rally at the preordained ORP, or Operational Readiness Position, rendezvous with the SEALs, then proceed as a group the ten miles back to Echo Outpost. Lieutenant Pete "Bingo" Robbins and crew would extract them from there, dropping the SEALs back at Camp Casey and returning Justice and her guys to the *Richard.*

Then it'll be bye-bye to you again, Petty Officer Knight.

Although maybe this time they could indulge in a Bo-gart-style goodbye, *We'll always have Paris*, and all that.

Except they didn't.

They had a fucked-up post-BUD/S separation, and the thought of another farewell with everything still a mess of macaroni between them was re-enlivening her *what-to-feel-now?* confusion.

Bad timing for emotional havoc.

It was going to make for an interesting mission.

She concluded with, "Any questions?"

"Prowords?" Knight asked. *Procedure words* were a way to communicate in code over the radio.

She hid her surprise behind a moment of silence. Keith was taking point on this?

Bigfoot appeared to be the senior Team Guy. But probably the misogynist refused to work closely with a creature who had no right being out in hot and foreign climes, polluting the battle space with the stench of reproductive pheromones and fishy vaginosis, even if the female in question was just trying to make a contribution to the free world.

No, said female should be barefoot in the kitchen and, when not baking cookies, down on all fours sucking dick.

Justice *did* make a mighty fine batch of snickerdoodles, and her blow jobs were legendary, but Bigfoot could take his mopey attitude and shove it where the sun didn't shine.

"No prowords," Justice answered Keith. "Just one non-verbal signal. If you hear three clicks on comms, it means SOS."

Chapter Fifty

THE FOURTH-STORY ROOM in the guard building was furnished sparsely with a plain modern desk and a high-backed chair. This was set to the right of the main door, nose to the wall. To the left of the door was the only window—and why the desk didn't take advantage of the view was strange.

Glinski seated himself at the desk while Morris moved to the window to keep watch.

Justice stood off Glinski's shoulder.

Light from the computer screen cast a bluish tint over Glinski's features. "Something's wrong," he told her, searching the files.

"No, it's not."

Because, see, statistically speaking, yesterday's goatfuck mission should be protecting them from this one going bad. What was it…a hundred thousand-to-one odds two missions would go wrong right in a row?

Glinski made a few more clicks with the mouse, intent on the screen in front of him, then shook his head. "It's nothing overly obvious—call it a gut thing—but these launch codes aren't right."

Justice bent over and read the string of codes. They looked okay to her, but then she didn't have Glinski's genius. "What's hinky?"

"They're missing chunks of sequence."

She straightened. "They're defective?"

"Yeah."

"So they won't work?"

"Correct. They won't work."

She crooked her brows. "Are you saying that North Korean incompetence has done our job for us?"

Hope springs eternal. All North Koreans in the entire country are IT idiots—hope immediately dashed by Glinski's dubious expression.

"So why have fake codes?" she asked. "Wait." *Fake.* "I think I just answered my own question. They're decoys."

"Maybe, yeah."

"Have you checked all the files? The real codes might be mislabeled."

"I've opened everything on this computer. There aren't any other launch codes."

"Guys," Morris interrupted. "The guards are one-quarter of the way through their perimeter check."

Justice set her hands on her hips and exhaled. They had very little dicking-around time scheduled into this op. "If these codes are decoys, then where are the real ones?"

"Beats me." Glinski shrugged. "Maybe already underground. Maybe intel was wrong."

Always the first to pucker when things went wrong, Morris said, "We need to scrub the op."

Except the job of decommissioning a silo of first-strike missiles sat pretty far beyond the edge of Super Important. "Before we call it quits," she said, "let's do a quick recon of the room. Going with the decoy theory, do you two see anything in here that could hide the codes? Something disguising a flash drive or a disc? Anything."

They glanced around.

On top of the desk there was the one computer, a mouse with a mouse pad, a carved wooden box—empty—and a bamboo pencil holder with two pencils. Glinski confirmed these were real.

"Anything inside the desk?" Justice asked.

Glinski opened the one drawer. "Only a backup wireless mouse." He closed the drawer.

She searched underside surfaces of the desk. Nothing.

"Place is sparse," Glinski commented.

Hmm. Same thing she'd thought—pictureless walls, carpetless floor, careless attitude about the view…almost like this wasn't a real workspace.

Morris took a visual tour of the room. "There's not a lot of square footage to work with."

Justice narrowed her eyes. No, there wasn't. She visually measured the space. The square footage of this room didn't match the total square footage of the fourth floor. "I bet there's a hidden room."

She started knocking softly on the walls.

Morris and Glinski watched her.

Wall to the right of the desk: solid thump.

Wall to the left of the desk: hollow echo.

Glinski's eyes rounded.

"Maybe we're not dead in the water yet," Justice said. "*If* I can find a way in."

"Why not bust in?" Morris spun his M-4 around so the butt of the weapon was aimed threateningly at the hollow-sounding wall.

"That would sort of negate the *covert* part of this covert op."

"Oh, yeah." Morris blushed.

Hurrying back to the desk, Justice picked up the pencil holder, upending it. Nothing else inside. She snatched up the carved box and checked for a false bottom.

Morris returned to his vigilant watch of the grounds.

Glinski kept his hand resting on top of the mouse,

tension showing in the ligaments of—

Justice stilled. "Wait a minute. Let me see that backup mouse."

Opening the desk drawer again, Glinski handed her the second mouse.

She flipped it over. *Yes!* "This is a magnet." She rushed over to the hollow-sounding wall and began to drag the fake mouse along the edges. At the upper right corner, a *snick* sounded.

A sliver of an opening appeared in the wall.

A secret door.

Morris gave her an awestruck look. "How do you always know these things?"

She opened the door the rest of the way, exposing a secondary room. Now *here* was an office, replete with low-pile commercial carpeting, a four-drawer wood filing cabinet, a picture on the wall of the Tree of Life, a cushioned swivel chair in front of a large desk of wood-toned laminate, the top of it hosting a fancy pen, a writing pad, two celadon teacups, a candle with Asian characters on it, and a bonsai plant. The interior smelled like a new car.

A low hum emanated from the computer tower.

She gestured at it. "Do your thing, Ron."

Glinski sprang into action. Plunking his butt down at the new desk, he nudged the mouse. The screen lit.

Thank God. The computer was already booted up, just running at idle.

"Found the codes," he said. "They're the real deal." He inserted a flash drive into the USB port.

"Hey," Morris warned from the outer room. "The guards are over three-quarters of the way done."

Justice and Glinski's eyes connected.

"How long is it going to take to upload the false launch codes?" she asked.

Glinski's Adam's apple bobbed. "More time than we have."

Shit. The ticker had ticked down.

"All right. I'll stick around until the codes finish uploading. You and Charlie go."

Glinski gaped at her. "You can't do that."

"We can't leave a flash drive sticking out of the computer tower. That will also negate the covert part of this covert op."

"So would leaving *you* here," Glinski countered.

"Nobody will see me. Office space like this is only used during normal working hours."

"You *think*."

It was a risk she'd have to take. "I'll sneak out with the morning shift change."

Glinski's mouth fell into a frown. "That's twelve hours from now."

"I know, but I don't have a choice, Ron. These are first-strike missiles." She pushed the speak button on her throat mic. "Whiskey One, Bat Three Actual. We've hit a mission glitch, and are now running behind schedule. We're diverting from the original operational plan. Glinski and Morris are exiting now. I'll leave with the next shift change."

Keith's voice sounded in her earpiece. "Repeat last, Bat Three."

She sighed. "Did you really not hear me?"

Pause. "Recommend aborting."

"Negative. This is the only way to complete the mission."

The muted sounds of Korean yibber-yabber floated up from outside in the courtyard area.

Morris careened into the hidden room. "Hey! The guards—"

"Out," she growled. "Both of you. Now!"

The Alpha Dog growl sent Morris shooting off right away.

It took an extra narrow-eyed glare to get Glinski off his ass.

He cursed once but left, worry lines furrowed above the bridge of his nose.

As Glinski and Morris's stealthy footsteps faded down the stairs, Justice shut herself inside the secret room. Darkness enclosed her, broken only by the impersonal whitish glow of the tower. The computer whirred, and four stories down, she heard the rumble of voices.

One batch of guards was turning over with another.

Jesus. Her guys had barely made it out.

She paced the room for a bit, then stopped. Time to make herself comfortable. She had a long wait ahead of her. She unzipped her sleeveless vest—more pockets for the myriad supplies she liked to carry—then sat down next to the desk. Bending her legs, she rested her forearms on top of her knees and pondered her supplies.

She had one energy bar in her fanny pack and a small flask of water in a lower pocket of her pants. That's it. For twelve hours. She would also eventually need to go to the bathroom. *Where?* The bonsai plant? If the bonsai stank of urine when the morning sentries came on duty that would also negate the covert part of this covert op. She would have to hold it.

Wonderful.

The computer stopped whirring.

She plucked out the flash drive and stuck it in her rear pocket.

Leaning back again, she stared at the nothingness. Now what? Napping wasn't a good idea, which meant she'd be staring at nothing for twelve interminable hours.

On any job, you must settle your mind, Justine. Fear makes for slippery fingers.

Yeah? What does skull-crushing boredom make for, Dad? Or bladder bust? She sighed. It was good advice, though. She should practice her meditation or…

Or she could toss aside boredom altogether and go for outright fear.

Because…because, yeah….

Footsteps were heading up the stairs. More than one set.

She shifted her weight forward and listened with focused attention. She *had* to be hearing things. No way was her luck this bad.

Her throat muscles spasmed.

Those were footsteps, all right, clear and purposeful.

She double-checked the room through the shadows, confirming that the only place to hide was under the desk. Not optimal—the open part of the desk faced the door. Good chance she'd be spotted if the guards came in here, and then she'd have to initiate combat with them from a wedged-in position.

Combat…

She kneaded her brow, her fingerless gloves lightly chafing her skin.

The Special Missions units are noncombative. Ideally, they will only be sent into cleared areas.

Why did this issue keep coming up, Mr. Dawson?

But, hey, maybe the top floor wasn't the guards' destination.

Voices grew louder…

Or maybe up here was exactly where they were headed.

Her belly cramped, and icy barbs ran up and down her spine. She brushed her fingers over the Sig Sauer strapped to her side. It was getting pretty old, tackling the moral dilemma that went along with enemy capture for her.

She checked her breathing, keeping her lungs functioning at a normal, steady pace.

"Whiskey One?" she said quietly, pressing her speak button.

"Solid copy," Keith came back. "What's your status, Three?"

"I…I wish…" She trailed off. *I wish things hadn't ended the way they did between us. I wish we had time to figure out what we might've meant to each other. I wish I'd been given the chance to get to know you better—all of you.*

She felt a catch in her chest.

Dying utterances were such a cliché.

"Justice." Keith made her name a calm and firm statement. "What's going on?"

"I just wanted to tell you to remind me never to try my luck at Vegas. Okay?" She licked her lips. "Because I don't have any."

North Korean chatter entered the outer room.

Her heart jumped into a few arrhythmic beats.

Coming to her feet, she yanked her KA-BAR out of its sheath.

Seemed like the only way to avoid dying utterances was not to die.

The secret door went *snick*.

CHAPTER FIFTY-ONE

TWO NORTH KOREAN guardsmen entered the room, and Justice lunged at the first man to step inside, jabbing her knife into his carotid.

Tip first.

Straight on.

In-out. Squeegee sound. *Yuck.*

Blood gouted from his artery in a pressurized jet, splattering the wall, the carpet...her face. She ducked under the red stream and came up kicking the second guard in the stomach. The blow hurled him back through the secret doorway into the outer room. He landed flat on his back with a *thud*, gasping.

Adrenaline at full pump, Justice scrambled on top of him, setting the tip of her knife at his jugular and—

A pair of wide, terror-filled eyes stared up at her.

Not Haunted House terror.

Brain stem terror.

She froze.

Moment of truth time—could she kill an enemy while staring into his eyes? Eyes that belonged to someone's son...maybe someone's brother or husband...

She didn't move.

The man underneath her writhed and bucked, knocking the knife out of her hand.

Her KA-BAR skidded across the room.

Well, now don't you feel extra-stupid?

She crawled after her weapon.

Her adversary tottered to his feet and let out a eardrum-piercing war bellow.

Shouts of alarm erupted from the first floor guardroom.

Fuck!

With the hue and cry now raised, she gave up on her knife and sprinted for the window. *I'm outta here, you piece of shit.* Yanking an egress hook off her belt, she quickly attached a long length of rope to the hook and—

Her adversary abruptly shut up.

She glanced at him.

He was scowling at her open vest, clearly taking umbrage with being brought down by the owner of breasts instead of a fellow testicle-bearer. Why this was the case was a mystery to her.

If she was a lightweight, okay, maybe…although she knew some kickass petite women. But she topped this guard by three inches and probably outweighed him by ten pounds.

Still.

He was insulted down to the core of his male ego.

Brows bunching into a spikey scowl, he charged her.

The thanks I get for sparing your life.

She swung her egress hook at him. The claws embedded near his left ear and ripped half his face off as it tore free.

He shrieked in falsetto.

Now, see, *that* noise could be considered an embarrassment to his manhood…although the injury was extremely shriek-deserving.

Jamming the bloody claw into the underside of the sill, she leapt out the window and whizzed down the rope so fast her fingerless gloves smoked.

Her heartbeat thundering in her ears, she landed soundly, then whirled around, and—

Wham!

She rebounded off a man's solid chest. "Holy shit," she gasped, stumbling backward, losing her footing.

The man's hand shot out, grabbing a fistful of her vest to keep her from falling over.

Keith Knight.

"What the hell are you doing here?" She'd never sent him the SOS signal.

Luke Skywalker to Princess Leia in her Death Star detention cell: *I'm here to rescue you!*

Okay, yes. It was clearly that.

Gunfire roared.

A firefight between the other SEALs and the silo guards had started near the front gate.

"Come on!" Keith seized her arm and hauled her into a run toward the rear wall. "We'll have to exfil out the back."

"Glinski and Morris okay?" she asked breathlessly.

"We got 'em."

Three North Korean guards ran after them, rifles raised.

Keith spun around, running backward while raking them down with his M-4, one-handed.

Well, damn… Where was this guy earlier when she'd needed him in the secret room?

She and Keith pounded up to the back gate, panting.

"I'll have to pick the lock again," she said.

"No time."

Two more guards were coming for them.

Wresting her out of her vest, Keith flung the garment over the triple layer of barbed wire topping the stone wall.

She intertwined her fingers into a makeshift stirrup. "You first, then pull me up." She didn't have the upper-body strength to offer Keith the same favor. His current weight probably sat somewhere between a pregnant moose and a titanium boulder.

Keith stepped into her hands, vaulted to the top of the wall, then spun around, lying belly-down over the vest-covered barbed wire. He reached down for her.

She jumped up and grasped his hands, wall-walking up to—

Rat-a-tat-tat.

The wall exploded around her from a rain of bullets, a few pieces of stone flinging into her bare arms.

She grated a breath—*ouch!*—and increased her rate of ascent.

Clambering over the wall at full-tilt, she flew off the top and hit the ground in a hard roll.

Flopping to a stop, she caught back a moan and stared blankly at the sky. Stars twinkled before her vision...from inside her head or up in the galaxy, she couldn't entirely tell.

Keith hopped off the wall, yanking her vest down with him. It came off the barbed wire with a *riiiip.*

Korean shouting arrived at the spot where they'd just escaped.

One beat. Two.

A grenade soared over the wall.

It hit the ground near Justice with a dull *thud.*

She bug-eyed it.

Keith rushed her, jerking her up by the scruff of her T-shirt and urging her along, *fast.*

The grenade went off—*wa-boom!*—and the pressure wave lifted her into the air. Her boots did a little twinkle-toes number across the ground before she landed back on earth in a spin-out of limbs. She blinked up at the swirling stars again.

Not a good night for her health and well being, this night.

Keith scrambled over to her, his brows down. "You okay?"

A red neon bonfire had been lit on her right side. Maybe she should tell him how bad off she really was.

Don't try to be Superwoman…

Except they'd lost this sort of intimacy long ago.

She opted for being a duck. "I'm good."

He helped her to her feet.

Pea-soup waves of green passed over her eyes.

Keith handed over her vest. Hunks of fabric had been torn off, creating several air vents. She put it on and zipped it up.

Keith radioed his men, ordering them to bypass the ORP and go directly to Echo Outpost, then RTB from there. Keith and Lieutenant Hayes would arrive later and exfil via a different bird—the back route they now had to take would tack on a couple of extra miles to their journey.

Goody for her.

They took off together, settling into a steady jog.

Justice was semi-okay at first, but under the relentless passing of miles, the world became a runny ocean of pain. The ground turned gooey beneath her boots. Pinecones on branches sagged into lumpy mashed potatoes. The churn of wind, the annoyed call of a disturbed loon, the occasional scattering thump of deer hooves—all the night noises sounded as if they were accompanied by a whoosh of sea noise, like everything was passing through a conch shell into her ears.

Fighting dizziness, she had to slow her pace twice.

Both times, Keith checked on her, but the darkness hid her face, the strained—surely bloodless—nature of it, and the bout of sweating going on, reminiscent of her BUD/S days.

By the time she and Keith finally reached a dingy shack embedded in some woodland, she felt too lousy to hide her lousiness anymore.

She staggered the last few feet to the door.

"What's up with you, Justice?" Keith shoved open the door. "You used to run circles around us at BUD/S."

She wobbled inside and immediately propped her shoulder against a wall. Her breathing sounded like it was coming out of a broken respirator. "Yeah, well…"

Keith clicked on a nearby hanging lantern and got his first good look at her. He exhaled sharply.

With a weak curve of her mouth, she let her weighted eyelids sink shut. "At BUD/S I wasn't running after I'd been shot."

CHAPTER FIFTY-TWO

KEITH'S TORSO WENT loose. He saw it now.

Blood.

It covered Justice from hip to leg to ankle to boot, looking like no more than shiny wetness against her dark clothing. But…

It was definitely blood.

His brain spun out of his skull, his mind reeling back to all the other hurts—Instructor Hill jamming her face in the sand…Brantley Shaw kicking her over during Egyptian push-ups…every man on the Knight boat team leaving her floating in the Pacific Ocean all by herself…Brayden rejecting her.

Justice isn't the right woman for me…

Asshole.

And the worst—that big, longhaired terrorist at SERE hitting her face…pounding away on top of her.

Motherfucker had deserved some serious payback for that. So one Friday after SQT, Keith grabbed Dog Bone and Ziegler as backup and drove out to Warner Springs. Seething in his car outside the Navy Remote Training Site's front gate, he waited for the motherfucker to drive out. But when the guy finally did, he was in a Honda Odyssey—a fucking *family* car.

Keith couldn't bring himself to thump the SERE instructor.

He left, still seething.

Had seethed for the entire year.

And now here it all was—every wild, raging emotion, exploding out of him.

He snatched up Justice by the upper arms. "How the fuck am I supposed to help you," he growled at her, "if you don't tell me anything?!" He gave her a single shake, his vision blanking over with the sudden image of Ryan, his hockey buddy from high school, bumping lifelessly down a cliff.

Justice's eyes edged open fractionally.

They probably would've widened further if she had the energy.

"We had to get the hell out of Dodge," she said. "There wasn't time for a patch job." She blinked sluggishly. "I'm thirsty," she informed him in a weak tone.

The skin on his face tightened, putting pressure on his cheekbones. "That's from blood loss." He forced himself to check the tension in his shoulders. He inhaled a breath. Oxygen burned going down. *Fix this. Make her better.* "I'll patch you up, then take you to a hospital."

"I don't need a hospital."

He gave her a *don't-argue-with-me* glower.

"It's a through-and-through," she snapped. "I felt the wound earlier."

"Damned lot of blood for a through-and-through." He wrested her shirt out of her pants and bent down, inspecting the wound. Blood was seeping steadily from twin holes on the right side of her waist. Okay, she was right. "Not too bad," he agreed. "The bullet would've passed through your fat if you'd bother to have any."

He took her by one arm—more gently this time—and led her over to the far side of the room. Leaning his M-4 against the wall, he removed his flak jacket, then handed her his canteen.

While she drank, he unrolled a sleeping bag on the floor.

Turning back to her, he reclaimed his canteen and set it down, then unzipped her vest. He flipped it off her shoulders, tugging it down her back—momentarily tugging her against him.

His stomach bottomed out as her breasts bumped his chest. They were the best of both soft and firm. She smelled like trees. With a bitten-off curse, he urged her down on the sleeping bag.

She gingerly settled onto her butt and leaned back against the wall.

He headed off to the pile of supplies, rifling through the contents until he came up with the first aid kit he'd donated earlier. He strode back to her and squatted down, pulling out a square of gauze. "Here." He handed it to her. "You might want to clean off your face. It's covered with blood."

She took the gauze with an unsteady hand. "It's not mine."

"I figured." He searched the kit for more supplies. "You want to tell me about it?"

"I had a job to do," she said simply. "I did it." She wiped her face with the gauze.

It was probably more than that to her, but who was he to probe? He'd say the same thing.

He concentrated on organizing his supplies, laying out antiseptic wipes, bandages, and tape.

She tossed aside her dirty gauze, then swatted a gesture at the first aid kit. "You got any pain meds in there?"

This was a SEAL first aid kit, customized for combat wounds, so, yeah, it came stocked with the big guns of drugs. He found a syrette of morphine. "Lie down," he instructed.

She scooted her rump until she was lying flat on her

back.

He pushed the hem of her T-shirt up enough to expose her wound.

Damn, what a waist. The muscles of her abs were defined, but mostly only visible in their washboard state when she flexed them or was exhaling. Otherwise her belly was an expanse of smooth, satiny skin, calling for lots of touching and kissing and—

His groin tightened.

He was officially a lunatic.

He popped the syrette into her belly, then tore open a packet of antiseptic wipes and started to clean her wound as gently as he could with his tense fingers.

Justice's hand slipped around his wrist.

He jerked his eyes up.

"Good ol' Hero of the Day," she murmured.

Her lashes were fluttering.

The morphine was already taking effect.

"Man of the Hour and all around Hunk-a Chunk-a." She gave him a wistful smile. "That was some rescue at the silo."

Heat surged up his nape. "Was it?" He tried to sound noncommittal.

She lightly fingered his pulse.

It tripped out of rhythm.

"You're such a…" She heaved a sigh. "I've always respected you so much."

Warmth fisted up his heart. *She's in awe of you, Keith.* "Yeah?" He returned to his supplies, arranging them into a neater line. "I respect you back."

"Do you? I've always wanted you to. It's why…it's why I didn't come to you after SERE."

He stilled.

"I thought about coming to you." Her voice took on an

aching note. "I wanted to. But, uh, I was afraid if I did you'd think I was weak or loose or something."

He sat back on his haunches and closed his eyes. Well, there was that question answered. Horribly. He *had* blown it with her by keeping his mouth shut. Because if he'd been more open about his feelings, she never would've worried about what his opinion of her was.

"But then you thought bad about me anyway, so it was wasted effort."

He popped his eyes open. "I did what?"

Her lashes lowered. "You were disappointed in me when you saw me with Brayden."

"The fuck I was." He snatched up the spool of medical tape. "You really need to learn to read me better, Justice. I was *concerned* about you." *And out of my mind with jealousy.* "I thought Brayden was taking advantage of you when you were vulnerable. And just to clarify, I *never* would've lost respect for you if you'd come to me. I was at SERE. I saw what happened to you. I would've done whatever it took to help you." He ripped off a strip of tape with his teeth.

She angled a look at him. "You would've been my cure-all fuck, huh?"

The tape tangled on his fingers. He gave his hand a hard flick to get it off, his fingers *thwapping* together. "A listening ear, a drinking buddy, someone to give you a hug, someone to be your *best* fuck—whatever you needed."

Their eyes connected, and the moment they did, all the bad washed away and left only the good. Everything they'd conquered together: eight-foot waves and endless push-ups and mean-ass shouting and rubbery mess hall burgers and freezing surf torture and the vile dip tank and…and managing to toss out a joke or two or more through it all.

She was a great teammate, the best.

An awesome friend.

The best-matched woman in the world for him.

She fit perfectly into his heart.

He quickly dropped his focus and went back to work, unwrapping four gauze pads and stacking them on top of each other. He set the stack on her wound, then secured the whole thing with fresh tape.

She studied the end result. "Petty Officer Keith Knight," she sang softly, "king of the patch 'em up."

His pulse thudded at the side of his jaw. There she was again, inside his memory, sitting at the officers' dinette table, her shirt up...

Patch 'em up time!

Something caught in his gut. He slowly spread his fingers open on her belly until his palm lay flat on her supple skin.

Flesh made for touching and kissing...

Justice set her own palm on top of the back of his hand, her fingers resting between his.

A knot lodged under his solar plexus. He lifted his chin to search her expression.

A raw look was in her eyes. She was remembering that day too.

"God," she whispered. "It's been such a long fucking year." She lurched to a sitting position.

He started to move back from her, but she took his cheeks between both hands and stopped him, her palms rasping over his beard.

A shudder wracked him.

She slid her fingers over his temples and threaded them into the sides of his hair.

Another shudder, a stronger one.

She urged him toward her.

"Justice," he protested. "You're injured."

She brought him to her lips.

"Justice…" It was a final attempt at a protest and mostly half-assed. After the *long fucking year*, there wasn't much left in him able to stop forward momentum.

When she kissed him, he let her.

No—he kissed her back, and not with the usual teasing explorations of a first kiss…discovering a new mouth, growing to know it, then coming to own it.

None of it.

He couldn't.

Not after wanting this woman so much and for too long.

He latched onto her lips with hard possession and plunged his tongue aggressively inside her mouth, slashing and demanding and consuming and…

He growled.

Doing battle with him right now was a dangerous occupation, but she was going full-bore with her usual *in-your-face* style, meeting him stroke for stroke—pushing his tongue away, then coaxing it nearer, then fighting it off again.

His cock rose up thick and rigid against his camos. His muscles loaded with energy.

Justice exhaled breathlessly against his mouth. "I need you *now*, Keith. Be my best fuck."

Control evaporated.

That fast.

In one brainless instant.

Tipping her back onto the sleeping bag, he reared between her parted knees and went straight for his zipper.

She tugged off a combat boot and flung it aside.

Clump.

He worked his camos off with one hand while fumbling at her pants with the other, making a mess out of undressing her. He only managed to remove one leg from her pants before he saw her bare sex—wet and glistening, pink lips nestled within a soft triangle of curls. *God, yes.* She kept herself natural.

He lost it.

She was naked enough.

In the next second, he was on her.

Get inside you… Now.

Yesterday. A year ago. Always.

With a heave of his entire body, he thrust into her, and a jolting spike of excitement went through his belly. A groan wrenched out of his throat. He should've known this woman would be as tight on the inside as she was on the outside. His remaining brain waves jammed up.

He levered onto straight arms and started to pump his hips, hard and fast.

Justice gasped and dug her fingers into his butt.

The tendons at the base of his neck throbbed as the instant, massive friction slammed pleasure into him like a body blow. Fisting his hands into the sleeping bag, he closed his eyes, letting it all boil out of him—everything he'd felt for her from their first handshake at BUD/S till now. Maybe his internal warrior also unleashed because suddenly he was plunging into her body with wild, pistoning force, with all the power inside him…with an insatiable need to claim her.

The sleeping bag bunched beneath them.

The shack filled with the rhythm of his grunts and Justice's low cries of pleasure.

She was everything—soft, wet, tender, tight, forceful, welcoming, strong… The ecstasy of being inside this woman who'd been out of his reach for a year became too much. A coil of climatic anticipation built at the base of his cock. Sweat flooded off his brow.

Too much…

The anger, the regret, the passion, the fun, the laughs,

the craving over the past year…it all coalesced into a single ball and gathered strength…energy…size…and finally burst into the rapture of an orgasm. *Dammit*, Justice hadn't come yet…

But then she did.

Her hips rose to meet his in a take-charge claiming of her own orgasm, and her sex became a wet, flexing muscle around his cock. He felt his balls pull in. His back muscles went rigid. Ecstasy streamed from his pelvis to every compass point in his body. He clutched Justice's shoulders, shouting raggedly, the edges of his vision partially closing off.

With a final shudder, he collapsed on top of her, gulping for oxygen, his heart roaring like thunder. He sucked in breath after breath.

The wait is finally over…here she is…I have her now…

But the mind-blowing aftermath was short-lived—some part of his brain heard footsteps approaching.

In a blink, he was rolling off Justice…tugging his pants up and springing to his feet…buttoning and zipping and snatching his M-4 off the wall.

He planted his legs wide for balance, braced the weapon against his shoulder, and aimed at the door.

The man who entered also carried an M-4. The moment he stepped inside, he put his free hand up in a gesture of *Whoa, man, hey, it's only me!*

Rick Sickmeir.

Keith swallowed down two breaths.

Rick pointed his thumb in the direction of the door behind him. "We came to get you."

Now Keith heard the distant, muffled *thump-thump-thump* of a helicopter. "Christ." Stepping out of his shooter stance, he lowered the barrel of his rifle. "Am I glad to see you."

Rick's mouth curled into a serene smile. "Are you?"

Keith's nape heated. He somehow resisted the urge to tuck in his shirttails and smooth down his hand-ravaged hair. "Yes, dammit. Justice has been shot." He stepped sideways to reveal a better view of her.

Rick's eyebrows eased up—*Justice, huh? Not Lieutenant Hayes?* He strolled over, checking out the open first aid kit, its contents knocked into a jumble, and Justice's boot, still strewn aside, looking guilty.

Justice had managed to pull up her pants—they were zipped, but not buttoned—and her T-shirt was tucked in, although her black dog tags were flopped out in front. Her bun, which Keith had known to endure flood, famine, and pestilence, lolled at the side of her neck in a half-knot.

Rick rolled his lower lip out at her.

Justice cocked her head. "Does Santa know you're out past curfew?" Then she followed the lean of her head and toppled into a faint.

CHAPTER FIFTY-THREE

Camp Casey Medical Clinic

KEITH SET HIS palm on the exam room door and gave the back of his hand a long stare. Lots of shit he could do well with his hands—shoot a weapon, build a house, fix a car, punch a face, gut a fish, pet a dog. It was his damned mouth he was having trouble putting in working order.

Be nice if he could produce some words with it.

Good words.

The right words.

He was a performer, not a talker, yeah, but even *he* should be handling things better with Justice than he had been so far. Growling, yelling, threatening, and criticizing weren't going to convince the woman he loved to love him back. Oh, and let's not forget the hard-fuck he could now throw onto the pile of ways he'd been bungling everything.

His endgame totally blew chunks.

He needed to stop blowing chunks.

He pushed inside the room.

Justice was sitting up on an exam table watching television. Onscreen a Korean newscaster talked in rapid-fire indecipherable. Justice was in a hospital gown, with an IV line trailing out of her left wrist, and her bun was still squashed to the side of her neck. Besides those things, she seemed good.

All things considered.

Hitching his backpack higher on his shoulder, he strode

up to her bed.

She clicked off the TV.

"So…" He grinned. "Where did Becky go during the bombing?"

The edges of Justice's mouth tipped up. "Uh-oh."

He widened his grin. "Everywhere."

She made a *hmm* noise. "You joke to release tension."

"Naw. What do I have to be tense about? I just berserker-fucked an officer in a military outpost where we could've been caught at any moment—almost were—all the while showing little to no regard for her gunshot wound. That wasn't piss-poor headwork at all."

She considered him. "Don't forget the lack of protection."

He breathed heavily down his nose.

"Diseases and pregnancy…these things don't bother you?"

Oh, good. This was starting out really well. "Obviously I was out of my mind."

She scratched behind her bun. "Well, I didn't say anything either."

"At least you have the morphine to blame."

She waved that away. "I was feeling no pain, Keith, not minus my decision-making faculties."

"Okay." He waited. "Then how are we assessing what happened at Echo?"

She picked at the tape securing her IV needle.

Shit. "Regret? Big mistake?" *Kill me now.*

"No. I've wanted to fuck you for a long time."

Heat shot up his neck, then slinked back down. *That's it? Just fuck him?*

"Do *you* regret it?" she asked.

"Only if I hurt you."

"You didn't, but…"

His stomach slipped sideways. "But what?"

"I'm just wondering if that berserker-fuck might've been overlaid with some lingering anger."

He jerked his chin in. "What?"

"For my walkout a year ago."

"Absolutely not," he returned. "That was pure lust, not some kind of...of punishment." He was going to throw a fucking party on the day she finally learned how to read him correctly. "Look, I understand now why you left BUD/S the way you did. If I *had* betrayed you in the way you thought, then I would've deserved it. I just..." He traced the ball of his thumb along one side of his mouth. "Someday, I'd like to understand why you didn't trust me not to screw you over."

A tinge of pink touched her cheeks. "Here's the SparkNotes version: I don't know you—not really."

He stared at her for an astounded beat. "How can you say that after everything we went through?"

"You mean surf torture and Log PT and IAD drills? I know what it's like to perform with you, Keith, or learn from you, but I don't know anything meaningful about you. Oh, wait. Yes, I do. I know that when you were growing up in Wyoming, nothing was ever hard enough for you. It's why you joined the SEALs—for the challenge. When you were fifteen, you got in a rock climbing accident, and one of your friends died. You blame yourself."

Oh, Christ. He took a noisy step backward.

"But I know those things from *Brayden*. Not you."

A testy burn of defensiveness rode up his throat. "Maybe that's because you and Brayden got to spend downtime chatting it up on a deck with a fucking ocean view. You and I were never alone together. So tell me exactly when were we supposed to have all these magical, meaningful conversations? When we were up-chucking between Log PT and surf torture or sweating our balls off on the way to IAD drills?"

"We were alone on top of that hill at Mountain High," she pointed out. "And you used the time to quiz me about everything I could *do*: whitewater rafting and camping and skydiving and—"

"I was trying to make a point," he cut back in, curling his hands into loose fists. "To show you how well-matched we are." They'd also had a personal conversation about her Uncle Alistair, which she wasn't giving him any credit for— but the hell if he was going to remind her about it. That convo was the reason she thought he'd narked on her about her arrest record.

She turned toward her IV bag and watched it. "It's just…" *Drip…drip…drip.* The bag was almost empty. "I think for two people to work well together, at least one person in the pair needs to be a good communicator— someone has to *press* sometimes." She looked at him again. "I'm not sure either of us is good at that."

A cold lump settled in the pit of his stomach.

Some vehicle with a squeaky wheel rolled by out in the hall.

Eee-throp-throp. Eee-throp-throp.

Maybe it had a fucking flat too.

"At Echo," Justice went on quietly, "you saw blood on my face. You knew the missile silo op had gone wrong, but you didn't press."

"I *asked* you if you wanted to tell me about it."

"And I gave you a trite answer. There was a chance for something deeper between us, but I brushed it aside, and you let me."

He fought not to squeeze his eyes shut. She was giving him one rat fuck of a headache. "I didn't press because I figured you're like me—you'll talk when you're ready."

"I *am* like you. And that's the problem."

He pushed air between his teeth.

"Tell me something about yourself. Your faults? A fear?"

Thorns stung the back of his neck. Nothing like having your back shoved up against a wall during one of life's more unstable moments. "I don't operate that way," he retorted. "Shit happens. I deal with it. I move on. Women need to talk. Fine. But men work out their own problems. Don't jam me somewhere I don't belong, Justice."

After a moment, one of her hands lifted off the exam table in a hopeless gesture. "How can I connect with you if you don't give me anything to connect to?" Turmoil surged like dark groundswell into the depths of her gaze.

The room shrank.

He flexed the muscles in his face.

A female corpsman wearing field utilities entered and strode to Justice's IV stand. "I see you've finished your fluids, Lieutenant Hayes." The corpsman unhooked the wrinkled plastic bag from the standing pole. "How are you feeling?"

"Like I want to get out of here."

Keith chewed his teeth together. Maybe that would somehow masticate the lump at the back of his mouth down to a more manageable size. "Here." He plunked his backpack down on the bed. "I brought you a clean set of camos."

The corpsman started to remove the IV needle from Justice's arm. "Actually, Lieutenant Hayes's own gear just arrived from her ship."

Justice frowned at the corpsman. "Why would the *Richard* send over my gear?"

CHAPTER FIFTY-FOUR

JUSTICE STOMPED UP the C-130's loading ramp, her mood sitting somewhere between grumpy and vile. Her bullet wound ached, but other than that *she was fine*. Would anybody listen to her and just let her get back to work?

No.

Because God forbid—

She came to an abrupt halt in the belly of the cargo plane.

Four men occupied the jump seats on the left side of the aircraft.

Whiskey.

Aw, fuck. "What are you doing here?" she demanded.

"Deployment's over," Keith answered evenly. "We're heading back to San Diego."

She set her jaw. The idea of spending a long flight sitting across from the source of her raw glop's rawness was really not a pleasant thought.

She jerked her ire over to Digger, whose favorite habit was still staring at her. "You got something to say to me?"

"Ah, don't take Digger wrong," Mitch Nickelson stepped in, his collar buttoned up to his chin like a boarding school prefect. "You're not even his type. Dig's into ample women."

"Yeah." Digger's teeth flashed. "I like flesh."

Justice snorted. That was something, at least. She marched over to the right side of the plane.

"What are *you* doing here?" Digger asked. Absent his boonie hat today, he was showing off a mop of thick, black hair.

"Navy's sending me stateside for three months to recover from my bullet wound." She slammed her duffel bag down near a jump seat.

"*Three* months?" Nickelson's voice rang with surprise. "I thought it wasn't much more than a bug bite."

"*Thank* you." She made a flip gesture. "But apparently this is standard protocol for all gunshot wounds."

Rick the Elf bulged out his cheek doubtfully.

"Yeah." She snorted. "Standard protocol, my ass." This was SERE aftermath rising up to fuck up her life again. God forbid the Navy should make another misstep with her health and well-being.

She flopped down in the jump seat across from the elf and locked her arms over her chest.

The loading ramp began to crank up.

She started to shut her eyes, paused to throw Keith a *don't-even-think-about-talking-to-me* look, then closed them all the way.

There wasn't anything to talk about, anyway. The two of them were pretty much a lost cause. She wanted things from him he couldn't give, and, honestly, probably vice versa. They would just have to settle for that Bogart-style goodbye when the plane landed.

We'll always have this mess of macaroni…

An hour later, the plane had been humming along nicely, lulling her into thinking she'd escaped any more Big Discussions. Then Keith trod all over her peace with, "Can I talk to you?"

She opened her eyes a slit.

Three hammocks were strung up behind him, gently rocking with the weight of his sleeping teammates.

"No," she answered shortly.

He gestured toward the front of the aircraft. "We can find some privacy up there."

She flattened her lips. Back to the habit he had at BUD/S of ignoring her basic human rights, was he?

Official statement on the record: being ignored was one of her biggest pet peeves. "Remember what I said about it being a long fucking year? I meant it, Keith. I'm sick and tired of the pain." She was beaten down by it. Bludgeoned. Exhausted. A wet tarp.

He planted a hand on the wall just above her head, which put a very delectable bicep in her periphery, and leaned his face close to hers. "You wanted to hear about a fault of mine. How the hell am I supposed to tell you that? I want to *win* you, and confessing my faults doesn't exactly seem like the best way to go about it. Especially..." He edged back, his jaw shifting. "Especially when one of my worst fuckups has to do with you."

"For the love of everything, we don't need to keep covering this ground. I believe you didn't betray me to Sherwin."

"I'm referring to *SERE*." He straightened with a curt motion, his eyes flashing. "I did exactly what I shouldn't have done—I cracked when I saw you hurt. I was supposed to do what Brayden did and stay calm. But I didn't fix things for you that day, and then...when you needed someone, you turned to him."

"I told you why I didn't come to you, and it had nothing to do with anything you did or didn't do that day. Turning to Brayden was also convenient. He was the one who came back in the barracks that night."

"None of that matters." A rough note entered Keith's voice. "It still kicks my ass that you didn't come to *me*."

The pain in his voice and eyes caught her off guard.

She'd never realized how much it meant to him, her seeking him out for help. But then… "I never knew you had feelings for me, Keith."

"I know you didn't. That's because you wanted me to treat you like a professional at BUD/S. So I did. Are you really going to make me pay for giving you exactly what you asked for?"

"No. I appreciate that you honored my request. But our issue is with the *here and now*." She lowered her voice. "You're not sharing yourself with me."

"Yeah, you're probably right—I could stand to talk more." He gestured up front again. "But that's exactly what I'm trying to do."

She paused.

Well, hell.

Coming to her feet, she strode toward the front of the aircraft, passing the toilet on the way.

Keith followed.

She came to a halt next to a stack of crates held in place by nylon netting.

He stood facing her.

They stared at each other. The metal clasps on the nylon netting tinkled.

"I'll start," he said. "Here it is, straight out: I'm crazy about you. I've been trying to tell you that from the beginning, but I keep hosing it up." His lips formed into a droll line. "Little things like fighting and fucking keep getting in the way."

She swallowed hard. *I'm crazy about you.* "And? What does all that mean?"

He raised his brows, like the answer was obvious. "I want a relationship."

"A full-on one? Commitment? Monogamy?"

"Fuckin' A." He braced is legs wider against the shift of

the aircraft. "What about you?"

She stared at him through the shadows, her heart slowly pushing into her throat. Some of the shinier strands of his hair were picking up the dim light, and it reminded her of the morning she'd met him, mustering at dawn next to the pits on day one of First Phase BUD/S—the dark stubble on his head had been glinting under a halo of lamplight. She'd immediately been drawn to how ruggedly handsome he was, and taken a full hit of his vitality and power when she shook his hand. *So the rumors are true…*

You're doing good, Hayes. Just keep working hard like you are. The men will come around.

You're not getting pulled off my team.

Circle of trust here. Total cone of silence.

You go against Hayes, you're not a Team Guy.

Maybe she'd been building toward a total raw-glop takedown for a long time.

Hayes is going to be on your boat team…

The words that had started it all… And now here the Hero of the Day was, wanting to be with her. So why was she standing here like a lump and *questioning* if she wanted him too?

Her heart fell down and hurt.

"Yesterday at Camp Casey medical," Keith went on, "you said you've wanted to fuck me for a long time, but…is that it?"

"No. But I think…" She hesitated. "All along I've wanted you, but the idea of being with you makes me nervous."

His eyebrows dipped into a faint frown.

"You and I are both doers, Keith, and I worry that everything will become about doing with us—and I don't want to be *all* that." Old emotions stirred in her belly, sloshing acid against her esophagus. "Growing up, everything was about performance for me. Crack a safe.

Neutralize an alarm. Scale a building. Whatever tasks my dad put before me. I also watched him run his team through their paces, constantly testing them to make sure they were always up to par. For my whole life, that's what I saw—do or die. And now with you…it's like it's the same. That day at Mountain High, when it seemed like you were auditioning me, it felt like the most important things to you were action-related. And I just…" She scrubbed her index finger across her upper lip. "I need to be wanted for *me.*"

"You don't think I…" Keith looked down, pinched the bridge of his nose briefly, shook his head, then looked back up. "I'm going to tell you something I kind of don't want to say because it's a little embarrassing, but here goes."

She kept her focus on him. He definitely had her attention.

"The Knight boat team struggled during Hell Week while you were away—more than I thought we would, at least. It seemed like sometimes the only thing keeping the guys on track was my threat to make them explain themselves to you if they quit. No one dared. When you were with us, you made us stronger, and not only from being a great athlete—although I give you credit for that— but because…I'm not even sure how you pulled it off. It was just you being *you.*"

Her lips parted. She pressed her mouth closed and rubbed her lips together. That was probably the best thing anyone had ever said to her.

"No auditioning is required with me, Justice. No need to re-prove yourself—I'm already sold. And if you think I'll ever send you packing, like your dad did to your Uncle Alistair, for a mistake or for *any* reason, you're fucking crazy. That's not the kind of man I am."

She drew in a full breath, the expansion of her lungs bumping into a heart that was suddenly huge. No, he wasn't a cut-and-run man, was he? He was solid and dependable Keith Knight.

She *did* know him in a lot of important ways—in all the ways that really mattered.

"And by the way," he went on, "I'm into low-key stuff too. I like to read and watch movies—although I prefer action flicks, yeah, and you should know I'm a big James Bond fan. I also like to eat a good burger and just bullshit about the day."

She tried to imagine what it'd be like to just kick back and be chill with him. A small smile touched her lips. It'd be very cool. "All right. You wanted to know what I'm looking for between us? Here it is. I want monogamy too. Dedication. Sex. Beer and baseball. Picnics. Dinner by firelight. Fishing for trout. Snorkeling in Hawaii. Hand in hand on a beach at sunset. More sex."

A deep chuckle rumbled in his chest. "Christ, woman, you don't need to keep selling what's already sold."

"But there's a catch. I also need to know you, what you're thinking and feeling. I'm not saying you have to gush. Just clue me in."

"I can do that."

The plane went over a bump of turbulence, sending her lurching back against the crates. Keith swayed forward, grasping the netting to keep from crashing into her, but—

He was suddenly very close.

Power and vibrant energy rolled off him...heat rising from desert sand.

Keith's focus lowered to her mouth, and his eyes smoldered. He angled his jaw, moving in for a kiss.

She stopped him with a palm on his chest, glancing at the swaying hammocks.

"A kick to the head is the only thing that'll wake those guys." Keith came forward again, his kiss soft and light, his lips barely touching hers with gentle brushstrokes. His solid pecs skimmed over her breasts, just a touch, but her nipples instantly tightened into erect, shivering peaks.

She pressed closer.

He parted his lips.

She parted hers.

His tongue stole inside her mouth. The silky friction of it caressed her own tongue with teasing hunger.

Her womb contracted around a sultry coil of need. Warmth eddied down her spine and—*damn.*

She nudged him back, sucking in a few short gasps as she tried not to hyperventilate.

Keith's smoky gaze slipped from her wet lips down to her erect nipples.

"Come on, Keith. Guaranteed Santa's elf has a radar for this kind of monkey business." And Rule Number Primo of their relationship was secrecy…unless they were both okay with being court-martialed.

Keith snorted. "Probably accurate."

The airplane jerked beneath their boots as it went over a jarring bump of turbulence. If they'd still been kissing, they would've clacked teeth.

Keith gestured to a couple of jump seats opposite the stack of crates. They moved over to them, sat, and strapped in.

The walls vibrated, the metal clasps on the nylon netting rattled, and the floor shimmied. Behind the closed door of the cockpit, Justice heard muffled voices. A second later the plane started to ascend. The pilots were probably trying to find smoother air.

"What happened on the missile silo op?" Keith asked.

She shot him a look.

His focus was steady on her. "I want to hear about it."

She faced front again, consulting the steel walls, a line of packed parachutes, a temperature gauge, then the toes of her own boots. Her stomach was very cold by the end of the circuit. "I killed a man. Maybe two."

"I didn't hear a gunshot."

"No. I was trying to take care of it quietly, so I...I stabbed the first guy in the throat." She felt a trembling in her chest. "I should've killed the second guard right away, but..." She looked at Keith. "I couldn't. I froze. It's a miracle I didn't die—I probably would have if I hadn't escaped out the window so quickly."

"Fear lock you up?"

"No, it wasn't that. It was because he was...he was a *man*, you know." She tucked her hands under her legs. "I realize there are bad men in the world, but how do I know if he was one of them?"

"He was trying to kill you."

"And I was trying to kill him back, but *I'm* not a bad person. What if that guy was a good man just doing a job? Like me." Grit filled her mouth. "And I killed him."

Keith exhaled a long breath. "Stock answer is: it's war, it's ugly. Thinking about it too much will mess up your head."

But she couldn't get rid of the images. "How do you deal with it?"

"I figure if a man picks up a weapon, he's fair game. You didn't waste a civilian, Justice. You killed a *soldier*, someone who knew the risks of the job he took."

She rubbed her knuckles under her nose. "Yeah, I guess."

The sound of the plane's engines down-shifted to a softer whir.

"I'm sorry that happened to you. Killing shouldn't be a part of your job on Special Missions—it's not what you signed up for. Next room you go into, I'll make sure I go in with you."

She smiled. "You can't go into every room with me."

"I can try."

As unrealistic as that was, it was also very sweet.

He wrapped his arm around her shoulders and tugged her against his side.

She rested her cheek on his chest and just breathed for a while, letting herself absorb his solid, reliable strength. He smelled good: warm and soapy, a bit like cedar.

He kissed the top of her hair. "We should hang out while you're med down. I'll be taking leave when I get back, so why don't we head out of San Diego, get away together?"

The idea perked her up. "Where? Hawaii?" She'd mentioned snorkeling.

"I actually had someplace else in mind…"

CHAPTER FIFTY-FIVE

Jackson Hole, Wyoming

THE KNIGHT FAMILY home was built in the tradition of a mountain log cabin, although this house was far from a mere cabin, but rather an expansive, two-story structure with sloping roofs and large mullioned windows affording views of some of Wyoming's most stunning countryside.

Fronting the property was a thick grove of pine trees rolling up to uneven peaks along the horizon of the Grand Tetons. Behind the house a good acre of land stretched out, with a barn and a split-rail corral. The sky was the kind of infinite, crystal-clear blue that would've challenged a poet to capture adequately, and the air tasted like it came directly from heaven.

Justice met Keith at the trunk of their rental car and grabbed her bag.

"Nice house," she commented, starting up the walkway with him. "Your dad obviously doesn't do half-bad."

"He manages Jackson Hole Mountain Resort." Keith grinned. "Now if Dad *owned* it, you'd be looking at a mansion right now."

"And you'd probably be a starchy pain in the—"

Three strapping young men exited the house and stopped on the porch.

Keith's brothers. No doubt about it.

To a man, they were attractive and dark-haired, with bodies that looked to have been built through conquests—of rocks, mountains, whitewater rapids. And women. The three stood proudly steroid-free in their virility: buff Wyoming outdoorsmen all, each giving off a vibe of being solid and dependable, like they could withstand anything from a hurricane to a pregnancy scare. There wasn't a black sheep among them.

Justice and Keith slammed to a halt at the same time and cursed, although for different reasons.

"Shit," Justice repeated hers. She wasn't supposed to be meeting family members yet. Her relationship with Keith was too new.

The only reason she'd agreed to come to Wyoming—other than the beauty of the place and all the cool stuff to do in that beauty—was because Keith's parents were out of town.

Granted, he'd made no promises about his three brothers, who all lived *in* town.

The tallest one had to be Walt. According to Keith, Walt, younger by eighteen months, was a ski instructor at several local resorts and partook liberally of the snow bunnies. What was a man to do?

Thad was a sophomore at a local college, studying to be a park ranger, and, oh, what a smile. It was lopsided and boyish and a little shy, and it said that he had no idea just how good-looking he was. Walt's exact opposite.

The youngest, Adam, still had a bit of a wonder-of-the-world aura about him, which he tried to cover with too much cockiness. He was a junior in high school, still living at home, except when his parents went away. During those times he was required to bunk with Walt. A wild party thrown—property damage, sheriff called, etcetera—was behind the mandate.

So Adam wasn't staying in the Knight family home this week.

Which meant Keith and Justice could make all the noise they wanted during sex.

And now Keith repeated his own curse. "Fuck." He'd clearly been planning to start making all that noise as soon as they entered the house. "I'll get rid of them," he told Justice in an undertone.

"Hold on a second." She stopped Keith. "Your brothers are loaded down with climbing gear." She was coming to embrace the idea of meeting them, *if* those three wanted to do something fun. "I've been cooped up for way too much time with medical rigmarole. Let's go out and play."

Impatience edged Keith's jawline. "Over these last three days, you and I haven't been able to see each other at all."

Keith had been checking out on leave—debriefing his deployment and squaring away his gear and weapons—and she'd been…well, mired in the rigmarole.

"Hey, Keith," Thad called out. "Welcome home from deployment."

"Aw, listen," she crooned. "Your brothers want to spend time with you too. Duty to family cannot be ignored."

Keith's eyes narrowed. "Those three would understand my motives for telling them to get lost, believe me."

"Play first," she coaxed, "then fuck. All night, if you want."

His eyes seamed tighter. "*All* night?"

She gave him a silky smile.

"You two ready to hit the cliffs?" Walt held up a bundle of belaying ropes and clasps with a *rattle*.

"Definitely," she called back.

She and Keith strode the rest of the way up the front walk and stopped at the foot of the porch steps.

She waited the requisite two-count while all three masculine eyebrows rocketed sky-high—the Knight men were getting an up-close look at her now—then introduced herself.

"I'm Justice."

"Well, well, what a sight you are," Walt drawled, giving her a bold once-over. "A woman who can finally keep up with us."

It was summertime; she was wearing shorts and a tank top. Walt's inspection lingered places.

"Are you as good as you look?" Walt smirked.

He was rapidly earning himself the nickname Walt the Womanizer.

Maybe she needed to prep her psycho eyes. "I'm an advanced climber, if that's what you're asking."

Walt's expression lit. "Well, hell, let's head over to Blacktail Butte then, climb some five-point-eleven or five-point-twelve courses, make this day interesting."

"We'll go to Rock River Buttress," Keith stated in a tone of authority. "Justice is still recovering from a gunshot wound."

She threw an irked glance at Keith. She'd been hit nearly a week ago, and it was only a through-and-through, not a—

"I'm not a virgin anymore," Adam the Adolescent blurted out.

Keith hovered with one foot on the bottom porch step. He stared at his younger brother for an elongated beat. "Great, Adam," he said dryly. "Thanks for sharing."

Behind Adam, Walt rolled his eyes. "He feels the need to share that several times a day."

"I'm just saying," Adam defended himself. "You guys always think you're the only ones doing stuff…but…you're not." Adam darted a look at Justice.

She maintained a neutral mask. The kid didn't deserve her psycho eyes, but if she smiled, she might put the poor young'un into a terror-lock that lasted into his thirties.

Blushing, Thad cleared his throat. "How's Brayden,

Keith? Did you see him over there?"

"Yeah. His squad relieved mine." Keith continued up the steps. "He's good."

"Two SEALs for brothers." Walt pursed his lips at Justice. "How does a man compete? He probably needs to be really good at—"

Keith whammed his shoulder into Walt's on the way past.

Walt lurched back a step, his face splitting into a grin that said he clearly understood the man-speak: *Watch how you deal with my girlfriend, dickhead.*

Keith opened the door and gestured Justice inside. "I'll show you where you can change."

THE CRAGGY STONE face of Rock River Buttress dropped steeply into a sprawling plain of woodland and rugged boulders, the vista bound by a sparkling blue ribbon of waterway—Rock River itself.

Justice and the four Knight brothers climbed mostly in silence, aware of each other but respecting the individual zone—the headspace a climber drifted into when he or she was one with nature. Only the occasional *pop!* echoed when one of them fixed an anchor with a bolt gun.

Inhaling a deep, invigorating breath of fresh mountain air, Justice took in the scent of pine and almost reached a hand out to touch the clouds. This high up, it felt like she could.

It was one of the best parts of rock climbing, being so close to the sky, and there was nothing better than seeing so much natural beauty from on top of the world.

Slick with sweat, Justice was almost to the crest of the cliff. But—*shit.* She'd veered too far right to avoid running into the four Knights.

Now she was under one of the buttresses this climbing

spot was known for, the outthrust of rock running along the entire top edge of the cliff where she was. To scale it would require her to climb around and over the outcropping, instead of going straight up.

To do that, she would have to dangle midair for a period of time.

Not a pleasant prospect.

Her only other option would be to climb sideways left toward where Keith and his brothers were. But she didn't like climbing sideways, and she'd have to go a fair distance in that mode to get free of the buttress.

Besides, the buttress wasn't impassable, just difficult.

She placed the nose of her bolt gun against the underside of the buttress and—*pop!*—set an anchor. The sound echoed into the vastness of nowhere. Birdsong halted mid-chord, then, after several beats, restarted.

She hooked herself to the anchor, and—against her survival instincts' better judgment—let herself swing clear of the cliff face, her legs doing that midair-dangle thing. A trace of fear skittered down her spine. If her anchor didn't hold, she was toast. That was always the case with an anchor, but it felt like a more dire absolute while floating out in space very, very high above the ground.

Grasping the edge of the outthrust, she gradually hoisted herself up, thanking God for her upper body strength. She set herself belly-down on top, scooted forward, then unhooked from her line and stood.

Good. She'd made it.

Wait… *Not good.*

Bad news, in fact.

She was cut off from the mainland.

This rock formation was shaped into an L. Justice had just climbed up onto the long end of the L—an arm of land stretching out from the main cliff into open space, nothing but steep drops on either side. The short end of the L was the mainland, the flat top of it expanding back for about twenty yards before it hit a trail leading down to the ground.

Climbers scaled up the front but didn't have to climb back down—they could take this path instead.

The Knight brothers were just now topping the short L—straight up, no buttress to contend with—and for Justice to meet up with them, she would have to traverse the length of the long L. Normally, no big deal; the leg wasn't treacherously narrow or anything. Problem was, rock erosion had created a gully in the long leg, cutting it in half.

To get from long to short, she would have to jump the gully, and it was a big jump…maybe not even jumpable.

Setting her hands on her hips, she pulled oxygen steadily into her lungs and analyzed her options. All around the edge of the cliff was buttress. If she didn't jump, she'd have to shimmy back down and around the outthrust, dangling midair again—very unappealing—then make that sideways left-hand climb she hadn't wanted to make in the first place.

Or she could jump the maybe-unjumpable gully.

Jump the gully or tackle the buttress?

Neither was inviting, so…*fuck it.*

She launched into a fast run, her rig *jangling*, her lungs pumping full force, and—

"JUSTICE!" Keith bellowed.

She took flight, soaring over the gully, her heart booming fast and loud. She thrust her chest out, like a runner passing a finish-line tape, and finally landed with a jolt on the opposite side.

She—*ahhh!*

She didn't land true. She teetered with her insteps on the edge of the gully, the weight of her equipment pulling her backward toward a steep, ugly fall—one that would kill her.

Fear dumped adrenaline into her bloodstream. Her lungs bucking, she frantically cycled her arms, the motion sending pain searing through her partially healed bullet wound. Somehow—after several grave, horrible seconds—she managed to propel her weight forward.

Stumbling free of the gully, she staggered along the long leg of the L for a few paces before stopping to brace her hands on her knees. She panted for air.

Holy fuckity shit. That had been close.

She collected herself for two more seconds, then straightened and ran down the long L toward the Knight brothers.

Walt, Thad, and Adam stood clustered in a group, looking sickly.

Keith was charging at her, his brow thunderous.

"I know, I know." She held up a hand. "I should've dropped my rig before jumping."

Keith slammed to a halt in front of her, stopping so close he clacked toecaps with her. His teeth were gnashed, his eyes fierce. He raised tautly curled fingers to a spot near her throat, like he was imagining ripping her to pieces.

"Keith," she began. "I—"

His hands lashed out to seize her arms. "You go climbing with me, *safety* comes first. Always." His hands convulsed into a firmer grip. "Don't you *ever* pull a stunt like that again? Do you fucking hear me?"

She drew in two shallow breaths. "I hear you."

Keith let go of her and stalked off.

Walt, Thad, and Adam shuffled by. None of them seemed able to look at her.

She turned to watch Keith's retreating form, studying his tense shoulders and the rigidly furious lines of his back.

CHAPTER FIFTY-SIX

IF A MOVIE set designer had been directed to come up with a *typical masculine bedroom of a sporty teen*, Keith's childhood bedroom would've fit the bill perfectly. Decorated in basic blues and browns, the room was furnished simply with a double bed, a nightstand, and a floor-to-ceiling bookshelf. The latter was overstuffed with framed pictures of sports teams and other guy friends, plus lots of ice hockey paraphernalia and a staggering number of sports trophies.

Completely blowing Justice's image of Keith, this bedroom was not.

Sitting on the edge of the bed, she scanned the contents of the shelf again. Her focus settled on an ice hockey team pic, and a heavy weight settled around her heart.

The only thing bothering Keith from that day is his conscience. He was leading us on the climb, so he blames himself for what happened…

How had she not seen this before? It was so obvious.

Shit happens. I deal with it. I move on. Men work out their own problems.

Except when a man didn't work it out.

I don't think he's ever gotten over the accident…

No judgment. She wasn't exactly the poster girl for how to deal effectively with pain.

But then sometimes action people needed help working things out.

Keith did now.

The difficult part would be convincing him of that.

She heard the shower turn off in the bathroom down the hall.

Standing, she changed quickly from her climbing clothes into jeans and a plain white T-shirt. She needed a shower too, but it'd have to wait.

She sat down again, this time facing the door.

Keith entered his bedroom, a towel wrapped around his waist, his hair wet but combed. He gave her a dour look. "I'm assuming I shouldn't bother leaving my pants off."

Faced by a towel-clad, very chiseled Keith, it was tempting to put off the unpleasant convo and instead tumble around on the bed having a bunch of hot sex. His powerful chest was lightly dusted with dark hair that forged a path down the steely muscles of his six-pack—no *eight*-pack—to the edge of his towel and parts beyond. Very sexy.

But ignoring emotional demons only worked in the short term.

In the long run demons destroyed.

She'd also like to think she'd learned something since BUD/S. Namely, that running away from problems didn't solve them.

As Confucius liked to say, *Wherever You Go, There You Are.*

"I think we should talk," she said.

His lips curled sardonically. "Exactly what I like to do when I'm naked." But he rammed himself into a pair of Wranglers and jerked on a blue T-shirt.

Staying by the door, he set his hands on his hips. "I really don't know what there is to talk about, Justice. I'm not going to apologize for getting pissed at you. You completely ignored your own safety today." Raw tension crackled from him, his jaw dead-set. "Do you have any idea what it was like for me to watch you almost fall off a fucking cliff?"

No, and she didn't want to know what it would be like to see Keith almost die. "I'm sorry. I didn't mean to put you through that. And you're right—I should've climbed back down instead of jumping the gully. But that's not what I want to talk to you about." She tucked one leg underneath her bottom. "When do you think you first fell in love with me?"

That threw him. His eyebrows inched together. "Why do you want to know?" he asked guardedly.

"I'm curious about something."

He paused another beat. "I can't remember, exactly. It was sort of a process. I was *compelled* by you at first sight, but...probably a lot changed for me the day of Extraction Swim when you asked for help doing the sidestroke in combat boots. You finally let me in that day, and it got to me."

She smiled a little. He'd told a joke to lessen the tension with her boat team, and she remembered being all hero worshipful about him. Maybe something had started for her then too. "What about by our first evolution of surf passage, when I cut my head open? How did you feel about me then?"

"More hardcore."

"And by SERE?"

"A goner."

She nodded. "I think you don't want to lose me."

"It's not a matter of want. I *won't*."

You may not be entirely, completely off base about some overprotectiveness on my part.

And here was the crux of the matter. "I don't want to lose you, either. No one wants to lose someone they care about. But those times when I've been hurt or close to it, it pushes you someplace over the top—surf passage, SERE,

Echo Outpost when you found out I'd been shot…hell, even keeping me out of the middle position during Land Portage. And now today's climb."

He glowered. "You almost *died* today. It's not over the top to get wound up about that."

"I saw the crazy look in your eyes, Keith. You'd lost control."

His mouth hardened.

She pushed to her feet and moved to the bookshelf, picking up the ice hockey team photo she'd focused on earlier. She searched the two rows of jersey-clad players until she found Brayden and Keith in the back row, smooth-cheeked, their features still rounded by youth.

She chuckled. "God, but you and Brayden look so young here." She glanced up. "You made the varsity team your freshman year?"

Keith didn't answer at first, maybe trying to figure where she was headed *now*. "Yes."

"Impressive."

He didn't comment.

"You played a lot of ice hockey."

"It's kind of a big thing around here."

Circling the bed, she strode up to him and angled the photograph in his direction. "Which player is Ryan?"

Keith stiffened.

"Brayden told me the kid who died in your rock climb-ing accident was on the ice hockey team with you. He's in this picture, isn't he?"

Grooves dug into the sides of Keith's mouth. "I see where you're going with this," he said in a restrictive tone. "A friend who I was leading died in a climbing accident years ago; you almost died today during a climb. It's all one big, unhappy, cosmic freak-out, right?" Keith made a rude noise in his throat. "Totally fucking unoriginal."

"Yes," she agreed. "It's very simple." She hugged the photo against her breasts. "Brayden also said you didn't go to Ryan's funeral. Why not?"

Keith's complexion darkened. "I don't want to talk about this."

"I can see that. But sometimes someone has to press, and today that's me. I'm pressing."

"I don't need to be *pressed*," he bit out. "I work out my own shit."

"Except you haven't worked this out."

"Really? I didn't realize you could see inside my head. Now *I'm* impressed." He took a step back from her. Half of him was already out the door; the rest of him was about to follow.

"Go, if you need to," she said in a level tone. "But won't that be post-BUD/S bullcrap for us all over again?"

A tic on his cheek jerked. "What the fuck do you want from me?"

She sat down on the mattress again. "I want you to listen to the difficult stuff I have to say." She ran her fingers along the edge of the frame and steeled herself. Bringing up the memory of her mother's death was going to be the height of no fun, but she didn't see any other way.

She swallowed. "Do you remember on day one of BUD/S when Chief Tanner broadcast to the class that my mother died?"

Keith paused a beat, then gruffly said, "Yes."

She set the team picture on the mattress beside her. "I'm the one who killed her."

Keith stilled.

"She died giving birth to me." A fist pushed cotton wadding into her throat. "She shouldn't have. Her pregnancy was perfect. No prenatal problems at all. But during labor she suffered a placental abruption and ended up bleeding to death. Just, you know, a freak accident."

Keith's eyes closed in an extra-long blink.

"I thought she died in a car accident—that's what my dad told me. I never would've known the truth if I hadn't overheard him arguing with my nanny about it one night. It was…" Her throat grabbed the cotton wadding. "Well, actually, I don't have words for how it felt to discover I killed my own mother."

Lines speared out from the corners of Keith's eyes.

"I never talked about it. Just started acting out and screwing up my life, making lots of bad decisions and doing messed-up things. Nanna Rosemary finally figured out what was going on, sat me down, and told me I needed to say a proper goodbye to my mother. She told me to write a letter to Mom, s-saying—" Justice set a palm over her mouth, swallowing twice to fight back the quaver in her voice.

A vein pulsed visibly at the base of Keith's throat.

"You see, um… People need rituals to help them get closure. That's what Nanna told me. It's why we have things like retirement ceremonies and funerals. Nanna said writing a letter would be a ritual for me." Justice took in a deep breath. "And she was right. It was one of the toughest things I've ever had to do, but doing *something* helped."

She placed her hand on top of the hockey team photo. "You never said goodbye to Ryan, Keith. You didn't go to his funeral, and so, no, you haven't worked this out. I see what it's done to you. Be in charge. Stay in control. Keep everyone in your sightlines. That's Keith Knight—always the leader, trying to look out for everyone all the time. Except you can't." She slowly shook her head. "You can't go into every room."

Keith's lips pressed together.

"And I'm afraid…I'm worried that if you keep trying to do the impossible, you'll eventually burn out. Then you'll have nothing left for your own happiness. For a family maybe, someday. For a future." Her voice slipped into a hollow space in her larynx. "For me."

Keith turned his gaze up to the ceiling. His chest rose and fell.

"A moment ago you asked what I want from you. I want you to heal this wound." She stood. "So we're going to do a ritual." She crossed to the bookshelf, grabbed a hockey puck, then returned to Keith. "We're going to go to Ryan's gravesite, and you'll set *this* on his headstone." She held out the puck. "You'll talk to him. Ask for his forgiveness, if you think you need to, let him know how much you miss him, tell him about the man you think he'd be today if he'd lived—whatever you want. But make your final goodbyes, Keith. It's past time."

Keith stared at her for the longest seconds she'd ever withstood. Finally he said something thickly under his breath, blinked hard, and reached for the puck.

CHAPTER FIFTY-SEVEN

JUSTICE FOLLOWED KEITH into the Knight family kitchen an hour and a half later. The room was bright and cheery, decorated in autumn shades of brown and gold. The countertops—made of granite in a mauvey-rusty-swirly design—formed a U with a double sink positioned in the scoop of the U and a large plate glass window affording a spectacular view of the Grand Tetons. The longer arm of the U would be used for food prep—chopping, mixing, rolling, and the like. The shorter arm ended at a side-by-side stainless steel refrigerator and freezer unit.

Keith went directly to the fridge and opened it. "You want a beer?" he asked, speaking for the first time since the two of them left for Aspen Hill Cemetery.

"Sure." She leaned against the counter across from the fridge.

Keith found a couple of cans and handed her one.

She read the label. "Rainier." She arched a brow. "Isn't this Longmire's brand?"

"My father's a fan," Keith said with a brief laugh. Popping the tab on his beer with a *shhhhht*, he downed a few good swallows, then leaned against the counter across from her. "Dad read the whole book series and threw a party to celebrate Longmire being named *Walt*."

She smiled. "I bet you can't think of anyone here in Wyoming who doesn't love the show."

"Probably not." Keith drank more beer, seeming glad to

relax into everyday-speak.

She opened her own can and took a sip.

If a lot could be learned about a man by spending too much time with him under a large rubber boat, more from the touch of his hands, and even more from seeing his dark side emerge at a POW camp, then the whole kit could be learned when his aqua eyes unblocked from a certain resistance to intrusion.

And Keith's eyes were an endless blue right now, more open than she'd ever seen them.

Warmth welled in her.

She had helped make that happen and by doing nothing more than letting Keith feel her love and support. It was the first time in her life she hadn't had to perform to succeed. No obstacle course to overcome, no contraptions to outsmart, no booby traps to defuse. *No auditioning required with me, Justice. No need to re-prove yourself.* She was beginning to believe him.

"You doing okay?" he asked her.

"Me? Why wouldn't I be?"

"You had to dredge up a lot of tough memories today to prod me into moving my ass. It must've been hard on you." He sloshed the beer around in his can. A bubble rose into the opening and popped. "*I've* been hard on you."

"Nah. You were just trying to get out of dealing with some messed-up shit. Totally understandable response."

He met her gaze. "I don't mean being a pain in the ass." His mouth twisted into a grimace. "At Rock River Buttress, I grabbed you. And back at Echo Outpost—"

"Come on, Keith. Knock it off. I can take it." She gave him a cavalier smile. "Hooyah, tits in the sand and all that."

He gave her a half-smile but also shook his head. "Point is, you shouldn't have to. And I'm sorry."

"Well, don't be. One of the things I love about you is

that I know you're here for me when I need to go extreme and blow off a head of steam. I'm here for you in the same way. In fact"—she set aside her beer can—"discussion time is over. It's been a long, hard day, and at some point in a long, hard day, action people need to get back to what they do best—*action*." She cocked an eyebrow. "You ready to blow off a head of steam?"

He breathed out a laugh and glanced at the plate glass window. The sun was dropping steadily behind the Grand Tetons, burnishing the mountainside a brilliant copper. "What do you have in mind?" he asked, tipping his beer can up and taking another drink.

"Getting naked."

He jerked the can away from his mouth and double-swallowed to get the beer down.

She forced back a smile. One of the more amusing terror-reactions she'd witnessed. "You've never seen me completely naked."

"No." He licked his lips and swallowed again. "I haven't."

"An inexcusable lack in our relationship to date." She sauntered toward him.

He set his beer on the counter without taking his eyes off her. "I've also never seen your hair down," he told her.

"Absolutely unforgiveable." She reached for the band at the end of her long braid and tugged it off.

He watched her avidly while she wove her fingers into her braid to unravel it. When the rope was all the way undone, she shook her head to scatter her hair over her shoulders.

"Holy fuck," he rasped, his eyes locked on the sight of her braid-wavy hair. "Now I know why you always kept your hair up at BUD/S. None of us would've ever gotten any work done."

She chuckled.

"And you've got the hot-girl head toss move down solid too." He made a growly noise. "That one gets me."

"Does it? Check out this move then." She tugged her T-shirt off and tossed it aside, standing before him in her bra. It was plain, basic white—donned without thought of a moment like this when she hastily changed out of her rock climbing gear—but what her bra lacked in frills, it made up for in plenty of cleavage.

Which she increased now by scooping up her breasts and pressing them together.

Keith's eyes glazed over in what looked like a moment of gray matter shutdown. He repeated his growly noise and surged toward her, sliding a muscled arm around her waist. "Big fan of that move." He pulled her against him and bowed his head, placing a warm kiss in the valley between her breasts.

A tremor rushed through her pelvis. "Hey, big boy," she murmured, burrowing her fingers in his hair. "Is that a hockey stick in your pocket, or are you just glad to finally be getting laid?"

He answered by tightening his arm around her waist and tracing his tongue in a silky path along the rounded edge of a breast.

Her nipples flushed with eagerness. "I'm still sweaty from earlier," she warned huskily.

He said, "Mmm," and nuzzled one of her taut nipples through the fabric of her bra.

It tautened some more. Heat grabbed her loins.

"You taste perfect." Keith nudged the cup of her bra aside with his nose, freeing the puckered nipple. "I wouldn't want you any other way." His fingers crept up her spine to her bra clasp.

"Um…but still…" Tingles paraded up her back. "No

doing my favorite thing till I've showered."

He stopped in the middle of curling his tongue around her nipple. His focus inched up to her face. "What's your favorite thing?"

She gave him a heavy-lidded look. "It would require you getting down on your knees, frogman."

He straightened abruptly, his pupils large. "You better shower then." He took her by the hand and led her to the stairs.

On the trip up to the second floor, she watched his muscle-bound ass flex against his Wranglers. The way his jeans clung to his powerful hips and thighs brought back the memory of how Wyoming Man had moved those hips with such vigor at Echo Outpost. A frisson of eagerness ran through her.

She reached out and seized one of his firm butt cheeks, giving it a good squeeze.

He stopped halfway up the stairs and shot a heated look over his shoulder.

"Mine," she said, continuing past him. "Me. Want. Now." She backed through Keith's bedroom door, eye-locking him as he stalked in after her.

Reaching behind her, she unhooked her bra and flung it across the room.

His eyes turned to smoke. He tore off his shirt, revealing four black Chinese characters running a vertical path down the left side of his ribs. His arm had covered these when she saw him bare-chested before, post-shower.

"You have ink now."

"I do." He wrenched his pants open and took out his erect cock.

A breath left her on a small groan. "Ho, boy." She stared at the thick appendage jutting from a patch of dark pubic hair. "Boy, oh boy, I so want to defile you in your teenage bed right now."

He smirked. "You'll be the first."

"Such a liar."

He walked out of his pants and grabbed her hips, smiling languidly. "*Real* young men in Wyoming have sex in their trucks." He slid his hands upward, stroking over the indent of her waist, the small rills of her bullet wound scar, then up her ribcage. He stopped just below her breasts and caressed both thumbs across the rounded undersides of her flesh, his nostrils flaring. "Another thing that gets me."

"What's that?" Streaks of hot pleasure raced through her. "Under-boob?"

He grunted.

"Hmm. I guess I'll have to stock up on crop tops."

His eyes collided with hers. "I'd kill-fuck you in one of those."

She laughed. "Not going to win any Poet of the Year Awards with that one, Knight."

"The day you see me trying to"—he undid her pants—"you have my permission to shoot." He pushed her jeans and undies down her hips.

She obliged the completely naked agenda by stepping out of them.

He took air through his nostrils for a couple of breaths, then crowded against her, a territorial move that hammered her pulse. His hard cock brushed over her mons, and her heart tried to make a break for it through her chest.

Perfect-placement fit.

He cupped one of her breasts with a powerful hand while the other pressed flat against her lower back, urging her forward into his touch as he molded and massaged her breast.

A moan spilled out of her. Her neck went weak, and she leaned her cheek to her own shoulder.

Keith kissed the exposed length of her throat, his rough breaths warming her flesh.

Rising tension locked up her abdominal muscles. She moved in reverse until she was at his bed. She sat, leaning back on her elbows.

Keith followed her down.

She scooted toward the headboard, using the dig of her elbows and small hip rotations to help her progress.

Keith's hands lightly rode her waist and hips through the twists and turns of her body. He gave her a dangerous look.

Lightning strikes of sensation hit her low in the gut, and by the time she was at the pillows her lower region was in core meltdown.

Keith fit himself between her legs, his naked flesh warm and slick, his weight a welcome heaviness. He smelled like soapy cedar. His eyelids were lazily half-closed, offering a mere glimpse of smoky blue. He took hold of her wrists and pressed her hands to the mattress on either side of her ears.

She gasped slightly, her breath hitching out of rhythm.

Her wrists…

It was the dominant hold she'd fantasized about when he grabbed her wrists in the officers' barracks on patch-'em-up day. And now here he was…her Man of the Hour…her Undisputed Hero…gazing down at her with the singular, most extraordinary look she'd ever received in her life.

I'm crazy about you.

Her lips trembled with a sudden and uncharacteristic shyness. *Is this real?* Here was the man she'd watched conquer the world—face down huge surf, hold his own against Tanner and Clark and Hill, crush the O-Course, pound out soft-sand runs at top speeds, charge to her rescue twice in North Korea, take on his emotional demons at a cemetery and defeat them.

"Are you real?" she croaked out.

He freed one hand to slide his fingers through her hair. Cupping her head, he lowered his mouth and sought out her lips. Kissing her deeply, he entered her with a slow, smooth push, and proceeded to show her just how real he was.

CHAPTER FIFTY-EIGHT

KEITH HOVERED ON top of Justice, crudely dripping sweat on her, his breathing hectic and his heartbeats deafening. His vision was still half whited out from a body-slam of impossibly intense pleasure—like a neutron bomb had gone off in his nuts and dick.

Moaning, he sagged his dead weight on shaking arms—not shaking from any trouble supporting his own bulk but from the sheer impact of what had just happened.

If he was ever going to use the term "making love"—and he'd have to press his tongue to a hot stove burner if he did—it's what they'd just done…eyes locked, fingers entwined, hips slowly rocking together…

First time ever for him.

He couldn't seem to recover.

Maybe he never would.

"Well, that was fucking amazing." Justice's legs went slack on either side of his hips.

He finally managed to lug himself off her. "Accurate to the extreme." He sprawled on his back with his arms flung over his head.

She released a sigh. "I came three times."

"I noticed."

"I never do that." She settled onto her side facing him. "Not with straight sex, anyway."

His smiled at the ceiling, a great, satiated languor stealing over him.

At some point in a long, hard day, action people need to get back to what they do best—action.

She'd been right about that.

In fact, she'd done everything right to help him through this long, hard day, starting at the cemetery. When he'd knelt at Ryan's burial spot, she stood three graves over from him, not trying to talk to him or touch him, just giving him space while still letting him feel her presence.

Head bowed, Keith didn't utter a single thing for the first ten minutes with Ryan. Only to spend the next ten minutes babbling out a steady stream of words, half of which he couldn't remember, but by the end of it, he felt like Ryan had released him. Keith could almost swear his friend told him to quit being such a douche, worrying about shit that was long done and over with.

When Keith finally came to his feet, Justice moved to stand beside him, still silent. He pulled her into his arms and hugged her for five minutes, feeling better…lighter…almost like, yeah, he'd finally thrown off a hefty weight and worked out a lot of stuff.

So the ritual of saying goodbye to Ryan with the hockey puck had been a good idea. Although maybe hearing Brayden accept some responsibility for the rock-climbing accident helped too. Probably a combination of both. But whatever the whole reason, he couldn't have done it without Justice.

"I'm hungry," she told him now.

He grunted.

"Half a beer isn't enough calorie compensation for what we just did."

"If you can get up, be my guest. I'll take a turkey and provolone on wheat, no skimping on the mayo."

"Can you call one of your brothers? Have him bring a pizza over?"

Keith laughed outright at that. No way was he involving one of those three in this night. After some sustenance and a rest break, he planned to dive into round two.

She reached across his body and tickled her fingers over his tattoos. "What do these mean, by the way?"

He stretched and grabbed a pillow. "Honor. Courage. Integrity."

"Very Knight-like," she approved. "There are four symbols, though. What's the last one?"

He tucked the pillow under his head. "Family."

She struggled up onto an elbow. "What kind of Team Guy adds 'family' to his battle tats?"

"This one does." He fiddled with some of her hair. She had an amazing amount of it. "I'm under no illusions about where my real strength comes from."

She sat up all the way, pressing the bedsheet to her breasts. "Oh, Hunk-a Chunk-a," she purred, slanting her lashes at him. "I'm so into you."

He chuckled. "Yeah?" *I also need to know you, what you're thinking and feeling.* "There's more. Remember how you said I went into the SEALs for the challenge?"

"Yes."

"That's not the whole reason I joined. It was partly for my mom."

Justice lay back down, resting her cheek on folded hands and focusing on him.

"Mom's a lobbyist," he continued, "always off to Washington D.C., campaigning for one thing or another, trying to change the world. I thought I might give it a try too—changing the world."

"A tall order."

"Yeah, but." He rearranged the pillow, shoving part of it under his neck. "It seemed like the right way to give my mom the recognition she deserves. She...my dad doesn't love her. He's not a bad guy. He tries to love her—I give him credit for that. He just never got over Brayden's mom. And…actually, I think my mother leaves town so often to escape that fact."

Justice made a quiet sound.

"When you said…" He stopped, took a breath, and restarted. "When you said I might not have anything left to give you someday, that's what convinced me to go to the cemetery." Something squeezed his lungs. He forced in a deeper breath and looked at her. "I didn't want you to end up like my mom because of me, getting only half of what you deserve."

Justice blinked a couple of times, a tender expression hazing her eyes. "Who knew you could be so sweet?"

Am I? He laughed softly. "Don't let it get out." He turned back to the ceiling. "I only wish it hadn't taken me so long to deal with Ryan. But, uh, according to Brayden, my dad never helped me figure out how to let things go."

He settled his attention on a scatter pattern of dotted brown stains on the ceiling. He and Walt had wrestled over the last Coke in the house after hockey practice one evening, and the can exploded all over the damned place. "I saw Brayden at Echo when his squad relieved Whiskey, and we talked out a lot of shit. Bray thinks that because Dad is still bunched up over losing Marsha, he never taught the rest of us how to come to terms with loss."

After Ryan died, did Dad say anything to you? 'It wasn't your fault' or 'It was just a horrible accident' or something like that?

A strange emotion lodged in Keith's chest. Disappointment, it felt like.

In his father.

Justice said, "I think I sort of know what you mean."

He turned his head toward her.

Her mouth curved at the corners. "My dad didn't help me come to terms with my mother's death, either."

"He didn't?"

"My Nanna Rosemary had to step in."

"Ah, yeah."

Justice's focus searched the empty space over his shoulder. "Maybe it's why we're overachievers."

"How do you figure?"

She shifted back to him. "Maybe we interpreted our fathers' distance like withdrawal on some level...and maybe that made us feel like bad kids...like we'd failed. So now we keep tackling the biggest and hardest goals so we can prove to ourselves and everyone else that we're good."

Keith squinted, trying to see it. Was that true? Did he really do that?

"Question is, when does it become enough? At what point are we able to think we're okay, even when we're not performing?"

"How about now?" he suggested. "With each other?"

Her eyes softened. "I like that idea."

Anything was doable with this woman in his life.

"Easy to slip back into old habits, though, right?" she added. "So if either one of us gets caught up in an internal rat race, the other should call foul on it."

"Roger that." He wrapped an arm around her shoulders and tucked her against his side.

She rested a hand on his chest.

They lay in relaxed silence, shadows taking over the room as the sun made its final descent behind the mountains. Dark shapes leisurely climbed the walls, and the trophies on his bookshelf gradually morphed into distorted blobs, faceless beings with frozen limbs extended.

Justice angled her head to look at him, her lashes casting shadows over her cheeks. "You can stop trying now, you know."

He tipped his chin down. "To do what?"

"To make me fall in love with you." Her eyes were radiant in the last glow of twilight. "I'm sold too."

He laughed low in his throat, but it was a cover-up for the actual goofy, nutso shit going on inside him. It felt like his heart was rising up to the ceiling. Probably higher, but since he didn't say things like "to the moon," he was going to stick with *up*.

"Good," he said. Because he couldn't do life without this tough-on-soft woman. "Then there's something I want you to do for me."

"Name it."

"I want you to start thinking of us as a forever proposition."

She froze for two beats, then flopped onto her back. "Keith." She moaned his name like a plea for him to stop being a noob.

"See a problem, fix it. Want something, obtain it. That's how I operate. And I want you. You make me feel good."

She glanced slantwise at him. "You make me feel good too, but we just got started. It's too early for a proposal."

"I didn't propose." *Not yet.* "And we've known each other for a year and a half."

"We've been *apart* for a year," she countered. "Before that we were together for six months of torture, and we just traveled the rockiest road ever to arrive *here*."

"All good points. Don't care. I lived a year without you, and I don't want to live that way anymore. Ever."

Her expression turned droll. "You do remember I'm going back on deployment in three months, right?"

"Besides that." And he planned on having her Missus unit attached to Whiskey. *No more gunshot wounds for her. No more having to stab bad guys.* He needed to be able to protect her in the field.

She gave him a pained look. "Please don't make me feel like a crap-bag for needing time."

He smiled slightly. No, he didn't want that. Kind of stole the cool parts away from *forever*. "How about this? We come up with a signal you can give me when you're ready to take the next step."

"Yeah?" She rolled toward the nightstand and clicked on the lamp. "Like what?" She sat up, this time not holding the bedsheet to her breasts.

Her hair was a wild tangle around her face, a just-been-fucked look that made him want to get back to the business of messing her up some more.

"Oh, I know. This—" She stuck her hand out and gestured.

Her nipples were an awesome rose color.

"Are you paying attention to me?"

He wasn't.

"Keith!" She drew the sheet up to cover her breasts.

"Hey."

"*This.*" She put her hand out, her pinkie and thumb stretched wide, and made a swimming motion with her palm.

He gave her an astounded look. "*Chalmers'* fish-hand from surf torture?"

"It's perfect," she said with a low, soft laugh. "It's BUD/S. And that's where everything started for us."

Hayes is going to be on your boat team…

The words that had changed his life…months of wanting…of deprivation…

How could he have known way back at dawn muster it was going to be so difficult, but that the triumph of finally winning her would be all the sweeter for the tough road?

He grabbed her fish-hand. "All right. But since I want

you to give me the go-ahead sooner rather than later, I'm going to have to engage in a daily operation of convincing you." He stood and tugged her to her feet.

"What? Wait...what are you doing? Ugh, what happened to being a couple of post-coital slugs and not moving?"

He led her toward the door.

"Keith... If you're thinking about traipsing off to Vegas..."

"First off, I don't *traipse*. Second, I'm taking you to the shower." He grinned. "Time to show you that your favorite thing is my best thing."

Epilogue...

Wait!

Before you read on to find out more about Justice and Keith's happily ever after…

To obtain a FREE <u>authentic</u> copy of the military <u>evaluation</u> Petty Officer Keith Knight received following his deployment with Justice in Korea.

tracy.link/keith

Epilogue, Part 1

Eight months later
McP's Irish Pub, Coronado
Reunion Party, BUD/S Class 684

RUDY DUNBAR LEFT BUD/S Class 684's reunion party in a hurry.

His rapid departure had everything to do with Justice driving him off the premises, with insults like *shit-talking little dick-fuck* spewing from her mouth as she barreled at him with plans to do him bodily harm.

She'd found out that Rudy Dunbar was the rat fink who'd told Admiral Sherwin about her arrest record.

She'd got the lowdown on this from Brayden.

When she'd returned to Korea, she sought out Street—his squad was still in-country—to talk out BUD/S graduation. Over ice cream cones in the Camp Casey mess hall, she apologized to Brayden for the way she'd left. He accepted, then they both wished each other well for the relationships they were now in.

After that, she asked him if he knew anything about how Sherwin discovered her arrest record.

Guess what?

He did.

Brayden had caught Rudy in the officers' barracks one day opening a letter addressed to Justice—the letter informing her that her arrest for solicitation had finally been expunged from her record.

Rudy leaked this info to Sherwin, along with all the other salacious details of the "conduct unbecoming" he'd witnessed the night before graduation. This led to a lot of extremely bad things happening in her life.

So it'd required two men to hold her back from showing her displeasure to the true turncoat in the most violent terms possible. Not that she could've beaten the shit out of a SEAL, but she hadn't been able to control herself…and there were plenty of men at McP's Pub who would've backed her efforts, so…

Rudy left.

As the bar door closed on his sorry ass, Brayden's girl-friend—no, *fiancée*, as of yesterday—sidled up next to Justice, bringing the scent of her trademark rosy perfume with her.

Charlotte was dressed in what could be termed as "casu-al bar wear," except that Charlotte never did anything causally—her jeans were designer, her cream blouse was silk, and her blond ponytail looked like golden frosting had been piped down her shoulder and chest in a curvy line.

Justice had never pulled off a ponytail like that in her life.

"Are you okay?" Charlotte asked her.

"Yeah, thanks. Some old business I needed to address is all. Hey, I hear congratulations are in order." Justice raised her Collins glass.

"Oh, yes." Charlotte fluttered her left-hand fingers to show off her engagement ring, the diamond catching sparks of light.

"Have you and Brayden set a date yet?" Justice asked.

"We're hoping for April of next year." Charlotte glanced across the bar.

Justice followed the direction of Charlotte's gaze to Brayden.

He was talking to Omar Boyd—High School Crush Lookalike—who'd ended up graduating with the BUD/S Class after 684. Boyd had joined Zack Kilgour, a legit sniper now, over at Team Three, sister squadron to Team Five on San Diego's Naval Amphibious Base.

"Hey, um…" Charlotte turned back to Justice. "Can I ask you something?"

"Sure."

Charlotte chewed one side of her lower lip. "Was there ever anything between you and Brayden?"

"God, no!" Justice added a *hah-hah!* for good measure. *Why, what a silly girl you are, Charlotte!*

Charlotte's forehead crinkled doubtfully.

Justice shut off her laugh and rattled the ice in her glass. Just what she needed, Charlotte's womanly intuition getting in the way of a perfectly good lie—at Camp Casey over those ice cream cones Justice and Brayden had also agreed to lie shamelessly about their post-SERE near-oops.

Keith gladly jumped on board with the plan to erase it.

The only other person who knew the truth about what had happened that night was Rudy Dunbar, and he was no longer available for comment.

"Brayden and I are good friends," Justice assured Charlotte. "That's all."

"I just…" Charlotte spun her engagement ring. "I get the sense…" She trailed off.

Pesky woman's intuition. "All right, look. I'm going to tell you the real deal here, Charlotte, but I need you to keep it a secret, okay?" If Charlotte wasn't a good secret-keeper, Justice supposed it didn't really matter. This particular secret would soon be moot. "I'm with Keith."

Charlotte's chin popped up. "What? Oh, Lord!" A hand flew to her breast. "Keith! Of course. That makes perfect sense."

Justice smiled ruefully. "Makes perfect sense to me too, but the Navy doesn't agree—Keith is enlisted and I'm an officer, and according to military regulations, us being together is a big no-no. We could get in a lot of trouble if our relationship got out."

"Oh, don't worry, I won't tell." Charlotte's brow puckered again. "You must really miss him."

"Yeah. I do." Justice watched the ice melt in her glass.

After spending an amazing three months with Keith during her med-down break—part of the time in Wyoming, part of the time in San Diego—she'd returned to Korea to finish the three remaining months of her deployment. Keith stayed in San Diego at Team Five. The two of them kept in good touch via FaceTime for the first month they were apart. Then Keith got pulled back into the field on a super-secret assignment—Justice had no idea where he'd gone or how long he would be away.

She hadn't seen or heard from him for four months—the last two of her own deployment plus the two months she'd been back in San Diego. She tried to stay busy with training and preparing for her new life, but still…

To say she missed Keith was to put it mildly.

Justice shrugged. "It's nothing we don't have to get used to dealing with as women with Team Guys, right?"

Charlotte sighed. "That doesn't make it easy." She reached out and touched Justice's arm. "Thank you for everything you told me." Smiling sunnily, she bounded off toward Brayden.

Justice ordered herself another Tom Collins, then made another round of the bar, catching up with Dog Bone and Brad Ziegler, both stationed at Team Four in Little Creek, Virginia.

While she chatted with Dog Bone, she watched him eat an entire plate of onion rings one-fisted and suggested he contact the Guinness Book of World Records. He didn't get it, and she didn't push it.

Hairy Arms Ziegler had done the impossible and grabbed himself a girlfriend. His lady love was stationed at a military base close to Little Rock—Naval Air Station Norfolk—where she was an AM, or Aviation Structural Mechanic. Which was a fancy way of staying she fixed and maintained jets.

Everyone asked about Keith.

No one was particularly surprised to hear he was deployed—such was the life of an operator—although everyone was bummed he wasn't there.

A Class 684 reunion party wasn't the same without the leader of the Knight boat team.

It's nothing we don't have to get used to dealing with as women with Team Guys, right?

Intellectually, Justice understood this. So she thought she'd been prepared for life without him. But emotionally…she hadn't expected the hole inside her to be quite so big.

Out of sorts and reserved, she left the party by ten o'clock.

As she drove toward home, she pissed and moaned mentally about how bad she'd been shafted. Most military girlfriends had at least *some* contact with their boyfriends during a deployment. But she wasn't able to talk to Keith *at all*. It was stupid. She was in SOF. She had all kinds of security clearances. Would it really be so bad to let her have one damned phone call with the guy?

She parked in her reserved spot and headed up the walkway to her apartment building. She lived in a converted loft in the gentrified Normal Heights area. Her street was—

A man materialized out of the shadows.

She jumped out of her skin and thrust her house key

between the fingers of the fist she made, ready to punch the fucking skinhead who—

"Hey." He stepped closer. "Sorry. I didn't mean to startle you."

She squinted through the darkness. "Keith?"

Her insides did a weird up and down toggle—upward toward the joy of seeing the man she loved again, but downward with an unexpected weirdness. Because this man didn't altogether look like Keith. And he definitely didn't *feel* like Keith. His high energy was battle-ravaged and hard, his eyes holding something dark, like he was still carrying a lot of in-country nasty.

"Uh…wow." She tucked her keys away. "I can't believe you're finally back."

She stood mutely in front of him. She didn't know what to say to this version of Keith.

And here was another thing she hadn't prepared herself for—a total stranger for a boyfriend.

She asked, "What happened to your hair?" He was minus several pounds of body weight too.

He rasped a hand over the stubble on his skull. "Me and my guys spent almost all of the past four months moving from one bush to another in the dirt, tracking some asshole HVT. By the time we got back to base, we were all covered in lice and fleas. They shaved our heads and burned our camos." A moth circled his bare skull once, then decided not to stick around. "I must look fucked."

She brought up a smile for him. "You look like you did at BUD/S." Although not really.

Silence spread between them and hovered, like it didn't know what to do—be companionable or awkward?

He tilted his face up to the moon. His eyebrows were formed into harsh slants. "Maybe I shouldn't have come."

"No," she countered quickly. "I'm really glad you're

here. I'm just adjusting to you being on my doorstep so suddenly, without warning." She started for her complex's main doorway. "Why don't you come in, and I'll make you something to eat?"

He followed her into her building. "That'd be good, thanks. I haven't been home yet. I came right here."

Her heart turned over. To see *her.* "How long have you been waiting for me?"

He shrugged a single shoulder.

"I'm sorry. I wish I'd know you were home. I would've bagged on McP's."

They stepped up to the elevator, and she pushed the call button.

"You just getting home from the reunion party?" he asked.

She tugged her keys out of her pocket again. "You knew about it?"

"We were given our personal cell phones back when we returned to base. I saw the invite text then."

"Why didn't you come?"

They stepped inside the elevator.

In the severe fluorescent light, Keith looked frightening. Part Black Mamba, part *Jacob's Ladder.* Wes Craven meets Son of Sam.

"After four months under a bush, I'm not fit for civilization." He gave the elevator wall a hard, detached stare. His jaw was stone-like. "I never thought I'd grow to hate my Whiskey brothers, but the thought of spending even one more second with those jackasses makes me want to hammer something. I figured that was a good indicator of how I might do in a crowd."

Her heart slid into the pit of her belly. Whatever Keith's assignment was, it clearly hadn't been fun and games.

Inside her apartment, she made them both sandwiches

while he sat at her square dining room table and waited in a state of unnatural stillness and quiet.

She came out of the kitchen with two plates. "Turkey and provolone on wheat, no skimping on the mayo," she said as she set his sandwich in front of him.

The tautness in his face finally cracked a bit into a faint smile.

She sat kitty-corner to him.

He started to eat.

Her refrigerator *ticked* as it switched out of energy-conservation mode—it always did that after she'd opened and closed it several times.

"So how are you?" he asked.

"Good. Been keeping busy with work mainly, and in between, playing beach volleyball with my friend Chloe and other girlfriends." She took a bite of sandwich, chewed and swallowed. "Bat Three was called out on a short assignment to South America to help with a counter-drug op. Incriminating intel on a major drug lord was hidden in some saint's tomb inside a Catholic church in Colombia—everything wired to blow. The local populace would've hated America's guts if I'd failed to defuse that properly."

Keith finished off one half of his sandwich.

She wasn't sure if he was listening, but she had the sense he was—he was just out of practice about how to express the usual cues to make that clear.

"I've done a lot of training at Camp Pendleton," she added. "The usual stuff."

"Prepping for your next deployment?" His nostrils tensed. "I just got back, and off you go. We knew it would be like this, but…" His tone was bitter. "I didn't expect it to be *this* much of a fucking bitch." He picked up the other half of his sandwich and glowered at it. "I was right—life without you is miserable."

Her heart turned over again, a double flip this time. "Actually, I'm leaving the Navy."

His head swiveled around. "What?"

She twisted her lips. "Rear Admiral Joseph Sherwin's wishes and dreams have finally come true. He's managed to dissolve the Special Missions program and revert SOF to an all-boys club."

Keith's expression darkened. "Are you shitting me?"

"No. The intel-gathering operations Special Missions conducted will now be farmed out to a civilian contractor. Specifically, Conroy Dawson's company, Sevette Security and Investigations. I suspect this was the secret plan all along."

"Those fucks," Keith growled. "After everything they put you through."

"Ah, well, it's working out pretty fine for me, actually. I was given the option of joining the regular Navy or getting out." She finished her sandwich and sipped some water. "Seeing as I'm the only woman ever to make it through BUD/S, plus my, *ahem*, special skillset, I'm considered a hot commodity in the civilian sector. The moment I chose to drop my letter, Dawson pounced. He offered me a job with his company earning a cool six figures." She buffed her nails on her shirt.

"Whoa." Keith's eyebrows jacked up.

"I'd like to accept the position but wanted to talk to you first. I wasn't sure," she added in a playful tone, "if you'd be okay with me making more money than you."

Keith chuffed. "A shiny new speedboat ought to soothe my male ego just fine." He gave her a probing stare. "You sure you're okay with this?"

She dotted some crumbs up with her fingertip. "I'm going to miss the guys."

Glinski and Morris, Willie and Wild Man Pete.

"Our run was short," she went on, "but really great, and I'll never forget it." *I'll never forget that this crazy experience brought me you.* "But working for Sevette Security means less time away from home—I'll head overseas only for contracted jobs—and less chance of having to kill again." She traced her forefinger around the rim of her water glass. "I don't like that part."

"I know," Keith said quietly. He ate the rest of his sandwich.

She watched him wipe his hands on a paper napkin.

I think for two people to work well together, at least one person in the pair needs to press sometimes...

But then there was also knowing when *not* to press. And it was obvious Keith wouldn't benefit from a lot of "processing" right now. He'd either strike out or shut down. Neither was desirable.

It's been a long, hard day, and at some point in a long, hard day, action people need to get back to what they do best—action.

"So are you up for doing something tonight?" she asked. "Or is it too late?"

"I'm up for something." Sitting back, he ran his tongue around inside his mouth. "Would taking this into the bedroom be an option?"

She laughed in a burst of air. *Not with your eyes looking like that.* "I'm afraid I'm not really ready for that yet, so we're still on a breather." She stood. "Besides, I think what you need first is some lighthearted fun. Come on."

EPILOGUE, PART 2

JUSTICE DROVE KEITH north to the nearby town of Clairemont Mesa and parked in front of a Chipotle Mexican Grill.

He ducked his head to peer out the windshield at the restaurant. "Didn't we just eat?"

"This isn't our final destination," she said, climbing out of her car. *Never park in front of the scene of the crime* was another inviolable thief rule.

She led Keith a couple of blocks to an amusement park called *Boomers!* on Clairemont Mesa Boulevard—mini golf, an arcade, a go-kart track.

The place was dark and shut up for the night.

Keith set his hands on his hips, his T-shirt hanging loosely on his overly lean torso. "It's closed."

She drew a lock pick out of her backpack. "Not to me, it isn't." Waggling her eyebrows, she spun the metal instrument smartly on the palm of her hand.

"What the fuck, Justice?"

She just smiled and put her skills to work, snipping the alarm wire and opening the lock. They were inside in under thirty seconds. "This way." She aimed for the go-kart track.

About ten carts were parked near the start line, gleaming in the moonlight.

"We'll only have time to make it around the track once," she warned as she grabbed the large on-off handle that controlled the electricity. "As soon as I flip on the lights, someone in the neighborhood will call the cops."

Keith seamed his lips, but he didn't say anything to stop her.

She flipped the switch.

The overhead lights blared on.

They flew into the carts like a couple of crazy kids and took off at maniacal speeds. Zooming around the course, they bumped into the track's rubber sidewalls and bumped into each other...and laughed their asses off.

Keith was making an unbridled charge for the finish line, nearly skidding up on two wheels around the final turn, when she saw a flash of blue lights in her periphery.

"Keith!" she called to him. "Hold up!"

He braked and looked at her.

"The police are already here! We gotta split."

He jumped out of his cart and raced over to her. "You just didn't want me to win."

She snorted. "More like Grayson Hayes's daughter doesn't want to get arrested." She threw her backpack on. "Let's go—the back way out." She leapt onto the rear chain-link fence and shimmied over it.

Keith said, "Christ," but made the same climb.

They hopped to the ground and escaped at a fast run.

"Times like this," she said breathlessly, "I wish I had a getaway driver."

Keith laughed.

They found their way back to Chipotle Mexican Grill and dove into the safety of her car.

"You're fucking nuts," Keith panted.

"You had a blast," she lobbed back.

"Yeah," he said, his eyes more vivid and human than she'd seen them since he emerged from the shadows in front of her apartment building. "I did."

Chuckling, she put her car in gear and pulled out of the

parking lot. She drove south but didn't aim directly for home. She still wasn't entirely sure what to do with Keith; he'd been so completely out of her life for so long, the idea of getting naked in front of him still felt weird.

Ten minutes into the drive, he pointed at a passing building. "Hey, let's go there."

She parked down the street, and they walked back.

The sign on the building said Kearny Mesa Pool. Not a single light shone in any of the windows.

"Can you bust in there?" Keith asked.

"Of course." She bent her lips into a ghost of a smile. "You want me to?"

"Uh…" His own smile was uncharacteristically sheepish. "Yeah. This sneaky shit is kind of addicting."

She let loose with a big laugh. "Tell me about it."

It took her a little longer to break into the rec center— she had to connect a couple of motion sensor wires into a feedback loop—but she still was inside in under two minutes.

They wandered together toward the indoor Olympic-sized pool and stopped at the edge. The pool itself was unlit, but there were small bulbs of security lighting in each of the four corners of the room.

The scent of chlorine hung in the air, along with moisture. The silence was weird. Like, because this was a place normally alive with the noises of playful splashing and kids' laughter, now that it wasn't, it felt ghostly and empty.

Keith crouched down at the edge of the pool and stuck his hand in the water, swishing it around. Coruscating pinpricks of diamonds and stars jumped across the surface of the rippling water.

"The temp's good." He glanced up at her. "Are the cops going to show here?"

"They shouldn't." She'd left the security system looking

and acting normal.

He straightened. "I'm going in." He shed his shirt and dropped his jeans, undressing so fast she didn't have the chance to remind herself to breathe before he was diving into the pool, his body barely disturbing the surface of the water.

So…apparently they were doing the naked thing now.

She'd caught only a glimpse of his bare body, but it'd been a long-enough peek to see that his powerfully muscled physique didn't have an ounce of fat on it—a man who'd been living off MREs for four months and hating it.

She watched the shadow of his body glide beneath the surface.

He swam with unhurried strokes and without purpose, cocooned in the peace and quiet of the water. She sensed he would've stayed underneath for a week if he could have.

She dropped her backpack, took off her own clothes, and slipped into the water.

She swam toward him.

His head appeared above the surface. He swept water out of his eyes and looked at her.

She treaded water across from him.

The scent of chlorine was heavy in her nose.

They circled each other.

He dove under.

In the next second, his solid thigh grazed her leg.

Her belly jolted. She swam away.

He chased after her.

She felt his hand wrap around her right ankle.

Her pulse leapt, but he let go right away, his fingers skimming over her foot.

She swam to shallower water and stood with her breasts bobbing just below the surface. She was breathing deeply.

He swam into position across from her and stood, too,

wreathed in a vague shimmer of light, pool water lapping gently at his sculpted pecs. He lowered his focus to where her nipples were making periodic appearances above the surface. He slid toward her, water eddying around him.

Her nerves jumped, but she stood still.

His hands found her waist and squeezed the indent, as if testing the circumference. "If we'd been like this during BUD/S surf torture," he murmured, "I might've stayed in the water."

She exhaled softly. "It was cold."

"Not so cold now." His hands smoothed toward her breasts, his fingertips brushing over her flesh. His erection nudged her hip.

She sprang backward, throwing up gouts of water, then touched bottom again, several feet away from him.

He stood unmoving. Darkness and light made up his features, geometric shapes, cubism and surrealism in form and line.

Her heart was skipping every other beat. She had no idea what that meant.

"Still on a breather?" he asked quietly.

"Still on a breather." She swam off.

He followed.

They plunged low into the water and arced high over the surface, swimming together like playful dolphins. Finally they met at the deep end. She climbed up the pool ladder first, then Keith.

They tugged their clothes on over their wet bodies.

"You're so beautiful," he said.

She paused in the middle of picking up her backpack. Her smile felt lopsided with embarrassment. "Thank you."

"No." He shook his head. "I know you hear that from guys all the time, but I mean you're really beautiful. *All* of you."

She checked the zipper on her backpack, tears gathering in the corners of her eyes. "You, um…do want to go back to my place now?"

"Up to you."

She worked the zipper tab back and forth. "I read there's a James Bond retrospective playing tonight. A marathon showing of every movie in order of release. I thought we could watch it together."

He laughed softly. That probably wasn't what he'd been hoping to hear.

"You once told me you love James Bond flicks," she said.

He rolled with it. "I do. It's a great idea."

Back at her apartment, she clicked on the television located at the foot of her bed and found the right channel. The retrospective had started as six. *Dr. No* and *From Russia With Love* had already come and gone. *Goldfinger* was halfway through.

"Get comfortable," she told Keith. "I'm going to pop some popcorn."

Keith lounged back in her bed with his hands behind his head.

When she returned with a full bowl of popcorn, he was out cold.

She stood at the edge of her bed and gave his sleeping face a tender look, then scooted in next to him.

Mumbling, he rolled toward her, shoving his nose against her hip and wrapping a heavy arm around her waist.

She smiled, relaxed against her pillows, ate popcorn, and watched *Thunderball.*

She'd just started in on *You Only Live Twice* when Keith blearily came up onto an elbow. He squinted at the TV. "Is that *Octopussy?*"

She scoffed. "What kind of James Bond aficionado are

you? That's Sean Connery, not Roger Moore."

"I…just…" He rubbed his face as he pushed to a full sitting position. "It feels like I slept for a week, not a couple of hours. I can't remember the last time I slept so soundly." He peered at her. Television light flickered over one side of his jaw. "Thank you," he said, his voice deeper than usual, more resonant.

She brushed a speck of pillow lint off his eyebrow. "I didn't do anything."

"You being you." His lips formed a warm half-smile. "You've learned how to read me exceptionally well, by the way."

She gave him a fleeting return smile. He was going to make her cry again.

"I hope the same can be said about me. Because here goes…" He reached down to the floor by the bed, grabbing the backpack he'd brought in from his car. He dug something out of it and set that something in the nearly empty popcorn bowl still on her lap.

It was a ring box.

Her heart melted down to sap. "Holy smokes. Keith!"

"Open it."

She did. "Dear God." He'd bought her a single teardrop diamond set in gold. "Look at the size of that sucker! I'll be catching it on all kinds of trip wires, for sure."

His expression shone with satisfied pride. "My hazardous-duty pay came in handy." He took the popcorn bowl and set it on the nightstand. "Here's the thing, Justice. I know you haven't given me the Chalmers' fish-hand yet, so maybe you're not ready for this…and maybe I'm jumping the gun because you're leaving the Navy and so I *can* ask you to marry me. But the time we spent apart solidified a lot of things for me, and I want to know we're heading in this direction." His eyes moved back and forth over hers. "So please say yes."

"Yes."

He started to smile, then hesitated. "Real yes, or you're-pacifying-me yes?"

She laughed. "Absolutely, one-hundred-percent real *yes*. The time apart solidified a lot of things for me too, Keith. I'm ready to take the next step."

He grinned fully now and plucked the ring from its box. "So this guy's digging in his garden, right?" He grabbed her left hand.

"What? Oh, no way. Do not ruin this moment with one of your stupid jokes."

Keith slipped the diamond on her finger. "He finds a trunk full of gold coins."

"No, no, no." God, the ring was even more beautiful on her finger.

"The guy gets so excited he's about to run home to tell his wife, but then"—Keith's grin grew—"he remembers why he's digging in his garden."

"You—" A laugh erupted from her. She couldn't help it. "A preview of what our marriage is going to be like, I take it?"

"Nope. Not us. Our marriage is going to be monogamy. Dedication. Sex. Beer and baseball. Picnics. Dinner by firelight. Fishing for trout. Snorkeling in Hawaii. Hand in hand on a beach at sunset. More sex."

She gaped at him. "You remember what I said to you perfectly. Word for word."

He bobbed his eyebrows.

"Aw, frogman." She peered at him through her lashes. "You're a very romantic guy."

"Yeah?" One side of his mouth climbed. "Well, don't let it get out."

With a brief laugh, she edged toward him, twining her arms around his neck and pressing her body close to his. "I love you," she whispered.

"Love you back." He kissed her lightly, once, then gave her a questioning look. "Breather over?" His eyes were the bluest she'd ever seen them.

"Oh, definitely," she said.

His eyelids lowered halfway as he urged her down on the mattress and climbed on top of her.

The strong arm that slid around her waist was solid and true.

The scent that stole into her senses was soapy cedar.

This was *her* Keith whose heart was beating with such power against hers.

Her Hero of the Day—of her *life*—was home.

A BIG, HAPPY SIGH…

Now that Justice and Keith have enjoyed their happily-ever-after, you're probably sitting back and sighing with contentment.

But…

Are you also wondering how Justice's life might have turned out if she'd chosen another man?

How about Brayden Street, the gallant with dimples?

Or full-of life, fun-loving Pete Robbins?

You can find out!

Just **Choose Another Hero** and keep reading…!

If you'd like to read **Brayden Street's story**, go to page 465.
If you'd like to read **Pete Robbins's story**, go to page 605.

BRAYDEN STREET'S STORY...

He watched her walk away once, twice…he's not letting her go again.

Honorable and courageous, Lieutenant Brayden Street has never been afraid to lead with his feelings when it comes to Justice Hayes. Crazy in love with her since the day they met, he plans to wine 'n dine his way into her heart once they're no longer teammates. But a single act of caring the night before BUD/S graduation backfires on him, and he loses the only woman who's ever understood the shattering wounds that both constrain and strengthen him.

He drowns in regret but doesn't chase after her, because he learned from his father that relationships are unfixable – you lose, you lump it. But then a startling confession from his brother changes everything.

Now he's laser-focused on earning back Justice's trust and making her fall in love with him. It's going to be a helluva challenge to find his way past her conviction that a thief isn't meant to be with a so-called "Golden Boy," but he'll stop at nothing to convince her.

Cracks begin to show in her defenses from his relentless pursuit, but then he succumbs to a moment of weakness one night and does something that just might ruin his chances all over again…

CHAPTER FORTY-FOUR

Late June
North Korea
Near the AH6 Highway between Najin and Sonbong

BRAYDEN STREET HAD dropped shrooms in college.

Did he admit this to the Navy? No, he did not. Did that mean he lied on his application? Why, yes, he did. But he hadn't planned on continuing his drug-taking behavior, so the past seemed irrelevant.

College was a time of...change for him. He'd gone from never backtalking his father—for fear of losing what little regard the man had for him—and rarely fighting with his four half-brothers—for fear of losing his inroad into the Knight family unit—to arguing with everyone.

Not the best way to stop feeling like a doormat.

Unfortunately, no one in his dorm had wanted to hang out with him for a while, and he was lonely until he figured out how to balance himself.

Dealing with his loneliness through drugs wasn't the healthiest choice, and the shrooms experimentation had left behind some lingering weirdness in his brain—but only when he first slapped on a pair of Night Vision Goggles.

As the world changed into a surreal collage of greens, it was a bit trippy—the moon looked like a ball of cabbage, the trees in the forest like upright asparagus stalks, and the asphalt highway like a river of puke.

He had to reassure his mind that, *No, this isn't a drug*

trip, just a different shade of real.

His brain got right on board with the thought this time.

The truck now arriving on the AH6 Highway looked exactly like what it was—an olive drab, standard-issue Army vehicle.

"Target's right on time," Chief Madden observed in a quiet tone. He was lying belly-down next to Brayden on the east side of the highway, hidden in the forest running along both sides of the road.

This part of the wooded highway was flat, but about a hundred feet down the road the sides were hilly, creating a perfect spot for the team's sniper and spotter, Rongo and Boomerang, to set up shop.

Brayden checked in with Rongo now. "Foxtrot Three," he said, pushing the speak button on his shoulder mic, "Foxtrot One. We have a visual on target. Entering kill zone in a hundred meters."

Thunder boiled out of the clouds.

Rongo answered, testy, "I'm going to be no joy for this shot if it starts to rain again."

Chief Madden exhaled a short, hard breath. "Dickhead needs to get used to it. It's fucking monsoon season."

In the little over a week that Foxtrot had been in-country, the six men had spent roughly seventy percent of their time wet. Uncomfortable, yeah, but not a huge deal for Brayden, who'd grown up in Wyoming, where the harsh winters were legendary. But Rongo was Samoan. Korea's summer heat and humidity, the sniper could handle. Constant rain was definitely not his jam.

Brayden spoke into his mic again. "Kill zone in three. Two—"

The Army truck drove into the circle of dim light cast by a streetlamp.

"One—"

Zzzzt was followed by *thwat.*

The truck's windshield splintered, and the driver slumped over the steering wheel.

Through his NVGs, Brayden watched the vehicle continue to lumber forward, then finally crawl to a stop.

Brayden almost snorted. Not very dramatic. Then again...maybe the bad shit was about to come. He maintained his position, watching the truck. No horde of North Korean soldiers jumped out of the back.

"No movement," he murmured.

"Nope," Madden agreed.

Didn't mean the horde wasn't in there, waiting to spring out. But lying belly-down in a forest wasn't going to find that out.

"Rongo and Boomerang," Brayden said over comms, "maintain overwatch. Kopeck and Wrigley, move in from the west. Chief and I, approaching east." He rose to his feet and carefully advanced toward the truck, his strides soft-kneed and fluid, his M-4 raised.

The other three men did the same from different angles.

They entered the streetlamp's ring of light.

Brayden flipped his NVGs to the top of his combat helmet. He reached the hood of the truck, peering through the front windshield.

There was only one person in the cab, and it was the dead driver.

Brayden continued toward the back of the truck, rifle stock braced against his shoulder. He aimed at the rear door.

Wrigley and Kopeck did the same.

Brayden nodded to Madden, and the chief eased forward, pulling the door open and—

Brayden held his breath.

But no one jumped out.

He exhaled. *Good.*

But also bad.

Because there also wasn't a single assault rifle inside the truck on its merry way to a North Korean Special Forces training facility.

Two such enemy facilities had recently been discovered: one on the outskirts of Pyonggang in the south, but Foxtrot had blown this one to smithereens during a rescue operation their first day in-country.

The other was here in the north, just outside of Sonbong.

The objective of this mission had been to intercept a weapons shipment headed to the northern facility, but evidently…

"We hit the wrong truck," Wrigley grated. The man had a voice like sand gravel on any given day, but his gritty vocals sounded even rougher when overlaid with things like blame and criticism.

Brayden's ears heated, and his stomach dropped. Wrong truck equaled wrong North Korean driver just killed.

Fuck.

Lowering his weapon, Brayden stepped back and stiffened his jaw.

He'd boned up the mission.

Dammit, he wasn't even supposed to be in charge of missions yet, not as a first-fucking-tour Lieutenant JG. What he was *supposed* to be was the assistant to Foxtrot's Assistant Officer in Charge. But the AOIC, Lieutenant Havcheck, had taken a bullet during the rescue operation in Pyonggang, and SOF command, who didn't like to overload their teams with brass anyway, decided not to replace him.

Instead they moved up Brayden to lead SEAL Team Five's Foxtrot squad and assigned him an experienced chief to help him not bone up missions.

That chief was Shane "Mad Dog" Madden, a dark-haired salty dog out of South Boston with a scar ruining the entire left side of his face. "Experienced chief" would be understating matters. Madden was a legend in the SPECWAR community.

Back in the days when he was attached to Team Three, Madden had been on a hostage rescue mission in Pakistan when his helicopter was shot down. The only member of his SEAL chalk to survive the crash, he ended up taking three bullets on a week-long run for his life across the country. He was hit by a fourth while stealing a helo from a Pakistani Air Force base, which was, in itself, ballsy as shit.

Following his recovery in the States, Madden was sent back to Pakistan but in some nominal job as punishment for—and the Teams could hardly believe this—sexual misconduct aboard the USS *Mercy*. During this second tour, all hell broke loose again, and Madden did additional heroic shit, making even more of a gnarly-assed name for himself.

So as babysitters went, Madden was a good man to have around—a knowledgeable veteran who wasn't arrogant or pushy. He offered his opinion only when asked for it, and otherwise never countermanded Brayden in front of the men, showing him the respect that was not yet his due.

Rank counted for very little in the Teams. The other men on Foxtrot were only giving their wet-behind-the-ears leader half a chance to *earn* their respect because of Madden.

In fact, the chief stepped in now to back up Brayden. "It's not the wrong truck," he contradicted Wrigley. "The vehicle's specs match our intel, including the license plate number. The North Koreans must've pulled a switch."

"So what now?" Wrigley growled. "Just leave the truck here, dead in the middle of the road?" Wrigley had a habit of directing his questions at Madden while really challenging Brayden.

Paul "Wrigley" Dolinski, and his best friend on the Team, Joe Kopeck, were hard-bitten men of Polish decent, hailing from Pennsylvania working class. Their fathers had toiled a lifetime in the Pittsburgh steel mills, good fathers, to hear Wrigley and Kopeck tell it, but men who ruled with their fists. Wrigley and Kopeck laughed that *fuck up and feel it* was the way things went around their households. Neither of them had ever gotten away with shit, and in return they didn't forgive much.

Getting assigned to a team with those two on it was a bit like a baptism by fire for Brayden.

Both had faces only a mother could love. Wrigley might possess a few redeeming qualities from his Slavic ancestors, but Kettle-Faced Kopeck was hopeless, his smashed-together features making him look like a B-grade movie leg-breaker for the Polish mob.

Foxtrot had actually been dubbed Team Five's Brute Squad. Because—while Wrigley and Kopeck might be naturally ugly—there wasn't a single attractive man on Foxtrot. All of them were well-seasoned veterans who'd seen a lot of action and looked it, almost as if at some point a wrecking ball had rolled through the five, leaving behind a collection of scars, lumpy joints, and some attributes permanently mashed out of whack.

Brayden's "pretty boy" face was just another thing he had to overcome to get his teammates to take him seriously. If his men ended up fragging him for any reason during this tour, they could probably make a solid case for it in the SOF community based on his dimples alone.

"Hold up," Brayden said, stepping closer to the truck and peering in the back.

There was a computer inside. Not a mere laptop, either, but a complex setup: tower, screen, and keyboard attached to a built-in desk with a small generator.

"This might not be a total loss." Brayden gestured at the computer. "There could be some valuable intel on that." He pushed his speak button. "Three, One. Truck is a bust for weapons. Maintain overwatch and report incoming while I check in with Base."

"Roger that," Rongo confirmed.

"Pull back to cover," Brayden told the others.

The four of them returned to the trees while Brayden took the SAT phone off his belt.

"Base," he spoke into it, "Foxtrot One."

"Lima Charlie," a voice answered. *Loud and Clear.*

"Target truck has been engaged," he reported, "but weapons are a no-go. We've spotted a large computer inside that appears operational. Awaiting your orders."

"Roger, One," Base came back. "Hold for mission parameters."

"Copy that."

Another rumble of thunder rolled across the sky, and a few patters of rain came down, then stopped. *Strange.* Usually once the rain started, it fell in sheets.

"Foxtrot One," a voice came through the SAT phone, "Base."

"Go for One," Brayden answered.

"Be advised: the computer may be of high intel value. Do not attempt to move the truck or touch anything inside. A Special Missions unit is floating nearby in the Sea of Japan and is en route. They will arrive via airlift at an inlet in the Unggi Bay, three klicks away from your current location, and hump in to your position. Copy?"

Base waited for Brayden to confirm.

He didn't.

He held the SAT phone to his ear and stared at the trees in front of him, his stomach rolling into a tight knot.

A Special Missions unit is floating nearby…

The only in-country Special Missions unit was Justice's.

Brayden had found that out the hard way a week ago when Foxtrot was called in to rescue her unit in Pyonggang.

And for the second time in his life, he'd just let her walk away…

CHAPTER FORTY-FIVE

One week ago

"STREET."

Someone nudged Brayden's hammock, sending it into a gentle sway.

He opened his eyes, finding Lieutenant Havcheck's mangy face above him—guy never managed better than a patchy beard.

"Sir?" Brayden swung lithely out of his hammock and came to his feet, his combat boots clomping solidly on the C-130's metal floor.

"We're touching down at Camp Casey in ten," Havcheck told him. "Pilots want us to strap in for landing."

"Roger that." Brayden packed up his hammock while the other men of Yankee Platoon woke and did the same.

Gear stowed, Brayden found a jump seat near the aircraft's loading ramp. Setting his duffel between his legs, he strapped in and rested his rifle across his lap.

Minor G-forces tugged on his stomach as the cargo plane made its final descent into Camp Casey, the U.S. Army Base in South Korea closest to the DMZ, or Demilitarized Zone. All SpecOps operating in Korea worked out of Casey. At any given time a mix of Delta, Rangers, Force RECON, or SEALs could be at Casey, but right now the only in-country unit was Keith's—SEAL Team Five's fast-action guys, call sign Whiskey.

Foxtrot squad was Whiskey's relief.

As luck would have it, Brayden and Keith had ended up in San Diego together, both assigned to Team Five's Yankee Platoon—Brayden on a six-man squad, call sign Foxtrot, Keith on the four-man "element" built for rapid deployment.

After BUD/S, Brayden had followed the officer track and gone to JOTC, Junior Officer Training Course, while Keith headed directly into SQT. By the time Brayden made it through his own six months of SEAL Qualifying Training and arrived at Team Five, Keith had already pinned on his trident and deployed to Korea.

Brayden and Keith had only maintained spotty contact during Keith's six-month tour, so it'd be good to catch up with him again.

Last time he actually saw his brother was a year ago, right after BUD/S graduation.

A horrible fucking day.

Brayden had been sitting slumped on the couch in the officers' barracks community room after the ceremony, dressed in his cleaned and pressed camouflage uniform, his Certificate of Completion hanging limply from his fingertips. His throat was sticky with unspent emotions— the same way it'd felt during the whole time he stared at Justice's white-painted flipper prints, standing sickeningly empty on the grinder.

She was gone. Like, *gone* gone.

Off to her crypto school without speaking to him first.

He was stunned.

Last night had been a bag of shit, no denying it. Getting caught in the act—or near-act—had been an asshole mess. But as bad as the embarrassment was, he and Justice had just spent the last six months becoming close friends.

He couldn't believe that she wouldn't talk things out with him before she left.

"Did she say anything to you before she PCS'd?"

Brayden jerked his head up.

Keith was standing at the end of the couch, dressed the same way as Brayden. His left temple and cheek were darkened with bruises. Evidence of their throwdown last night—more of yesterday's horrible.

Brayden's own face still felt swollen and thick where Keith had punched him. "No. You?"

"No." Keith raked a hand over his hair. "Do you believe what Chief Tanner said about an ORDMOD requiring Justice to leave for her crypto school immediately?"

Brayden set his certificate on the couch. "No."

Keith glanced aside.

Brayden followed his brother's stare.

Someone had left a box of Honey Oh's cereal on the kitchen counter.

"You shouldn't have slept with her," Keith said, still focused on the cereal.

Brayden lowered his brows. "I didn't. I was in the process of telling her no when you busted in and made things worse."

Keith brought his focus back around. "From where I was standing, it didn't look like a whole lotta *no* was going on." He set his hands on his hips. "Justice wasn't in her right mind after SERE, Brayden. She was vulnerable as hell."

"No fucking kidding." Brayden stood abruptly, the couch cushion letting out a bilious wheeze. "Of course I knew Justice was hurting. But there she was, telling me that what she needed to feel better was for me to fuck her—and I should stick it up my ass if I tried to say otherwise. She's shoving her tits in my crotch and kissing me everywhere, while I'm struggling to figure out how to make her stop without being a jerk, because I don't want to hurt her even more. What would you have done, Keith? Please, bestow your infinite wisdom on me."

Keith didn't say anything.

"You've spent your whole life around me," Brayden snapped. "When have you ever known me to mistreat a woman?"

"Then why the hell did she bail?"

"Maybe because *you* acted like a jealous dipshit."

Keith scowled. "I did what?"

"*You're* in love with her," Brayden accused, the words a blade to his heart. Wasn't it an unspoken rule among brothers that they weren't supposed to fall for the same woman? Because, yeah…then throwdowns happened.

"The fuck I am," Keith shot back.

"You tried to kick the shit out of me."

"Because I thought you were taking advantage of someone on my boat team."

"In all the years we've been best friends, you've never once hit me, Keith."

Keith exhaled a harsh breath. "Did I notice Justice is a beautiful woman? Damned right I did. Did she and I become good friends over the six months of BUD/S? Without question. But if anything more than friendship ever tried to happen, I squashed it. I decided coming into the Teams that relationships were going to take a back seat to my career. I have designs on Green Team someday, hopefully Tier 1, and to achieve that level means constant deployments, which is no life to offer a girlfriend. I'm not in love with Justice," he repeated firmly. "So get off it."

Brayden stood in place, jealousy and uncertainty still a cold knife in his chest. He replayed BUD/S, seeing Keith and Justice together every day. BUD/S might've been a torment of punishment and pain, but at least Keith got to spend *every minute of it* with Justice.

"Does Justice know you're in love with her?" Keith

asked.

Brayden jerked his gaze up. He hadn't realized Keith knew.

The ceiling fan rattled as its whirling blades stirred up the hanging metal chain.

Brayden finally let go of a huge breath—and his jealousy. His brother wasn't the type to back down if he really wanted something. Okay, he believed Keith about Justice.

"Yes," Brayden answered, "I told her last night." And then she ran away.

"What are you going to do?"

"Now? Go get a drink." *About Justice?* Brayden had no idea. "You want to join me? It's our last chance for a while." Tomorrow the two of them would be heading off in separate directions.

"Yeah, that'd be good." Keith held out his hand. "Bury the hatchet?"

Brayden shook. "Definitely. I'm ready to be done with smackdowns."

They started toward the main entrance together.

As they passed Justice's open bedroom doorway, something caught Brayden's attention, and he stopped abruptly.

"What's wrong?" Keith asked.

Brayden stepped inside Justice's room and flipped on the light.

On her bunk was a T-shirt, brown with white lettering showing across the back.

H-A-Y-E-S.

Both men walked over to Justice's honorary brown shirt and stared at it.

"She didn't just forget that," Keith said.

"No." It was folded too neatly.

"Why the hell would she leave it behind on purpose?"

"Maybe she thinks she doesn't deserve it anymore."

Brayden inhaled a breath that ached in his chest. "She came to me for help last night—she never liked doing that."

Keith nodded. Slow. "True."

The pain in Brayden's chest worsened until he felt hollow. "And I never got the chance to help her." Rudy and Keith barged in, and everything went to shit.

"You should probably get in touch with her, Bray. Figure out what drove her off. Fix it."

"Yeah."

And he *had* tried. Many times.

He'd left message after message for her at her crypto school, but she never answered. Finally seeing the writing on the wall—she was done with him—he stopped trying to contact her. It was a completely rotten way to end things, but her mind was clearly made up.

The screech of the C-130's wheels touching down on the runway broke through Brayden's depressing thoughts.

Camp Casey in South Korea.

Real-world shit. Not training.

His heart hurried through its next couple of beats. The start of his first deployment was happening *now*.

He checked on the other men of Yankee Platoon, twelve total—a platoon consisted of sixteen men, but Whiskey's four were already in-country.

Team Five's AO, or Area of Operation, included Korea and the Northern Pacific, so after Foxtrot was dropped here in South Korea, the C-130 would take off again to bring Yankee's other squad, Romeo, to China.

The six men of Romeo were slouched in their jump seats, their MWD, or Military Working Dog, sacked out at Giddiup's feet. Giddiup had gone through BUD/S with Brayden.

Romeo was still partially bombed out on Ambien, and as soon as the aircraft took off, they'd be back in their hammocks.

The men of Foxtrot were ready to depart, looking relaxed and business-as-usual. Wrigley was picking food out of his teeth, and Kettle-Faced Kopeck was rearranging his balls. Rongo had his precious sniper rifle cradled in one arm like a baby and was using his other hand to fix his long, wavy hair. As if that could make a difference in his appearance. Boomerang sat in his usual way, his legs veed wide.

The C-130 landed with a jolt and a roar of reversing engines, then taxied briefly and lurched to a stop. The cargo door started to lower with a loud, *cru-shu-shu*, *cru-shu-shu*, gradually revealing an inky night sky full of metallic clouds.

The ramp clunked to the earth, letting in a blast of oppressive humidity, the cloying stench of fish, and a man wearing a gold clover leaf on the collar of his jungle camos.

"Lieutenant Commander Diako," he introduced himself, stopping halfway up the ramp. "Vacation's over, gentlemen. Jock up." He waved a closed iPad at their group. "Got an emergency exfil going down *right now*. Whiskey's off hunting an HVT, so Foxtrot's the in-country shit." He turned and strode back down the ramp. "Shift your asses."

Brayden jumped up and hotfooted it down the ramp with his teammates, every cell in his body suddenly hyperaware.

Jesus Christ, he was heading into enemy territory *tonight*.

"Lucky fucks," Giddiup called after them.

Chapter Forty-Six

THE MEN OF Foxtrot followed Commander Diako toward a squat building at the end of the runway. Lightning strobed in a double-flash, turning the building's walls an eerie shade of white.

"Get used to that," Diako warned.

"Who's the HVT Whiskey's after?" Lieutenant Havcheck asked the commander.

"Dr. Hyeong."

Havcheck nodded his approval. "A big catch."

Dr. Hyeong was North Korea's head nuclear physicist—Foxtrot had been briefed about him pre-deployment.

The CIA had been picking up some disturbing chatter about the scientist. Apparently, Dr. Hyeong was planning something big in a southern city of the U.S.—Atlanta or New Orleans or maybe Dallas. All in-country assets were under standing orders to grab the scientist if they spotted him.

He would be an easy ID. The guy had the most peculiar birthmark in the world on his right cheek: a red blotch in the shape of a third eye.

Their group entered the squat building, stepping directly into a briefing room furnished with an eight-man conference table surrounded by cushioned roller chairs, a white board up front, and a coffee-colored sofa in back.

Diako set his iPad on the table, opened it, and brought up an image.

They all gathered around.

Sweat rolled under Brayden's arms and down his temples. A short walk from the cargo plane to this briefing room, and he was already sweating from the humidity as if he'd just run three times the distance.

"We lucked out," Diako said. "When the shit hit, a satellite was in the right position out in space to give us some valuable imagery of the target location. As you can see"—Diako pointed at the iPad screen—"we've got three of our own trapped in a small cluster of trees at the bottom of a canyon. A fuckload of enemy gathered along the ridge."

"Those dead guys?" Wrigley sandpapered out, indicating the human-shaped lumps scattered on one side of the hill, their heat signatures faded to a dull white.

"Affirmative," Diako said. "Our guys fought off an initial assault. But the enemy has the high ground and superior numbers. It won't take them long to regroup and calculate their odds of success."

"Where the hell did all these fuckers come from?" Wrigley asked.

"According to our guys, this is a faction of North Korean Special Forces who they spotted at a nearby training site. Part B of this mission is to blow that site. But first we have to figure out how to extract our people." Diako changed pictures on the screen. "Last image of the location showed the enemy moving to surround the canyon completely. Not good for this op—Foxtrot won't be able to set up an effective firing position."

"How 'bout we lob mortars at 'em from an outer perimeter," Wrigley suggested through the rust and gravel living in his throat.

"Too risky." Lieutenant Havcheck ran a hand over his scraggly beard as he contemplated the screen. "To do real damage, we'd have to hit the ridgeline. Live mortars could easily create a rockslide and take out our friendlies."

Rongo made a dismissive gesture at the screen. "There's no ground high enough for a good shot."

Commander Diako grunted. "What I'm saying."

"Go low," Brayden recommended, "not high."

The group looked at him.

Brayden pointed at a waterway on the screen. "A river bisects the canyon, entering west and exiting east, and it runs right beside the small woods. Three of us can swim in and escort our people out via that river. Risk is minimal. Our guys will have to haul ass from the woods to the river, but they won't be exposed for very long."

Havcheck shook his head. "It's too far down the river from the point of contact at the woods to the east-end exit. The enemy will pop you as soon as you come up for air."

"We don't come up for air. We use these." Out of his pack, Brayden pulled a small scuba canister, one foot in length with a rubber mouthpiece attached to a valve on top.

Operations in Korea consisted mostly of *land* not *sea*, but SEALs arrived on deployment equipped for both—all the men in his squad would have two such metal canisters in his gear.

"Two minutes of breathable oxygen," Brayden added, "should give us enough time to swim the required distance."

"*If* we've got some good swimmers." Havcheck glanced at Diako. "Who's trapped in that canyon? They got any E&E skills?"

"Missus unit," Diako answered.

Brayden's pulse jacked up, then settled when the commander added, "Lieutenant Browning's team. Short timer's bad luck for him and his guys. He was due to roll tonight."

Havcheck smirked through his spotty beard. "That should motivate them to swim fast. Rongo and Boomerang, you're with me. We'll approach from the outer perimeter and pepper the bad guys with fire, create a distraction." He gestured at Brayden. "You take Wrigley and Kopeck to extract the Missus."

I take? Brayden stilled. *On the main rescue mission?*

Outside, the sky let out a surly grumble.

Havcheck gave Brayden a firm nod. "This is your idea, Street. You get the honors. I'll inform the Missus via SAT phone of the plan, let them know to watch for you with their NVGs. You'll signal them with an IR Illuminator"—which used infrared light, only visible through Night Vision Goggles—"when you three are in position to extract them."

Commander Diako grunted his approval of the plan. "Black Hawk helo is spun up on spot four right now, waiting to transport you to Echo Outpost—SpecOps rendezvous point right on the DMZ."

They concluded the brief by determining a set of prowords—code words said over comms to mark each step of the op successfully completed. Theirs were based on Family Guy characters.

"Roger that," Havcheck said. "All right, men, hightail it—hard and fast run time. We've got four miles to cover once we get to Echo."

They hustled from the briefing room and jogged outside.

With a thunderous clap of sound, a jagged shard of lightning tore open the sky in a blaze of white fury, and rain slanted down.

BRAYDEN'S HEART HAMMERED, matching the rhythm of the buckshot raindrops denting the river water. The deluge was nearly blinding, and the water temperature was cooler than he would've expected in the summer. Had it been winter, this op wouldn't have been doable without wet suits—and who knew if any of those were just lying around at Casey?

A small point in their favor, this happening in June.

Brayden would take any he could get.

The number of bad guys wasn't a point to their advantage. There *were* a fuckload. Brayden couldn't see them very clearly since he couldn't wear NVGs with a dive mask, but he could hear their shouted crosstalk over the flurry of the river and the pelting rain—and if he could hear them over that shit, it meant there were a lot.

Gunfire *pop-popped*, the occasional illuminated tracer round streaking the air.

Havcheck, Rongo, and Boomerang were engaging the North Koreans.

Wrigley, swimming on point, raised his IR Illuminator out of the water, judging the physics of the current expertly. The first Missus, a short guy, darted out of the woods with just enough time to arrive at the edge of the river the exact moment Wrigley did.

Wrigley gestured him forward.

The guy quickly slid into the water.

Wrigley connected him to a buddy line, handed him a scuba canister, then stuck a second canister into his own mouth.

The two submerged.

Nobody shot at them.

Havcheck's distraction was working.

Kopeck arrived on target, gesturing a second man to—

Brayden's heart seized.

The moonlight silhouetted enough of a curvy figure to assure him that the person approaching Kopeck was no man. Rounded breasts, a tautly indented waist, the gentle flare of hips—the quintessential hourglass shape of *woman* but with tight athleticism drawing the lines. The body provided a big clue about who the person actually was, but the bun on the back of the head was a lock.

Justice.

Brayden's lungs emptied of air.

Kopeck didn't hesitate over the unexpected appearance of a female in the middle of a North Korean firefight. He attached her to his side—and didn't the man's ugly face need pounding now?—and handed her a scuba canister.

They submerged.

Brayden collected his Missus guy—a large man with glasses—and arrived downstream of the volatile canyon moments after Kopeck and Wrigley had climbed onshore with their two charges.

Brayden came out of the river with water flooding off him and felt the skin across his chest split as a door opened inside him, releasing a deep-seated pain.

The agony of losing the woman he'd fallen in love with on sight had never fully left him during the past year. Sometimes it hibernated, other times it roared, but the dogged craving for her was always there.

And now here she was, smiling at her rescuer and shaking his hand.

Kopeck was blinking at her through the rain and pumping her arm on repeat.

Brayden couldn't clearly see Kettle-Faced Kopeck's expression, but he could guess well enough that the man had never been within twenty yards of such a beautiful woman's mere airspace, much less experienced the touch of her hand.

And even as a drowned rat, Justice was something to see.

A sudden hot pressure pushed at Brayden's ribs.

"Thank you!" Justice shouted to be heard over the battering rain. "*All* of you." She turned to meet his stare but squinted through the deluge without recognition. "You saved our asses."

The SAT phone at Brayden's waist vibrated. He jerked

it off his belt and unwrapped its plastic covering. "Foxtrot Two," he answered.

"This is One," Havcheck said, sounding out of breath and strained. "Status report?"

"Phase Stewie secured, sir, but it's Lieutenant Hayes's unit, not Browning's."

"Affirmative. Browning and Hayes made a last-minute swap we weren't informed of—Browning's wife went into labor, and Hayes took the op for him."

And since comms were dark during the underwater part of the op, this was all such a nice surprise for Brayden.

"Uh, yes, sir," Brayden said. "Roger that. Moving on to Phase Lois." Lois meant Brayden's team would escort the Missus to Echo now.

"Negative, Two. I've been shot."

Brayden stiffened. "Sir, are you okay?"

"Mostly dinged up, but out of commission. Unable to move on to Phase Peter"—setting charges to blow the North Korean SpecOps training facility—"so I need you to take point on this part of op."

And leave Bat Three? Brayden stood in place and stared at Justice.

"Two? You copy?"

"Yes, sir. Solid copy. Advancing on your position now." Brayden resecured his SAT phone to his belt.

Wrigley jerked his chin at his waterlogged charges. "You want me 'n' Joe to get Oscar Mike with these three to Echo?" Wrigley had heard Havcheck's order.

Brayden nodded rigidly. "Affirmative. Exfil from there."

"Roger that."

The five took off into the woods.

Brayden watched them go, one hand clenched around his SAT phone, a year's worth of silence still lodged in his throat.

CHAPTER FORTY-SEVEN

ECHO OUTPOST WAS a slapped-together, windowless wooden shack hidden in the forestland of South Korea, but practically sitting on the North Korean border. A SpecOps hangout, it was a place to kick back, tell war stories, get high on Red Bull, and argue about whose beard was the longest— not Brayden's, he kept his trimmed short. Whiskers itched like fuck.

Basically, a place to regroup and recharge.

Wrigley and Kopeck and their three Missus were already gone by the time the four remaining men of Foxtrot arrived—Brayden, Sniper Rongo and his spotter Boomerang, plus an injured Lieutenant Havcheck, who'd ridden most of the way on Brayden's back.

Brayden called in a dust-off for Havcheck, but the bird that arrived out of Camp Casey was a Huey, too small to carry all four men with the load it was already hauling.

Boomerang and Brayden agreed to take a later transport while Rongo hopped on board with the wounded lieutenant.

Brayden tramped back to the shack after seeing the helo off and crashed down onto a stool outside—a shack without windows was probably a sauna inside. Tipping back on the stool's rear two legs, he leaned against the wall and blinked heavily.

A four-mile hard run from Echo Outpost to the canyon in Pyonggang, a half-mile swim to rescue the Missus, a quasi-meetup with Justice for the first time in a year and not saying anything to her, a one-mile run to a North Korean SpecOps training facility to blow it, a five-mile run back to Echo Outpost humping Havcheck…

Very exhausting shit.

Boomerang came out of the shack with a couple of cans of Coke. He held one out to Brayden. "It's warm." He angled his head back at the slap-together. "No electricity it this shit-pile."

"Got anything stronger?" Brayden asked sardonically as he accepted the Coke. "It's been a helluva first night."

Boomerang's lips twitched. "It's caffeine."

Point. They were all still on California time.

Boomerang took a seat on another stool and sat with his legs in an extra-wide spread, probably making room for what were considered to be the biggest balls on Team Five—not based on anything visually confirmed but because he was always the first man into all the nastiest places.

Rangy, with dark eyes and a lantern jaw, Boomerang was a man of action. He didn't talk as he drank his Coke.

Which was fine by Brayden right now.

He popped his soda with a *fzzzz* and drank a large swallow. Lightning streaked in noiseless darts between oily clouds, the sky endlessly wrapping the earth.

His mother was under this same sky—was she painting right now?—and his brothers. What were they doing? Was Walt trying to hustle some woman into bed? Was Adam going extreme on his skateboard?

Booted footsteps crunched the earth, approaching the shack.

Boomerang snapped alert.

So did Brayden, dropping forward on his stool and lifting his M-4.

He was stopped by a low whistle of greeting.

Four sweaty men wearing jungle camos appeared out of

the night, rifles slung over their shoulders.

Whiskey's fast-action guys.

Keith smiled, his teeth showing white against his dark beard. "Well, look what the fucking cat dragged in."

Smiling back, Brayden shoved up from his stool, his shins protesting the pressure. "Well, look who needs a fucking shower."

His brother was carrying a heavy layer of grit on him, although it was the grit of experience as much as anything. And, yeah, knowing Keith, he'd just completed a kick-ass deployment.

Brayden would have some big boots to fill.

As usual.

A spot heated in the middle of his chest as the familiar self-doubts rose, and with them, the hated questions. Had he genuinely been outperformed by Keith all these years? Or had he subconsciously let himself be beaten to get along? Did Keith take on the role of leader—when, as eldest, Brayden should've been the one in charge—because their father put Brayden in a one-down position? Or by his own doing?

"'Bout fucking time our relief arrived." A dark-complexioned man wearing a boonie hat instead of a combat helmet let out a hiss. "We've been—" He stopped talking and squinted at Boomerang. "'Rang, that you, man? What the hell you still doing alive?"

Three of the Whiskey guys moved forward to join Boomerang.

Keith stopped in front of Brayden. "Think I'll pass on the brotherly man-hug myself." He gestured at Brayden's soaked clothes. "You're going to want to avoid the downpours as much as possible. Your clothes never fully dry in this humidity."

"It's partly river water," Brayden said. "Just finished

hauling the Missus out of a clusterfuck."

"You're kidding?" Keith laughed. "How long you been in-country?"

"Oh, I don't know…" Brayden glanced at his watch. "A few hours."

Keith shook his head. "Fucking Browning. What kind of deep shit did he get himself into this time?"

Brayden sipped his Coke. "It was Justice's unit, actually."

"Yeah?" Keith took off his helmet and tucked it under one arm. "I heard her team was due in-county any day. Didn't think she was here yet. So you saw her?"

"Yep."

"And?"

"And what?"

"And… What do you mean, *and what*? What did you say, what did she say?"

"We didn't talk."

"You didn't…" Keith frowned. "Why the fuck not?"

"We didn't have the chance."

"You didn't have *the chance* to finally get some answers out of her?"

Brayden's face tautened. "We were sort of in the middle of an E&E inside enemy territory," he defended himself. "It wasn't that simple."

"Probably wasn't that complicated, either."

A muscle spasmed in Brayden's cheek.

More questions.

Did he not talk to Justice post-rescue because there really hadn't been an opportunity? Or because he knew she'd reject him and so he'd pussied out?

One of the Whiskey guys let loose with a ribald laugh, and Brayden glanced over. The guy looked so young he probably still had amniotic fluid in his ears.

Keith gestured Brayden to move farther away from the shack. "Don't hose this up, Bray. This is the woman you're crazy about."

"I'm well aware of that," he said stiffly. "Doesn't matter. The sentiment's not returned."

"How the hell do you know? You haven't talked to Justice since BUD/S."

"You don't think I've tried to talk to her," he clipped out, a sour taste sitting on the back of his tongue. "She never answered any of my messages. I think that makes it pretty damned clear she wants nothing to do with me."

"It doesn't make fuck-all clear," Keith argued. "You remember how tightly wrapped she was the first week of BUD/S?"

He remembered.

"Locking down is how she deals with life's crap, and having me and Dunbar see her trying to smoke your pole clearly wasn't a banner moment for her."

Brayden's face flushed. "Nice way to sugarcoat it, Keith."

"You don't need sugarcoating. You need a kick in the ass to get over your own shit."

He cooled his voice. "My own shit?"

His brother paused. "Fuck," he muttered, rubbing a hand over his beard. "I've never told you this before because I didn't want to add fuel to the fire, but..." He hesitated again, as if weighing his next words. "You doubt yourself too much."

The tic started up in Brayden's cheek again. "Ah. Okay, thanks." Nothing like having one's own inner worries spoken aloud. He started to back away.

"I'm not trying to be a douche here, Bray. I get it. Dad messed with your head. He ignored you." Keith's eyes darkened, clouding with shadows of the past. "I've spent a lifetime watching you question your decisions because of that."

Brayden stood rigidly in place. A mosquito buzzed the opening of his Coke can.

"But the thing you don't get—the part you *need* to get—is that Dad treats you the way he does because he's taking out your mother's rejection of him on you."

A bucket of cold water poured over Brayden. The mosquito moved to fly in tight circular patterns at the back of his neck.

"There's nothing fucking wrong with you. Dad being an asshole toward you is on *Dad*." Keith gestured in a general way with his M-4. "So work up your nut and confront Justice. She's still in lockdown—even now—and you won't know how she really feels about anything until you shake her loose."

Just what he wanted—to deal with Justice's rejection face-to-face.

Brayden chucked his Coke toward a half-full Hefty garbage bag near the shack. "There's just one problem with your plan."

The can landed on its side and began to urp up brown liquid.

"I have no idea when I'm going to see her again."

CHAPTER FORTY-EIGHT

Present day
North Korea
Near the AH6 Highway between Najin and Sonbong

LYING ON HIS belly, Night Vision Goggles dropped down over his eyes, Brayden watched the three human forms thread through the trees—two with billed caps on, the third with a bun at the back of her head, and…

The quintessential hourglass shape of woman.

Brayden's pulse fired in rapid bursts through his veins, pumping heat throughout his entire body.

Second-chance time, bonehead. It's a miracle you got it. Blow it with Justice again, and you'll turn into what Keith said you are—an insecure little pussy.

And the fuck if he was going to be that.

He'd done a lot of thinking over this past week—ever since Keith dropped his payload of hard-speaking, just-keeping-it-real-dawg, brotherly-love wisdom on him—and had come to several conclusions.

First and foremost: Keith was wrong about him. Just because he doubted himself sometimes didn't make him a candy-assed decision-maker.

Second, Keith was correct about the situation with Justice: she *was* still in lockdown, and Brayden would have to shake her loose from it if he wanted to get anywhere with her.

Fate, the Universe, God, the Olympians, Buddha…all

and whoever…were on his side in the matter. The North Korean Army truck Foxtrot had taken down had a *computer* onboard, not weapons.

And so now Justice was headed his way.

The hard part was that the two of them were on a mission again, not tucked away in some private corner. All of Foxtrot was around, and his teammates' ears tended to grow as big as Dumbo's when it came to listening in on shit that was none of their damned business—eager to overhear any info they could use for jokes and ribbing for years to come.

Justice's long, loping strides ate up the distance between them in no time.

Brayden lifted his NVGs and pushed up onto one knee, resting the stock of his M-4 nose-down on his thigh.

Justice drew up to his location and took a knee, her two guys doing the same a couple of paces behind her.

"Foxtrot?" she confirmed quietly, tucking her GPS into her back pocket and sweeping off a pair of strap-on NVGs.

"Roger that," Brayden verified.

The sound of his voice slammed a steel rod into her backbone.

He hesitated.

Work up your nut and confront her.

Right. *Make* the chance.

Brayden pretended not to notice her reaction. "These are the guys," he introduced his men, first indicating the chief, still prone. "Chief Madden."

Madden glanced up at her with a "Hey," then went back to keeping track of the truck through his rifle scope.

"Over there are Wrigley and Kopeck." The Polish twins were kneeling two trees over. "Rongo and Boomerang are on overwatch."

Justice unlocked her stare from Brayden long enough to nod a brief greeting at the men, taking an extra moment to squint at Wrigley and Kopeck, possibly wondering what the hell kind of creatures she'd suddenly found herself alone in the dark with.

Like something Mary Shelly and Bram Stoker might've invented in a condemned lab, probably.

"You already know Joe Kopeck," Brayden went on, still being matter-of-fact. "A week ago he swam you out of some trouble in a canyon."

Kopeck smiled, exposing teeth spaced like broken barrel slats.

"And, of course, you know me." Brayden laughed off-handedly as he tossed over his shoulder to his men, "Lieutenant Hayes and I went through BUD/S together."

His men looked on silently, no doubt fascinated by watching pretty boy's ship sink. *Lusitania, Titanic, Costa Concordia*—all famous sinking disasters. Plus him. *Save yourself!*

Justice's lashes were starting to spike and quiver. She wasn't blinking much.

He moved on to explain the current situation with the truck—it was supposed to have been transporting weapons, turned out to be harboring a rather big-ass computer, yadda, yadda.

Justice peered at the truck.

Funny how she was such a sturdy woman in many respects, yet the bones in her profile looked almost delicate.

She started to drill questions at him. "Have you been inside? Touched anything? Flipped any switches?"

"Negative. We were ordered to wait for your unit."

She nodded briskly.

"Ma'am?" The biggest of the Missus—the guy with glasses, who Brayden rescued from the canyon last week—asked, "You want me to go check it out?"

"No, Ron, I don't want you to do anything of the sort."

Brayden looked between the two, then lifted his brows. "Why not?" *Isn't that what you're here for?*

"I've got a strange feeling about this," she answered. "Something's hinky."

The shorter Missus guy turtled his head in, like the moment Justice pronounced herself to have a strange feeling something nasty would strike.

Brayden, for his part, didn't hear either the high-pitched whistle of an incoming mortar or the low but distinctive sonic percussion of an arriving bullet. "About what?"

Her mouth turned down. She glanced again at the truck, still sitting on the road encircled in a halo of streetlight. "How easy was it to disable that truck?"

He shrugged. "Easy."

She made a *hmm* sound.

"And?"

"This might be a trap."

He smiled broadly, letting his dimples rip. He generally didn't use his dimples for purely manipulative purposes— like softening a woman's attitude toward him—but he needed every advantage he could get with Justice. "Or maybe my guys and I are good."

She scowled at him.

"Uh…" he backpedaled. "It's not that I'm not taking you seriously. But wouldn't we have been ambushed already, if this was a trap?"

She gestured stiffly at the truck. "There's a computer onboard, Lieutenant. What does that tell you?" She didn't let him answer. "The enemy has baited their trap for *us*, not you—or not *only* you. Special Missions has been causing the North Korean nuclear program a lot of problems lately. Lieutenant Browning's unit for the past six months, and now mine. My guess is that the truck is rigged to blow. The moment we turn on the computer, it'll be Goodnight

Gracie. Maybe even the moment we step onboard. I need to examine the undercarriage to confirm it's safe."

"Okay." If she knew what needed to be done, why wasn't she doing it?

"*Not* okay. The hinky part is that I feel like we're being watched."

"We're not." Brayden shook his head. "We cleared the area."

She didn't move. Her eyes reflected pinpoints of light from the moon, making it difficult for him to get a full bead on her reaction. Probably a good thing. The tension rolling off her was about as thick as it got.

"All right," he said. "Stand by." He pressed his speak button. "Foxtrot Three, One. You got any contacts?"

"Negative," Rongo answered.

"No heat signatures anywhere? On either of the hillsides?"

"Nada. All's quiet."

"Roger that." Brayden disengaged comms. "You're good," he told Justice.

She still didn't move.

Brayden scratched the back of his head. The motion tipped his helmet forward. He straightened it.

Justice's jaw knotted. "Look, I don't know how to explain this to you. Call it a thief's Sixth Sense for knowing when we're being watched. But I believe my gut more than your overwatch."

And he believed in what his sniper could tangibly see through a magnetized scope more than in the crystal ball speakings of *anyone's* gut. But he said, "All right," anyway, because he respected Justice, and also there was, you know, the whole *I-wanna-get-back-to-what-we-were-doing-the-night-after-SERE* motivation for keeping the peace.

I love your happy trail. I love where it goes...

He cleared his throat. Squirming in his pants probably wouldn't be a smooth move right now. "I'll call in EOD."

Her eyes narrowed. "So *they* can get shot at or blown up? Never mind. I'll go." She thrust to her feet in a sudden burst, slapping wet mud off her knee.

Brayden came to his feet too.

"Just tell your overwatch to make sure I don't get fucking killed." She started for the truck.

He fell into step beside her.

She stopped.

He smiled. "Seems like I should stick close." Seeing as she was really serious about this.

She pressed her lips together and gave him a look that proclaimed she thought he'd be more of a nuisance than a help. He also noticed she didn't express any concerns about *him* getting shot at or blown up.

They continued together toward the truck.

Clacking his NVGs down, he knelt at the outer edge of the halo of streetlight, off the rear of the vehicle. He pointed his attention toward the hills, scanning back and forth, while in his periphery he saw Justice circle the truck, inspecting it from every angle.

She stopped at the hood, spun her fanny pack from back to front, then dropped onto her spine and began to work her way under the truck's engine block inchworm-style.

A Naval intelligence-gathering expert wouldn't do this. No, such a person was *supposed* to go inside the truck and boot up the computer.

So when Justice instead scooted under the truck, whomever was watching—and, damn, she was right about that—obviously figured the jig was up about their ambush—and, yeah, she was right about the trap too. More than a half dozen enemy combatants materialized on the west side hill, appearing as if by magic when they threw off heat-shielding blankets.

Shit!

"Contacts!" Rongo's voice blasted into his earpiece.

Brayden got off a couple of shots, his spent brass *chinking* across the asphalt, before chaos erupted.

The human forms started shooting back, bullets zinging everywhere, *thwatting* into the asphalt of the road and *dinging* directly into the truck.

Blam! Blam! Blam!

The rest of Foxtrot joined the firefight.

"Get out of there!" Brayden shouted at Justice.

If the truck was rigged to blow—and she'd been right about everything else—then a bullet in the wrong place would detonate the explosives on board.

Justice rapid-scooted out from under the truck.

Zzzzt.

Zzzzt.

More enemy down, thanks to Rongo.

Hopping to her feet, Justice sped for the trees.

Machine-gun fire roared, and—just like a scene right out of a classic Red Baron movie—mini mushroom clouds of dirt chased after her boots.

Fuck!

She wasn't wearing a single bulletproof item of clothing to keep her from getting her ass shot dead.

Brayden ran after her, veering across her path. He put himself between her and enemy fire to—

Lightning flickered.

For a moment he thought he'd been struck by it. A searing pain socked him in the middle of his back. He was suddenly being picked up off the ground, his feet racing along the topsoil. With a shout, he crashed into Justice.

She twisted as if to catch him, but the abrupt turn of her body sent him pitching sideways.

He grabbed for her.

They spun in a half circle, tangling together. He went down first, hitting the ground on his back with a *woof* of expelled air, and she came down on top of him.

Panting, they lay where they'd landed in what could only be described as Inside-Out Missionary Position—his bent legs were spread wide while her hips were nestled between them.

I'm very clear about what I want, Brayden, and it's sex…

Clang! Didn't the male brain pick the damnedest moments to remember certain things?

Had the two of them been naked, there was no way he could've gotten his dick inside her in their current position, but her crotch was snugged up next to his package and he felt…movement down below.

He groaned, although the noise was partially due to pain.

He'd been shot.

A few raindrops sprinkled down, and he squinted. Any second he'd have enough oxygen in his lungs to ask Justice if she was okay.

She sprawled motionless on top of him, clearly stunned by their fall. Her nose was half-mashed into the area between his ear and shoulder, and…and *her crotch was snugged up next to his package*.

She sure as hell felt okay.

Madden's face appeared above them, backdropped by the cloudy night sky.

Brayden heard an owl hoot, and it dawned on him then that the gunfire had stopped.

Madden idly scratched his scarred cheek, like it was no big deal to find Lieutenants Hayes and Street locked together in a sex clinch during a gun battle…or that neither of them had made any attempt to untangle themselves. Navy

Chiefs probably figured it was best not to question the crazy-assed way officers did things—such was the kind of wisdom that earned them a place as Navy Chiefs.

"The rest of the bad guys squirted," Madden informed him.

Brayden opened his mouth, but only air poured out when Justice lurched to get off him and accidentally kneed him in the ass.

She stood on braced legs, glaring down on him. "You still think I'm *good*, Street?"

Well now...couldn't that question be answered in myriad ways?

CHAPTER FORTY-NINE

THE USS *BONHOMME Richard's* briefing room was furnished with six rows of cushioned, burgundy faux leather armchairs set in a semi-circle of stadium seating. Down front was an oblong wood table surrounded by more comfortable armchairs. Thick tan carpeting softened the thump of booted footsteps, and a small bar portside of the table was outfitted with a coffee urn, mugs, pastries and snacks, along with a fruit bowl, plus a mini fridge.

The needs of important strategists obviously sat high up on the *Richard's* priority list.

The briefing room was built for comfort.

The oblong table was undoubtedly reserved for bigwigs, but Brayden grabbed a seat there anyway. He needed to be able to brace his elbows on a tabletop and lean forward. The bullet he'd taken to his back was embedded in his flak jacket, not his flesh, but considering the round's velocity when it hit him, the ouch factor was a motherfucker.

The other men of Foxtrot took his lead and dropped into the remaining chairs surrounding the table.

The two Missus guys sat in the front row of the stadium seating. As soon as their butts hit the faux leather, they had their cell phones out and their noses glued to the screens.

"How long we gotta wait here?" Kettle-Faced Kopeck wrenched his helmet off, revealing streaks of discoloration on his forehead and cheeks where sweat had met dirt and mingled.

Brayden didn't answer, too preoccupied with tracking Justice as she made her way to the small bar.

No longer concealed by night, no longer a drowned rat, she was now on full display, and, *holy shit*, but she was even more beautiful than before.

Minus the stress of BUD/S, her figure had developed into something more womanly. Well-shaped shoulders still complemented a flat belly and sleek hips—and these she wore with the same attendant athleticism—but now there was an added sumptuousness to her body. Her breasts were more voluptuous, her hips riper, her legs—already her tour de force—so nubile that Brayden couldn't look at them without imagining how they'd feel wrapped around his waist, squeezing him tight to urge him on.

"Lieutenant?" Kopeck butted back into Brayden's thoughts. "How long?"

Justice dropped her fanny pack on the floor next to the bar and opened the mini fridge, crouching down in front of it to…

And there it was.

Her ass.

Brayden tensed his stomach muscles as he began to harden.

Her butt's shapely proportions were outlined against her black-and-gray camo combat pants to perfection. He was being given unimpeded access to the view—he was seated at the head of the table directly across from the small bar—while the other men had to turn their heads to look.

Which they did.

Except for Madden. The chief snapped open the action of his M-4 and peered inside. Being married with a kid on the way probably had something to do with it.

Kopeck kept at him. "Hey, boss…"

"Until we've been debriefed," Brayden said shortly.

The truck-switcheroo-plus-ambush twist on their mission had wadded up a bunch of superior officers' undershorts. The CO of the *Richard* was being flown over to the battle group's carrier USS *Theodore Roosevelt* to report to the admiral, and the skipper wanted a full accounting of the details before he went.

"Anyone want water?" Justice asked.

"I do," Rongo answered in a velvety rasp, his inspection of her turning smoldering.

A nerve pulsed in Brayden's cheek. He forced himself to inhale a calming breath through compressed nostrils. All men eyeballed Justice. *Understood.* Most men merely stared—with fascination, interest, astonishment, hunger: the usual gamut. Some followed up with flirting. Others couldn't stop a steady flow of crude comments from coming out of their mouths, like the Brad Zieglers of the world.

But Rongo was his own breed of problematic.

He was the type of fucked-up guy who would take advantage of a crowded bus to rub his dick against a woman and assume two things: One, there wouldn't be any repercussions for his behavior, because two, the woman would be complimented by his attention. This attitude was born from arrogance—the sniper was all but infallible in the field. And while Brayden slept better at night knowing Rongo was on his overwatch, in all other respects the man was a real tool.

Justice stood, holding two water bottles. "Sorry, there's no ice for your back."

It took a beat for Brayden to realize she was talking to him. How nice. "I'm good."

Justice fired one of the water bottles at Rongo.

The sniper caught it one-handed, never taking his eyes off her. "So…" He cocked his head. "What's the deal with your name?" He smiled a languid, sideways smile—the one that meant he was about to say something oh-so-clever. "Your dad a judge?"

Justice opened her water bottle. "No."

"So Justice is a nickname?"

"Yes."

Rongo treated her to his patented moue. Probably it was supposed to be sexy.

Wrigley glanced at Kopeck and smirked.

On the Universal Scale of Female Hotness those two had developed, a five was about the highest number the men of Foxtrot could bag—with the exception of Madden. He was married to a pretty Navy corpsman, although the chief was really more scary than ugly.

When it came to Wrigley and Kopeck, neither man ever hunted outside of his feasible number zone. Those two knew exactly what their limitations were, and it was a source of endless amusement to them that Rongo should be so clueless about his own.

The arrogant sniper operated under the misconception that he was good-looking, even though he wholly deserved to be on the Brute Squad. His forehead was too broad, his nose too flat, his lips too full, and his too-long, dark, curly hair only heightened his overlarge features. His right shoulder also sat permanently higher than his left. Not from faulty DNA, but from an old injury. Still…even if a woman could see past all the other ugly, the biological drive not to breed the qualities of Quasimodo into her offspring would send her in the opposite direction, fast.

"What's your real name?" Rongo set his water bottle on his lap—directly on top of his dick.

Brayden narrowed his eyes.

Justice watched Rongo.

The men watched her watching him.

"Julianne?" Rongo guessed. "Janet?"

Madden pulled an oilcloth out of his back pocket and began to polish his rifle.

Justice tilted up her water bottle and drank for a long moment.

"Jocelyn?"

"Justine," she finally said.

"Hey, I like that name!"

Justice blotted water off her mouth with the back of her wrist. "I don't."

"Aw, why not?" Rongo stroked his thumb up and down the length of his water bottle.

Up. Down.

A stream of boiling air leaked slowly from Brayden's nostrils.

"Is it a secret?" Rongo asked, all coy-like.

Justice gave him a flat look.

Wrigley smirked again at Kopeck. Talk about disasters at sea. Rongo's sinking ship was about to break records for how fast it hit bottom.

"Is it?" Rongo pressed.

"No. Just not a topic of conversation." Justice turned around to search through the fruit bowl, giving Rongo her back—unfortunately, that meant another gander at her ass. Her body language clearly sent the message: *discussion over.*

Wrigley pantomimed laughter at Rongo, then mouthed, *Loser.*

Rongo's nostrils flared. "There's a good story behind how Dolinski got the nickname Wrigley. Tell her, Paul."

Justice turned back around, holding—of all things, *dear God*—a banana.

The men froze.

Beat.

They all unfroze.

The entire table, in fact—minus the oblivious chief—

did an anticipatory forward-lean, waiting for Justice to peel that banana, maybe slowly, then eat it, maybe even more slowly, then…do sexed-up things with the phallic symbol that would spin way off the rails.

It was the kind of wishful thinking that completely ignored the fact that this wasn't *Penthouse Forum*. Or *Maxim*.

"What's the story?" Justice asked.

"Ah…yeah." Wrigley cleared his throat, although that did nil to smooth out the concrete mixer his larynx used to produce sounds. "Me and Joe here"—he gestured at Kopeck—"were out booming one night with a coupla girls. We all got really wasted, right? And on the drive back to our place—to take the party to the next level, see—one of the girls barfs in my lap. After that, the mood starts to, you know, die down. But Joe here doesn't get laid very often, and I didn't want him to lose his chance. So I gave my girl a stick of Juicy Fruit, then made out with her to keep the night moving along."

Justice's brows lifted. "Why didn't people nickname you Juicy Fruit then?"

Wrigley laughed. "Probably because they value their teeth." His smile showed his own teeth, dingy gray and probably unflossed since the age of ten.

Boomerang leaned back in his chair, broadening his wide spread. "You end up getting laid?" he asked Joe.

Kopeck lit up and nodded vigorously. "Oh, yeah."

At that, Big Missus and Little Missus popped their heads up. They studied Kopeck, then exchanged glances. *What in ungodly fuck had that woman looked like?*

Justice peered down at the banana in her hand, considered it a moment, then put it back in the fruit bowl.

The room deflated a bit.

"Now, me," Rongo took charge again, "my name is one-hundred percent Polynesian." He thumped his chest. "Rongo Tonono."

Justice's lips slanted. "Well, that's a mouthful."

Winking, Rongo purred, "Just like I am."

Madden stopped polishing his rifle.

The fuse burning down to Brayden's brain-blow of temper cooked faster.

Rongo lounged indolently in his chair and smirked. "Now Boomerang here got his nickname because he always comes back. No matter what. He's been shot, stabbed, burned, fragged, and broken into pieces, but he's made it back every time. He's got a fuckload of scars. Show her, 'Rang."

"No."

"Oh, well." Rongo gave Justice another flirty head-tilt. "You got any scars? I mean, I see the one on your forehead, but...anywhere else?" Rongo's brows slid into a lecherous angle.

Brayden slammed to his feet.

CHAPTER FIFTY

"ATTENTION ON DECK!" the ship's XO barked as he barged inside the briefing room.

Already standing, Brayden snapped into a rigid posture, while the others rose to their feet and came to attention.

The CO of the *Bonhomme Richard*, Commander Abe Cardoso—with a face he'd left out in salt spray a couple of cruises too long—strode inside. He told them to relax.

The debrief commenced.

Brayden and Justice, as the two officers, did most of the talking.

During it all, the edges of Brayden's nostrils flexed tight on each grab he made for air.

That's a mouthful.

Just like I am.

Up. Down.

By the time the brief concluded, the skin on Brayden's nostrils felt stretched too tight and the lower rims of his eyes, overheated.

The CO left, and the XO dismissed them.

Justice picked up her fanny pack. "Catch you later, gents," she said to the men of Foxtrot. "Nice working with you." She left through the east-side door.

The two Missus guys headed out the west exit.

Rongo stretched, tendons in his humped-up shoulder popping. "Well, time to hit the hay."

Foxtrot had been assigned temporary beds onboard the

ship for the night.

But Rongo clearly had no intention of heading to his own rack—otherwise he would've departed west, like the Missus guys, in the direction of the enlisted quarters.

He started east.

Brayden stepped into the sniper's path.

Rongo drew up.

"You're not going through that door."

No need to indicate which door. Everyone in the room—Brayden, Rongo, their audience—knew he meant Justice's door.

"Yeah?" Rongo tossed back flippantly. "What're you going to do about it?"

A direct challenge to Brayden's authority—it had to come at some point.

Rongo sneered. "Kick me off Foxtrot?"

"This isn't about rank," Brayden said in an iron voice. "It's not about an officer throwing his weight around. It's about being a Team Guy, Tonono. Lieutenant Hayes is a member of our squad. For one mission or a dozen, it doesn't matter—she's one of us. You want to be the type of man who backs up his team members?" Brayden vised his focus in on the sniper. "Or who fucks them over?"

The inevitable stare-down commenced, the silence stone-cold, the tension thick.

After a couple of crackling seconds, Rongo finally sniffed and stepped back. "Whatever," he said, snatching up his pack. "I don't have a condom on me, anyway."

Brayden gathered his own gear, attaching his helmet to his pack, then hiking the bag onto one shoulder, his rifle on the other. All the movement elevated the pain in his back from motherfucker to cocksucker while his skull split open and spilled lava over Rongo's *condom* comment.

Brayden aimed for the east-side door. It was where he

needed to go to find his temporary rack in Officers Country, but he also had every intention of hunting down Justice.

Did he feel like a hypocrite for telling Rongo he couldn't go after Justice, then going after her himself?

Not a bit.

Don't hose this up, Bray. This is the woman you're crazy about…

A year of silence was about to come to an end.

JUSTICE CLOSED THE door to her stateroom.

She didn't slam it.

She applied firm, steady pressure with her palm until she heard the latch *click* into place, the door snugging up flush against the jamb. *Good. Okay. All secure.* Precision in certain things kept the mind from splintering to pieces over other things. *Right?*

Right.

Leaning back against the door, she stared across the room at the set of bunk beds. She and her roommate, Marine Corps First Lieutenant Tiffany Tesarik—the *Richard's* meteorological officer—hadn't done much to liven up the functional-only atmosphere of this stateroom with "womanly touches."

A rainbow afghan was draped across the foot of Tiffany's bottom bunk, and a pinup calendar of horses was thumb-tacked over her metal desk.

On Justice's desk there was a small, clear plastic bowl with a fake goldfish in it. Press a button on the base, and the fishy swam around for thirty seconds—a joke gift from her dad, so Justice would have a "pet" on cruise. Next to the spindly desk lamp was a bar of French *Fer à Cheval* soap, emitting a slight lavender scent.

What is it?

Soap. Some French kind.

Why?

What do you mean, why? What is soap used for, Justice? Jesus Christ.

Sticking a fist to her mouth, Justice lurch-stepped over to her desk chair and sat. Plunking her elbows on her knees, she covered her face with her palms.

The damned gallant hadn't changed a bit in the past year, had he? Mister Consummate Gentleman…giving her gifts…opening doors for her and trying to carry her bags…bringing her ice cream at the end of the day to make sure she decompressed…cooking lasagna for her when she'd been done-in from the Down Dog push-ups beating…

And tonight he'd thrown himself in front of a bullet for her!

Fucking damsel-rescuer.

Always on his white horse, looking out for her…

Except when she'd needed him most.

Take me to a hotel and roll around on the sheets with me all night.

Thanks, lady, but—*makes car horn noise with cheek*—pass.

Humiliating much?

She dug her fingers into her forehead. She didn't need these memories. She'd spent an entire year working to—

A knock sounded.

She dragged her fingers down her face and peered over the tips at the door.

It can't be.

Pushing to her feet, she crossed the room, opened the door, and—

It was.

Brayden slapped a hand to her door, stopping her from closing it in his face in case she had a mind to do so.

But also putting himself very close to her.

The spicy flavor of his aftershave wafted over her, striking a direct hit to the memory center in her brain.

With lightning speed, she was back to the night she'd knelt between his strong thighs, feeling the warmth of his body, smelling the All Man scent that was so inimitably *him*, seeing the desire in his eyes, reveling in the feel of his delectable happy trail beneath her nuzzling lips.

But of all the things she remembered about him, there was so much she'd forgotten too: how broad and big he was, how handsome, just how toe-curling his dimples were— God, how it'd pissed her off when he flaunted those on the op tonight—how strikingly blond he was. His hair was longer now, the strands just touching his collar, and he also wore a short beard, his whiskers darker than the hair on his head.

"Why did you leave BUD/S without a word to me?" Brayden pushed inside her room.

She stepped swiftly backward. "What the fuck do you think you're doing?"

"Finally getting a long-overdue explanation. Answer my question, please."

She didn't.

He planted his hands on his hips, the barrel of his rifle sticking straight up his back. "Yes, you were embarrassed about us getting caught—I get that—but you and I were *best friends*. Were you really so upset that you couldn't come to me and work things out before you left? Or what about later? Why didn't you answer any of my messages?"

Recriminations and blame and hurt feelings.

My. Catching up with Brayden was turning out to be as much fun as she thought it would be.

"What the hell did I do to deserve such a total shutout?"

"You want to know what?" she bit out. "Here's what: I missed one of the most important days of my life because of you."

He frowned. "What day?"

"BUD/S graduation."

"What? How did I make you miss that?"

"You didn't go to a hotel room with me when I asked you to. If you'd bothered to do that, then I wouldn't have had to waste time seducing your sorry ass, and no one would've caught us. And getting caught wasn't just *embarrassing*, Brayden. It got me called into Admiral Sherwin's office bright and early the next morning to face a slew of 'conducting unbecoming' charges." *And other humiliations.*

Brayden visibly startled, his hands slipping off his waist.

"I wasn't on the grinder that evening for graduation because Sherwin *forced* me to leave or get slapped with punitive charges." She shoved past Brayden and grabbed the doorknob. "Now, go. I've answered your stupid, fucking questions."

He didn't move. His eyes clouded. "I'm sorry all that happened to you with Sherwin, but there was no other decision I could've made that night. If I had sex with you and ended up hurting you, I *never* could've taken that back."

Her heart lurched. But a man who said those words wouldn't have hurt her. *No way.*

"Even at my most gentle," he went on, "I couldn't see sex not being a rough go for you. Not after what you'd been through at SERE."

She swallowed hard. "All right. Got it. All cleared up." She swung the door with a juddering motion, strongly urging him to go. His presence was just bringing back all of her painful need.

A stitch formed between his eyes. "I told you I was there for you."

"*Stop* seeing everything from your own viewpoint!" she

snapped. "You were there for me in the way *you* thought I needed, not the way I truly wanted, so that makes you think you were there for me, but you weren't."

Cherish me, care for me, celebrate my femininity…

"I asked for your *help*," she continued, hot and accusing. "Do you know how difficult it was for me to do that? And you pushed me away. You let me down. You broke my trust. So that's it."

Done with needing.

Done with trusting.

Done.

"It's over, Street. Find the door behind you."

He still didn't move.

A *grum, grum, grum* filled the silence between them. She was never sure what that sound meant. The bilge pump coming on? It didn't make her feel good to hear it.

"I'm sorry," he repeated. "I didn't mean to hurt you. I tried to stop you the best way I knew how, and…I *wanted* to help you." He drew in a breath that swelled his chest. "But my intentions don't matter. I've heard you say that. You don't trust me anymore, so I'm going to work hard to earn that back."

Her belly clutched around a knot of panic. "I forgive you," she returned quickly. The ways and means a consummate gentleman might use to earn back her trust weren't things her raw glop could effectively fight off right now. "You don't have to earn anything back."

Brayden stared at her for a long moment, his whiskered cheek moving, like he was working his tongue against it. Finally, he smiled. "Okay. Awesome. Let's go to the wardroom together, grab a cup of coffee, and hash out the particulars of our relationship." His dimples appeared and danced. "I'm partial to the left side of the bed, by the way."

She blushed. A bona fide heatstroke in her face. She

didn't need to hear talk of *bed* right now.

Out of character for her, the damsel-y blush, but her emotions had been extra-gloppy ever since a few hours ago, when she'd squinted at a face hidden in the shadows of a combat helmet and found a familiar lean jaw; the jaw that'd been flexing vigorously the first day she met him at BUD/S; the jaw that'd been braced into a tight ridge when she tried to seduce him after SERE; the jaw that jerked slightly when he confessed to being in love with her.

The suddenness of seeing Brayden Street in a North Korean woodland had left her unprepared to fight back a flood tide of memories. What a great friend he'd been. Their easy conversations. His unstoppable chivalry. *Her confidant, her ice cream-eating buddy, her only-child comrade…* Noble, good, honorable Brayden—all the qualities she admired in him but that destined them to fail if she was ever stupid enough to get into a relationship with him.

A guy like Brayden Street with a woman like her?

Golden Boy with Grayson Hayes's daughter?

Please.

"I'm not going to be your girlfriend," she told him. "The situation is forgiven but not forgotten."

"Ah," he said, his voice going soft. "That doesn't sound like true forgiveness to me."

She pressed her lips together. She was just the world's biggest bitch, wasn't she? "I don't mean to be a hardass, but I can't help the way I think. One of the first things I learned at my father's knee was mistakes kill."

His brows arched. "You can't expect to go through life without making any mistakes."

"I'm not talking about perfection. But what I do expect—from myself, at least—is not to make the same mistake twice. And aren't you glad I feel that way? We'd both be blown up by a booby-trapped truck right now if I was cavalier about life's lessons." She made an impatient noise in her throat. "This isn't a new concept to you, Brayden. *No margin for error* is something the BUD/S instructors pounded into our heads."

"They also pounded in the concept of *no pain, no gain.*" He waved it aside. "But it doesn't matter. That's work. This is life. Relationships aren't booby-trapped trucks, Justice. Mistakes lead to figuring shit out, to learning how to do things better the next time. They're actually necessary. How else can you expect to grow?"

"From some mistakes maybe, but others…" She trailed off.

Excuse me, Officer, but you misspelled my name on the arrest report. It's Justine, not Justice…

She caught back a swallow. "I will never again allow myself to be subjected to the kind of pain you put me through—that would be making the same mistake twice." She gestured at the corridor. "Now please go. There's nothing more to discuss."

After tense seconds of silence, he finally moved into her doorway. He stopped there. "There's a lot more to discuss, actually, and I'm going to say it all. I've been benched for an entire year because I figured your rejection was a done deal. And now here you are"—he inhaled a quiet breath— "rejecting me."

She flinched.

"And you know what? Screw it. I don't give a fuck. For six months of BUD/S, I was deliriously in love with you. All the great conversations we used to have on the deck while scarfing down ice cream. All the bullshitting we did side by side in the decon shower. Or how about stirring up cans of stew or franks 'n' beans over a campfire at the end of a vile day on the rock, not saying much, just enjoying each other's company?"

She took a halting step back. She remembered it too—all of it.

"I spent a lot of sleepless nights trying to figure out how to get you to understand that all the ways we connect make us perfect for each other. But you were so determined to remain only friends I thought it was a lost cause." His voice dropped, and his eye color deepened. "I never imagined I would ever know the feel of your body against mine, or the touch of your lips, or the sound of—"

"Stop it." It was a shaky hiss.

"No. Never." He leaned toward her. "I'm not backing down this time. We have a difficult road ahead of us. I understand that, and I'm ready for it. After all..." He stepped into the corridor and flashed her a big smile. "The only easy day was yesterday."

CHAPTER FIFTY-ONE

THE *BONHOMME RICHARD'S* fancy-pants comm center was an IT geek's paradise—knobs, buttons, dials, screens, consoles, all of them blinking prettily with colorful lights. Techie enthusiast that Justice was, she swore to figure out how everything worked one day.

Not today.

Today was for figuring out why Mr. Garcia, the CIA executive who'd once hired her, was standing near an illuminated map table next to Commander Cardoso, Pete Robbins, and—more to the point—Brayden Street.

Why, in fact, were all of Foxtrot still on board, making pests of themselves by interfering with her daily life? This morning she'd missed breakfast to avoid running into Mister Consummate Gentleman in the officers' wardroom. At the gym, she'd backed out after entering to see More-Than-A-Mouthful Rongo Tonono pumping iron. She hadn't been able to joke around with Pete in the hangar because the rest of the Foxtrot screamers were using the space for a game of basketball.

For fuck's sake. Was it too much to ask for a few stress-free hours on her own ship?

"Lieutenant Hayes." Cardoso beckoned her over.

"Skipper." She joined the group, nodding hello to Pete—resplendent in a flight suit—but altogether ignoring Brayden. As far as she was concerned, he was a potted plant.

She reached out to shake Mr. Garcia's hand. "Good to

see you again, sir. How's the shipbuilding business treating you?"

Garcia chuckled. "You can speak openly about my real job, Lieutenant Hayes. I'm here in that capacity."

"Yes, sir."

"The agency has a mission for Bat Three, in fact." Mr. Garcia gestured them to gather around the illuminated map table.

Their group surrounded it—all *five* of them.

She cast a pointed glance at the potted plant, who was *not* a member of Bat Three. "Are we expecting trouble on this op, sir?"

"We are, yes." Garcia leaned over the table, the light from below hitting his face in a way that made it look he was holding a flashlight under his chin, about to tell a campfire ghost story. "Our in-country assets have uncovered another uranium lab. There." He pointed to a spot on the 3-D image of North Korea. "But unlike the last bunker your team breached, this one is heavily guarded. You'll need the way cleared before you can enter. Foxtrot will do the honors."

"I see," she said, her stomach rolling.

"The upper echelons of SOF," Commander Cardoso put in, "have actually been talking about attaching Special Missions units to SEAL squads in order to conduct ops just such as this one—where firepower is needed to gather intelligence effectively." The skipper indicated the potted plant. "To that end, Lieutenant Street has volunteered Foxtrot to be a test case."

Prickles of heat needled Justice's cheeks. *Oh, he has, has he?*

She addressed Mr. Garcia. "With all due respect, sir"—*I really can't spend time around the potted plant, around his dimples and his aftershave and his aqua eyes and his ways and means; my raw glop is too gloppy*—"if Bat Three enters the compound with guns blazing, the North Koreans will know their computers have been tampered with. They'll hunt for a bug, and in all likelihood find it."

"Correct," Garcia agreed. "Which is why we'd like one on your team to implant a decoy bug in a computer while the other two attend to the *real* mission of rigging a microwave antenna to the satellite on top of the bunker. Via this secret antenna, our intel assets will be able to keep a close watch on what the North Koreans are doing, and we can disrupt matters as the situation warrants."

Mr. Garcia claimed a manila folder from off the ledge of the table. "Once the North Koreans find the decoy bug, we're banking on them not searching further." He held the folder out to her. "Here are the specs."

"Yes, sir." She accepted the folder and opened it, glancing down at the top sheet, but the earthquake of her inner emotions shook the letters into nothing but a Word Find game.

"Any questions?" Mr. Garcia asked her.

"No, sir." She showed him a tight discipline of teeth. "I'll need to confer with my men."

Commander Cardoso nodded. "You're dismissed."

She left the communications center with Pete and the potted plant, the three of them heading down the outer corridor in the direction of the briefing room.

The potted plant turned to Pete. "Will you be able to make a sundown departure? I saw some mechanics working on your bird."

"No prob," Pete answered. "Routine phase maintenance. My crew will be finished by—"

Justice cut off Pete by stepping in front of him—in front of both men.

The two came to a halt.

She narrowed in on the potted plant. "Since this is a test

case, Lieutenant Street, you might be a little foggy on how things run with Special Missions. Allow me to clarify. We are about stealth. Which means I don't need a bunch of Pipe Hitters clomping around my workspace and ruining my op." *Ruining my life. Get it?* "After you've cleared the way for me and my men, stay on the perimeter." *Of my life—message received?*

"Sure," he drawled. "I'll stay out of your way." He smiled.

On the op.

The next morning
5:30 a.m.

JUSTICE THUNDERED DOWN the second deck corridor of the USS *Theodore Roosevelt*, Pete and the potted plant flanking her.

Yesterday's mission had gone off without a hitch: bad guys were run off by Foxtrot, decoy implanted, antenna affixed in place, timeline maintained, no causalities suffered.

One would think such a picture-perfect op would earn their team a *hooyah!* or two, not an o-dark-thirty summons to the battle group's carrier to stand tall in front of Admiral Dirk Rosen, the carrier's commander, and also—

Wonderful.

Admiral FuckOver himself: Joseph Sherwin.

The two admirals were seated at the wardroom's large oval table, mugs of coffee—the Navy staple—in front of them. They were talking but stopped when the three junior officers entered and came to attention.

Neither admiral directed them to relax into parade rest.
Shit.

Had something gone wrong with the mission after all?
Admiral Sherwin lifted his coffee mug and took a sip.

"I'm attaching Bat Three to Foxtrot."

Justice sucked in a breath. Holy shitballs, did FuckOver have no concept about how to deliver bad news effectively? *Ease your way into it, you insensitive dickwad. Don't just outright crush every hope and dream a woman has of preventing her raw glop from getting smushed.*

Meanwhile the potted plant next to her played pine tree and lit up like Christmas.

"I want this unit to be a well-oiled machine before I send it downrange again," Sherwin added. "To that end all of you will be pulled off station, *effective immediately*, and transferred back to the States to train together for two months."

What?! But Bat Three just got here.

Admiral Sherwin took another sip of coffee, then set down his mug. "Lieutenant Browning's Bat Two unit and Yankee Platoon's men from Whiskey will be extended on-station to cover the two-month training cycle."

Justice tightened her jaw. *Oh, perfect.* Lieutenant Browning was going to hate her guts now.

You want out of this? her raw glop sneaky-voiced. *Tell Admiral FuckOver about how two nights ago Lieutenant Potted Plant threw himself in front of a bullet to save your life. Remember how stick-up-his-butty FuckOver gets about you being a "liability in the battle space?"*

Except that tattling wasn't exactly a team player thing to do.

"This combined unit will be stationed in San Diego," Sherwin stated. "Bat Three will be given two weeks of leave to move from their home port in Little Creek, Virginia, to SEAL Team Five's base of operations in Coronado."

Now Pete lit up.

Justice glared across the room. *So many men to kill, so little time…*

Admiral Rosen concluded this horror show with, "A C-130 is scheduled to transport both your teams out of South Korea at eighteen-hundred tonight via Seoul. That is all." Rosen waved them off. "Inform your men and pack your gear. Dismissed."

"Yes, sir," they intoned, then about-faced and marched out of the wardroom.

As they started down the hall, Pete clapped Brayden on the shoulder. "Oorah, man! Thank you very much for volunteering for this gig. Back to sunny San Diego. Back to living close to my LA-based girlfriend. *Yes.* I was getting sick of FaceTime sex." Pete stopped and clapped a hand on Justice's shoulder now, too, grinning brilliantly. "You and I owe Street a drink."

Brayden shifted his focus over to her. "An ice cream works for me." His blue eyes shone as bright as Pete's sparkling fucking veneers.

She concisely picked up Pete's hand and removed it from her shoulder.

"Hey, what's wrong?" Pete asked. "You look pissed."

A master at reading the subtleties of body language was Robbins.

She said, "Career advancement in the Navy doesn't happen for someone who never leaves homeport."

Pete gave his head a *nah* shake. "This is actually a great career move for us. We'll see a lot more action attached to a SEAL squad."

Oh, shut up. "And what about Lieutenant Browning? He's already been away from his family for six months. This'll tack on two more."

"Browning will be okay. He likes being deployed."

"His wife just gave birth."

"Yeah, I know, and I know Betty. She'll be cool with it."

No one else was in this corridor right now. Justice could

grab Pete and Brayden by the backs of their skulls and smash their heads together. Right? Because everyone acting carefree and offhand in the midst of her life falling apart wasn't working for her.

She pivoted toward Brayden. "Well, daaaamn. I gotta say…now I *really* wish I'd gone to Pete after SERE instead of you." She smiled sweetly. "I considered it, you know."

Brayden went very still.

"What's this?" Pete asked.

"Pete would've given me exactly what I wanted: a good fuck with no aftermath bullshit." She touched the tip of her tongue to the bow of her lip. "Wouldn't you have, Robbins?"

Pete shifted his chin sideways as he glanced between Justice and Brayden. His focus finally settled on Brayden. "Is there any correct way I can answer this?"

"Not on my end."

"Right." Pete lifted a hitchhiker's thumb until it was directed over his shoulder down the hall. "I think I'm just going to…" He turned and strode away.

She stared at Brayden.

He smiled amiably at her. "I wanted to spend some quality time with you. That's not going to happen while you're floating on the *Richard* and I'm based out of Camp Casey. So I had to get creative." His smile broadened, freeing a dimple. "See you on the C-130."

CHAPTER FIFTY-TWO

One week later
Little Creek, Virginia

JUSTICE HAYES'S HOUSE was a two-story Victorian with dark green shutters, ruffled curtains in the windows, and a green lawn dotted with waving dandelions, a light breeze occasionally plucking gossamer seedheads from stems and sending them off in flight. The place didn't seem to match Justice's personality, but from the research Brayden had done to unearth Justice's whereabouts, he discovered that she roomed with two other women.

The decorative choices were probably theirs.

The front door swung open, and two guys in coveralls hauled a couple of cardboard boxes labeled *Hayes, Kitchen* to the moving truck parked out front.

Brayden sipped his Starbucks coffee, watching them from his seated vantage point on the next-door neighbor's front porch steps.

After loading the boxes into the back, the guys banged the rear door shut.

At last. Justice's packout was complete.

The two men hopped into the cab and drove away from the curb.

A moment later, Justice stepped outside. She dropped a duffel bag at her feet and turned to lock the door.

Brayden stuffed his to-go cup in his own duffel and came to his feet. Slinging his bag on his shoulder, he crossed from the neighbor's yard to Justice's.

An Uber ride had dropped him off an hour ago, and he'd been waiting ever since for her to come out. And now…*wow*.

She looked great.

He'd seen her in civilian clothes before, of course. After she'd returned to BUD/S following Hell Week, she started going out for drinks with him and the other candidates on the occasional weekend. But that was during the winter months, when full-coverage clothing—like jeans, boots, turtlenecks, and jackets—was required.

July in Virginia was hot and humid, and Justice was dressed accordingly in clothes of the barely-there summer variety.

Brayden nearly tripped over his own feet at the sight of her in a pair of frayed denim shorts, a light gray tank top, and sparkle sandals.

The shorts she'd worn at BUD/S had been the khaki UDT shorts all the candidates wore—built for men—and *clearly* had lacked the curve-hugging design necessary to display her attributes to their absolute best. Because these jeans shorts were…Jesus, *these* shorts were showing off her round, tight ass and her bronzed and toned quads and hams to ball-gripping perfection.

Cursing under his breath, Brayden untucked his polo shirt and let it hang over his crotch. What a slick dude he was, arriving at Justice's house with a boner leading the way.

She finished locking the front door, dropped her key into a small mailbox tacked to the wall, and turned around.

"Holy shit!" She fumbled to keep the pair of sunglasses propped on her head from toppling off.

"Hey." Even that one syllable required effort to push out. Her long brown hair was caught in a high ponytail, and as she stood there staring at him in utter shock, a gentle breeze stirred several strands across her soft mouth—stirred memories of the only time he'd seen her hair down. The night their relationship had bitten the dust…but not before she rocked his world with her lips on his belly, kissing a path toward his crotch…

I love your happy trail. I love where it goes.

Heat shot through his testicles and clear up into his diaphragm.

"What the *hell*, Brayden?" she exclaimed. "How did you get here?" She peered over his shoulder, like maybe she expected to find a spaceship or a sleigh parked out front.

"I flew here." Exactly what he should've done after Justice ran off to Pensacola a year ago and didn't answer his messages—hopped on a plane and chased her down.

Then he would've found out way sooner than a week ago that she'd interpreted his refusal to have sex with her post-SERE as flat-out rejection rather than the effort to protect her from a bad decision he'd intended it to be.

She was not horribly embarrassed.

She was hurt.

And now she had it in her mind that he was bent on hurting her again.

I will never again allow myself to be subjected to the kind of pain you put me through—that would be making the same mistake twice.

Nothing could be further from the truth. Getting together with him would *not* be a mistake. First mistake, second mistake, the same mistake twice—any way you sliced it, no mistake. He needed to prove to her that she could trust him to be there for her. And the only way to do that was to actually be here.

So here he was.

Justice's focus jerked back to him. "*Flew* here?"

"You don't have to sound so surprised. I didn't fly here

on my own." He smiled. "I came via airplane." He reached down and scooped up her bag.

She tried to take it from him, but he angled it out of her reach. She could go for it again but would have to bump chests with him.

She dropped her arm and narrowed her eyes. "What are you up to, Brayden?"

"I'm not *up* to anything." *Except earning your trust back and making you fall in love with me.* "I'm merely here to help. You have to drive your car cross-country, right? I thought I'd join you."

"I don't need your help."

"I know, but it's a long trip. It'll be nice to have some company."

Her face reflected how mortifying she found the idea. "I'm not spending three, four days straight in a car with you."

Because if he bombarded her with his presence and made sure she knew how crazy he was about her, maybe she couldn't stay in lockdown? His very plan.

He gave her an *it'll-be-all-right* shrug. "We can talk about work. I'll fill you in about Team Five, so you can hit the ground running when you arrive in San Diego."

Putting her future competence on the job at stake was a move in the right direction.

She wavered.

He gently wedged the car keys out of her hand. "I'll take the first shift."

Justice owned a black Chevrolet Tahoe, nearly brand new. While he threw their bags in the back, she grudgingly settled into the passenger-side seat, sitting with one elbow propped on the elbow rest. She shielded herself behind her sunglasses and stared out the open car window.

Brayden didn't try to talk to her at first. He tuned the

Spotify on his cell phone to classic rock and left her alone to get used to the idea of him. The wind whipped her ponytail around, and he snatched glances of that, also periodically trying to sneak peeks down the front of her flapping tank top.

Well.

In reflective silence, he watched the world roll by. Thick groves of trees passed into patchwork fields, some bare, others stubbled with summer-brown wheat stalks, some with well-tended farmhouses and barns rising up behind them. He listened to the Eagles sing about having a peaceful, easy feeling and Don McLean warble about driving his Chevy to the levee but finding the levee was dry, and he thought about how nothing much ever got accomplished through silence, either living in it or creating it.

You won't know how she really feels about anything until you shake her loose.

"So are you dating anybody?" he asked.

Lifting her sunglasses, Justice turned to stare at him. "*That's* the topic you're kicking off with? Seriously?"

He shrugged. "Just wondering."

"Well, you can keep wondering." She looked out the window again.

"What do you want to talk about?" A car ahead of him hurried across several lanes to make an exit, and he braked.

"How about *work*?" she shot at him pointedly. *Like you said we would talk about.*

He catalogued the possible choices. *The CO of Team Five is a decent guy, the Master Chief is the lifeblood of the place, Romeo squad is known for partying all the time, Foxtrot for being a bunch of guys you'd never want to meet in a dark alley—or a candlelit bedroom, for that matter—Whiskey for having the hardest-working sled dogs.*

All standard, straightforward stuff.

Boring.

"I'm not dating anyone either. Not since you left."

"Did I ask?" Her jaw was set in an obstinate line. "And if you're about to tell me you haven't been with anyone this past year *because* of me, you can save it. Your lack of action is your own damned fault."

"I know. But I don't like hooking up with strange women." The number of potential lays he'd turned away over the years drove Keith nuts, but as much as Brayden tried to talk to his dick about it, the thing refused to get hard over someone he didn't know. "It's been a busy year."

"Here's a solution: get back together with your ex." Justice jammed her window all the way up and fiddled with the AC. "Problem solved."

"Who?"

"Charlotte."

"*Charlotte.*" He weaved sharply between an SUV and a hay truck.

Justice's chin rose a notch, and she adopted a highfalu-tin tone. "Oh, I can just see the happy Lieutenant and Mrs. Brayden Street now. The spiffy Charlotte's makeup will always be so properly applied, her hair perfectly coiffed when she meets her husband's commanding officer. Her holiday table will be set with sprigs of holly and name cards written in well-spaced calligraphy. She will bear you two fine sons, who she'll dress in matching sailor suits when she struts them around Saks Fifth Avenue, and she will never, ever refuse to bear your weight when you crawl into bed to mount her after a long, hard day of SEALing."

Brayden's knuckles hurt. He glanced down at his hands and saw he was gripping the steering wheel too tightly. "Yeah, Charlotte only wants me for the prestige of being a SEAL's girlfriend"—*or wife*—"someone she can display in a perfect little box on her mantelpiece." He'd been in a similar box of his own making his whole life. He didn't need more of that crap. "So I think I'll pass on her."

"Fucking stupid." The obstinate set of Justice's jaw turned downright mulish. "She's perfect for you. I thought it the second I saw her in the barracks community room. Compared to her pedigree, I'm a mongrel."

"A what?" He took his eyes off the road to frown at her. "What the hell are you talking about?"

She *tsked*. "The day a Golden Boy like you hooks up with the daughter of an infamous cat burglar is the day you've decided to go slumming." She gave the A/C knob an aggressive spin. "I'm going to take a hard pass on our inevitable breakup, thank you very much."

He bit down hard on his teeth, flexing his jaw. "I can't believe you just said that." He jerked the steering wheel over hard, veering off the freeway to a cacophony of honking horns.

Skidding to a halt on the shoulder, he slammed the car into park and rounded on her. "I'm the man who laid on a couch with you when we both smelled like sewage." He clutched her headrest. "I'm the man you watched throw up half a gallon of chlorinated water after lifesaving drills. From day one, you and I have seen each other at our worst, and we still became best friends." He grabbed her arm.

"Let go."

"No. How can you be such a colossal ignoramus about this?"

She glared at him and didn't answer.

The only sound between them was their heavy breathing and the roar of vehicles speeding by the Tahoe.

The windows started to fog.

One passing car tooted, the driver probably thinking the two of them were gettin' busy.

Brayden took another moment to breathe—long inhale,

long exhale—then let go of Justice's arm, but slowly, letting his fingers slide along her tricep. "You don't put me in a box. You free me." He turned back to the steering wheel. "And you're a thief who steals intelligence to stop *terrorism*. The fuck if that makes you a mongrel." He jacked on the air conditioner and put the car in gear.

Hitting the gas hard, he peeled back onto the freeway.

CHAPTER FIFTY-THREE

THEY DROVE THROUGH lunch.

Justice's moving company had used up most of the morning loading her household goods, so they decided to make up for lost time by snacking in the car on potato chips and beef jerky bought from a gas station minimart.

By eight o'clock they reached Knoxville, Tennessee, and Brayden was starving. "I need real food for dinner."

Justice pointed to a roadside sign. "Next exit there's a diner."

Brayden slowed and took the off-ramp, driving until he found a restaurant with a red-and-white-striped awning hanging out front. He parked in the attached lot.

They climbed out and stretched.

Brayden bent over and massaged his sore shins.

Inside, a hostess led them through country western music to a blue booth about mid-restaurant. If they'd been in a movie, the music would've squealed off as everyone stopped eating to observe the passage of two people who definitely hadn't just come off the farm...although no one seemed particularly interested in him.

Justice had thrown on a white, button-down shirt, jacket-style—even though it was still hotter than the devil's ringus outside—but still. Men drooled, children gaped—probably suspecting Wonder Woman in their midst—and the other women were...

Hey. Was the napkin in that cowboy's lap moving on its

own?

Jaw tight, Brayden set a palm at the small of Justice's back and guided her into the booth.

She glanced back at his hand, then studied his unruly expression as he sat across from her. "You're not going to start beating your chest and howling, are you?"

"If necessary." He opened a laminated menu.

She opened hers.

Chicken fried steak, Monte Cristo and BLT sandwiches, biscuits and gravy, standard burgers.

Justice briskly flipped a page. "You know you're completely full of shit when it comes to me, don't you?"

He glanced up, turning a page, even though he wasn't looking at the menu anymore.

A middle-aged waitress wearing a blue nurse's smock-like uniform with a white apron over it dropped off a couple of waters. "Anything else to drink?" she asked, touching the side of her hair, a French knot held in place by half a can of grocery store hairspray.

"Coffee for me, please," Brayden said. "Black."

Justice gestured at her glass. "Water's fine."

"Be back in a jiff." The waitress bustled off.

"Your last comment probably warrants an explanation," he told Justice.

She kept scanning the food choices. "Earlier in the car you said you can't get excited about strange women." She peered at him over the top of her menu. "Except you once told me that you fell in love with me the first day you and I met. Do you see how that doesn't compute? When I walked into the officers' barracks you didn't know me at all, so the only things you could've fallen in love with were my tits and my ass."

"I *did* know you," he countered, taking a moment to relive seeing her for the first time. How her long stride had eaten the ground, making it look like Captain Eagen was struggling to keep up. How Brayden's first *good* look at her, when he came out of attention, was like a heaven-sent slap to the heart. "I saw the strong set of your shoulders and the intense determination in your expression, and I knew you were exactly like me."

Justice scoffed. "You knew I was an only child?"

"No." He smiled. "I didn't know that till you told me. You looked like someone with something to prove. Like me. And the similarity linked us right away."

The waitress returned, setting a mug of coffee in front of him. "Here you go." She pulled out a pad and pencil from her apron pocket. "You two know what you want?"

"What's good here?" he asked.

The waitress smiled, showing a smudge of lipstick on her front tooth. "We're known for our cheeseburgers."

"A cheeseburger work for you?" he aimed at Justice.

She closed her menu. "That's fine."

The waitress scribbled on her pad. "Two cheeseburgers, comin' right up." She left again.

Justice picked up their menus and tucked them behind the condiment caddy. "So what is it you think I have to prove?"

He shrugged. "What are we all trying to prove? That we're good enough. Your dad's an infamous cat burglar, and you're in a similar business. It probably isn't easy living up to his expectations, right?"

She didn't answer, but her silence pretty much spoke for her.

"But, hey, same with me. I'm sure the confusing mess of a relationship I have with my dad is one of the reasons I went into the Teams."

She drew a line down the tabletop with her thumb. "Because your dad treats you like one of his son's friends instead of his own son?"

"I'd say that's probably it, yeah."

Justice carefully unfolded her napkin and laid it in her lap. "I don't think you're trying to prove you're good enough to your dad, but to Keith."

Brayden froze.

A teenager entered the diner with a squeak of tennis shoes. A bell dinged *order up!*

"What do you think I have to prove to Keith?" he asked.

"Nothing, according to me—you and Keith are both top performers. But you seem to let him overshadow you."

Brayden's face heated. He looked down and edged his napkin over an inch. "Keith is a better leader than I am."

"No, he's not. You two have different leadership styles, is all. Keith is aggressive and forceful. You're firm and steady. A good leader takes care of his people, Brayden, and you excel at that. Remember how you snuck Power Bars to my team after my Extraction Swim fuck-up, and how you cooked lasagna for me when I was zoxxed from the Down Dog push-ups beating, or how you used to slip me dry socks on my worst days at the rock after I made too many trips to the dip tank? That's leadership. But…it's almost as if you hide how great you are."

A stronger wave of heat burned Brayden's cheeks.

Was I genuinely outperformed by Keith all these years? Or did I subconsciously let myself be beaten to get along? Did Keith take on the role of leader because our father put me in a one-down position? Or by my own doing?

Questions answered.

He *was* good.

"Thank you." He cleared his throat. "I've never thought of it that way before."

One side of Justice's mouth angled up into a half-smile. Maybe a full smile was on the way, but the waitress arrived just then.

"Food's here," she said cheerily, placing a plate with a burger and French fries in front of each of them. "Can I get you anything else?"

"No, thanks," Brayden answered. "We're good."

The waitress checked his mug. "I'll be by with more coffee in a bit."

"That'd be great." Brayden grabbed the ketchup from the condiment caddy and unscrewed the cap. Upending the bottle over his plate, he shook it a couple of times and some ketchup plopped out next to his fries.

Justice cut her burger in half with a butter knife. "You done with the ketchup?"

"Oh...yeah." He angled the bottle at her.

She took it from him. "Thanks."

Normal stuff.

Everyday interactions.

If they could just share this one meal where they were relaxed and natural with each other, it would be a huge step forward.

Brayden drank some water.

CHAPTER FIFTY-FOUR

THEY REACHED NASHVILLE at eleven thirty, but even though it was late, they kept going to make up more of the time they'd lost in the morning. Their goal was Memphis.

They didn't make it.

At a little after one in the morning, too tired to keep driving, they stopped for the night at a roadside motel in Jackson, Tennessee, and lucked into the last two available rooms.

Fresh from a shower, Justice plopped down on the edge of her bed and brushed her wet hair. Steam was still wafting through the open bathroom door, and the humidity of it heightened the smell of the place—like someone had stomped through here at one point with cow dung on his boots. The mattress was also a little lumpy, but other than those things, the room was decent, only lacking in one thing.

She stared at her door.

Him.

The man with a thousand-pound heart—*If I had sex with you and ended up hurting you, I never could've taken that back*—nine-hundred-ninety-nine pounds heavier than hers—*It's over, Street. Find the door behind you*—and a hundred degrees warmer—*For six months of BUD/S, I was deliriously in love with you.*

Her confidant, her ice cream-eating buddy, her only-child comrade…

The man she connected with over shared commonalities and mutual understanding.

You looked like someone with something to prove. Like me. And the similarity linked us right away…

Breathing deeply, she tightened her grip on her brush. Her vision blurred.

Steal this with panache, and everyone will envy your glittering talent!

Save the free world from nuclear annihilation, and you can wear a sable mantle of pride!

Knit one, purl two, be happy as a clam!

It wasn't exactly working out that way.

She hadn't lived up to the world-class Hayes image. Not by a mile.

Excuse me, Officer, but you misspelled my name on the arrest report. It's Justine, not Justice…

She swallowed hard.

How long would she keep trying to make up for that? When would she allow herself to have more than just the satisfaction of excelling at a job?

To love and be loved.

Shouldn't that be the real goal? Wouldn't achieving that pinnacle be the true measure of a life's worth?

Except…

Love hurt.

A heart-breaking fate with Golden Boy lay in wait.

It'd be incredibly naïve of her to let him talk her into a relationship.

Except…

Every hour that passed, he became more mouthwatering, and the lure to step into the circle of his caring arms grew stronger.

Mr. Consummate Gentleman with his ways and means. Mr. Smarty Pants who'd volunteered to be a test case for a combo unit, and now she was in this pickle, stuck driving cross-country with him, no other pulls on her attention like there had been at BUD/S.

Just him and her. Together. Constantly.

Her confidant, her ice cream-eating buddy, her only-child comrade…

He would make her feel warm and valued and ridiculously glad for being part of a team again.

She was so damned sick of solitude.

She set her brush on the nightstand and stared at it. Wheels hummed on smooth asphalt across the street, like a vehicle was pulling into the all-night convenience store she'd spotted earlier. A car door banged shut. Two people laughed with each other in a friendly way.

From day one, you and I saw each other at our worst, and we still became best friends…

She and Brayden were still friends on some level, weren't they? So, why couldn't she go to him as a *friend*?

No relationship in the offing.

No declarations of love.

No risk of pain.

Just two people coming together from a foundation of friendship and affection.

They could do that, right?

I'm not dating anyone either. Not since you left.

See? They were both lonely.

All she had to do was leave this room and walk to the one next door…

She glanced at her duffel, clothes spewing passed the open zipper, then stood abruptly. She put on shorts, a tank, and sandals, and gathered her wet hair into a ponytail.

Grabbing the small, zippered canvas bag containing her wallet and hotel key, she crossed to the convenience store. She bought ice cream and booze, then headed back to the motel, this time aiming for the room next to hers.

She knocked.

A second later the door swung open on Brayden. He was wearing a pair of long khaki shorts and—

Bong. Jaw drops.

Nothing else.

She fumbled her armful of snacks.

Holy mackerel. He was huge now!

Somewhere along the way after BUD/S, he'd traded in his runner's body for a more bulked-out version. His shoulders now looked like something you might find on a defensive end whose hobby off the field was bare-handed logging, and his hairless chest was carved with contours of raw, imposing strength.

"Hey!" His brows shot into the stratosphere at the sight of her.

English words came, but not in any discernible order. "I…you have…me stuff…"

Well, hell.

It was just that he was the incarnation of godly male beauty, standing there in bare feet with his naked upper body slimming to a narrow waist, the loose waistband of his shorts sagging deliciously low on his lean hips.

Funny, how she'd never seen him shirtless until now…besides his alluring happy trail. But all training exercises at BUD/S had been conducted in either full combat gear or T-shirts, and Brayden, like her, had been careful not to go around unclothed in the officers' barracks.

Arranging her eyes into a less buggy shape, she presented two paper cups covered with plastic domes, balanced on one palm. "I've got ice cream." She lifted a plain paper sack with her other hand. "And beer."

Brayden broke into a huge smile, granting her a sexy peek of both dimples through his whiskers.

Uh-oh. "Unless you think it's a bad idea to let me into your motel room in the middle of the night to ply you with alcohol." It probably was.

"What?" He laughed. "No. Sorry. I'm just surprised to see you. Come in." He cleared the way for her to enter.

She went inside.

He closed the door behind her, then reached into the duffel sitting open on his bed, hastily pulling out a white T-shirt and shrugging it on.

Probably a good idea. But still…

A pity.

He turned around to find her holding one of the ice cream cups out to him.

Smiling again, he accepted it. "Come and sit." He plucked the paper sack out of her arms and headed toward a table and two chairs. He put the sack on the table, then waited until she sat in one of the chairs before taking the other.

She put her canvas bag on the table, then pried the dome off her ice cream cup.

Brayden did the same.

"Not very inspiring," she apologized. "The store only had soft-serve vanilla, but I was able to drum up some sprinkles."

"It's perfect."

She reached into the sack and pulled out two plastic spoons, handing him one.

She used her own spoon to scoop up a bite. As soon as the vanilla hit her tongue, it was almost as if she could smell the briny scents of the Pacific Ocean. She couldn't believe she was eating ice cream with Brayden again. How many great conversations had they enjoyed on the barracks' deck, winding down after a grueling day of BUD/S?

"The ice cream's good," Brayden assured her.

Must be—it was disappearing fast from his cup. "I feel a little guilty eating it," she admitted.

"Why's that?"

"We're not supposed to be here right now—in the States, in air conditioning, eating ice cream and burgers." She took another bite. "Do you think Keith is pissed, being stuck in Korea when he should he home?"

"Nah. Keith doesn't get spun up about shit like that." Brayden scooped up a large spoonful of ice cream—large enough to almost be worthy of Dog Bone. "Besides, Keith's always had the better deals, so if it's my turn, I'm not going to feel bad about it."

She gave her vanilla a stir, the sprinkles smudging rainbow colors across the white. "What kind of better deals?" Sibling dynamics were always so fascinating.

"Like…" Brayden scraped his bowl. "Summer jobs, for one. Our dad manages Jackson Hole Mountain Resort, and he would always arrange for Keith to teach rock-climbing classes during summer breaks to earn extra money. Dad didn't arrange dick for me, so I got stuck babysitting a bunch of snotty kids at camp."

Justice arched a brow. "You were a camp counselor?"

He finished off his ice cream. "Not my finest hour."

She stopped stirring. Her ice cream was purple. "You've never figured out why your dad treats you like that?"

Brayden reached into the sack and grabbed a beer. Cranking off the beer's cap, he took a long draw on it before answering. "Keith recently suggested that Dad has been taking my mother's rejection of him out on me."

"Really?" *How shitty.* Justice set her ice cream cup on the table. "Do you agree?"

"Well, consider this: Keith and I are only fifteen months apart. So that means Dad moved on from my mom's rejection to marry Keith's mother and get her knocked up within six months. What does that tell you?"

She twisted her lips. "He's pretending it doesn't bother him?"

"Exactly. Trevor Knight has never dealt." Brayden produced another beer from the sack and offered it to her.

She accepted the bottle. "You know what's funny?"

"What's that?"

"Not only are we both only children, but we were raised by opposite sex parents—you by a mother, me by a father."

"Hah. True."

She ran her fingers around the scalloped ridges of her bottle cap. "Do you ever feel weird because of that?"

"I dunno," he mused, drinking his beer "Maybe." He abruptly pulled the bottle away from his mouth and chuckled. "Shit, I knew the diner waitress was wearing grocery store hairspray. Damn." He laughed some more. "Maybe that's why I went into the Teams—to prove I'm a real man."

She watched the strong muscles in his throat work as he drank more beer and felt her raw glop slide into her vagina. "Men don't come much more real than you, Brayden."

He cast her a quick sideways glance, a flicker of surprise in his expression.

She opened her own beer and sipped it. The alcohol glided coolly down her throat…and her focus slipped slowly along Brayden's broad shoulders. The light cotton fabric of his T-shirt hugged the heavy pads of his chest muscles and the vivid strength of his biceps. "You've gained weight," she murmured.

He snorted, a near laugh. "Is that a crack about all the ice cream I eat?"

She lowered her voice to a deeper note. "I mean muscle weight."

He seemed to falter. His tongue made a brief pass over

his lips.

"You've packed on more since BUD/S."

"Yeah, well…" His fingertips kneaded his beer bottle. "I've never been a big fan of mess hall food. It's probably why I ate so much ice cream at BUD/S."

"And you always invited me along," she reminded softly, "making sure I de-stressed." *Mister Consummate Gentleman and his ways and means.* "I owe you thanks for that."

"Nah." He stared down the neck of his beer bottle like he was trying to figure out how a penny got jammed down there. "It was my pleasure."

She gazed at the side of his handsome face and felt her loins clench. He wore just enough scruff on his lean jaw to turn his appearance slightly criminal. Thief that she was, it was a look that really lit her jets. "I owe you thanks for saving my life too."

His chin came around. "Saving your life?"

"In North Korea. The night of the truck ambush. I never thanked you."

"Oh, that."

"Oh, *that*? You threw yourself in front of a bullet for me."

He shrugged. "I was wearing a flak jacket, you weren't."

Just another day at the office for Mister Consummate Gentleman…

Warmth suffused her. A lot of it. She set down her beer and rose.

Brayden started to hasten to his own feet, but she moved to stand right in front of him.

He sat again, peering up at her—surprised, uncertain, searching.

"To answer your question of earlier…no, I'm not dating anyone. I haven't since BUD/S, either, and I'm…" She couldn't say, *I'm lonely.* "I'm not shaken up post-SERE right now, Brayden, so you don't have to worry about me not thinking clearly when I ask you to go to bed with me."

The muscles riding the length of his neck contracted.

"Will you?"

"I…" His throat worked one, but his voice still came out a little gravelly. "What about trusting me?"

"We were once best friends, and sitting here tonight eating ice cream together has brought that home to me. Yes, I trust you, but…that doesn't mean I want a relationship."

His eyelids sank shut.

"I'm sorry. I just…I'm not good with complications. We can have some great sex from our foundation of friendship, but…no strings, no commitments."

Brayden slowly dragged a hand down his face. "I'm not sure I can do that."

She swallowed heavily, a cold lump settling in her belly.

"I'm not rejecting you," he added hastily, coming to his feet. "The total opposite. I don't think I have it in me to go to bed with you, then just walk away."

"I understand. I wish…" She turned aside, looking at her reflection in the TV. The dark screen drained her image of color. *How apropos.* "I wish I was the type of woman who could jump into a relationship with both feet, but I have a lot of Hayes family rules in my head to follow. Never let 'em see you sweat," she recited. "Never completely trust. Never—"

"Never make the same mistake twice," he filled in for her.

She looked at him.

There was a tinge of pain in his eyes. "And getting together with me would me making the same mistake twice."

She pulled a breath through her nose.

"I won't hurt you," Brayden said in earnest. "How can I

prove that to you?"

"You won't *mean* to hurt me," she conceded. "I believe that much." She picked up her canvas bag, a wave of regret rushing up and over her. Who would've thought The BUD/S Woman feared the *no pain, no gain* concept?

She walked toward the door.

She heard Brayden follow.

She grabbed the knob, pulled the door open, and—

Brayden's hand landed on the top part of the door and shut it again.

She turned around, her breath catching, and peered up at him.

His gaze was a deep, dark blue. "One night with you," he said softly. "Okay. If that's what you can give me, then I accept."

CHAPTER FIFTY-FIVE

JUSTICE'S PULSE JUMPED.

Her belly loaded with butterflies, a fluttery nervousness the likes of which she hadn't felt since her first double-whammy break-in. That night she'd taken down the Walkers—stealing a coffee can from them—and the Haywoods—who'd ended up being minus a stapler thanks to her.

There'd been lots to think about the night of her first twofer.

Lots to think about now too.

Faced with the prospect of having sex with Brayden from a foundation of friendship but not letting it go further, her big question was: *can I?*

Or would she do the stereotypical chick-thing and become emotionally attached to a man she'd slept with. Pretty fucking gooey, although maybe impossible to prevent, like succumbing to an unavoidable biological stew.

Put one cup estrogen, two tablespoons pheromones, and a couple of generous squirts of dopamine from the brain's pleasure center into a pot and get stupid.

How stupid? That was the real question.

"I'm noticing that neither of us is moving," Brayden commented.

She met his gaze.

His eyes crinkled at her.

Quintessential Brayden Street Nice Guy.

"Maybe someone should," she suggested.

"All right." He strode to the end of the bed.

She left her canvas bag by the door and followed him there.

They stood across from each other, holding gazes again.

The air conditioner ticked. Somewhere down the street a small dog yipped.

"Maybe," she said, "someone should undress now."

"Mmm. I'd like it to be you." His focus drifted down her body in a slow, savoring fashion, like he was reveling in the freedom of finally being able to observe her with open want.

A tremor tumbled down her spine. "Okay." She removed her shirt, revealing a bra that was nothing special—serviceable beige, lacking in lace or bows.

Brayden didn't seem to care.

He drank in the sight of her with dark eyes. "Keep going," he urged roughly.

"Shouldn't it be your turn?"

His pupils widened into aggressive pits.

Hmm. Best not to press it.

Reaching behind her back, she unhooked her bra and let it slide down her arms to the floor.

He hissed. "Jesus H."

She snuck a peek in a downward direction, trying to be inconspicuous about checking out the activity going on at his zipper. And...*wow*. Difficult not to go saucer-eyed over *that*. He was already erect.

Instantly and hugely.

God love a man in his prime.

"Your turn now," she insisted. "Start with your—hey!" She tried to sidestep his forward charge, but he caught her by the shoulder and stopped her escape.

Turning her toward him again, he scooped a breast into

his palm, lifting it as he bent his head. His mouth latched onto a nipple, and he sucked hard.

Teetering on her feet, she grasped fistfuls of his blond hair. "Oh, God." A steamy ribbon of fire stirred to life low in her belly, flickering hotter and hotter with each caress of his mouth. Her nipple jutted excitedly against his tongue.

He kissed the top of her breast, his short beard rasping lightly over her flesh.

She pressed into his kiss.

"Fuck," he growled, his breaths hot and swift against her skin. "You're even hotter than I imagined." He thumbed open the snap on her shorts.

She moaned. "What happened to your turn?"

"Later." His hands stole around her back, sliding inside her waistband to cup her buttocks.

She wriggled against the pleasure of his powerful grip.

A coarse noise vibrated out of him. Not at all gentle-manly, that sound.

She felt her pulse throbbing at the tip of her clitoris.

He gave her shorts a push, and they fell to her ankles.

"You're such a cheater," she breathed.

He back-stepped her to the bed. "You want me to get naked?" He sat her down on the foot of the mattress, then took a small step back. "You got it." He unbuttoned and unzipped and shoved. His shorts dropped. The thick pole of his cock bobbed once, heavily, then stuck straight out from his body.

By a looooong ways.

Blood roared through her veins. "Holy fuck!" She scrambled back across the bed, knocking his duffel bag to the floor.

He laughed in his throat. "You're The BUD/S Wom-an," he said, seizing one of her ankles and hauling her back toward him. "You're not allowed to be afraid of my cock."

"No? Have you seen the size of that thing?"

With an amused expression, he removed his T-shirt.

"Uh, you know…" God, his chest was amazing. "You can't use The BUD/S Woman excuse to do anything you want to me."

"Hey, you don't like something I do," he said, "you just let me know." He yanked the bedspread down halfway, exposing the sheets. "Hop in."

She paused another second, then scooted toward the headboard. She was going to choose to find comfort from the fact that this wasn't Brayden's first rodeo with his cock. He undoubtedly knew what to do.

He set a knee on the bed, the mattress briefly indenting with his weight, and climbed toward her.

Lying down, she let him settle comfortably between her legs.

He sank down on top of her with care, his solid cock pressing her inner thigh, his chest a pleasant weight against her breasts.

Her flesh hummed. Her bones ached for him, her marrow, her cells, the mitochondria in her cells.

Brayden carefully tugged the band off her ponytail, his eyes turning inky black as he spread the mass across a pillow. He lay unmoving for a moment, just breathing, just looking at her. Then he delved his fingers into her hair and gently held her head. Angling her into the best position to receive his lips, he kissed her, slow and sweet, his lips caressing hers with such touching tenderness and genuine care her eyes actually stung behind her closed lids.

The savoring process awoke unpracticed nerve endings all over her body. Shivers chased along her hair follicles. Her insides grew warm and eager, and her core, wet and swollen.

He gradually built the contact to a deeper intimacy, his solid chest rocking against her breasts. His tongue probed inside her mouth. She tasted vanilla ice cream, cool and fresh, and a hint of ice-cold beer.

She flitted her tongue over his with urgency and wrapped her legs around his waist. Locking her ankles against the small of his back, she ground her crotch against his.

His jaw went loose around their next kiss, a low groan spilling out of him. He left her mouth to go on a journey down her body, his lips flowing over her throat and collarbone, then kissing a path between her breasts. He traveled farther downward, licking warm, swirly patterns near her navel.

A rivulet of honeyed juice trickled out of her entrance, and she clenched her inner muscles, moaning quietly. His talented tongue-caresses on her belly hinted at his potential skill elsewhere. Her core shivered in the greedy hope for her favorite thing.

"I thought you'd be hard," he murmured, nuzzling her flesh.

Her spine dissolved into the mattress. "What am I?"

"Soft. Very firm, but soft." He brushed his open mouth across the sweep of her belly. "And you taste as good as you feel."

"Oh, Street. If tasting's your goal, you're not at all where you need to be."

His head came up, one eyebrow slanting. "Permission to go south?"

"God, yes. Why wouldn't you?"

"Some women are shy about that."

"Not this woman."

She caught a glimpse of his crooked smile just before he disappeared between her legs.

She gladly spread her knees wider to accommodate his broad shoulders, her flesh thrumming in anticipation of—

"H'oh!"

His tongue slid down the entire line of her sex.

Her butt went tight, and her thighs flexed as another sound of pleasure escaped her. Shy women were really missing out on the goods.

Brayden took another leisurely taste of her, the soft, moist heat of his tongue gliding up and down her inner lips, while his thumbs traced along the edges of her outer labia. At the top of her sex, he parted her, exposing her clitoris. With just the tip of his tongue, he tickled her clit. Flicker, flicker, flicker—directly on her most sensitive nerve endings. Her sheath snapped taut around a fierce pulsation.

"Brayden!" She slapped her hands on the mattress. "Slow down, would you? I'm going to come too fast."

He chuckled, sending warm breath flowing over her swollen flesh. But he moved off direct contact. His tongue circled in tormenting and torturing ways all over her sex, the velvet burr of his beard sometimes grazing the entrance to her body. Her nipples stood on end. Her sex was drenched and engorged. The lights in her brain flickered on and off while Brayden steadily teased her toward climax.

"Oh, God, oh, God." She tensed and arched and scrunched her toes, but there was no hope for stopping where this was going. It was just too good. Fluttery clenches rolled along the length of her sheath. A throaty noise spilled out of her, and she flung one leg over Brayden's shoulder.

Clearly sensing that he had her, he honed in on her clit, lapping there with total focus.

Her entrance pinched tighter and tighter, then exploded into rhythmic throbs. *God! God!* "Ah!" She surged her hips up, working herself against his face. "Brayden," she moaned, ecstasy continuing to crash over her in wave after inexpressible wave. Her lungs expanded toward bursting. Her heart raced toward breakdown.

As her convulsions tapered off, he gave her a last kiss, tenderly, like the way he'd kissed her mouth.

Sweat-slicked, he sat back on his heels between the vee of her spread legs. "Where are my shorts?" he asked hoarsely, breathing hard as he glanced around.

"Why?" He didn't think he was going anywhere, did he?

"I need a condom." Hopping off the mattress, he found his shorts on the floor at the end of the bed and tugged his wallet out of the rear pocket. Opening it, he searched inside and—

He looked up, his mouth screwing into a small grimace. "I don't have one. I've, uh, sort of been in a dry spell."

"My wallet," she said. "In my canvas bag. By the door."

He found her bag and dug out a condom. Unwrapping the foil on his way back to the bed, he repositioned himself between her splayed thighs and unrolled the rubber onto his—

His cock split right through it.

"Shit." He shot her another grimace. "You don't happen to have a magnum, do you?"

"Jesus, Brayden." She shoved onto her elbows and gaped at the ragged remnants of the condom. "Your cock is a monster!"

"Well," he said simply. *What's a well-endowed man to do?*

"Do you...want to go without?" she asked. Stopping altogether sounded like a terrible option. "We were both tested for STDs before going into BUD/S, and it sounds like neither of us has been with anyone since then."

He gave her a small smile. "Okay." He removed the torn condom, tossed it aside, and lowered himself on top of her again. Resting his weight on one elbow, he reached down between their bodies and set his member at her entrance, then resettled onto both forearms.

His hips flexed.

Her nether lips stretched taut around the wide head of his phallus. She breathed steadily as he kept pushing.

He paused partway in. "You okay?" His voice was low and tight, achy with urgent need. "You should be—you're wet as fuck."

"I'm good." Except…*how far in are you, exactly?*

"You're on birth control, right?"

"Yes."

He smiled again and kissed her. And kept advancing.

In, in, in.

She closed her eyes at the feel of everything that was Brayden, both power and gentleness, entering her. By the time he was settled deep inside her, her body was open and accepting of his size.

He hovered over her, breath leaving his nostrils in rapid gusts. "Jesus, that's good. You okay?"

Sexually? Perfect. Physically? Things were odd. She could no longer tell where he ended and she began, and…she'd never lost herself so completely to the feel of a man before.

And if this was the biological stew at work, she wasn't going to think about it.

Because emotionally? It felt like her heart was about to burst—it was beating so fast it seemed to reverberate off the walls of the room. And it was probably a good bet this motel was too cheap to have a defibrillator stored in the nightstand drawer next to the Holy Bible. In case of an emergency, that was unfortunate.

"No more stopping," she told Brayden softly.

He made a partial grunt. "If you say so." He launched right into solid thrusting, his hip movements perfection, his strokes long and deep. Skin-on-skin was fantastic and the level of friction astonishing.

The lingering aftershocks of her oral-sex orgasm brought her swiftly peaking to another precipice. "Faster," she urged him on.

He increased his tempo, and her sheath gave a preemptive pulse. "Yes," she gulped out. "I'm going to come again."

Brayden thrust twice more, then pitched to a complete stop.

She waited for a few seconds, but he remained still. She peered at him through her sweat-spiked eyelashes. "Should I not?"

"No. Of course, uh… It's just when you said that, it got me…um…I think I'm going to come now too."

She chuckled breathlessly. "For God's sake, go ahead. Don't worry about me. My orgasm is a bonus one."

"No, no, I got this. Just give me a second."

He was being silly. She was thoroughly satisfied. She squeezed her inner muscles around his erection.

"Ah!" he blasted. "Hey, don't—"

"Listen, Brayden, we can be together more than once tonight, okay?"

He blinked twice, then an expression emerged, something charmingly happy, and—something she didn't need to see right now. That, or any underpinnings of yearning.

She hid her hot face in the side of his throat.

"Glad to hear it," he whispered. "Because I *don't* got this."

Her eyes burned behind her lids again. She gripped his flanks with the strength of her thighs to encourage him back to business.

He started to thrust, and almost immediately she felt his spine tauten. He kissed her again, this time not gently. Demanding. Relentless. Deep. His hips slammed into her. She dug her fingers into his shoulder muscles, and—although unplanned—she climaxed again, crying out.

His cock lurched in spasmodic ejaculation inside her. He threw back his head, tendons corded against the strong column of his neck, and made a sound of such low-moaning death it could only be a noise of absolute ecstasy. Two more jerky thrusts brought him to a final stop.

Lungs pumping, he sank onto his elbows, sweat leaking down his temples.

She met his gaze across the short space between them, and in that moment, everything came together: their friendship and affection and caring for each other, their mutual understanding and shared commonalities.

Cherish me, care for me, celebrate my femininity…

He'd done all that.

Nothing but warmth and contentment enveloped her entire being, and a laugh of pure joy poured out of her.

The corners of Brayden's eyes creased, and he laughed too. "Wow," he said.

CHAPTER FIFTY-SIX

THE LANDSCAPE UNFOLDED into portrait-perfect country-side images, sprawling pastures of late-season crops giving way to undulating cornfields, then green, open meadows of ranchland with grazing cows and horses. Brayden drove through the beauty with one hand on the wheel, the other elbow propped on the open window, and one eye aimed sidelong at Justice.

He was slightly nauseous and entirely heartsick.

No strings. No commitments.

What kind of idiot was he, agreeing to that?

Part of proving he was here for her—and actually *being* here for her—was to get her into a relationship. He was supposed to have stood firm on the issue of a commitment.

I don't think I have it in me to go to bed with you, then just walk away.

Absolute truth.

He didn't have it in him.

Trouble was, last night he hadn't been able to let her walk, period.

When he saw her striding for the motel room door, he'd seen his chances to make her his heading right out the door with her. Impossible to face, not after he'd come so far with her in a single day—she trusted him again. So he'd convinced himself that having sex with her would be the next best step toward persuading her to become his girlfriend.

And then he fucked her.

Twice.

He'd awakened from a short nap to find Justice riding his dick through another round of ecstasy. He didn't stop her or complain. Just the opposite. With both hands on her hips, he urged her toward deeper depths—willed her to become as lost in sensations as he was.

She met him full-on.

He'd never come so hard in his life.

He fell asleep after that in a state of unprecedented bliss…only to wake this morning to an empty bed.

He was now driving next to a traveling partner who was silent and withdrawn, her face pointed out the side window.

They'd come full circle.

Justice was locked down again, tighter than ever, and he couldn't think of anything to say.

I've spent a lifetime watching you question your decisions…

He wasn't being hesitant, dammit—he wasn't that man anymore. Hadn't he challenged Rongo in the *Richard's* briefing room, not a single worry in his head about getting along or making waves or saying the wrong thing? He'd just stepped in to stop a man from being an asshole and got the job done.

He knew what needed to be done now—he had to say something brilliant and wise to get Justice around all the Hayes's family rules blocking her. He just didn't know what, exactly. What might help her versus what might drive her deeper into withdrawal?

Rocking his hand on the steering wheel like he was revving a motorcycle throttle, he stared at a cornfield, the ears bowing in the breeze, his mind hopping from one answer to another like it was running over a bed of hot coals. No thought was useful, or even clear, and an unpleasant sense of powerlessness crept over him, like when he hadn't been able to help her at SERE.

He gritted his teeth, his lungs constricting as a wave of dizziness hit him, sweeping him back into hell. The smoke-choked, armpitty stench of the POW camp…the spine-scraping music…the horror of what he'd been forced to watch through the one-way glass of his "special" interrogation room.

Justice.

Being beaten.

Suffering a violent pounding between those beautiful, strong legs of hers.

"What are you going to do about it, Ensign?" his captors had taunted him.

"I'll tell you everything you want to know" was the answer that finally got him released to charge to Justice's rescue—although he suspected he was only allowed to join the others because the SERE instructors thought he was going to blow it.

He hadn't screwed up. He'd even earned high marks at the debriefing for the way he handled himself.

At the debriefing was also where he learned that Justice's rape was fake.

But the thing was, it *wasn't* fake…not her strangled-red complexion, not her bruised and swollen face, not the flow of tears down her cheeks that no BUD/S instructor had ever been able to get out of her. She'd cried real tears at SERE, and the flashback images that woke him in the middle of the night writhing with a nameless horror felt real too.

Brake lights flared in front of him, and he darted around a meandering Honda, cutting back into the lane too close to the car's bumper.

Justice glanced briefly at the road ahead, then returned to staring out the side window with faraway eyes.

Just talk to her…say something…

Mute and strangled, he kept driving.

You doubt yourself too much…

Well, there was a lot of tangled wretchedness inside his head right now, so *fuck off*.

He passed the state line into Arkansas.

He passed a grove of poplars.

Then clarity struck.

When he doubted himself, he got defensive, and when he was on the defensive, he stopped listening, adopting an unhelpful *I'm-right-you're-wrong* position.

Just look at how he often dealt with Keith when he felt like his brother was out-performing him. Any time Keith tried to give him pointers, he came down with a case of cotton ears.

Don't fucking tell me how to swim, Keith.

I'm not fucking telling you how to swim. I'm fucking telling you how to navigate…

He needed to stop worrying and over-thinking this.

It was time to just listen.

To Justice's silence, to her body language, and to whatever she finally had to say.

BY FIVE O'CLOCK they'd reached Little Rock, Arkansas. It was too early for dinner, but after only eating dry sandwiches on the go in the car, Brayden needed caffeine. He pulled into a service station.

While he put fuel in the car, Justice went inside to buy coffees and pay the gas bill.

She was still inside after he filled the Tahoe's tank, so he moved the car next to a set of air hoses and topped off the tires. He popped the hood and checked the oil.

Everything looked good.

Wiping his hands on an oil rag, he searched for Justice again and spotted her by a vending machine.

She was holding two takeout coffee cups and gazing vacantly at the selection of junk food.

Exhaling, he tossed the rag aside. He couldn't stand much more of this. Banging the hood closed, he started for—

A man in an oil-stained John Deere ball cap veered across Brayden's path, aiming for Justice, his focus laser-locked on her ass.

She was wearing shorts again, white and fringed with lace, very feminine, the trim cut making her ass and legs look stupendous.

John Deere was staring at—*bam!*

He walked right into the vending machine.

Slammed into it, actually, so hard a Mars bar tumbled loose and the man's ball cap got bonked onto the back of his head, the bill now facing skyward.

The candy bar hit the dispenser shelf with a dull *thud*, and Justice gave John Deere a bland look.

Brayden stalked up to him. "Hey, man, thanks." He slapped John Deere on the back. Not altogether gently. "Mars is my favorite." He tugged out the candy bar and tucked it into his back pocket.

John Deere stepped away with a frown. Adjusting his cap, he looked Brayden over, then strode inside.

You've gained weight… Yeah, he tipped the scales at about two-twenty, two-thirty now. John Deere clearly wasn't down for tangling with that kind of poundage.

Justice handed Brayden one of the to-go cups. "You're going to exhaust yourself if you confront every man who's curious about me."

Yeah? Too bad.

He couldn't help himself.

Justice went back to staring at the vending machine.

Brayden rotated the to-go cup once in his hand. "Justice…" he began.

She pulled something out of her back pocket and waved it at him in a general way. "His wallet," she said.

John Deere's.

Brayden blinked. How the *hell…*? "Both your hands were holding coffee cups."

She offered up a languid shrug. "Magic." She let the wallet tumble off her fingertips. It *thumped* to the asphalt among a foliage of candy wrappers, old lottery tickets, crumpled tissues, filter tips, and condom wrappers.

"That's some talent you've got there."

"As you said, my dad was a world-class cat burglar, and he trained me in his image." She peered down at her coffee cup, her loose bangs sliding almost demurely over one eyebrow. "So you were right—I *was* expected to live up to his expectations. I was on track to become his partner, until…the incident happened."

Brayden nearly stopped breathing. *Incident…*

"Then that plan got derailed."

He played it casual with a, "Yeah?" and took a sip of coffee—burnt-tasting, like the pot had been sitting on a hot plate since nine this morning.

There was a drip of coffee on Justice's plastic lid, and she dotted it off with a forefinger. "I found out that—"

John Deere showed up.

Dammit. Justice had just been about to say something very important.

John Deere scowled back and forth between Brayden and Justice.

Brayden pointed at the wallet nestled in the pile of trash. "That yours?"

Scowling some more, John Deere bent over and snatched up the wallet. Saliva gathered at the corners of his mouth. Dude was about to say something.

Brayden gave the guy a fuck-off smile. "It must've fallen out of your pocket." *Get lost. I don't have time for your shit.*

John Deere's lips sucked in, and he stomped away.

Justice exhaled a scratchy laugh. "Watch out, Monsieur Top Hat. Hanging out with a thief is turning you into a rather gifted accomplice."

"What incident?"

"Ah." Justice tilted her head to one side. "Golden Boy thinks he wants me, but he doesn't know who I really am."

Brayden started to argue, then stopped. *Just listen to her.* "So tell me who you really are."

She edged her thumbnail along her cup's plastic lid. "Remember at BUD/S when I told you my mom died giving birth to me?"

"Of course."

"I only found out when I was sixteen. Before that I thought she died in a car accident—it's what my dad always told me. But then one night I heard him and my nanny arguing. They used to argue about me all the time." Squinting at the vending machine, Justice rubbed a smudge off the window with her thumb. "Nanna Rosemary didn't care for the way my father was raising me. Immoral, wicked, depraved, corrupt—these were the usual adjectives bandied about."

Brayden felt his forehead tighten. "That's what you heard said about you on a regular basis?"

"Yes."

Jesus Christ.

"I wasn't supposed to hear them, of course, but they would start shouting, and... During one of these epic arguments, I found out about my mom, and...it..." She gave him a look heavy with grief. "It pretty much devastated me."

Brayden's heart squeezed. "I can imagine," he said softly.

"I'm sorry."

She accepted his apology with a vague nod. "I didn't know how to deal with it, so I ended up doing the typical teenager thing—I acted out. But I did it Hayes style." She gave him a close-lipped smile. "I robbed a bank."

"You…" Brayden nearly dropped his to-go cup. "You did what?"

The lean of her mouth steepened. "I just wanted to get in and leave the vault open, prove I could do something really badass. But I was sixteen and not exactly ready for such a big job, especially on my own. I got busted on the way out."

"Holy crap," he breathed. "What happened?"

"Since I didn't have anything in my possession when I was nabbed, the DA believed I was just trying to pull an elaborate prank. He was willing to negotiate." She toed a flattened box of shoeprint-stamped Good & Plenty. "He said he would release me from juvey with a clean record, but *only* if my father retired."

Brayden paused. "The authorities knew your dad was a burglar?"

"Oh, yeah. They just couldn't prove it. Drove them nuts."

A tinny voice came over a loudspeaker by the gas pumps, complaining to someone that a lever needed to be lifted before the nozzle would work.

Justice turned back to the snacks.

Brayden hovered on the balls of his feet. "Did your dad agree?"

Justice tapped the tip of her fingernail against the window of the vending machine two times, as if coming to a decision. *Milk Duds, yes, those are the ones.* "Dad took the deal." She flipped her hand over palm up. "I still remember how badly my hand was shaking when I signed my release papers in the police station. The desk sergeant had misspelled my name, subbing in a 'c' for the 'n.' *Justice.*" She dropped her hand. "From that day forward, it's what I called myself. So I'd never forget."

Sweat drizzled down the valley of Brayden's spine.

What's your real name?

Justine.

Hey, I like that name!

I don't.

"Never forget what?" He was barely able to ask the question. A part of him really didn't want to know.

"So I'd never forget that my father's beloved career ended not because *he* made a mistake. But because *I* did."

Brayden closed his eyes in a slow blink.

"Dad left me after that." Justice threw her full coffee cup into the overstuffed trashcan. "Went off to Monte Carlo and was gone for three months."

Her dad left her…

I'm going to take a hard pass on our inevitable breakup, thank you very much.

Her eyes suddenly seemed way too young for her face. "Do you mind taking another shift driving? I'm a bit sick to my stomach."

CHAPTER FIFTY-SEVEN

WAS JUSTICE SUPPOSED to be enlightened now?

Confession was good for the soul, right? People said that. Probably it was supposed to lend a body an aspect of lightness, or maybe provide a heretofore undiscovered clarity about a problem.

If any of that were true, Justice wasn't feeling it.

Unless she was feeling it, but couldn't tell because she was too busy trying to claw her way out of the biological stew.

Because, yeah. *Gotcha!* and all that.

She'd let herself get emotionally attached to a man she'd slept with.

Undone by her female gooey factor.

Estrogen, pheromones, dopamine—get stupid.

Stupid enough to have fallen in love with Brayden?

She rubbed her lips together.

How could she not? What wasn't there to love about Brayden Street? His big heart? His handsome face and toe-curling dimples? His gallantry? The care he'd shown her from day one?

The instructors are going to try and eat you alive…

Why don't you come out on the deck, sit and stare at the beach for a bit? Down some extra calories and decompress.

It's either up on your own, or I carry you. Like a damsel.

Whether you realize it or not, you're hurting right now, Justice, and I can't do this while you're hurting. I'm in love with you.

She squeezed her eyes shut.

What is soap used for, Justice? Jesus Christ.

She'd kept his soap...all this time.

Dragging the back of her wrist over her mouth, she swallowed twice. Some large, deep place inside her was hollow and unhappy, and it was a scary thing, not knowing if she'd ever figure out how to fill it.

"You okay?" Brayden asked.

"Uh, yeah." She coughed once. "Just a little tired." She peered past the pie-slice of visibility cast by the car's headlights, checking out the serrated skyline of mismatched towers, lights twinkling with the pulse of a metropolis. "What city is that?"

"Dallas."

She glanced at the dashboard clock. Nine o'clock. They were arriving a good hour ahead of schedule—the result of Brayden driving like a maniac ever since they'd left Little Rock.

He was clearly upset about everything she'd told him at the gas station, but being upset the guy way—letting his subconscious work a problem while his conscious attended to handling a physical challenge. Like not fucking killing them. This was how a guy could think about upsetting things without admitting he was actually upset.

But Brayden was driving over a hundred miles an hour for no good purpose.

Justice had ruined her father's career, and that was that. There wasn't anything Brayden could do to change it.

Done is done.

There's no going back.

Insert other relevant platitude here.

"Do you mind if we stop for the night?" She *was* tired, actually. The job of trying to sort out all her emotions—or repress them...or whatever she was doing—was exhausting.

"I don't mind."

"Maybe we could stay someplace a bit nicer, if that's okay too? The mattress in that last motel was lumpy."

"Works for me." He punched up hotels on the GPS.

Ten minutes later they were parking in the garage of the Hyatt Regency Dallas, the car and its passengers miraculously scratch-free.

They each grabbed their bags from the trunk, then headed into the lobby, navigating through a mass of milling people.

All of them looked like computer geek brethren with their polyester clothing, eyeglasses, and office-colored complexions, many smooth hands clutching the latest electronics and gadgetry.

Justice's interest got piqued.

"Good evening," a blonde greeted them at the front desk, speaking in a refined Southern accent. Her name badge identified her as *Madison*.

"Hello," Justice said, then gestured at the lobby. "What's going on? Looks like half of Dallas is here."

Madison smiled. "A huge science symposium is taking place at the convention center just down the road from us. Many of the participants are staying here as our guests."

"Sounds cool." But *uh-oh*. "Does that mean you're fully booked?"

Madison consulted her computer screen and brightened. "You're in luck. There's a room available on the tenth floor."

A room? As in, *singular*? "Only one?"

"Um…" Madison glanced between Brayden and Justice. "Yes, I'm sorry."

Brayden dug the car keys out of his pocket. "We can try to find another hotel."

A less than thrilling option. Justice didn't want to go back on the road with Brayden tonight.

"I doubt there will be any other vacancies," Madison

warned. "We only have this room available because one of the conventioneers left this evening ill."

"Are there two beds?" Justice asked.

Madison consulted the screen again. "There's one king, but it can be made up into two twins."

Justice looked at Brayden. "I think we should take it."

"Your call." He was acting remarkably casual about how easy it would be to fuck again if they were in the same room.

Justice told Madison, "We'll take it."

"Great. How many nights?"

"Just tonight." One was plenty.

Brayden handed Madison his credit card.

She *clacked* at her keyboard. "I won't be able to send staff to make up the twin beds until shortly after eleven this evening. I know that's late, but we're at full capacity. Is that okay?"

"Yes. We'll still be up." *Probably circling the room and side-eyeing each other.* Justice panned the lobby again while Madison checked them in. "What kind of scientists are here?"

"Oh, all kinds, from what I understand. Nuclear physicists and rocket scientists, biologists and chemical engineers." *Clack, clack.* "Put all those geniuses together in one room, and they'll blow the roof off with their combined IQs." Madison chuckled at her own wit. "Here you go." She placed two plastic keycards plus Brayden's credit card on the countertop. "You're in room 1014."

"Thanks." Brayden grabbed the cards, then picked his duffel up off the floor.

"Have a nice stay." Madison set her hands on the counter, one on top of the other, like she was posing for an ad. *You're in good hands with Allstate.* "The elevators are to your right."

Brayden and Justice joined two people already waiting, suitcases beside them, their chins lifted slightly while they watched the indicator light steadily blink down from the sixth floor.

Justice stared mindlessly at the two other hotel guests in the reflection of the elevator's metal doors.

One hotel room.

To share.

With a man of godly male beauty.

We can try to find another hotel.

Might've been the better choice. Justice could already feel her vagina and her raw glop—two very subversive characters—conspiring against her rational mind. Her heart, if consulted, would make a further mess of things.

She returned to studying the hotel guests. One was a plain-faced woman in a plainer taupe dress who was half-asleep. The other was a chubby Asian man with black hair sticking up on his forehead. He wore horn-rimmed glasses, and on his right cheek Justice could just make out a—

Her pulse skidded off track. *Holy shit!*

The elevator dinged, and the doors spread open.

As the Asian man and the sleepy woman collected their suitcases and started to step inside, Justice lurched against Brayden's back, propelling him toward the rear of the elevator.

"Oh, James!" She giggled. "I've missed you so much."

Brayden spun around with a flabbergasted expression. Maybe wondering what was up with the "James" moniker. But more likely because she just made a noise she'd never uttered before—a giggle.

She gave Brayden a steady stare. *Go with this.*

He immediately murmured, "I've missed you too, baby."

His tone was unexpectedly sultry. Chills rippled through her, and her nipples puckered. She did some internal fast-talking to bring her nipples in off the ledge. This was no time for lust.

She moved her eyes at Brayden in a deliberate way, indicating the Asian man behind her. She discreetly tapped her right cheek, *look here*, then turned around. "We should order champagne."

"Definitely." Brayden studied the Asian man's reflection in the elevator doors, and Justice felt the wave of tension pass over him the moment he recognized the man who all of SOF had been briefed about—one of the CIA's Most Wanted.

Dr. Hyeong, the scientist in charge of North Korea's nuclear program, owner of the human race's most distinctive birthmark: a third eye dropped down onto his right cheek, Picasso-style. Normally red, the mark was now shaded to a hazy brown by an attempt to conceal it with pancake makeup.

Justice carefully surveyed Dr. Hyeong, roaming her eyes down his portly body. He was holding an overnight bag in one hand and a metal briefcase in the other. Near the handle of the briefcase there was a steel panel secured in place by small screws—a setup generally used to conceal a special lock.

A special lock meant that something very important was inside that briefcase.

A secret formula for the next energy-efficient fuel?

Or…

Something bad?

The roots of Justice's hair stood on end. Stupid question to ask about a scientist whose expertise lay in making nuclear bombs.

The elevator doors opened on the fifth floor, and Dr. Hyeong stepped off.

The sleepy woman stayed on.

Adrenaline kicking into high gear, Justice slipped her hand in Brayden's and pulled him with her after the scientist.

CHAPTER FIFTY-EIGHT

AT THE FIRST door Justice came to—Room 508—she flung down her duffel bag and snatched up Brayden by the shirt collar. "Oh, James." She hauled him with her as she backed up against the door, stage-whispering loud enough for Dr. Hyeong to hear, "Hurry up with the key."

The scientist shambled down the hall toward his room, whichever one that might be.

Brayden rumbled out a low laugh that had her nipples crinkling into another pucker. Dropping his own duffel, he braced his hands on either side of her, enclosing her between his thick arms.

Her senses reeled. A delicious thrill rushed into her groin. Lord, but if the real hotel guests in Room 508 should happen to open the door right now, they would get treated to quite a sight. Six feet three inches of solid, heavy muscle, loaded with an impact of presence that had grown tenfold since BUD/S.

Justice dug her fingers into Brayden's shirt while she waited, her blood throbbing in her temples. This close, his aftershave was working its magic on her, along with his body heat, flinging her back to memories of last night—his weight on top of her, the rhythm of his body, the strength of his muscles…his face between her thighs, then the power of his cock inside her.

She muttered a curse. "Is this guy's room on the third planet from the sun?"

It was taking forever for Hyeong to find it.

And Justice and Brayden were just standing here in a frozen tableau—probably looking very fake.

She clasped her palms around Brayden's nape. "Oh, James," she gasped, then let loose with another inane giggle.

Brayden leaned in close, like he was going to steal a kiss.

Her heart picked up its beat.

"When this is over," he whispered, "promise me never to laugh like that again."

She crossed her eyes at him and mutinously giggled again.

He gave her a hooded look.

They waited.

The hallway was starting to feel sapped of oxygen.

Her pulse ticked down the seconds.

Brayden's focus latched onto her mouth. *Should I keep going with the playacting and kiss you?*

Justice blinked very slowly.

And they say penises were notorious for making bad decisions. Really, the female anatomy was no better. She was on the verge of letting Brayden kiss her—*more*—and to hell with whatever Dr. Hyeong was hiding in his briefcase.

She licked her lips.

A door down the hall *clicked* shut, and she darted her focus over.

Dr. Hyeong was in Room 515.

"Okay." Brayden said softly. "What do we do now?"

They both went very still as it seemed like each of their brains now jumped off-track from What do we do now—*about the North Korean bad guy?* to What do we do now—*about this sexy stuff going on between us?*

Justice used her tongue to toy with her upper lip. From a vaginal perspective, the answer was obvious.

The door to Room 515 opened again.

Shit! Justice hugged Brayden closer, pressing her face against the strong pillar of his neck. She rolled her eyes up into her head. He smelled so ridiculously good. "Where's the key?" she whined urgently. "Come on, James."

"Hey, baby, you're distracting me." Brayden laughed low again, the rumble passing from his chest to hers, and now her erect nipples were interfacing frantically with her vagina about what the real plan needed to be.

Brayden made a pretense of searching his pockets as Dr. Hyeong sidled past them.

The scientist was no longer carrying either his bag or his briefcase. He stopped in front of the elevator and pushed the button to call it.

She clamped her jaw. Was the stupid elevator on the *fourth* planet from the sun? She made an eager sound and canted her hips forward, pressing her crotch against Brayden's.

His eyes slammed to hers and darkened, a muscle along his jaw tightening to the snapping point.

Oops. She made an apologetic face. Playacting Gone Too Far—that's what the headline would read.

Two Special Operations Forces personnel were found stuck together by their own bodily fluids late last Thursday night, when, while on a mission to save the city of Dallas, they—

The elevator finally arrived, and Dr. Hyeong got on.

Justice and Brayden stepped apart.

Their gazes clung.

I spent a lot of sleepless nights trying to figure out how to get you to understand that all the ways we connect make us perfect for each other.

Justice tore her focus away and picked up both their duffel bags, handing Brayden his. "We need to get inside Dr. Hyeong's briefcase."

They stole down the hall to Room 515.

Squatting in front of the door, Justice set her duffel bag by her side and tugged out her fanny pack of tools, finding her "ghost" keycard. She lay some "reader" tape across the magnetic stripe, then stuck the card into the door's lock slot. Extracting the card, she peeled off the reader tape. Now her ghost card was programmed for Room 515. She stuck the card back into the lock slot. The green light blinked, and she pushed the door open.

Reclaiming her bag, she entered.

Brayden followed.

Dr. Hyeong had left the bedside lamp on—add non-conservationist to the scientist's list of sins—and the metal briefcase was practically glowing at the foot of the bed.

Justice walked to the end of the mattress, crouched down again, and inspected the steel panel. It appeared to be secured with normal screws. She could probably get into it without mishap.

Probably.

That was the trouble with her game. A lot of uncertainty always threatened to end a woman's day in a mahogany box.

Retrieving a small screwdriver from her fanny pack, she carefully undid the four screws, then eased off the panel, revealing the innards. Her blood got a good dousing of adrenaline. "Ho boy," she said, sinking back on her heels. "This is going to be tricky."

Very, very tricky.

"What is it?" Brayden asked.

She pointed at two wires leading to the interior of the briefcase. "The same detonation system triggers the briefcase lock *and* whatever is inside the case. If we mess this up, we'll not only be denied access into the briefcase, but we'll be incinerated." She peered up at Brayden. "Along with God knows how many square blocks of Dallas."

Brayden's eyebrows dipped down. "You think there's

something that powerful inside?"

"It's Dr. Hyeong, isn't it? I doubt if he's just carrying around his tax returns." *Not with this lock.*

Brayden's expression remained skeptical.

"A handful of Russian backpack nukes disappeared when the Soviet Union fell. Dr. Hyeong could've got a hold of one and modified it, made it small enough to fit into a briefcase."

"We're in a *Hyatt Regency*," Brayden argued.

"With many of the world's greatest minds in this hotel right now. Get rid of a chunk of them under a gigantic radioactive haze, and you'll cripple the future scientific discoveries of other nations for decades. North Korea will emerge as the front-runner." She shrugged. "Only guessing, though."

Brayden heaved a breath. "No, I think you're right. When the CIA briefed Foxtrot about Dr. Hyeong, they told us they thought he might be planning something nasty in a southern city of the U.S.—Dallas was mentioned." He filled his cheeks with air. "We need to call in an expert."

"I *am* an expert."

His eyes blanked for a couple of beats—he was probably thinking about all the eggheads milling about in the lobby five floors below—then the glimmer of a dimple peeked out. "Oh, yeah."

"I'm going to need your help, though. The disarming process has been reversed. Instead of cutting wires to deactivate the bomb, you have to meld two together. Those—" She pointed at two dangling wires. "See?"

Brayden leaned over her shoulder to take a closer look, treating her to another whiff of his aftershave.

She swiped the back of her wrist across her nose, wiping away traces of *that*. This was no time for lust and presumptuous raw glops and disobedient vaginas to get involved.

"Is that unusual?" he asked.

"Very. Most people wouldn't catch it. They would merrily start snipping away at wires, and then…"

"Go boom?" Brayden supplied.

"Exactly. Moreover, even if the reverse process was caught, who carries a soldering gun around in his bag?"

Brayden's lips twisted. "You do?"

In fact, yes. She pulled her soldering gun out of her fanny pack and held it up, probably in a good mimic of Charlie's Angels. "This is a two-man job. So…" She found a couple of paperclips in her pack and unbent them. "You and I need to practice. The two wires and the weld must come together at exactly the same moment, otherwise…"

"Boom," Brayden guessed correctly again.

"Right." She handed the two straightened paperclips to Brayden. "On the count of three, put the ends of the paperclips together as I bring the tip of the gun up to them."

She counted down to three, and the two ends of the paperclips slipped past each other.

"Shit," Brayden said.

They tried again.

And missed again.

"Is this the tricky part you mentioned?" Brayden asked.

"This is it."

He exhaled loudly. "Maybe we should just jump two hundred feet in the air and scatter ourselves over a wide area now."

"Let's try switching jobs. I think your hands are too big for the delicate work." *And masculine.* But she wasn't going to think about that either. She gave Brayden the soldering gun and took the paperclips. She counted to three.

Success.

They practiced twice more and scored each time.

"Okay," she said. "I think we should go for the real

thing now."

Brayden studied the briefcase intently. "You sure about this, Justice?"

"Yes," she said with a stilted smile. "Time is sort of, uh, of the essence, because…I think this is on a remote detonation system."

Brayden's attention whipped back to her. "So you're saying that *any second* this thing could blow?"

"The moment Dr. Hyeong gets far enough away, yes."

"Holy crap. What the hell are we doing practicing?"

She gave him a droll look.

"Oh, yeah. The tricky part."

"Don't worry. We've got this. No biggie. Exactly like we've been doing with the paperclips. All right?"

"Right. No biggie."

She took a moment to steady herself. Inhale. Exhale. *Stay calm*. She moved to grab the two loose wires, then paused to look at Brayden. "I'm glad you're here."

He held her gaze for several seconds, then he smiled.

She drew in a final lungful of air. "Ready?"

He nodded and raised the soldering gun.

CHAPTER FIFTY-NINE

BRIEFCASE NUKE SUCCESSFULLY defused!

Justice whispered, "Hooyah," to a stunned-looking Brayden, then stood up, contracting her knees to keep from swaying off her feet and toppling to the floor in an ignominious heap. An unusual reaction for her, but then this was her first ever nuclear bomb—probably best not to focus on the *nuclear* part.

In a sudden motion, Brayden dropped down onto the edge of the bed. While he sat there, looking equal parts dumbfounded and worn out, she put in a call to Mr. Garcia at Langley, briefing him about everything that'd just happened.

Ten minutes later FBI agents from the Dallas field office arrived, and while several feds thoroughly questioned Justice and Brayden, others discreetly removed the briefcase nuke from the premises.

Might've been a good idea to evacuate the hotel before doing that, but the on-scene agents seemed satisfied with Justice and Brayden's work, and, moreover, they wanted to keep the situation on the down-low.

Made a soul wonder how often these "near misses" happened unbeknownst to average, just-going-about-his-business Joe Citizen.

The Dallas suits also apprehended Dr. Hyeong on the city streets and immediately hustled him onto a plane, shipping him off to Virginia for a long-overdue chat with

Mr. Garcia.

It was close to eleven thirty by the time Justice finally unlocked Room 1014 and entered a space of warm grays, pelmetted curtains, and the scent of pine cleaner. She was so tired at this point, she was beyond caring that she was sharing a bedroom with Brayden. She plopped her duffel bag beside the bed and stared at the trellised wallpaper. It looked like chicken wire.

"I get it now."

She turned toward Brayden, yawning. "What's that?"

He was standing very still in the middle of the room with his duffel bag still on his shoulder.

"What you've been trying to tell me about not making mistakes."

She came fully awake. "What do you mean?" She focused all of her attention on Brayden's duffel bag. He hadn't put it down, yet. That fact seemed very important at this moment.

"If you'd messed up anything with that briefcase op, a lot of people would be dead right now. Us included. So, yeah…" Muscles shifted in his jaw. "I get it."

Her mouth went dry. "I don't…I'm not sure I understand what you're saying."

He hiked his duffel higher on his shoulder. *Higher.* Like he wasn't going to stay. "You learned not to make the same mistake twice and…" He trailed off, as if his next words were too difficult to say.

I will never again allow myself to feel the kind of pain you put me through—that would be making the same mistake twice. Now please go.

A thick breath caught in her throat, a cold realization gripping her.

This was a goodbye speech.

Brayden was about to give her exactly what he thought

she wanted—his departure from the scene—exactly what she'd been pushing for—a preemptive breakup in order to save herself the pain of a real one later.

Except this wasn't saving her from pain.

This was agony.

"I did a lot of thinking on the drive from Little Rock," he went on, "and—"

"Don't!" She leapt forward, panic exploding in her heart. All the precarious pieces she'd been barely holding together this last year crumbled—the miserable excuse for a human she was while she was alone…all the vital rules she had stuffed inside her head that locked out happiness except she didn't know any other way to live other than to abide by them…her growing love for Brayden in spite of how much she'd been trying to block her feelings for him.

All those pieces just shattered apart at the thought of going back to life without him.

"Please." She seized his arm. "Don't go!"

His eyes flared wide.

"I can do better. I…I…" But what if she didn't have it in her to jump into a relationship with both feet, to manage commitments and complications?

What would that mean?

Answer: sprawling emptiness. Because when it came to all or nothing, the other side of *all* was *nothing*.

I don't have it in me to go to bed with you, then just walk away…

She burst into tears.

"Hey, whoa!" Finally dropping his annoying duffel bag, Brayden lifted both hands in a placating gesture. "Don't cry. I'm not going anywhere."

Slumping her shoulders, she just cried harder, clasping both hands over her face. It felt like she was wringing her heart out with her own fists, squeezing out emotions that'd been trapped inside her raw glop for a decade.

"Aw, hell, Justice, you're killing me with this." Brayden wrapped an arm around her and shuffle-stepped her over to the bed, urging her to sit on the mattress with him. "I was just going to tell you that I think I know why you've been pushing me away."

She leaned more deeply into his embrace, sniffling and scrubbing her nose. "I'm so sorry. I don't mean to keep rejecting you."

"I know." He rubbed her back. "I have an idea about that, although you might find it a bit mind-blowing."

"I'd like to hear it."

"Okay. Here it is: what if messing up that bank robbery didn't screw over your dad but actually helped him?"

"What?" She left the sanctuary of Brayden's chest to peer at him. "How?"

"Your dad was the best, right? He was never caught, which means he made few, if any, mistakes in his career. But here's the thing, he *would* have slipped up at some point. It's just not possible for a person to stay sharp forever, even the best in the game. He would've eventually grown too old or too shaky or too tired, and he would've lost his edge." Brayden brushed some lingering moisture off her cheeks with his thumbs. "The way I see it, you did your dad a favor by forcing his retirement. Cutting a deal with the DA allowed him to quit while he was still on top, to help you out and save face while doing it."

She opened her mouth. That's all she could do. No words came. *A favor?*

Brayden smiled gently. "And the stuff about your dad going off to Monte Carlo for three months? Typical man-cave maneuver. He wasn't leaving *you*, Justice—not in the sense that he was punishing you by taking his love away. He probably figured he was leaving you in the care of a loving nanny while he went off to come to terms with his decision. Because even though it was the right choice for your dad to get out of the game, he was still leaving a career he loved. He would've needed time to accept it. Normal retirement transitional stuff, you know. Any man would've gone through it. But...I think you were so weighed down with guilt, you didn't see it that way."

She still couldn't speak. This was amazing and... Was that what actually happened?

"And all this talk about being a dirty thief compared to 'golden-boy' me. You've been feeling unworthy, yeah, but not of *me*. Of love. I think in your mind—probably your subconscious—you figured you messed up your dad's career, so you didn't deserve love, or you weren't allowing yourself to feel love to punish yourself, or something along those lines." He took her gently by the chin, making sure she kept her focus on him. "But you didn't screw up your dad's life, Justice. I firmly believe that." He let go of her, lines creasing his brow. "Does any of this sound right?"

"Yes." Everything he just said actually made perfect sense. "Sitting here now and thinking back, I can't remember my dad giving me a max amount of shit over the failed bank job." The lion's share of recriminations had come from herself. "So..." She squinted at Brayden. "This is why I've been pushing you away? I needed to forgive myself?"

Brayden took her by the hand, lacing their fingers together. "There's nothing to forgive yourself for, okay? Remember that."

Right. A *favor*.

Mind-blowing might be understating matters. She might not have a single neuron of gray matter left inside her skull.

Total flabbergasted head disintegration was what it was.

A knock sounded.

Brayden stood, strode for the door, and opened it.

"Sorry for the late hour, sir," a man in a hotel uniform said. "I'm here to separate the beds for you."

Justice got to her feet and went to Brayden's side, sliding her arm through his. "Thank you," she told the hotel guy. "But that won't be necessary anymore."

CHAPTER SIXTY

"I WANT TO ask you to do something for me," Justice told Brayden, urging him toward the bed.

He glanced once at the mattress. "Yeah?" He smiled broadly. "What's that?"

She let out breathy laugh. "Don't get too excited, big guy. I was just going to ask you to lie down with me for a bit." She suddenly felt about as stuffing-less and brainless as Dorothy's Scarecrow.

His brow knitted. "Are you okay?"

"For the most part. It's just been a long day, all told— emotional confessions and hundred-mile-per-hour car rides, topped off with a shared hotel room, scary nukes, a stressful bomb-dismantling op, and brain-splat epiphanies. Everything has sort of caught up with me all at once."

"Hundred-mile-per-hour car rides?" Brayden asked, a trace of confusion in his voice.

"It's how fast you were driving."

"I was not. Was I?"

"Yes." She climbed onto the bed, crawled to the center, and lay down. "It's just until I stop shaking," she told him quietly.

It was what he'd said to her after the Down-Dog pushups annihilation, right before he lay down with her on the barracks' community room couch.

His gaze softened, and she could tell he remembered too. Climbing onto the bed, he curled himself around her.

He was a marvelous big spoon. She knew that from napping with him before, but here in the Hyatt Regency, he didn't stink, and at least twenty extra pounds of sheer muscle was pressed warmly against her.

Her entire body relaxed into bonelessness.

He draped one arm over the indent of her waist, a solid weight. "I'm here for you, no prob." He kissed her ear, then rested his chin on top of her head.

Her raw glop liquefied and ran out from between her fingers.

WHEN JUSTICE WOKE, the nightstand clock read three in the morning. Her wits-gathering lie-down with Brayden had stretched into a three-hour nap. Everything was quiet. Birds were asleep outside, and hotel staff at rest inside, but more than that, *she* was quiet in a way she'd never been before.

Inner peace. That's what it was.

She had Brayden to thank. He'd never lost patience with her, never stopped loving her through all the difficult times, and he cared enough about her to have thought through, solved, and then redefined one of the most tragic episodes of her life.

What if messing up that bank robbery didn't screw over your dad but actually helped him?

She owed Brayden so much.

Owed him for showing her the way through her guilt. Owed him for not giving up on her and tracking her down in Virginia. Owed him for a chance to live life as a new her.

How could she make him understand how much he meant to her? How special it was that he treated her the way she'd always wanted to be treated but never thought she deserved? How could she ever express what a gift it was to have the ability to love him back freely and openly?

She didn't have his ways and means.

She owed him *too* much. There was no place to begin…

She smiled to herself.

Or…

She could start simple. Get back to basics.

Help him understand her feelings for him with *doing* rather than *saying*.

She rolled over in his arms, her movement releasing his All Man scent, now flavored with a cozy warmth.

He stirred and his lashes shifted.

She sat up, took him by the shoulders, and urged him to lie down flat on the mattress while she swung a leg over his hips.

His eyes lazed open, the blue of his irises soft with sleepy curiosity. *What are you up to?*

Straddling him, she scooted back to his thighs. "I was just thinking that I never got the chance to finish what I started the night after SERE." She unbuttoned his shorts. "I owe you a blow job."

BRAYDEN'S HIPS AUTOMATICALLY lifted to allow easy removal of his shorts and briefs—he hadn't given his hips the command to do that. They just did. In fact, if he had any control over his brain right now, he might've decided to pause, long enough to confirm, *Yes, we're together now.* Because no words of commitment had actually been spoken, even though he and Justice had just traveled some very important steps forward these past few hours.

But he wasn't without his caveman tendencies, no matter how much Justice liked to call him a gentleman, and one of the ways he was a typical male was…

Well, he was a whore to the blow job.

So when Justice kneed his legs apart to make room for herself, his thighs happily spread wider to accommodate her.

And when she encircled his sex with her lithe fingers—*Christ, yeah*—he made no move to urge her off.

He instead twisted his hands into the bedsheets and bit his teeth together, watching her prop his hard-on upright with a grip at the base.

"Hair," he croaked.

She glanced up. "What?"

"Take your hair down."

Her mouth eased into a smile as she slid the band off her ponytail. Her hair tumbled down around her shoulders, and, as always, the change was astounding.

Hair up: beautiful but no-nonsense Justice Hayes.

Hair down: instant fucktoy.

She bent toward his cock—the thing was practically purple from the rapid influx of blood—and he held his hip flexors rigid in suspended anticipation.

Soft strands of her hair slithered across his belly and thighs.

He moaned, then hissed when she teased her tongue along the little slit at the top of his member.

Muscles all over his body tensed as one.

She attentively lapped her tongue all over his glans.

He watched her, pulling air between his teeth, fast and hot. It sounded like he was breathing enough for four men.

Her lips enfolded him, her mouth riding down his length, and—

He flung his head back. He couldn't watch anymore. The sight of his cock disappearing into the suctioning power of her lips was too much. He arched his neck. He twined his fingers tighter, bunching up the sheets.

Her lips met her hand at the base of his cock, then she sucked her way back up, this time dragging her fisted hand up with her mouth. She paused at the top to dispense more saliva onto her fingers, and the next trip down was an extra-smooth, gliding stroke.

Oxygen backed up in his lungs. A pleasure point beneath his balls began to throb violently.

She set a perfect rhythm—suck and stroke, suck and stroke. At some point he let go of the sheets and dug his fingers into her hair, his biceps flexing. He didn't try to control her—what idiot would interfere with a perfect performance?—he just needed to touch her during this, to feel her long, silky hair sifting through his fingers, the heat coming off her flesh, and the hypnotic up-and-down bob of her head.

"Yeah," he growled. "I'm going to—" He shook with a ferocious spasm of muscles.

Come!

Pleasure shot through him like sexually charged electricity, and he let out a guttural moan as the forceful geysering at the end of his cock pumped hot liquid into the back of Justice's throat.

She drank him down.

Ecstasy crested into the death throes of rapture, the whole-body convulsions damn near ripping him apart. The arches of his feet contracted through to the end, and finally his climax released him. He sank into the mattress, panting, his heart reeling, groaning again.

Justice gently laid his spent cock on his hip. "Wow, Brayden, you're gonna get blow jobs all the time if you're always so easy."

Still gasping for air, he cursed once, then pried an eye open and peered down at her. She looked sexy as hell sprawled between his thighs, even fully clothed. "I might've been thinking about that for an entire year." *I love your happy trail. I love where it goes...* Sweat slid down his temples. "*And* you suck really hard."

She chuckled with a funny little cockeyed look of piratical pleasure. Evidently she was happy to discover that she possessed such an effective implement of torture on her person.

He flopped back onto his pillow. "Give me fifteen minutes, woman, then I'll screw your godless brains out."

Impatient little upstart crawled up his body anyway.

He partially un-sagged his eyelids to see what she was doing. She sat up on his lap, divested herself of her T-shirt and bra, then pushed his shirt up and stretched out fully on top of him, settling her soft, naked breasts against his bare chest.

"Make that ten minutes," he murmured, skimming his hands up her back.

He caressed the tips of his fingers along the length of her spine, then swept the pads of his thumbs over the plumped-up sides of her breasts. She was so hot. How had he lived one room over from her for six months and not jumped her? "Although I'm beginning to think five is doable."

She smiled lazily down at him. "I owe you something else."

"Quit it, would you?" He could feel her nipples hardening. He felt extremely good right now.

"I owe you a declaration of love."

He stopped what he was doing and flipped his eyes up to hers, a full breath arrested somewhere mid-throat.

She looked accessible in a way she never had before, her expression completely open and warm. "I love you, Brayden."

His throat swelled to monstrous proportions. Shit, that better not be visible.

"I'm ready to be a team now. All in. Both feet. And you're just the type of leader I've always wanted to be with."

The words hit him dead center and with such impact the backs of his eyeballs burned. He rubbed his thumbs across his lids. Only a little dust in 'em, that was all. *Hell.* She was making a mess out of him, a genuine, turn-in-your-trident-at-the-desk basket case.

She kissed him lightly and, with a slinky move of her hips, stripped herself out of her shorts. "How does three minutes sound? Doable?"

A laugh of spontaneous happiness burst out of him. He flipped her onto her back and settled between her thighs.

"How about *now*?" he asked, a smile against her mouth.

Epilogue...

Wait!

Before you read on to find out more about Justice and Brayden's happily ever after...

To obtain a FREE authentic copy of the <u>Bronze Star</u> Lieutenant JG Brayden Street received for his daring rescue of Justice in North Korea.

tracy.link/brayden

EPILOGUE

Eight months later
McP's Irish Pub, Coronado
Reunion Party, BUD/S Class 684

A COLLECTIVE GASP of excitement went up in the bar, then a wave of whispers passed from one person to another.

Dog Bone's girlfriend, Karen, grasped Justice's forearm and let out a *squee!* that nearly sent Justice jumping out of her socks.

"It's Marilyn Dower!" Karen exclaimed.

"What?" Justice turned toward the front door.

Pete Robbins had just entered the bar, a knockout blonde on his arm.

He was making a path for himself and his date through the crowd with the force of his gleaming smile.

Justice laughed under her breath.

Leave it to Pete to pull off a grand entrance in a room full of operators.

Karen switched to clutch Dog Bone's arm. A young woman with a rosy face and dumpling cheeks, Karen had an undying smile for Dog Bone that likewise kept the gentle giant in a state of starry-eyed bliss.

"Let's go meet her!" Karen hauled her boyfriend off.

Dog Bone waved goodbye to Justice.

Justice waved back, then threaded her way to the bar for a fresh drink. She found Keith Knight sitting on a stool, a bottle of beer in front of him.

"Hey," she said.

He looked scruffier and tougher than his BUD/S days, more rugged, if such a thing were possible, like he should be wearing leopard pelts, boots made of scorpion skins, and nicknamed Grizzly Grizzle…or something with Grizzly in the title.

She and Keith were on good terms again.

After her two-month training cycle in San Diego with Foxtrot, she'd returned to Korea to continue her deployment, and sought out Keith before he left for home. Over coffee in the Camp Casey mess hall, she apologized for leaving BUD/S the way she had, explaining about Admiral Sherwin driving her off, and…by the way, what did you two talk about the morning after your brawl with Brayden?

Keith had shrugged. "Sherwin warned me to keep my temper in check. The Navy doesn't want to lose a good man like me, yadda, yadda."

"Nothing else?"

"No. Why do you ask?"

She'd answered, *No reason*, not really seeing the point of stirring the pot about her arrest record at this late date. She had the information that mattered—Keith hadn't thrown her under the bus. Somebody did, and hopefully someday she'd figure out who.

"What's all the noise about?" Keith asked her now, aiming his head back toward the bar's main crowd.

"My pilot, Pete, just arrived with his girlfriend." Justice caught the bartender's attention. "Marilyn Dower—she was in the latest Avengers movie."

One of Keith's eyebrows hiked up. "A movie star is dating a Navy pilot?"

Justice shrugged. *Why not?* Pete looked like a movie star himself.

The bartender arrived, and Justice ordered a Tom Collins.

"Welcome home, by the way. You've been back for, what, three days now?"

She slid onto the stool next to Keith. "Yep"

"I hear you and Bray kicked ass over there. You two make a great team." Keith gave her a knowing smirk. "In a lot of ways."

She chuckled. Everyone on Team Five knew she and Brayden were dating, and, you know what? *Oh, well.*

The bartender set a Tom Collins in front of her. She nodded her thanks.

Keith slugged back some beer. "He wants to ask you to marry him, you know?"

"Yeah?" She kept her tone casual, even though her heart was suddenly doing a weird dance. "Why doesn't he?" She glanced over at Brayden.

He was in conversation with Brad Ziegler, who'd finished a deployment in the Middle East with a medal on his chest for doing some unpublicized, heroic shit. No girlfriend yet for Hairy Arms, not that he lacked for wannabes to judge by the entourage of lash-flutterers surrounding him.

"He's afraid you're not ready," Keith said.

She sipped her cocktail. *Brayden, you dope.* "How about you? Anyone special in your life?"

"Nah. Too busy."

Keith had always been a hard-charger and always would be. "I've heard rumors that you're an early select for Green Team."

He smiled vaguely. "We'll see."

A cheer went up in the bar as a couple of new celebrants arrived.

She glanced over. One of the men was—"Hey, it's Omar Boyd!" *High School Crush Lookalike!* "I never heard what happened to him."

"He ended up graduating from SWCC."

"He never made it back to BUD/S?"

Keith finished off his beer. "He joined Class 685, but he couldn't get through Hell Week then, either."

"Ah, well, SWCC's probably a blast." Special Warfare Combatant-Craft Crewmen were in charge of inserting special operators into out-of-the-way places via fast boat.

She hopped off her stool and tossed some money on the bar. "I'm going to go say hi."

Keith shoved her money back at her. "I've got it." He showed his empty beer bottle to the bartender, indicating he wanted another.

She tucked her money in her pocket. "Thanks." She swept her drink off the bar, then leaned toward Keith and smiled. "Tell Brayden to ask."

She caught up with Boyd, then Zack Kilgour, who'd realized his career goal of becoming a Team sniper, then she talked to Giddiup, Hooper, and Sanchez. Rudy Dunbar joined the party toward the end of the evening. He didn't say *hi* to her, just glanced at her once, awkwardly, and kept to a group at the far corner of the bar. Rudy still believed Justice and Brayden had slept together during BUD/S.

She waved down Brayden and pointed at the door. The thought of being around Rudy's sour-lemon face for the rest of the night meant *time to go.*

She and Brayden strolled outside together and crossed the parking lot, making their way to the Acura Brayden had borrowed from a friend—he'd sold his own car predeployment and hadn't bought a new one.

Unlocking the passenger side door, Brayden started to open it, then stopped. The door *snicked* shut, and he turned to face her. A halogen streetlight illuminated his eyes. "So…do you want to have kids someday?"

A surprised laugh spilled out of her. "Wow, Keith already talked to you, huh?"

Brayden rotated the car keys in his palm and grinned. "How many do you want?"

"Oh, no, not those." She pointed an accusing finger at his dimples. "Put those away while we're discussing kids. I won't be talked into six."

His grin widened, then he caught himself and wiped the smile off his face.

His fake-sober expression was even more endearing than his dimples. Well, not *more*, but close.

"But you *do* want some?" he asked.

"Yes. Two."

"Hmm, how about maybe three, like, you know, if we have two girls and want to go for a boy, or two boys and want to try for a girl?"

"Maybe," she said. "I just don't want an only child."

"Ah." He nodded. "And when, you know…" He scratched the side of his jaw. "When were you thinking about having these kids?"

"This is really the full-court-press convo, isn't it?" Next topics would be religion and in-laws. "Let's see…depends on how long I'm in the Navy." She was obligated for four years, and hadn't decided if she would re-up her commitment at that point. The Special Missions job required a lot of time away from home and a lot of hard work. "About three or four years, probably."

"Right. Makes sense. Or—" He gestured in the general direction of nowhere. "Maybe sooner."

"It's kind of difficult to have kids when one is deployed all the time. Besides, I'm only twenty-four years old. What's the rush?"

"There isn't one. Except…*I'll* be home."

She didn't see how that was possible. "Last I checked we were a combined unit, which sort of puts you on the same deployment schedule as me."

"Yeah, well…There's something I've been wanting to talk to you about that."

She frowned at him. "What?"

He watched several moths circling each other inside the beam of streetlight. When he looked at her again, his expression was solemn. "I want to med-out of the Navy, Justice."

"Why?" Her stomach jerked. "What's wrong?"

"My shins. I'm sorry I didn't talk to you about it sooner, but…the truth is, they never fully recovered from the beating they took during Hell Week."

"Oh, God, Brayden…" After all his hard work. "I'm so sorry."

"I'm actually okay with it. I joined because I wanted to be a good leader, and I've led Foxtrot pretty well."

More than *pretty well*, she'd say. Brayden had been awarded the Bronze Star for the part he played in developing and executing the dangerous mission to save Bat Three from a canyon in North Korea.

"I needed to prove something to myself and…" He drew in a ragged breath. "I think I have. I'm good. I don't have to be a Team Guy to know it. I mean, don't get me wrong— I'm going to miss the job and the guys. But I can't run the risk of ever letting down a Team brother out there because of my shins. I'd never forgive myself."

She reached out and squeezed his arm, her heart full. Such quintessential Brayden.

"So I'll probably be out by some time next year." His smile returned. "That means we could start a family."

"Are you saying you want to be a house daddy?"

He thought about it for a moment, then laughed. "No."

She chuckled too. "Okay."

"But I'll be around, so…it's something to think about."

"All right, I will."

He opened the car door.

She started to climb in, then stopped. "So, um…aren't you going to ask me?"

"What? *Now?* Fuck no. These things have to be done right. I need the ring, and candlelight and champagne, before getting down on one knee to—"

"You don't have to kneel."

He looked appalled. "The hell I don't. There are certain traditions a man holds to. I'll also be carrying you across the threshold." He pointed a finger at her nose. "No arguments."

She held up both palms. "Okay, okay." Far be it from her to get between Mister Consummate Gentleman and his ways and means.

He paused. "Actually, I do have something I've been wanting to give you." He headed toward the back of the car. "We can consider it a pre-ask gift."

She followed.

He opened the trunk, revealing an assortment of guy stuff inside: combat boots and a pair of camos, a hockey stick and clunky ice skates, a six-pack of Gatorade and a duffel bag. Shoving the car keys in his pocket, he reached into the duffel and pulled out a wrinkled brown lunch sack.

She took it from him and examined it. "This has seen better days." She peered inside. "A brown rag?"

"Jesus." He yanked out the brown rag and held it up to her with both hands. The cloth unfurled into a T-shirt with white letters across the back.

H-A-Y-E-S.

The earth rocked. She lost her breath. "Oh, my God," she whispered. "It's my honorary brown shirt."

He said quietly, "You left it behind in the barracks."

"I know, I…" The old emotions crashed over her, the

wretched disappointment of missing BUD/S graduation, the loss and betrayal of two best friends, the hollowness to follow, and the despair and defeat that'd led her to spend a year living inside a shell, empty and miserable.

The line of Brayden's mouth softened. "Remember when you came back to BUD/S after Hell Week and you told all of us that you'd learned how to do things your own way?"

Unable to find her voice, she nodded.

"From then on you kicked butt at BUD/S. And it's the same now. I've seen how you've been with me these last months, and…you've changed. You're not operating off Hayes family rules any longer, but your own."

"Yes," she said through the tight constriction of her throat. She'd realized a while back that she'd been following her dad's rules to honor him, but…since she hadn't ruined his life, she didn't need to do that anymore.

"You earned this shirt, Justice. You *deserve* it. If you accept it now, you're also saying you deserve everything I'm offering you. A house with a pool in the back, kids and little league, watching the sun set together every day…even when we're a couple of old farts in rocking chairs."

A laugh hitched out of her. She stared misty-eyed at the shirt—one of her crowning achievements—and her heart melted for this man all over again. It was *Brayden* who'd asked the BUD/S instructors to reward her with this symbol of achievement. The damsel-rescuer on his white horse, looking out for her, falling in love with her right from the beginning.

"If I take this shirt," she said, her voice coming dangerously close to breaking, "it means my answer is *yes*."

"Ah. Then I guess I better do this." He went down on one knee before her and held the brown shirt up high, his eyes brilliant—with moonlight and halogen and love.

She smiled through a sheen of tears.

Top rule she followed now: whenever given the chance to love or be loved, *take it*.

She accepted the shirt and hugged it to her breasts.

His eyes still bright, he came to his feet and framed her face between his palms. "Let's go get some ice cream to celebrate."

We romance readers love our happily-ever-afters, don't we?

But what if there was another chance at happiness waiting along a different track?

What if wild mand Pete Robbins's girlfriend wasn't a movie star, but he BUD/S woman he really always wanted?

What if Justice was the one woman who could save Keith Knight from a career-only path?

Wouldn't that be fun to read about?

The story doesn't have to end…

You can **Choose Another Hero**!

If you want to find out how Justice's happily-ever-after turns out with **Keith Knight**, go to page 325.
If you want to find out how Justice's happily-ever-after turns out with **Pete Robbins**, go to page 605.

PETE ROBBINS'S STORY...

Has he finally met his match…? *What, are you kidding? Of course I'll get her.*

Busted off flight status for disobeying an order, Lieutenant Pete "Bingo" Robbins has nothing but time to dedicate to his "Operation Get Justice" scheme. But the gutsy BUD/S Woman won't be an easy mark – even for this consummate player.

So when the CIA dangles an exciting undercover mission before him, he jumps at the chance to up his game and take advantage of his enticing role as Justice's husband.

The role actually lands him at a sick, secret club with the Russian Minister of Defense – Pete must survive a barbaric contest or put Justice's life in jeopardy.

His usual devil-may-care charm deserts him, and he turns to Justice to help him recover. Who would've guessed that experiencing his raw side is exactly what she needs to finally lower her guard? She starts to see him as a solid boyfriend candidate…but did she put her trust in him too soon?

Out of nowhere comes the ultimate test of his ability to stand by her. He must dig deep within himself to find the right stuff, but will he get his act together before Justice's life is thrown into utter chaos…?

CHAPTER FORTY-FOUR

Late June
South Korea

A NIGHT CREATURE of some sort skulked out of the stand of dark trees circling the parked helicopter. Moving with a waddling gait, its fur like polished ink in the moonlight, the thing was about the size of a possum or raccoon or maybe even a beaver.

Did South Korea even have rodent-y animals like those?

Tracking the mystery beast from beneath flagging eyelids, Pete slouched in his jump seat. Poss-coon-eaver shambled under a bush.

Pete kept his focus on where it'd disappeared, readying himself. Any second now the creature would prove to be a Transformer and change into a monstrous creature that would try to eat him, Willie, and Ketchup.

Probably wasn't much fun to be eaten, but at least fighting off a monster would give Pete something to *do*. Some kind of freaking damned excitement.

Pete drummed his fingers on his thigh and rapped his bootheels on the floor, rattling the flight helmet propped on his knee. Here he was, on his first in-country op with his Bat Three Special Missions crew, and he was stuck only providing taxi service.

Yeah, okay, so his job in general was to transport Justice, Glinski, and Morris wherever they needed to go to do their job, but the *where* of that was supposed to be someplace more challenging than a tranquil wooded clearing in friendly territory where he would be bored out of his skull just sitting.

Sitting and waiting and sweating and waiting some more.

And if you were Nate "Willie" Wojno, you'd be drinking lots of water and overusing the piss-tube.

No engine running at idle meant no A/C blasting cold air meant an interior cockpit as sticky as Stormy Daniels's bedroom floor.

Sweat slithered steadily down Pete's brow and temples. He just let it. Bouncing his knee again, he scanned the dashboard. He'd already pre-flighted the bird and gone over the Alert Condition Checklist for a rapid restart. So…

There was *nothing to do.*

By the dim red light coming off the dash, Pete peripherally saw Willie using the piss-tube again. The fourth damned time.

He rammed his gloved fingers through his hair.

A stiff evening breeze swept by, tousling the leaves on the trees and whistling through the motionless rotor blades. The scent of cooking meat swirled around Pete, beef or pork—locals making mandoo, or Korean dumplings. The scents were homey. Pleasant. Out of place.

His stomach growled. "I need a drink."

Willie held out his gallon jug of water.

"Not that kind of drink." And not to be a germ-a-phobe or anything, but wasn't that the same hand Willie used to hold his dick in the piss-tube?

"Ah." Willie nodded. He was wearing his helmet, Night Vision Goggles down, and Pete could almost hear the thing sloshing back and forth on Willie's sweaty skull. "You're talking shots of mezcal. Yeah."

Pete stopped his fidgeting and stared at the unmoving

altimeter gauge. *Mezcal…*

He'd been holding a bottle of that particular brand of tequila when he showed at Justice's Pensacola BOQ room a year ago—he and his crew had been temporarily assigned to Pensacola while Justice and her guys were at crypto school so they could train as a team on the weekends.

He'd presented the tequila to her with a flourish. "Time to start up a new bottle!" He bobbed his brows. "And maybe this time I'll get stuck eating the worm." And if things went as planned, Justice would suggest that they share the worm—like he'd offered to share *her* worm the night of their lingerie prank—and the sharing would lead to kissing would lead to touching…

Would lead to falling into bed together and burning up the sheets.

A major goal of his from the first moment he'd seen her stride like a Valkyrie invader into the HSC-85 hangar.

How the incredible hell would a body like *hers* perform in bed?

Never in his life had he imagined a woman could look like Justice did. Her looks went so far beyond the norm, he couldn't even describe her. Muscular, strong, hardy, determined, hardworking—made her sound like a plow horse. And, strictly speaking, labeling her with all the applicable adjectives *should* have landed her somewhere in the animal phylum of species rather than *homo sapiens feminam*. But she was most definitely a woman. Every soft, smooth inch of her. Every dip and valley on her body, every rounded curve.

Best way he could think of to describe her was striking…but in a way that could kill you. Which only missile-locked him on wanting to fuck her even more. Because no matter how commanding and gutsy a woman was in daily life, she changed in bed—at least when he got his hands on her—and it was a special kind of fun to watch her melt.

But there would be no bed with Justice. No sheets-on-fire. No together, even. She'd greeted him at her BOQ room door with dead eyes and her bun—which seemed to be an indicator for just how well or badly her day was going—looking like an unleavened dinner roll.

"I've given it a lot of thought," she said, mincing no words, "and I've decided not to date military men."

Well…shit.

That wasn't supposed to happen.

Justice was supposed to have stepped up and been the real deal for him.

Relieved him of all the game-playing it took to hook up with a woman.

Saved him from conversations that were almost exclusively bar banter.

Nice shirt—wink—*looks like boyfriend material.*

Is it hot in here—arm squeeze—*or is it just you?*

I'm not wearing any socks—hair flip—*and I have the underwear to match.*

Was it fun to hear stuff like that from women? Sure. And getting laid was better than sitting at home watching the History Channel. Well…unless you were talking a six-part series on WWII.

But after a nice rollicking roll in the hay, his insides always seemed to go flat with boredom…or something worse than boredom. He wasn't sure what.

Maybe sort of a doldrums of the spirit—like windless waters.

Not when he was around Justice, though.

But oh-fucking-well.

Shit happens and etcetera.

When Justice shut her BOQ room door on him a year ago, that gesture turned out to be an analog truth in every sense—she'd shut him out of her life.

After an initial *WTF?* bump over her rejection, he'd taken it in stride.

The last thing he needed was to get his heart crunched. And, yes, Justice Hayes had the ability to crunch him.

Not at first.

In the HSC-85 hangar, he'd just wanted to fuck her. Sex only. But then he saw how she was with her guys.

Dedicated.

Protective.

Committed.

Figure it out, Pete.

That's all he himself had ever heard from his parents growing up. *Got a problem? Figure it out, Pete!* Nice for Mom and Dad to have such confidence in him, and he supposed their hands-off style of parenting expanded his innovative problem-solving skills.

But going it alone all the time was also a pain in the ass. People sometimes needed advice and help. He could've used a little support now and again.

So when he saw how resolved Justice was to help Glinski fast-rope effectively—to make sure her guy didn't go it alone—it'd touched a chord.

And the more time he spent with her, the more he got a kick out of her—and the more he'd grown to really like her. He'd been dead serious about wanting to date her—as her boyfriend.

It was a damned shame they hadn't worked out.

But the hell if he was going to stress over it. She did her thing, he did his, and somewhere in the middle, they managed to maintain a solid working relationship. That was the most important part.

Funny, though…he'd never touched a drop of mezcal since. Wonder if that meant anything. Or if—?

The knee holding his flight helmet crackled.

Willie turned to him and tapped the side of his own helmet. "Call coming in."

Pete was already wedging his helmet back on.

It squished in place over his sweaty hair, reminding him of the time his little sister had put Jell-O in the straw hat he wore out in the field. She'd deserved a good smack or two over that, but of course he wasn't allowed to scrap with her. *Use your words to convey your displeasure, Pete.* His parents were so Zen about everything, maybe he'd actually been raised by a couple of potheads. He hadn't been. They weren't. But still.

Justice's voice came through his earpiece. "Chaos One, this is Bat Three Actual. How copy?"

Pete keyed the comm trigger on his stick. "Loud and clear. You ready for onload, Three?" *Please say that you're all done with your uranium bunker op.* He was hungry and dreaming of a shower. "I don't have a visual on you yet." He combed the forest. No Bat Three squad. No Transformers. No poss-coon-eaver.

"Roger. We are mission complete but need to be picked up from a new extraction point. Mark these grid coordinates." Justice began to rattle off numbers.

Willie punched them into the Multi-Purpose Display.

Pete switched to inner-cockpit comms. "Let's initiate startup." He buckled back into his five-point restraint.

"Roger that," Willie said.

"Ketchup," Pete called to his AW in back. "You awake, man?"

"Locked and loaded, sir."

Willie opened the three-ring binder on his kneeboard and flipped to the Engine Start Checklist. "Battery," he said to Pete.

Pete flipped the battery switch. "On."

"Fuel pump."

Pete flipped another switch. "On."

"Auxiliary power."

"On."

"Number one engine."

"Start." The jet engine growled to life.

"Number two engine."

"Start." The growl roared louder. Pete scanned the dashboard. Everything looked good. "Gauges in the green. Rotor brake off." He grabbed the lever overhead.

"Uh, Bingo…"

Pete glanced at Willie from underneath his raised arm.

"The GPS coordinates Lieutenant Hayes gave us are across the DMZ." His copilot was staring at the map that'd popped up on the MPD. "Bat Three is inside enemy territory."

CHAPTER FORTY-FIVE

PETE JACKED HIS brows up. "What?"

Willie began to repeat himself, but Pete gestured for him to stop.

Justice was speaking again.

"Interrogative," she said. "Are you able to fly in and exfil us from this new location?"

Pete engaged the trigger for external comms. "The coordinates you gave us are inside North Korea." At the bottom of a canyon by the look of it.

"Affirmative. Be advised we're pinned down by a large force of hostiles and unable to move."

You're...? Pete blinked so hard his sweaty eyelashes squished together. *What?*

Willie pointed to the stick between Pete's knees.

Pete glanced down. He was squeezing the comm trigger, holding it in the *on* position. He released it, then turned to Willie. "How the hell did those three get pinned down by a large enemy force? Isn't this a covert op? Sneaky shit being done sneakily?"

Willie scrunched his face at him and shrugged.

Well, fuck a duck.

"Chaos One," Justice said. "Do you—"

"Stand by," Pete interrupted. Changing frequencies on the radio, he called the *Bonhomme Richard*. "Chaos One to Combat Control."

"Roger, Chaos One. Loud and clear."

He explained the situation with Bat Three, concluding with a request to cross the DMZ, or Demilitarized Zone, which marked the border between South and North Korea.

Base said, "Stand by while we coordinate with South Korean air traffic control."

"Roger." Pete said to Willie, "Continue Engine Start checklist." Pete grabbed the brake lever again. "Rotor brake off." This time he released the blades. A *whop-whop-whop* joined the growl of the jet engines. He eased the engine power control levers to "fly" while observing the gauges. "One-hundred percent NP/NR," he reported.

"Mission systems, on," Willie reported back. "Generators, on."

Everything was perfect. Pete radioed the ship. "Combat Control, Chaos One. All systems green, ready for takeoff."

"Chaos One," a voice answered. "You are ordered to stand down. You've been denied clearance to cross the DMZ."

Pete stared at the radio. *Denied?* But…he was ready to go, one hand on the cyclic, the other on the collective, both feet on the pedals. "Whiskey Tango Foxtrot?" he returned. *What The Fuck?*

"A nearby SEAL squad is on the way," Combat explained.

Pete glanced again at the map on the MPD. It was a four-mile hike to where Bat Three was trapped, and that was starting right at the border.

"Maintain your present position," Combat instructed. "The SEALs will bring Bat Three to your current coordinates for exfil."

But…that's going to take too long.

"Chaos One, do you copy?"

Yeah, yeah, you putz. "Roger that, Combat. Standing down. Out." Pete sat for a second, thrumming his fingers on the stick, then looked at Willie. "Is *anyone* on our ship more than an empty fucking uniform?"

Willie scrunched his face again. It was his *I-agree-with-you-man-but-what-can-we-do-about-it?* expression.

Pete switched the radio to Justice's frequency. "Bat Three," he said into his mic. "Exfil is a negative. I've been denied permission to fly into North Korean airspace." The words were like mashed-up rotten eggs in his mouth. "Hold your position. There's a SEAL squad inbound on your location."

"Roger that," Justice answered. "Standing by. Out."

Pete heard comms click off and stared out the front windshield. His rotor wash was whipping the treetops into a frenzy and kicking up dust and grass. The subsonic oscillation of the beating blades vibrated his jump seat, jarring his vision as he scanned the gauges. Everything still in the green. He flexed his toes in his boots. *Four miles...*

"Do you think they're taking on fire?" he asked.

Willie grunted. "If they're not now, they will be at some point."

Not a big glass-is-half-full kinda guy was Willie.

"Chaos One," Justice called in, "Bat Three Actual. How copy?"

"Go ahead, Bat Three."

"Update on that Team rescue?" Her voice was rough.

She sounded scared. He squeezed the comm trigger extra hard. "Stand by." He switched radio freaks to the *Bonhomme Richard.* "Combat Control, Chaos One. You got an ETA on those SEALs?"

"Negative, Chaos One. SEALs have gone dark during the op."

How very cooperative of them. Pete formed a pistol with his fingers and shot out the radio. "Copy that." He switched back to Justice. "Bat Three, that's a negative on info.

Comms are dark."

She didn't respond.

Only empty static answered him.

He maintained a steady scrutiny of the Master Caution Panel, staring and waiting, waiting and staring, as if any second Justice's voice would come out of the panel, tell him, *Oh, whew, the enemy decided to bug out, shuffle home to eat the Korean dumplings all their wives are cooking right now.*

Celebratory drinks would be on Pete at their first port call, his wallet falling wide open in *thank-God-you're-still-alive* relief.

Justice would go out with their group, as she sometimes had while they were stationed together in Pensacola, her smile genuine but distant.

And as always, he'd end up leaving with another woman, thinking, *What a waste.*

"I'm checking in with them again," Pete told Willie.

His copilot's face was no longer scrunchy. Just intense.

Pete keyed comms. "Bat Three, SITREP?"

No answer.

A hiss and a pop, but no words.

We're pinned down by a large force of hostiles.

Do you think they're taking on fire?

Pete's abdominal muscles cramped. "Bat Three—"

"Chaos One, overwhelming enemy forces are imminent on our position," Justice came back, her voice raw and low. "This is my final transmission."

The radio clicked once, then went silent.

No more sound at all.

No crackling. No hissing.

Only dead air.

Pete was reasonably sure his heart just threw up.

Willie turned to look at him. From his periphery, Pete saw his friend wet his lips. "The SEALs will get there in time, Bingo, don't worry. I mean…don't you think?"

Pete had to force his answer out. "No. I don't think." He stared straight ahead with pulsing vision, his spine full of ice.

I could go on thinking of you as Bingo the dog.

Why do I always feel like you're seducing me?

Do I need to give you my Don't Get the Wrong Idea speech?

This was such a blast! Do you have any idea what I just did?

You really helped me, Pete. You showed confidence in me.

The flood of memories hurt his chest. He and Justice had always got along so well—talking easily, enjoying the same reckless style of fun, and for sure they would've been awesome in the sack. One kiss from her on the *Bonhomme Richard* and he'd gone hard enough to pound rocks.

But when it came time to make a choice about her— *them*—he'd picked a non-heart-crunch option. Safety protocol of that kind, unfortunately, lacked total situation awareness. Because on the opposite side of crunch was big, sexy love.

And *big* rewards took *big* effort.

Women like Justice didn't come along every day. No one was going to just hand her to him. He had to work for her. Risks would have to be taken, yes, but why did that have to be a drag? Winning Justice could be fun. Hardbody Hayes would be no easy mark—he'd have to be at his best.

'Course he couldn't ply his magic on a woman who'd been overtaken by *overwhelming enemy forces.*

Pete glowered at the radio. *Combat Control limp dicks.*

With a forceful jerk of his wrist, he cranked the radio dial over to the *Richard's* frequency. "Combat Control, Chaos One. Situation with Bat Three is now critical. Need for exfil is immediate. Request change in mission parameters."

"Denied," Combat came back. "You're not authorized to cross the DMZ."

Pete set his jaw. Could you at least *pretend* to think about it for a second?

Poss-coon-eaver lumbered out of the woods and stopped to stare at the big, ruckus-making machinery, its face scrunched up like Willie's.

Something in the pit of Pete's stomach knotted—an inexplicable urge to rush out there, scoop up poss-coon-eaver, and bring the poor little guy back to the aircraft, tuck the creature in a life jacket or the raft bag, snuggled up safe 'n' sound from all things bad in the world.

Pete made a coarse noise in his throat. "You know what? Hellwithit." He keyed comms. "Coming in broken," he told Combat. "Understand mission is approved, and we're cleared to cross the DMZ. Roger and out." He turned off the radio.

Stand down, my ass.

Pete drew in two measured breaths. *Alrighty, then.*

He spoke through inner-cockpit comms. "Everyone in this aircraft knows exactly what I just did. Depart the bird now if you have a problem disobeying orders because I'm flying into North Korea to save our people. Anyone?"

No one.

No big surprise. Pete was pretty sure both Willie and Ketchup had written off their careers when they decided to fly combat SpecOps with the notorious Lieutenant Pete "Bingo" Robbins.

"Roger that. Call the altitude," Pete instructed Willie, "and watch for obstacles. We're flying in under the radar on this one." Electrical wires, trees, and mountainsides were not friends of a low-flying helo.

"Roger," Willie piped back, a lot of *tally ho!* in his tone, although Pete would lay ten bucks down on Willie's sphincter already having suctioned half his seat cushion into his inner bowel cavity.

"Ready for takeoff," Pete said, adding power. The *whop-whop-whop* of the idling blades whined into a fast-moving *whip-whip* as the helo lifted off the ground.

Pete slapped down his NVGs and thrust the stick forward, setting off at high speed into North Korean airspace.

CHAPTER FORTY-SIX

"NOTHING DOING ON a strafing run, boss," Ketchup assessed over inner-cockpit comms as soon as they arrived on scene. "Truckload a contacts."

Yeah…so…turned out *a large force of hostiles* actually meant *hundreds* of North Korean soldiers, too many damned "truckloads" to cut down to size with a machine gun.

It would take at least half a dozen flybys with Ketchup firing nonstop on the M-60 to make an appreciable dent in the enemy's numbers…and on every pass, they would run the risk of taking on catastrophic return fire.

Ketchup's exact point.

But landing in a canyon with the current truckload within firing range would be equally suicidal.

Pete could launch missiles at the enemy first, decrease their numbers that way. But once Hellfires were brought into the equation, so did a myriad different ways for friendlies to get snuffed accidentally.

And killing Justice, Morris, and Glinski would pretty much cancel out the whole *rescue* part of this rescue op.

So how did he pull out Bat Three safely?

Figure it out, Pete!

Yeah. He really needed to do that.

Getting his ass in a sling for disobeying a direct order all for nothing would go down in aviation history as a Class Alpha Stupidity.

Pete cranked the aircraft around, circling the canyon out

of range, keeping an eye on wind speed and…

Wind.

An idea sprouted. He gauged the velocity and direction of the wind and—*all right.*

He knew what to do.

"Ketchup, prepare a full complement of smokes. When I fly over the south ridge, drop those smokes like they're your granny's titties."

"Roger that," Ketchup confirmed.

Willie adjusted his NVGs. "What's dropping smokes on the ridge opposite to the enemy going to do for us?"

"The wind will push the smoke into the canyon, creating soupy coverage for us to land in." Pete checked the distance from the small woodland where three green heat signatures were hunkered down to a spot in the canyon where he could safely land. They would have a very small window to make this happen. Once he landed, the rotor wash would blow out the smoke, clearing the way for that potential catastrophic return fire he was trying to avoid.

He engaged external comms. "Bat Three, Chaos One. If you can read me, I'm dropping smoke canisters in approximately three mikes. As soon as you see the canyon basin fill with smoke, head east, and don't take your time about it."

"Roger that, Chaos One," Justice responded. "Read you loud and clear. Confirm last."

Pete grinned. So Justice wasn't dead. *Oorah.* That was good news. Exceptional news. "Commencing smoke run," Pete told his guys.

"Yo, Bingo!" Ketchup called. "Got a visual on some bad guys prepping a shoulder launched surface-to-air party-ender."

Shit. There went a regular landing. He wouldn't have time to circle back around, not if he wanted to avoid a blown-to-smithereens fate. "Roger that. Prepare to do a rotor-over to land."

"What?" Willie squeaked. "But you won't be able to see the ground." *And there are already enough blind moments during a rotor-over.*

That last part was implied.

Yeah, this was going to be…er, a mite challenging.

"Call the airspeed and altitude, Willie," Pete said in an even tone. "And quit talking like Mickey Mouse."

He raced down along the south ridge of the canyon.

"Last smoke away!" Ketchup reported.

"Roger that. Hang onto your nuts." Pete yanked back on the stick and dropped the collective, rapidly bleeding off power as he swung the bird nose-up, angling nearly ninety degrees into the sky—this was one of those heebie can't-see-nuttin' moments. A swath of glittering, NVG-emerald stars swept past his vision.

"Thirty knots," Willie called the air speed. "Twenty…"

Up, up, up…speed continued to reduce drastically. As the helo closed in on a hammerhead stall, Pete stomped on the right pedal and wrenched the stick hard right. With a shudder and a groan—neither of which were especially confidence-inspiring—the aircraft arced over to starboard and plunged toward the earth like a stone in a well. The pull of G-forces sucked Pete back in his seat.

"Sixty feet! Fifty feet!" Willie shouted. "Airspeed fifteen knots!"

Pete ran his focus over the gauges, checking Doppler radar for drift and angle. He was too far to the right. The ground was coming up fast. His heart tried to leap from his chest.

I need some freaking damned excitement!

It might've been better if he hadn't wished for that.

"Drifting right!" Willie barked.

Yeah, got it, Nate.

A loud *snat!* sounded from the north ridge, and inside the cockpit the missile lock-on alarm shrieked.

Eeeeeeeeee....

"Incoming!" Willie bawled.

"Release chaff and flare," Pete ordered.

Willie pushed a button, and light exploded from the side of the bird. Chaff would misdirect the missile.

The flare burst apart in a showy display of lights and fire just as Pete scooped into the soup of smoke. The pyrotechnics would buy them some time—the enemy would think they'd hit the helo and hold off on firing again.

But not for long.

"Ground contact!" Ketchup was hanging out the side door, checking for tree stumps and rocks. "Visual reference."

The smoke whooshed apart, revealing the sandy earth. "Bat Three," Pete clipped through external comms. "Prepare for running landing." He flared the helo and landed in a skid...and kept skidding.

If Justice, Glinski, and Morris were Johnny on the Spot with their running landing—and they sure as hell should be after practicing so many back when their team was avoiding fast-roping the first time on the *Richard*—then they'd be hopping onto the aircraft any second now, like hobos onto a freight train.

"Three souls, safe on board," Ketchup relayed.

"Roger that." Grinning, Pete took off, keeping low in the smoke for cover. "Navigating west along the river."

"Trees! Trees!" Willie yelled. "Pull up!"

Pete flew out of the smoky fog, adding power. The engines roared as he climbed to a safe altitude and finally leveled off. No one spoke for a moment, then—

"Holy freakout, Bingo." Willie mouth-breathed into the mic. "I think I just pooped myself. Wait. Did I say poop? I'm so scared, I've regressed!"

Pete laughed. "No Wet Willies allowed in the copilot's seat, man." He glanced over his shoulder at the cabin. Justice and her guys were strapped in, and wasn't that the coolest sight ever? He scanned the gauges. Nothing was reading as over-torqued or over-heated. The aircraft hummed along nicely.

They were in the clear.

Or…not quite.

"Chaos One," a brand-new man grated into Pete's earpiece. "This is the air boss of the USS *Theodore Roosevelt*."

Oh shit, an air boss…and that explained the menacing voice.

Pete had never met an air boss who wasn't scary as fuck, something about the massive stress and responsibility of being in charge of all flight operations around a carrier contributed to molding the man's features into boiled glue and his voice into something resembling cement being ripped apart by a pickaxe.

The air boss went on. "You are ordered to divert immediately from your present course toward the *Bonhomme Richard* and make directly for the carrier."

Bummer. Being redirected to the on-station carrier meant Pete was getting his ass in the aforementioned sling.

He'd soon be standing tall in front of the big guy himself, Commander, Carrier Strike Group Seven, Admiral Dirk Rosen, and eating a Big Snot Sandwich as he tried to defend his actions.

And probably couldn't.

Rosen would schedule Pete for an immediate FNAEB.

It wouldn't be the first time Pete had been forced to defend his wings in front of a Field Naval Aviator Evaluation Board, but this time *flagrant disregard of a direct order* would be the charge.

His goose was pretty much cooked.

He sighed another private *bummer*. He really did love flying for the Navy.

"Roger that, *Roosevelt*," Pete said, keying comms. "Checking off station with the *Richard*." He switched over to his ship's freak. "Combat Control, Chaos One. Changing course. We've been ordered to the USS *Theodore Roosevelt* by—"

"Negative, Chaos One," a voice cut in. "Belay that order."

Pete snapped his finger off the comm trigger and raised his brows. That voice wasn't whichever Ensign Wienie was on duty in Combat Control right now. It was Captain Eagen, Naval Special Warfare Group One Commander.

The captain had deployed with Bat Three on their inaugural cruise—since Special Missions was a new SOF concept, he wanted to be nearby to oversee potential problems.

Like…?

Flagrant ordinis disobeyance?

Yeah, like that.

"Inform the carrier that you have a left engine fire warning light," Eagen instructed, "and you've been instructed to conduct an emergency landing on the *Richard*. On *my* orders."

Ho, neat. Pete was about to get himself in the middle of a pissing match between an air boss and the head of SPECWAR. "Yes, sir."

But the carrier released Pete without argument, allowing him to go home to his own ship.

He landed and shut down, then expelled a long breath. His fingers were stiff. He might have been gripping the stick a tad bit harder than usual.

It's not just a job, it's an adventure!

Great motto!

Everyone should live by it, up to and including Admiral Rosen and Captain Eagen. Yes, it would be very nice for Pete if those two men could embrace that standpoint especially closely right now and, you know, motivate themselves into a forgiving mood.

Pete tugged his flight helmet off, then hopped out of the aircraft, and—

"Oh my God, Pete!" Justice was standing right in front of him.

Her bun was an exhausted fallen soufflé, but her face was all smiles.

"Totally amazing flying," she complimented him. "Thank you so much for coming to get us." Her torso leaned slightly forward, like she was on the verge of giving him a big hug. But then she caught herself.

Too many flight crewmen were around. And, *oops*, remember, she wasn't supposed to be into him, right? She'd shut him out of her life.

Yeah, well. Not anymore.

Not after tonight.

He hated to be a cliché and do a complete attitude turn-around in response to a near-death experience. But Justice had, in fact, almost died. And since he'd already been dealing with her rejection in the uber-cliché way of sleeping with a lot of nameless, faceless women, why not continue along?

So, yeah, he was Going Big, saying *hellwithit* to the potential heart-crunch and officially putting himself back in her life.

Commencing Operation Get Justice.

Step one: he stuck out his hand, offering her a handshake.

Not a tongue kiss.

Not a little much-needed decompression, reconfirm-life

calisthenics in his stateroom.

No. Hardbody Hayes had a fully operational bullshit meter. Finesse was everything.

"You're welcome," he said.

She shook his hand, and although she didn't drop her panties for him on the spot—following his expectations of her to the letter—she did spend more time than was required shaking his hand.

And staring at his mouth.

The ship's master-at-arms, Gunnery Sergeant Walck, materialized, wearing his usual jungle utilities, but instead of a billed cap, he had on ear protectors.

He saluted Pete. "Lieutenant Robbins!" He shouted to be heard over the noise on the flight deck. "You and your crew are ordered to report to Captain Eagen's stateroom immediately."

Walck didn't particularly like Pete, but if the gunny felt any glee over Pete's upcoming trip behind the woodshed, he didn't show it. He didn't show much of anything, though. His expression never changed from frying-pan flat. Break a pickle jar across the man's nose, or order up a little tootsie to give him a hand job under a table—same expression would meet both acts.

Their group jogged across the flight deck, and once they were inside, where shout-free conversation was possible, Justice pulled up next to Pete in the corridor.

"What's going on?" she asked.

"Time to kiss the don's ring," he answered. "Try to convince Eagen not to put one behind my ear."

Justice frowned. "What does that mean?"

"I wasn't given clearance to cross the DMZ to come get you."

Her eyes did a double-blink. "Oh, crap."

Yep.

They turned toward Officers Country, and their six-member crew arrived at Captain Eagen's stateroom. Even though Pete was the only one whose ass was in the hotseat—in fact, he'd make sure of it—they all waited at attention outside the captain's door.

Gunny went inside to inform Eagen of the insubordinates' arrival.

The SPECWAR commander appeared in the doorway, his brows set in a stern bar over his nose. "Lieutenant Robbins and Lieutenant Wojno inside. The rest of you are dismissed."

Willie blanched.

Justice gave the two of them a forehead-wrinkly expression, then left with Glinski, Morris, and Ketchup.

Pete and Willie marched inside. "Mouth shut," Pete snarled softly into his buddy's ear.

They came to attention in front of the captain's desk.

Eagen's stateroom was wood-paneled and nautical-themed, with an old-timey schooner's steering wheel tacked onto one wall and a picture of a compass hanging on another. Behind the desk was a bookcase stuffed with novels of the sea and one brass sextant. Everything in the room—besides the sextant—was wood.

The room was like the Toontown version of a ship's interior—if the *Bonhomme Richard* should sink, this stateroom in its entirety would bob to the surface, probably Eagen still sitting at his desk, bent over paperwork. Pete was betting the captain hadn't made any of the decorative decisions. He gave Eagen credit for being more interesting.

Eagen took a seat at his desk and leaned back in the chair. Wood cracked under the strain of his muscular weight. "Tell me why I shouldn't have both your wings on my desk right now?"

Gulp. People in China probably heard Willie swallow

just now.

"Sir," Pete answered. "I, and I alone, am responsible. Lieutenant Wojno tried to depart the aircraft prior to the op, but I couldn't fly the mission without a copilot, so I ordered him to remain onboard. *He* actually follows orders."

Not a big appreciator of irony was Captain Eagen.

His steely gaze chilled. "And you?"

"Permission to speak frankly, sir?"

"I think you'd better, Robbins."

Pete looked Eagen directly in the eyes. "Sir, Special Operations Forces hired me to do *exactly* the kind of balls-out flying I did tonight. A major SOF asset would be dead right now if I hadn't made the judgment call I did."

A muscle in Eagen's jaw went rigid. "You made a judgment call based on knowledge of your limited view of the op, Lieutenant. Your superiors have the big picture in front of them when they issue orders. Do you think it's too much to ask for you to *follow* those without us having to explain ourselves first?"

So, okay, sarcasm was definitely in Eagen's repertoire.

"Your wings are the least of your worries." Eagen stood. "Disobeying a direct order is an actionable offense under the UCMJ." The captain crossed to his door and opened it on Walck. "Gunnery Sergeant, take Lieutenant Robbins into custody and escort him to the brig."

Willie exhaled a big, spluttery breath.

Shit. Pete squeezed his eyes shut briefly. *Fuck and shit.*

Walck strode toward Pete with a firm sense of purpose, and as the gunnery sergeant seized Pete by the arm, the only thing he could think was, *Are we going to make a pit stop on the way to my jail cell?*

Because suddenly he had to take a leak really bad.

CHAPTER FORTY-SEVEN

One week later, early July
USS *Bonhomme Richard*
Sea of Japan

THAT SHAVING NICK on Mr. Garcia's chin? *Total spook trick*. Made Garcia look like a regular guy. Any Old Joe from Plain Town Everywhere. Mr. Don't Mind Me, I'm Only Here for the Doughnuts.

Smiling to himself, Pete reclined in his chair where he was seated in his regular spot at the wardroom table to the left of Commander Cardoso, Justice across from him.

At the other end of the table, the head chair was empty of Captain Eagen. The SPECWAR commander was instead on his feet, standing next to the ship's esteemed guest.

Mr. Garcia.

No first name given.

Slick James Bond type for a spy? Nope. That was total Hollywood hype. Actual spies were all about blending.

Like this dude from the CIA.

Garcia comma nothing.

Pete would go one step further and say being a good spook was also about *charm*. About being a *go-ahead-and-talk-to-me-about-anything-because-I'll-make-you-feel-so-great-about-sharing* kind of guy.

Pete could be a spy. *Definitely*. How many times had he teased an exhaustive amount of information from a woman on his way to getting laid? Every woman had a line she drew in the sand. Some women needed to say a lot about herself to feel close to a guy, others a little—the ones who informed Pete they weren't wearing any panties were usually the quickest sells. But once that certain amount was reached, the line was crossed and—*Ding!*

Intimacy was formed.

Sex was a foregone conclusion then. Intimacy was all a woman needed to fuck. It was *easy* from that point, although he never made her feel easy for it. In the sack, he gave her all the closeness she craved. Total attention. Complete ga-ga-eyed adoration. He was not a selfish prick. He figured she deserved everything he had to offer for all the great gifts she was giving.

It was the afterward part where he fell off.

He didn't really have the call-back thing going on. The intimacy had only been perceived, after all, and follow-on boredom was another foregone conclusion.

Or maybe…maybe the sensation was an overall lack of fulfillment. His dick had fun, yeah, no complaints there, but all the other parts of him were left suffering from a massive case of blue balls.

"The Russians have developed a new missile," Mr. Garcia told the wardroom, bumping Pete out of his thoughts. "All Russian cruise missiles, as you all know, fly under the radar and follow the nap of the earth on their way to a target."

Missiles like these were called—*put the drums away; no drum roll, please*—nap-of-the-earth missiles. Totally dull title. Wholly uninspiring. Why not be honest and call them Shit-Your-Pantsers Missiles or Here-We-Go-Man-Hold-Onto-Your-Sac Missiles? Because that's what a guy would have do when a nap-of-the-earth missile entered American airspace undetected by radar.

Hard part for the bad guys was *launching* the suckers

unnoticed. The U.S. of A. kept a vigilant lookout for enemy ships and subs floating within a fifteen-hundred-mile firing range.

"The Russians have invented a technologically enhanced propulsion system," Garcia went on with his doom and gloom, "which has made possible a long-range nap-of-the-earth missile." He selected a doughnut from the sideboard.

Pete smirked. Mr. Don't Mind Me, doing his shtick.

"Theoretically, one could be fired right from downtown Moscow."

Well, now. That *was* a skid mark-maker, for sure.

Garcia moved back to the end of the table and set his doughnut on a napkin. "None of these missiles have been built yet, but construction will begin shortly. Our in-country assets report that the Minister of Defense is cutting the ribbon on a new factory early next week. Before that happens, we want those missile plans out of Russian hands and into American possession." Garcia nodded toward Pete and Justice's end of the table. "The agency is asking for Bat Three's assistance in stealing the documents."

The word *stealing* brought Justice forward, her elbows on the table, her bun electrifying with little spikey hairs.

Pete swallowed a smile. She was such a kick.

"Ask?" Justice clarified.

Right. Military personnel *take orders*, Mr. Charlie India Alpha. Didn't you know that?

"Your team may feel free to refuse our request," Garcia offered. "This operation sits outside the normal purview of a Special Missions assignment."

Purview. No. Not a good word choice. I'm-Only-The-Wallpaper-So-Don't-Worry-About-It-Guy wouldn't use a word like that.

Captain Eagen explained further. "This op won't be conducted in the usual covert manner."

Pete smoothed a finger over his lips. *Uh-huh.* Now, see, Garcia wasn't eating his doughnut, more proof that he'd grabbed it just because that's what normal people did.

"For this mission," Garcia stepped back in, "the CIA will need Lieutenant Robbins to play the role of an American State Department employee in order to infiltrate the Russian diplomatic scene. Lieutenant Hayes will act as his wife."

What's this? Pete brought his chin up. *Wife?* He smiled his ass off over that—on the inside—savoring the possibilities. Set a palm at the small of Justice's back, brush his lips over her ear as he whispered a little nothing nonsense to her, hold her hand... So many subtle, nonsexual touches were at a "husband's" disposal, things a spouse could do to his wife in public—*should* do—that a regular smorgasbord bonanza of opportunities to forward *Operation Get Justice* would be laid out before him.

Pete lounged deeper into his chair. *Oorah.* This op was shaping up to be awesome.

Justice asked, "Why aren't you using regular agents for this op, or your in-country assets?"

"The missile plans are stored on a red-and-yellow striped flash drive locked inside the Russian Minister of Defense's office," Garcia explained. "The minister's inner sanctum can only be accessed by way of a state-of-the-art security system—our intel is solid on that. From there, unfortunately, we have no idea how the flash drive is kept secure. Under such circumstances, we feel *you* are the only person capable of breaking into anything."

Justice's lips slanted. "I appreciate the vote of confidence, sir, but even I can't guarantee success going into a job cold. Unless," she added wryly, "I can bring an entire bin's worth of equipment with me."

Garcia spread his hands. *Well, you can't.* "We don't

believe our confidence is unfounded, Lieutenant Hayes."
His eyes crinkled in fatherly approval. "The CIA wanted you
for exactly missions like these."

Pete did a double-take of the spook. *Wait.* Who wanted
which for what?

Justice exhaled a short breath. "So how state-of-the-art
are we talking for outer security? More than fingerprint or
retinal recognition, I'm assuming."

Garcia nodded. "Access into the minister's office spaces
is through DNA."

"Blood?" Justice verified. "Via a finger pinprick?"

"Saliva," Garcia corrected. "The Minister of Defense
uses something similar to a Q-tip to swab his inner cheek,
then inserts that into an inlet on the panel outside his office
door."

"Inventive," Justice approved.

"Yes, but unfortunately we can't mimic the activation.
We'll need the minister's actual saliva." From his back
pocket, Garcia pulled out a small pack of what looked like
rolling papers. "This is special absorbent paper that can be
used to gather saliva remnants."

Justice glanced once at the pack. "We can't just nab a
glass the minister drinks from?"

"No." Garcia shook his head. "That won't provide
enough DNA for our scientists to model a substitute cotton
swab. We also can't just swipe one of these papers along the
rim of a glass or bottle the minister drinks from. The paper
only works on porous surfaces. The best way to gather the
necessary saliva will be for a woman to kiss the minster, then
kiss the paper immediately afterward." Garcia set the pack
next to his doughnut—his *untouched* doughnut—and
tapped it with a forefinger.

Justice turned her gaze to the ceiling, clearly not a fan of
the plan.

Because it was obvious which woman would have to do the kissing.

Pete barely caught back a *hah-ha!* although the warmth in his eyes was probably giving away how much he was still smiling his ass off on the inside. It couldn't be helped. Watching Justice wrangle a kiss out of a stodgy Russian diplomat was going to be legendary.

He laced his fingers behind his head and stretched luxuriously. "And I take it my job is just to sit back and enjoy the show?"

Captain Eagen cut a sharp glance at Pete.

Pete unlatched his hands long enough to gesture at Justice. "Lieutenant Hayes is going to get a kiss out of this minister guy in under five minutes." In fact, Pete should start a pool on it. *Stay tuned.* "And after that, she's the one on tap to do all the breaking and entering. Nothing much more for me to do other than watch her six." *And you, Cap'n Eagen, had better give me massive points toward earning my flight status back for such a snorrendous assignment.*

Pete had been bored out of his gourd ever since Eagan grounded him a week ago, right after Pete spent a night in the brig—only one night, probably just so Eagen could make a point.

A no-fly status meant Pete was back to having *nothing to do.*

"Actually," Garcia interceded, "due to a certain reputation the minister has, we wouldn't be able to assure Lieutenant Hayes's safety with him. It turns out the Minister of Defense—although married for twenty-one years to a rich and politically connected socialite—is a rather…aggressive womanizer." The agent turned on Pete. "That's where you come in."

Pete blinked. *Me?*

"The CIA is aware of your own proclivities in this regard, Lieutenant Robbins."

Justice's expression went flat.

Pete dropped his arms.

Garcia gave Pete an unreadable look, a look probably taught at spy school, then practiced in the mirror for hours and hours, until it was the perfect amount of vanilla pudding. "Your part of the mission would be to inveigle your way into being the minister's philandering companion."

Proclivities… Inveigle… Philandering… The agent's word choices were really going down the shitter, and—w*a*it. Pete squinted. "You want me to…?" He stopped talking; he couldn't say it.

The CIA wanted him to go out on the prowl with the Russian Minister of Defense and pick up chicks with him. And what did a "philanderer" do when he picked up a nameless, faceless woman?

He fucked her.

But I don't wanna.

Pete almost said it aloud.

Because he didn't want to.

Call him silly, but wouldn't banging another woman— even to save New York from being flattened someday—put a serious crimp in his mission to *Get Justice*?

Over the last week he'd come so far with her, knocking down her defenses and drawing her out of her shell, getting her talking again and making her laugh, reminding her of what a great time they always had when they were together.

Pete sat back. "Huh."

So this was how female agents felt when they had to sacrifice their bodies for God and country.

Pretty damned rotten.

CHAPTER FORTY-EIGHT

July 4th
Moscow, Russia
Marriott Hotel

PETE MCNAMARA.

Really?

The CIA couldn't come up with a better alter ego for him than McNamara, capital "m" capital "n," Pete, owner of the fruit stand with the juiciest peaches?

See? Fruit Stand Owner. Not Suave Man About Town, licensed to carry and kill. The spooks should've gone for something like *Pete Buckstone*.

Or even better—*Pete Striker*.

How about just plain *Spike*?

Maybe *Thunderballs*.

Pete chuckled as he adjusted his tie in the hotel mirror. His name might not be anything special, but he sure as hell was. Thanks to the CIA's makeover team, he was shaved and styled, daubed with expensive cologne, and swathed in a perfectly tailored dark gray suit.

Daub and *swathe* weren't his words, by the way.

If you would stand still for a moment, sir, we will daub you with this herpy-derpy and swathe you in that dillyfuck… Yeah, a lot of *whatever* spoken by the head makeover artist.

Pete was too busy formulating strategies to really listen to the guy: Plan A, Plan B, and always a backup Plan C about how to charm his way into being the minister's new best pal at the Fourth of July party today.

Embrace the challenge!

That was now his going-in attitude.

Because it turned out—to his total relief—he wouldn't have to *really* sleep with a nameless, faceless woman.

The CIA had constructed a fake dance club for this mission, *The Diamond Czarina*, and populated it with their own people. Namely, any number of sexy female operatives on hand to seduce the minister and obtain his saliva.

If Pete needed to bag a babe while at *The Diamond Czarina* to maintain his cover, he could simply disappear with an undercover agent and have fake sex with her. Although problems might arise if the minister was into doing a group thing in the same room. Pantomiming the act would be tricky, not to mention a huge ouch to the balls. All the more reason to have a backup Plan C.

Maybe he needed a Plan D too.

Crossing to the hotel mini fridge, Pete grabbed a bottle of water, then checked the time. *All good.* Justice was still being worked on by the makeover staff in the adjoining room, but she and Pete weren't due at the Fourth of July party for another hour. This was the one time of year when all manner of Russian diplomats were invited inside Spaso House, the United States ambassador's luxurious mansion.

Mr. and Mrs. Minister of Defense, Viktor and Alyona Sokolov, would be in attendance.

So would Pete and Jennifer McNamara.

Best to stick with actual first names, according to Mr. Garcia, when agents were on a short-term op, and so lacking the years put into establishing an identity. So Pete was Pete and Justice was Jennifer because Justice couldn't go by Justice—the strangeness of that name would invite too many questions—but every time Pete had tried to call her Justine—with an "n"—he flubbed it and called her Justice.

Excuse the fuck out of me, but the two names were really damned similar.

No worries about the rest of their backgrounds, though. He had that info down solid. He'd diligently studied their dossiers over the course of the last day and a half of travel, a journey that'd started via skiff boat from the *Bonhomme Richard* to a sea port in Vladivostok—a small Russian town butting up against the northernmost part of North Korea. From there, they took a taxi to Vladivostok International Airport and hopped on an eight-hour flight to Moscow.

During the plane ride, Pete read all about himself, learning that Pete McNamara was being groomed for the position of head of the Political Military office, or POLMIL, in Latvia. So he was relatively small potatoes—Latvia being a small country—but who was on his way to being a big potato—because *head*. It was a perfect mix of nobody and somebody. Nobody enough that Russia's Foreign Intelligence Service, SVR—formally the KGB—wouldn't dig too deeply into his identity, but important enough for it to make sense that he would travel to Moscow to hobnob at this Fourth of July bash.

His wife, Justice/Jennifer, was a former college track star who spent all her time in the gym—*some* explanation had to be given for her body.

But herein lay a possible mission glitch. One glance at such a stunning example of womanhood, and who would believe McNamara was a cheating louse? Wouldn't Pete be too bushed from partaking nightly of *that* to off-road?

But Pete's suggestion to give Justice a wee bit of a mustache fell on the makeover team's deaf ears.

Justice needed to stay hot-looking in case Pete failed to engage Sokolov. Then she'd be on tap to obtain the man's saliva.

No longer an amusing thought.

Now that Pete had read up on the minister, he knew just how much of a womanizer the man really was. Sokolov acted discreetly for the sake of his politically advantageous marriage, but that didn't stop him from racking 'em up. In fact, compared to Sokolov's bedpost notches, Pete might as well have spent his dating years hanging out with Julie Andrews at a convent singing *Do-Re-Mi*.

The Russian wasn't exactly off the charts in the attractive department, either. From the photo on file, Sokolov was in his early forties, tall and lean—though not skinny—with dark brown eyes and black hair. He wore a goatee, the mustache part twirled at the ends in a Mr. Monopoly look. Not a stodgy, musty, dusty thing, no, but not a ten, either.

So how did a guy like that manage to fuck so many women? The *aggressive* part Mr. Garcia had mentioned, that's how. Sokolov wasn't opposed to forcing himself on the reticent types.

Due to a certain reputation the minister has, we wouldn't be able to assure Lieutenant Hayes's safety with him...

Less and less amused by this guy was Pete.

Rape-y men were nothing but weak little dicks.

Pete could spot a true weenie a mile away—he hung out with Naval aviators and had long ago learned how to tell genuine confidence from the showboat dick-swingers.

Sokolov was a showoff.

The minister's dossier was littered with all the ways he constantly tried to prove his manhood. He'd tackled just about every high-risk activity on the planet: whitewater rafting, sheer granite rappelling, hang gliding, bungee jumping, cliff and sky diving, high-speed alpine skiing, waterfall kayaking, ice climbing, wingsuit flying.

Some might say the minister was an adrenaline junkie, but throw in the rape-y tendencies, and you got a man who was obsessively and diabolically competitive. But guys who tried to prove their manhood all the time were really fakes.

And every time Sokolov saw himself in a mirror, he knew that deep down he was an insecure little mole-rat.

And thus we have arrived!

Here was the key component to Plan A of Pete's "inveigling" scheme.

What did an insecure little mole-rat do when he came face-to-face with a man who *did* have an actual set? He got obsessively and diabolically competitive, that's what.

So despite the CIA thinking Pete's primary tactic was to become Sokolov's philandering companion, there was no way a Russian diplomat—who wanted to hide his whore-monger reputation from his wife—would go out on the prowl with an unknown, potentially untrustworthy American just to get laid.

Pete would have to turn a night on the town into a competition. Which one of them could bag the most women? Seduce 'em the fastest? That type of thing. Which meant that with every word and gesture today at the Fourth of July party, Pete was going to have to relay the message *I'm-better-than-you.*

Good thing the makeover team had made him look like the shit.

Pete checked himself in the hotel mirror again and flashed his best wall-banger smile—so named because women tended to walk into walls when they saw it—making sure it was fully operational.

He would need it working at optimum devastation mode when he reeled in women this afternoon.

A ladies man like Viktor Sokolov wouldn't give an amateur a second glance.

A knock sounded.

Pete opened his hotel room door, and Tiffany Tesarik and Willie entered—the op's extra eyes and ears.

Tesarik was Justice's shipboard roommate, a young Marine Corps officer built by her maker into the image of Tinkerbell. Pert personality, perky body, animated eyes, freckled nose, coppery red hair cut in a short, offhand style—most days she ran just shy of ridiculously cute, despite the jungle utilities she wore, which were a frank joke on Tinkerbell.

Today, she'd gone heavier on the makeup and was wearing an emerald cocktail dress, short-sleeved, but high-necked, sort of a tie-dye flowery pattern on top, but plain green from the waist to the knees. Today, she looked straight-up beautiful.

Willie—pretending to be a State Department account-ant, also out of the Latvian office—was also looking mighty fine in a navy blue pinstripe.

Tiffany's eyes were practically spinning in her head over that. She'd been working on a scorching crush for Willie ever since Bat Three checked onboard the *Richard*.

Willie pretended not to notice. Willie owned a fully-functioning hetero heat-seeker, so he did notice. What Willie *was* could be summed up as this: petrified of pretty, lively, sweet, smart Tinkerbell. He'd never dated all those qualities in one woman before.

Tesarik wasn't handling the rejection well. This led to the unfortunate habit of her dragging Pete into private huddles to lament her unrequited love and ask for advice. Dealing with two people being idiots about each other wasn't Pete's idea of a wild kegger. In fact, it could be counted as the definition of a wild kegger's antithesis.

"Hey," Willie said. "Where's Justice?"

The adjoining door *squeaked* open behind Pete.

"Is she—" Willie stopped talking and focused wide-eyed on a spot over Pete's shoulder. His mouth crashed open. A piece of bubble gum rolled off his tongue.

"Oh!" Tiffany gasped. "You're so pretty!"

Pete turned around to—

Holy Cow.

My God.

And FUCK.

He stood frozen. Riveted to the spot, the sides of his vision sparking out as blood sped too quickly from his head to the center of his body.

For a moment he thought he might have to pull a Fred Sanford and clutch his chest, stagger around a bit. *Ow, my heart. This is the big one! I'm coming, Elizabeth!*

For Christ's sake, this wasn't fair. It just wasn't damned fair.

His first time seeing Justice look sexy on a level he hadn't even known was possible and he was without his smorgasbord bonanza—it'd been blown all to shit by him having to be a cheating louse. No light touching, no whispered nonsense. He had to show his wife nothing but attentive disinterest—if that wasn't an oxymoron for the ages.

If Pete acted like a doting husband, Viktor wouldn't give him the time of day.

How the *hell* was he supposed to act apathetic toward Justice when she was in a *dress*. Not just any old dress, but a slinky, silky, clingy cocktail sheath number in mossy green with a scooped, rhinestone-edged neckline sweeping low enough to show the deep valley between her breasts. The moss color brought out the green in her eyes, though so did her makeup, perfectly applied by the CIA team. Her features were now seductively feline. Half her hair was pinned on top of her head while the other half flowed around her shoulders in silky curls.

Curls and cleavage. He would've lost money on this bet: could Hardbody Hayes look *this* amazingly feminine?

She started to walk toward him.

The water bottle in his hand let out an *oomphy* wheeze. He was crushing it in his fist.

The dress hit her mid-thigh, making her skyscraper legs appear even longer and more shapely, her high-heeled sandals showcasing the muscles in her calves.

He was a leg man, and watching those sleek, perfectly developed muscles perform with such beautiful and well-defined proficiency washed heat through him from scalp to toes. The majority of it landed in his crotch—and good thing his suit jacket was buttoned shut.

She came to a stop in front of him. The makeover team had daubed her with a scent too, something fresh and female. Or maybe the female part was her.

"You okay?" she asked.

"I think I just swallowed my fillings," he said, his voice rough and raspy. "Can I get lead poisoning from that?"

Her eyes sparkled with amusement. She smiled. "Let's go kick the shit out of this mission."

CHAPTER FORTY-NINE

JUSTICE TOOK A sip of champagne and savagely chewed the bubbles.

A crowd of primped diplomats mingled and kvetched around her, the subtle play of light from the chandelier dancing off the beadwork and rhinestones on women's dresses and splintering in brilliant rays along cut crystal glasses.

Spaso House's Chandelier Room was a picture of decadence, lavishly decorated in blue-and-cream floor tiles with gilt-framed paintings and baroque wall sconces. The entire room was bordered by shiny white pillars and lorded over by its namesake lighting apparatus, made of glittering crystal in both clear and gold.

Waiters liveried in black and white drifted through the crowd with near invisibility, carrying silver trays with champagne, vodka as smooth as water, and appetizers of every sort.

A musical quartet added jazz to the ambience, while the wife of the Russian Minister of Defense, Alyona Sokolov, droned in Justice's ear about fashion and interior design. The woman might as well have been talking about the merits of prosecutorial overhaul and prison reform for thieves for all the interest those topics held for Justice.

Introductions had been made between the McNamaras and the Sokolovs by the current American head of POLMIL in Moscow.

Justice immediately huddled up with the minister's wife to talk about interior design, doing her part to keep Alyona's focus off the direction her husband's attention was wandering, so it could, in fact, wander toward Pete's shenanigans.

Pete and Viktor had chatted about this and that...until a thirtyish blonde with sparkly eye shadow and wearing a form-hugging gown strolled by.

Pete watched her pass with smoldering eyes, then said, "Excuse me," to the minister and sauntered after her. The second before he said hello to the blonde, he cut a sly smile at Viktor, a sort of buddy-buddy look of *watch how easily I snare her, dude.*

Ten seconds later the woman had her hand on Pete's forearm and her head tossed back with a laugh so huge it bounced her breasts.

Fucking man-slut.

Justice gripped her champagne glass in a rigid fist. *Just ignore him.*

If only.

This past year she'd managed a certain immunity to Pete Robbins solely because of their physical distance. At crypto school she'd seen Pete only on the odd weekend to train, and post-crypto school—when Bat Three began working up to deploy—she saw him more often. At the end of every day, she'd still been able to say goodbye and escape his tempting flash and infectious vibrancy.

But now that the *Richard* was home to the Bat Three team for the next six months, there was no escaping him, especially lately—it seemed like wherever she went on the ship, Pete appeared at the same location soon afterward, a ball of unspent energy, moving, talking, and making her laugh.

His mood was perpetually good, even when it shouldn't

have been. For a man like Pete, who loved to be in the thick of everything, being off flight status should've put some serious grump in his state of mind.

It hadn't.

He'd received a Nonpunitive Letter of Caution as punishment and accepted the slap on the wrist in stride—*Hey, at least I didn't lose my wings!*—sauntering around the ship in his usual sexy, gunslinger way.

Impossible to ignore.

Under the onslaught of his endless, boisterous energy and his *take-life-serious-and-life-gets-serious* attitude, Justice had steadily been shedding her shell and coming back to life. His attention made her feel good. Special, even.

And now here she was, standing under a sparkling chandelier and feeling like a complete ninny.

No woman was special to Pete the Penis.

Every female he encountered wore a target, and seeing him work the room like a pro was flinging Justice right back to Pensacola…back to those nights when she'd gone out for drinks with the gang and had to watch Pete seduce a parade of Hostess snack cakes—Twinkies and Ding Dongs and definitely Ho Hos.

While he royally ignored her.

"Zee lamp vas made from zee shell of a tortoise, if you can believe…"

How to playact interest when one's eyeballs are boiling in their sockets?

Justice glared at Pete's ass.

Swaggeringly sexy in a flight suit, drop-dead gorgeous in black jeans and a button-down shirt, casually hump-able in nylon basketball shorts and a Stone Temple Pilots T-shirt, Pete was—in his suave suit-and-tie guise—currently hot enough to melt the stitches right out of his clothing.

In fact, how was he not standing in the middle of the

room naked?

Or maybe he was—to her.

Jesus Christ. What was her fucking problem? What kind of woman was she, lusting after a man who was such a skankface mcwhorebag?

"Zee wainscoting vas zee most divine…"

The side of Justice's brain closest to Alyona went numb. The other side started to busily invent all manner of especially cruel methods of torture to use on Pete, anything that would have him drinking his dinner through a straw by the end of the night.

Justice clenched her teeth around another sip of champagne. Pete was on the move again, adeptly making himself the center of attention among a group of women in the far corner of the room. Using his smile like a weapon, he bowled them all down—one, three, a dozen, more! He collected two marriage proposals, four offers to bear his children, and innumerable proposals of a more spurious nature.

Okay, so maybe Justice couldn't tell exactly what the women were saying—stuck as she was listening to Alyona drone—but if she was even remotely good at reading expressions, then her guesses were spot-on.

The arteries in Justice's brain dilated, putting enormous pressure on her skull.

Viktor Sokolov was starting to look bristly.

Right. The mission. Pete's trying to nab Sokolov's interest…focus on that…get a grip on yourself.

An hour later, the party finally broke up, and Justice was still without a grip.

Her eyeballs were cooked, her jaw needed a week in traction to loosen, and at some point during a rambling description of the merits of minimalism versus mid-century modern, she'd bitten her tongue.

Pete shook Sokolov's hand goodbye, the tendons in both men's hands flexing up as they gripped each other's palms extra-hard.

Pete politely gestured Justice out the door. "Let's walk," he murmured.

The walk from Spaso House to the Moscow Marriott would take about twenty minutes, and she was in heels, but they couldn't talk privately in front of an unknown Russian cabbie.

Their hotel room was safe. The CIA had given them a "bug-buster"—a machine that created static on listening devices and snow on cameras—but until they made it to their room, it was better to stay outside if they wanted to talk.

They strolled at a measured pace as dusk fell over the city. The air stank of ozone and was sticky on Justice's bare shoulders, although after Korea's eighty percent humidity, Moscow's sixty was almost like a breath of spring. Mercedes and Rolls and BMWs and other gaudy, flashy cars cruised by on the street.

"Good news," Pete said. "I convinced Sokolov to give us a tour of the Ministry of Defense building tomorrow. If I finagle my way into his office, I can recon his inner security for you."

She stopped. "You think you can *finagle* your way into a place guarded by a DNA-activated system?"

Pete's mouth slowly curved.

Her face flushed. "Ah, yeah. Of course you can. Stupid me. You can connive your way in anywhere." *Oh, to have a glass of champagne right now.* She would dump it on Pete's arrogant head.

One of Pete's brows jumped up. "Something wrong?"

"Just getting a little sick of the show, is all."

"The show?"

"Your manipulative charm."

Pete scratched the side of his jaw. "Wasn't I *supposed* to be charming and manipulative today?"

"You didn't have to be so damned good at it." Justice gripped her clutch purse to her side. Because that's what you did with a clutch purse. *Clutched* it. "You always know the exact right thing to say, don't you? To bend the human psyche to your will. To change any creature that doesn't reproduce through asexual means into a hunk-drunk drooling loon."

Even *she'd* fallen for his slick tactics, becoming all sappy-eyed over him a year ago at Nicky Rottens.

I remember looking around at other kids my age and wondering why their experiences were so totally different from mine. A lot of times my life didn't feel real, either.

Played by the player…

She ground her teeth. She couldn't trust a single word that came out of this fucking guy's mouth. Nothing was real to him. Everything was a game.

"Ah," he said.

"*Ah?*" she shot back. "What the hell does *ah* mean? Everything is so clear to you, and I'm just a Hostess snack cake?"

"Actually, right now nothing is clear to me. Why are you so pissed?"

"Excuse me, but I'm having trouble understanding you." She placed two fingers behind her ear and angled her head toward him. "Shouldn't you be mimicking Kermit the Frog or quoting Spock now that we're talking about something serious?"

He paused. His brows lifted. "Wow."

"Exactly. You're never serious." She seamed her lips. "I need to know who I'm dealing with in a partner…a teammate."

Pete pushed back the sides of his suit jacket so he could tuck his hands in his pockets. "Truth is, I don't know what I'm dealing with either, Justice. Maybe you and I would do better if you'd teach me the dance steps to this hot-then-cold number we keep repeating. You want to be with me—that's clear—but for some reason you're not letting yourself. I'm getting a little motion sick from all the starting and stopping."

More heat boiled into her face, her throat constricting around a conflicting turmoil of emotions, all of them churning up to yank her in different directions.

He was right. A part of her did want to be with him. He was the man who'd believed in her during BUD/S and showed confidence in her abilities when she'd needed it the most. Pete knew how to have a great time. Escapades with him had always been barnburners, and always would be. Sex with him would be...was inconceivable. Like aliens—no human brain could imagine the existence of something so amazing...only experience of the phenomenon could prove its mind-boggling reality.

These were the pulls—the draw toward him.

The constant craving to be playful and free.

To live her days full of games and fun, just like life with Dad had been.

But ah. That was the kiss of death as much as the jaws of life. She also hated the way she'd been raised.

And *that* was the push-away.

She met his gaze again, her tight lips dangerously close to trembling. "Thing is, Pete, sooner or later someone has to be the adult in the room, and I'll grow sick of it always having to be me."

He exhaled a long breath. "That's unfair."

"Is it?"

A yellow sedan slowed at the curb, the driver peering at

them. A random cabbie searching for a fare? Or a Russian spy curious about what Pete and Justice/Jennifer McNamara were doing?

"Remember when you dropped by my apartment on your way back to BUD/S?" Pete curtly waved off the cabbie. "You did that to expressly tell me you'd been unfair to me—so this seems to be a pattern between us." He watched her with an intense stare. "What is it about me that makes you want to only see the worst?"

She moved her jaw around. "You're all flash, with your buffed-out smiles and your glib charm." And she'd spent a lifetime around flamboyant thieves, who were all about deception—who all too often looked like more than they really were. Maybe even her father included. "And guess what, Pete? Sometimes life isn't a game. Like…like when…"

Like when one male friend didn't give her what she needed when she needed it, and another threw her under the bus with Admiral FuckOver. Or how about the man who hadn't overtly betrayed her like the other two did, but still wasn't there for her when she needed him because *he was too much fucking fun*.

Her voice suddenly went hoarse. "I could've used your help last year. Something happened, and I needed to come to you, but I couldn't."

His brows lowered. "Of course, you could. I told you if you ever needed a break from getting your balls busted, I was here for you, ready to make things better."

"This was more than typical ball-busting BUD/S crap," she bit back. "What happened to me at SERE school was serious. I needed someone *to be serious*."

A shadow crossed his expression. "What happened at SERE?"

Acid washed into her mouth, her stomach balking at the question…at the memories. The weight of Lieutenant Gavin between her legs, the burnt-smoke smell of him, the drip of his sweat on her nipple, the loss of control, and the keelhauling her spirit had taken over everything.

She gave her head an unsteady shake. "Nothing I want to rehash with Chuckles the Clown."

"Justice—"

"You said it yourself—if you take life serious, life gets serious. That's your motto." Moving a step back from him, she turned and continued down the sidewalk.

CHAPTER FIFTY

The next day

SLAVING IN THE fields under a hot sun to harvest the soy for tofu wasn't fun. Listening to Old Shaw tell one of his long-winded stories about his younger days when you'd rather be loafing around and watching a DVD was a ball-ache, and so was practicing Latin instead of playing the board game Life—which forwarded capitalistic ideals and *we don't subscribe to those, do we?* Spending the weekend performing as Smacky the Rabbit in a homemade theatre production instead of hanging out with school friends was the ultimate trip to Snooze Fest.

Pete knew what it was like not to have fun—*the fuck he did*. He'd spent his entire childhood stuck in the wrong life.

Was it really so bad that he wanted to avoid being serious now?

Answer—*No*. It wasn't. Fun didn't equal flaky. He wasn't undependable. Justice had it all wrong. She *could* count on him. She should've come to him after SERE.

Now he just needed to plan his next move for how to change her attitude.

First: convince her to tell him what happened at SERE. She clearly still needed to work through that. People who were hunky-dory about things didn't get so temperamental about them. But during the cab ride to the Russian Ministry of Defense building, when he tried to figure out *what* could've possibly happened to her, he came up with zip.

Nothing bad should have happened to her.

Yeah, the POW camp was a huge fucking drag, too many days spent immersed in stink and noise and violence, along with lengthy stints jammed into cold, damp, dark places—his fun-meter definitely hadn't been blinking while he was there.

But SERE was governed by rules, all kinds of strictures that should've made SERE manageable, especially for a woman who'd managed BUD/S. But she *was* the woman who'd survived BUD/S—so if Justice Hayes said something was serious, then it had to be a shitpile's worth of terribad.

That thought kept him distracted, and his mind was still elsewhere when he and Justice/Jennifer arrived at the Ministry of Defense building for the tour.

Viktor and Alyona Sokolov were waiting for them in a ground-floor courtyard, a forty-by-forty tiled square bordered with sculptures of historically important Russians and leafy plants in oversized pots. Four stories up, yards and yards of red and yellow bunting along with the Russian flag were strung from one building to another.

"How festive," Justice remarked.

Viktor gestured offhandedly at the decorations. "This Saturday night there is a gala here to celebrate the Prime Minister's birthday."

"It looks like it'll be a lovely affair," Justice said, then gave Viktor a coy glance. "I've always wanted to meet the prime minister."

Broad hint for an invitation—smart woman.

She was trying to engineer her way into the building later for a shot at Viktor's office.

Office…

Pete almost shook himself—he needed to get his head back to business.

"He won't be in attendance," Viktor told Justice/Jennifer. "But we will celebrate anyway."

"Security vill not be so strong wizout the Prime Minister here," Alyona said to her husband. "So ve can invite zem to attend, Viktor." Back to Justice/Jennifer. "And *'tis* a lovely affair."

"Yes, of course, attend," Viktor offered magnanimously. "I will put your names on the guest list."

"How wonderful," Justice enthused. "I love dolling up for a party."

Their group set off on the tour, gradually making their way up from one floor to the next. On the fourth, they entered a rotunda with a large bronze statue. The figure was a soldier with a Charlie Chaplin mustache sitting in rigid pride astride a horse.

Viktor explained who the dude was.

Pete nodded attentively and planned what he would have for lunch. *Pierogis.* He was in the mood for those.

"I can think of nothing else to show you," the minister concluded. "So this ends the tour. Would you perhaps care for a drink now?"

At eleven in the morning? Russians sure did love their vodka. "We haven't seen your office," Pete pointed out.

"I am sorry, but that area"—Viktor gestured toward a door made of thick wood—"is off limits to the public."

"Ah, too bad," Pete said. "At the Fourth of July party yesterday you mentioned that there are pictures in your office of some of your greatest conquests. I was hoping to see them." *Then I can give your ego a good, hard poke.* "You said you climbed the Matterhorn, but I wasn't sure if you meant the one at Disneyland, haha."

Justice joined in with the laughter.

A light stain of color spread across Viktor's cheeks.

Justice glanced at Alyona. "Didn't I read about there being a room here with twelfth-century antique furnishings?"

Alyona perked up. "*Da*." She flapped a hand at her husband. "Zere is no harm in showing Mr. McNamara a few pictures, Viktor. I vant to take Mrs. McNamara to zee Blue Room."

Alyona and Justice trooped off.

Pete gave Viktor a sideways smile. "It appears the women have abandoned us, Mr. Minister."

Viktor sniffed. "We shall adjourn to my office to see the photos. But just for a moment."

"Great." Pete approached the thick wooden door, but hung back while the minister extracted a clear plastic vial about the size of a tube of lip balm from his inner jacket pocket. He pulled out a Q-Tip look-alike, used this to swab his inner cheek, then stuck the cotton head into a hole on a glass panel to the right of his office door.

Well, CIA intel was right about that.

A *tick* sounded.

Viktor pushed the door open and gestured Pete through.

They walked down a corridor lined with doors.

The Minister of Defense's office was last on the left, furnished simply with a set of shelves—populated only with books—a table with a tea set on it, and also—*ah ha!*—an eyesore of a safe made out of bulky metal.

Photos of Viktor, wide-smiled in triumph and posed in every conceivable "extreme" situation, covered the walls.

"Hey, these pictures are great." Pete kept up a desultory conversation about the photos as he moved from one to another. "You climbed the Fitz Roy in Patagonia... Awesome... I spend summers in California... You should join me there sometime... We can climb El Capitan together... It'll take us four or five days to make it up the sheer granite, so we'll have to sleep in hammocks strung from pitons on the rock face along the way, but you don't mind that, do you?

"Oh, you want to climb the Totem Pole? In Tasmania, Australia, right? I'm interested! Afterward we can surf Shipstern Bluff. Massive swells there… 'Course lots of great white sharks too… Probably best to surf with a knife strapped to your leg, haha… You'd be down for that too, right?"

By the last photo, all of Pete's subtle challenges had worked—Viktor was thin-lipped and defensive.

"You have clearly been on many great adventures too, my comrade. I would like to see pictures of you."

Uh oh. "Absolutely! I left my cell with Jenn, and the pics are on my phone, so we'll have to get together later for me to show you. In fact…" He rubbed his jaw. *Here goes.* "We could go out tonight. Jennifer goes to bed early—she's a bit of a bore—and I like to head out on the town after she's asleep. Just for a few drinks. That's all. Unless, well…" He caught the Russian's gaze and arranged a smirk on his mouth. "Sometimes I meet people. Anyway, I asked around and was told some place called *The Diamond Czarina* is the best. Have you ever heard of it?"

"No."

"It's supposed to be where the most beautiful women in Moscow hang out."

Viktor scoffed. "If that were so, I would have heard of it."

Pete shrugged. "It's apparently Moscow's newest hotspot."

Viktor snorted. "Someone is telling you tales about this club, comrade."

"Yeah, probably. But I'm going to go, anyway. I somehow always manage to have a good time wherever I am." Pete smirked again.

Viktor's nostrils flared. "I should go with you."

Should you?

"To make sure you are not being duped."

"Ah, okay. And who knows? Maybe you'll find out this place is your next favorite club, and then you'll have me to thank for it."

The Russian's lips stretched into a forced smile. "Indeed."

Chapter Fifty-One

The Diamond Czarina

AW, SHIT. PETE barely stopped himself from venting a huge sigh. *The CIA totally blew it with this place.*

The agency had definitely pulled off a club that looked like the "new hot commodity," with the throb of electro music and stripes of red and orange lighting on the walls—like a prison cell in Hell. It created a surreal backdrop to the undulating silhouettes of several hundred people.

The dance floor was packed, mostly women dancing with other women, rubbing up so close they were glistening with each other's sweat—and not a single one of them didn't looked primed for sex.

The most beautiful women in Moscow where here all right, but they were too beautiful—too plastic, too tantalizing, too fucking *accessible*.

For a man who was obsessively and diabolically competitive, a club like this would be about as yawntastic as—

"These women are hookers!" Viktor's smile was maliciously gleeful.

Yeah…a whorehouse.

"Just as I thought!" Viktor exclaimed. "You've been duped, comrade."

Pete kept his own smile in place and went for the save. "When I asked around for a hot club, why would anyone suggest a place with prostitutes?" He offered Viktor his best *gimme-a-break* expression. "Do I look like a man who has to pay for sex?"

"No. But someone is trying to fleece your pockets none-theless."

A woman wearing a dress up to the crotch slunk over to them with an exaggerated sway of her hips. Her lipstick was so red it hurt to look at it. She stopped in front of them and said something sultry.

She spoke in Russian, but that didn't stop Pete from smacking a hand to his face—mentally.

Obvious much?

Viktor laughed at her. "Come," he said to Pete. "I know a better place."

"Wait," Pete called after Viktor. "Let's at least have a drink first." *If I get you drunk, maybe you'll change your mind about sleeping with one of these super snazzy undercover agent women…*

But Viktor was already out the door.

Shit.

Curbside, Viktor hailed a cab, and the two of them hopped in, Viktor giving the driver instructions in Russian.

Pete tried not to sit with rebar up his spine, even though the mission had just gone off the skids in a bad way.

They were now heading outside of a controlled zone.

How was Pete going to get the minister's saliva now?

If Viktor banged a woman at this *better* club, Pete couldn't see asking her—a stranger—to kiss a piece of absorbent paper after she got busy with the Russian Minister of Defense.

When it came to weird, that was all the way at the top.

He needed to call a time-out and discuss next-move options with the CIA. Too bad he couldn't—he couldn't say anything, actually, and be heard. For safety reasons, Pete had opted not to be wired.

A group of handlers were keeping tabs on him,

though—Justice among them—and hopefully even now they were stuffing a passel of secret agent beauties into a van with plans to follow Pete and Viktor to the new club, then discreetly drop off the beauties there.

Tricky part would be spotting the undercover women. Maybe one of them would slip him a secret handshake…

Ten minutes later he and Viktor arrived in front of a low-slung building with no windows and no sign out front.

As they strolled for the door, Pete checked both ways on the street but didn't see any van arriving in hot pursuit.

The new club had a trippy, psychedelic atmosphere, lit with an array of long, thin tubes of neon lights—pink, blue, green, yellow. The tubes lined the ceiling, the walls, the underside of the bar, and the dance floor. When a person stood next to a particular shade of neon, it turned his or her face that color, so stepping into this club felt a bit like entering a bar from a Star Wars movie.

And when it came to the most beautiful women in Moscow, *a better place* this club was not.

Men and women alike were hard-jawed and cool-eyed, wearing aggressive leather clothing, their bodies covered in piercings and tats and scars.

Pete and Viktor stood out like sore thumbs in their suits and ties.

A woman who outstripped Pete by two inches, both in height and width, stalked by, inspecting him with a whetted look. No red lipstick for this lovely creature. Black. She wore black eye shadow too, which didn't help matters in the attractive department.

"Not exactly a target-rich environment," Pete commented drolly to Viktor.

"Forget these women," the Russian said. "I am member of a special club in back. Come." He was off again, weaving his way through the crowd.

Pete followed.

They arrived at a black door guarded by a man who stood in the kind of arms-splayed stance that resulted from having too much muscle.

Typical bouncer tool...except this guy had eaten a Sherman tank for dinner.

Viktor spoke to the guy in Russian.

Bouncer Tool assessed Pete, then took a hand-held radio off his belt and spoke into it. He waved them both inside.

Pete walked into a wood-paneled room about the size of a two-car garage. Cold air was blowing thin strips of cloth into undulating ribbons from two vents high on the far wall, but the A/C was doing little to disperse the pungent stink of sweat. The noise was just as loud in here as out in the main club, although in here the racket wasn't from music.

It was from yelling.

A horde of men was gathered in a ring around some spectacle going on in the center of the room. If there were any women present, Pete couldn't see them. Unless they were part of the spectacle...

A sense of unease spread across Pete's flesh. *Oh, crap*. This was some kind of *Eyes Wide Shut* sex club, wasn't it, with a live sex show going on in front of these shouting men, and the only thing missing were the creepy masks.

Pete's scalp tingled. Shit, now that he was outside of the CIA-controlled *Diamond Czarina*, the possibility of having to screw a faceless, nameless woman was back on the table.

To prove his *I'm-better-than-you* status, Pete might be pushed to fuck a woman in front of this audience, maybe side by side with Viktor. Who had the biggest cock? Who could last the longest? Who could make his faceless, nameless partner climax the quickest?

Who could projectile vomit the farthest?

Viktor looked at Pete with a second dose of malicious

glee. "Here is a place where we can partake in the ultimate test of manhood."

That made Pete feel so much better. He put his brain to work coming up with an excuse to avoid performing at a live sex show but kept bumping up against his cover story. Would a cheating louse and a womanizing pal really refuse the chance to headline his sexual prowess?

How about just slipping out the door?

Dear parents of everyone living in the Russians' bull's-eye zone, sorry that your loved ones have disappeared under a cloud of missile dust. Pete "Bingo" Robbins ran away from his op…

He exhaled. Why couldn't he just be some regular guy—Wal-Mart greeter, weekend mechanic, beer connoisseur, and armchair sportsman? A guy living in blissful ignorance of all things bad in the world.

No. He had to be the guy out to save thousands from long-range nap-of-the-earth-missiles, a pack of absorbent papers burning a hole in his front pants pocket, just dying to be passed off to Viktor's "date" for the night and used.

The crowd roared, and the uptick in noise jerked Pete's attention back to the blocked scene. "What kind of club is this, Viktor?"

Viktor gestured him toward the horde, smiling. "Go see for yourself."

As Pete started forward, he spotted another bouncer against a wall. This man was no tool. He stood in a pose of utter confidence, one hand clasped around the opposite wrist, sleek and fit, hawk-eyed for the first sign of trouble. An honest-to-God badass. He wore a shoulder holster with a Russian-made GSh-18 pistol in it, the standard sidearm for all Russian Armed Forces.

The badass was probably ex-military, and a guy being armed in this uncontrolled environment, and likewise trained to use said weapon, pretty much took a huge dump on Pete's fun-meter.

He arrived at the edge of the spectators and peered over the tops of their heads to where all the commotion was—

Huh.

This was no sex show. Not even close.

Two men sat across from each other at a scarred wooden table, each holding a stick about the size of a dollar store flashlight. A push-button switch was near the thumb, electrical wires trailing out the other end—these plugged into a metal box about the size of two stacked shoeboxes set on the table. A cheap ceramic bowl with several small pieces of folded paper in it was on the table opposite the metal box.

Sticky pads like those used to take an EKG were secured to the forearms of both men, more wires trailing out from the pads. These wires plugged into the metal box, too, but into different input portals.

A lighted number on the box was steadily counting higher.

The higher the number rose, the more the two men sweated…swore…gritted their teeth…shook.

Higher…higher…

Both men were shaking so much now that the ceramic bowl was rocking.

Viktor spoke close to Pete's ear. "Those men are being electrocuted."

Pete's chest went cold. "Oh, yeah?"

"Every thirty seconds the odds change. See?" Viktor pointed to an electronic scoreboard tacked up mid-wall.

Dimitri was favored to Yeorgi three to one.

With a piercing scream, one of the men at the table thumb-punched the button.

The number on the box flicked out, and both men slumped forward onto the table.

A mini red lightbulb on the side of the box nearest to

the man who'd tapped out started blinking.

Viktor made a sound of disgust. "Yeorgi has failed."

A man with a pencil-thin mustache stepped up to the table, stuck his hand in the bowl, swished it around, and came out with a folded piece of paper.

"Now Yeorgi must pay for his weakness," Viktor explained.

The man with the pencil-thin mustache opened the paper and read its contents in Russian.

Loud murmurs raced through the crowd.

The loser went pale.

"What did he say?" Pete asked, his unease fanning into a full-blown case of the *this-is-bads*.

"They will break Yeorgi's left arm."

Pete whipped his head around. "What?"

Two more bouncer tools stepped up to the table. One held the loser down, practically sitting on him, while the other guy stretched out Yeorgi's left arm.

Pencil-Thin Mustache Guy came forward with a cudgel.

Bile reached gluey fingers up Pete's throat as he watched the man raise it.

Pencil-Thin Mustache Guy slammed the club down on Yeorgi's extended arm with a brittle *crack!*

Skin split, serrated bone punched up, blood sprayed.

Yeorgi shrieked.

Heart pounding, Pete rounded on the minister. "Holy Jesus Christ, Viktor!"

Viktor shrugged in a bland way. "The bowl holds an array of consequences, some easy, some difficult. Yeorgi was unlucky."

Ya fucking think?

The two bouncers hauled off the injured man.

"They will take him to a hospital now," Viktor assured Pete.

"Ah. Well. Then it's all okay." Pete's sarcasm was lost on Viktor.

A man with a black widow's peak arrowing back from aquiline features had just walked up to them. "Comrade Sokolov," he greeted Viktor in a cool tone.

Viktor was just as chilly. "Comrade Chekov." Viktor gestured at Pete. "English, please. My friend here does not know Russian."

Chekov looked at Pete with dark, lifeless eyes. To Viktor, he said, "We have not seen you here at *Drugoe Mesto* in many months."

Viktor made a languid gesture. "Why come when no one will compete with me? I am here tonight only because I have found a man who will." Viktor's palm landed on Pete's shoulder.

Pete blinked. *I'm going to do what?*

Chekov peered at Pete again. "Brave man. No one has ever defeated our Minister of Defense."

Pete's heart stalled out.

Danger, Will Robinson! Danger!!
Get the hell out of there!

CHAPTER FIFTY-TWO

"I GIVE YOU luck at being the first to break Comrade Sokolov," Widow's Peak continued to Pete, then he gave them both a hooded look. "I am one of the men in charge of the bowl this night, so I hope you two are feeling at your best." He sauntered away, pulling out his cell phone and putting it to his ear.

"That guy's a real hoot, isn't he?" Pete said, then added dryly, "A friend of yours?"

"A political rival," Viktor corrected. "Chekov will make sure a heinous choice is in the bowl for us."

Oh, good. I was worried this night was becoming a bore. "There's no *us*, Viktor. I'm not playing that fucked game."

Viktor gave Pete a level stare. "Once a man enters as a competitor, he cannot leave until he has competed—it keeps fear from making decisions. I told Boris at the door we were competitors, and he has declared us as such."

"Well, you didn't exactly tell me that, did you?"

"I didn't think I needed to," Viktor drawled, his tone edging toward disdain.

The room suddenly quieted.

Pete turned to look.

The crowd had parted, opening a passage for Pete and Viktor to make their way to the scarred table, now puddled with sweat.

The two of them had been announced. Their names were lit up on the scoreboard.

Viktor was favored fifteen to one over Pete.

Dear CIA operatives who are supposed to be keeping me under surveillance, please read the Morse Code my heart is banging out and haul your asses in here NOW.

His idea of a fun night on the town *so* did not include being electrocuted.

Last-ditch effort: "Let's at least have a drink before we do this." *Because my brain isn't dishing up anything other than the repeat plan of trying to get you drunk on the way to getting some of the old in-out...*

Viktor swept the idea aside. "We can drink plenty afterward."

Sure, sure—that is, you know, if no one's on his way to the hospital.

"Come now, Mr. McNamara. The chance to prove which of us is the stronger man awaits." Viktor started toward the table.

Pete hesitated a beat, then followed. If he stuck this out, then there was a good chance he and Viktor would be sloshing back drinks afterward, yukking it up over what a riot that electrocution-thing had been.

And then Pete would finally be able to drive this op where it needed to go—toward saliva collection. After Viktor got a little buzz on, Pete could press the Russian into the arms of a secret agent woman—after receiving a double wink and a finger-beside-the-nose from her, of course.

Pete moved to stand across the table from Viktor, taking comfort from his cover story. "Pete McNamara" was an American diplomat. These Russians would know that. Nothing too *heinous* could end up in that consequence bowl, no matter what kind of bone the zombie-eyed Chekov had to pick with the Minister of Defense.

Pete sat.

Viktor sat too.

One of the tool bouncers attached two EKG sticky pads to each of Pete's forearms.

Viktor was wired the same.

The minister lifted his push-button stick and showed it to Pete. "When it becomes too much for you, you may press your button to make it stop." He smiled.

Pete picked up his stick and smiled back. "Same goes for you, Mr. Minister."

Viktor's eyes flashed, a dangerous undercurrent in his gaze.

Five Russians stepped out of the crowd, including that schlub Chekov.

A guy missing a front tooth read the consequence he'd written on his piece of paper. "Take all money from loser's wallet." He folded the paper and tossed it in the bowl.

Some air eased out of Pete's lungs. *See? Not so bad.*

An acne-scarred guy was next: "Burn house down."

Hmm, okay, that consequence was worse but still not a big deal for Pete McNamara, whose house in Latvia was pretend.

Pudgy guy: "Must have sex with Helga."

The crowd rumbled loudly.

Viktor's lip curled back.

Pete's forearms twitched under his sticky pads. *Uh…*

Bald guy: "Loser must eat a dog." Then he added wickedly, "Raw."

Yuck. *Hell no, fuck you very much.*

Chekov came forward, his soulless eyes sweeping the crowd. He held his piece of paper up high, paused a long moment for dramatic effect, then said, "Kill wife."

The crowd sucked in a communal breath.

Pete snapped his attention to Viktor. *What the…?*

Silence hung in the air, the muted beat of the club's music the only noise to cut through the base astonishment—

clearly this was a new and unexpected consequence.

"Is this some kind of sick joke?" Pete demanded of Viktor.

"No." Color was rapidly bleeding out of Viktor's cheeks.

The skin on Pete's stomach crawled. "Well, it is for me." He started to tear at his sticky pads. "I'm out."

In the next second the iron sight of a pistol was jammed against Pete's temple.

It was the Honest-To-God Badass with his GSh-18.

Put a gun to a guy's head in the movies, and the hero faces it with stoicism, maybe even a lot of *fuck-you!* in his expression.

That was make-believe.

In real life the smell of cordite and gunpowder and the feel of cold steel right next to your brain, a nine millimeter Parabellum a mere trigger-squeeze away from instant and ugly death was nothing short of terrifying.

Ice washed from Pete's stomach into his bowels, and his sphincter pumped a couple of times. He sat very still.

"Fear is not allowed to make our decisions," Viktor reiterated in a hoarse voice. "We compete or we die."

Pete licked the sweat off his upper lip. "Another rule it might've been nice to hear about beforehand, Mr. Minister." He cut his eyes sideways. "Get off me."

Honest-to-God Badass lowered his weapon but didn't back away.

Chekov—that rank prick—looked between Pete and Viktor with his bleak, merciless eyes. "I have called my men on the phone and have instructed them to wait outside of Comrade Sokolov's house and Mr. McNamara's hotel, ready to strike at one of your wives on my bidding. There will be no chance to warn your women beforehand, gentleman— only winning this challenge will save her."

Viktor's lips folded inward, disappearing from view.

Pete's heart faltered. "Is this Chekov douche serious?"

"He is."

It was a shock like flying into wind shear and suddenly finding your helo being driven uncontrollably and inescapably toward a crash landing—almost too absolute to believe.

So Pete wasn't going to believe it. No way would these guys really kill someone.

Skin splitting, serrated bone punching up, blood spraying…

Okay, so this *was* real. "Do something," he spewed. "Stop this."

"I cannot." Beads of sweat speckled Viktor's mustache and goatee. "Fear is not allowed to make our decisions."

Stop saying that, you psychotic lowlife! Pete wasn't too manly to release the yell—his neck muscles had simply locked up and incapacitated his voice box.

I have called my men on the phone, and they wait to strike at one of your wives…

Justice…

Her name pushed against the back of Pete's teeth.

His wife wasn't a no-name CIA operative he'd met yesterday.

His wife was *Justice.*

His brain went squiggly. He couldn't think anymore. His lungs didn't seem to want to work either. He was caught in the wind shear again, falling toward an unknown, dark place of ending.

Justice… Her name brought him pulling upright before impact.

Keep your shit together.

He conducted some private calisthenics, flexing and releasing muscles all over his body to relieve the tension in them. *Justice's death isn't a given, all right?* The consequence bowl held four chances in five that Justice wouldn't be killed.

And then there was always Pete's ability to outlast Viktor. "Fine, let's do this." He cut another hard look over his shoulder at Honest-To-God Badass.

The man finally holstered his weapon and resumed his position against the wall.

Pete narrowed his eyes on Viktor. "I'm going to kick your fucking ass, you turd." Not one of his better insults, but he was rapid-cycling between the need to piss and to hurl everything he'd recently eaten in a corner.

Electronic numbers on the odds scoreboard flipped in a blur.

When they stopped Pete had gone from fifteen to one to twenty to one.

Viktor laughed darkly. "They know your outburst has only made me more determined to best you." He stood and unbuckled his belt.

Pete watched Viktor undo his pants and shove them down to his knees.

Jesus, now what?

"The electrodes will be attached to our inner thighs instead of our forearms," Viktor told him. "So our testicles may take the worst of the abuse."

The crowd buzzed.

"Sounds like a real honky-tonk," Pete drawled. Standing, he dropped his own pants, then sat back down.

The table was shunted out from between them so they could see each other better.

One of the tool bouncers switched the sticky pads from Pete's forearms to his inner thighs.

The other tool rewired Viktor.

While this was going on, the crowd shouted at Pencil-Thin Mustache Guy, placing their bets with him like this was the New York Stock Exchange.

Pete clenched his fist around his safety stick and kept his

focus on Viktor.

Pencil-Thin Mustache Guy made a betting-closed gesture, like an umpire calling "safe," then stepped up to the metal box and set his thumb on the on/off switch.

One corner of Viktor's mouth flicked up a bare inch.

Pete's Adam's apple grew two sizes too big for his throat. All this time, he thought he'd been playing the Russian right into his hands.

But he hadn't.

The Russian had played Pete into his.

CHAPTER FIFTY-THREE

FIGURE IT OUT, Pete!

Pete's body lurched in his chair and hot spikes drove through his nuts.

Fi-fi-fi-figure it out, Pete.

His leg muscles grabbed onto his thigh bones. His spine jellified. His nuts dropped into a pot of boiling water.

Fi-fi-fi-figure it ow-ow-ow-out, Pete!

Sheet lightning speared through his pelvis, and the hair on his nuts scorched off.

Fi-fi-fi-figure it ow-ow-ow-out, P-P-Pa-Pa-Pete!

Across from him, Viktor's eyes were red with ruptured blood vessels. Drool trailed from his elastic lips down to his lap, where his undershorts were now stained yellow from when his bladder had released thirty seconds ago.

Every thirty seconds the odds change…

Last Pete saw, his odds had dropped to ten to one.

He had no idea what the standings were now.

He couldn't see clearly anymore.

Sweat streamed down his brow into his eyes, and his eyeballs were bouncing around the room like rubber balls.

Viktor was equally showered in sweat, and if the man's nuts felt anything like Pete's, then they'd scampered up inside his abdominal cavity some seconds ago to escape this agony.

Seconds…

Each one felt like a small eternity.

Pete glared swimming eyes at the Russian.

Tap out, you dick face!

The minister wouldn't.

And Pete couldn't figure out what to do about it.

He felt like the lead pilot in the cockpit of an Airbus. Panic was trying to set in, and he was darting his focus everywhere. A pilot couldn't fly everything. Maybe he thought he could—a lot of gauges were the same—but when it came right down to it, every aircraft handled differently, especially fixed wing versus helicopters. And right now Air Traffic Control was screaming at Pete to land this air cow, but he didn't know how.

Justice…Justice…Justice…

He could only say her name over and over in his mind.

I have called my men, and they wait to strike at one of your wives…

I really don't want you to die, little sailor.

But…if I could just—

"Ah!" His entire body locked into catatonic rigidity, his heels jerking off the floor.

B-but if I could tap out for one second…just for a short rest, okay?

Saliva drained between his teeth.

Justice…Justice…Justice…little sailor…

I can't take much more of this.

Viktor's shoe heels did a jittery tap dance on the floor. A dot of blood appeared in the opening of his nostril.

No, no, no, I won't tap out…I'm here for you…

But I want to tap out. I really do. My nuts hurt so bad. All of me does. A-a-and—

The lights suddenly clicked off, dousing the room in darkness.

Pete slumped in his seat as the grip of electricity released him.

The spectators let out an angry shout.

Pete slithered out of his chair, landing face-up and loose-boned on the floor.

Bump. That had to be Viktor falling out of his chair too.

Rushing footsteps…hawked orders…the flatline hum of Pete's brain dying…

The door into the main club flew open, letting in some talcum powderlike light. He peered at the jamb, seeing human-shaped forms coalesce in and out of the rectangle. It all seemed so far away…

He should probably move. Go on a saliva-hunting expedition and that sort of thing.

He craned his neck back and found Viktor's amorphous shape.

The Russian wasn't moving either.

So maybe Pete would just rest here for a bit more, wait for his vivisected muscles to come back together and his nuts to stop hating him.

Dear parents of everyone living in the Russians' bull's-eye zone, Pete "Bingo" Robbins just charred his testicles for no good reason…

Grinding his teeth, he hefted himself into a roll-over. The expected javelins of pain stabbed through him. His follow-on moan sounded like a toad with a bad case of bronchitis. He wobbled onto his hands and knees, gave himself a second to crap out his liver, then with his pants around his ankles, shuffle-scooted over to the fallen Russian.

The minister was insensible, his head lolling back and forth, his eyes rolling toward his hairline.

Easing onto his heels, Pete dug a palsied hand into the front pocket of his pants—not the easiest thing to do with them down—and pulled out the packet of absorbent paper. He carefully withdrew one of the papers and wiped it across the drool on Viktor's lips. He had no memory of how he managed the intricacies of slipping the paper into a small plastic holder.

He was suddenly just jamming everything back in his pocket and…

And falling over once more.

He crashed to the floor again, his mouth drooping open as an adrenaline hangover hit him hard—irregular heartbeat, bulging orbital veins, numbness in the extremities. He croaked out another moan.

A shadow darted across him a second before a woman crouched at his side.

One of the clubbers.

She wore the typical black eye shadow and lipstick, although atypically she was wearing baggy clothing. Whatever hair she might've possessed was stuffed under a black beanie cap. Maybe she was going to steal his wallet.

Oddly, Justice's voice came out of her mouth. "He cannae take any more, Captain. He's gonna blow." She grinned at him.

The expression lit her eyes, and he hoped to God he wasn't hallucinating her. Because that smile was really cool. He blinked a couple of times. "Little sailor?"

She lifted a pair of electrical wire cutters in front of him and snapped the jaws. "At your service."

CHAPTER FIFTY-FOUR

JUSTICE STOOD MOTIONLESS in the middle of her hotel room and quietly observed the strange primate behavior.

Pete was squatted down in front of her mini fridge and rapidly clearing it of its cache of Stoli.

"This vodka isn't the industrial waste shit America stocks, you know." Straightening, he dropped a double handful of mini bottles on top of the fridge. "That crap isn't truly imported, by the way, but manufactured in the U.S. of A. using Russian grains. Total bull." He turned a bar glass right-side up. "This vodka is *Stolichnaya*, made right here in Mother Russia." He cracked open a mini bottle. "The good stuff."

Justice tugged her beanie cap off, releasing her ponytail. Pete seemed all right on the outside, but otherwise his energy was off, sort of a strange erratic volatility edging his normal gamboling vibe.

Understandable considering what he'd just been through…although the exact nature of what he'd experienced while inside *Drugoe Mesto*—which basically meant *The Other Spot*—she didn't know. The CIA had unearthed the *what* of the special club—it catered to men wanting to challenge their manhood—but not the *how*.

Pete grabbed his cocktail glass and gestured to her face with it. "You look like hell, by the way. Goth really isn't your thing." With his other hand, he upended the mini vodka into the glass.

"Awfully big talk from a man who was rescued with his pants around his ankles."

He laughed.

It was a big laugh, but still…the usual jubilation was missing from his eyes.

"You want one?" He plucked a second bottle off the pile he'd made.

"Maybe now isn't the best time to be drinking a lot, Pete."

He looked at her like she'd just asked him to urinate all over his freshly detailed Mustang. "Are you fucking kidding me?" He dumped the second vodka into his glass. "There *is* no better time."

"What are you trying to drink into oblivion, Pete?" She sat on the edge of the bed. "I'm guessing you weren't invited to kick up your legs with a bunch of other Russian dudes at a Cossack folk-dancing show."

"Definitely not." He shot back the double vodka and swished the alcohol around in his mouth, bulging his cheeks in and out.

Avoiding talking.

She used her beanie cap to wipe off her black makeup. "Our intel assets told us that *Drugoe Mesto* is some kind of special club."

Pete swallowed the vodka and smacked his lips "*Special.* I love how everyone keeps calling it that." He held up a third mini bottle and admired its clear contents. "Let's not tap dance around truth, shall we? The place was a torture club."

"Oh?" She held her next breath as she quick-scanned his body, double-checking for bruises and swelling. She still didn't find any. "How?"

"Electrocution." He gestured absently with the third bottle. "'Course your average, everyday Russkie gets to put the electrical pads on his *arms*. Our pads were put on our thighs." He drained the third vodka into his glass. "A special tweak of Viktor's to focus the ouch-factor on our nuts." He poured in a fourth vodka. "It worked. My nuts got fried to extra-crispy." He drank down the two shots in a single gulp. "Which is really too bad. I liked my nuts." His jaw hardened. "Not that I was using them much."

He snatched up a fifth vodka.

"Hey." She stood and walked over to him. "I think four's enough, Pete."

Apparently this statement was hilarious.

He threw back his head and belted out a laugh, a huge, rollicking laugh that ended with a *ho, ho, ho*. "It's not enough until I *forget*." He started to unscrew the fifth vodka.

She grasped his wrist. "I'm sorry you had such a rough time."

"Oh, the electrocution part is only the half of it." He removed his wrist from her grip and reclaimed his cocktail glass.

She swallowed carefully. "What else happened?"

"*You* happened, that's what." He lifted a single forefinger off his glass and pointed it at her. "You."

She didn't understand. "Was I not supposed to break into the lockbox and cut the electricity?" There'd been no other way to save him—the entrance to *Drugoe Mesto* was too well-guarded.

He tipped the fifth mini bottle into his glass. "There was a bowl of consequences. Five potential horrors for a man to endure if he tapped out first." His eyes emptied of color. "One of the consequences was you being killed."

"What? Me?"

"Yes, you. As in, Pete McNamara's wife."

She couldn't believe... *No way*. "No one would've actually—"

"You weren't there," he cut her off sharply. "You didn't

see the things I saw. Those assholes were dead serious about their threat. Some creep was even staked out in front of the Marriott, ready to off you if I fucked up. And I…I almost did."

She shook her head. "I was with the CIA backup team the whole time—a group of operatives. I would've been fine."

He clonked his glass down. "No, you wouldn't have," he snapped. "It was up to me to keep you safe, Justice. *Me*. And I…" He looked away, an array of tics playing musical chairs around his face. "I wanted to tap out. Even though your life was on the line, I wanted to make it stop."

She stared at his ear, salty with dried sweat…his hair was crusty too. He'd really gone all out for her. "Pete," she said. "Ease up on yourself. Electrocution is no party, and the thing about torture is it hurts like nothing else. *Everyone* can be broken."

"Well, no man wants to know what his breaking point is." Pete's Adam's apple rolled in his throat. He stared at her for a long moment. "I almost tapped out."

"But you didn't."

"I *wanted* to."

"No one loses cred for something he wanted to do but never actually did," she argued. "You're not being fair to yourself."

"How the fuck do I even know what I would've actually done? You cut the electricity before I knew if I—" He bowed his head, pressing his eyes with thumb and forefinger. "I wanted to save you."

She stared at the top of his head, his short hair such a mess, flecked with dirt along with old perspiration. The collar of his dress shirt was also turned up along one edge, and his suit jacket was stiff and wrinkled from being drenched with sweat.

Nothing ever got to Pete, but this mission had gotten to him, and she'd never seen him so rattled…so real.

And serious.

This man who was supposedly never serious had just withstood torture. For her.

Her heart expanded in her chest. Her first introduction to Real Pete was one helluva whopper.

He swirled the vodka in his glass near his nose, inhaling.

"Why don't we order something to eat?" she suggested. "Room service is twenty-four hours here."

"I don't need food."

"What do you need, then? Tell me."

"How about proof positive my fried nuts haven't been incapacitated by—" He suddenly stopped swirling and lowered his glass. He gave her a speculative once-over and said, "Hmm." Putting down his drink, he latched an arm around her waist and drew her against him.

"Pete," she breathed, setting her hands on his chest.

His eyes glittered beneath the ebony sweep of his lashes.

Her pulse quickened. He smelled of vodka, expensive cologne, manly sweat, and—as usual—of mayhem and Big Trouble…*trouble, trouble, trouble*. Her balance wavered, rocking her onto the backs of her heels.

Push…pull…

"What I *need* is a new memory," he told her. "Pleasure instead of pain."

A new memory… Her belly fluttered. The same thing she'd needed from him after SERE—a new memory for the area between her thighs.

Out with an old memory, in with the new…

She shifted her feet, distributing her weight evenly. It didn't help. She was still off-balance and tumbling to…somewhere…falling into eyes that were Real Pete's right now.

This was no player holding her in his arms.

Tunneling his hand into the hair at the base of her skull, he tipped her head back. The large barrette holding her ponytail *ticked* open and *flumped* to the carpet, releasing a flood of her hair over his hand.

He rumbled a sound low in his chest and burrowed his fingers deeper, sending a seismic shudder racing down her spine.

A lambent burn lit his eyes the moment before he captured her lips with his. Soft. Moist. Masterful. He kissed her with partially parted lips and the commanding movement of his jaw, taking the kiss where he wanted it to go. All over. New places. Exciting realms. He urged her lips farther apart so he could sinuously entangle his tongue with hers. Seductive fire. More dizzying need.

She groaned and dissolved against him, her womb going as languidly compliant as the rest of her.

Push… Pull… Do-si-do and around we go.

She was in full pull-mode now.

CHAPTER FIFTY-FIVE

A FUNKY LIGHT-HEADEDNESS spilled over Pete, the hotel room dropping sideways for a moment, like he was in the middle of flying one of his infamous rotor-overs. From the vodka? Or a near bone-cracking relief? Probably not the vodka—those mini bottles were pretty mini—so from relief.

At *last*, after waiting a year for Justice, he was on final approach to big, sexy love, and *Operation Get Justice* was in its ultimate round of negotiations.

And he was an excellent closer.

The timing couldn't have been better either. Yeah, he probably stank up a storm, and two achy hot spots still lingered where the EKG pads had been stuck to his inner thighs, but otherwise he was fired up to prove that his nuts hadn't been fried completely off.

He hiked Justice off the floor by her ass—*such fucking resilient flesh*—and was at the bed in three strides, bringing her down on the mattress with his hands still in place. He tilted her hips up to meet his, fitting their bodies together. He exhaled haltingly as blood surged into his loins. His cock hardened against her, and it was okay—full steam ahead and man the torpedoes! Everything was functioning properly and without pain.

He closed his eyes to prolong the moment, to keep exorcising his demons…Viktor's macho game night…and a year spent with a door shut in his face.

No doors now. The gutsy woman was doing her melty

thing, her entire body humming with the need to switch up a little new-memory-making into full-out, balls-deep sex. Her strong legs were gripped around his waist like he was an exercise ball she was trying to pop.

How the incredible hell would a body like hers perform in bed?

He was about to find out. His pulse kicked at his wrists and throat, and a droplet of warm pre-come seeped to the end of his—

Uh-oh. He stared at the bedspread. That was…*huh*. He might be in less control than he'd thought.

Normally a suave devil in the foreplay department, the throbbing eagerness in his cock was warning him that once he began exploring the sheer stupendousness of Justice's body, he might do something unprecedented, like—*no, not prematurely ejaculate, get real*—but, like, go blind and stupid.

He'd better get the condom ready now.

Twisting his hips off her a bit, he fished into his back pocket.

Justice clutched his belt loops. "You're not stopping, are you?"

He smiled. "Try naming something that could make me." He snagged a square foil out of his wallet, set the condom on the bedspread, then chucked his wallet in the general direction of the bedside table.

Justice gazed at him through half-lowered lashes. "Do we have to use a condom?"

He froze. He stared. He squinted. He thought *real* hard. *Trick questions for five hundred, Alex.*

She unknotted his tie. "I don't like them."

In this day and age wasn't that kind of a *too bad*? He cranked his mouth sideways. "Why, you little anarchist."

She gave him a smile. It was a sensual, sultry thing that nearly had him jumping off the bed and racing to the nearest condom factory to burn the damned building to the ground for her. Not that *he* minded condoms. *No, really.* So what if latex separated him from the best part of a woman. Did it matter if intimacy was only perceived in the first place?

Cymbals clapped inside his head. *BONG!* A broadside epiphany, slapped right into his brain. The latex separation *did* matter with Justice. Because she wasn't just some pickup. This was warm, nubile, uniquely ass-kicking Justice Hayes, the woman he'd been trying to make his for a long time.

The woman who was taking care of him tonight, making sure he didn't go it alone.

"All right," he said. "You've convinced me."

Eyes sparking, she loosened his tie into a broad circle. "Good."

"I only require one thing."

"A clean bill of health?" She unlooped the tie from his head and tossed it across the bed. "I have one." She raised a single brow into a wry arc. "Do you?"

"Shocking though it may seem, I do. Because I *always* use a condom. Except under one condition."

"Birth control?" She pushed his suit jacket down his back. "That's also covered."

"Nope." He tugged his arms free. "Although it's nice to know."

"What then?"

"A monogamous relationship."

She froze for a loaded moment of silence, her eyes darting to the side.

A fist right to the balls, that. He was back to pain.

"I—" she started to explain.

He didn't let her. He climbed off, the crunch in his chest just about pulverizing bone, and crossed stiffly to the mini fridge.

She sat up. "We're stopping?"

"We are." Apparently there *was* a force strong enough to make him stop: his—*what's the word, what's the word?*—*feelings* for her.

"Okay, fine, Pete. We'll use a condom."

He sucked hard on his teeth. Did the woman have no idea what she'd just said? "Better a hateful rubber than be my girlfriend, is that it?"

The truth of that slid between his ribs like a blade. He didn't think his ego had ever taken a more profound hit. "Change in plans. I'm not fucking you without a commitment. Period. The prophylactic issue has been rendered irrelevant."

She scooted across the mattress, rearranging her jeans as she came to the foot of the bed. "Would you please dial it down? I only just arrived at the point where I want to be with you, so I'm taking things one step at a time. That's all. No offense intended."

"Offense taken," he retorted. "Clearly I'm good enough to be a lay but not a boyfriend."

"No."

"Yes." He laughed hollowly. "I'm Chuckles the Clown, remember? Bobby the undependable Boob. Totally unreliable. Someone you can't count on to step up and be there for you. I wasn't there for you after SERE, so—"

"I'm not saying that," she interrupted. "You just went through torture for me tonight. I *wouldn't* say—"

"It's *SERE* wedged between us, Justice," he interrupted back. "You never gave me the chance to support you after SERE, so let me support you now."

"I don't need your support."

"The hell you don't."

A small muscle flashed in her jaw. "Tonight is about *you*, Pete. Not about—"

"Great. What *I* want is to know what happened to you

at SERE School a year ago."

She looked away, blanching. If her hair had been in a bun, it would've been trying to fold in on itself right now. She was running away from this thing, and if she kept running, he would never catch her—not all of her. "I told you about what happened to me tonight when you asked. Now it's your turn."

She jerked back to him. "You're really going to pull a move like that on me?"

"Shamelessly."

She just stared at him, no color in her lips.

"What happened?" He crossed his arms over his chest. "I'm happy to stand here and wait."

She scrubbed her knuckles over her mouth.

"What. *Happened?*"

Her throat convulsed. "A rape happened."

He seamed his eyelids into a thin line and rotated his jaw in a slow circle. *Take life serious and life gets serious!* And then there were those times when a Zen outlook was utterly impossible.

The fully actualized male plummets from Maslow's Hierarchy of Needs, falling from dispassionate intellect to his basest, most cave-dweller impulses. To hunt. To shelter. To protect. To defend what was his own. And he found his most beast-like potential. To rend and tear and disembowel. Pete probably should've been appalled at the darkness he discovered inside himself in that moment. He wasn't particularly.

"Who?" he scraped out. "Who hurt you?"

She shook her head. "You're not allowed to be angry. Sorry. I'm not, either—that's the messed-up part."

He gathered his brows into a frown. "What are you talking about?"

"It was all a fake. A setup. The military's tall foreheads

wanted to stage a rape at SERE to push the other BUD/S candidates. They asked me to agree to it, and I did." She bared clenched teeth. "I *agreed.*"

Cold water gorged Pete's stomach. It felt like an absolutely endless flood.

"My attacker was never *inside* me, so, haha, it wasn't real." She gestured choppily. "He beat me, he ripped my clothes off below the waist, he held me down by my throat, he shoved himself between my legs and pounded against me."

Pete inhaled air on a hard draw. How much of a security deposit would he lose if he destroyed this hotel room right now?

"But it wasn't *real.* See? I should be okay. Right? But…but…" She put a palm up to her eyes and bowed her head, her shoulders tensing.

Another rush of cold anger jolted down Pete's spine and crashed to the floor. They'd fucked her up good by stealing her right to work this out. "Those dicks."

"I-I'm the one who screwed up," she wobbled out. "I never should've agreed." She lowered her hand but didn't lift her head. "The tall foreheads said the training exercise could save the lives of my guys, so what was I supposed to do, Pete?" She peered up at him now, her eyes dark with haunted bewilderment. "What was I supposed to do?"

Lungs seizing, he dropped to his knees in front of her, fierce pride swelling his heart, love like a lump in his throat. "You did the right thing, little sailor." He set his hands on her knees. "They're the ones who fucked up."

Justice blinked several times, a glitter of moisture appearing along her lower lashes.

Some of the foundational roots in him wrenched up and tore free. It was weird—never before had he wanted to take care of a woman. Not that he was an insensitive prick who would stand around picking a hangnail while a woman sobbed her guts out, or who wouldn't step in if some guy was hassling her, but...this was different. This was him wanting to tuck Justice away somewhere, snuggled up safe 'n' sound from all things bad in the world—yeah, just like little poss-coon-eaver in a life jacket.

"He *could* have raped me," she said thickly. "My attacker. At the moment of truth during the training exercise, I was powerless to stop it—everything was up to him—and that left me so...so...broken." She moved her teeth back and forth over her bottom lip. "Afterward, I needed to be, I don't know, pampered. What you said a minute ago about wanting a new memory was what I felt; I wanted a new memory for my, uh...my area down below, you know."

Had he said that only been a minute go? It seemed like a lifetime. He supposed it was—between then and now, *wham*, a certain belief in mankind, lost. He was a different man.

"I thought about coming to you, Pete. I really did—just jump in the car and show up on your doorstep." She looked into his eyes with an earnest gaze. "You once told me to 'drop by anytime,' remember?"

"I remember."

"But, I was..." She smudged a couple of fingers across an eyebrow. "I was too raw, and you were...weren't..."

"Wasn't serious enough for what you needed then," he provided, a tangle of rusty wires sitting in the middle of his chest.

"Yes." Her gaze dipped. "So I turned to someone else—I ended up seducing a fellow officer at BUD/S."

Pete's throat splintered.

"You probably don't want to hear that, but it's part of the whole horrible story." She pinched her nose for a second. "Two other candidates caught us. Things got ugly from there—a fistfight, nasty accusations.

"I was called into Admiral Sherwin's office the next morning and told that one of my best friends from BUD/S gave Sherwin the ammunition he needed to kick me out of SOF. After some back-and-forthing, the admiral and I ended up coming to terms, but I was so hurt by my friend's betrayal, I walked away. Nothing ever got worked out. The pain lived in me, and I couldn't manage it, so I ended up cutting everyone out of my life. You became collateral damage in that emotional apocalypse."

Pete dropped back onto his haunches. So this was why Justice's eyes had looked dead that day at her Pensacola BOQ. "I'm so fucking sorry, Justice," he said, air gusting out of him. "As a man, I never really understood what it'd be like to feel powerless and out of control. But I do now." *We compete or we die.*

He shoved his fingers through his hair. "Tonight at the club with Viktor, all control had been taken out of my hands. But here's what I'm realizing about it—and I think this is something you should put into your head too. I was on a *mission.* Same for you a year ago at SERE—you were on an assignment. You *agreed* to put yourself in danger. If not for that, there's no fucking way you would've gotten yourself into a position where you could be overpowered. Just…no way."

She stared at him with huge pupils.

"But that doesn't mean what happened at SERE wasn't real—having control taken from you made it that way. It was real and it was traumatic. Let yourself hurt over it."

She kept staring at him, more dampness sliding onto her lashes.

"Okay?" he pressed.

She paused another moment, then nodded, her lips trembling a little.

He nodded back. A veritable powerhouse of psychological analysis he was.

Big words. No strength to back them up.

Because when her lips trembled a lot more and the tears on her lashes spilled down her cheeks, his belly went loose. And when those tears kept falling, he lost all remaining confidence in his ability to handle this like a bold and fearless pilot-man.

"Hey," he whispered. "Hey, hey." Pushing to his feet, he sat on the bed next to her and pulled her into his arms.

She buried her face against his chest and cried quietly.

He closed his eyes and held her as tight as he dared. And that was all he could do—hold her—the pure, heavy rhythm of his heart beating steadily against hers.

CHAPTER FIFTY-SIX

NOW JUSTICE KNEW what a potato felt like. Or a carrot. Or any one of the class of vegetable able to have its protective fibrous skin stripped away by a sharp peeler. She was without skin now, her raw glop as exposed and sore as it'd ever been. She could count on one hand the number of times she'd cried in her life, and now Pete had borne witness to one of them.

He was still patting her back.

She was still sniffling into his shirtfront.

How to disengage without revealing what a complete numbskull she was about him right now? He'd shown reliability and authenticity and been sweetly supportive of her when she should've been taking care of him.

Was that any call to let herself start falling for the guy?

Leaning back in his arms, she said, "Uh…" Transfixed by his eyes, a deep and dark brown within impossible lashes, that *duh*-utterance was about all the brilliance she could muster for the length of time it took her to screw an awkward smile onto her mouth. "Tell me you didn't drink all the vodka."

He chuckled. "I didn't, but I think you're right about food." He helped her off the bed and urged her into a chair at a small round table. "I'll order some room service."

He went for the Russian essentials—borscht soup, pierogies, and tea—then popped through their adjoining hotel room door to change.

She stared out the hotel window at several smoke stacks, the billows of steam drifting into different shapes against the starry sky—cupids and hearts and cherubs and angels…and *this* was why a woman needed a properly fortified raw glop. Because, *yeesh*.

Just as the food arrived, Pete returned, wearing clean shorts and a T-shirt, although his hair was still a mess. He sat down, spread the cloth napkin over his lap, and picked up a fork. "By the way, I haven't had the chance to tell you yet, but I spotted a safe in Viktor's office this morning while I was checking out his adventure photos. It has to be where the flash drive is stashed. Not much else was there."

She lifted her tea, a clear glass cup set in a curlicue metal holder. "What did it look like?"

Pete used the side of his fork to cut a pierogi in half. "Like the same one Commander Quinn has in his office at HSC-85."

She sat bolt upright, rattling her teacup in its holder. "Sokolov has a Ward-Lock 2000?"

Post cry-slump over!

Holy shit, she was going to get another chance at battling it out with the big dog of all safes.

"Looked like it, yeah." Pete pointed his fork at her face. "You're wearing your Punky Brewster expression again." He regarded her with a gleam in his eyes. "Should I take that as a good sign you'll be able to rock this thing?"

"Are you kidding me? Hah! Since I was able to practice on a Ward-Lock during the Quinn heist, I'm going to crush it." She knew exactly how to listen for a decoy tumbler.

Pete gave her a droll look. "It was a *prank*."

She rolled her eyes and drank her tea.

Pete poked his fork into one of the pierogi halves and swished it around in the sauce. "Your Punky Brewster face is one of my favorites." He popped the halved pierogi into his mouth, smiling close-mouthed as he chewed. "It's a happy expression."

A blush rode up her nape. Somehow Pete's assessment felt like more exposure. She hitched a shoulder. "I like my job."

"Do you?" He sipped his tea. "You once told me you thought your love of excitement was an unhealthy compulsion."

She flashed her eyes up. "When did I say that?"

He stabbed the other pierogi half. "A year ago over Reuben sandwiches and beers at *Nicky Rottens* on the Island."

Had she? "I don't remember."

His mouth quirked up at one corner. "You were a bit bombed at the time."

She squinted at the past. *Oh, yeah*. It was coming back to her. "We talked about leaving no challenge unmet, right?"

"Yep."

"You said you do the same thing."

Now it was his turn to look surprised. "No, I didn't."

"Actually, you told me that while I was eating the mezcal worm in my North Island BOQ room." She scooped up some borscht soup. "And I was *not* drunk then, so I remember it clearly." She ate the soup. "Why?"

"Why what?"

"Why do you leave no challenge unmet?" She knew why she did it—her father had thrown challenges at her on a regular basis and rewarded her lavishly for conquering them. "Is it just the inevitable result of you being an alpha fuck?"

He barked out a laugh. "Save that descriptor for your SEAL pals." He sat back, his mouth angling down in a considering way. "I think more than half the crazy shit I did in my life was to rile a reaction out of Mom and Dad. I guess I figured if they blew their tops that meant they loved me. Sounds corny, maybe, but my parents never criticize me."

She arched a brow. "And that's not good?"

"Not particularly. Not for me, at least. I love my folks— they're great people—but seriously? Fate landed me with the wrong parents. I needed excitement, not peace. I needed my butt kicked around on occasion, not just always 'whatever you think is best, Pete.'" He stabbed another pierogi with his fork. "It didn't help that I was raised in a commune, where *everyone* was practically in a Zen coma."

She scooped up another bite of soup but didn't eat it. "A commune?"

"More like a community—an ecovillage, to be exact. I lived on five hundred acres of land in Virginia."

"What's an ecovillage?" She continued eating her soup.

"*Not* a cult, if that's what you're thinking. It's a place for people to live who want to be outside the mainstream, but not completely isolated from it. Like, I wasn't homeschooled but went to public school, and although we didn't have television, we rented movies. Everyone shared everything, including income, which came from farming the land for the soy to make tofu. The people were peace-loving and nonviolent and…your mouth is hanging open."

It was. She couldn't help it. Movie-star gorgeous Pete Robbins had grown up on a *tofu* farm? "Sorry. I, uh, was just wondering what your parents think about you being in the military. Peace-loving and nonviolent seem counterintuitive to your profession."

He shrugged. "Your guess is as good as mine. As I said, they never criticize."

"I think I can sort of relate. More than half the crazy shit *I* do is to make sure I impress my dad, like I'm some sort of dancing monkey, you know, holding a coin cup out to him."

"Really? Looking at your résumé to date, I'd think your dad would be plenty proud of you—no extra effort required."

She set down her soup spoon. "If I'd gone into the family business, probably. But I had the audacity to go legit." She stood.

Her sudden movement caught him by surprise—his chin pulled in.

"I think I should head off to bed now." This cucumber didn't need to be peeled any more than she already was, and a discussion about her complicated relationship with her father would scrape off another layer. "I have an early appointment with the makeover team tomorrow for a ball gown fitting." She started across the room. "I'll see you soon, all right?"

"Hold up a second."

She turned around at the door. "Are you okay?" She checked eyes with him. "I don't mean to leave if you aren't."

A small smile toyed with his mouth. "I'm good, thanks. I just want to ask you out on a date."

"A what?" It was like he'd dropped a beehive on her head—the question set off a frantic buzzing in her ears.

"A *date*." He chuckled, the flecks of gold surrounding his irises dancing. "I'll define it for you: not slinging back drinks at a military bar. Not scarfing down a drunk-prevention Rueben sandwich. Not boring room service. But a bona fide go-out-to-dinner date. Candlelight. Wine." He grinned. "Pete Robbins at his most charming."

A tinge of panic squirmed through her belly.

Trouble, trouble, trouble…

"The Ministry of Defense ball isn't till Saturday night, which leaves tomorrow night free. How about it?"

The idea whisked around her mind, making her feel like she was a doll that'd been put together incorrectly: the wrong head on the correct body. Because why would she hunger for risk in her profession, but then be so afraid of it in her personal life?

"I'm not asking for any big commitments to a relationship, Justice. Only the next step."

She clasped the doorknob and smoothed her hand over it. She *had* told him she was taking things one step at a time—and a date was a reasonable next step. "Well…" She gave him a slow perusal. "Will you have taken a shower by then?"

He grinned, a whole lot of Brad Pitt socking her softly in the gut.

CHAPTER FIFTY-SEVEN

SHOWERED, SHAVED, AND wearing dark slacks and a Navy blue button-down, Pete combed his hair in the bathroom mirror and considered options for taking Justice out tonight. Probably be a good idea to ask the hotel concierge for a restaurant recommendation, since he knew fuck-all about Moscow's fine dining scene. Planning for a porterhouse and ending up with the equivalent of a Happy Meal would be the kind of rookie mistake he hadn't made since…well, ever.

Someone knocked on his door.

He looked at his watch—too early for Justice. "Dumb-ass," he muttered, tossing his comb on the sink.

Willie had gone out to pick up their tuxedos from the CIA makeover team and forgotten his keycard.

Pete strode out of the bathroom and crossed his bed-room.

The room was nice, actually, although a bit uninspiring with the décor running along the color wheel from brown to beige. Two cushioned armchairs plus a lamp on a low table were assembled in a conversational grouping a few feet inside the main door. Beyond that arrangement were two king-sized beds—set more to the left side of the room. To the right was a mini round table and two ladderback chairs. More to the right was the bathroom he'd just exited.

Pete opened the main door and—

Tiffany Tesarik reeled inside. "He won't go out with me!" she wailed.

Jay-sus. Pete stuck a finger to his ear, then swore under his breath. *Shit, a Tesarik meltdown.* He didn't have time for one. He still needed to make a dinner reservation and buy some flowers, but Tiffany's face was red and bloated, sure signs she was already three-quarters of the way into a full tailspin.

Sniffing and snuffling, she stomped over to the comfy chair setup. "Here we are in Moscow, at a nice, romantic hotel, and Nate won't even go out for one drink with me. *A drink!*" She emphasized this offensive word in air-raid decibels that made Pete's ears bleed and his sinuses explode.

He popped his jaw and peered at the hand he still had wrapped around the doorknob. Maybe if he just pushed the door shut, Tiffany would cease to have entered.

"Why, Pete, *why?*"

Casting a last longing glance at the hallway of freedom, Pete closed the door. "Have you told Willie you like him, Tiffany? Directly. He's the type of guy who needs a two-by-four smacked across the top of his head."

"Yes." Tesarik marched farther into Pete's room, stopping near his bed. "Last time you and I talked, you told me to tell him, so I did. I…I-I…" Her eyes grew liquidy.

Here come the floodgates, opening wide.

Her lips wobbled. "I don't get it. Nate's such a nice, sweet man to everyone else. Why isn't he nice to *me?*" Tiffany dropped her face into her palms and sobbed, the whole deal—shoulders shaking, tears dripping through her fingers.

Pete went to her. "All right, now, come on." He pulled her into a comforting hug.

"What am I going to do?" she asked, weeping louder.

Pete didn't know about her, but *he* was going to rip Willie's balls off, hold them out to the dumb-ass, and ask, *Do you want to give these jobbies some relief or not?*

And, by the way, there were other people around here

with balls in need of tending—balls recently sacrificed to God and country—who should be concentrating on *that* instead of your stupid love life.

Pete gave Tiffany brotherly pats on the back as she had herself a good cry. He studied the carpet pattern—it looked like a kid's game of Pick-up Sticks had been steamrolled into the low pile—and made sure to murmur the occasional *there, there now.*

Squeak.

The noise brought Pete's focus up.

Hey! Justice!

She was standing next to Willie near the comfy setup, but who cared about his copilot. *She* looked amazing, a flowy miniskirt showcasing her awesome forever legs—God help him—with a form-fitting green shirt on top, her hair gathered in a sleek braid.

On its next beat, his heart bounded forward. Holy fuck, she'd dressed nicely for their date—she was taking it seriously! His chances of successfully nudging her in the direction he wanted her to go—toward a relationship—just rose a couple of notches.

Oorah! He would've pumped his fist in the air if he wasn't still holding onto Tiffany.

Oh, yeah…Tiffany.

He gently set her aside. "Hey-oh-ay." His upbeat greeting dropped into the lower regions of his voice box, like a *Happy Days* Fonz doll running out of battery. He'd just noticed Justice's expression.

Thunderous.

Storm clouds roiled on her brow, lightning forked in her eyes, and her stance was wide and combative.

Next to her, Willie's complexion was bilious.

Tiffany made a sound of dismay.

Oh, shit. Pete held up a single finger to them. "No."

Justice sneered. "Pete the Penis."

CHAPTER FIFTY-EIGHT

PETE TURNED HIS upraised pointer finger toward Tiffany. "That's not what it looked like."

"Of course not," Justice shot back in an acid tone. "Guilty people never say that."

He shook his head. "You're not going to do this, Justice. Tesarik came here to talk to me. She's upset about this dumb-ass." He flung a gesture at Willie. "And I was helping her. Nothing more."

Justice's chest heaved through a couple of breaths. "Was anything you said and did for me last night real?" Despite her rage, her voice came out a little cracked.

His chest jerked. It felt like she'd hit him—he would've rather she *had* struck him than say that. "You think what went on between us over SERE was some kind of game?"

"*Everything* you do is a game." A pinched line throbbed on her forehead, the natural human cover-up for pain returning—fury. "Played by the player," she hissed. "Never again."

Turning abruptly, she aimed long, aggressive strides for the door.

He chased after her. The fuck if he was getting shut out of her life again.

Grabbing her arm, he spun her around.

She wrenched out of his hold and glared at him.

He manufactured a tone of excessive calm. "Let me talk to you about this. Five minutes. Two."

"I'm too angry to talk."

Yes. Clearly. The riot of emotions in her eyes was at full boil. *Let her go and calm down, talk to her about it later.* Yeah. Sounded reasonable. The right choice. Except another part of him was like *screw that!* He'd already waited forever for her behind a shut door, and tonight she was damned well wearing a miniskirt.

She turned toward the door again.

I walked away without a word to anyone. Nothing ever got worked out…

He seized her arm once more.

She spun back around, but this time her fist swung up too. *Wham!* She plowed a solid punch into his left eye.

He *wuufed* a breath and rocked back on his heels, the strength behind the blow sending him into a stagger. Flinging an arm out in automatic search for balance, he connected with the lamp on the low table. It hit the floor with a loud *smash!* and broke apart.

Tiffany screamed.

Still stumbling, Pete clattered through the tiny porcelain pieces as he fought to find his feet. He'd spoken too soon about wishing Justice had hit him instead of casting aspersions against his good character, because *ow!*

"Jesus Christ, you hit hard!" Pain was radiating from the back of his abused eyeball and pounding through the entire left side of his face.

"Oh, my God, stop!" Tiffany bawled. "Please don't. Pete's right—it's not what you think."

"Shut up," Justice growled. Brows down, she turned back around and continued her charge for the door.

Willie dashed out of her way.

Pete sprinted past her, arriving at the door first. His breaths coming quick and ragged, he body-blocked her way out. "You're not leaving here thinking what you're thinking, Justice. Forget it."

She gave him a dark look of warning. "Move away from the door, Pete."

"No."

She stepped back, her nostrils going white at the edges.

All the fine hairs on his body rose as she looked him over with cool precision, clearly planning to do something to take him out. He'd never been looked at like that before, like maybe she was measuring him for a body bag.

He held out a staying hand. A calming hand. A hand in possession of all the powers of Superman and Batman combined. There was always hoping that, at least. "All right, now. All right. Whatever it is you're planning on doing, don't do it."

She tilted her head to one side, a cunning, ominous glint in her eyes. "I was just going to show you what you're missing by being an asshole."

"I'm not an asshole."

She untucked her T-shirt.

He stilled.

"Are you watching?"

He was. Warily. But also with a throat full of *oh-God-yeah-baby* when she hooked her thumbs into the bottom hem of her shirt and started to lift it.

She bared her waist.

His mouth came open for a second before he caught himself and shut it with a *click* of his teeth. He'd never seen a waist like hers before, taut and flat and curvy. Defined muscles showed with her deeper intakes of breaths, but the whole beautiful sight was covered with honey skin that was one-hundred percent womanly smooth.

"After my gown fitting, I went out shopping," she told his googly brain, "especially for *you*. I found this at a store selling kitschy American paraphernalia." She lifted the shirt up past her breasts.

His eyes popped wide enough to eject from their sockets.

She was wearing a Budweiser bikini.

Holy Jesus Christ on high. She'd made herself into a Budweiser bikini contest girl.

For *him.*

His esophagus closed around an unrecognizable emotion. "We can…" He cleared his throat. "We can work this out."

"You want to see more of what you're missing?"

Willie crab-shuffled over for a better view.

"Get out," Pete snapped.

One of Justice's eyebrows rose.

Not you. "Willie, Tiffany. Go." Pete cracked the door wide enough to rid the room of the only two witnesses to his murder.

Banging the door shut, he gave Justice a level stare, although not *that* level, because her tits were right fucking there, and *come on.* "I know you said you're angry, and it's clear you are, but this is something we can easily work out if you would *listen* to me."

Down the hall, he heard Willie and Tesarik yelling at each other.

Justice tugged her T-shirt off.

Pete's eyes crossed; saliva filled his mouth; his pelvic bones locked up.

A full view of the bikini top showed it consisted of not much more than two small triangles covering her nipples. The rest of her breasts were visible, and very bouncy-looking.

The muscles around Pete's battered eye throbbed. He was clenching his jaw too tight.

A door slammed down the hall. The arguing cut off.

Silence…except for the *hishing* of what sounded like a wet-vac working at the other end of the hallway.

Justice sauntered a couple of steps toward him.

Pete narrowed his eyes at her. "Stop."

Draping her T-shirt over one wrist, Justice unbuttoned her skirt.

"Don't make me pull rank on you," he threatened.

A peek of the Budweiser logo showed at her open zipper.

It was like when he opened his mouth only little birdies came out.

"Here's more of what you don't get." She turned around and pointed her fanny at him, dipping her waistband down just enough to show the part of her bikini bottom traveling along the line of her butt.

God All-Fucking-Mighty. He wrapped a fist around the doorknob and chewed on the air in his mouth.

"It's a thong. See?"

Heat rushed from his groin down his thighs. He saw the firm globes of her naked ass peeking above the droopy waistband. He saw the shapely swell of her hamstrings. A low moan climbed his throat. His hand went numb around the doorknob.

"Do you see?"

"I see." His voice was low and husky. Forcing in a short breath, he made sure to firmly plant all four points of his feet on the floor. He was about to fall on her like a sex-starved beast-thing, and he couldn't do that. There were still important things to discuss. Very important things. Any second now they would come out of his mouth, and all would be resolved.

Hiking up her skirt, she turned back around and fastened it.

Well, she'd done it—applause all the way around—she zapped his brain of all functionality. When she sauntered toward him again, twirling her T-shirt, he was in no fit state of mind to see her trap.

Not until it was too late.

CHAPTER FIFTY-NINE

PETE JOLTED HIS chin back but not fast enough.

On the next twirl of her shirt, Justice whipped the material around the back of his neck, then grabbed the free end and crisscrossed the shirt in front of his throat in a stranglehold. Dropping her weight down, the tails of her garrote held strongly in her fists, she jerked him off the door.

The Valkyrie was as fast as she was strong, and only his years on the high school wrestling team enabled him to clap an arm around her waist before his right shoulder slammed to the carpet—karate and boxing hadn't been allowed, but for some reason his parents let him wrestle.

Coughing instead of breathing, Pete performed a reversal-and-escape and surged to his feet.

Justice hopped upright too, immediately launching herself at the door.

He caught her in a bear hug, trapping her arms against her sides.

She growled and arched, pushing him into an arch with her. "Let me fucking leave!" She cocked her legs back and slammed her feet into the door. The psi of force her strong legs were able to produce sent him hurling backward at a tearing pace.

He tripped and fell.

They hit the carpet in a mix-up and rolled across the room, not stopping until they crashed into the mini dining setup. The ladderback chairs exploded out from the table, slewing across the floor at odd angles, one toppling over with a sickening *crack* of breaking legs.

Justice and Pete flew apart in a carpet-burning skid-out.

Justice sprawled on her back with a moan.

He struggled up on his knees, yanking off his shirt garrote. His head was hammering. He'd skull-rammed the base of the table.

Justice swayed to a sitting position, fumbling to adjust her bikini top. Her braid was sprouting hairs at haphazard angles. She peered at him with glassy eyes, blinking to clear her vision. The table base hadn't been nice to her either—blood suddenly flooded from her nose.

"Shit." He shoved himself to his feet. "Dammit, Justice!" Hoisting her up, he sat her on his bed, then stalked into the bathroom. He came back out with a hand towel and thrust it at her.

She took it and pressed it to her nose.

He inhaled a great breath—deep, deeper, deepest—then leaned into her face and exhaled the full lungful of air in a raging bellow. "*Why don't you ever believe in me?!*"

Her eyes widened above the towel.

Yes, very non-Pete behavior, the full-on bull-bellow. But the usually no-stress Pete Robbins was very much full of stress at the present moment. "After everything you and I went through about SERE, after I was *there* for you, you see me with Tesarik, and you think the worst."

"You were hugging her," Justice muffled from behind the towel.

"We were fully clothed," he countered. Which a lame argument—he'd been known to undress at record speeds. "She was crying. I was comforting her."

Justice lowered the towel. "So, let me see if I've got this straight. You're saying I'm allowed to hug a man, alone in my hotel room, if I'm only offering him comfort. That's okay with you?"

He lashed the sweat off his brow with his forearm and glowered. *Don't put it that way, damn you…putting it that way is very fucking aggravating.*

"Besides, just because you weren't screwing Tiffany a few minutes ago doesn't mean you haven't been screwing her all along. My *roommate*," Justice added savagely.

"I have not."

"I see you two together all the time, wrapped around each other in chummy huddles."

"Tesarik and I are not *wrapped*. She's always bugging me for advice about Willie. She's been in love with the donk ever since we boarded the ship. Which is something you would've clearly seen if you didn't always see the worst in me." He exhaled a harsh breath. "What do I have to do to convince you to trust me, Justice? Tell me. I'm the man who defied orders to fly into unauthorized airspace to rescue your ass. I'm the one who withstood torture to stop you from being murdered. What else do I need to do on top of that? *What?*"

"I…" Her face flamed. "I don't know. Nothing. I…" The next words burst out of her. "I'm just incredibly insecure around you!"

Pete braced his hands on his hips. "Why?"

"*Why!*" She clenched the towel in her fist. "You're a total player, Pete."

He threw his arms out from his sides. "Why do women always think that a player wants to stay a player? Maybe he's just waiting for the right woman to come alone."

"Is that supposed to be me?"

"Yes! For Christ's sake, I've been trying to get you into a relationship practically from the start."

"That doesn't fucking matter."

He blinked at her. "How the hell do you figure that?"

Her throat jerked. "I may be able to *get* you, Pete, but I won't be able to keep you. You get bored at the drop of a hat. And I'm not... I don't want to have to be a dancing monkey for you too." Her lower lip suddenly looked a little swollen.

He stared at her—at the filaments of fragile hair swaying up from her head, like spring's first tender shoots waving gently in a field, and gooseflesh sprayed over his forearms on a sudden flush of cold realization.

Oh, shit. Oh, crap. This *was* bad on him. He saw it so clearly now, why Justice had such a hard time believing in him, why she immediately jumped to seeing the worst in his behavior, why she was insecure about his intentions.

Because she was right; he *had* been playing her. He'd been handling her like any other conquest to land in the sack—negotiating situations to his best advantage, leveraging her emotions, directing her where he wanted her to go...*Operation Get Justice.* What the hell was that, anyway?

He'd forgotten to just make her feel like what she was to him: special.

Everything you do is a game!

Just getting a little sick of the show, is all.

You always know the exact right thing to say, don't you, to bend the human psyche to your will?

He'd blown this. Very badly.

He opened his mouth, but his tongue tangled around what he should say now. He had to get this next part right. It was very important. "You need ice for your nose," he said abruptly. "It's swelling."

Frowning, Justice touched her nose experimentally.

He grabbed the ice bucket off the nightstand.

She watched him with an uncertain look.

"Wait here." He headed out the door.

In the hall, Willie was leaning against the wall outside of

Tiffany and Justice's hotel room next door.

When Pete approached, Willie pushed straight. "Hey, wow, lotta noise coming from inside there, Bingo. You okay?"

"Yes." *Ish.* Echoes of pain were still tugging the corner of his left eye into a wince, and the bump on his head felt as big as a pomegranate. He stepped past Willie and knocked on the door.

It opened on Tesarik's cautious face. Her brows jumped when she saw it was Pete.

"Please grab Justice's things for me," he said to her.

Tiffany's focus shifted briefly to Willie, then she nodded and ducked back inside, leaving the door open a crack.

Pete strode farther down the hall to the ice machine.

Willie observed him, his hands jammed in his pockets.

Pete scooped cubes into the plastic bucket.

Nothing ever felt real when I was growing up. Not my upbringing. Not the flashy, notorious man my father was…

You're flashy and larger-than-life, and being around you pings the side of me that wants to be flashy and impressive too…

More than half the crazy shit I do is to make sure I impress my dad, like I'm some sort of dancing monkey, you know, holding a coin cup out to him…

I don't want to have to be a dancing monkey for you too…

My mother died giving birth to me.

Pete paused in the act of scooping and closed his eyes. He'd just put it all together, the real reason Justice kept pulling away, and it wasn't about him. She was trying to find a large part of who she was and chasing after an impossible way to get it—and it was this very chase making it so difficult for her to relax into a relationship with him.

He slowly shut the ice machine lid. Tucking the plastic bucket into the crook of his left arm, he walked back to Willie and grabbed his friend by the shirtfront in his right fist.

I may be able to get you, Pete, but I won't be able to keep you...

Pete hauled Willie inside Tesarik's room.

Tiffany gasped and froze with Justice's suitcase clutched to her breasts.

Pete released Willie but spoke to Tesarik. "Nate keeps saying no to you because he thinks that even if he gets you, he won't be able to keep you. You want him, Tiffany, you need to convince him that's not true."

Tiffany bit her lip.

Pete rounded on Willie. "If she can't do that, then find another room to stay in tonight. I'm taking ours. But"—he looked between them both—"I really hope the two of you can finally quit being idiots."

Pete took the suitcase from Tiffany and left, closing the door securely behind him.

CHAPTER SIXTY

PETE THUMPED THE ice bucket back on the nightstand and stood in front of Justice with his hands on his hips. "This is all my fault. I fucked up."

Justice didn't say anything. She eyed him warily, like any second a Chucky-faced Jack-in-the-box would sproing out of his mouth, screaming a maniacal *haha, JK!*

"Played by the player," he said. "Okay. No denials. You're not totally wrong. Yes, I've been playing you, although I didn't mean to—I wasn't aware of what I was doing until a few minutes ago. I've been so intent on getting you, I was using all my best techniques to make it happen instead of just being myself. So, yeah, I guess on some level you've been dealing with a fake Pete, and I'm sorry. I don't want to be that way. You might not believe it, but I'm sick of all the game-playing it takes to be with a woman. The obligatory arts 'n' crafts and finagling a man has to do out there. I want to be real with a woman—with *you*. If you'll give me the chance, I think I can."

He went into the bathroom to give Justice a few seconds to absorb that. He wetted two hand towels, then returned to the bedside table and filled both with ice. He handed her one.

She pressed it gingerly to her nose.

He applied the other to his left eye. "Your dancing monkey worries? Set those aside. The idea of me ever getting bored with you is laughable. Just thinking about you is better than my best day in a cockpit. Being in the same room with you is like a ride on the space shuttle. A man doesn't tire of a woman who has that kind of effect on him. It means she's the one. It means he loves her."

Justice's eyes widened.

"But here's the real money shot—the truth about the dancing monkey worries. Prepare yourself, Justice. This one's going to pack a wallop."

She blinked rapidly.

"You're not trying to impress your dad or me or yourself with all the flashy shit you do. You take on impossible challenges to please your *mom*." He gentled his tone. "She died giving birth to you, so…so I think you want to prove to her that you grew into the kind of daughter who was worth a mother giving her life for."

Justice's mouth fell open as her hand dropped down from her nose. Ice cubes rolled out of the towel and thunked to the floor, skipping across the carpet before spinning to a stop. She gaped at him, all big eyes and pale skin.

It was the reaction he'd expected, but it was still a bitch to watch. "The thing you need to remember, though, is that if your mom were alive today, she would love you no matter what—warts and bad breath and mean right hook and all. She's not around to tell you, which sucks. It means you have to find a way to accept it on your own."

His left eye was going numb. He switched the ice towel to the bump on his head. "Sit back. Live in the moment. Relax, and realize that there isn't a damned thing you need to do. Not for your mom *or* your dad." He lowered his voice an octave. "Not for me."

The sides of her nostrils fluttered.

"You don't have to be alone in this, either. Have you ever heard it said a person can't be fully with another until he or she really knows themselves? I think that's why you've been shying away from a relationship with me—you've needed to figure yourself out. But why can't it actually be *better* for you to work on your stuff with someone at your side, supporting you, helping you make sense of shit? No one should have to deal with their crap single-handedly." He lowered the ice towel. "That's my opinion anyway. What do you think?"

"I…I don't know." She hefted a breath.

Considering she was practically bare-breasted, he was very proud of himself for not looking down. Well, he might've peeked. A little.

"I guess…" Her expression turned thoughtful, then she smiled unsteadily. "I guess I think *thank you*. You've really opened my eyes, Pete. It's clear I've got a lot of stuff to work on, but…you're right. I don't want to do it alone."

His heart tripped out of rhythm. "So does that mean we're together?"

"If you're sure you still want me."

"Of course, I do." He couldn't remember a time when he hadn't.

"I just punched you a minute ago." She grimaced. "I'm sorry."

He waved it away. She *had* told him numerous times that she wanted to leave.

"Well, okay, then. You've got yourself a girlfriend, Pete. God help you."

"Yeah? Oorah."

She snorted and rolled her eyes. "You say that just to annoy me."

"True." He paused a brief second to pinch himself internally to make sure he wasn't dreaming. *Nope.* Hot Stuff Hardbody Hayes had just said *yes* to a relationship. "Alrighty then." He tossed aside his ice towel. "Time to have at that awesome ass." He took her by the shoulders and turned her around, then grabbed the back of her skirt and hiked her up to the middle of the bed, laying her flat on her belly.

She released a surprised breath but didn't say "no" or "stop" or "ouch, my nose."

He reached around to the front of her waistband, undid the button, then tugged her skirt down to her knees with a single pull, exposing that hot-as-fuck Budweiser thong and a full view of the exquisite globes of her ass. A deep sound rumbled from his throat. Same as with her waist, her ass was unlike any he'd ever seen. Curvaceously rounded muscles resided beneath nubile flesh, and—

She wriggled her hips to get her skirt the rest of the way off, and he went erect so fast stars swam across his vision. He staggered back, blinking hard. More un-Pete-like behavior, but in his defense, this was hard-on number three when it came to her. First was in her stateroom on the *Richard*, second, in her hotel last night after Viktor's torture club—so *twice* now, he'd popped a raging boner and hadn't been able to use it.

If he was left hanging this third time, the damage might be extensive enough to prevent him from ever siring children. Considering all that, the extent of his control was already pretty much *gone*.

So…

He dove right in.

Leaping on her, he buried his face in her crotch in a move more worthy of a frat boy than the almighty Pete Robbins, but damn…*her ass*. He did a scrambling, knee-shift shuffle onto the bed, cranking himself around so that his chin fit neatly into the valley of her butt and his mouth came to rest against her Budweiser-covered sex. Inhaling the sweet scent of her natural perfume, he went to work on her, licking and probing and exploring.

She moaned and squirmed and arched her hips, the sexy

pleasure-fidgets electrifying his cock and weighting his balls with steel. He lifted his face, breathing roughly. The line of her thong was riding deeply into the folds of her labia and the whole area was soaked.

"Don't stop," she groaned.

He hopped off the mattress.

"And here I thought I'd spoken in English," she said.

"Stay right there." It was one of the faster times he stripped out of his clothes.

Bending over her, he glided his hands up her hips, sliding his fingers under her bikini's side-ties. With the strings lying across the backs of his fingers, he eased her bottom off, then tossed the garment aside. He straightened, taking in the sight of her labia peeking out from the wedge formed by the juncture of her thighs.

Best f'ing sight in the world.

His cock grew so heavily engorged the tips of his fingers tingled from lack of blood flow. It looked like she was a tight fit, too, and—

A mutinous swell of ejaculate rushed up his shaft.

He quickly grabbed his member and gave it a good squeeze. *Knock it off.*

"You okay back there?" she murmured.

He quickly let go of himself. "'Course."

"Do you want me to turn over?"

"Definitely not."

Balls throbbing, he climbed onto the bed and buried his face in her crotch again, but this time head on, his nose coming to rest near the bud of her ass. He began an unhurried devouring of her, tasting her more thoroughly without the thong in the way. She was zesty and tangy, like the woman herself, and her aroma was clean—even the musk of her butt.

Need ached in the pit of his belly as these basic human

smells nestled deep into his nose. If a woman smelled right, she was right, and Justice smelled perfect.

Using long, downward reaches of his tongue, he slid the length of her slit all the way to her clitoris, lingered there for a few flickering caresses, then dragged back up and suckled her opening. It was a signature skill of his, being able to do both tongue-moves and sucking-action in such a synchronized way, and Justice didn't disappoint in letting him know how much she appreciated his unique talent.

"Oh-oh-oh-oh-oh-oh-oh," spilled throatily from her, nonstop. Her all-over body tension heightened, her hips trembled, and her fists closed and released around the bedspread. When her juices ran freely into his mouth, he knew he had her.

He pushed up onto his knees.

"Pete," she gasped. "Why do you keep stopping? I'm about to come."

What, was he an amateur? Like he couldn't tell? "Thanks for the info, hot stuff." Seizing her by the hips, he lifted her onto her knees. "Press your chest flat to the mattress, but keep your ass up."

A shudder ran through her. "What are you doing?"

"You'll see."

She did as he asked, presenting her backside to him.

A white-hot bolt lanced through his balls. Taking a strong grip on her waist, he pushed inside her, hissing a stream of air all the way in, his head falling back on his neck. He'd forgotten how great flesh-on-flesh was. He hadn't been condom-free since his last monogamous relationship, eons ago, but this... Justice felt even better. Like the way her inner muscles clutched him was somehow both tender and strong.

Maybe this was what having sex with a woman you were crazy in love with felt like.

Maybe he loved her even more than he realized.

Maybe she was just tight as fuck.

He sucked a breath through his nose and moved inside her, normal at first, lubing up his cock, getting a sense of her, but it didn't take long for his balls to start thrumming. *Get going, man.* Because…*argh…ho, damn.*

"Stay like that," he panted. Stretching up high on his knees, he pounded into her at an angle—scientifically proven to hit her G-spot on every penetration.

"Oh, God!" she shouted. "God!" She screamed louder when her inner muscles clamped down around his dick and strangled it.

"Grunch," he said.

Grunch? His lungs expanded with pleasure and laughter, and for a fleeting moment he wondered where the hell hotel management was. A lamp had been broken, a ladderback chair, Willie and Tesarik had yelled at each other, and now Justice was screaming in orgasmic bliss, and—

"Ah!" And now *he* was making strange, loud noises, digging his fingers into her hipbones as he surged into her with his most powerful thrusts. His balls wrenched into his body and his pelvis lit up. *Yeah…fuck, yeah…* His member bucked convulsively, each eruptive spasm sending ecstasy racing throughout his entire body. He shouted even louder and bumped his hips jarringly against Justice's ass, plunging as deep as he could go for the last—

Suddenly his lungs congested. *Too good…too good…* He jammed his eyes shut. Spots danced behind his lids. He uttered a few untranslatable words, then reared up and fell over backwards.

Flinging his arms wide, he inhaled a long shuddering breath…then everything went dark.

Chapter Sixty-One

JUSTICE CUDDLED HER naked backside closer to Pete's warmth. He had bestirred himself enough to assume the big spoon position, and the rhythm of his breathing was also steady and even, so she supposed he was all right. *Still.* Oddest conclusion to sex, ever.

Leave it to Pete.

The guy never did anything normally.

He was a man of great contrasts, operating at either one end of the spectrum or the other, and rarely languishing in the mundane middle.

He was all about a good time—fun and jokes and pranks.

Until.

He was blowing her away with the depth of his wisdom.

But that doesn't mean what happened at SERE wasn't real—having control taken from you made it that way.

I think you want to prove to your mom that you grew into the kind of daughter who was worth a mother giving her life for.

He never took life seriously.

Except.

When he did.

It was up to me to keep you safe, Justice. Me.

Who hurt you?

He was an unreliable goof, messing around and pushing her buttons.

Unless.

He chose to be utterly and totally there for her.

I'm the man who defied orders to fly into unauthorized airspace to rescue your ass.

I wanted to save you.

Sighing, she drew Pete's forearm more snugly around her waist.

Pull…

…and more pull.

She was finally out of the square dance.

Her tummy gave a testy grumble, and she checked the bedside clock. It was past dinnertime, probably too late to make a dinner reservation. They'd have to settle for room service again. She reached for the menu next to the ice bucket.

"What's going on?" Pete asked.

No hint of sleepiness was in his voice. She glanced over her shoulder and saw his gaze was clear. He wasn't even rumpled, just ready to go, and, er, a bit bruised.

"I was going to order food. We could both use some sustenance after all that." She felt the corners of her mouth twitch. "Especially you."

"*Especially* me?"

"You fainted."

He laughed. "Nuh-uh. That was a post-romp nap."

"A rather sudden one."

"Ah, well…" He propped his head on his hand. "I'm what you might call a sex narcoleptic."

She rolled over to face him. "You mean you do that all the time after sex?"

"Pretty much."

"But then…how do you have sex in an elevator or on the beach?"

"I don't."

"But…" She hesitated. *But you're Pete the Penis.*

"Yes?" he drawled.

"I just always imagined you doing it everywhere. You know, behind vending machines or on the back nine or at the La Brea Tar Pits."

He laughed. "I do it wherever I can give my woman the best attention." He nudged her shoulder. "That would be you, by the way." He rolled her back over and clasped an arm around her waist, pulling her against him.

"Hey. Food."

"Fuck again first, then food." His hand smoothed down her belly to her mons, his fingers brushing through the trimmed hair there. "Have you ever considered shaving this?"

She rolled her eyes. "Since I'm neither a porn star nor a pre-pubescent female, the answer to that would be *no.*"

"Hey, no need to go all Gloria Steinem on me." He nuzzled her nape. "It's just so I can get at you better for certain things."

Dear God. Like what? "You get at me plenty well enough as it is." Although, *what a way to die.*

He laughed. It was his barrel-like laugh, the one that conveyed all sorts of knowledge beyond the normal pale, certainly way outside of her—apparently—ignorant sphere.

He fit her butt more neatly into the cup of his hips.

Her body immediately sent up signals of agreeing with his plan to wait on food. She traced the raised veins on the back of his hand. "You do realize I have a decent front side, too, right?"

He hummed in his throat. "Not done with your back-side yet." He nipped her ear. "I was thinking a little rear entry action might be—"

She blasted away from him.

His fingertips hooked her hipbone, stopping her. He

laughed deep in his throat.

She looked over her shoulder at him again, her heartbeat bouncing around at a crazy tempo. "Are you fucking nuts?"

He peered at her from beneath his dark lashes. "I know how to make it feel good."

"Oh, I bet you do." She'd always known this man was going to be out of her league, although she should've guessed by just how much when it turned out Pete had no appreciable terror-lock, not even a millisecond's worth. *No.* Pete Robbins of the movie-star smiles didn't go into terror-locks.

He put others into them.

She was in one now.

He towed her persistently back toward him.

She scrabbled her feet on the sheets. Didn't work. She was against him again, the solid prod of his erection bumping her butt cheek.

"How the hell are you already so hard?" she asked, still looking over her shoulder.

"Well, uh…you know…you obviously have a virgin butt." He smiled bashfully. "It's really turning me on."

"That's right…I'm a virgin…or, uh, my butt is…my butt's a virgin…" *Ladies and gentleman, this is what it looks like to grasp at straws.* "I'm thinking maybe I'm not ready for this. You know, maybe after you, um…"

"Buy you dinner first?"

She snorted. "I was thinking more like a *car*."

Chortling, he rolled away from her, dug something out of his suitcase, and rolled back. It was a packet of lubricant.

"You keep lube in your bag?"

"A Navy man's best friend on long deployment." He tore the packet open with his teeth, then conducted covert operations behind her back and below her waist.

Her breathing sped up. "What are you doing back there?"

"Did you go to the bathroom today?"

She assumed he meant *numero dos*. "So you're going to throw in sexy talk now, are you?"

He laughed.

Nice to know he was having such a good time.

His lubricated fingers slid along the cleft of her butt, and she stared at the hotel wall with wide-open eyes. His fingers remained at her anus for extra lube application, inserting inside her a bit.

She stiffened.

"Hey." Setting his other hand on her hip, Pete whispered into her ear, "Relax, hot stuff, you're going to like this. Anything happens you don't want to have happen, say 'bananas' and I'll stop." He pulled her thighs apart a bit and caressed her sex with his finger.

She forced herself to relax, but the *forcing* part didn't work, so her muscles remained clenched.

Pete teased her with his touch, running figure-eights through her folds, sweeping around her opening, then over her clitoris. His skillful caresses built pleasure on top of her tension. Nothing was happening in or near her butt, so her muscles finally loosened.

He stimulated her to the crest of climax, again and again, never letting her fall over the edge. A guttural sound broke from her. This man was the Supreme Grand Master Wizard of all-things-sex. She writhed and squirmed, her spine flexing. Perspiration filmed her body. Her core was desperate.

The blunt tip of his cock nudged her anus, but she could only care tangentially about her butt in her desperation. The head of his cock entered her—just the head—and a sharp burn flared as the ring of muscle gave way. She released a gritted-teeth groan.

Trailing kisses down the side of her throat, Pete carefully

worked his lubed cock inside her, all the while lightly caressing her clitoris, scattering her focus between the clench of her sex and the developing fullness behind her. His hips finally seated flush against her ass, and he uttered a low groan against her nape. The entire length of him was inside her, his chest heaving against her back. He paused, giving her time to adjust...maybe to say *bananas*.

The word never made it anywhere close to being uttered. Within two heartbeats, the pain faded to a vague discomfort, leaving behind the discovery of new nerve endings.

Pete began to slide slowly in and out of her, gradually increasing his tempo.

She tucked her chin down and fisted up a wad of pillowcase. The feeling of it was so intense it went way beyond the simplicities of pain or pleasure—the fullness was just too vast.

He escalated his attention on her clit, massaging the sensitive nerve endings.

Her breath stuttered. Her hips hitched.

"I'm going to make you come now," Pete told her in a husky voice.

If he said it, it happened, and as the first flush of pleasure overtook her, Pete dipped a finger inside her core and pumped in and out of her as he rocked his hips against her backside. A strained cry threaded between her teeth. The fullness behind her was ramping up the ecstasy of her orgasm to an uncharted high. Her body torqued beyond her control. The fullness wrapped from her behind to her front, and back again, all becoming one.

She'd never felt anything like it. She cried out again.

He finished with speed and power, his hips plunging vigorously, his breath ragged. He gave a hoarse shout, froze for a moment of full-body tension, his legs quaking against her hamstrings, then slumped onto her shoulder. His body weight squished her for the length of two gulped breaths, then he slid out of her and collapsed onto his back.

Panting, she tipped forward, landing face down in a spread-eagle position. *Oh, God... Oh, God...* Her brain seemed to be stuck in a stupefied do-loop. She fought for oxygen and maybe drooled. Her muscles were so relaxed now they were jelly.

I know how to make it feel good.

Holy wow. Yeah, he did.

No *bananas* for that rear entry action. None.

"Pete..." She turned toward him. "That was—"

She popped her eyebrows up.

He was face-jammed in a pillow, snoring softly.

She studied his handsome profile for an affectionate moment, then rolled over and pressed the back of her wrist to her mouth, laughing quietly.

Chapter Sixty-Two

THE RUSSIAN MINISTRY of Defense's ballroom was decorated with a bunch of garish swank, yards and yards of red bunting everywhere, miles and miles of tables with food displayed on silver trays and covered plates, candles flickering beneath chafing dishes almost in time to the music. A trio of Russian musicians were strumming *balalaikas* off a parquet dance floor placed center stage. A champagne fountain was at one end of the room, a chocolate one at the other, and the whole place smelled of money and corruption.

Pete switched his champagne glass from one hand to the other. Switched it back. Stuck a hand in his pocket and rattled his change. Fought the urge to rub off the itchy pancake makeup the CIA makeover team had troweled over his black eye.

He adjusted his belt, fighting another urge, this one to shove his waistband lower and give his nuts more room to breathe. The makeover team had tailored the tuxedo perfectly to his measurements, so it wasn't like his nuts *needed* room.

It was just that whenever Viktor cast Pete a penetrating look across the crowd of high-ranking guests, his balls creeped with the memory of being a couple of briquettes.

Maybe Pete's hands also itched a little with the urge to throttle the Russian. Last night the selfish asshole hadn't lifted a pinkie finger to try and save his wife—and his whole *fear-is-not-allowed-to-make-our-decisions* stance also put Justice in danger.

Selfish asshole was being too nice.

Pete had exchanged only a terse greeting with the Russian right after he and Justice/Jennifer arrived at the gala.

Viktor had demanded, "What happened to you Thursday night?"

Pete had put the smirk on his face he knew drove the Russian's ego crazy and drawled, "I didn't see the point in sticking around after you'd *fainted*, Mr. Minister, so I left *Drugoe Mesto*"—*I didn't hobble at all*—"and caught a cab back to my hotel."

Not a huge fan of that response, Viktor had stalked off to mingle and—

In his periphery, Pete saw Justice give him a subtle nod.

The makeover team had engineered a complicated up-style hairdo for her—a quasi-bun with a few wispy strands left to trail down the sides of her face—and stuffed her into a strapless black silk gown cut low enough across the tits that one wrong move and she'd be reenacting her own version of a Super Bowl nip slip—and making his night. For the entire party he'd been in suspense, just waiting for...*oh, yeah, right.* A nod meant she was sneaking upstairs to Viktor's office.

Dear Mr. Garcia of the Langley Garcias, sorry you weren't able to flex the CIA's might by getting your hands on Russia's long-range nap-of-the-earth missile plans. Pete "Bingo" Robbins was too much of a horn-dog to stay on task.

Earth to Pete...

Time to step up to the plate for his part of the job.

Distraction.

This time when Viktor glanced over, Pete slowly curled his mouth into his special ego-poke smirk.

That's right, buddy, keep your attention on me, not on the sneaky going-ons my un-wife is up to... And guess what, you weak little mole-rat? You didn't beat me.

Viktor's intense expression took on a dark edge of an-noyance.

No one has ever defeated our Minister of Defense…

Hah!

Jaw tight, Viktor made his excuses to the politician he was talking to and wended his way toward Pete.

What the man planned to say, Pete couldn't wait to hear, but the minister's progress was stopped by a uniformed lackey, who leaned toward Viktor's ear and spoke quietly.

Off Viktor's right shoulder, Pete spotted Willie, pre-tending to talk to some diplomat wearing a gold sash, while really eavesdropping on the convo.

Then—*bammo.* Lots of stuff happened right in a row.

Viktor frowned.

Willie gave Pete a mini-scrunch face.

Viktor strode off toward the elevator.

Willie made for Pete at a rapid clip.

"Whiskey Tango Foxtrot?" Pete asked his copilot in a low tone.

"That guard guy just told the minister he saw Mrs. McNamara on the fourth floor of the building."

The fourth floor was where Viktor's office was.

"Shit," Pete said.

"Yeah, Justice is going to get caught if you don't do something, Bingo."

JUSTICE STOLE SOUNDLESSLY down the corridor toward the Minister of Defense's office, tucking the Q-tip infused with Sokolov's DNA back into a small vial next to two tubes of lipstick. Should anyone have asked, the cotton stick was a special lipstick applicator. A bit strange? Yes, and, luckily, no one had even bothered to open the vial.

The guards who searched her purse on her way into the ballroom *did* examine with interest her mini listening cone. But she'd jammed a cigarette into one end to make it look like a cigarette holder, albeit an odd-shaped one. Thankfully, the guards let it go at that, probably having no idea what on earth else it could be.

Justice thanked God, or Pete, or thanked God that Pete had been able to recon Sokolov's safe prior to this job. The kind of small, beaded purse a formal gown required left little room for spare tools. Knowing that she only needed her listening cone had saved her from trying to figure out how to smuggle in lock picks or wire cutters…or how to explain *those* to the guards.

She ducked into Sokolov's office and instantly homed in on the monstrous steel safe located to the left of a large desk. A smile pulled at her mouth. "Come to mama," she whispered to the Ward-Lock 2—

An entire lungful of air spilled out of her.

Holy fuckity shit. The safe had two dials on the front.

Two.

It wasn't a standard-issue Ward-Lock 2000.

A heat-flash rippled along the entire length of her vagina.

It was a Ward-Lock 2000 *Class A*, even more difficult to burgle than the standard version: If the Ward-Lock 2000 was the Saint Bernard of all safes, the Class A was a Mastiff.

"Dear God," she hummed with a grin. "I think I'm going to wet myself."

This was *it*. The challenge of a lifetime. Never again in her career would she encounter such a profound test of her worth and skill as a thief.

Gathering up her skirt, she made for the safe and hunkered down in front of the big, beautiful beast. She inhaled a slow, deep breath, taking control of her nerves and settling her heartbeat.

Delicate work lay ahead.

Not only did she have two dials to tackle, but the Class A came with a time-lock feature. If she missed a decoy tumbler and pulled the handle while the tumbler sat in a fake slot, then the safe would be rendered inoperable for the next twenty-four hours.

Which would pretty much classify this as a Flop Op.

No pressure, right?

Yeah, except this kind of pressure was cool.

Fishing her listening cone out of her purse, she set it near the top dial and leaned her ear against it, hearing—

"What do you think you are doing in here?" Viktor Sokolov demanded.

Justice jolted back, spinning on her heels as ice clutched her spine. But—

She was alone in the room.

"What do you mean?" Pete answered down the hall. "You signaled for me to follow you."

"I did not."

"I thought… Well, anyway. I'm here now. It's time for us to settle the score, Viktor."

"You must wait a moment," Viktor returned. "I have to check something in my office."

Oh, shit. Someone must've made Justice on her way up to the fourth floor. *Shit, shit, shit.* She crab-walked on her haunches as quietly as she could with a rustling skirt, tucking herself into hiding behind Sokolov's desk. Anyone walking into the office wouldn't see her.

If that someone should happen to walk over to the safe, he'd see her clear as day.

"Are you avoiding me, Mr. Minister?" Pete goaded.

Footsteps stopped their progress toward the office.

Pete was buying her time. *Good.* Justice shuffled back to

the Class A.

"Let's go," Pete snapped out. "There's a window in the office across the hall where two metal bars are suspended from one building to another above the courtyard. I noticed banners hanging from the bars on the day Jennifer and I came for the tour."

Justice set her cone in place again, listening intently as she spun the top dial.

"You and I," Pete continued, "can compete in a little something called highlining."

The safe's tumblers whispered to her.

"What is that?" Viktor asked.

The first tumbler murmured into place. Justice slowly spun the dial in the other direction.

"It's tightrope walking," Pete explained, "but very high above the ground."

The second tumbler—

Justice stopped dialing. *Wait, what?*

Pete drawled, "You want to prove which one of us has the biggest balls. This is the ultimate test—no net, no safety ropes, no one else but you and me. First one across his bar to the other building wins."

Justice frowned. Was Pete off his fucking rocker? It was a four-story drop from up here. And as far as she knew, Pete had never practiced the art of highlining a day in his life.

Pete taunted, "Are you going to let fear make your decision, Mr. Minister?"

"No." Viktor gave his answer in clipped syllables. "I accept your challenge."

"Good," Pete responded. "Let's take off our shoes."

Shit. What was she going to do?

Work fast, that's what.

She flexed her fingers a couple of times but still didn't touch the safe.

The sound of clothes rustling as the two men took off their shoes and socks brought her back to the last time she'd battled it out with a Ward-Lock—Pete flinging women's lingerie around Commander Quinn's office, her with a pair of women's panties draped over her head.

The two of them had been having the time of their lives back then—a vastly different vibe from now.

Now, she faced real-world danger. Lives were at stake. Nations stood in the balance...

Right. Get to it.

The greater good trumped danger to one man.

At least that's what all the politicians in DC and the agents at Langley would say.

But those politicians and agents hadn't laid in Pete's arms last night, had they? They hadn't learned how Pete could take life seriously and be totally there for a person when necessary or how incredibly wise he truly was.

They hadn't met and fallen in love with Real Pete.

"You ready?" Pete asked Viktor.

A chill stroked Justice's spine. She had two dials' worth of decoy tumblers to get through, plus a time-lock feature hanging over her—this wasn't a fast safe crack. She wasn't going to be able to do this job quick enough to save Pete from climbing out that window.

A four-story fall might not kill Pete, but it would definitely break bones. And what if those injuries didn't heal completely? If he was permanently disabled, he'd never make it back into a cockpit.

I was the kid always at the top of the tallest tree or jumping off a roof. My whole life, I wanted to fly...

She swallowed tautly. How could she let him risk sacrificing such an essential part of himself?

Because he knew the risk he was taking?

But did he? Or was he being a dancing monkey too?

I think more than half the crazy shit I did in my life was to rile a reaction out of Mom and Dad. I guess I figured if they blew their tops that meant they loved me.

Justice closed her eyes against a timeless pain. How could she leave Pete to a fate that hit at her worst sore spot: You wanna be loved? Better perform well, then.

Pete needed to know that he didn't have to *do* anything to be loved either. No crazy-shit challenges required. *Relax, and realize that there isn't a damned thing you need to do. Not for your mom or your dad. Not for me.*

She opened her eyes.

Same goes for me, honey bunny.

Politicians and agents could require *her* to make sacrifices—but don't ask her to put those on the man she loved.

Springing to her feet, she gathered up her long skirt and dashed for the door.

Later she could figure out another way to pinch the missile plans.

For tonight the man meant more than the mission.

CHAPTER SIXTY-THREE

JUSTICE BURST INTO the office across the hallway and skidded to a stop. "What's going on?" she demanded.

Pete and Sokolov, hovering near an open window in their bare feet, snapped their gazes to her at the same time.

"Jennifer…" Pete began solicitously.

"You'd better not be up to one of your crazy stunts, Pete." She glowered at his bare feet. "What have I told you about that?"

Sokolov scowled. "How did you enter here?"

"The outer door was left open."

"Impossible."

Justice thunked her hands on her hips. "How else could I have got in?"

Eyes narrowed, Sokolov snatched the desk phone out of its cradle and barked Russian words into it.

Pete's focus edged over to her.

She shook her head in a nearly imperceptible motion.

He squinted a teensy bit. Uncomprehending.

Sokolov put his shoes and socks back on.

Pete did the same.

By the time the two men were put back together, three uniformed guards marched inside.

"Keep watch over Mr. and Mrs. McNamara," Sokolov charged his men, "while I verify all is well with my safe."

"Your safe?" Pete exclaimed, sounding affronted.

With a guard each escorting Justice and Pete across the

hall, the six of them assembled in Sokolov's office.

Sokolov bent to his safe, opened it, and riffled through the contents.

Pete stood erect, a vein in his temple visibly throbbing. He assumed Sokolov was about to find himself missing one red-and-yellow striped flash drive, but…

"Nothing is amiss," Sokolov declared with relief, some of the tension easing from his shoulders.

A shadow of a frown clouded Pete's face, and he flicked another glance at her.

She didn't offer him a reaction this time. She stayed focused on the minister.

Sokolov removed several items from his safe and tucked them inside his inner coat pocket.

"I don't understand what's going on," she said, adding a fair amount of peeved to her tone. "I came upstairs to use the bathroom, and when I saw my husband enter this office, I followed him in. That's all."

Straightening, Sokolov came to stand in front of her. "Why would you come to the fourth floor to use the bathroom?" he interrogated. "There is one near the ballroom."

"I know, but I wanted to go someplace private where I could be sick, and I remembered a bathroom being up here from the tour." She set a hand on her abdomen. "I'm in the early stages of a pregnancy." She rounded on Pete. "And if you think I'm going to sit around puking while you run off with you little friend to—"

"Honey, I—"

"No! I mean it, Pete!" She shoved him, then pretended the sudden movement knocked her off balance. She stumbled into Sokolov and gasped. "Oh!"

The minister grabbed her by the elbow and helped to right her.

"Excuse me." Lashes downcast, she said with the slightest quaver, "I-I want to go home."

Sokolov held up a staying hand. "You will go nowhere until my man Sergei confirms the integrity of my safe."

Every muscle in her body tightened. Would Sokolov's man be able to tell that she'd settled one tumbler into its spot on the top dial?

FORCED TO SIT mutely next to Justice on a bench in the rotunda room, the statue with the Charlie Chaplin mustache staring down at them with stately disapproval, Pete tried to use the stress-ridden downtime to figure out how to salvage the botched mission.

He came up dry.

No way could either he or Justice get near the missile plans tonight. There was just too much activity concentrated around Viktor, his office, and the monster safe.

Another night?

He didn't see that happening, either. Not with Viktor suspicious about Justice/Jennifer's foray to the fourth floor. Not now that Justice/Jennifer had scolded Pete for playing dangerous games with Viktor.

So where did that leave them?

Pete bounced his knee. Brilliance wasn't within his reach right now. His heart was still missing every other beat, which wasn't helping his ability to think. Mere minutes ago he'd been sure that he and Justice were well on their way to Siberia to be thrown into a secret prison and beaten with rubber hoses until one or both of them fessed up to where the stolen missile plans were hidden.

But then…

Nothing is amiss, Viktor had said.

Whiskey Tango Foxtrot?

Thirty minutes later, the minister finally released the McNamaras.

Pete exchanged a stiff farewell with Viktor, then flagged down Willie and Tiffany, those two looking a little drawn, and their group made a quick exit.

Outside the Ministry of Defense building, Pete had every intention of pulling Justice aside and strategizing a way to fix this catastrophe, but she set off rapidly on the twisty and turny route leading to their rental car, strategically parked for a speedy evac—should there have been need of one.

Which there wasn't.

The sound of four sets of shoe heels rapped loudly on cobblestones, echoing down a dark alleyway with muted, almost ghostlike resonance. Their swiftly moving legs churned steam billowing from a rusty wall pipe.

Well, their getaway was cinematic at least, if not totally unnecessary and stupid.

They arrived at the rental a little out of breath.

Pete popped the trunk on their suitcases—now was when they were supposed to change into casual traveling clothes.

Justice set her small, fancy purse inside the trunk and began to unzip her suitcase.

Pete didn't go for his own bag. "What the hell happened in there?"

Justice stopped unzipping and turned to face him. "I aborted the op."

"Aborted?" Absolutely last thing he'd expected to hear. "That botch-job was *on purpose?*"

She steadily held his gaze. "The safe was going to take me too long to open. You would've had to go out that window with Sokolov. So I made a call."

"And the call you made was to *no-big* New York being

flattened someday, just so I wouldn't have to walk across a metal bar?" He was astounded and wasn't even remotely trying to hide it.

On the other side of the car, Willie and Tiffany exchanged glances, then angled away, as if to give Pete and Justice some privacy. An utterly ridiculous move. Those two could still *hear* everything.

Justice asked, "How many times have you gone highlining, Pete?"

He didn't answer. Of course, his silence spoke the truth: zero.

"You don't think that call was hard for me to make?" She cut a gesture at the alleyway. "Do you have any idea what I gave up to prevent you from falling four stories, landing on your fool head, and killing yourself? A Class A, pal. Two"—she held up two fingers—"dials' worth of decoy tumblers and a time-lock feature. A fucking Mastiff."

He paused to stare at her Punky Brewster face, then strangled on a laugh that ended on a groan. She'd just taken all the wind out of him by being so damned adorable. "Everything you just said sounded like Charlie Brown's teacher to me, but…" He released a breath and added rawly, "nap-of-the-earth missiles with long-range capabilities."

"I know," she said. "But I figured we could come up with a way to steal the missile plans later."

"Really? Got any ideas on that you'd care to share?"

She smiled. "A plan isn't necessary anymore. When Sokolov was worried about the integrity of his safe, he removed several items from it. I saw him slip those things inside his coat pocket for safekeeping. So I stumbled into him and lifted them." She picked up her fancy purse from beside her suitcase and took out an envelope, handing it to Pete.

Brows high, Pete opened it and pulled out a stack of

photographs.

Willie and Tiffany crowded close to see.

Tiffany gasped.

"What the fuck?" Willie mused aloud. "Dick pics?"

Pete flipped through the photos. The pictures were of more than just Viktor's dick. They were of the minister in pornographic poses with a variety of women—none of whom were his wife.

Justice pointed at the envelope. "There's more."

Pete peered inside and—

He inhaled a sudden breath. A red-and-yellow-striped flash drive was tucked into the bottom corner of the envelope. He plucked it out and held it up.

"Oh, my God!" Tiffany jumped up and down, clapping. "You did it, Justice!"

"*We* did it," she corrected, smiling.

Willie hooted and punched Pete in the arm.

"Holy shit." Pete laughed from deep in his chest.

Several hairs in Justice's quasi-bun were swaying as if in time to a 21-gun salute of victory. "Little did Mr. Garcia know that something as simple as my pickpocketing skills would save the day."

"Why, you sneaky little pilferer," Pete drawled. "I should kiss you." *Well, hell.* Why wouldn't he? Clasping Justice around the nape, he tugged her forward and gave her a big ol' smackeroo on the lips.

She kissed him back, then looked up at him with little twinkles lighting the depths of her hazel eyes. "Sokolov is eventually going to realize the missile plans have gone missing from his pocket. So, you know...I'm thinking we should change clothes and beat feet to the airport now."

Pete wiped the grin off his face and adopted his gravest expression. "An excellent idea."

CHAPTER SIXTY-FOUR

Three weeks later
USS *Bonhomme Richard*
Indian Ocean

"WHAT'S THE DEAL, Bingo?"

Pete didn't look up from his computer screen. He just kept scrolling rapidly through the timeline on his Facebook page. *A huge bore.* One of the few times he had access to social media on the ship, and everyone was posting pics of what they ate for lunch. "You're going to have to be more specific, Willie."

The ship leaned hard to starboard, and Pete's chair skidded sideways. He quickly grasped the edge of his desk to prevent a collision with his bunk.

Yesterday the *Richard* had left the relatively protected inlet of the Sea of Japan for the open waters of the Indian Ocean, and they'd run into a fucking hurricane.

"Did you piss off Justice or something?" Willie kept at him.

"No," Pete said. "She's not hanging out with me because she's seasick." Which was why he was looking at someone's half-eaten burrito.

"Well, she must be doing better because one of the Marine pilots is spinning up to fly her on a mission."

That got Pete's attention.

"What?" He snapped his chin around. "Bullshit." If there was a mission to be flown, *he* would be the one flying it.

He'd been back on flight status ever since returning from Moscow, returning as he had looking like a military man who'd given his all for his country—with a lump on his head, a black eye, and bruises around his throat.

No one on Pete's team had seemed particularly interested in telling Captain Eagen the real reason behind Pete's injuries. And it wasn't like Pete *hadn't* given his all. If the SPECWAR commander needed more proof of Pete's dedication to the mission he could take a gander at Pete's roasted nuts.

Willie pointed an accusing finger at the door behind him. "I just came from the hangar. The pilot prepping for takeoff relished telling me that Lieutenant Hayes asked for him specifically."

"Nuh-uh," Pete countered. No way would Justice do that; she knew he was antsy to get back in the game.

For the past three weeks, there hadn't been even a whiff of trouble anywhere, and Pete was bored stiff…besides all the fun—and sex—he'd been having with Justice.

Willie made an exasperated sound. "I saw a bird being pre-flighted with my own eyes, Bingo."

"All right. Jesus." Pete stood. "I'll go talk to Justice." It being clear that his copilot wasn't going to quit harping on this. "Where is she? The hangar?"

"In her stateroom."

Pete made his way down the hall, veered right, then let himself into Justice's stateroom. Normally he would've knocked in case Tesarik was inside in some stage of undress, but since Willie was prowling the hangar, Tiffany had to be on duty and unavailable to hang out with, either—after a marathon date in Moscow, those two idiots were finally together.

Justice was bent over the bottom bunk, fiddling with

something, but when Pete stepped inside, she straightened abruptly. Her complexion was Kelly green.

Poor little sailor. She didn't have her sea legs on her today—which was kind of weird. The ship had sailed through rough weather before, and it hadn't fazed her. But earlier today, she got so woozy, she did a full rollout in the wardroom, landing smack on her ass.

After that Commander Cardoso had ordered her to report to the ship's corpsman, posthaste.

"Hey, hot stuff," he said. "Not feeling any better?"

"Uh…no. Not really."

"Aw, sorry. Can I bring you anything?"

The ship tilted. She slapped a hand on the upper bunk's railing while her other palm clutched her stomach. "Ugh, no. Thank you."

He leaned his mouth into a crooked slant. "I *thought* the idea of you heading out on a mission was crazy."

"What?"

He gestured dismissively. "Willie, spouting off about—" And that's when he saw what she'd been fiddling with on the bottom bunk.

Her sea bag.

It was packed.

"Wait." He frowned. "*Are* you leaving the ship?"

"Um, yes. I was just coming to talk to you about it." Her knuckles blanched white on the railing. She widened her stance.

Hold on. "If you're leaving the ship, why aren't I flying you?"

She didn't answer.

He deepened his frown. "Well?"

She cleared her throat. "For safety reasons."

"For…*excuse* me?"

"It's not—"

"I'll have you know," he cut her off snappishly, "that I've flown in foul weather *numerous times*. Way more than any other dingus pilot on this fucking tug boat."

"I know. It's not that."

He planted his hands on his hips. "What, then?"

She rubbed her lips together.

He checked out her duffel bag again. It was stuffed to the gunwales. Wherever she was going, it required all her gear.

"You need to start talking, Justice. Right now. Where are you going, and for how long?"

The deck swayed. He set his hand on the narrow metal standing locker that served as her closet.

Damned weather. Hurricanes were such a—

Fire ants suddenly crawled up the back of his neck.

Flying in extreme weather was only allowed in two cases: for a mission-critical situation or...

For a medical emergency.

A balled rock moved into the center of his chest. Justice wasn't heading out on a mission. So... "The corpsman found something wrong with you, didn't he? You're being MEDEVAC'd off the ship."

She winced.

Jesus Hell. "And that's why I'm not flying you, right?" He was beginning to talk too fast. "You don't think I can keep a clear head flying my girlfriend for emergency medical reasons." *The audacity. The absolute gall.* He pinched his lips together. "What's wrong with you?"

"I'd really rather...I don't have all the facts yet, Pete. So I'd rather talk to you about this when I have the full picture. If you don't mind."

"Ah, well, actually, this is the kind of thing I mind down to my toes."

Her lips quivered once, then held. She turned and

grabbed the strap of her duffel bag.

"Do *not*," he spat.

She kept hold of the strap but didn't move otherwise. "I don't want to worry you until…until I know if this is going to be a problem or not."

He laughed. The noise was laced with undertones of marbles-not-all-there. "We're *way* past worry, Justice. I'm officially out of my mind with terror right now. What's *wrong* with you?"

Her throat undulated but failed to produce any words.

The pit of his stomach made a grab for his intestines. "You want to play Twenty Questions?" he asked, his voice thick. "Or maybe Charades. We could do Pictionary, if you have a pencil and some—"

"I'm pregnant."

CHAPTER SIXTY-FIVE

PETE BLINKED. HE wasn't aware of time passing, but he must've closed his eyes for a long span of a hard blink because when he opened his eyes again, he was seeing spots.

"Don't flip out," Justice urged him.

She was here in the stateroom. Right? *I mean...*he saw her standing there. Saw her lips moving when she spoke. Except...her voice sounded distant and reedy, like it was coming up from the bilge of the ship.

"I have an IUD," she rushed to say, "and there's a chance the fetus will spontaneously abort when the doctor removes it, so, you know, this might turn out to be...uh..."

He put a fist to his mouth. Words meant to reassure him burned a hole through the middle of his heart instead. Sudden panic rose, the non-hysterical kind, but panic nonetheless. Buildings crumbling, fires burning out of control, fields rotting away to seed—a world falling apart around him, the screams of innocents clogging his ears.

There were things he needed to take care of, important people in his life to make sure were okay, to save, people he loved.

"Spontaneously," Pete asked roughly, "but not on purpose?"

"What?"

"When the doctor goes in to take out your IUD, you're not going to ask him to take the baby, too, are you?" The words hurt his throat. "On purpose?"

Two clicks of heavy silence went by.

"You've had ten seconds to think about this," she said, "and you already know that's what you want?"

"Yes." *Cue laugh track.*

No. Don't laugh. The *yes* was real. He didn't know why, but it was.

Justice turned aside and stared at a horsey calendar tacked on the wall. The edge of her jaw quivered. A hair clip tumbled out of her saggy bun and *tinked* mournfully to the floor. She looked down at her hand and noticed she was still holding the strap of her duffel. "I have to go," she said leadenly, hoisting the bag onto her shoulder. "The helo's waiting."

She headed across the room.

Pete followed.

At the door, he pressed his hand to the back of it so she couldn't leave. He met her gaze deeply, achingly. "Not on purpose?"

Tears gathered in her eyes. "No, Pete, not on purpose." She grabbed the doorknob, stared at it, then looked at him.

Her expression of utter panic nearly folded his knees out from under him.

"What am I going to do?" she whispered. She waited a beat, then pulled on the door, forcing him to lower his arm.

She left.

He stood riveted to the spot, his boots stuck to the floor by the blunt force of her emotions. The last time he'd seen her this upset was after she told him about SERE. But then… This was its own kind of impactful, wasn't it?

Talk of worlds crumbling…

Life, as Justice knew it, had just ended.

Her journey to her position as Special Missions leader had been brutal. She'd gutted out the worst the Navy had to throw at her, fighting her way through BUD/S to the premiere Special Operations Forces. And now, after everything she did to achieve her dream job—*bammo!* Gone. Other military women might be able to deal with the challenges of deployments and motherhood, but Special Missions was *all* deployments. There was no job to do domestically.

This pregnancy meant SOF was over for Justice.

Meanwhile, he was going to click his heels together and bound off to the next party now, thanks.

At least that's what his biographer would write about his story at this point. Chapter Heading: Pete Runs For The Hills…bailing on stinky, shitty diapers, the mortgage he'd have to sweat, and the horror of sending his Mustang off to live with a new owner so he could buy a minivan.

It was his expected next move as the Clown, right?

The Player.

Maybe deep down he was those things.

It was just…he didn't feel like those things.

Being a player had always felt more like something to do than someone to be, and clowning around had just been a way to chase off boredom.

When the chips were really down, he'd never failed to step up.

He was *Bingo*, the guy who landed below mandatory fuel reserves to save his people.

So what the hell was he doing, just standing here like his jaws were wired together? So, okay, no, he didn't have any answers to give Justice right now, but that didn't mean he had to leave her to figure everything out on her own.

Because that sucked. He knew that better than anyone.

Hauling the door open, he bolted from the room and careened the hallways until he spotted Justice up ahead. She was about to exit onto the flight line.

"Justice!"

She stopped and turned. Her complexion had gone from Kelly green to shamrock ghastly, though her lips were stark white.

He caught up to her. "What are you going to do?" he repeated her question back to her. "I'll tell you what you're going to do." He took her by the upper arms. "You're going to count on me, that's what. Your job on Special Missions? No worries. We'll find something even better for you than SOF. And…and the baby part? Well, let me tell you this—I know how to make a mean mud pie and a killer tree fort and Christmas wreaths out of popcorn, and you'd be amazed at the staggering variety of lizard species I'm conversant in, and…oh, wow."

He stopped reciting the finer points of his childhood as a full lungful of air slid out of him. "Epiphany time. I get it now—what my parents have been trying to do for me my whole life." He *got* it, in the way only impending fatherhood could lock it in. "Do you know why my mom and dad lived the way they did?"

She stared up at him.

"Because everything was about family to them. They wanted to live someplace where they could raise their children away from the daily grind, where they could focus all their attention on me and my sister, and…as crazy-making as that simple lifestyle was, I realize now what it gave me. Mom and Dad taught me to love family."

Justice blinked twice.

He had to swallow before he could go on. "All this time, I haven't been about the party. I've been gathering people around me like I was creating my own family unit. It's what…what's comfortable to me. I see that now. It's what I've always wanted. This news…the baby… It's not dragging me down. Just the opposite. I feel nothing but profound relief." He finally had a reason to become the man he was always meant to be. "And you? Maybe you're not sure about all this now, but stick with me, okay? I'm going to take care of you…you and the pipsqueak…and it's going to be super fun and cool. I'll make sure of it."

Her arms trembled beneath his grip.

The wind outside picked up, blowing with such violence he could hear it making a weird keening sound through the radar tower.

Finally, a small, uneven smile crept across her mouth. "Your speeches are really growing on me."

He laughed in a ragged gust.

She reached up and touched his face searchingly, as if checking for droid parts. "You really *are* that man, aren't you?"

He inhaled and nodded. "Not part-Zach Galifianakis and part-Chris Hemsworth, but one-hundred percent Clark Griswold, Family Man."

He watched the process happen—gradual, dawning—but then there it was: the full and complete belief and trust he'd been waiting for Justice to find in him…that meant everything.

The flight line door burst open.

They stepped apart as an AW stuck his helmeted head inside. "Lieutenant Hayes!" He yelled to be heard over the thundering rotor blades and howling wind. "We're ready for you!"

Justice gave the AW a thumbs-up.

"Hey!" Pete called to the guy. "You flying to the Naval hospital in Yokosuka?"

"Roger that, sir!"

"Okay, thanks!"

The AW ducked back out. The door swung shut.

Pete said to Justice, "You and the pipsqueak hang on, all right? I'll be at the hospital as soon as I can."

Her brows came down. "How are you going to do that?"

"I'm going to talk Cardoso into pulling into port at Yokosuka."

She snorted. "The skipper won't agree to that."

Who in the hell did this woman think she was about to marry? "I'll be there. You just concentrate on getting to the hospital in one piece."

She nodded and grabbed the handle, then let go and turned back to him. Dropping her duffel, she threw her arms around his neck and hugged him tightly. "I've never told you that I love you," she muffled against his throat.

No, but his little sailor wasn't one to gush. "I guessed."

Her chest moved shakily against his. "You know I'm a fighter, right?"

He smiled. "None tougher."

She leaned back in his arms. "I'm going to fight for the pipsqueak, Pete."

His ribs closed around his heart. He heaved in a full breath.

"Okay?"

He tried out a nod, but it just felt like his head wobbled around. Good call on him not being in a cockpit right now. "Okay."

"Remember that night in Moscow after *Drugoe Mesto* when you said you wanted to save me?"

"Yes."

She set a hand on his cheek, her heart in her eyes. "You just did."

His jaw went unsteady beneath her palm. He quickly leaned forward and kissed her hard. Messily, too, because, *well, shit*, she'd made a complete, fucked-up wreck out of him.

She picked up her duffel, gave him a smile he'd never forget, then flung the door open and rushed out into the storm.

CHAPTER SIXTY-SIX

U.S. Naval hospital
Yokosuka, Japan

A TROLLEY FULL of food trays rattled by in the hallway.

Justice watched it pass until her view was blocked by the entrance of a stoutly built nurse with bright Clairol-blond hair.

She was wearing scrubs and holding a clear plastic IV bag. "The doctor has ordered some meds to make sure your uterus doesn't contract, Lieutenant."

Justice gave a clumsy nod of acknowledgment, her throat too thick to maneuver out a response—unless she was okay sounding like SpongeBob.

An afternoon spent in the stirrups had been followed by tears and a maelstrom of emotions she'd never expected to feel.

She'd spotted after the procedure to remove her IUD, then surprised the hell out of herself by feeling grief and devastation over that.

During the horrible hour of bleeding to follow, none of the shakeup her life was undergoing mattered an iota. Leaving SOF shrank down to a minuscule issue. She was done with trying to impress, anyway. *Needed* to be done.

All she wanted was for the pipsqueak to be okay.

A *baby*.

She and Pete had come together and created a precious being, and she hadn't had to strategize or plan or dance around like a monkey to make it happen.

The most beautiful thing she'd ever done in her life was this child, and it was the most natural thing in the world.

The danged kiddo just needed to hang on.

Her chin quivered from her struggle not to cry. Her efforts failed, and tears streamed freely down her cheeks. "Ugh. *Why* does this keep happening to me?"

"Oh, it's okay, honey." The nurse gave her arm a reassuring pat. "It's just the hormones."

If only things were that simple.

"Hey," someone whispered. "Hey, hey."

Justice turned toward the door—and gaped. It was *Pete*. "Holy mackerel," she squeaked, then cleared her throat. "You really did make it."

He was still decked out in a flight suit, gorgeous and… She sniffed. It was so good to see him.

"'Course." He set a small, olive green flight bag on the floor beside her bed and sat on the edge of the mattress. He took her hand in his, the expression on his face stripping down to raw emotion as he studied her tear-streaked cheeks for a gathering-himself moment. "Not good?"

"No, no. The pipsqueak's hanging tough. They've put me on bed rest, and I…." How could she put into words all the changes she'd undergone in a mere few hours? "I'm just a mess."

A small smile touched his mouth, relief glowing from every pore. "You're allowed to be. And don't worry about thinking right now. I've got everything covered." He made an expansive gesture meant to include everything. "First, this—" He reached into his flight bag and brought out a manila folder stuffed with papers. He set it carefully on her lap. "Research I've done on civilian security firms who would—and I quote—*die* to have a woman of your skillset on staff. I've already contacted a few in San Diego via email, and they're very interested in meeting you."

She glanced at the folder a second time. The file was half an inch thick. *Research and then some.*

"Next—" Pete reached into his flight bag again, this time pulling out a ring box.

Ring! She tugged the blanket up to her collarbone and widened her eyes.

"I made a pit stop at the base jewelry store on the way here." He opened the box, revealing a beautiful solitaire diamond set in white gold, smaller diamonds trailing down from either side of the main event along the ring band.

"Jumping jiminetty," she exclaimed.

Laughing softly, Pete took the ring out of the box and slipped it on her finger. "Never thought I'd hear you say something like that."

"Well, I'm extremely weird right now, okay? I told you." She gazed at the beautiful engagement ring through a renewed wash of tears. *Is this really happening?*

Pete spoke to the nurse. "Do you know if there's a chaplain on duty right now?"

Justice blinked. *Right* now?

"Well, sir"—the nurse plumped fists on her rounded hips—"seems to me like I don't recall you actually *asking* the girl to marry you."

Pete grinned, unleashing a massive dose of Hugh Jackman on the nurse. "That's because I'm not taking *no* for an answer."

The nurse swallowed visibly and slid her eyes toward Justice.

Yeah, totally irresistible, isn't he? "I'm going to say yes," she assured the nurse. "Especially now that I have proof positive my future husband did not, in fact, overly fry his nuts to extra-crispy."

A barrel laugh exploded out of Pete—he almost fell off the bed.

The nurse gusted a soft noise from her nose. "You two are cute together. All right." She breezed for the door. "I'll see if I can track down the chaplain."

"What's the big hurry, anyway?" Justice asked Pete once he quieted down.

"I want you taken care of before I set sail again—to make sure you're on my medical insurance plan since you'll probably be discharged from the military before the baby comes, and also so you're on record as the beneficiary of my survivor benefits in case the worst happens. We can have a full-on wedding later, if you—" His brows drew inward. "I'm sorry to bring all this up."

She was crying again. "It's just…look at you! Pete the Penis has left the building and Practical Pete is now in charge."

He snorted out a laugh. "Not sure I'm a fan of either nickname."

"Well, I'm not calling you Bingo."

"How about Thunderballs?" he suggested, a wicked sparkle leaping into his eyes.

"I'm beginning to suspect an unnatural obsession with your testicles, Pete Robbins." More tears fell.

"You going to be okay, hot stuff?"

She swiped the back of her wrist across her cheeks. "We were supposed to deploy together, and now we're going to be apart for five months, and the next time you see me I'll resemble something out of a Barnum & Bailey catalog."

"I was thinking more like a Thanksgiving Day float." Pete gave her tummy an affectionate pat. "And so cute."

She drew in a shuddering breath. "I'm going to miss you so much."

He smiled into her eyes. It wasn't Bradley Cooper or Ryan Reynolds or Hugh Jackman.

His smile was one hundred percent Pete Robbins, and it was all for her.

Epilogue...

Wait!

Before you read on to find out more about Justice and Pete's happily ever after…

To obtain a FREE *authentic* copy of the <u>Nonpunitive Letter of Caution</u> Lieutenant Pete Robbins received for flying into unauthorized airspace to save Justice in North Korea.

tracy.link/pete

EPILOGUE

Eight months later
McP's Irish Pub, Coronado
Reunion Party, BUD/S Class 684

JUSTICE EASED HER bulk onto a barstool at the high round table and concentrated on breathing with lungs compromised by at least one small foot lodged against them…maybe a tiny fist too. "Mumph," she said. The pipsqueak was active tonight. Probably dancing to the bar's rock 'n' roll music.

Pete set a Perrier in front of her. "You ready to head home?" he asked, sitting on the stool across from her and plunking down a draft beer.

"Mumph," she repeated. "But no. Just taking a break from making the rounds."

She'd already chatted with Sniper Kilgour, Dog Bone, and Ziegler. All three were here with girlfriends, Ziegler's a perky blonde who appeared to be a Normal.

Justice had scrutinized the woman intensely, searching for something wrong with her, but it looked like Ziegler had landed himself a good one—someone who was obviously having a positive influence on him. Ziegler hadn't made a single inappropriate comment about the beach ball Justice was hiding under her shirt, or, *hmm*, how it might've come to be there.

Justice took a swallow of the Perrier. "How are you doing?"

"Me?" Pete's brows rose in a questioning arc. "Why wouldn't I be okay?"

"You don't know anyone here."

He answered with a languid laugh. "Pete Robbins knows how to manage himself at a party, hot stuff."

True enough. Although he was no longer much about the party anymore—he didn't need to be. Pete Robbins found fun in everything he did, whether he was at home making sandwiches for them, or lazing in front of the TV watching The History Channel, or out playing softball with his aviator buddies, or partying at a bar. Anywhere. Anytime. Anything. He found a way to enjoy it.

Married life hadn't been a bump in the road at all for him.

Married life hadn't been a bump in the road for her, either. She'd gone from feeling insecure about Pete to totally trusting him.

I'm going to take care of you, and it's going to be super fun and cool...

He was right—being wed to a combination of lively and reliable had allowed her the freedom to finally let loose and play. For the pure joy of it, not from an unhealthy compulsion to impress anyone. She anticipated the next chapter—motherhood—with hardly any nerves at all.

Excitement, laughter, orgasms galore! Beach bonfires, T-ball, Legos, late-night feedings, Oorah! Together, she and Pete would do it all, and keep each other laughing and on their toes the whole way through.

"Well, well, someone's been tampering with government property," a voice drawled from behind Justice.

In the next second, a handsome Black man with a small mole near his lip appeared at her table.

High School Crush Lookalike! "Omar Boyd! Hey, congrats on earning your trident." He'd graduated from BUD/S

Class 685, the one right after hers.

"Thanks." A beer in one hand, Crushy Boyd pointed the forefinger on his other hand at the large mound of her belly. "You do this?" he accused Pete good-naturedly.

Pete smiled. "Guilty as charged."

Boyd said to her, "That looks uncomfortable."

"Better than Log PT."

"You sure?" Boyd huffed a laugh. "When are you due, anyway?"

"Two weeks."

"Shit, Hayes, you look it."

"It's Robbins now." She gestured at Pete. "This is my husband, Pete Robbins. He's the pilot of my former Special Missions squad."

"Former?" Boyd kept his focus on Justice as he shook Pete's hand. "So the rumors are true? You're out of the Navy now?"

"Yep." Justice had been shipped back to San Diego directly from Yokosuka Naval Hospital and signed her discharge papers there.

"Too bad," Boyd said. "We'll never get the chance to work together." He drank some beer. "You miss it?"

"I miss the guys, yeah. But I've actually headed off in a cool direction work-wise."

"What's that?"

"My father and I are opening a security business." Grayson Hayes had, *ahem*, plenty of money squirreled away to invest as startup capital. "We're going to offer to test a business's security system, and if we can break in"—haha, *if*—"then we'll advise them on how to fix their problems."

"No shit?" Boyd chuckled. "Sounds like a blast. Right up your alley."

More than that, the extra time spent with her father was smoothing some things out for her. She'd made a point of not acting in ways to impress Dad, all the while suspecting she'd catch some subtle flak for it.

Not even a little bit. All these years of her thinking her father's love was performance-based... Turned out the misunderstanding was on her.

The wrong impression had probably been helped along by a father-daughter relationship based more on doing stuff together than talking things out. But in the end, she was coming to believe her dad loved her, warts and bad breath and mean right hook and all, and no matter what.

Just like Mom would have.

Boyd glanced across the room. "Cool. Knight and Street just arrived."

Justice followed the direction of Boyd's gaze, and her stomach clenched.

Keith and Brayden.

She set a hand on her belly as the baby kicked her. She hadn't seen those two men since her inauspicious departure from BUD/S almost two years ago.

Pete leaned toward her. "Hey, you okay?" he asked quietly. "You seem intense all of a sudden."

Boyd was talking to a waitress.

"Remember how I told you one of my best friends from BUD/S betrayed me to Admiral Sherwin after SERE?"

"Yeah." Pete studied Keith and Brayden.

"It's the dark-haired guy."

"And the good-looking blond? Lemme guess..." Pete turned back to her. "He was your comfort bang."

She exhaled a hard breath. "I never actually fucked him, Pete."

Pete seesawed his head, like *tomato, tomahto*. "You want to go over and talk to them, work things out?"

"I probably should." The scene with Sherwin still niggled at her as being not-quite-right. "I just wish I could have a drink first. Oh, hey, look! The balloon guy is here."

"Balloon?" Pete sat up straighter on his stool. "What balloon?"

A man stood at the front door with a silver, Mylar helium balloon floating above his head on a string.

She waved him over. "After the sonogram today, I asked my OB to call in the sex of the baby to a party store that does special balloons. Inside, there's either blue confetti or pink."

The delivery guy arrived at their table.

"I thought we decided to wait till the birth," Pete said to her.

"You seemed to be hemming and hawing over it."

"We only have two more weeks to go."

"So don't pop the balloon."

Crushy Boyd had turned his attention back to them, and he was now observing their exchange with the kind of expression he might've worn listening to a couple of Mary Kay consultants talk shop.

"Do you want to pop it?" Pete asked.

"Do you?"

"So, hey," the balloon guy butted in. "I got other deliveries to make."

"Together?" Justice suggested. "On the count of three?"

Pete nodded. "I'm in."

"One," she said.

"Two," Pete counted off.

"Three!" They slapped their hands around the balloon at the same time, and it burst.

A rainfall of pink confetti drifted over them.

"Hey!" Pete whooped. "It's a girl!"

The bar exploded in applause.

Pete jumped off his stool and swept her into his arms, his face alight with joy. "I love girls!"

Justice tipped back her head and laughed.

I'm actually the best fucking guy who could be in your life right now...

Nothing had ever been more true. Blinking confetti out of her lashes, Justice squeezed Pete as tight as her big belly would allow.

Now and forever.

There's nothing like the joy of a happily-ever-after. But as delighted as Justice is with Pete Robbins, there are other happily-ever-afters waiting for her.

How would her life have been different if she'd ended up with Brayden Street or Keith Knight?

You can send Justice on a different life path and find out...all you have to do is **Choose Another Hero** below and immerse yourself in an exciting new story!

If you want to read **BRAYDEN STREET'S** story, go to page 465.
If you want to read **KEITH KNIGHT'S** story, go to page 325.

Keep reading for author's notes...

Author's Notes

The BUD/S curriculum is constantly changing, in large part due to the wishes of whoever is in command of Special Operations Forces at any given time, but the training program in this book is depicted to the best of my extensive research at the time of publication. The exception would be the Extraction Swim—I took great liberties when describing this exercise to best fit the story.

Regarding timing issues, the training cycle required for a SEAL to go through before he's ready to head out on deployment is much longer than one year.

Regarding Keith Knight, he wouldn't have entered the Navy as a Petty Officer but would have moved up to this rate very quickly as a college-educated man. He also wouldn't have trained to be a medic (as mentioned in his story) at the same time he went through SQT. He would've been required to go through a separate training track.

SERE School exists, although the unorthodox exercise that Justice endured would never have been truly allowed.

The HSC-85 *Firehawks* is an operational squadron on North Island, the I-Bar is an actual aviator hangout (as described), and the Naval Amphibious Base (NAB) in Coronado does house BUD/S training (as well as odd-numbered SEAL Teams, One, Three, Five, and Seven). However, no character in this book is based on anyone factual.

All flight operations depicted are pared-down versions of how Naval aviation is genuinely conducted. A "rotor-over" is an actual high-risk maneuver that is prohibited by regulation but is at times practiced by aviators who want to push the envelope of the aircraft and their own abilities.

"Fighter Alley" exists—it is an unofficial "playground" off the coast of San Diego, created by aviators wanting to practice impromptu but unauthorized air to air combat maneuvers while en route to other missions.

The missions that took place in North Korea in this book are wholly derived from my imagination. This is due to the fact that crossing the DMZ on the ground or via the air is not permitted, is considered extremely dangerous, and isn't something normal military units would consider. However, U.S. Special Forces secretly operate in nearly every corner of the globe.

There is no intel-gathering asset known as Special Missions that is part of American Special Operations Forces (SOF). This is my own invention.

This is a work of fiction. All mistakes are my own.

ABOUT THE AUTHOR

Tracy Tappan is a bestselling and award-winning author of gritty romance and the creator of the Choose A Hero Romance™ reading experience, a brand-new concept in storytelling where the reader controls the ending. You can find out more about this exciting new trend at www.chooseahero.com.

Tracy's books in paranormal and military romance have earned both bronze and gold medals in the Readers' Favorite contests, have finaled for the USA Book News and Kindle Book Awards, and won both the HOLT Medallion and the Independent Publishers Book Award (IPPY) bronze medal for romance.

Tracy holds a master's degree in Marriage, Family, Child Counseling (MFCC), loves to play tennis, enjoys a great glass of wine, and talks to her Labrador like he's a human (admittedly, the wine drinking and the dog talking probably go together).

A native of San Diego, Tracy is married to a former Navy helicopter pilot, who retired after thirty years of service and joined the diplomatic corps. He and Tracy currently live in Rome, Italy.

Visit her website and join the gang on her monthly newsletter for giveaways, publication updates, and other fun and sexy news. www.tracytappan.com.

www.ingramcontent.com/pod-product-compliance
Lightning Source LLC
La Vergne TN
LVHW010859070325
805299LV00001B/7